FOR THE PRINCE! FOR THE QUEEN!

THE CONFLICTS: BOOK I

ZACHARY T. SELLERS

Contents

Dedicated to Clark and Pam Sellers,

For always supporting me.
For always being proud of me.
But most of all,
For always loving me.
You are both my dearest blessings.

BOOKS BY
ZACHARY T. SELLERS

THE CONFLICTS

THE NEW HARTLAND
CIVIL WAR
1109 N.F. (E.Y.) –

For the Prince! For the Queen!

DESRYOL WARS OF
REUNIFICATION
1109 N.F. (E.Y.) –

For the Bloody Marquesa!

Acknowledgements

This book has been a long time coming. The roots of this story go back all the way to 2006 when I wrote my first book in high school. From there, the world and characters that originated from that story blossomed, if not in a convoluted way, into this one. I say convoluted because the story presented in this book wasn't even conceived in the original story. Rather, it grew out of me going back and trying to redraft it. From one book came a plan for five. Then, as more plans and outlines were made to flesh out the world, the individual plots, and characters, one book with multiple storylines had to be split into three. Three stories. Three fantastical historical events, all happening simultaneously across a fantastical world.

Thus, the very identity of this book and my hopeful series at large was born. This process took over a decade from the original idea to be worked into a fully realized story. Through that time, many people heard of my ideas, read previous conceptions and old chapters, and wondered if I would ever have something official to put in their hands to read. This is a thank you to them.

First, to my parents, Clark and Pam Sellers, whom this book is dedicated to. They have always been by my side, supporting me in every endeavor, challenge, achievement, and failure in life, and this book is no exception. They were both inspirational in helping me seek a sustainable, independent career while always allowing me to pursue my dreams, as well. No one could ask for more loving and supportive parents, to my mother who was always eager for updates, even though she didn't understand my love for fantasy books, to my father who was my first yet unofficial beta reader, eager to read my stories. I say unofficial because I knew he would love whatever I wrote, but he swears the story is great. And he doesn't use that word often.

Next, I want to give a big thank you to my beta readers: Emily Carrol, Nita Fowler, Donald Gooch, Matt Light, Victoria Medina, Zachary Musgraves, Hayden Redd, Brett Roberts, Clay Sapp, Kirsten Simmons, James Stayton, Forrest Stobaugh, and Elizabeth Talkington. Thank you all for taking time out your busy lives to read my story and provide me feedback to help make this book even better.

And a special thanks to my fellow attorney at law, Ryne Johnson, who allowed me to use the spelling for his name when I was drawing a blank and needed a name one night. He understands I just wanted to borrow the way his name was spelled and the character does not reflect his true personality or characteristics at all. I would have had to have created a much more awesome character to capture those qualities.

Also, this book would not be publish-ready and as polished if it weren't for the excellent work of my editor, Kristin Campbell at C&D Editing. Kristin did a marvelous job taking my book, which had by then gone through multiple drafts, and editing it with care, professionalism, and reverence. I believe she grew to love the characters as I do and wanted to ensure their story was told as clear and concisely as possible, while also making sure the story's core remained intact. For that, I feel blessed to work with her.

I wish to recognize the artists who brought their talents into this book. Doan Trang brilliantly provided the gorgeous illustrations for each character's chapters as their individual symbols. The master map designer, Tracey Porter, aka Pixeleiderdown, took my years-old doodle of a map and patiently worked through a mountain of corrections and added details to bring a corner of my world to life. Micah Epstein created the masterpiece for this book's cover art, bringing my characters to life. James T. Egan of Bookfly Design who created the cover of this book's edition and brought all the pieces together to make a great design for the overall cover. A grateful thank you to all of them who made this book more beautiful than I could have imagined.

And lastly, to everyone else whose names are beyond counting who were there for every update, gave me endless words of encouragement, and showed boundless enthusiasm to one day finally read my stories, I thank you all from the bottom of my heart. This has been a long time coming for us all. So, to them, to everyone I mentioned above, and to you, dear reader, welcome to my world.

Map

The Kingdom of New Hartland
(Northern Provinces)
Timsberg
Inglworf
Siegmun's Success
Enderval Keep
North Bog
(Siegmun's Failure)
N
E
S
W
Renwood
Amadas's Manor
Daincastle
Tradon
Kanestown
Daincliff
Vorge Township
Ralmae River
0   100 Miles
Disputed Territory
as of 1104 N.E. (w.y.)
Haemsville
Sevier Township
To Silkhaven

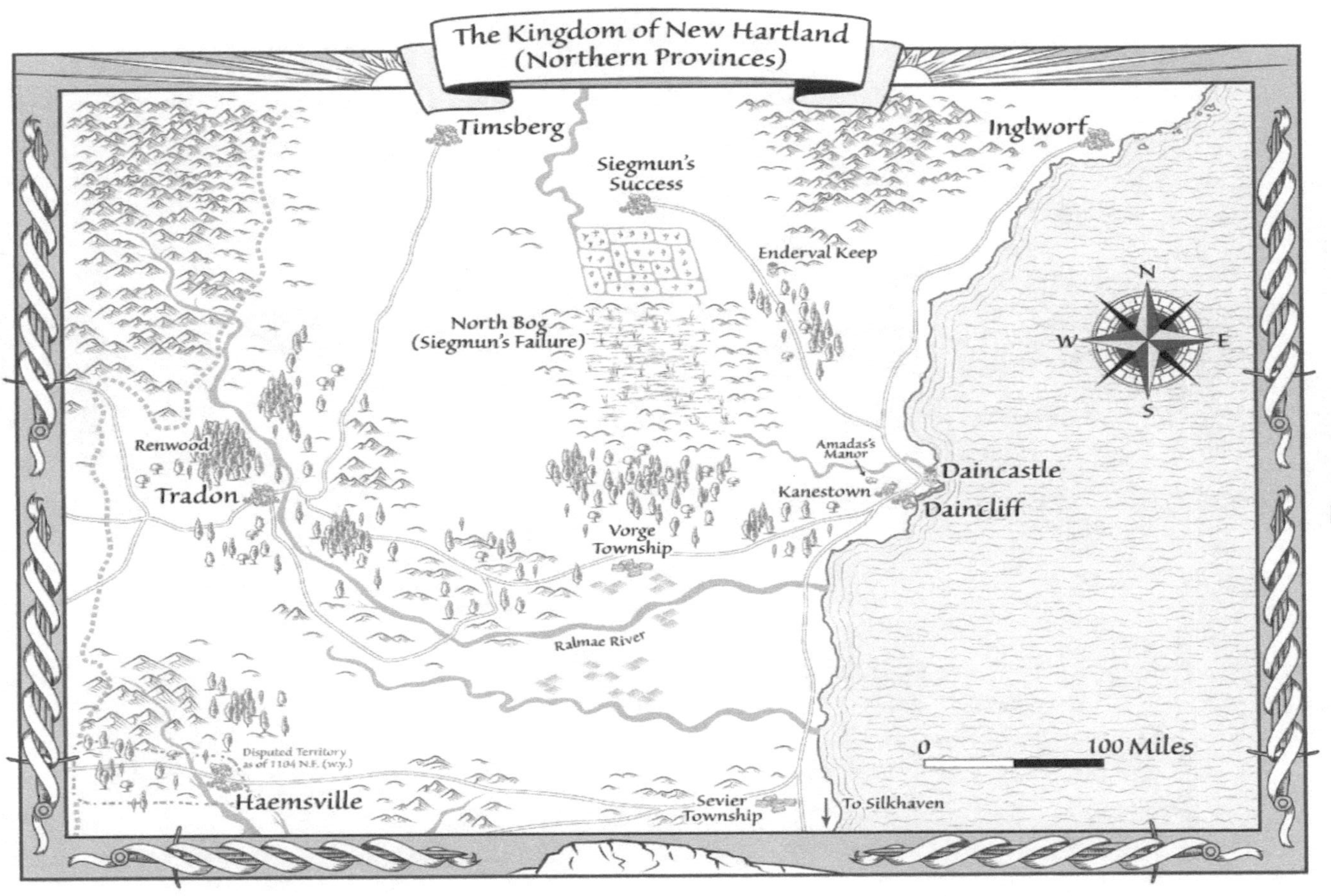

Prologue

18th of Benjamine, 1104 N.F. (w.y.)

Kalleb Kane slowly stirred awake as the early morning sun's warmth grew on his face. He groaned and shifted in his bedroll. The pleasant call of having a comfortable spot on the ground after weeks of riding was too hard to resist. But the bright, white rays from the Westerly Sun slowly grew brighter against his closed eyes and became impossible to brush off.

In protest, Kalleb rolled over.

And planted his face into cold water.

"Ah!" he yelped in surprise, jumping fully awake with a start.

Blinking and rubbing the sleep out of his eyes, he looked around and found the ground, the top of his bed roll, and his saddle that he had used as a pillow covered in dew. He wiped his face in frustration, his bristly stubble pricking his hand, and threw off his bedroll.

Red Eye, his horse, aptly named due to the large patch of red around his left eye, bayed.

Kalleb squinted at the gelding staring at him and shaking his mane. "That wasn't funny," he told the horse, ruffling his blond hair, shaking the dew out.

Red Eye bayed again.

"I know, I know." He pulled on his boots then pushed his saddle aside to get his provisions. He propped his curved saber against the saddle before he dug around and found a large, sagging sack. It had been full of apples when he had left Tradon, but as he reached in and fumbled around, Kalleb found only one left.

"Last one, buddy," he said with a sigh as he got to his feet and brought out the squishy, bruised fruit. He held it out for Red Eye, and the horse sniffed it then shook his mane, as if he knew it wasn't the best of treats. He ate it, anyway.

Kalleb watched his fingers as the horse took the apple, easily crunching and chewing it down. Then he rubbed Red Eye's mane, and the horse's large, dark eye blinked at him as he swallowed his morning snack.

"Sorry." He patted the horse's neck. "But that's the last of 'em. And you ate all the grain last night, so if you want any more grain or apples, we better make it to Haemsville today, or you're going to have to make do with grass."

Red Eye just blinked at him again.

Kalleb heard his own stomach growl and turned back to his meager camp. Red Eye's provisions weren't the only one's running low. He went back to dig through his saddlebags, finding some jerky, now rock hard and near impossible to chew. Not wanting to waste any more time, though, he rolled up his bedroll and provisions while gnawing on the tough meat.

They barely weigh anything now, he thought, piling his roll and saddlebags together.

Kalleb had thought he had brought enough food to last him, but he had also thought he would have reached Haemsville by now.

He threw his saddle across Red Eye's back then tied the girth straps around the horse's belly as the month-old proclamation rang in his head.

The Téions, whom the aristos called Téionaropi, but Kalleb and other common folk called them Téions, were marching on Haemsville. Prince Adam Dain had gone against the king and was riding to defend the boarder, with a thousand royal men-at-arms and an additional five-hundred-man contingent of Storm Cavalry. The prince had sent word that he would accept any able-bodied man who wished to join.

"A fool's errand." Amanda's words still stung. *"Lord Haemin brought the Téionaropis' wrath when he raised his illegal army and invaded them. He made war on them by himself, he can make peace by himself."*

It had been presumptuous of Kalleb to ask her if any in Tradon were allowed to go, especially with him a lowly lieutenant and she a princess, but he had known her most of their lives. His pa had been her retainer for as long as he could remember, until she announced her . . . engagement and moved to Tradon. He had figured she would give him leave.

He had been wrong.

The order came that night, after he had spoken with her—*no one* was allowed to ride to Haemsville. For most, it was a simple matter of following orders. Not to Kalleb. His pa was leading the Storm Cavalry contingent with Prince Adam, and Kalleb was certain Kenith, his oldest brother, was with him, as well. He couldn't let them ride to war alone, and he couldn't ask his squadron to disobey orders. So, here he was, alone in the middle of the woods, riding south.

Red Eye's baying made Kalleb blink, snatching him from his daydream.

He patted the gelding's neck again. "You're right; we need to get a move on."

He tied his saddlebags and bedroll onto the back of the saddle then clipped his saber to it, hanging the over three-foot-long metal sheath against his horse's left flank. Red Eye snorted as Kalleb tried to fit the bridle over his head. It took a few tries before the horse settled down and let the leather straps slide around his face and into his mouth.

In his hurry, it wasn't until Kalleb was settling in his saddle that he realized he had forgotten to gather the reins, still dangling down to the ground.

"Dammit," he cursed, reaching for them. It took a few reaches and coaxes for Red Eye to turn his head just so before Kalleb caught them and was able to guide the horse where he wanted him to go.

"Okay." He sighed as he brushed the horsehair from his wrinkled, burgundy coat then nudged Red Eye with his boots to get him moving. "To Haemsville."

Despite the early morning, the forest was quiet. Its foliage was slowly returning as the ferns grew new stems, and the grass was starting to green. Many of the trees, however, had yet to bud, and several of the pines were brown.

This second winter had been the coldest that Kalleb could remember, so he was glad it was finally over. Its snows had even reached Silkhaven this year. Second winter, which happened once every four years, was the only time snow ever fell but rarely reached that far south. This forest hadn't fared well from it, either.

As the day wore on, Kalleb rotated from riding to walking Red Eye through the hauntingly silent woods. Occasionally, a sharp chirrup or low honk broke the silence, making him and Red Eye pause to look around cautiously. He worried the lack of wildlife meant a predator stalked nearby and feared the next distant sound he would hear would be the gurgling yawl of a gorro.

He was thankful when they came upon a trickling brook winding through the trees and ferns. He hopped off Red Eye's back and ripped his leather water bag from the side of the saddle. Then he leapt over the brook, unplugging the bag's cork, and dunked the bag into the stream. Red Eye dipped his head down and pushed Kalleb's hand away as he drank.

Kalleb grunted and pushed against the horse's nose. "Don't be a—"

He froze. A faint, low rumble had run through the forest. He bounced his eyes here and there, peering through one clump of trees to another while remaining crouched and low.

Hooves!

Kalleb's heart began to beat harder as realization struck. For a moment, the vision of riders bursting through the undergrowth popped into his mind. He had defied orders and taken a horse to come this far, anyway. His captain, or the major, could have sent his squadron after him.

But no riders came charging through the trees.

A bubbling gurgle came from his water bag as the last bit of air escaped, indicating the bag was full. Kalleb sighed and shook his head as pulled the now heavy bag out. His arms trembled as he lifted it to his lips, the cool water a welcome relief against his dry throat. He then pulled it away and gasped, water sloshing inside as he twisted the cork back on.

"All right"—he coughed as he stood up—"you've had enough."

Kalleb reached down for Red Eye's reins then stopped. The gelding eyes were wide, his ears up and twitching, his legs stiff. Kalleb followed the horse's ears.

South!

He turned his head slightly, and the low rumble returned. A picture of hundreds of horses entered his mind.

There's only one reason so many horses could be just ahead of us.

He leapt back over the brook then hastily tied the water bag back onto the saddle. Red Eye snorted at him as if Kalleb's hurrying made him nervous.

Kalleb threw his leg over the saddle then kicked the gelding into motion. His heart began to race, beating in time with the horse's gallop, as they crashed through half-dead underbrush and rode under bare tree limbs. The sound of hooves became louder and, growing under it, there was a low hum of thousands of shouting voices.

Kalleb sat forward in the saddle and charged Red Eye through a thick bush . . . only to be greeted with the sudden burst of sunlight. He was blinded momentarily before realizing the forest had fallen way.

Red Eye bayed in alarm, and Kalleb's throat clenched at the sight of them charging straight toward a great drop. He pulled back hard on the horse's reins, and Red Eye screamed from the sudden jerk, his hooves beginning to slide against the rock. He reared up, and Kalleb's training and instincts kicked in. He leaned forward while tightly gripping his saddle horn, squeezing his legs against the horse's flanks and keeping his boots in the stirrups so he wouldn't be thrown. Red Eye danced about before finally got his footing under him.

Kalleb wiped the sweat from his brow, his heart pounding as he glanced to see the ground suddenly drop off some forty feet. Then he gaped at the view below him.

"Where is everybody?" He looked around frantically, refusing to accept what he was seeing.

A battle raged below on the western side of a river.

Through his training, Kalleb always thought battles consisted of men marching in long columns and formations with cavalry wheeling around them, looking for the enemy's cavalry or their exposed flanks. This battle didn't resemble that at all.

A barricade of spikes lay over a recently made road, which curved around a large hill and led back to a stone bridge over the Temins River. A line of soldiers huddled behind broad shields between the spikes, with an entire Knights Brotherhood, wearing divided green and yellow tabards over plated armor, in defensive lines, thrusting halberds and pikes at the oncoming harassers. Horse riders, thundering in perfect formation, charged the barricade and hurled long spears at the shields and men behind them.

Javelins? Kalleb pondered, confused. *Cavalry using javelins?*

He had never met a Téion before, even though he had lived in Tradon for over a year now. He had heard old Kanes describe them as a race of perfection made flesh, but he had never thought such tales could be true.

Each rider rode in a column of eight, the sun gleaming off their silver and bronze armor. As each forward line charged up to the barricade, the riders would throw their javelins, puncturing shields or sliding between the gaps to find the man behind. In mere seconds, after the riders threw their javelins, they would turn their horses and ride off to the sides, four to the left, four to the right, before any of the crossbowmen hidden among the knights' ranks could return fire while also allowing the riders behind them to charge in.

The persistent yet methodical patience of the Téions reminded Kalleb of a water wheel bringing up a small amount of water, one turn after another. Individually, small, but all those turns together amounted to a great, unending flood. By the number of staggering knights and men crawling away from the barricade, that flood threatened to soon break the barricade defenders. That would allow the column of pristine infantry waiting behind the attacking light cavalry to march in and remove the spikes unless the knights were reinforced.

But, as Kalleb followed the battle lines south, the knights at the barricade were not the only ones in need of reinforcements. Stumps of freshly felled trees still dotted the three large hills that the defenders of Haemsville were deployed on. The city's banner, a green "*X*" on a field of yellow, waved on the center hill, while dozens of smaller banners, Kalleb assumed represented other Knight Brotherhoods, fluttered about on the others.

A pitched battle raged on the slopes of the southernmost hill. Groups of men were urgently pulled away from the northern hill and sent to the southern. Soldiers on the central hill piled logs that they had failed to plant as stakes before the battle, around the crest of the hill to form some form of defense.

Waves of perfect infantrymen were marching out of the barren woods below the southern hill and up its slope in perfect step, their spears held in the same height. When they met the defenders waiting at the top, the front line lowered their spears and acted as one, while the rear lines halted and waited, instead of crowding in from behind. And they were gaining ground.

As the southern hill teetered on collapse, the column Téion infantry which had been guarding the light cavalry attacking the barricade moved off and began marching up the northern hill's slope.

Where's the prince? Kalleb thought furiously.

There couldn't be more than two thousand men defending Haemsville, and none fought under the royal banner. The Storm Cavalry was missing, as well.

Pa, where are you?

A hundred bowstrings snapped at once. Arrows streaked through the sky then curved down into the frontlines of the column marching up the northern slope. Here and there, Téions fell, but most of the arrows landed either between gaps in their lines or made metal pings as they bounced off their armor. The remaining Téions marched over their fallen comrades without pause.

More arrows fell on them, and yet the Téions continued up the slope. They leveled their spears as one when they reached the defenders then waded into them.

Kalleb gritted his teeth as he watched the defender's line bulge and pull back. By the way the battle was going, if Kalleb stayed on the cliff for much longer, it would be over by the time he looked for a way down.

I have to get down there!

He took quick stock of his surroundings, searching for a path that he could lead Red Eye down. The forest continued to his left, and the cliff didn't appear to slope downward. However, to his right, the forest thinned, and he could see the ground sloping.

He grimaced, studying the ground to the right. *That'd take me behind the Téions' lines.*

A bugle's high-pitched reeling cut through roar of battle below.

Kalleb snapped around at the familiar signal.

Across the river, mounted knights and lancers streamed out of the distant, unwalled city of Haemsville. Despite the distance, Kalleb's chest swelled as he made out the banners at the column's head.

His family's banner, the banner of the Storm Cavalry, golden horses riding over clouds, flew at the front of the column, surrounded by lancers in burgundy armor. Beside them rode men-at-arms in full plate armor, over gray and blue gambeson livery, flying the royal Sunrise banner of the Dains; a banner depicting the Westerly Sun rising over a gray cliff that looked like the prow of a ship.

Prince Adam had arrived.

Men appeared from behind the southernmost hill and roared up into the melee for the crest of the hill. However, even with the added men from below, the Téions' line didn't budge a step back.

The mounted column rushed over the bridge then split into two. Storm Cavalry followed the road, charging toward the besieged knights at the barricade.

The Téions' cavalry's constant harassment halted upon seeing the more heavily armed lancers riding up behind the road. The remaining men at the barricade scrambled out from behind the shields and pulled the spikes back as crossbowmen took the reprieve to fire bolts at the reforming Téions.

Kalleb expected the Téions to flee once they saw five hundred lancers bearing down on them, while the knights parted and cheered them on. Instead, the Téions' light horse reformed, leveled their short javelins, and countercharged.

The storm of hooves rolled up the cliff. Their crash drowned out the sounds of battle on the hills. Lances snapped. Armor cracked. The screaming of men and horses pierced over it all.

The Dain men-at-arms wheeled south upon crossing the bridge. Kalleb followed the Sunrise banner as it disappeared behind the southernmost hill. Moments later, the Téions' infantry, still pushing up the southern hill's slope, buckled for the first time as the point of the Dain charge cut through its center, halting the Téions' advance.

"*Yes!*" Kalleb whooped, jumping in his saddle, almost giddy with excitement. He reached for his saber but remembered how high up he was.

Shortest way would be best, he thought, looking back at the easiest way down and figuring his kin's numbers were pushing the Téions' lighter cavalry back.

I should be able to join Pa and Kenith then. He grinned, imagining Kenith's face.

Kalleb turned Red Eye to the right then kicked him into gallop. He lost sight of the battlefield as he urged his horse back under the trees and through the undergrowth. The sounds of the raging battle hounded him the deeper they pushed and as the forest floor started to slope downward.

Kalleb's excitement grew with every step. He could make out the beating of horse hooves in front of him and knew, once he cleared the trees, he would see his fellow Kanes wheeling around the Téions' rear, finally forcing those perfect columns into disarray.

He could just see the surprise on his pa's face upon seeing him. He couldn't wait to find Kenith and burst into laughter as they rode side by side, as they were always meant to—

Red Eye burst through another grove of trees, and Kalleb jerked back the reins, causing the gelding to bay loudly and rear up. He kept his grip and saddle, but lost his excitement, his blood running cold.

"By the Last God," he whispered in dismay, running a hand through his hair.

Cavalry were waiting for him.

But they weren't Kanes.

Kalleb gazed over column after column of heavy Téion cavalry. He wouldn't have believed it possible to outfit five thousand riders in full plate armor and heavy lances, but the Téions apparently had. Their silver armor gleamed together, as if a piece of the Westerly Sun had fallen from the sky and was now a mounted nightmare.

He was close enough to hear the individual horses snort and stomp their feet in expectation of a coming charge. Each horse had armor over its head and flanks, with red caparison cloth under the armor.

In the center of their huge column waved a long banner depicting a silver diamond with three golden wings on each side of the diamond on a field of white.

Chanting snatched Kalleb's attention away, and his heart fell. Squares of Téion infantry waited beyond a tree line to the south, around the winding road. They stood at attention, easily over thirty thousand strong, waiting to file into the trees and make their way into the battle still raging beyond.

Between each column stood robed figures, chanting and holding up long staffs with glowing stones on their tips. The stones reminded Kalleb of the stories about the Téions. They were a race of wonders, but no wonder more coveted than their ability to make crystals glow and perform the miraculous. However, no amount of gold or promises would make a Téion relinquish the secret on how the crystals worked.

The sound of clanging metal tore Kalleb's gaze away from the ominous sight of the chanting, robed figures and back to the column of heavy cavalry not a hundred feet in front of him. A few of the riders stared at him through their helmets' vizors.

Kalleb smiled weakly. "Right. Heavy horse in front of me." He glanced at his saber hanging off his saddle. "Like *shit* that'll help!"

He jerked Red Eye's reins, wheeling the gelding violently around, and kicked him to bolt back into the forest, the way that they had come.

His heavy breathing matched Red Eye's. He didn't take the same care in going around trees or going through the easiest thicket. He simply knew he had to put distance between him and that army.

The sounds of the battle began to grow louder as he got closer, and a dark realization hit him. *They've just been probing the lines!*

He clenched his jaw tightly as he ducked under a low-hanging branch. *They almost took a hill and the road and haven't even begun to attack!*

And his pa and brother were in the middle of it now.

Kalleb whipped Red Eye with the reins, but the horse just screamed and suddenly planted his hooves into the ground, leaning forward as he skidded along the ground. Kalleb tried to hold on, but he felt his rear leave the saddle and his feet slip from the stirrups.

He yelped in surprise as he flew over Red Eye's head then crashed through thick ferns. He hit the ground hard on his right shoulder then rolled into his fall like his pa had taught him. The impact drove his breath out as he rolled through another thicket and onto the cliffside overlooking the battle.

The world spun around him, the clouds above blurred with the Westerly Sun's white rays, and his head began to hurt as he lay on top of the hard rock.

As he regained his senses, he slowly pushed himself up with a sharp grunt. He clutched his throbbing shoulder and groaned at the sight below.

"This is"—Kalleb's breath staggered—"madness."

The Sunrise banner was planted firmly on the southern hilltop. The Dain men-at-arms had pushed the Téions' infantry off the crest and were fighting on foot, alongside knights of various brotherhoods and Haemsville levees.

The Téions' advance had halted on both the northernmost and southernmost hills. The Téions on the southernmost hill were trying to fight back up, while those on the northern hill fought a defensive battle, surrounded by the Haemsville defenders on top of the hill and Storm Cavalry below.

The entire northern half of the field was utter chaos. The Storm Cavalry's column had broken into different squadrons; some harassed the Téions on the northern hill's slope, others attacked another infantry column on the road to block them from moving up, and the rest chased the remaining Téions' light cavalry, attempting in random groups to get behind the defenders' lines.

Some of the knights had dragged a few of the spike barricades back over the road, but their line was too wide and the knights too few to man it fully.

"They think they're winning," he groaned out.

Kalleb would probably believe the same, if he were down there, but he knew it was a lie.

As his faculties fully returned, he saw the huge, open corridor to the center hill, with the fighting split between the field's north and south ends.

"I have to warn them!"

Kalleb tried to jump to his feet but gasped from the burning pain in his right shoulder, making him fall back down to the ground. He clutched his shoulder again, feeling how sore it was, but it wasn't dislocated, and no bones had been broken. He struggled more carefully to get to his feet and found Red Eye behind him, munching on a tall patch of grass.

"Red Eye," he groaned out as he walked up to horse, firmly holding his shoulder, "a warning would have been nice."

Red Eye snorted at him, as if he didn't care since he had found something to eat.

As he munched on the crunchy stems, Kalleb heard Red Eye breathing hard and saw foam around his mouth. "I'm sorry, boy," he said sympathetically, rubbing the horse's neck. He had pushed him hard today, and they both had barely eaten.

He shuffled around to Red Eye's left side and made three attempts before finally dragging himself back up onto the saddle.

"Come on, Red Eye." He nudged the horse with his knees and lightly pulled of the reins, but the horse didn't move. "I know you're hungry, but we have to get down there." He pulled harder on the reins. Red Eye snorted and shook his head, refusing to leave. Kalleb growled in frustration. He knew if he tried to be more forceful, Red Eye would buck him off.

The sound of running horses from down below caught Kalleb's attention. The Téions' light cavalry was leaving the field, and instead of pursuing them, his fellow lancers were pulling back. Some of them were pulling back across the bridge to the east side of the river and dismounting, probably to rest their horses. Others formed a column where the old barricade stood so the remaining knights could reform the levees into ranks behind them.

The defender's line began to ripple across the three hills. Ranks of men pushed in from the back, trying to get to the front, as men at the front tried to withdraw. The Téions' infantry on the hill slopes seized the initiative and attacked.

An officer galloped up the ranks of the lancers in front of the barricade, swinging his saber toward the northernmost hill. As the lancers began to turn their horses toward the hill, another Téion infantry column marched down road. The officer barely swung his saber at the column before the infantry charged. The lancers wheeled their mounts around, but only a few were able to lower their lances before the infantry made contact.

Kalleb gritted his teeth. "Cut your way out!" he yelled, his officer instincts flaring. "Drop lances and draw sabers and maces!"

His shouts, however, were swallowed up in the roar of the battle below.

He grimaced as he watched lancers frantically fight off the Téions' spears and bounced helplessly in his saddle as several were pulled from their saddles.

Kalleb drew his saber and ignored his sore shoulder as he waved the curved, three-foot-long steel in the air in the vain attempt to get someone's attention. "*Get out of there!*" he roared.

He couldn't tell if anyone could see him. From his height, he could barely make out individuals in the mad press below.

If they can't disengage . . .

Kalleb pulled Red Eye's reins hard and, fortunately, the gelding reared his head. Kalleb nudged him forward and walked the horse over to the edge of the cliff, in an attempt to make himself more visible. Then he waved his saber in the air and yelled, "Fall back! Heavy horse is aiming for your center! *Fall back!*"

The battle continued, with everyone deaf to his yells.

His throat grew hoarse.

A thunderous rumble made him go silent. Even on the cliffside, Kalleb could feel the ground shake. He dared not look west, hoping if he averted his gaze long enough, the rumbling would stop.

But it only grew louder.

The Téions' heavy cavalry charged in from the northwest, straight into the open corridor, to the center hill that their infantry had left for them. The defender's line in the center was a mass of confusion, as ranks of men moved between the other two hills.

Now they were all scrambling. Some were being pushed into lines at the front of the hill, whereas a few others made mad dashes down its eastern slope, toward the bridge. Soon, more joined them in flight. Even men from the northernmost and southernmost hills followed, ignoring the shouts from their officers.

Kalleb watched in awestruck horror as the Téions' heavy cavalry flowed up the center hill's slope and its front lines dropped their lances in unison. They rolled over the Haemsville defender's mangled line in an unyielding wave. The Haemsville banner fell under their hooves.

The center crumbled.

The sounds of war swallowed everything again. Men and horses screamed over the clanging of swords and the rattling of lances and spears.

Kalleb dropped his arm limply and watched the Téions' heavy cavalry ride down men running for the bridge. Divisions splintered off from its massive column, around the north, south, and toward the bridge.

The strength in Kalleb's fingers gave out, and his saber slipped from his grasp, to *clang* against the rocks, as the southernmost hill was surrounded then ingulfed by the Téions' tide. A hoarse wail escaped him as the tide swallowed the Sunrise banner.

As the northern hill met the same fate, the remaining Storm Cavalry and knights guarding the road tried to charge toward the river and back to the bridge, but the Téions had the numbers. All who didn't flee to the northeast and out of Kalleb's sight were slain.

A rolling, warm sting of tears ran down his cheeks as the last remaining lancers were unhorsed. The Storm Cavalry banner, *his family's banner*, was trampled in the dirt.

As the Téions began crossing the bridge in force, the lancers on the other side fled.

Kalleb folded in on himself, leaned down, arching his back, and pressed his head against Red Eye's neck. "Pa!" he gasped. "Kenith!"

They were dead. They had to be. He couldn't imagine either of them leaving the field with lancers still on it.

"I didn't make it." He trembled in his saddle. "*I didn't make it!*"

Chapter 1

11th of Petrarium, 1109 N.F. (e.y.)

Lady Tory Syros basked in the Easterly Sun while on the forecastle of her family's yacht, a sleek, two-mast ship, built for speed.

A gust of wind whipped her hair around her face, and she spat and pulled damp, bloodred strands away from her mouth, softly growling in frustration. Then she raked her hair back just as another gust of wind flung ocean spray over the yacht's bow and misted around her.

A storm's on its way, she thought, looking up at the rolling gray clouds moving toward Daincliff, *either tomorrow or the next day*.

Regardless, the wind was helping to push the yacht toward the capital's Old Harbor.

A high-pitched trill came from above and behind her, and she turned to find Harpo, her pytre hawk, hanging upside-down on the foremast. He looked down at her with his large, brown eyes as he twitched his black, scaled head from side to side. He dug his talons and forewing claws into the mast as he hugged it. The bright red feathers on his forearms and thick hind legs stood out, fanning against the mast's black wood, and his long tail feathers stood rigidly in the air to keep his balance.

"You should be below!" Jerro shouted.

Her nonchalant, second eldest brother waved at her while clomping up the forecastle's steps. Like her hair, the breeze whipped his long, flaming red braid hanging from his chin, as the sun reflected off his clean shaven, ebony cheeks. He dressed a bit flamboyantly for a ship's captain, but it was Jerro's sense of style, being the son of nobility. His white, sleeveless shirt was tucked into his black trousers without a wrinkle, and his red vest, with gold buttons, fluttered in the wind, like his chin-braid.

"It's stuffy down below," Tory replied, reaching up to scratch the top of Harpo's head.

Harpo chirped happily as she lightly pushed aside his coarse feathers to reach the scaly skin underneath.

"I'd rather watch the docking, too." She kept her eye on Harpo, prepared to pull her hand back at the slightest twitch. His soft twitter was a sign he enjoyed the scratch, but his sharp, needlelike teeth could rip her fingers to shreds with a few quick bites, if she wasn't watchful.

As if to mock her, the yacht pushed through another wave, and the ocean sprayed more mist around her. Harpo ruffled his feathers and squawked in protest, causing Tory to jerk her hand back. Goosebumps ran down her bare arms as the water, cooled by the wind, landed on her arms. She wrapped her arms around her waist, pressing her white, sleeveless blouse against her as she attempted to rub the goosebumps away.

"Why is it so much colder here?" she complained as Jerro walked up beside her, his tall figure blotting out the sun.

"Colder?" Jerro asked, puzzled. "The crew would disagree with you on that. They're drenching my decks with their sweat while securing the sails."

"All the while, their captain leisurely strolls under them without a care." Tory pursed her lips and gave her brother an upward, sideways glance.

"My first mate can handle yelling at them over the rigging," Jerro replied, not taking the bait. He folded his thick, muscular arms across his broad chest and turned to admirably gaze upward. "It's still as fascinating a sight as when I first saw it."

Tory followed his gaze upward to the great cliff that gave the city its namesake.

Rising over three hundred feet and gently curving to extend over the ocean below, the cliff's gray stone cut up into the sky like the bow of a ship, able to cut through the tallest ocean wave. And built squarely on its slopes was Dain Castle.

The tops of the castle's six towers and the main hall could be seen rising over its walls, even from the harbor. Her sister had told her that the lights from its glass windows could be seen for miles around.

A great stone wall surrounded it, and upon each of its ten turrets flew the Royal Sunrise banner, depicting a blazing white sun rising to shine over and outline great cliff. Legend told that the banner depicted how the royal family, the Dains, first sighted the cliff, with the Westerly Sun breaking the dawn and rising over it. Therefore, the Dains had put the image on their banner.

"Just imagine hauling all that stone up that slope." Jerro shook his head in disbelief.

There were no castles where they came from, on the Syros Isles. Their people lived in black wood homes, while Tory's family had built their mansion and estate in the Red Mountain's crater. Her father always told them that the Syros Isles' greatest defense was the Black Syros fleet, and if anyone got past it, even the Last God's mercy wouldn't be enough to save them from the island's jungles.

"Too bad they couldn't spare some of that stone for the rest of the city," Tory said with a sigh, looking down the slope and back to the city.

At the base of the slope was another stone wall, with a deep moat in front of it, filled by the ocean. A draw bridge linked the wall to North End. Tory could see the rooves of the three- and four-story manors peaking upward from behind the stone wall.

"*Only the wealthiest and oldest families live there*," Serina's, Tory's sister, voice echoed in her head from Serina's repeatedly gushing about it for over two months since receiving Her Majesty's invitation to court. "*The manors and townhouses are splendid, and invitations are required to visit any shop, which I have.*"

I hope she visits so much that she stays there and forgets about me.

Passed North End and Old Harbor was Alpheaus Square, commonly known as the square, where the Last God's grand cathedral towers casted shadows on the smaller ministry buildings, banks, and the Ministry of Justice. A large market and heavy traffic lined this part of the shore, where merchant ships came to unload their goods and fisheries prepared their day's catch.

Farther down the shoreline, the city became less extravagant and well-built. Another stone wall divided this portion of the city from the square. Its houses and buildings were poorly built and stacked close together, with narrow streets and alleys. Its docks were shabby, and the vessels moored there gave off an appearance of ill repute. Lastly, its walls were covered with ivy, missing stones, and large cracks ran up from the base where it touched the ocean.

"It looks like they ran out of stones," she said, pointing at the neglected part of the city.

"Don't worry," Jerro said, "you won't be going there. Nothing but cheap inns, cheap taverns, and . . . places a young lady shouldn't go, is all."

Tory gave him a sly look. "So, I suppose you're going to be spending a lot of time there?"

Jerro pursed his lips to stop himself from grinning, but Tory could see a gleam in his eye.

"Harbor pilot coming up the port bow!" the lookout yelled from the mast nest.

A single-mast cog was looping through the choppy harbor waves toward them.

"What an odd little ship," Tory commented. "It doesn't have any iron on its railing or a ballista mounted on it."

"Too much traffic in the harbor for serpent whales," Jerro said. "I'm just glad someone finally saw us waiting out here. If we had to wait another hour, Serina would've been storming my deck, and my crew would mutiny."

Tory giggled as she watched the cog's crew struggling to get the sails under control because of the uncooperative winds. The cog raised three small flags—one yellow, one half-red and half-white, and the other a light blue. Tory's brothers had been teaching her signal flag messages ever since she could sail with them. The message read, *"Prepare to follow."*

"Signal *Standing By!*" Jerro ordered, finally acting like a ship's captain.

A crew member hurriedly ran up two small flags—one black and the other orange—under the Syros family's banner—a black ship on a sea of red.

"You better get below now," her brother told her. "Serina will skin both of us alive if you're seen dressed like this by mainlanders."

"What's wrong with the way I'm dressed?" She raised an eyebrow at him then glanced down at her white, sleeveless blouse and loose, black silk leggings. "I'm the picture of modesty in the Isles." *Especially considering some of Serina's wardrobe.*

"Not up here. Here, you'd pass for a . . ." His words died on his lips as he gave her a sideways glance. A hint of a blush even cut through his dark cheeks. "It's unladylike up here."

Tory narrowed her eyes at him. While her brothers still treated her like an innocent, she knew what he was calling her.

"Fine." She turned and walked away in a huff. "Wouldn't want to upset Serina, would we?" Tory's bare feet slapped against the deck's black wood as she stomped away. Harpo squawked loudly after her, annoyed that she didn't have a treat for him.

Once down the forecastle's steps, she dodged shirtless sailors, walked around the main mast, and passed under the shadows of the ballistae on the stern to make her way to the steps leading to the aristo quarters.

Her clothes immediately clung to her once she stepped into the yacht's humid corridors. They were tight and didn't help the air circulation, either. Worse for Tory, she knew she had to pass her sister's cabin—the great cabin, reserved for the highest-ranking passenger, of course—to get to hers.

"One does not wear black to court! And red is too bold!" Serina shouted, her loud, frustrated voice echoing down the close space.

Tory paused, grimacing at the tone. Her courage to pass by the great cabin was diminishing with each second.

"I hate our family's colors!" Something slammed against a wall. "They're just not suited for these noble functions. Nina! Put those things away, stupid girl! I don't need *all* my jewelry laid out."

Tory's breath caught. Nina was *her* maid.

She felt her cheeks flush as her apprehension for her sister turned into anger. Serina displayed joy in treating everyone else as her servant, despite having her own myriad of personal maids. She only tempered her behavior around their father, while her mask slipped around everyone else.

Tory always felt her older sister delighted in taking Tory's things for her own whims, and commandeering Tory's servants was her oldest pastime.

She marched down the corridor, finding the great cabin's door half open, and barged in . . . right into a maid carrying a load of skirts, spilling them onto the cabin floor.

"Idiot!" Serina stood in front of a large mirror, wearing a black corset and white under-skirt, with another maid brushing her fiery red hair. She looked back at the spilt skirts with disdain on her heart-shaped face. "If even one of those skirts are ripped, I will dismiss you and send you back to the Isles with the assurance that the only work you will find is either in the sugar fields or whore houses."

"Serina!" Tory protested.

Serina glanced at her, as if finally seeing she was in the doorway, and just as quickly dismissed her.

"Oh, Runt, what do you want? We will be docking soon, and I must be perfect when I present myself to Her—Not green, you fool!"

The maid holding a green dress bowed apologetically then left to find another dress.

Tory fumed at her sister, balling her fists with the urge to throw something at her. Her sister always resorted to mocking her whenever she felt Tory was irritating her, like now, because Tory was shorter than the rest of her siblings. While Jerro and Andre both loomed head and shoulders over her, Serina was only half-a-head taller. Even so, she took pleasure in continually pointing out that Tory didn't match up to her.

Other times, it was her hair. Her siblings all had flaming red hair, the most prized and notable status in the Isles. Tory's, though, was dark, bloodred with traces black strands among them, common and dirty in Serina's view.

But, if Serina felt particularly nasty, she would mock Tory for being too thin or not as pretty. Serina was prideful of her angelic face and delighted in alluring men with her supple curves and ample figure.

"Well, it's hard for me to get ready when you've stolen *my* maid," Tory replied, looking over Serina's seven other maids, each either holding a different dress or doing some menial task, until she found Nina in the back. The poor girl was sorting through Serina's inordinate amount of jewelry laid out on the cabin's dining table, looking back and forth nervously between the two sisters.

"*Ugh!*" Serina dramatically rolled her eyes then waved away the maid brushing her hair. She turned and gave Tory a condescending look, propping her left hand on her hip in preparation to deliver a scolding. "If you cannot keep track of your servants, you should not be surprised when someone, who actually needs them, makes use of their services. That is their purpose—to serve. Not to lollygag in their cabin as their mistress frolics away on . . ." Serina pursed her lips and critically looked Tory up and down as her pout turned into a scowl. "You are *not* wearing that to court! If you dare embarrass me, and our family, before Her Majesty, I will send you back with a long letter to Father that you should never be out in public again!"

Of course this is all about you, Tory thought as she blankly stared back at her sister. *You only notice* now *that I need to change. How flippant can you be?*

"I would change faster with my maid," she replied dryly.

"Take her, then," Serina sighed out dismissively, waving her hand again. "But your nasty beast stays here! I will not have that smelly, noisy thing stinking up Her Majesty's castle."

She turned back toward the mirror then gave her maid with a brush a disgusted look. "Well? It's not wavy enough!"

The maid squeaked and bowed her head apologetically before resuming her gentle brushing.

With Serina's back turned, Tory waved to Nina, who hurriedly walked past Serina's servants. A couple of them watched Nina go with painful envy, but Tory could do nothing for them. She wrapped her arm around her nervous maid, and they shuffled out the great cabin.

Nina pressed herself close to Tory as they turned and walked down the steps to the lower deck. "I'm sorry, Lady Tory," she whispered. "Lady Serina summoned me, and I couldn't refuse her."

Tory shushed her and smoothly stroked the woman's brown hair. Any other time, she would have felt silly comforting a woman at least ten years older than her in such a way but knowing how intimidating Serina could be made Tory try even harder to relax her servant's fears.

"I know," she whispered back. "I'm back now, and I won't leave you alone where Serina can order you about."

"Thank you, My Lady."

Tory patted her on the back. "We're docking soon. Help me change, and then we can get off this ship and see if we can be quartered far away from my sister in that big castle we're going to."

That brightened Nina's spirits. She shot her head up, her eyes wide with excitement. "Not to be disrespectful, My Lady, but I would really enjoy that."

Tory giggled. "Then I'll insist they put us in a whole other tower!"

That set off a whole round of giggles from them both as they found Tory's quarters and went to change and ready the luggage.

Chapter 2

Prince Alindale Dain paced back and forth in his father's study, waiting and hoping one of the royal physicians would come out and speak with him. He wasn't sure how long he had been waiting, but he suspected over an hour by the window drapes' shadows.

How long does it take to tell me something? he fumed.

His father had been sick for over a month now. At first, they had kept him sequestered in his chambers, not knowing what it was. Now the physicians were completely secretive, refusing to let anyone know about his father's condition.

Alindale being the royal heir was the only thing granting him admittance into his father's chambers. The Sunrise Guard, the personal guard to the king and queen of New Hartland, had given him the choice of waiting to speak with one of the physicians in either his father's study or in the hall. The study was the only choice. It at least had books, shelves and shelves filled with books from across the kingdom and centuries, written by his ancestors, deceased lords, master knights, historians, ministers, and even humble, common playwrights.

Alindale paused his pacing and looked across the leather- and wood-bound covers. *If only one of them had all the answers*, he thought longingly.

A thin manuscript, dividing two thick, wood-bound tomes, caught his eye. Out of a mixture of boredom and curiosity, he fished the manuscript out, its yellow-stained parchment crinkling in his hands. His eyebrows shot up when he read the title, *The Three Tragedies of the Wandering Boy.*

Old memories drifted back to him—the ink blot on the title page, multiple page corners folded in, and the crease down the center of the manuscript. This was his old copy of Machel Avel's two-hundred-year-old play.

"How did you get here?" he asked aloud, flipping through the first pages. He sat in a chair in the corner of the study, mesmerized by the familiar story and the memories while he thumbed through the pages.

It was a story about a young boy who leaves home at a young age, and in each act, he would go through a tragedy, which ultimately forced him to go home and find that home was no longer how he had left it. Alindale had many of Machel's plays in his own library and had even recited a few to his little brother when they had been younger.

"Adam!" he realized, lifting his head out of the pages.

His brother was notorious for avoiding things he didn't like, and Alindale remembered he *hated* this play. So much so that Alindale would read it to him as punishment if he found Adam's demands annoying.

"He must have stolen and hidden it here, thinking I would never find it," he mused.

Alindale sighed as he sat back. He ran his fingers through his black hair and grimaced at the oily, stiff texture. The ticking of the grand, two-faced clock to his left filled his ears, making his head pound from the clockwork's steady rhythm.

What do I do? He turned to the door beside the clock, the one to his father's bedchamber. *I should just knock and demand to be let in.*

He let his arm fall away, and the manuscript flopped closed in his lap. He knew if he did, though, the physicians might tell his mother that he had caused a disturbance. Then the Sunrise Guard would have their excuse to keep him out, along with everyone else.

What do I do? He clenched his eyes closed. *What would Adam have done? Maybe I should see Amadus—*

"Your Highness."

Alindale spun toward his father's chambers, but no one was there. He then turned to his right and found a Sunrise Guard in his silver plate armor, from boot to helmet, with the golden sunset cliff crest on his breastplate and gold cap down his back, standing at the door at the other side of the room.

"Yes?" he asked wearily.

"Someone wishes to speak with you," the Sunrise Guard replied, his voice muffled behind his visor. "A Mr. Rigsby."

Alindale frowned. *Julian's secretary?*

"Send him in."

"Pardon, Your Highness," the guard started, "but he cannot enter the royal chambers. You must speak with him outside, if you wish."

Alindale frowned and glanced back at his father's chamber door. On the other side of that door lay the answers to his worries, if only he could get word of what was going on in there. It seemed everyone was conspiring to keep him from it.

"Fine," he sighed out heavily. "I shall step out."

The Sunrise Guard led him through the royal meeting and sitting room, both empty, even of servants. He opened the door for him then led him down the entryway to the hallway and stairs beyond. Alindale caught sight of his Storm Cavalry retainers, waiting with a sharply dressed man in black and green.

A chill ran down Alindale's spine at hearing the door shut behind him. It was if they were locking him out from his father.

His retainers snapped to attention as he walked down the entryway. They clicked the heels of their shiny, black boots together, and their curved sabers rattled on their dress uniform's belts. Lieutenants Holt and Malory rarely stood on ceremony, but Alindale figured they didn't wish to appear unprofessional in front of the Sunrise Guard.

"Your Highness." Mr. Rigsby bowed deeply from the waist, his curly, auburn hair waving as he did so.

"Mr. Rigsby," Alindale greeted. "It is not often you run errands personally. Is Julian all right?" Alindale knew he better be, for his sister and the kingdom's finances' sake.

"Pardon me, Your Highness"—Mr. Rigsby took a step closer—"but my Lord Renald told me it was urgent you receive this." Mr. Rigsby held out a neatly folded parchment, clutched tightly in his pristine white glove.

An urgent message? Alindale arched an eyebrow as he cautiously took the parchment. Everything about this felt off. It wasn't like Julian to send him clandestine messages.

He unrolled the parchment and read: "*Come quickly. Her Majesty has announced she will personally hear a petition. C.R.*"

Alindale frowned. *Mother can't hear petitions.*

He reread the message two times, thinking he had read it wrong, before letting the message drop.

Court's not in session. Emergency or not, she doesn't have the authority. It didn't make sense.

"Did Julian send you from the throne room?" he asked.

Mr. Rigsby nodded. "Yes, Your Highness."

Mr. Rigsby looked him up and down then instantly went to straighten Alindale's wrinkled tan and silver doublet. Failing that, he tried to straighten Alindale's hair, but Alindale knew that was a lost cause and slapped his hand away.

"This will have to do," he said, walking around Mr. Rigsby, with his retainers on his heels.

~~~

Where is everyone? Alindale thought as he and his group entered the curving, stone corridor outside the throne room.

For the past three days, his mother had been welcoming various lords, ladies, dignitaries, knights, merchants, and a few township mayors to court in place of his ailing father. Ministry officials, pages, and castle servants had congested corridors around the throne room, sorting out where everyone was staying and filing their pre-petitions before the start of session to the point they were nearly impassable. Now the corridor was eerily silent.

Sunlight streamed down on them from the slanted windows in the ceiling and divided it between broad strokes of light and small patches of shadow.

Alindale stopped in the middle of the corridor when they found the throne room's wide double doors shut.

Session isn't supposed to start until tomorrow!

He eyed the two castle guards posted beside the doors cautiously. The streaming sunlight gleamed off their helmets and shoulder pauldrons. The Sunrise crest eyes emblazoned on their uniforms. They stomped to attention at Alindale's approach, slapping their halberds against their pauldrons.

"Has the throne room been ordered closed?" he asked.

"No, Your Highness," the guard to his left replied.
~~~

Alindale took a deep breath before pushing open the doors and stepping into his worst nightmare—hundreds of eyes turning as one and staring at him, freezing him at the entrance. The courtiers packed the stands between the limestone pillars that held up the oval-shaped room. One pair of eyes, though, made him sweat.

His mother, Her Majesty, Queen Avera Dain, stared disapprovingly from her throne on the royal dais. His father's throne sat gleaming and empty beside her. Seven Sunrise Guards ringed the bottom of royal dais.

"Prince Alindale," she said, projecting her voice to the back of the room, "you honor us with your presence, but you are late."

Alindale swallowed, his legs beginning to shake, but it was too late to turn back now. Thus, he summoned all his courage and focused on following decorum, to ignore the judgmental stares of the attendees. He walked as calmly as he could to the center of the room where he bowed deeply, followed by his two retainers, who knelt behind him.

"Forgive me, Your Majesty," he said. "I was just informed—"

"Yes, Your Highness," she interrupted, loudly opening her fan, "something of the utmost importance has come to our attention, and the crown wishes to address the matter before session begins. We are gladdened His Highness has taken an interest in the affairs of the state. Please, take you seat."

The hairs on the back of Alindale's neck stood up. *Something's wrong.*

"Thank you, Your Majesty," he replied then went to his reserved seat—a lone wooden chair with a tall back in front of the left pillar by the royal dais.

He tried to straighten his doublet and trousers as he sat, but they both felt suddenly tight. He hesitantly tried to straighten his hair again when his mother gave him a long, irritated look over her fan. She then closed the fan with a *slap*, getting everyone's attention.

"My lords and ladies," she began, "we have called this gathering because a matter of grave importance has come to our attention. We find the severity of this petition be brought before us now, to emphasize its need to be resolved when session is called to order tomorrow."

A rumble went through the courtiers like a wave.

Alindale frowned. It was just as Julian's note had said. She was actually going to hear a petition before session had been called.

Session was the executive forum of the kingdom, where ministry policies were set and petitions to consider policy changes and complaints were lobbied. Only during session could petitions be made and, according to the Carta, only the king had final decision power to grant or deny them.

Alindale looked around the room and saw some of the courtiers looked as confused as him. Some seemed excited.

I should say something . . . He gripped the arms of his chair but had no strength in his legs. *Shouldn't I?* But the mere thought of standing made his legs shake even more.

"Your Majesty!" Lord Bernold Vanni, First Minister of the Table of Ministers, shouted. The stout man then stepped out from the crowd, the thin tips of his oiled mustache quivering, and hastily bowed to Her Majesty.

She raised an eyebrow at him. "The crown recognizes First Minister Bernold Vanni."

"Thank you, Your Majesty," Bernold said as he rose. "This comes as a complete surprise to all of us. We were all hoping for good news of His Majesty."

"His Majesty still remains confined to his bed," Her Majesty replied. "The royal physicians assure me that he is recovering, but they are still unsure of his ailment, and so he will be unable to attend session."

Bernold's mustache twitched, and his broad brow furled in confusion as he tried to keep a diplomatic look. "And we all pray for his speedy recovery, Your Majesty. However, it is my duty to remind the crown that the court cannot hear petitions until in session and those petitions are scheduled to be heard. To hear a petition now, when Your Majesty is welcoming people to court is"—Bernold shook his head and rubbed his palms together as he searched for words—"if you will pardon me, out of order."

Alindale tensed, as did many of the other courtiers, and watched his mother. Her face remained a cool mask. Her practiced smile didn't even twitch.

Careful, Bernold. He was an old friend of his father's, but Alindale knew his mother didn't like to be told she couldn't do something.

"First Minister, thank you for your concerns for custom," Her Majesty stated calmly, "but the severity of this petition heeds an emergency, which we will not ignore. Please, step aside."

Alindale made out Bernold's darkening face and quivering chin from how tightly he kept his mouth shut as he returned to his seat.

"The crown recognizes," Her Majesty projected, "Lord Rudmund Fauman, Lord of Silkhaven and Province Governor of Siodina."

Fauman! Alindale sat up straighter as Lord Fauman approached the royal dais from the back of the throne room. *Haemin's friend.*

The Lord of Silkhaven's red sash shimmered in the rainbow light from the throne room's stained glass ceiling as he bowed before Her Majesty. A man of middle years, his hairline was receding, and the edges of his brown hair were turning gray. His sash wrapped over his silver embroidered, violet doublet that bore the white shield pin of Siodina on his shoulder.

"I thank Your Majesty," he said. "And I apologize to the court for bringing my petition now, as some may see it out of order and not ripe for discussion. Except, I believe my province can't wait months before new petitions are given their fair due in session."

Alindale looked across the room to Bernold, who glowered at Lord Fauman, his darkened face hidden from Her Majesty's view by the pillar. His right leg bounced irritably while he sat with his elbows against knees and hands clasped together in front of him.

Urwald, Alindale guessed, knowing the troubled province had been the first minister's greatest burden since before his father had fallen ill.

"The Province of Siodina is facing a crisis," Lord Fauman continued. "Our westward border with Urwald is in near lawlessness. Township mayors have requested I levee soldiers to protect their crops, livestock, and even their lives. I've turned to the various Knight Brotherhoods of Siodina, and they tell me they need more men and demand for more food and provisions."

That's because using the Knight Brotherhoods as cheap peacekeepers is futile! Alindale leaned against his arm propped up on the chair's arm and rubbed the side of his temple. *They'll never have the resources to meet the demand.*

Lord Fauman turned and addressed the courtiers. "Every week, there are more reports of crop looting and banditry. Every week, groups of ragged peasants fill into our towns and demand food and shelter. Our magistrates' dockets never seem to empty, and Siodina merchants fear using the roads."

Still sounds like problems for the province governor to deal with. Alindale squirmed in his seat, irritated that he had rushed to hear *this,* irritated he had left his father, and irritated because he knew where this was going. *Get to the petition already.*

"Just a few weeks ago, there was a riot in Silkhaven!" Lord Fauman shouted. "By the people of Silkhaven themselves!"

Alindale sat up again.

"Dozens were killed and nearly an entire ward was burned down," Lord Fauman described, unabated by the ladies' gasps or the lords' grumbling to each other. "The provinces neighboring Urwald can no longer wait and harbor the fleeing Urwald peasantry. Therefore"—he turned to Her Majesty and bowed—"I petition the throne to immediately act to appoint a new province governor to Urwald, who will restore order to the province."

"Here! Here!" an agreeing lord from the stands shouted, followed by applauds.

Alindale didn't join them.

Across the room, he noticed Lord Vanni shaking his head.

His mother raised her fan to silence the courtiers. "The crown calls First Minister Vanni to hear when such action can be taken."

Alindale looked up at his mother in disbelief. *You know what has to happen! Father must come back and appoint a new governor! This is pointless theater.*

He gripped the arms of his chair with the urge to storm out, but then he remembered all those watchful eyes, and the fear stopped him.

Bernold straightened his clothes before stepping back in front of Her Majesty, trying to smooth out the wrinkles in his coat from leaning forward while sitting. "Forgive me, Your Majesty," Bernold said gruffly, "but what exactly do you wish to hear? I'm afraid this surprise proceeding has me a little out of sorts." He tried to put on a faint smile, but Alindale could tell he was stalling. So could his mother.

"Why, when can order be returned to Urwald?" His mother's dark eyes flashed down at Bernold. Her practiced smile never wavered, but she did tap her fan against the arm of her throne. "Were you not listening to Lord Fauman describe this horrid crisis?"

"With all due respect to Lord Fauman"—Bernold took a deep breath—"the crisis he described to the court, while admittedly are great burdens, do fall under *his* jurisdiction and duty to mediate as Lord Governor of Siodina—"

Several of the courtiers groaned and booed, but Bernold spoke over them.

"—because those are problems within Siodina!"

"Do you deny the crisis we face in Siodina doesn't spawn from the turmoil of Urwald?" Lord Fauman asked furiously.

Bernold rounded on him, his mustache twitching as he glared up at the taller man. "No matter the local concerns of the individual provinces, it is still the duty of each lord governor to meet them. Help from the kingdom can be petitioned before the throne and table during session, as proscribed in the Carta of Unification!"

"Does it also proscribe that the Table of Ministers do nothing and let a whole province tear itself apart if His Majesty isn't present?" Lord Fauman shouted in Bernold's face.

"You dare insult His Majesty?"

"I'm insulting you, you wastrel!"

"Silence!" Her Majesty shouted, slamming her fist on the hard stone of the king's throne beside her.

A dull ring cut through the shouting, drawing everyone's attention back to the royal dais.

The Sunrise throne was larger and taller than Alindale's mother's throne, carved from pure granite, with its base fixed to the royal dais. A rising, golden sun crowned the top of the throne. Five crystal wedges protruded out of it, like the rays, with the center being the longest, and its end rounded off to have a ruby placed within it.

Alindale thought he saw a ray of light running down the long, narrowing veins of crystal and silver wedged in the back of throne and into the seat, but he dismissed it as a trick of the light.

He returned his attention back to his mother, who was rubbing her hand and degradingly glaring at the two lords before her.

"Bickering before royal presence?" she chastised. "People are dying in our kingdom, and we demand action."

"Yes, Your Majesty," Bernold agreed, humbly hanging his head.

"Apologies, Your Majesty," Lord Fauman added, hanging his head, as well.

"First Minister"—her practiced mask returned as she lightly fanned herself—"we wish for this to be the first matter that the table entertains tomorrow. Can we have your assurance that a solution will be found to this crisis?"

Bernold sighed, defeated. "I can assure Your Majesty that the Table of Ministers are doing everything we can to support the isolated magistrates and townships in Urwald—"

Her Majesty closed her fan with a loud *snap*, quieting Bernold instantly.

"Can you, First Minister, guarantee to call this issue before the table for the appointment of a new province governor?"

No! Alindale wanted to shout.

Bernold shook his head. "I cannot, Your Majesty. The Carta requires His Majesty—"

"Do not hide behind the Carta, Lord Vanni," she interrupted, leaning back in her throne. "It is unbecoming as First Minister."

Just then, she snapped her head to the left as one of her ladies politely walked up and whispered something in her ear. Then she took a deep breath, and her smile slowly returned. She waved the lady away, and Alindale watched her retreat down the line of his mother's ladies, standing off to the left beside the royal dais. The lady spoke to a servant, who rushed along the back of the room and out the doors.

"We shall take a quick recess," Her Majesty announced, "and cool our heads so we can think more clearly about this issue. More guests have arrived. And, since I invited one of them, it would be rude of me to make her wait." Her laugh was a bit showy for Alindale, but the other courtiers laughed with her, anyway.

"Lord Vanni, Lord Fauman, would you both step off to the side, please?" She pointed to her left with her fan. "I want to take good look at this one."

What's the point of all this? Alindale asked himself.

He studied his mother carefully as he turned over thoughts in his head. Her practice mask gave away nothing. Even still, one possibility did occur to him. It was an answer to something else that she had done recently that perplexed him. He shook his head, dismissing the thought, finding no other explanation as to why she continued to demand Bernold commit to doing the impossible.

She wouldn't do that, he thought. *She wouldn't welcome Haemin back and install him as Province Governor. He killed Adam.*

Even so, a pit was growing in Alindale's gut that told him *something* was dreadfully wrong.

Chapter 3

Tory pressed her head against the coach's glass window, trying to get an up-close look of Dain Castle as the coach slowly climbed the switchback road up the hill.

"Sit up straight," Serina snapped. "I will not have you being a distraction because of a wrinkled dress."

Oh no, what a horrible thing that would be, Tory inwardly groaned.

The steep incline of the road forced her to lean forward in her backward facing seat. Otherwise, it threatened to slide her out.

Two coaches, bearing the Sunrise sigil on their doors, had arrived for them when they had docked, much to Serina's delight. She had immediately taken charge, ordering the servants and coachmen on how to load her trunks. Once she had been satisfied that none of her luggage would fall off, she had hurried Tory to the front coach and forced their servants to all ride together. To Tory's relief, Nina got to sit up by the coachman and didn't have to stand with the coachman in the back.

As they passed the lavish mansions and townhouses, Serina happily gushed over North End, excitedly describing it as a place only suited for the nobility and elite. She giddily pointed out the few shops they passed and boasted on how those craftsmen were so renowned that one required an invitation from them to even be let in.

She also took the opportunity to brag that she had such an invitation.

Again.

Serina only remembered they were going to court when they crossed the drawbridge and started up toward Dain Castle. Then began the repetitious instruction on how Tory was to behave.

"Only speak if spoken to," Serina went on. "Being seventeen, you are *far* past due to enter *real* society, but it is important you do not speak out of turn or look foolish in any way. Do you understand me?"

Not wanting to argue, Tory indifferently replied, "Yes, Serina."

She stared down at her lap. She wore a light green dress, with only two skirts. Serina found the dress lacking, of course, but there had been no time to change, and Tory figured Serina didn't care because it didn't outshine the regal velvet and white dress that she had finally chosen.

Tory kept mentally reminding herself not to mess with the dress's short sleeves or kick her legs out from under the skirts. Otherwise, Serina would scold her for not acting ladylike, as these mainlanders expected, regardless of how hot or uncomfortable she became.

"We are only presenting ourselves to Her Majesty today, but the court will be in session soon. That means many important people are here now. Do not talk with anyone unless I introduce them to you, understand?"

"Yes, Serina." Tory had a thought and glanced up. "What if they introduce themselves to me?"

Serina gave her a blank look, as if she were stupid. "While I do not know why anyone would, just be as sweet and courteous as you can be. But *no* conversations. If a lady introduces herself to you, talk about her hair or her dress." Serina's expression changed, and her tone became serious. "If a lord, or any man, for that matter, tries to talk with you, however, just smile and excuse yourself the first chance you get and come find me. Understand?"

Tory swallowed then nodded. "Yes, Serina."

Serina reached down and surprised her by squeezing her hand tightly. "No matter who it is, even if someone claims to be a lord, no matter how important he claims to be, or if you find him charming, you must not carry on a conversation with them."

Tory was shocked from feeling of such a sisterhood bond from her. It was as if Serina was trying to look after her for once.

She squeezed her sister's hand back and smiled. "I won't."

"Good." Serina nodded, let go of her hand, and then sat back straight. "You are not experienced enough to talk with men yet. And I cannot have you become a gossip item while I am here." She leisurely looked out the window, glancing upward toward the castle. She pursed her lips and gave a narrowed-eye glance at the coachman's box, clearly becoming impatient at his speed.

Tory's smile slipped off her face, and she clasped her hands together to keep them from trying to rip out Serina's hair.

"No, of course not," she said, biting her bottom lip and staring back down at her lap. She would probably only mess up her hair and that would make Serina even more insufferable. "Wouldn't want them gossiping about anything else except you and Harris Fauman."

Serina sniffed disdainfully. "That's old news. Everyone knows we've been exchanging letters for over a year now."

"Over a year since his wife passed, too." She winced, instantly regretting saying that.

"Don't act like a prude to me, you little chit," Serina hissed. Tory could feel Serina's eyes boring into the top of her head. "Every unmarried twit was writing him condolences the moment they heard of his wife's passing. I knew him before he married, so who better to console him over his loss?"

"His mother, his father," she half-heartedly listed, "a friend not pursuing their personal ambition—*Umph*!"

Tory's breath caught as Serina seized her by the chin and made her look up at her fiery eyes.

"You think I'm the only one who pursues what they want, you scrawny twig? Everyone acts in their own interests. Do you think Father sent you with me because he wanted you to go off and see the world? Smarten up, Runt! He sent you with me, hoping that, with the match I'm making with Harry, other lords will see you as a good match for their sons.

"Everyone I introduce you to is going to have their own ambitions and interests. Jerro's not taking you daydreaming on his boats anymore. I am towing you along into the only world that matters. So, you can grow some ambition yourself, or I *will* lock you in the servants' quarters." Serina flicked her chin away and sat back, her eyes still fuming.

Tory rubbed her chin, certain if they weren't on their way to present themselves in court, Serina would have slapped her instead.

"If you're so proud of your ambition, why haven't tried to hook the prince?" she asked mockingly. She knew she should leave her sister alone, but Serina wasn't the only one who was mad. "He's unwed, and you've had *plenty* of time to write to him."

Serina's nostrils flared with rage, and her glare could melt iron. Tory glared back, but in her heart, she feared she might really strike her this time.

Jerro had told Tory not only had Serina and Harris been childhood friends, but Serina was infuriated that he hadn't married her the first time. For years, Serina had bounced from one suiter to the next but always broke their relationship before they could ask. She even instigated relationships just to break them off. That was until Harris's wife had died.

Serina surprised Tory yet again as her anger slowly cooled, and she even gave Tory a small smile.

"Good to see you aren't as meek as that useless maid of yours." Serina's smile slid away, and she became serious once again. "But do not press your luck too far, or I really shall have you locked in the servants' quarters. And don't waste my time talking about that useless dullard of a prince. He's not going anywhere." Serina looked out the window again. The edges of her lips curled in a small smile as she whispered, "Not like my Harry."

He's yours already, is he?

Tory figured she wasn't supposed to have heard that, but knowing her sister, this didn't surprise her. Whatever Serina wanted, she saw as hers. Everything else were things to play with, whether she wanted them or not. It was of small comfort that her vanity would accept no substitute, and Tory didn't have to worry about her setting her sights on being the next queen of New Hartland. It was well known that for the past month His Majesty was bedridden with sickness, and the prince was his only living male heir. Hardly worth referring to as a useless dullard, surely.

"Finally!" Serina excitedly looked about outside as the coach leveled off.

As a large shadow blocked out the Easterly Sun, Tory glanced out to see they were passing through a wide, arching gateway of stone.

Entering Dain Castle, the rocky road turned into cobble. Armored royal soldiers, with long halberds, flanked both sides of the carriage and marched beside it farther into the castle yard. Tory felt sorry for them in their armor. She couldn't imagine how unbearable the heat must be.

"Just goes to show how important I am," Serina mused, reveling in the reception. She glanced at Tory and shrugged. "You, too, dear."

Tory shook her head and looked out the other window.

The castle yard was filled with servants and groomsmen going about their tasks. Just in passing, she caught the livery of at least fifty different aristo families, along with royal servants. It finally dawned on her that Serina's talk wasn't an exaggeration.

The coach began to turn, and Serina's breath caught. The coach circled around a large fountain of white stone, filled with flowers.

Where does the water come from?

The coach then slowed to a halt and, a moment later, the door opened.

Serina took care with her skirts as she eagerly took the helping, gloved hand of the coachman and slowly climbed out. Tory followed and gasped, awestruck.

Dain Castle loomed over them, its towers easily reaching ten stories, with the main construction itself reaching twelve. No matter how far Tory craned her neck, she couldn't see their rooves.

"Tory!"

She jumped at her sister's low hiss and found Serina staring at her with narrowed eyes.

"Do not stare!" Serina chastised. "This shouldn't be anything new."

Tory gave a small nod and heard the other carriage with their servants and most of their luggage pull up. The two coachmen, who had been riding on the back of the carriage, were now jogging behind it, huffing and sweating profusely. It seemed they had to get off so the carriage could make it up the steep road.

"Ladies Syros!"

A line of male servants, wearing blue suits, trimmed with silver, and white gloves, marched down the steps toward them. They rushed by and began helping the coachmen unload their luggage.

The steps led up to a landing to the castle's great, golden double doors, and on the landing stood a tall, thin, older man in a black suit that had a velvet pattern traversing down his left breast. He wore white gloves, like the other servants, but in his left hand, he carried a tall, wooden scepter, the end capped with gleaming steal that clapped loudly against the stone steps as he walked down to them.

He made a deep bow once he was at the bottom of the steps. His wide sleeves flapped as he then extended his arms wide. His thin, graying eyebrows flickered in the light breeze.

"Her Majesty, Queen Avera Dain, welcomes you both to Dain Castle. I am Thomas Mel, royal steward and keeper of the castle. It is my greatest privilege to welcome such beautiful ladies to the royal capital." He then turned sharply and motioned toward the steps.

Serina took his meaning instantly and, picking up her skirts, began to ascend behind him. The steward turned as soon as she passed him and walked up the steps beside her, leaving Tory to follow along behind.

"Thank you, Steward," Serina told him. "I can hardly remember a more gracious welcome."

"It is an honor, Your Ladyship," Thomas respectfully replied. "Their Majesties expect nothing less."

When they reached the doors, Thomas struck the stone landing twice, and the doors began slowly opening inward. Tory found herself awestruck again. While the outside was gray, weatherworn stone, the inside was polished marble. Unlit golden candlesticks lined the walls, and velvet curtains hung beside each window that spilled in golden light from three stories to illuminate the grand foyer.

Thomas led them toward a large staircase that extended past the second floor, all the way up to the third. Blue carpet flowed down the steps, and its polished, wooden railings were smooth as silk. While taking it all in, Tory realized, with a castle this tall, it was probably full of stairs and instantly worried for her feet. She also realized that Thomas and Serina were going up the stairs without her, the tapping of the steward's scepter muffled by the carpet.

"Your rooms have all been prepared, Your Ladyship," Thomas assured. "We were also expecting your brother, Lord Jerro, to be with you. Will he be staying with us?"

"Lord Jerro is still shoring up his ship," Serina replied. "If Her Majesty asks, please assure her that he will present himself promptly as soon as he has seen to his crew."

"Yes, Your Ladyship."

Tory was several feet behind them, but the talk of rooms made her try to catch them. She tried to use the railing like a rope to pull herself up the stairs faster, but almost tripped when her shoe got caught in her skirt.

Fortunately, she caught herself and didn't hear anything rip. The near trip made her heart pound, and she winced, expecting to hear Serina yell down at her to be more careful. Yet, when she looked back up, Serina and the steward had continued without a glance back.

Well, that's typical.

"When can we expect to present ourselves to Her Majesty, Steward?" Serina asked as they got to the top of the stairs.

"Well, as you are aware, His Majesty is still stricken with a terrible illness." Thomas went on about how the castle was in grief and trepidation over the king's predicament. All the while, Serina nodded sympathetically, but Tory didn't believe it for an instant.

When she reached the top of the stairs, they were about to turn a corner, and she had to rush to catch up to them, just in time to hear Thomas finish.

"However, the duties of state must be tended to in His Majesty's absence."

"Of course," Serina agreed, fervently nodding. Tory was sure that was the first sincere thing she had said.

"Session will begin tomorrow. Her Majesty is tending court in His Majesty's place to settle certain affairs before then."

Serina's eyes lit up. "Her Majesty is tending court at this very moment?"

"Yes, Your Ladyship. I had planned on showing you to your rooms before arranging an audience with Her Majesty. However, if you wish, I can see if she will welcome you now if—"

"Oh, now!" Serina excitedly interrupted then immediately composed herself. "Pardon me, Steward, but we came prepared to be presented to Her Majesty, and it would not do to keep her waiting."

Thomas bowed. "As you wish, Your Ladyship. This way, if you please." His scepter clanged against the wood floor as he led the way.

Serina busied herself every step of the way, messing with her hair, adjusting her neckline to make sure some of her shoulders were exposed but not completely, checking her waistline, making sure nothing was on her skirts, and adjusting her jewelry.

Tory rolled her eyes at the display.

She noticed something, though, as they walked through the castle. They were all alone. Not a single servant, guard, or aristo had passed them since they had entered.

She walked closer to Serina and whispered, "Where is everyone?"

Serina's glare could have warped wood. "I told you to keep quiet," she hissed.

Tory bowed her head and, grimacing, moved back. Serina was fully engrossed with herself now, preparing for her grand moment. Tory might as well be a servant in her eyes.

She looked past the steward and finally spotted more people—two guards standing before wide double doors.

The guards' armor was more decorative than the soldiers' whom Tory had seen outside. The Sunrise seal, decorated in gold on their chests, gleamed off the sunlight streaming down from the slanted windows in the ceiling. Their helmets covered their entire faces, and gray plumes rose from the back to loom over the tops of their helmets. Even the shafts of their halberds glinted with gold ornament.

The hallway opened into a wide, gentle curve, bathed in sunlight, as the wall before them reached up to the level above and the wood floor changed to stone.

Thomas nodded to the guards, who nodded back.

"I will enter and inform Her Majesty that you are here," Thomas said. "When she is ready to receive you, I will announce you by striking my scepter, and then the guards will admit you." He raised his hand sharply and pointed at Serina. "I will announce you first, Your Ladyship, and then the younger. Do *not* enter the throne room until announced." He passed his blue eyes between them to make sure they understood. "And when you enter, you must first curtsy immediately upon crossing the threshold. Once you do, keep your head lowered and walk to the middle of the room. Upon reaching the Grand Sunrise seal, bow and wait to be acknowledged. Do *not* look up at Her Majesty until told to do so. You will also not be allowed to approach closer unless she wishes. Do *not* approach the royal presence without permission or step past the Grand Seal! The Sunrise Guard will restrain you and drag you from the royal presence if you do."

Serina appeared to be taking all the instructions in stride, but Tory's heart was beating faster and faster as she tried to keep all the steps and formalities in her head. The warning about the guards restraining her made mouth go dry, and she felt her knees start to shake.

Thomas gave her a reassuring smile. "Don't worry, Your Ladyship; the Sunrise Guard haven't tackled a lady in months."

Months!

When Thomas gave her another smile, she hoped he was joking. Glancing at the guards stationed at the door, though, and knowing the devotion her father's guards had for him and their safety, Tory could picture them tackling someone if they got out of line.

She suddenly pictured Serina taking one step too many and getting tackled. She almost laughed but managed to catch herself in time.

The steward must have taken her smile as assurance, as he gestured to the guard on the right. The guard opened the righthand door softly, just wide enough for the steward to slip in. Tory heard voices coming from inside, but the guard reclosed the door before she could make out what was being said.

Serina smoothed out the skirts of her dress and rhythmically breathed in and out, as if she was nervous, too. She noticed Tory watching her and gave her a warning look.

"Remember what I told you."

"Yes, Serina," Tory meekly replied, taking a step back. Since Serina would go in first, there was no need for her to stand so close.

The wait seemed to drag on. At first, she figured it must be a large room, considering the size of the castle, and Thomas was being diligent not to disturb Her Majesty while holding court. Then she thought they had been forgotten after a while. She could have sworn, by the shifting light, that the sun was going down.

CLANG!

The loud sound of metal against steel rang out so loudly that it made Tory jump. She barely had time to compose herself before both guards turned and opened the throne room doors.

"Presenting, Lady Serina Syros!" the steward's voice boomed, louder than Tory would have thought, from within.

Serina stepped through the doors and curtsied.

"Eldest daughter of Lord Guamalto Syros," the steward continued as Serina slowly walk into the room. "Lord of Blood Island and Lord Governor of the Syros Isles!"

Watching her sister walk in, Tory peered into the throne room. A rainbow of colors shined down from above and obscured much of her vision. She made out a line of silver-plated guards with gold caps aligned at the bottom of the dais. The steward stood off to the side, on one of the dais's lower steps.

Serina stopped and bowed, and Tory's breath caught again. With her view unobstructed, she caught sight of the royal thrones, illuminated by the wash of colors rather than obscured, as was the rest of the room. The empty throne, she surmised was His Majesty's, but her attention was instantly drawn to the occupied throne beside it. She could make out the gold glint from Her Majesty's crown and dark dress outlining her figure. And, while Tory couldn't see her face, she felt those eyes looking down and taking in the entire room from her perch. It was only then that she remembered she was not to look at the queen until granted permission and quickly looked away.

"The crown recognizes Lady Serina Syros of Blood Island and welcomes her to court." Her Majesty's voice echoed throughout the throne room, as clear as if she had been standing beside Tory when she had spoken.

"Thank you, Your Majesty," Serina called out, still bowed and head low. "It was an honor to receive your gracious invitation. I am humbly at whatever service Your Majesty requires."

Humbly? Tory snorted. As far as she knew, Serina hadn't been humble a day in her life.

"The crown accepts the lady's kind offer," Her Majesty said. "You may rise, Lady Syros, and look upon our royal personage. We wish to see if the stories of you are true."

Serina slowly straightened, and Tory was sure that she wasn't the picture of humble humility now. Her sister loved it when people fawned over her beauty. She was surprised Serina didn't twirl about so everyone could admire her from every angle.

"Lovely," Her Majesty said approvingly. "Very beautiful, indeed. We would be honored if you would join my ladies, Lady Syros."

"The honor would be all mine, Your Majesty." Serina curtsied and lowered her head again.

Oh, I'm sure it would be all yours. Tory bit her lip and told herself that she wasn't jealous but only annoyed at how obvious her sister was.

"Then, please, join my ladies, Lady Syros." Her Majesty gestured with something in her hand that Tory couldn't make out because she was too far away.

Serina curtsied once again then walked around the dais over to Her Majesty's left.

Three loud clangs rang out, startling Tory as she realized it was her turn. She felt her knees getting weak again.

"Presenting Lady Tory Syros!"

Tory couldn't move. She peered back into that large room, feeling sweat running down her back. A hundred worries ran through her mind as she pictured things going wrong—she could trip on her skirts again, she could talk out of turn, she could walk past her point and get tackled by the guards, she could look up when she wasn't supposed to, she wouldn't be able to speak when spoken to or, worse of all, she would just be told to stand in a corner somewhere.

The scraping of metal beside her brought Tory back to the present. She glanced to her left and saw one of the guards motioning with head, his helmet scraping against his shoulder plate. She swallowed and nodded.

Finally crossing the threshold, she curtsied and lowered her head, remembering what her sister had done. Then she slowly began to walk forward, keeping her head down and looking for the Grand Sunrise seal that the steward had mentioned.

"Second daughter of Lord Guamalto Syros, Lord of Blood Island and Lord Governor of the Syros Isles!"

As the steward listed her pedigree, Tory heard the throne room doors close behind her. She fought the urge to turn while also struggled to keep going. She could feel the eyes of everyone in the room upon her and didn't know what was worse: the fact that they were comparing her to her sister or that she didn't know how many people were actually watching her. It felt like hundreds.

The floor's white tile changed under feet to a bright blue, only to have a wedge of silver cut through it. Tory stopped in the center of the mosaic, the Grand seal, the Sunrise crest of the Dains, which encompassed the center of the room. The silver tiles of the depiction of the cliff were highlighted by gold tiles arrayed as the rays of a sun, with green tiles on either side of the cliff, symbolizing the land, and blue for the ocean.

"The crown recognizes Lady Tory Syros of Blood Island and welcomes her to court."

Tory breathed a sigh of relief that she had stopped where she needed to and wouldn't be tackled.

"Thank you—Uh!" Tory remembered she had to bow and hastily bowed as low as she dared in her dress and corset. "Thank you, Your—"

"Speak up, girl," Her Majesty commanded. "We understand that one's first time in the royal presence can be breathtaking, but you must project and enunciate clearly."

Tory cursed herself. "Yes, Your Majesty!" She winced when she heard her voice echo throughout the room and lowered her voice, so not to yell again. "For welcoming me . . ."

She suddenly found herself lost for words. Despite all her faults, Serina had impressed upon her the importance of this grant, but in all her time telling Tory not to speak, she had failed to mention what she should say when told *to* speak. Thinking of nothing better to say, Tory settled on repeating her sister's words.

"I am humbly at whatever—"

"Yes, yes," Her Majesty said, cutting in over her. "The crown thanks you for coming. May your first time at court be of great education for you. Please, join the other observers. This court has pressing business to tend to."

Tory knew a dismissal when she heard one. It raised another problem for her, though.

Where are the other observers?

She dared to glance to her left and saw many people sitting in rows of escalated wooden stands built among four great pillars, each with a guard, like those at the doors standing in front of them. Finding an open space, Tory shuffled out of the way and breathed a little easier, although still embarrassed, to be out from everyone's gaze.

"Now," Her Majesty said, "Lord Fauman, Lord Vanni, please return before me. We were discussing . . ."

While the court's attention returned its previous business, Tory maneuvered her way to an open seat, three levels up in the stands. She gravitated to a spot where most of the observers were ladies, and several appeared her age, likely here for their introduction to court, as well. They watched her from behind their feathered fans as she reached the open seat, close to the edge of the bench, and she could hear them whispering to each other.

She smoothed her skirts and sat, finally getting a good view, and her eyes were instantly drawn to Her Majesty.

Her dark hair was pulled back, partially braided and partially flowing behind her shoulders, kept out of her face by her golden crown. The light streaming down from the ceiling's stained-glass windows allowed Tory to see few wrinkles or age lines on her face. Her small smile appeared practiced, as she stared down her pointed nose at the two lords arguing over some famine in the mainland's interior.

There was a glint in her dark eyes to match the sparkle of her ruby, dangling earrings. She sat comfortably, even relaxed, on her throne in her dark green dress of silk, her skirts smoothed neatly, with her legs crossed as she tapped the end of her throne's armrest with her fan. The dress had a square neckline, revealing only her shoulders and loose sleeves.

To her left stood a line of ladies that now included Serina. They were all whispering to her, giggling and grinning behind their fans. Serina was clearly in her element. Fortunately, that meant she wasn't staring death at Tory from across the room.

"Enough!" Her Majesty slapped the end of her armrest with her fan then pointed it down at the shorter of the two lords, her small smile gone. From behind, he appeared stout and stocky and stood with a military bearing. "Lord Vanni, we are very displeased by this situation, but also very displeased that, as First Minister, you have allowed this issue to continue to this point."

Tory realized she had missed something, and Her Majesty's tone didn't bode well for Lord Vanni.

"Had this situation only just been brought to our attention, we would have left this matter to the table during session, but for it to be ignored for four months, since the Westerly Summer, we find that a gross miscarriage of duty."

"Your Majesty—"

Lord Vanni's attempt to protest was cut off with a flick of Her Majesty's fan. Then two Sunrise Guards stepped from around the dais, causing Lord Vanni to step back.

"I call for a vote of no confidence by the rest of the Table of Ministers against First Minister Lord Vanni and his removal from the table."

Gasps went up around her. In truth, Tory was more lost now than ever. While her mother had taken to educate her as a lady, to understand the proper forms of decorum and behavior, and her father some level of understanding of official duties, none had taught her the governing structure of the court.

As the ladies around her whispered back and forth behind their fans, and the lords milled about on the other side of the room, she sat with her hands in her lap, confused and too nervous to ask what was going on.

"Do we hear any objections?"

The room became silent as Her Majesty scanned the room. It seemed everyone was holding their breaths.

"I object!"

Another round of gasps went up as everyone's attention was drawn to the young man who Tory only now noticed had been sitting off on the far-right side of the dais in a separate seat. He looked a few years younger than her brother, Jerro. From the look of him, he didn't get enough sun, because his skin was pasty white. A sheen of sweat covered his forehead, and his black, ruffled hair needed a brush. His wrinkled clothes appeared to have been slept in. He could have been considered tall, if not for his stooped posture. Two guards in burgundy uniforms and curved swords—clearly unlike the rest of the guards in the room—stood behind the man.

"Who is he?"

Tory only realized she had asked her question out loud when a lady in front of her disbelievingly whispered back, "The prince!"

He's the prince? She raised an eyebrow. *He doesn't look it.*

Chapter 4

Alindale stared at his mother in disbelief. Inside, though, he was frantic. Her sudden call to remove Bernold out of session made him act without thinking, and now he struggled to calm his raging anxiety.

"*You* object, Prince Alindale?" his mother asked, her lips pressed in a tight, thin line while arching her eyebrows over a narrow-eyed stare. It was her warning look, hinting he was out of line. Alindale knew it well from observation, but this was his first time receiving it.

He glanced around. Everyone was looking at him. Those judging eyes, all waiting for him to make a fool out of himself and laugh afterward. They were probably laughing already.

He was the royal heir but knew he wasn't well-liked. He had known that since the day Adam, his younger brother whom he had abdicated to, had died defending Haemsville.

What should I do now? he thought. *Can I convince her this is wrong?*

Regardless, Alindale looked back at his mother, ignoring the onlookers the best he could. Part of him told him that he couldn't back down now.

"Yes, Your Majesty," he replied, "I object."

A flash of disappointment crossed his mother's face before her calm demeanor returned. She pointed with her fan to the center of the room, and Alindale understood.

Lord Fauman and Lord Vanni stepped aside to allow him to stand before his mother. He ran through what he wanted to say, bowed with a wince, and then waited.

"Her Majesty recognizes His Highness, Prince Alindale Dain," Thomas announced then struck his scepter against the tile, sending a sharp ring through the room.

Focus on your argument, Alindale told himself for courage. *Block everyone else out and focus on what you need to say.*

"Thank you, Your Majesty." He looked up and took a deep breath. His mother's stare made his mouth run dry. It took another deep breath to ease the tightness in his chest that threatened to suffocate him.

"Your Majesty, I . . ." Alindale swallowed. "I object because this isn't a good enough reason for finding nonconfidence in the first minister . . . and . . . respectfully, Your Majesty, you do not have the authority to call for such a motion."

Gasps went up around the room.

He glanced around, not daring to turn, but he saw enough. His mother's ladies chattered behind their fans and looked down at him with disapproval and disbelief. Lords to his right whispered among their groups, undoubtedly trying to form quick agreements among themselves should his mother call on them to take sides.

Lord Vanni and Lord Fauman, though, stood silently, trying their best not to let their reactions show, because Alindale's mother still recognized them. Nevertheless, Alindale could just make out drops of sweat running down Bernold's sun-weathered face.

"We will hear your explanations, Prince Alindale," his mother said coldly, pointing her fan threateningly at him. "But we warn you, test our patience, or if your objection proves frivolous, we will have you removed from this court! Do we make ourselves clear?"

Alindale nodded nervously. "Yes, Your Majesty."

His mother sat back in her throne and put her fan in her lap. "Proceed."

"Thank you, Your Majesty," he began. "And may I add that I meant no disrespect before. I meant to say Your Majesty doesn't have the authority *at this time* to—"

"We have given you permission to argue your objection, not repeat yourself!" she snapped. "We suggest you use this time wisely."

Alindale felt his legs weaken and remembered not to lock his knees and tried to relax. His body felt numb from all the tension. He shifted his weight from one leg to another but resisted the urge to roll his shoulders. Sweat rolled down his brow, and he cursed himself for not wearing something lighter.

"Your Majesty, First Minister Vanni's actions in responding to the famine and disease in Urwald Province have been thoughtful and justified in dealing with the province's ongoing situation. The province's problems started before the Westerly Summer when the province governor died. As Your Majesty is aware, by the Carta, only the king can name a replacement, and before any petitions could be heard, he was taken sick—"

"We know of His Majesty's ailment, Prince Alindale." His mother sounded annoyed, and Alindale could feel he wasn't gaining any ground. "All New Hartland prays for his recovery. Regardless, to say that a first minister's ineptness can be excused while his liege lies indisposed is not an excuse we will entertain."

"But, Your Majesty, without an appointment, First Minister Vanni and the table have had to divide any relief effort they could gather among numerous provincial lords, magistrates, and townships, which in turn have had no central leadership because—"

His mother waved her fan, and he sputtered his last few words. His thoughts had run ahead of him too quickly to articulate properly, and his final words had come out a gargled mess.

"Prince Alindale, for over a month, we have listened to this excuse." She talked down to him slowly, calmly, and condescendingly. Alindale knew his point was lost before she finished. "And we no longer accept it, because our subjects are suffering and spread their suffering to other provinces. Now, while we are hesitant to suggest this"—a few chuckles spread through the crowd—"and warn you again to not try our patience, move on or withdraw your objection altogether."

Alindale understood. She was giving him a way out and saving him from more humiliation.

But, if I do that, he thought, *I might as well have stayed quiet in the first place.*

"Yes, Your Majesty," he said, trying not to sound defeated. "My other point was that a first minister cannot be found and removed for nonconfidence unless the Table of Ministers is in session. And currently . . . they are not."

His mother stared down at him, dumbfounded. Her ladies stared at him, dumbfounded. The room became still. Alindale didn't hear a single snicker, whisper, or chuckle, like before. It was as if everyone were holding their breaths, waiting for his mother's reaction.

Then a wide smile crossed his mother's face, and she laughed loudly.

Everyone turned their dumbfounded stares to her and, as she continued to laugh and shake her head, their tension slowly fell away as they began to laugh with her.

Alindale watched the sorry display of everyone joining in on a joke that he didn't believe they understood.

It's not that funny, he thought sourly.

His mother waved her fan, and the laughter slowly stopped.

"Prince Alindale, your other argument is we made our motion too early? By a *day*?"

He had to admit the point did seem . . . pointless. Rather ridiculous, really. Since she wouldn't entertain reasons based on the circumstances of the plight of Urwald Province and Bernold's actions, a point of order did seem trivial. However, he didn't see a reason to withdraw his objection since he had come this far.

"Yes, Your Majesty," he replied.

The whispers and chuckles came from the crowd again. His mother's ladies watched him gleefully, undoubtedly from the quips they were telling each other behind their fans. As for his mother, she simply smiled down at him and fanned herself with gentle, smooth flicks of her wrist.

"Your point is noted, Prince Alindale, and the crown accepts it."

The room fell silent. Everyone gazed up at her in either astonishment or in disbelief.

Alindale was stunned, too. *You do?*

"But the crown will not withdraw its motion. We place our motion on hold, to be the first order of new policy for the session on the morrow." She rose, and everyone who was sitting did likewise. "I call this court adjourned until then."

"This court is adjourned!" Thomas announced, striking his scepter three times on the floor. "All bow to Her Majesty, Queen Avera Dain."

Alindale stepped aside, with Lord Vanni and Lord Fauman, and bowed with everyone else as his mother walked down the dais. She passed by him in a brush of skirts without saying a word, followed by her ladies.

His jubilation had turned sour. The motion would be brought again and, after that, he was sure who she would make first minister.

~~~

"She's going to make Haemin first minister!" Alindale shouted angrily, leaning against an unlit fireplace's brick mantelpiece. He had guessed that was what his mother was planning and was surer now after thinking it over for a few hours.

"With all due respect, My Prince," Bernold said, stroking one of the thick points of his well-oiled mustache, "that is a stretched assumption." He lounged off to the side in one of the sitting room's cushioned armchairs with his arming sword hanging off its back. He had spent more time in thought than contributing to forming a plan against the motion to have him removed. "Lord Haemin is still disgraced," he continued. "And, without his city lordship, he isn't a qualified candidate for First Minister."

"She welcomed him to court!" Alindale snapped. It turned his stomach thinking about it. "Remember what she said? *We have* missed *you!*" He balled his right hand into a fist and slammed it against the brick.

And instantly regretted it.

"Certainly not the welcome expected for a disgraced province aristo," Julian Renald agreed. Alindale's brother-in-law gazed out the window, swirling the wine in his glass. A tall man of middle years, candlelight reflected off his sandy-brown hair and the gold embroidery on his red silk coat doublet.

"I must concur with Alindale," Julian continued, motioning down at him with his wine glass. "Given the aristos staying at the castle now, Haemin's recent activities, and his inconspicuous absence at court today, I'm sorry, Bernold, but your replacement has already been decided. As is mine." Julian set his jaw and drank his wine.

"Yours?" Bernold asked, frowning in confusion. He twisted in his chair, attempting to look up at Julian standing over him. "That's *impossible*. The Ministry of Treasure would fall apart without you."

Julian was one of the richest men in New Hartland, from his family's lucrative trade that flowed through his province's seat—Tradon. Three
~~~

years ago, Alindale's father had appointed him Minister of Treasure, and he had rebuilt the entire ministry from its foundations to the top.

Some rumored Alindale's sister had married him for his wealth. Some speculated it was a power play because she became Lady Governor of her husband's former province after his ministry appointment. Alindale knew better. Amanda wasn't petty for wealth or power.

"It's not impossible, I assure you." Julian chuckled then finished his wine. He walked across the landing and followed its railing down a few steps to join them. "If we assume Her Majesty plans on making Haemin First Minister, then we can also assume Haemin will want the other ministers to accept and follow his recommendations. And, while he has been conversing with most of the ministers since his arrival, he hasn't approached me. Which leads me to conclude, if he *does* become First Minister, he's likely to replace me." Julian set his empty wine glass on the lampstand by Bernold's chair and looked at each person in the room in turn, clearly waiting for everyone to digest his words.

Bernold sat back and returned to stroking his mustache in thought.

Alindale was convinced. Haemin would want to remove the husband of the woman whose brother whom he was responsible for killing from the table. It made sense. Especially with the confidence and skills Julian had.

If I only had a tenth of such confidence . . .

He frowned, shoving such envious thoughts away.

He had never grown close to his brother-in-law, but Alindale wasn't particularly close with anyone.

"I suppose you also have an idea of who he would replace you with?" Alindale asked.

"Whom better than his friend, Lord Rudmund Fauman," Julian replied with a shrug.

"Of course!" Bernold barked with the spark of realization in his eyes. "What a conspiracy!"

Alindale saw it, too. The Faumans were wealthy but had also sheltered Haemin after he had been disgraced. Then Lord Fauman had brought up the plight of his province to be used by his mother as cause to remove Bernold. It all made sense.

"But, if this is Her Majesty's intention—to reshape the Table of Ministers—she is doing so with great risk of displeasing His Majesty when he recovers," Bernold said from over his shoulder to Julian. "Her emergency authority will be over then."

Julian tensed, and a serious look crossed his face. He flickered a glance over to a corner of the room, behind Alindale.

"*If* His Majesty recovers," came a craggily voice from behind Alindale.

A chill ran down his spine, and the room grew quiet.

If mother is reorganizing the table, then she's expecting father to . . .

He shook his head, refusing to complete that thought.

"No!" he said stubbornly and spun toward the man sitting in an armchair in the corner. "Mother would never plan . . . or even want such a thing!"

Amadus the Immortal sat slouched with his elbows propped on the armrests and his fingers laced together. The wide sleeves of his gray tunic hung off his limbs. His face was casted in shadow by the lamp beside his chair. Strands of his long, gray hair moved while he surveyed the faces of his guests.

"My, how innocent you are," Amadus commented, leaning forward. He was pale from lack of sun. He squinted his left eye at them, adjusting to the light. He had deep, aging lines running down the inside of his face, around his cheeks, making them almost hollow. His shockingly white beard and gray hair were wild and unkempt. "You've all been living in a world of set rules and laws for so long that you can't even consider the darker lengths people will go." Amadus chuckled and shook his head. "What a time."

Alindale wasn't sure if he was amused or disappointed. Amadus was a living legend. He had grown up on rumors of how Amadus had gained immortality, each one wilder than the other. However, all agreed it stemmed from Téionaropi magic.

Amadus had tutored Alindale when he had been younger, with his father's permission. Alindale had spent months away from Dain Castle, reading the books in his mansion. Then his mother had objections and ended Amadus's tutoring days.

Alindale had come, hoping Amadus would offer some insight, an irrefutable winning argument to take back to his mother tomorrow. He had yet to offer anything, and Alindale's hope was quickly diminishing with the conversation's current direction.

"His Majesty's death is too dark to laugh at, Amadus," Bernold said disapprovingly.

"Is it?" Amadus surprisingly replied. "Everyone dies." He paused. "Well . . . mostly everyone. And the death of a monarch can easily be expected as anyone else's. To say it's dark to plan for the eventuality is the same as saying it's dark to plan what to eat tomorrow." A distant look grew in his hazel eyes, and his brow furled. "Planning to *cause* a monarch's death, now *that* would be dark."

The room fell deathly silent again. Alindale was uncertain whether Amadus was merely making conversation, following his line of reason, or making an actual insinuation.

"Assassination!" Bernold hissed. His face turned red, and his thick, black eyebrows quivered. "Are you making jokes about assassination?"

Amadus stared back a Bernold, unmoved and uncaring about the man's disapproval.

It gave Alindale pause, though, when he failed to admit he was joking. Amadus's insinuation was inconceivable to him. His view of the aristos at court shook at the thought of one of them attempting to murder his father for their own ends.

"You're not seriously suggesting someone would go that far?" Alindale asked. "Right, Amadus? There hasn't been an assassination of a king in"—he searched his memory of New Hartland's history—"over two hundred years."

"King Richman Dain the First," Julian concurred.

"That would be interesting," Amadus mused, getting out of his chair and slowly stretching. Alindale winced from the several loud pops coming from his back. It appeared immortality came with its downsides. Despite being ancient, he stood straight, though, just a little shorter than Alindale, without a hint of slouching. "The third Dain to bear the Richman name follows in the path of the first. Someone might be trying to be poetic."

"I doubt it," Julian said with an impassive expression.

"Oh?" Amadus raised an eyebrow at him.

"Assassinations must happen fast before anyone but the conspirators can act," Julian explained. "His Majesty grew sick. He complained about pains in his side for weeks before he couldn't attend court and was sequestered to his chambers. It is more logical that His Majesty's illness is grave, and Her Majesty is taking this opportunity to shape matters of state the way she wants."

Bernold turned in his chair and looked up perplexedly at Julian. "Just a moment ago, you were suggesting there was a plot to kill His Majesty. Now you're saying there isn't? You should know better than to throw around wild accusations, Lord Renald, no matter what company you're in."

"I only suggested there were those planning for His Majesty not to recover," Julian replied, giving Bernold a bemused look.

Then he turned his attention to Amadus. "You turned the talk to assassination."

Amadus passed a gaze at his guests before giving them a small smile. "Forgive me. I just had to see your reactions to such an idea." He then folded his arms behind his back and walked slowly toward the opposite side of the room.

Alindale had always felt there was more to Amadus than he ever showed. Most around the castle considered Amadus a hermit, without a family or friend, spending his days wallowing in his manor, miles away from Daincliff. After years of tutelage, Alindale couldn't see Amadus wallowing in anything.

"Speaking as the only man alive to have known a time when such things were common"—Amadus snickered—"I had to see how men living such relatively peaceful, law-abiding lives reacted to the idea." He stopped by a small, red wood writing desk in the other corner and began looking through some scattered papers.

"You suspected we could be a part of such conspiracy?" Bernold asked, offended.

Amadus gave them a surprised look from over his shoulder. "One should suspect everyone when talking assassination. But no matter the problem, you should always do . . . what?" He raised any eyebrow at Alindale, his prompt flickering a memory alive in Alindale's mind.

"Consider every possibility so you don't overlook anything," Alindale recited.

"Well done, Your Highness." Amadus gave him a proud nod of approval, which made Alindale's chest swell, remembering the feeling of accomplishment when getting his lessons right. "Especially since you would benefit the most from the passing of your father. Inheriting the throne is a better solution to your problems than convincing your mother."

Alindale suddenly felt cold and shuddered. *If Father . . . If Father dies, then . . . I . . . I become . . .*

He couldn't complete the thought. He *refused*. His breathing quickened, and he started to pant. He forced his eyes shut and clenched his fists, trying to keep his composure. However, a part of him flailed in full panic, thinking about all those mocking aristos and hearing them in court day after day. They would come to overwhelm him with their demands and insufferable attitudes. And worst of all, his father would be gone.

"*No!*" he shouted. "My father is not going to die. He is going to get better and return to court. I don't want to hear otherwise!"

The other men watched him. Bernold hung his head, and Julien casually glanced off into the corner, but Amadus held his gaze.

"I meant no disrespect, Alindale," Amadus assured him. "I only meant to advise you." He patted him on the arm then looked him up and down. "I wish you'd have taken my instructions to keep fit and practice your argumentation, as well as remembering my proverbs, though."

Alindale consciously sucked his gut in. He wasn't going fat. He was just a little flabby from sitting, was all.

He clasped his hands behind his back to stop himself from adjusting his belt. He had changed into a blue doublet and shirt after sweating so much in court, but the garments weren't flattering on him.

"*Bah!*" Bernold barked. "Never mind him, Alindale. Nothing wrong with having a good gut." He slapped his own belly. Although being plump, it didn't jiggle, because Bernold was more muscular than he appeared. "A little exercise routine would tone the edges up; that's what I say. You'd be the most presentable prince I've ever seen."

Alindale frowned and shuffled his feet. He had never been as athletic as others had expected or wanted from their prince. He never took to the martial arts, the sword, or horseback riding. He preferred the indoors and comfortable surroundings.

"Wellness advice aside," Julian interjected, much to Alindale's relief, "we are still left with our original problem—defeating Her Majesty's motion tomorrow. I don't see any way to stop it."

He looked to Amadus. "Have you devised one?"

Amadus shook his head, which made his long hair swing about his face. "There is no way to defeat the motion."

Alindale was stunned by how simple Amadus conceded defeat and only realized, after a moment, that his mouth was hanging open.

"I sent invitations to five other ministers," Amadus continued, "and six other aristos who might know Avera's mind. Yet, only you three came this evening." He shook his head again. "Since only you, Alindale, objected to the motion today, none will object tomorrow. The table will vote and, without the opportunity to see where the other ministers stand, it is more likely you will be held in no confidence, Bernold."

Bernold slapped the armrests of his chair and sat back with a scowl on his face. Julian leaned on the third armchair with that passive expression on his face, as if he had resigned himself to the outcome and didn't care. Alindale looked at them, defeated, and couldn't accept it.

That's it? Haemin becomes First Minister, as easy as a wave of the hand, and everyone forgets what he did?

"What if you came to court tomorrow, Amadus?" Alindale asked desperately. "You could speak with the other ministers before session is called."

Amadus gave him a flat look. "Alindale, that is desperate, even for you. I have not been summoned. And, without a royal summons, I dare not show myself at court or have myself seen trying to influence ministers before they go into session."

By law, Amadus was forbidden from court or participation in official business of the kingdom, under penalty of banishment. Alindale knew it was the reason he invited people to see him rather than going to them, but something had to be done.

"That's it, then," Bernold sighed out, as if he was resigned to his fate. "Four and a half years, I have served, preserving the stability of the kingdom, making sure we didn't go to war with the Téionaropi after Haemin's debacle. Now I'll be replaced by that very man while Richman's sick in bed."

"And I'm afraid there're no procedures or stroke of luck that will delay it this time," Julian added.

Alindale's eyes went wide as a thought suddenly sprang to mind. "What if there was a way that might prevent Lord Haemin from taking your place?"

This brought light back to Bernold's eyes, and Amadus drew closer, clearly interested to here Alindale's idea. Julian's brow furled, though, in confusion.

"Before a lord is appointed as First Minister, by tradition, the other lords at court are allowed to voice their concerns and are given the opportunity to oppose the appointment," he explained, hoping they saw the chance there. They could argue together that Haemin was a bad choice because of his past actions, even if his mother removed Bernold.

Instead, the light of hope left Bernold, and Amadus shook his head dismissively.

"Alindale," Julian sighed out, "that's not a procedure; that's a curtesy. One not even provided for by law. I can't even recall an instance when concerns *were* voiced over the appointment of a new first minister." He turned to Amadus, who was still looking glumly at Alindale.

"When the Carta was ratified," Amadus explained, "the main concern of the nobility about the Table of Ministers was that the king would appoint and remove ministers at will. As a show of faith, a clause was added that ministers could only be removed for cause, to be found to have no confidence in their duties, and the other ministers must vote to affirm the finding. You're correct, Julian; there is no provision allowing for an objection to the appointment of a minister. The curtesy was invented by previous kings to judge who, if anyone, will openly oppose his appointees once they become ministers."

Alindale ground his teeth together and grimaced. *We can't just give up! Just accept that's it!*

"But this is different!" he shouted. "Mother is changing the ministers behind Father's back. She only has *emergency* powers! Someone should remind everyone that Father said he *never* wanted to see Haemin again, or at least at court. Surely someone would get angry or fear what would happen when his health returns . . . wouldn't they?" He gave them each a desperate look.

Even his epiphanies seemed useless, and Bernold's and Julian's doubtful faces weren't encouraging. Amadus, however, ran his fingers through his tangled beard with a thoughtful look on his face.

"To convince Avera against appointing Haemin or turning the court against her would both be extremely risky acts," he said. "To attempt either one would require tact so not to anger her or inspire the court to object too loudly. The argument must be precise yet effective." Amadus gave Alindale a long look then turned to Julian. "Could you do it, Julian?"

Alindale slumped. While he doubted he could pull off such a feat, it still pained him to be dismissed so openly.

It was my idea.

"It would be difficult," Julian replied, folding his arm, "and it would depend on a few other things." He thought for a moment then glanced at Alindale before saying, "I can try."

Alindale smiled. After all the dead ends, finally one idea might stand a chance. And it was his!

"Still"—Bernold rose from his chair with a groan. Being shorter than the rest of them, at full height, he only reached Julian's shoulders—"with nothing to stop Her Majesty's motion tomorrow, I might as well instruct my retainers to pack my things."

"Nonsense, Lord Vanni," Amadus interjected. "While Alindale's optimism might be misplaced, should His Majesty recover—and it would be best that he does—you must be there to explain your side of your removal. His Majesty won't be pleased to find Haemin elevated to such an appointment in his absence, and that should be all the cause he needs to remove him."

Bernold appeared satisfied with that and nodded.

"I'll be leaving soon after tomorrow," Julian said with a serious look on his face.

"I don't think there is any real need for you to return to Tradon so quickly, Julian," Amadus casually replied.

Julian's serious expression remained. "If all doesn't go well tomorrow, and I'm removed after opposing Her Majesty, then it will be best if I return to Tradon. It could be . . . unpleasant if I stay. Besides, Amanda has been insistent I return more, and I have spent far too much time away from my children."

"As you wish," Amadus accepted.

Alindale began to feel left out again. "I should do something."

"No," Amadus quickly replied.

"That won't be necessary," Julian added.

"But—"

Bernold took Alindale by the shoulder. "You needn't risk yourself in such a gamble as this. And you mustn't pit yourself against your mother.

No good will come of members of the royal family being at odds with each other."

"He's right," Amadus agreed. "After making your objection today, you must not personally oppose your mother in session tomorrow. Allow your vassals to fight your cause for you. Instead, you should attend early and try to mingle with the attendees. The other ministers especially. You need more connections in higher places."

"But . . ." Alindale's objection died in his mouth. It was clear they weren't going to let him lead. His shoulders sagged, and he sighed in agreement.

"Very well." Amadus clasped his hands behind his back and looked at them in turn. "Thank you all for coming. I wish you well tomorrow."

"We need all the well wishes we can get," Bernold mumbled.

That brought a small smile to Alindale's face, but he still felt downhearted. *It would be nice to be chosen to take the lead . . . for once.*

Chapter 5

12th of Petrarium, 1109 N.F. (e.y.)

Kalleb Kane hung on the edge of restless sleep. He thought the pattering of rain on the roof and against the windowpanes would help him relax, like so many other times back on the penal farm, but the waiting kept him on edge.

"Wake up!"

He jerked forward from someone slapping his foot, nearly spilling out of the chair that he had been leaning back against the wall, but he caught himself against the table. His wide-brimmed, leather hat, however, fell off his face and rolled around on the floor.

"Hearing's in ten minutes," Smit growled. "Stick your arms up."

Irritated, Kalleb frowned up at the narrow-eyed sergeant at arms. His burgundy Storm Cavalry uniform jacket was buttoned all way up this time, and his black trousers were brushed clean, trying to look nice in front of the officers. His golden lance pin glinted on his coat collar. He tapped the chain of the iron manacles against the saber hanging from his hip.

Seriously! Kalleb grimaced at the manacles but bit his tongue. He was a convicted deserter. It had taken him two years to come to terms with that. Still, he couldn't see the reason to be in irons.

He glanced down at his hat by their feet. "May I pick up my hat first?"

Smit snorted at the wrinkled, water-stained hat then kicked it away. "Hold up your wrists," he ordered, snapping open the manacles with a creak.

Kalleb gritted his teeth but kept his temper. *That* had taken him a year to learn. A bad temper only resulted in harder punishments, and harsh punishments where easy to find in Calore Province where days of over a hundred-degree heat could span weeks during the summers.

He held his arms up, his wrists together. A grunt escaped him as the heavy iron bit into them tightly as they were locked.

"On your feet," Smit ordered, dragging Kalleb by the chain without waiting for him to obey.

Kalleb's boots scraped across the floorboards, and he jostled to keep his balance. The manacle's heavy chains dragged his arms down and rattled loudly in the small room.

Smit took him by the arm, leading him out into the corridor. Two lancers waited in the hallway, taking positions in front and behind him as Smit led them toward the Drumhead.

The corridor was strangely silent. Even though a storm was rolling through outside, the inside of Storm Hall, the central command of the Storm Cavalry, was eerily quiet. Kalleb had expected it to be bustling with officers and their staff, yet the only thing he heard climbing the stairs to the fourth floor was the heavy footsteps of the lancers, beating like drums, leading him to the gallows.

The worst they can do is send me back to the penal farm, he assured himself. After having faced court-martial once, a parole hearing felt small in comparison.

Two more lancers waited for them on the fourth floor, standing guard by the double doors.

Smit marched him in front of them and said, "Sergeant at Arms bringing deserter, Kalleb Kane, before the brigadiers, as ordered."

Couldn't just say convict, could you, you prick?

Both lancers on guard looked at him as if he was horse manure on their boots. Then one stepped aside and opened a door, while the other remained at attention.

The Drumhead was a combination of a magistrate court and military display room. The walls were lined with old, tattered banners, most of which Kalleb couldn't place.

Not as big a crowd as last time, he noted.

The back seats of the room were filled with officers, marked by the knotted cords wrapped around the right shoulder of their uniforms, sitting together in order of rank.

For the hundredth time, Kalleb wished they had allowed him to clean and dress for the hearing. His shaggy hair hung over his ears, and his months-old beard gave him an unwashed look compared to the clean-shaven cavalrymen around him. The bristly line of hair covering his mouth gave him the appearance of one who had turned his back on his heritage compared to the older officers with their trimmed mustaches. He looked like a poor rice farmer who didn't have another set of clothes other than his dirt-stained shirt and knee-worn trousers.

He walked down the aisle with his head up so as not to look ashamed while also evenly because the right heel of his scuffed, wrinkled boots was more worn down than his left.

Smit led him to a chair in the center of the room and sat him down with a heavy *clink* from his manacle chains. A map of New Harland hung in the front of the room with the Storm banner standing on one side and the Sunrise banner on the other. In front of Kalleb was a long table with five chairs, each with a horse rearing before a lightning bolt engraved on their backs.

Smit finally left, taking the lancers with him, to stand against the wall. "Attention!"

Old instincts kicked in, and Kalleb leapt to his feet with the rest of the room. However, he almost stumbled when he tried to stomp his uneven heels together. His manacle chain rattled as he steadied himself and stood straight with his chest stuck out and chin raised.

The five brigadiers of the Storm Cavalry entered the room with little pomp, their sabers slapping against their legs. They were older, hard men. Save for the brigadier marshal in the center, the four other brigadiers wore the same dress uniform, except gold cords ornamented both of their shoulders and medals of rearing horse crossed with a thunderbolt hung on their right breast.

Kalleb's heart ached at seeing his uncle, Gerald, the second brigadier in line. Seeing him reminded Kalleb of his pa. His beard was thicker, and his hair grayer than the last time he had seen him. His face had more aging lines—wrinkles around the eyes and creases running across his forehead, as if he had been grimacing for years. Gerald winced at the manacles on Kalleb's wrists.

The brigadier marshal slammed a heavy book, bound in wood and iron, on the table. The book's heavy *ping* nearly threw Kalleb out of attention.

The commander of the Storm Cavalry was an old man, over sixty, but with the body of man still in his fifties, save for his white hair. His beard fanned out over his chest, and a tabard, depicting the Storm banner, he wore over his white dress uniform. His hard, emerald eyes looked at Kalleb with the same disgusted contempt that Smit and the other lancers had given him.

Kalleb groaned. *Grandpa Kane still looks to be the same mean bastard.*

The people of Kanestown jokingly nicknamed the brigadier marshal *Grandpa Kane* because he was the longest-serving brigadier marshal in the history of the Storm Cavalry. Except, for Kalleb, the old man *was* his grandpa.

"Sit!" Grandpa Kane barked with a voice like gravel.

The room filled with the scrapes of wood against wood as everyone took their seats, and Kalleb moved to join them.

"Not you!" Grandpa Kane pointed at him.

Then, why give me a chair?

He begrudgingly went back to attention in front of the meaningless chair behind him as the old man sat.

Once seated, Grandpa Kane unlocked the book's three iron clasps then tossed its wooden cover back carelessly. Then he gently eased the first, yellow-stained pages with his rough, callused fingers, showing faded ink on the first pages then becoming readable the further he went.

"Kalleb Kane," he grumbled, "former Lieutenant of the Eighth Lancer Company, Squadron Three, this hearing is called to order to decide whether you shall be granted parole." He sounded bored, as if this was wasting his time. "If denied, you shall be returned to Calore to serve the remainder of your twenty-year sentence."

Something's not right.

Grandpa Kane turned to his right. "What say you, Brigadiers?"

"Denied," the brigadier on the far left answered.

"Denied," the brigadier beside him followed.

What? Kalleb's eyes went wide.

His uncle was about to speak, but Kalleb couldn't keep quiet.

"Don't I get to *speak*?" he yelled. He tried to raise his hand but forgot about the manacles, and so they crashed together.

Grandpa Kane slammed his fist on the table. "You will remain silent! And at attention!"

Kalleb exhaled sharply through his nose, clenching his fists and teeth tightly, holding back five years of restrained anger. The hairs on the back of his neck stood up from the sound of steel sliding against leather. He glanced out of the corner of his eye and saw Smit with the first inches of saber out of his scabbard.

He looked at each brigadier in turn, and only cold eyes stared back at him, save for his uncle, who looked down at the table.

Begrudgingly, Kalleb returned to attention.

"Brigadier Gerald Kane," Grandpa Kane turned to Kalleb's uncle, "your vote?"

Gerald sat forward, leaning on his forearms while clasping his hands together. The room went silent as everyone waited.

"You won't have it," Gerald finally said.

Grandpa Kane blinked and raised an eyebrow. "What?"

Gerald sat back and folded his arms across his chest. "I will not sit by and let a lancer be dismissed without hearing him out first."

Grandpa Kane's face turned red. "Then vote to grant parole!"

"Why?" Uncle Gerald spat with just as much venom. "Just so you can deny it and that be it? Since when do Kanes not allow a man to speak his peace?" He glared at his fellow brigadiers and the people behind Kalleb before settling his challengingly eyes on Grandpa Kane.

Grandpa Kane drew himself up and gave Kalleb a sideways glance, his eyes burning. "Very well," he then grumbled. He leaned forward, his forearms resting against the open pages. "If we must go through with this, we might as well remind *everyone*"—he shot a sideways glance at Gerald— "why we're here in the first place."

He ran a finger along the open page. "Kalleb Kane, were you, or were you not, posted in Tradon in the year 1101?"

"I was," Kalleb replied.

"Did you leave your post on the second of Benjamine and ride to Haemsville?"

"I did."

"Did you have orders to do so?"

"Not from—"

"Yes or no!" Grandpa Kane's face was a thunderclap.

Stop riding me! Kalleb squeezed the manacle chain.

"Yes," he replied.

A murmur rolled across the room behind him. The brigadiers all sat up and shared confused looks.

Grandpa Kane snapped his head back to the book, furiously looking across the page. He ran his finger along the parchment so fast that Kalleb was surprised it didn't catch fire.

"By *whose* order?" Grandpa Kane demanded in frustration.

"His Highness, Prince Adam Dain," Kalleb proudly replied. "I answered his call for any able-bodied men-at-arms to join him in the defense of Haemsville." A lump formed in his throat from the brief memory of that day. "As my pa did."

"Don't mock us!" Grandpa Kane roared, slapping the table again. The veins on the side of his head bulged, his face darkened. "Name the *officer* of the Storm Cavalry who granted you leave to answer the call of a fool-headed, glory-seeking *child*?"

"You have no right to speak of Prince Adam like that!" he shouted back, ignoring the concerned looks of the other brigadiers. He glared at the old man, his own cheeks growing hot. "You will *not* insult the man my pa died defending!"

"Your pa was upholding his duty!" Grandpa Kane snapped back. "He was charged with the protection of the prince. Same as *you*"—he jutted his finger at him—"were a part of a company charged with the protection of the princess in Tradon. But the first duty of *every* Storm Cavalry officer is to the cavalry itself!"

Kalleb drew himself up, refusing to be shamed. "I have never abandoned that. I didn't abandon it when I went to Haemsville. I've kept it every day in the mud of the rice fields, cotton fields, wheat fields, and every other field I was worked in. I am a Kane!"

The brigadier on the far left threw his hands up. "This is getting us nowhere. I thought we were talking about his parole, *not* convicting him again."

"Brigadier Horus is right, Brigadier Marshal," Gerald agreed with a nod. "I request to ask a question of the convict."

Grandpa Kane snorted and waved his hand dismissively.

"Kalleb"—Gerald cleared his throat—"what would you do if given parole?"

Kalleb swallowed. He had been so caught up in arguing with his grandpa, caught up going over the same ground and accusation that he had rankled with for five years, that he had forgotten what he was really here for. He hung his head, trying to think. He had been going over what to say for over four months now, since he had heard they were giving him this hearing. Now words failed him.

"Well?" Grandpa Kane barked. "The brigadier asked you a question."

Kalleb peered through stray strands of hair to study the stern faces in front of him. *Doubt they'll care*, he told himself. *To Oblivion with it, anyway.*

He took a deep breath and threw his hair out of his face. "I have thought about it. Even though I honestly didn't think I'd get a hearing or have a hope of getting it."

The brigadiers all drew themselves up. Kalleb recognized their impatient looks. The stern, watchful eyes of superiors waiting for a chance to interrupt and demand a quick response. However, he didn't rush. If this was going to be his last say, he might as well say it all.

"At first," he continued, "all I thought about was just getting off that damn farm." He snickered and smirked, despite himself. "Never thought much about farming before I was sent there, but now I'm sure"—he looked down at his hands, at the dozens of different scars crossing his palms and fingers and multiple calluses, which made them look like brittle, wrinkled parchment—"I *hate* farming."

Someone grunted, and Grandpa Kane glared at whoever it was, keeping the room in nervous silence.

"But, in the past few days, I've grown to hate something more." Kalleb glared at his grandpa, grimacing at the anger still in his eyes. "I've been dragged from cell to cell, room to room, waiting for today. And everywhere I'm dragged, they yell, '*This is the deserter!*' And the people stop and spit and look at me like you do, like I'm shit to be washed out on the street!" He spat. His chin wobbled. He tried to draw a deep breath to calm down and speak plainly, but five years of boiling resentment twisted in his guts, and his breath came out ragged.

"You ask me what I want?" he yelled. "I want to come home! I want to be with my family again!" He wheezed and trembled, his arms shaking from gripping the manacle chains so tightly that they rattled. "But, if I can't be a lancer, and you hate me that damn much, I'd rather pick cotton until my hands crack and plant rice until I have feet rot for the next fifteen years than be paroled and you spit on me for the rest of my life!" He snickered again, feeling like a weight had been lifted from him. "You can even drag me through the streets on the way back, yelling, '*The deserter's leaving! Spit on the deserter one last time!*'" Kalleb threw his arm in the air and crashed the chains together in frustration. His breathing grew more ragged, his fire getting low.

"If anyone asks why I'm so special"—he gasped then took a few quick breaths—"you can say, '*There goes the Kane who went to war when he was told not to*'"—he swallowed, trying to get moisture back in his mouth—"'*and didn't get there in time to die with the rest.*'"

Kalleb suddenly felt tired, like those long days in the fields, hunched over all day as he walked down row after row, tilling, planting, fertilizing, and sowing.

I want to sit down.

The soles of his feet were burning, the balls of his feet felt like they were being bitten by the points of hundreds of small nails, but he remained standing.

A heavy air settled upon the room. A lancer to Kalleb's left shuffled his feet. A few of the brigadiers studied the table. Here and there, a cough broke the tense silence behind him. The air smelled stale and closed off.

"Does anyone else have a question?" Grandpa Kane asked lowly, passing a glance left then right to each brigadier.

They sat in silence. A couple shook their heads.

Grandpa Kane folded his hands over the book and asked, "Kalleb Kane, given the chance, would you disobey orders again?"

Kalleb opened his mouth to answer, but his quick response died on his lips. A simple *yes* didn't feel enough. Days in the beating suns had made him wonder if it had been worth it to begin with. Yet, he doubted he could have lived with the not trying to reach his pa.

"I would charge in whatever direction I'm ordered to, sir," he finally replied. "But a Kane always rides to family, even when told not to."

Grandpa Kane turned a few more crinkled, yellow pages before he slowly closed the book, his anger seemingly cooled. "Sergeant at Arms."

Smit stepped up and stamped his heels together at attention.

"Remove the convict," Grandpa Kane ordered, "while we discuss this further." Then he turned toward his grandson.

"Kalleb Kane, whatever we decide shall be final. You will be informed of our decision."

Smit clicked his feet again then took Kalleb by the arm.

Kalleb gave a weak nod to Gerald before he was turned and led back down the center aisle.

He tried not to make eye contact with any of the lancers. He felt a little silly, as if what he had really done was yell and complain like child in front of the adults, and now he felt a fool for doing so. Therefore, he tried to just face forward. However, when the Drumhead's doors were opened, his breath caught when light from the hallway revealed the officer sitting to the left.

Kenith!

His oldest brother sat with his arms folded across his chest. The five knots on the cord wrapped around his right shoulder marked him as a colonel. He had deeper age lines around his eyes and above his high cheekbones, and light sprinkles of gray were in his blond hair, but Kalleb knew him.

Kenith's green eyes lit up upon seeing his face, not a hint of shame or disgust to be found in them. He pressed his lips tightly together, and his trimmed mustache and tufted imperial under his chin trembled. He gave Kalleb a firm nod as he was taken past.

Seeing his brother gave him smaller comfort than it had five years ago when he had learned that he had been one of the few to escape the rout after the battle. He wanted his family to remember him being strong, like he had been at his court martial, rather than raving like he just had.

Kalleb felt the urge to reach out to him, yet he only nodded back on his way out of the Drumhead. At least one of them had made it home.

Chapter 6

"Why did it have to rain today?" Alindale grumbled. He wiped the sweat from his neck with his handkerchief, watching rain streak diagonally across the windowpane.

The typically splendid westerly view was cast in gray distortion. Despite the rain, Dain Castle was humid and the air stale. Most of the doors and windows that provided drafts to keep the air circulating were closed because of the storm.

"The throne room is going to be stifling." He ran his damp handkerchief across his brow, but it offered little help. Then he glanced at his retainers and realized his annoyance was likely a trifle. "Although, it's probably worse for you two."

Holt and Malory stood off to the side, as quiet as shadows, in their full maroon armor for the start of session. Their horsehair-plumed helmets outlined their sweat-sheened faces.

"Don't mind us, Your Highness," Malory replied with sweat dripping off his pointy, reddish-yellow beard.

Alindale looked to Holt. His freckles seemed to stand out more because his cheeks were so damp. "You'll both be dismissed after session is over today," he promised.

"Thank you, Your Highness," they said in unison.

It was a small thing, but it was the least Alindale could do for them. He knew he was a bore to guard. He never did anything, never snuck out of his room to venture to forbidden places. He avoided horseback riding if he could. His brother, Adam, had been the one who the cavalrymen had loved to guard. He had sought out trouble every morning that he had gotten up, yet Alindale had noticed how his retainers had been fonder of the lad more than they ever showed him.

Taking a deep breath, Alindale continued down the corridor, toward the voices of the gathering courtiers. First, there were the mangled whispers, but he could soon pick out individuals out of the mix. Then he came upon small clusters of people crowding the corridor circling the outside of the throne room.

Bureau aristos, ministry officials identified by the badges pinned to their clothes, from all the various ministries, huddled with their pages, giving instructions on what notes they wanted taken. Province aristos representing their lord governors talked in the small groups in their court finery. The odd couple of representatives from far-flung townships or land aristos stood against the wall, awkwardly trying to find commonality in their outsider status.

As Alindale passed them by, the small groups went silent, one by one, while lowering their heads in waves. He heard the odd, "Your Highness," here and there but spared them only passing nods.

How convenient, he noted. *You get to bow your heads and hide your smirks.*

He fought not to grimace. He knew he shouldn't think like that. Some of these people were mere representatives of their families and provinces, sent here in case some urgent matter suddenly arose back home and had to be brought to court. The officials were only doing their jobs. Most were merely observers.

Nevertheless, he couldn't help the feeling that his performance yesterday had made him look like a petulant child in their eyes. Or worse, an idiot.

How am I supposed to talk with any of them?

Alindale followed the curved corridor to the throne room's entrance, its doors held open by the castle guards. People moved in and out of the room at will, since Thomas had yet to call them to order, but parted for Alindale.

Upon entering, his eyes watered from a thick miasma of perfume, bath soups, and candles.

Great. When they shut the doors, we are all going to suffocate!

The crowd was larger. The stands on both sides of the room were filling up, even though plenty of people were still in the corridors outside. Today, however, they followed session protocol.

Bureau aristos sat on the throne's left with their pages hustling up and down the steps or behind the stands. Petitioners, representatives, and observers sat to the throne's right. The stand's far-left end was reserved for members of various Knight Brotherhoods, attending in case their services were required. In this day, however, that was rare. And siting in the center of the room was the Table of Ministers.

The heavy, rectangular table's head pointed toward the royal dais, with eleven empty chairs around it. The five on both sides were for ministers of each ministry, and the chair at the foot of the table was the first minister's seat.

Where are you, Julian? Alindale thought, glancing about but failing to pick out his brother-in-law.

He hadn't received any word if Julian had contacted any of the other ministers.

His attention, though, was caught by the sight of a lady wandering down the middle of the room, a couple steps behind the table, while looking up at the ceiling. Her dark red hair hung smoothly down back, her black dress had divided skirts meant for riding than an appearance at session, and she also didn't seem fazed by the room's humidity, as she was the only woman in eyeshot who wasn't fanning herself. Her matching jacket's long sleeves and high collar made Alindale sweat more just by looking at it.

Is she lost?

Alindale walked up beside her and asked softly, not wishing to be noticed by the other attendees, "Is something wrong?"

She was young. Younger than him, he guessed. Her thin eyebrows were furled, and her large, reddish eyes stared up at the ceiling with confusion. Her natural light brown skin, her hair, and her eyes all told Alindale that she was from the Syros Isles. Then he remembered his mother welcoming two sisters the day before.

She must be the younger sister, he told himself. His mind had been elsewhere when they had been presented, so he had ignored most of it. *What's her name again?*

"Is it a story?" the lady asked without looking at him.

Alindale followed her gaze up to the circular stained-glass mural in the ceiling's center. On a clear day, they bathed the throne room in a rainbow of light from the suns, but not today. Nevertheless, each mural was separated by the curving wooden beams of the room's supports that came together in the center.

"They are the greatest Dains in history," he replied, surprised by her lack of recognition, then added, "It could also be considered the story of New Hartland's discovery and founding."

She pursed her lips, studying them. "They look like the same man holding a sword up with different backdrops."

"No, they are different." He pointed at the first mural. "The sword is just a theme. You see—"

She gasped.

Alindale thought his mother was entering and looked over his shoulder, but neither she, her train of ladies, or Thomas were there. Confused, he turned back and found Lady Syros staring at him, wide-eyed and mouth agape.

"Is something wrong?" He took his handkerchief and wiped his brow, but her expression didn't change. *Did I just smear something across my forehead?*

"You're the prince!" she whispered. Then she suddenly lowered her head and began to curtsy, when her hand struck the first minister's chair. The short, loud *creak* of the chair legs grinding against the tile floor cut through the drone of the multiple, small conversations and echoed throughout the room. In an instant, all conversations died, and Alindale felt all the attendees watching them.

Alindale and Lady Syros both froze. She stared back at him with those trembling red eyes, watching his every move. It took him a moment to realize that she was waiting on him to do something. Maybe she thought he could snap his fingers and tell them all to continue their talks because he was the prince. He didn't know. The silence was paralyzing.

Sweat ran down Alindale's face, but he was too nervous to wipe it off. He noticed Lady Syros's cheeks grow red the longer they stood staring at each other, and he felt his own flush, as well.

Malory walked around them and moved the chair back into place. He conveniently blocked them both from the observers' sights, and conversations started up again here and there.

"Thanks for that," Alindale whispered.

Malory grunted back.

Lady Syros collected herself. She tucked a few strands of hair behind her ear while keeping her head down, as if afraid to look at him. "Pardon me," she said timidly, "Your Majesty."

"Your Highness," Alindale corrected her then winced regretfully at how forceful it had sounded. "Sorry, but only my father and mother are Their Majesties. Someone, a long time ago, made the distinctions for some reason."

"Your Highness, then. I didn't mean to disturb anything. I'll get out of the way." She turned to leave.

Alindale suddenly felt guilty. He had embarrassed her in front of most of the other attendees, and this being her first time at court, too.

"No, wait!" He reached out to her, and she stopped and looked back at him with a mixture of confusion and nervousness. Alindale swallowed and began again, slower. "I did not mean to embarrass you. Nor startle you. I can still tell you what the murals mean, if you want."

Lady Syros's nervousness slowly drifted away, and she looked him up and down, studying him. Alindale could only wonder what she thought of him behind those red eyes. Although she had only arrived a day prior, her opinion of him might not be much after his pitiful performance. Or maybe she had formed a poor opinion of him after hearing the other ladies' opinions of him. Or, perhaps, she was the type who judged a man by his wardrobe.

Alindale wore a light blue doublet with silver and white brocade. He had hoped it would make him appear more regal and help in his waistline while its thin, silk sleeves would help keep him cool and look formal at the same time. The rain had ruined that hope, but at least his clothes were wrinkle-free today.

Lady Syros looked around. Alindale thought she was looking for a way out and was about to say she should go, but then he noticed she was searching the crowd intently, as if she was worried someone was watching. He wasn't sure if she found them, or if she didn't. However, for a moment, she flashed a small smile before walking back over to him.

"Okay," she said, looking back up at the ceiling.

Alindale was again surprised. Most ladies would have taken the opportunity to beg his leave and scurry off to their friends, to chatter and giggle at their narrow escape.

At first, his heart beat a little quicker, as if thrilled, but then a whisper came from the back of his mind that something wasn't right. Ladies at court didn't dote on him because he was the prince. Experience had taught him that they always wanted something, and that little voice almost made him beg her leave. Something about her small smile, though, made him stop.

Maybe this once, he thought, *I'll just see what happens.* He had to ignore the doubt, though.

"The first one"—he pointed to the mural above and a little to the right of the royal dais—"is Simon Dain. Little is written about him, but they say he was the man whom the Last God chose to lead humanity from Oblivion to Salvation." The glass outlining Simon and his raised sword was pure white. However, behind that, the glass was the darkest black, preventing light from getting through.

"And beside him"—he pointed at the next mural—"is Edeaus Dain, who built the Great Fleet and urged humanity to strike out for new lands." Edeaus stood at the bow of a ship. Behind him were dozens of others, with blue glass underneath them to symbolize the ocean and a small dot of brown behind them to symbolize the barren land that they had left behind. "He never got to see it, though."

Alindale turned and pointed over to his right. "His son, Alpheaus Dain the First, discovered New Hartland. He landed right here at Daincliff." The man in this mural, with his sword raised high, was standing on a golden shore with greenery about him. There were fewer ships to his left than the last mural, but beside him was the tall, gray cliff of his city's and castle's namesake.

"How convenient he landed somewhere that bore his name," Lady Syros commented.

Alindale frowned. "Well, no, I think he named it . . ." He looked over his shoulder and saw her smiling. Only then did he realize she was joking, but he became too serious again. "Yes, it was. Very convenient."

Lady Syros giggled, but then her brow furled. "But I thought the First Ships landed in Crescent Bay?"

Alindale felt a chill run down his back at the prospect of remembering the history wrong. He thought fast but couldn't remember that detail.

"No," he replied, "I'm pretty sure the First Ships landed here. I may have some books in my chambers; would you like for me to find out for sure after session?"

Her smile was gone now as she shook her head. "That's okay, Your Highness. If you say the First Ships landed here, then I'm sure they did."

Do you have to be so serious and right all the time? he chastised himself, though he could have sworn he heard it in Amadus's voice. The part about being right was debatable, however.

"Who are the other three?" Lady Syros asked, returning her attention back to the murals, much to Alindale's relief.

Moving on to the left-side murals, he pointed to the one beside Alpheaus's and said, "The next one is Jamison the Conqueror. He conquered all the northern provinces and most of the interior." Jamison was the only king in full plate armor. Behind him were rows of infantrymen, waving the Sunrise banner.

"The man after him," he continued, "is Richman the Second, or Richman the Unifier." Richman was the only king who held his sword up with only one hand, while his left hand held a parchment. Behind him was the depiction of New Hartland on a map. "He signed the Carta that brought the rest of the southern provinces"—he glanced at her—"the Syros Isle included—"

She gave a faint nod at the mention of her homeland.

"—into the kingdom, creating the Table of Ministers and such. My father is named after him."

"How is His Majesty?" Lady Syros asked softly.

"Still . . . Still ill," Alindale replied. He had gone to his father's chambers again that morning, hoping he had recovered, but was turned away completely this time, on orders by the royal physicians *and* his mother.

"I pray he'll recover."

He turned to her and saw she looked sincere. Her words sounded comforting, too. Maybe there was at least one other person here who hoped his father would recover instead of happily thinking of new prospects after he was gone.

He shuddered again, the panic from last night returning. It took all his strength to choke it done. He couldn't look flustered. Not here. Not now.

"Thank you," he said.

She gave him a nod and a small, comforting smile. "There's still one more—can't tell a story without the ending. But I think they forgot to color the background."

"That's Adam the Great." The last mural depicted the same as the others—a king holding high a sword. However, this sword was gold, and a white sun beamed behind it, sending rays of light in gold and white around the man. "He was crowned king while the whole continent was at war, some five hundred years ago. He kept most of New Hartland unified and together, defending against the Téionaropi, the Dharcach, and even other human kingdoms. The histories say he was the greatest king to ever live." *And my brother's namesake.*

Some had hoped that his brother would be the next great king, yet now all they had was Alindale, and he doubted they held such hopes for him.

"Perhaps one day—"

"Your Highness."

Alindale jumped as Julian strolled by with two pages trailing him, carrying the kingdom's large ledgers.

"I need to speak with you before session is called," Julian said, directing the pages to place the ledgers in the middle of the table. "It's important."

"Of course, Lord Renald," Alindale replied, disheartened by the interruption. "Allow me first to . . ." He turned to introduce Lady Syros, but she had slipped away and was walking into the crowd, which had grown since Alindale had last checked. The stands were almost full now.

"Pardon me, Your Highness," Julian said, watching Lady Syros go, as well, while pulling off his leather gloves. "I didn't see you talking with the lady behind your guards." His smile seemed more calculating than appreciative, if that was his intention. Either way, Alindale found it annoying and slightly embarrassing.

"Gloves, Julian?" he asked to guide the conversation anywhere else. "Is the castle not warm enough for you?"

"It's plenty warm"—Julian folded his gloves into his belt—"but I was caught outside when this gale swept in and had to dress accordingly." His coat was dark green, and the legs of his trousers were stuffed into his boots. He looked more ready for travel than session.

"Your plans have not changed?" Alindale surmised. "You still intend to leave?"

Julian frowned as he stepped closer. "I tried to speak with some of the other ministers last night. A few sent their servants saying they had already retired. The ones who did receive me said they hadn't made up their minds on how they'll vote."

"But you do not believe them." Alindale could tell by his expression that hadn't satisfied him.

Julian shook his head. "Everyone knows the choice they're going to make when the choice is presented to them. They only say they need time for appearances, or they don't want you to know."

Alindale picked up on his implications. "And if they do not want you to know, they must think you won't like their answer."

"Maybe. But possible." Julian shrugged then looked after Lady Syros. "If I may speak plainly, Amanda always says you have a keen mind but need to stop doubting and assert yourself more. It's assuring." Even when speaking plainly, Julian still sounded calculating.

Alindale frowned, not finding his praise assuring.

"But not today." Julian gave him a serious look. "Say nothing, no matter what happens. Even if I don't speak."

"What?"

Two loud, metallic clangs rang out over the room.

"Attend!" Thomas shouted. "Attend! Her Majesty comes! To your places, Lords and Ladies. Ministers, to your appointed seats! The business of the kingdom is about to be called to order!" Three more metallic clangs sang out from the tiles.

The room became a whirlwind of movement as the remaining attendees rushed to fill the stands. Julian walked away before Alindale could question him further, and the other ministers approached. In frustration, Alindale retreated to his seat.

What do you mean, "Even if I don't speak?" he internally reeled. *Are you going to abandon us, too?* Alindale involuntarily snickered. From where he stood, there was no *us*, only himself.

When he reached his seat, he remained standing, waiting for Thomas to announce his mother. His retainers took up stations on either side of his chair.

As the last of the ministers took their places, Alindale looked across the room where a tall, lean man stood watching him, grinning as if he were about to burst into laughter. The man was at least head and shoulders taller than Alindale, though not heavily built, just tall and gangly. His clean-shaven face was long, but his nose wasn't too large to stand out. His shaggy, sandy-brown hair reached his ears. He wore a yellow coat made of silk, with lace and silver embroidery on the cuffs of his sleeves. His coat revealed his white shirt underneath, at his collar. His trousers were black, as were his boots.

What does he find so funny? Alindale felt uneasy about the man's amused smile, unable to put a name with the face.

Thomas slammed his scepter three times on the tiles. "All hail Her Majesty, Queen Avera Dain!"

Everyone who was standing, including Alindale and the ministers, went to a knee. The upper stands creaked from the remaining courtiers bowing as low as they could.

"Royal wife and consort of His Majesty, King Richman Dain the Third!" Thomas continued as footsteps, both from heavy boots and delicate slippers, entered the room. "Lord of the First Kingdom, King of New Hartland, and Defender of Humanity!"

Alindale listened as the Sunrise Guard marched through the throne room and filed along the bottom of the royal dais. One stopped just a few feet from Alindale's chair. Next came the swishing of skirts from his mother's procession of ladies. Alindale knew their course without having to look. They climbed up two of the dais's steps, turned to their right, and then filed a line off that side. Lastly came his mother. He listened intently while she climbed the steps, the fluff of her skirts as she sat upon her throne.

A long minute passed in silence before Thomas followed, and then the throne room doors were closed.

"Rise," his mother commanded.

Alindale rose to his feet with the rest and looked up at his mother. She gazed down impassively from her throne. She wore a smooth, silver, silk dress, accented in silver and black brocade. Her skirts were smoothed neatly over her legs. The square neckline was modest, and her hair was smoothed straight behind her ears to keep her face unobscured or get hung up in her crown. Alindale caught the blue glint of her sapphire earrings as she nodded to Thomas.

"Hear ye! Hear ye!" Thomas slammed his scepter again on dais's step, which was starting to give Alindale a headache from the ringing steel. "This session before the throne and Table of Ministers is called to order. All persons seeking to petition their claims before the throne shall be permitted to do so after Her Majesty concludes business with the table. You may all sit." Thomas paused for a moment. "First Minister, you may bring the first order of business." With that, Thomas walked off to sit beside a page.

"Your Majesty," Bernold said from beside his seat at the end of the table, "my fellow ministers, this session being called to order, I bring the first order of business."

Bernold snatched a paper from a small stack on the left corner of the table and read, "*By motion of Her Majesty, Queen Avera Dain, it is moved that a vote of no confidence be had against Lord Bernold Vanni, First Minister of New Hartland.*" He tossed the paper back onto the table. "Upon this motion, I, Lord Vanni, relinquish my appointed office to Her Majesty so she may preside over the table's vote." Bernold bowed then walked away from the table.

Alindale watched his mother's eyes follow him and could guess she was furious under that cool exterior because Bernold hadn't waited for her to dismiss him.

"It is with a heavy heart we bring this motion," she said, though her tone didn't sound disheartened. "But for mishandling the plight of Urwald Province—"

There was nothing else he could do! Alindale wanted to yell. *He only had limited authority to react to it in the first place!*

"—and ignoring the calls for assistance by the lords and officials of the surrounding provinces, due to the flood of people seeking food, shelter, and escape from lawlessness—"

Escape from lawlessness? He rolled his eyes. *Couldn't think of anything more dramatic?*

"—the crown cannot permit this to continue." She dipped her head, grimacing as if this was hard for her to ask. "I know many are concerned for His Majesty and his well-being."

Alindale sat up as his mother gave the Sunrise throne a sorrowful look.

"But, while the royal physicians assure us he will recover, the needs of the kingdom cannot be put aside." She raised her head with a composed expression. "We ask each of you to affirm our motion.

"Steward, we call upon you to poll the ministers."

Alindale glowered at his mother as Thomas began to call out the ministers by their name and office. *Seriously, Mother?* He gripped the arms of his chair tightly, turning his knuckles white. *You'll invoke sympathy for Father while undermining him?*

He rubbed his forehead as the first "Yea" came in, his frustration worsening the headache that Thomas's staff had given him.

Another "Yea," and then another.

He leisurely looked across the room at the courtiers who he could see. Most looked bored. He could guess a few of them had expected this as much as he had. The long-faced man in yellow and black directly across from him, though, was still watching him with same, bemused look.

What in Oblivion do you find—

"Nay," the Minister of Justice, Lord Justice Hugo Blakwell, said. He sat with his elbows propped on the table, and his fingers interlocked with the sleeves of his long, purple robes falling over the arms of his chair. Alindale could only see the back of the man's half-bald head.

He was a man passed the middle of his years and spent most of his time in the Ministry of Justice in Daincliff. The only times he came to the castle were for session or if he was ever personally summoned. In session, he spoke only to the legality of proposed policies, and little else. He had spoken out often on why the table couldn't take a more direct approach to the situation in Urwald Province, mostly because the authority of the king was required.

Alindale sighed. *At least one minister has read the Carta.*

His mother watched impassively, leisurely fanning herself.

Another "Yea" followed. The Minister of Ships and Harbors joined the Ministers of Ambassadors and Interior in favor of the motion. Only one more "Yea" was needed.

"Lord Renald Julian, Minister of Treasure," Thomas called.

Alindale held his breath. He could see a contemplative look on Julian's face. The fact that he had the opportunity for the decisive vote was undoubtedly plain to him.

Alindale turned back and forth between his mother and Julian. His mother's fan fell still, covering her face, while she stared coldly at Julian.

"Nay," Julian voted.

Alindale exhaled in relief while a murmur ran among the crowd. *He kept his word.*

His mother narrowed her eyes, but Julian kept his calm demeanor and avoided her.

The attendees' whispers slowly died down, though the implications of the queen's son-in-law voting against her would likely give them much to gossip about for days. The deciding vote, however, would have to go to one of the remaining three ministers, or one of the two who would vote.

"Grand Master Degaol Etcor," Thomas continued, "Minister of Knightly Orders."

Abstain. He laid his head back against the back of his chair. *They always—*

"Nay!" Degaol shouted commandingly.

Alindale shot his head up. Everyone in the room was stunned. His mother's practiced mask momentarily cracked from shock. Her hand fell, lowering her fan, to reveal her speechless expression.

The Minister of Knightly Orders was more an honorary position of a bygone era, to help coordinate the multiple Knight Brotherhoods around the kingdom. A tradition of abstaining from serious matters had grown out of the honor of the position.

Grand Master Degaol smoothed out his tabard displaying his Knight Brotherhood's coat of arms—the long sword crossed with the halberd against a red field—and sat back in his chair. His look of satisfaction came through the bristly mass of a beard hiding half his face.

A loud *click* from the royal dais got Alindale's and the courtiers' attention.

His mother's shocked expression was gone, though her left eyebrow twitched. She sat rigidly upright and glared fire down at the old knight. She held her fan in her fist like a dagger and tapped it against the end of her throne's armrest.

Thomas continued, and the Minister of Proclamations voted "Yea" before Thomas had finished naming his office. Her Majesty smiled in satisfaction.

Thomas polled the last minister, the Minister of Trade, and with his "Yea," the dreaded vote was over.

That was anticlimactic.

Alindale rubbed his forehead again. The vain hope that maybe the last ministers would follow Grand Master Degaol's unexpected example had died before it could fully form, and his frustration headache returned.

"Steward," his mother called, fanning herself, "count the votes."

The page handed Thomas a piece of paper, and then he read, "*On the motion to find no confidence in Lord Bernold Vanni, as First Minister of the Table of Ministers, the Table of Ministers voted seven 'Yeas' and three 'Nays.' The motion passes. The Table of Ministers finds no confidence in Lord Bernold Vanni and is forthwith no longer fit to the office of First Minister.*"

"We thank you, Steward." His mother was beaming now. "We thank the Table of Ministers for passing the crown's motion, and we thank Lord Bernold Vanni for his years of service."

The attendees clapped, and Thomas retreated, with his page, back to his seat.

Alindale lazily rested his face in his propped-up hand, leaning against the armrest. The farce was over. Now for the travesty.

The clapping ceased when his mother rose to her feet.

"The crown must now appoint a new first minister as the next order of business. As royal consort, I, Queen Avera Dain, stand as representative of my royal husband in this matter. We recognize these are demanding times. The plight of Urwald Province and the surrounding cities is not relegated to those areas. Overpopulation is an increasing problem across the kingdom. Food shortages and weak harvests threaten the balance of a peace that has lasted over five hundred years. To maintain that balance and solve our people's struggles, we must reach to explore new ideas and new ways to solve our mutual challenges." She paused and took a deep breath.

Here it comes. Alindale prepared himself. *Try to look shocked everyone. A prize goes to the most stunned expression.*

"For these reasons," she continued, "the crown calls upon a lord who has taken up the fight against these problems at great risk and personal sacrifice to himself and the kingdom. We call upon Lord Henri Haemin to serve as First Minister of the Table of Ministers and help guide the kingdom through these troubling times."

On cue, the ladies gasped and hastily whispered to one other behind the fluttering of their fans. The lords either stayed stoned-faced or turned to each other for a quick conference of nodding heads. They quickly hushed, though, when Haemin stepped out from the far back of the room and strolled to the center.

Haemin was a tall man, approaching his late forties, with broad shoulders and a narrow waist. Specks of gray sprinkled throughout his thick, dark hair. He held his prominent nose and dimpled chin in the air, calmly gazing up at Her Majesty with a natural smile, as if they were the only people in the room.

His wardrobe was as elaborate as his entrance. His bright red jacket fell well below his waist and stopped above the knees of his shin-length trousers. It hung open to reveal the white, lacy, linen shirt underneath. The high collars of both the jacket and shirt made Alindale sweat. The jackets lapels were popped to the sides and down the length of the jacket's front. On both sides were seven decorative, horizontal gold stripes. The sleeves featured a floral and vine pattern down to the laced cuffs.

Haemin reached the center of the room and knelt on the Sunrise crest. "You honor me, Your Majesty. I humbly accept the charge you have placed upon me and will serve the throne and kingdom faithfully."

Satisfied with her choice, Her Majesty looked about the room. "Does anyone here have a comment on the crown's choice of First Minister?"

Alindale sat up and stared intently at Julian. He motioned with his head up at his mother, signaling it was time. Julian, though, collectively glanced at his fellow ministers in turn as the silence dragged out. Finally, he turned back to Alindale and stiffly shook his head.

This can't be it. Alindale clutched the end of the armrests. His legs trembled, heels bouncing against the tiles. His heart said, *stand up,* but Julian's words echoed in his head to stay seated. He looked at Lord Haemin, still kneeling, but Alindale could see his smug face.

Is no one going to say anything?

"Very well." Her Majesty sat back down on her throne. "Lord Haemin, we—"

"Your Majesty!"

Alindale had done it again. He was on his feet in a blink and suddenly unsure how he had gotten there. He didn't know if he had meant to yell as loudly as he had, but his voice rang in his ears.

His mother fluttered her eyes, looking down at him. Her smile was gone, replaced by a tight frown. Her left eyebrow twitched for a moment. Alindale wasn't sure if she was upset because he had caught her by surprise or because he had interrupted her. She was displeased either way.

"Prince Alindale Dain," she said, finally recognizing him, though her voice caught a little like she was out of breath, "is there something so important you must say that you had to interrupt us?"

Alindale read her implications. She didn't like being interrupted at the moment of her political triumph, but he also caught the hint that she was offering him a way out again. And again, he chose not to take it.

"Yes, Your Majesty." He took a step away from his chair so everyone could see him, and then he bowed to his mother. "I wish to comment on Your Majesty's choice for First Minister."

He looked up at his mother's dark eyes, blood pounding in his ears. This was the most important thing he cared about today. The only decision he hoped his mother would grant.

She passed her eyes between him and Lord Haemin in thought. "Very well," she finally said, much to the other courtiers' wonder. "We grant you the opportunity to comment, Prince Alindale. Please, be brief."

Someone laughed, but Alindale ignored them.

"Thank you," he replied. "Your Majesty, I beseech you to choose someone else." He pointed at Lord Haemin. "This man is not worthy his title, let alone to be First Minister of the kingdom. As Your Majesty should remember, he went against the throne's wishes and personally invaded the Téionaropi homeland. There is no way a man who nearly dragged the entire kingdom into war can maintain the peace you spoke of."

His mother sat regally, listening to his every word. Then she glanced back to Lord Haemin and said, "Lord Haemin, His Highness has levied a grave point against you. Do you wish to retort?"

"If I am permitted, Your Majesty?" Haemin replied, still kneeling with his head bowed.

"We permit it."

Haemin rose smoothly to his feet, looming a head taller than Alindale, with his chin in the air. "I do not deny I sent an expedition and seized Téionaropi lands five years ago. I did so not out personal gain but to ease the suffering and homelessness that was rampant in my ancestral city of Haemsville and surrounding lands.

"Available land gets smaller and smaller with each passing year. With each passing generation! People—*families*—are being left without a stead to call their own! The crisis in Urwald Province, the crisis in Silkhaven, these problems aren't localized. They're in *every* city and province of the kingdom! Even here in Daincliff, in South End, a *quarter* of this city, stands on the precipice of overflowing."

Haemin paused and took several deep, loud breaths, almost theatrically. "It would have sparked a rebellion to seize and divide the homesteads of the farmers and landowners into smaller plots to house the homeless when, for a hundred miles westward, there were open fields and room aplenty. I seized those lands to house and feed the kingdom's people. If such a measure is not worthy of lordship, then perhaps His Highness can inform us what is."

I hate you. Alindale glared, from disliking the man and how sympathetic his reasoning was. *By the Last God, I hate you!*

"Your Highness," his mother started, "do you have something to say?"

Alindale failed to think before replying with, "You're a murderer."

As the court erupted in gasps, Haemin's confident smile disappeared into a hard grimace.

"Prince Alindale Dain!" his mother shouted.

He turned around to find her on her feet and her face red with rage.

"You dare bring such an accusation against a lord we have welcomed and whose past transgressions we have forgiven?"

"Yes!" Alindale shouted back. "This man started a war! Regardless of his reasons, he started a war without the endorsement of the throne. He swore to His Majesty to make peace with the Téionaropi, only to turn and ride out of this very castle with my brother. He led my brother to his death! For that, I call him, murderer."

"Lord Haemin"—his mother's voice came out strained—"His Highness accuses you . . . of murder. We will hear your answer."

Haemin's hands were balled into fists at his sides. His square jaw throbbed, and his eyes were thunderclaps. "The death of our beloved Prince Adam was not my doing. I did swear to His Majesty to seek peace with the Téionaropi, but I did not seek out the prince afterward. He sought me out and offered to stand with us when the Téionaropi refused us, which they did. Prince Adam rode into battle of his own accord, rejecting all council to stay out of the fray." Haemin shook his head, and his face softened. "There was not a man alive of any age who could hold his noble heart back."

Many of the attendees nodded in agreement, and Alindale could sense he was losing them . . . if he ever had them at all.

Haemin drew himself up and turned his attention back to Her Majesty. "It was the Téionaropi who slew our beloved Prince Adam in open combat. His loss will haunt me to my grave. But I never intended, nor wished, nor desired such a fate. I ask Your Majesty: can a man be called a murderer for this?"

Oh no, you don't! Alindale could tell he was playing at the sympathies of his mother and the court. He had to stop it.

"The Téionaropi were yours to negotiate with, and you failed," he said. "The death of my brother is still on your hands!"

"Silence!" His mother's shout echoed throughout the room. She was again on her feet, her fan aimed like a bolt at Alindale. "We have heard enough. Prince Alindale, we have welcomed Lord Haemin to court and forgiven him of his past transgressions, yet you accuse him falsely with no evidence to the contrary. You will apologize to Lord Haemin here and now."

Alindale's knuckles went white. He could feel Lord Haemin smiling smugly. Every rational thought in his mind told him to apologize and accept his loss, but his head was pounding at the thought of that smug look and the feeling of everyone mocking him.

He looked back up at his mother and said, "No."

She blinked. "What did you *say*?"

"I said, *no*." Alindale stuck his chest out and raised his head. "I will not apologize."

His mother drew herself up. For a moment, he thought she would call lightning from the storm above down on him. Then she regained her regal demeanor.

"Very well," she said, her voice carrying a judgmental tone, then sat back down on her throne. "Prince Alindale Dain, you have gravely offended us during this time of session by making what we hold as false accusations and contempt for this court. We, therefore, banish you from court for the remainder of this session."

Alindale's stomach twisted as if someone had punched him in the gut. He tensed until he began to tremble. He couldn't have imagined his own mother would go this far. He tried to breathe, but his breath caught. The sudden prospect of being thrown out of his own home brought a terror that he had never felt before.

"But Mother—"

His attempted protest was silenced by her raising her fan.

"We, however, will not remove you from this castle," she granted, much to his relief. "His Majesty is gravely ill, and we will not remove a son from his father's side. You will not be allowed to enter court until we choose to summon you."

She turned to the rest of the court. "We decree no one attending this session is to discuss matters of the kingdom with His Highness until that time, under penalty of sharing his banishment. Are we understood?"

"Yes, Your Majesty," the crowd echoed in response.

"Guards, escort His Highness out. This session has been delayed long enough." Finished, she leaned back against her throne and smoothed the front of her skirts.

Distraught, Alindale stood there, motionless, as two Sunrise Guards flanked him. He felt numb, as if his body wasn't his own when he bowed and followed them to the door, his own retainers trailing them from behind.

He kept his head up the best he could. From his periphery, he spotted Julian shaking his head impassively. He didn't bother to look at the other ministers or attendees, especially Haemin.

When the throne room doors slammed shut behind him, he dismissed his retainers with a wave, unable to speak. Alone, he walked down the corridor and stopped to watch the rain streak across a windowpane.

Chapter 7

Kalleb grunted, twisting the manacle on his right wrist. Smit continued to be a prick and left him to fidget against the damn torture contraptions. He had tried to push the manacle up a little because his right hand was falling asleep. In turn, the manacle's hard edge pressed against a bone in his wrist, and the pain proved to be worse than his hand falling asleep.

"Damn these chains," he growled under his breath. "Damn this room. Damn Smit." He grunted again as the manacle slipped down and off his wrist bone. He sighed in frustration and sagged against the back of his chair. "And damn the horse thief who *stole* my hat!"

Kalleb had searched under the table, around the chairs, and the corners of the cramped room, but the hat was gone. It had seen better days—the leather was wrinkled, peeling in several places, and had holes in the brim—but an old hat with a wide brim was better than none in the burning summers months.

He had lost track of time, too. Clouds still covered the sky, but he stayed away from the window. Little had changed in Kanestown in five years, but watching people go about their business had done little to help his mood. If he looked just right through the slanted rooves, he could pick out his family's old home. All the more reason to stay away from the window.

Approaching footsteps outside caught his attention. Few had come down the hallway in the time Kalleb had spent in the room. Each time, there had been a rumble of voices outside the door. He tensed and sat up this time, though. There was intent behind these.

They've reached a decision.

Someone stopped outside the door. Voices spoke back and forth.

Kalleb watched the door, expecting it to open any second and hear Smit tell him he was going back to the penal farm. Instead, the voices continued and grew louder.

What are they waiting for? He rubbed his hands on his knees, his rough calluses picking at his trousers.

"Open the *frickin'* door!" someone outside roared.

The door's lock clicked then slammed open. A yellow haze drifted around the head of the tall man who loomed in the doorway. His uniform was disheveled and wrinkled, and his saber hung too low on his hip. He snorted yellow smoke from puffing on a hela weed cigarette hanging from his lips. He glared at Kalleb, the thin scar on his angular right cheek trembling.

Kalleb remembered that scar. He had given it to him when his second oldest brother was thirteen and he was eleven. They had been playing with their pa's saber and had learned the hard way that it wasn't a toy.

"Hello, Konner," Kalleb greeted.

Konner took a long drag on his cig, his watery eyes flickering up and down.

"Smit," Konner rasped, digging a folded piece of paper out of his uniform's breast pocket, "take off those chains."

Kalleb straightened in his chair.

"Captain?" Smit questioned from the hallway, his narrowed eyes squinting tighter in confusion.

"You are relieved," Konner said, slapping the paper into Smit's chest. "I'm taking command of your charge."

Smit snatched the paper, hastily unfolded it, and then began to read. His eyes flashed over the words while he crinkled the paper. His cheeks then grew red as he reread the order.

"Captain, I must protest!" Smit crushed the paper in his fists. "This man is a convicted deserter! I've received no orders—"

Konner snapped around and loomed over Smit. He took his cigarette out of his mouth then blew yellow smoke down into the man's face. "Two colonels and a brigadier signed *that* order, *Sergeant at Arms*," he growled. "Take those frickin' chains off, or I'll rip the keys off your belt and throw you out the window!"

Smit's pinched grimace turned his face purple, but Konner only blew more smoke into his face. Smit coughed and waved the fumes away as he stumbled past him, dropping the crumpled orders onto the floor. He fumbled with the key ring from the tears running down the corners of his eyes.

Kalleb held his wrists up, trying not to smile. Smit yanked the chain, nearly spilling him onto the floor, and rammed the key into the manacles' locks, opening them with a *click*. Then Smit threw them onto the table with a *clang* and snapped to attention beside it.

"The manacles are off, *Captain*," Smit said, his lips twisting in a resentful sneer.

"Thank you," Konner said, taking another puff on his cig. "You're dismissed."

Smit snorted loudly. "Sir, I must still protest. This man is a convicted deserter! As Sergeant at Arms, I can't allow this man out of my—"

"Shut up," Konner said dismissively, picking up the piece of paper from the floor. "Convict Kalleb Kane has been transferred into my custody. You can piss off and take the other two with you."

Smit snapped his heels together then stormed out of the room with a retreating glare at Kalleb.

"Bye-bye," Konner said, waving.

Kalleb rubbed his right wrist then flexed his fingers as he listened closely to make sure Smit and his former guards were marching away.

"That was fun." Konner chuckled gleefully, rubbing his cigarette out against the door, grinning broadly, showing yellow teeth.

Kalleb folded his arms across his chest and sat back in his chair. "If you have a pair of horses waiting for me to make a run for it, you can piss off, too. And quickly, before that prick finds someone who knows you're not a captain."

"I am a captain!" Konner snapped, pointing at the triple knotted gold cord hanging off his uniform's right shoulder.

Kalleb stared back at him. Calling out Konner's jokes always led to a spiral of denials, but he remembered Konner couldn't keep a straight face for long, so he waited. Konner merely stared back, unflinching.

Kalleb blinked, finally realizing he was serious. He snickered then tried to keep from smiling, but another snicker followed and he threw his head back and laughed.

"They *actually* made you a captain!" he said. Tears welled up in his eyes as his shoulders bounced from laughing so hard, especially as Konner's face twisted as if he had eaten spoiled pork.

"It's not that funny," Konner said sourly.

"Yes, it is, Mr. Lieutenant-for-Life! And they made you a *captain*!" He wiped the tears out of his eyes. "Oh God, your poor company." He gasped and laughed harder, thinking of Konner commanding a company.

"All right, *all right*!" Konner barked. "Do you want to get out of here, or stay in this room for the rest of the night?"

Kalleb coughed then frowned, confused. "You sure you didn't forge those orders? Grandpa Kane ordered I was to remain here until they reached their decision . . . whenever that'll be."

"Well"—Konner unfolded the piece of paper, making a show of turning the paper over and looking it up and down—"these orders place you in my custody. They don't say anything about you having to stay until a decision is reached." He grinned broadly and chuckled, waving the paper in his hand.

"As great as that sounds, I'd rather not be found in a bar when the lancers are sent to take me back to the farm."

"Well, that's where they'd frickin' find me," Konner said, folding the orders back in his breast pocket. "I wouldn't be sitting in this back room, I can tell you that." He walked up and loomed over him with his hand out. "We're going to see Ma."

A cold sweat broke out on Kalleb's forehead. "I don't think she'll want to see me."

Konner slapped him on the back of the head. "Ma's been bawling her eyes out over you being brought back home, even though she's been trying to hide it. So, get your ass up; we're going to see her. I'm hungry."

Kalleb rubbed the back of his head before begrudgingly getting to his feet. He wobbled for a second on his uneven bootheels and frowned up at

Konner smirking at being half a head taller than him. He snorted, and his nose wrinkled at the hela weed's scent, a mixture of musk and mold.

"Konner!" He gagged and pulled back. "Why are you still smoking those damn things?"

Konner barked a laugh. "Because I like the pep they put in my step." He reached into his trousers then pulled out a tender box.

Kalleb stepped for the door before he could fish another cigarette from his breast pocket and light it.

"And blowing smoke at assholes."

Kalleb reached for the doorknob when something dawned on him. "The brigadiers may come to a decision any minute. How will I hear of it, or what will they think, if I'm not here?"

"Kenith's been sitting outside the Drumhead ever since your hearing." Konner clicked the tinderbox closed then patted his breast pocket with the orders. "He got these signatures together to get you out of here, and he'll bring word once the brigadiers reach a decision."

Konner took a long drag on his cig then puffed out a small, yellow cloud. "Come on," he said, slapping Kalleb on the shoulder before opening the door and pushing him out into the hallway. "I've got a buckboard waiting."

"A buckboard?"

"Well, we can't have a dangerous convict like you riding around," Konner joked, taking another drag. "And I'm not walking. You may have been away for a while, but Kanestown's streets aren't just muddy on rainy days."

Kalleb paused and glanced at his worn boots, recounting the multiple times that he had come back from the fields and poured brown sludge out of them. "That makes sense."

~~~

The buckboard rattled and bounced against the dugout ruts zigzagging through the street. Kalleb held on the best he could by pressing his back against the coachman's seat and his bootheels against the footrest. He missed the cobblestones of Kanestown's East Main the moment Konner had turned off into the narrower neighborhood streets.

For the hundredth time, he nervously checked over his shoulder, expecting to see lancers chasing after them. Fortunately, none were coming . . . yet.
~~~

People were taking advantage of the break in the rain. Wagons rolled by at the intersection of East Main's wide street and their narrow street. Runners raced down the sidewalks, hurriedly trying to finish their business before heading home.

"Will you turn around?" Konner grunted. "No one's riding after us."

"Well, I never thought I'd ride out of Storm Hall outside a barred wagon," Kalleb replied, Storm Hall's orange glow in the murky evening light still hanging in his mind.

The wide, four-story building loomed over Kanestown from the center of its wide, paved roundabout. Its dozens of lit windows stood out like watchmen over the borough, and he felt their gaze on his back as Konner drove him away.

The Storm Cavalry headquarters were still the same. The hall's multiple renovations over its four-hundred-year history showed on every floor. It shared the same rock foundations as the houses along Main Street. The six porch columns rose all the way to the fourth story were red wood trunks held up the slated roof. While the outside of the building was painted yellow and maroon, a closer inspection would reveal the windows were different sizes and the trim didn't always match. Three Storm Cavalry banners flapped in the southernly wind on long poles.

Above them, lights from Dain Castle, high in the distance, twinkled like stars.

His ear twitched, and he heard Konner mumbling under his breath.

"What's wrong?" he asked.

Konner grunted and gave him an odd look. "Oh, nothing." He rubbed out the butt of his hela cig against the side of the buckboard. "I'm just getting the curse words out now so Ma doesn't throw a skillet at me."

Kalleb snickered. "A lance corporal can be promoted . . ."

"Shut up," Konner said. "A couple of captains, who I was playing cards with an hour ago, could teach every lance corporal in this cavalry a few new words."

"Playing cards?"

Konner gave him a look. "I wasn't going sit and wait around Storm Hall all day, especially since Kenith was there to look after you."

"Thanks, Konner," Kalleb quipped. "Nice to know how much you care."

"You're welcome, baby brother."

Konner turned the gray-blue mare down another narrow lane. The creaking from the buckboard's wheels bounced off the close, brick walls and roared down the alley. Chimneys filled the air with the smell of a dozen cookfires and woodsmoke from families preparing dinner across Kanestown.

At least the rain washed out the crap.

When the alley opened wider into a round cul-de-sac, a lump formed in the back of Kalleb's throat at seeing the two-story house in the back. Yellow candlelight spilled out of the windows, casting dancing shadows on its porch and into the street.

Konner drove the mare up to the side of the porch and pulled up on the reins. "Welcome home. I'll stable the mare and put the buckboard in the back. You get off here and see Ma."

Kalleb hung off the buckboard's seat, suddenly losing feeling in his legs. He dug his fingers into the seat and shook at a shadow passing by the window.

Am I . . .? Am I really back? he wondered.

For the past week, he had followed the orders of his guards like he was still on the penal farm. The familiar sights and sounds of Kanestown had been dulled by the constant reminder of his crime and the looks of contempt he had received. Even in Storm Hall, he hadn't felt the same pride that he had felt when he had been younger. Instead, he had felt numb walking those hallways again.

Yet, with his feet hanging inches from the porch, the numbness burned away like a lifting fog. His breath labored, as if seeing the light streaming out of the windows for the first time. He dared not blink.

Countless times, he had dreamed of walking up that narrow road and onto this porch, reaching his hand out to unlatch the door, hearing his ma's and pa's voices on the other side . . . only to wake up and find he was still at the farm.

"Go on," Konner groaned out.

Kalleb was shoved from behind and stumbled onto the porch. He gave Konner a begrudging look, but Konner just chuckled and drove the buckboard around to the back of the house, leaving him alone on the porch.

The night was still, despite the hustle and bustle that they had left on the main streets. The circle of houses and few remaining old barns blocked off the noise as housewives prepared evening meals for their families.

He walked slowly across the porch, hesitantly approaching the door and trying not to disturb the night. The coarse calluses on his hand pulled and scraped against the doorlatch's rough wood. He instinctively remembered to lift the latch up, drawing it across at the same time, and the door creaked open.

The old smells of home hit him instantly—apples and cinnamon, varnished wood and comfortable leather, frying pork and chicken and baked bread. His stomach growled, and his mouth watered with his first steps inside.

It was just as he had left it. To his left, the door to Ma and Pa's room was closed. In front of him, the staircase leading up to the second floor and his and his brothers' old rooms. He walked into the common room and stopped. Three of his pa's old hats still hung on pegs beside the door. He instinctively studied the matted, leather hat in the middle, with its round crown and wide brim after his years of hard labor.

That's a good—

Kalleb tore his eyes away from the hat and cut off the thought. *I'm finally home again. For whatever time I have left, I'm not going to think like I'm on the farm.*

He walked farther into the common room, only to be drawn in by the small portrait oil-painting hanging on the bricks above the cold chimney. His pa sat regally, his blond hair combed back, and the pristine points of his bushy mustache perfectly captured. Those stern, Kane-green eyes stared down at him, weighing his worth.

Kalleb ran his hand through his stringy beard and wished again that they had cut his hair and beard before sending him back.

Below the portrait hung his pa's heavy, curved saber. Its scabbard reflected candlelight from the small tables around the room, free of dust, along with the chairs and tables.

He walked up to his pa's old rocking chair and smiled at the small, red, silk pillow sitting on it. He rested his arm on its back, slightly rocking it, and remembered his pa sighing whenever he would collapse in his chair and made sure that pillow fit just right in the small of his back. Kalleb could almost hear him clearing his throat with a small, satisfied gasp before he rocked himself to an early nap.

"AH!"

Kalleb jumped at the sudden yell.

His ma stood in the kitchen doorway, trembling, her hands over her mouth. With her wide, hazel eyes, she looked him up and down, as if seeing a ghost. Hints of light streaks of gray peeked out of her long, blonde hair that was pulled back in a tail. The lines on her face, from long days and nights keeping the house up and raising three children, had deepened around her eyes and cheeks.

"Hi . . ." Kalleb said weakly, not sure of what else to say. "Ma." He tried to smile, but his cheeks kept trembling.

His ma cautiously walked closer, as if she didn't believe her eyes. The sleeves of her faded blue blouse were pulled up to her elbows, and her white apron was damp and stained from water and cooking. She reached out to him, gently cupping his face with her wrinkly hands.

"Kalleb?" she asked softly, slipping her fingers through his beard and pulling it back, as if making sure it was him. Her eyes quivered and watered. "My baby boy?"

Kalleb choked up and nodded. "It's me, Ma. I'm home."

She gripped his face and pressed hers into his chest, bawling out, "My boy! My boy!" She dropped her hands to the back of his neck and clung tighter to him. "They gave me my baby back!"

Kalleb felt a pang, like a horse nail driven through his heart. He had built a shell around him from the long days of hard labor. It had been easy to believe that the only thing he had to live for was another day in the fields while on the farm. Now his shell crumbled from listening to his ma cry. He didn't have it in him to tell her that he was probably going to be sent back. Hence, he embraced her warmly and let her weep for joy for as long as she wanted.

~~~

Kalleb gobbled down the tender cuts of fried pork with little pause. The hint of pepper, salt, and spice barely touched his tongue before he swallowed one bite after another. He only paused either to eat a wedge of potato, or a bite of onion, or half a buttery biscuit, or drink a gulp of beer.

"Don't choke yourself," his ma warned, patting his arm.

He groaned from her repeated effort to baby him, which was more unfair after the amount of food she had put in front of him. As usual, Ma had fixed enough food for ten people.
~~~

Konner chuckled from the other side of the table. "You can always count on a lancer eating and drinking a beer hall down whenever they're let out of the stockade."

Ma slapped his shoulder with the back of her hand.

"Hey!" Konner grunted, splashing some of his beer on his shirt. "Ma!"

"Hush!" Ma snapped. "You know better than to talk about such things like that at my table." She gave him a warning look, hinting that she suspected Konner meant more from his beer hall comment, and Kalleb agreed. "And don't stain your shirt! I have enough of your laundry to take care of before you leave."

"Yes, Ma," Konner begrudgingly uttered, wiping the beer off.

Kalleb paused, another biscuit halfway to his mouth. "Leave?"

"They're making me a major"—Konner nodded—"and sending me, my old company, and another to go ride around Tradon for close to a year, doing God knows what."

"No lancer talk or taking the Last God's name in vain at *my* table," Ma warned before scooping a spoonful of rice and beans into her mouth.

Kalleb stared down at his plate, cluttered with half-eaten food. He ran his fingers through his beard and raked out the crumbs. Hearing Tradon mentioned made him think of the city for the first time in years. He always tried not to think of it, or his time there before riding to Haemsville. Thinking about it or wondering what would have happened had he not rode south could have drove him insane after the repetitive days on the farm.

"Kalleb," his ma called, giving him a worried look, "you okay?"

He tried to give her an assuring smile. "I'm fine, Ma. Just . . . thinking."

Ma gave him a sympathetic look, patting him on the arm again then squeezing it.

"Thinking about your princess?" Konner asked, chewing on a slice of pork.

"*Konner*!" Ma gasped.

"What?" Konner shrugged. "Lancers in the stockade always think of their sweethearts. And we all knew he was sweet on her growing up while Pa was guarding her."

Kalleb glared at him. "Watch what you say about Her Highness."

Konner barked a laugh and pointed his chewed-on slice of pork at him. "You still call her *Her Highness*."

Ma backhanded him again with a hard *slap*.

Konner grunted and dropped his pork back onto his plate before patting his arm. "Ma!"

"*Hush!*" She sternly pointed a finger in his face. "I should have spanked you more while you were growing up. You know better than to talk about a married woman like that."

"You have plenty of time to make up for it," Kalleb said, looking at the half a dozen iron skillets on the table.

Konner gave him a pained look. Before he could retort, though, the thumping of footfalls on the porch gave him pause. Then the door jolted on its hinges from three loud knocks.

Kalleb tensed.

"Come in!" Ma called.

The latch creaked aside, and then Kenith walked in. His stern expression reminded Kalleb of their pa's portrait above the fireplace, but it also reminded him of what he was waiting for.

I guess the home visit is over.

A small tremble ran through his body as that dreaded numbness began boiling up again.

"Kenith!" Ma said happily. She pushed away from the table and rushed over to him. "You're finally here! Is Hanna and the boys with you?"

"I'm afraid not," Kenith replied, wiping his boots off on the doormat. His gruff voice had deepened and, like his aged appearance, sounded eerily like Pa's. "I thought it was best for just us to be here tonight."

"Ah . . ." Ma pouted. "I was hoping to see my little men."

Kalleb gave Konner a confused look. "Little men?"

"You're an uncle twice over now," Konner replied, scooping up the grease on his plate with a potato wedge before popping it into his mouth. "Kenith's been busy carrying on the family name."

Ma slapped Konner's shoulder again while narrowing her eyes at him. "Unlike your other brother, who refuses to settle down even though he'll soon be earning a major's wage."

Konner defensively put his hands up, and Kalleb felt the urge to laugh, but Kenith's silence gave him pause. He couldn't hold it off any longer.

"Ma," Kalleb started, pushing his plate aside, "I have something to tell you."

Ma's brow furled as a concerned look crossed her face.

A lump formed in his throat. He could still see her smiling and hear her happy cries. His mouth was suddenly dry, and he had to take a swallow of beer, the fuzz bubbled in his throat, yet he still struggled to find the words.

"I'm . . . I'm not—"

"Before you get to that," Kenith interrupted, pulling out a fold piece of parchment from the inside of uniform jacket.

"What's that?" Ma asked.

Orders. Kalleb frowned and hung his head. *Parole is denied. Send the deserter back to the farm to rot.*

Kenith unfolded the paper and read, "'*It is hereby ordered that Kalleb Kane, convicted of desertion of his post, be granted parole.*'"

Kalleb sat up and looked at Kenith in disbelief. The small, satisfied smile on Kenith's face told him that he hadn't misheard. Konner raised his mug to him then took a long swig.

Ma gasped, dancing her wide eyes between him and Kenith with the realization that Kalleb hadn't been released. "You mean . . .?"

Kenith held up a finger. "One condition. '*Parole is conditioned that it be retained by the Storm Cavalry for the remainder of his original sentence. If agreed to, Kalleb Kane will be reinstated as a lance corporal of the Storm Cavalry.*'" His small smile slipped away. "'*He shall retain this rank for the duration of his parole, regardless of merits or the recommendations of his superiors.*'"

Kalleb felt hollow. The mere hope of parole had seemed beyond reach, especially after ranting at the brigadiers. He had meant it when he had told them he would rather go back to the farm than be given parole and spat on by everyone in Kanestown. Making a living seemed impossible with the cloud of his conviction hanging over his head, but this was something more.

I'll be a lancer again. With a rank. But the lowest one . . . for fifteen years. He hung his head again.

A lance corporal's main duty was to a troop of no more than twenty-five other lancers. They answered directly to their squadron's lieutenant but, in truth, took care of the troop's smaller needs. The rank was a mere steppingstone.

"Frickin' bastards," Konner growled, slamming his mug down on the table.

Kalleb jerked up and nervously glanced at his ma. She stood, shaking in place, and didn't seem to have heard him. Trembling, she slowly walked to pa's chair and sat down. She wrapped his small pillow in her arms and gently started rocking.

Kenith tightened his jaw and crinkled the paper in his hands. He narrowed his piercing eyes down at the words in smoldering anger. "'*If this condition is not agreed upon, the officer of the guard is to return the convict to complete the remainder of his sentence. Signed Komrad Kane, Brigadier Marshal of the Storm Cavalry.*'"

Kenith reached into his uniform jacket then pulled out another folded piece of paper and caught something sliding out as he unfolded it. He studied it in his hand for a moment then walked up to the dining table and laid down a bronze lance pin.

Kalleb hesitantly picked it up, rolling the bronze pin between his fingers, carefully avoiding the needle so as not to prick himself.

The Storm Cavalry was founded on promoting men based on merit, regardless of wealth. Each recruit started out as a lancer and worked their way up. Then again, family legacies also meant something to the cavalry. And, because of his family name, Kalleb had been made a corporal when he had first enlisted. It had taken him less than a year to make lance corporal and four years after that to be promoted to lieutenant.

"Starting over," he finally said, closing his fist around the pin.

"But not," Konner growled, his mouth twisted in a snarl. "Who'd ever heard of career *lance corporal*?"

Kenith dragged a chair out from the foot of the table, scraping its legs across the wood floor before he sat down. "I'm sorry, Kalleb. I should have read the orders when Gerald gave them to me. He said it was the best he could do, and I thought he meant he got the brigadiers to give you a fair parole."

"Nothing fair about it!" Konner spat. "He can be a lance corporal and make sure a troop's uniforms are clean for fifteen years or be a shit farmer. What kind of *fair* parole is that?"

"They could have just sent him back," Kenith retorted, "or thrown him out into the street. This way"—he slid the second piece of paper across the table—"you get a choice, Kalleb."

Kalleb stared glumly down at the table, still clutching the lance pin tightly in his palm. *They still have their pride*, he understood. He probably would have felt the same if they had given him the same choice five years ago. Except pride counted for nothing on the farm.

"I just want to come home," he said, spinning the lance pin between his fingers. "If this is the only way, then I guess I'll . . ."

He read the orders then paused. His brow furled as he squinted, reading a second time. Then he barked a laugh.

"What?" Konner asked. "They didn't assign you to *guard* the penal farm, did they?"

Kalleb shook his head. "No, they're not that cruel. But it's funny if you think about it." He held the orders across the table to him.

Konner snatched the orders then quickly read them. "They assigned you to Squadron Five." Konner gave him surprised look. "Eighth Company."

"Back to my old company," Kalleb said. "And look where they're sending me."

Konner read on. "Tradon? You're to report for muster in three days." He tossed the orders onto the table.

"Can you beat that?" he asked, passing a look between his brothers. "They return me to duty and send me to the same company and post that I left. Maybe Grandpa Kane has a sense of humor after all."

"The Eighth isn't the same company," Kenith told him, sitting back in his chair with his arms folded. "Your former company was retired and most of the lancers transferred. You've been assigned to the *newly* formed Eighth Company. Gerald and the other brigadiers may have convinced him to grant you parole, but if Grandpa Kane had a hand in deciding your post, he probably saw it as an alternate form of punishment."

"Your commanding officer will be punishment enough," Konner said, taking another swig of beer.

"Yes, having *you* as a major will be torture," Kalleb joked.

Konner didn't laugh. "Not half as much torture as Cutter Vallant will be. He's the new Eighth's captain."

The name stirred old memories, causing Kalleb to groan. "That ass-kisser made captain, too?"

Konner shrugged. "He kissed the right ass somewhere and got assigned a company. The Eighth's mostly new recruits, too. Guess someone thought giving him command and keeping him stuck in training for a while was a good idea."

Kalleb ran his hand over his face. *Six months of training drills, at least,* he thought. *No, it'll be longer. Vallant will run practice drills until the entire company is the best parade company in the Storm Cavalry. And be a smug asshole about it, too.*

The brothers sat quietly around the table, each drawn in by their own thoughts. The creaking of wood rocking on wood caught Kalleb's attention, and he noticed one person had said anything. He peered past Konner's shoulder and saw his ma rocking in Pa's chair, his pillow still in her lap as she gazed up at Pa's portrait with her head leaning against the back of the chair.

"Ma?" Kalleb called.

She didn't look at him.

Heavyhearted, he got up from the table, leaving the lance pin, and walked around to kneel beside her. "I'm sorry, Ma. I should have said something before—"

"You'll need his saber," she said softly, still staring up at the portrait.

"What?"

"You'll need your own saber," she replied. "It'll take you too long to save on a lance corporal's pay, so you'll need to take your pa's instead."

Kalleb gently touched her arm, his confusion shifting to concern. "*Ma?*"

She looked down and gave him a small, warm smile. Then she reached out and stroked his face. "I'll cut your hair before you muster out." She tentatively brushed the long strands of hair out of his face as tears welled up in the corners of her eyes. She blinked, and couple of them ran down her cheeks, but she kept her smile. "My baby boy . . . but you're your pa's son, too." She then leaned back in chair and started rocking again, pulling Pa's pillow close as she looked back up at his portrait. "You're all Kanesmen," she said softly.

Kalleb remained kneeling beside her. That heavy weight pressed in on his chest. It made it difficult to breathe. He wanted to tell her everything would be okay, that his orders had assigned him to Tradon for now but not for the full fifteen years. However, as tears silently rolled down her cheeks, he knew there was nothing he could say to give her comfort.

With all the strength he could muster, he grunted as he stood back up and joined his brothers back at the dining table.

"Does Konner return me to Storm Hall tomorrow?" he asked, picking up the bronze lance pin. "Or do I wait to report in three days?"

"Report to Storm Hall tomorrow," Kenith replied. "I'll take care of things from there. Keep your orders and parole papers with you." He tossed the parole papers on the table.

Kalleb gathered them up, his parole and orders, and folded them together before setting them aside.

"Well," he said, holding up his mug, "here's to us riding again."

Konner's eyes lit up, and a gleeful smile spread across his face as he lifted his mug. "Ride, Lancers, ride!" he bellowed before throwing his head back and downing the remainder of his beer.

Kenith grunted and nodded.

"Ride, Lancers, ride," Kalleb said then drank.

Chapter 8

Alindale stared vacantly out his open window and into the black night. He slouched further into his chair, his arms hanging over the arms. The cushions in the back of the chair pushed his head forward until his chin pressed into his chest, but he ignored the growing stiff crick in his neck.

Not a single wisp of the whistling southeast winds swooped into his window to relieve him of the night's muggy atmosphere. The lone candle flickered beside him, and he briefly hoped the wind had changed, but those hopes died, like all his hopes of late, when the flame straightened.

Someone pounded on his door, rattling its iron hinges irritatingly.

"Go away!" he yelled. "I'm not hungry, need my bed turned, or my chamber pot changed!"

I would have called for someone for that last one.

The servants had tried that one already, but he had locked himself in his room upon returning from making a fool of himself, much to the servants' dismay.

More rattling came, and Alindale sighed and rolled his eyes. *They're more determined this time.*

The screeching of the latch being pulled up made him jump and immediately regret it as his neck and back popped. He had to rub the stiffness out of his neck before he could turn to see a hunched figure in a leather hood and weathered cloak stepping into his room and closing the door.

"Who are you?" Alindale shouted, having leapt to his feet. He searched quickly for anything to use as a weapon, but the only thing in easy reach was the tall, brass candlestick lit on the table.

"Just a curious, old man," came a familiar, gravelly voice from under the hood, "come to survey the carnage after the battle."

Amadus's straightened his back as he pulled back his hood and tossed off his leather cloak. He gave Alindale a disappointed look as he folded the cloak in the crook of his arm. "Alindale," Amadus started, "why couldn't you have kept quiet?"

Alindale's face felt on fire. "Julian didn't keep to the *plan*! And how'd you get in here?"

"I was here when the first stone of this castle was laid and know more about its passages than even the architects. But that's beside the point. Julian *urged* you not to speak!" Amadus shouted with more ferocity than Alindale would have thought possible for a man of his years. "He warned you, but you didn't listen!"

Alindale stepped back from shock. Gone was the frail, unkempt old man from yesterday. As Amadus stormed toward him, he appeared at least twenty years younger than when Alindale had last seen him. His gray hair and beard were neatly trimmed, he stood with his back straight and without a pause in his step, and he looked fit enough to travel instead of lounging away in his mansion.

"All you had to do was *sit* there and say *nothing*!" Amadus yelled, jutting a finger into Alindale's face. "Instead, you not only embarrassed yourself, but you *disgraced* yourself! Did you even consider the consequences of accusing an aristo, welcomed to court, of such a high crime with nothing to stand on but your dislike for the man?"

"Haemin *is* a murderer," Alindale replied, grinding his teeth together. After sitting locked away for so long, he had to concede what he had done was reckless but still right.

Amadus squinted at him, as if inspecting his face. "You don't see it, do you?"

"See what?"

"That taking that very position was pointless."

Alindale gaped. *"Pointless?* He's the reason my brother is dead! He started a war."

"Ah!" Amadus excitedly wagged his finger at him. "There! Right there. He started a war, but why?"

Alindale waited, confused, expecting Amadus to provide an answer. Then he realized Amadus expected him to have an answer, but he wasn't in the mood for games.

"It doesn't matter," he frustratingly replied. "He *killed* my brother!"

"Enough!" Amadus threw up his hands and stomped away to pace around the room.

Alindale's brother had once described their rooms as shaped as large pieces of a cake—the back wall rounding with the curve of the tower, and the two other walls coming to a point together. Alindale's rooms were larger than most of in the castle and connected to a separate sitting room, wardrobe, bedroom, and private dining room. With so much space, his sitting room was sparse, filled merely with two couches, his armchair, and a sitting table.

Amadus paced around the couches with his hands clasped behind his back, muttering to himself. He gave out a loud sigh when he finally stopped, keeping his back to Alindale.

"You need to accept something, Alindale," Amadus said before turning around with a pitiful look in his eye. "No one cares about your brother, or how he died."

"But . . ." Alindale stammered, "everybody loved him."

"Loved," Amadus pointed out. *"Loved* in the hope he would be the ideal ruler others envisioned in their own imaginations. *Loved* for a mythos created in their own minds. *Loved* for their own ambitions." He waved his hand, as if blowing away a wisp of smoke. "All of which ended with his death."

Alindale frowned. "People aren't that shallow." *They wouldn't compare me with Adam if they didn't love him.*

Amadus rolled his eyes. "That's a different argument. The most important thing about your brother's death was how it was viewed by the throne at court. Your father banished Lord Haemin from court and, afterward, everyone knew to avoid the subject. The moment your mother *welcomed* Haemin back, however, everyone viewed your brother's death as a closed matter and Lord Haemin absolved." He stared intently at Alindale. "Do you understand now why accusing was a wasted effort?"

Alindale felt his stomach turn. "In other words, my mother . . . *forgave* him when she welcomed him."

"Absolved would be a better word, but"—Amadus shrugged in agreement—"from a certain point of view, forgave would be correct, too."

Alindale slumped and flopped back down into his armchair. "Then it really was all for nothing."

"This is not the time to wallow, Alindale." Amadus grinned. "In fact, this is an opportunity."

Alindale got the impression the immortal was up to something.

"In case Julian left out a detail, I'm banished from court, Amadus." He slapped the arms of his chair in frustration. "Mother even ordered everyone not to speak with me, or they would be banished, too. Wallowing in my chambers is all she has seen fit to allow me to do!"

Amadus growled, disgusted, and surprisingly marched up and grabbed Alindale by his collar, jerking him back to his feet. "You're a Dain!" Amadus yelled. "Heir to the throne. It's time you live up to your heritage. And at twenty-one years of age, you should be prepared to accept your inheritance. Fortunately, your mother has given us the perfect opportunity to continue your education and prepare you without any unnecessary distractions." He let go of Alindale's collar and began walking toward the door.

Alindale straightened his clothes then rubbed his neck. "My education?"

"Correct," Amadus called back. "I didn't finish your tutoring when you were young, and your fitness is also something that needs taking into account."

Alindale sucked in his gut on reflex as Amadus opened his door and motioned to someone. Then a tall man with a black cross-skull boar's skull before a broadsword on his yellow surcoat, identifying him as a knight, stepped inside. He quickly surveyed the room and instantly bowed when seeing Alindale.

"Your Highness," the knight said, "I am Brother Marc Revel, Knight of the Enderval Brotherhood, and humbly at your service."

Alindale turned questioningly to Amadus. "At my service?"

"Brother Revel trains recruits for the Enderval Brotherhood," Amadus explained. "He has agreed to assist in your training during your banishment."

Brother Revel rose from his bow, standing head and shoulders over Amadus. The candlelight reflected off his brown hair, with only a hint of gray at the temples. His physique was a model of a man-at-arms—muscular, broad at the shoulders yet narrow at the waist, a square jaw that looked as rough as iron.

"Are you trying to get me to learn swordsmanship again?" Alindale groaned. "You know I have no talent for it." Several masters-at-arms had tried to teach him how to use a sword and had always found him a disappoint.

"Brother Revel won't be training you in the sword," Amadus replied.

"Amadus has asked, on your behalf, that I train your body to become stronger, fitter," Brother Revel added. "Master Montaigu will teach you in the sword."

Another knight entered Alindale's bedroom. Rather, he stalked into the room without a sound. He wore a white surcoat with the Enderval emblem on his chest. He was shorter and stouter than Brother Revel. Half of his bald head was scarred a reddish pink, while the other half was only suntanned.

Alindale grew stiff and felt a chill run down his back when the knight's dark eyes fell on him. They were more the eyes of a predator than a man, as if he could tell everything about you from a single look. The master bowed but didn't say anything.

"Please excuse Master Montaigu's silence, Your Highness," Brother Revel said. "Forty years ago, a group of outlaws tortured him and"—he hesitantly glanced at the disfigured knight—"his throat was cut. He lived, but he can't speak now."

Master Montaigu rose back to his feet, and Alindale noticed the jagged scar under his jawline and around his neck.

"But," Amadus interjected, "Master Montaigu is possibly the best swordsman among the Knights Brotherhoods, even possibly the entire kingdom. There is none better to teach you the sword than he."

Master Montaigu placed a hand over his heart and nodded to Amadus.

"Forgive me, Amadus," Alindale said with concern, "but I am still confused as to why I need their services."

Amadus squinted at him and frowned. "Because you need more than a few extra lessons in politics. You need to become more presentable, more capable, especially if you accuse a renowned duelist like Lord Haemin again."

"What?"

"Oh yes"—Amadus nodded—"Lord Haemin has a steady sword hand and has chosen to defend his honor with a blade more times than take the offender to a magistrate for slander these past five years. Your personage, and the fact you accused him in open court, are probably the only things that saved you from a challenge. Now, with you banished, at odds with your mother, and short-tempered when it comes to Haemin, it's best you learn to defend yourself, even though you're the royal heir."

"But my father—"

"Your father's condition aside," Amadus cut him off as he approached him, "you must look to your position. And it is very tenuous. If we don't do something quickly, it may be irreparable." Amadus shook his head discouragingly.

"And training as a knight is supposed to help?" Alindale frowned, deeply disheartened. It didn't seem likely that swinging a piece of metal around would improve either his situation or his disposition.

"You won't be training as a knight, no." Amadus took Alindale by the shoulders and gently shook him. "We must use your banishment as an opportunity to prepare you for the throne."

Alindale shrugged him off. "Amadus, my father is still alive!"

Amadus nodded. "And all pray that he remains so, but his condition and fate are in much more capable hands than ours. Your fate is in yours. You didn't want to hear it last night, but you *will* be king, possibly very soon. It's time for you to accept the fact that, at any moment, *all* the responsibility of the kingdom may be placed in your hands, as well! We must take this chance to raise your position in the eyes of everyone in the castle and at court."

"But I'm not allowed at court."

Amadus raised a finger. "Tell me, Alindale, how does a person outside a house get the attention of someone inside, who does not want to have anything to do with the person outside, to open the door and acknowledge them?"

Alindale remembered when he was under Amadus's tutelage that he would ask similar questions. Amadus would smack the back of his head if he answered wrong.

He thought for a moment but failed to see the greater point that Amadus was trying to get across.

"Knock loudly?" He shrugged shyly.

Amadus frowned and gave him a look that made Alindale fear for the back of his head. "The servants have been knocking on your door all day. Did that get them anywhere?"

Alindale rolled his eyes.

"The person outside must make so much noise that everyone inside has no choice *but* to acknowledge him."

Alindale raised an eyebrow at that. "You mean, I should make a nuisance of myself?"

"Some may find what I have in mind as a nuisance. But"—Amadus held up a finger like he was instructing again—"the main thing will be that you are seen and heard. Every morning, Brother Revel will wake you for morning exercise. On your way, you shall go with your guard to your father's chambers and demand loudly to know of his condition."

Amadus waved his concerns away before Alindale could voice them.

"Whether they have an answer is irrelevant. It is only important others hear that you are *constantly* and *personally* checking on your father, which you must also do each night before you retire. The courtiers will hear of this, they will see you training with two knights, and then they will begin to talk."

"And I suppose you have a master plan in guiding what the courtiers talk about."

Amadus smiled and made a high-pitched chuckle. "It's best they whisper and gossip among themselves in speculation. Let them make up as many wild ideas as they can come up with, just so long as you are seen out of this"—he glanced about the bedroom in distaste—"drab prison cell you sleep in."

Alindale contemplated Amadus's plan. "And you think that will be enough?" He doubted it would have the success that the ancient probably hoped for, but the idea of those in the castle talking and wondering what he was up to, instead of merely mocking him, sounded worth the effort.

"Depends." Amadus ran his fingers through his beard.

"Depends on what?"

"Timing, your effort"—Amadus glanced at him—"and progress. Some luck would be nice, too."

The old man smiled, and a twinkle entered his hazel eyes. It might have been excitement. "What do you say, Alindale? Would you prefer to stay in your room alone, or would you prefer to let all those mocking courtiers whisper and worry that you're up to something?"

Alindale looked about the room and sighed. "Start in the morning?"

Chapter 9

14th of Petrarium, 1109 N.F. (e.y.)

Sleeping in would have been much better than this. Tory sighed as she gently swirled the brown contents, which *she* wouldn't describe as tea, in her small, silver teacup.

"It is so wonderful for all of you to find the time to have morning tea with me," Serina said cheerfully to the gaggle of ladies crowding her sitting room. "I hope you accept my apologies for not inviting you all sooner. Unpacking and settling in can take such a frustrating amount of time."

We've only been here two days!

A chorus of understandings, and a wave of nods followed from the other ladies sitting in a large oval of cushioned armchairs and lounges. Their morning gowns were far less elaborate than their court dresses, but the amount of brocade, lace, and embroidery on their linen skirts and thin sleeves made them far too showy for Tory's taste. Serina, however, lavished at the head of her gathering.

She had stolen Nina again before Tory had woken up and had forced her and the other maids to move her sitting room furniture around to make the prefect shape for all her guests to face her, no matter where they sat or lounged. All save for Tory. Serina had reserved her a special seat off to her right, nestled in the corner, near the balcony.

"Think nothing of it," Lady Regina Malthas, the slender woman lounging to Serina's left, said. She shrugged, bouncing her chestnut curls off her shoulders. "Why, most of us barely had our rooms lavishly arranged as you do when we first arrived."

"Why, thank you, Regina," Serina gushed, pressing her hand to her chest. "I cannot express my gratitude to all of you for making me feel so welcome in the short time I have been here. Why, I almost feel right at home."

Serina giggled at another encouraging chorus from her guests.

I'm sure you do, Tory quipped internally. Despite all the smiles and warm gestures, she didn't believe any of them were sincere.

Tory grew more and more uncomfortable while watching the little interactions between the ladies, their whisperings, their sideways glances, their stifled giggles. Nothing the other women did felt real to her, especially her sister.

She had seen Serina put on a face before with their parents when she lied, but not like this. Serina's smiles, her kind words, even the act of listening gave Tory the impression she was watching a play being performed instead of friends talking with each other over morning tea.

"Now," Serina said eagerly, "who has the latest gossip? I have been preoccupied with my family, and we do hear so very little on the Isles."

Tory rolled her eyes as the ladies clambered over themselves to share first. *Preoccupied with Harris Fauman, you mean*, she wanted to scoff.

A lazy gust rolled in from the open balcony, around the blue and gold linen curtains, and whipped up the back of her chair. Tory sat up stiffly from the chill. Goosebumps ran up her arms. She gritted her teeth, and her hands trembled, tapping her teacup against the saucer. She winced, whereas the rest of the ladies chattered on unflinchingly, or perhaps the backs of their cushioned seats blocked the morning chill. *Is no one else cold?*

She shook her head and rubbed her arms, one after the other, while balancing the teacup in her free hand. She tried to avoid the mornings. A livable heat settled in just before midday and made the day enjoyable. Before then, however, Tory preferred to stay indoors and away from any opened windows. Yet another reason to make her miss her ever warm Isles.

As the curtains rustled in the telltale sign of another gust approaching, Tory looked to ask a maid to close the balcony doors, but they were busy prepare snacks at the other end of the room.

I could do it myself, she thought, but then she was hit with a sudden worry of drawing attention to herself.

The curtains rumpled again, and she bit inside of her cheek and rubbed her arm, watching the fabric sway. She glanced hesitantly at Serina, who was softly laughing and listening to Regina and didn't appear to be watching her at the moment, so Tory took a chance to slowly get out of her seat. She lightly set her teacup and saucer down before daintily attempting to draw the curtains.

"Dianna Hollister got betrothed to a knight," a curly-haired blonde, sitting with her back toward her and whom Tory hadn't been introduced to yet, shrilled mockingly.

At the round of contemptable laughter, Tory paused her tugging on the stubborn linen.

"I heard the betrothal was rather sudden, too," Regina added, receiving a few excited awes for her contribution. "She probably agreed to cover up the product of her latest flirtation."

"It was bound to happen with her," Serina said, cutting off the rising giggles. "She always flirted with the marital types too much. Why, I even warned her myself once that the athletic boys are good to look at, but men with prospects, names, and friends are the ones a woman of quality gives her favor to."

In unison, the ladies nodded agreeingly, which encouraged Serina to carry on.

"I told her to enjoy the knight-seekers all she wanted"—Serina shrugged—"but she should save herself for a man with status, as any fine woman of quality, like us, would." She smiled as her audience giggled approvingly. "And, if the match didn't work, take a knight as a lover every now and then, and she would have been happy *and* content for the rest of her life."

Serina and the ladies erupted with laughter. Regina kicked her legs while laughing, nearly flinging off her slippers. Another woman's cackle bordered on obnoxious. One lady snorted tea out of her nose then hurriedly covered it with her hand and turned red while waiting for a maid to rush in with her handkerchief. The other women laughed harder.

Serina sat back in her armchair, smiling so wide in satisfaction that her lips twitched. It was as if she took pleasure watching the other ladies laughing at the degradation of another. She shot glances from one lady to the next, taking in the sight of each of them laughing and agreeing with her, as if each sight were a treasure to behold.

Tory stood stunned. Her arms trembled as she clutched the curtain's rough fabric and looked down at her sister. She had never seen Serina act or talk like that before. Tory knew she was often selfish, even dismissive and cold. But this was worse. As if Serina was a different person.

Or maybe, she worried, *this is who she really is—unsatisfied and selfish—and just can't show it back home.*

She knew their father wouldn't allow this.

Serina glanced her way, and Tory shivered as Serina's smile dropped from her face.

"Tory?" Serina said with hinting annoyance. "What are you doing?"

Tory jerked as the rest of the ladies shifted in their seats to stare at her. The curtain had draped in front of her while she had been distracted, stunned by her sister's comment.

"The . . ." Her mouth went suddenly dry, and she hastily swallowed. "I felt a chill and thought I would"—a few ladies snickered behind their hands, making her pause. She looked between their smirking faces and Serina's annoyed expression—"draw the curtains."

Serina's lips trembled, as if holding back a sneer. She took a quick sip of her tea, and then her composure returned when she lowered her cup. "Leave the curtains alone."

Serina returned to her guests. "You must excuse my dear sister, ladies. She's yet to embrace the small blessing of the morning cool."

Tory's cheeks warmed as the other ladies nodded. Their grinning eyes watched her from over the rims of their teacups.

She sat down hurriedly and folded her hands in her lap. She twirled her thumbs and dropped her head to avoid the judging eyes. Strands of her hair fell across her face.

The room fell quiet and still. The rolling flap of the curtains and the ladies' sips were as loud as crashing waves in Tory's ears. She stared down to her white slippers that suddenly felt tight. She wiggled her toes in the unfamiliar confines in the vain hope they would stretch.

I miss not wearing shoes.

It had only been a few days ago that she had been on her brother's ship, running along the deck barefoot, excited to catch sight of a pod of snake whales sunbathing at the ocean's surface. Despite first seeing the city and

Dain Castle's throne room, she had found more thrills sailing to Daincliff than being here.

She gripped her hands tighter. *I want to go home.*

"It's really too bad," Lady Malthas said. "If your mother had allowed her to attend Faultaire University, Serina, she would be well-accustomed to such things now."

Several ladies hummed in agreement.

Faultaire University was a school for young ladies in Silkhaven. It mostly accepted pupils from aristo families but would accept other young women from wealthy and newly elevated families. It taught arithmetic, penmanship, etiquette, and culture. However, Tory had heard her mother complain about Serina's only interest in learning court culture and refused to send Tory when she had come of age.

"Quite," Serina agreed. "I warned Mother neglecting her education would make her ill-prepared for public life, *especially* here at court." She sniffed in disdain. "After witnessing Jerro trying to teach her to be a deckhand, I knew someone had to look to my dear sister's proper future. And I believe she is happy for the opportunity to come to court under my supervision. Are you not, Tory?"

Tory bit her lip. *I'd rather be a deckhand.*

She took a deep breath and composed herself before forcing a small smile and lifting her head. "Mmhmm . . ." she hummed with a nod.

Holding the smile made her grit her teeth. She felt herself start to shake and desperately tried to fight it.

Look away. Please, just go back to talking among yourselves and stop staring—

"What are your impressions of court life, Tory?" Regina asked, scooping up some loose grapes from a bowl on the sitting table in the center of the group and rolling them in her hand. She smiled mischievously as she keenly watched her.

Tory glanced at Serina out of the corner of her eye, but her sister sat, half-turned, leaning against her side and happily watching her discomfort at being the center of attention. She swallowed, trying to think of a quick response.

"Different. I'm adjusting, but I'm afraid everything is still too new." She shrugged and prayed they found her reply boring enough, or perhaps not flattering enough, to ignore her again.

Regina popped a grape in her mouth. "Met many interesting people yet?"

"Well . . ." She turned to Serina hesitantly, careful with her words after her sister's warning.

"I have taken a careful hand in whom she is introduced to while she is here," Serina interjected. "I could not risk her entry into public life being mired by meeting the wrong sort."

I've been miring with the wrong sort all morning.

"So, *you* introduced her to the prince?" Regina asked.

Tory blinked, and Serina's smile slipped completely off her face.

Regina rolled over onto her side, a bemused light flickering in her eyes while passing a look between Tory and her sister, still rolling the remaining grapes between her fingers.

"The prince?" Serina chuckled halfheartedly, trying to recover her practiced smile. "Why would I introduce her to His Royal Dullard?"

Serina's smile widened as the other ladies in the room erupted in another round of cackling laughter. Tory, on the other hand, sat stunned once again. Calling the prince a bore to her in private was one thing, but these were ladies of the court openly mocking royalty.

"*Serina,*" Tory whispered, shaking her head in concern.

Serina waved her away. "Oh, do not worry, dear; we are among friends."

Tory frowned and sat back.

Regina ate her grapes as the laughs faded. "I was just wondering, because I could have sworn I saw His Highness in a deep conversation with our young Tory the first day of session."

Tory sat back up, straighter than before. Her eyes went wide as she stared at Regina happily biting her last grape in half. A cold sweat broke out on her brow as she slowly turned to face her sister.

Serina's smile was gone. Now she glared back at Tory with a restrained smolder simmering in her eyes. Her lips were pursed, as if holding back a fiery tirade, which Tory could imagine. She had hoped the drama of Her Majesty barring the prince from session would sweep away their small conversation from Serina's notice.

"*And?*" Serina insisted, her voice strained, almost coming through clenched teeth. Her eyebrows twitched, and she tapped the arm of her chair with her fingernails. "What were you and the prince discussing?"

Tory clasped her clammy hands together and struggled to think of a safe answer. Her right leg began to tremble, and she had to stop it before her heel began to thump on the carpeted floor.

"Well, his family," she finally replied.

Serina arched her brow, almost menacingly. "Oh?"

"Yep." Tory nodded fervently. "I was looking at that beautiful mural on the ceiling, and he suddenly appeared and asked if he could tell me who they were." She gave Serina an apologetic smile, wishing she would accept it. She expected to be yelled at later, though.

"You poor thing," a lady in the back said. Her long, narrow face was framed by long, brown hair that gave Tory the impression of an oval mirror from how pale her skin was. "It must have been an awful bore."

Tory shook her head. "Not really. He seemed to know what he was talking about. I guess he would, being it is his family and all. Although"—she giggled, remembering the talk—"we did have a little disagreement that he took a *little* too seriously."

"Oh really?" Regina inquired, sitting up. "Do tell."

"It was just a little thing. He was certain we discovered Daincliff first when I'm fairly sure we found Crescent Bay first." She shrugged and giggled, but none of the ladies joined her.

Regina slumped back on her lounge, her interest and amusement gone as she lazily reached for more grapes. The other ladies stirred their teacups with bored frowns and refused to make eye contact with her.

"Fascinating," Serina groaned, rubbing her temples. "Clearly, Her Majesty's decision to throw that useless excuse of a prince out of session was the proper one, getting into such a *pathetic* debate as that." Serina shook her head, and the other ladies harrumphed in agreement.

"And I'm sure he recited a quote from each of those old men," Regina said, rolling over on her back and studying her new clutch of grapes as if she were bored.

Serina rolled her eyes dramatically. "He has always done that. Just another example of how weak he is. Remember, ladies, confident men don't recite other men as if they are poetry. Her Majesty will guide us through these trying times. She knows how to rule the table properly."

Tory felt uneasy, despite finally not being the center of the conversation. She had barely spoken to the prince, and his outbursts in court hadn't been impressive. They had reminded her of a child playing a game and complaining about a small rule not being followed.

But he still doesn't deserve this.

"Serina," she said softly, "you shouldn't speak of His Highness like that. He *is* the prince, after all."

Serina gave her a blank stare before barking a laugh. "So? A birth title is meaningless if the person is unworthy of it, and His High Dullard is certainly unworthy."

"But Serina, His Majesty—"

Serina dismissed her with a wave. "The king is only ill. We are in good hands with Her Majesty. *Better* now that she has appointed the right ministers."

Tory knew from her smile that the right ministers to whom she was thinking was Lord Rudmund Fauman. She had been ecstatic by his appointment as the new Minister of Treasure and continuously boasted to the other ladies how she had been in constant correspondence with his son.

"But Serina, dear, don't you think you are being a *little* bold?" Regina asked. "His Majesty is ill, and any moment, the physicians could proclaim some terrible news. His Highness could be the new king by tonight." She shuffled around on her lounge, coyly smiling up at Serina, while Serina passively stared back.

The other ladies fell silent, watching them. Tory, though, watched her sister. Of everything spoken this morning, this was the first thing that remotely came close to challenging Serina's hold over the conversation.

"Not at all, Regina dear," Serina finally said. "Because, as we have all witnessed, Her Majesty has everything well in hand. And if the prince were suddenly the king tomorrow, she would still have everything well in hand. He can slouch in and take his seat up there on the dais, but we all know he would not even know the first thing to do without Her Majesty helping him. And if he refused her help"—Serina snickered—"the kingdom would go so poorly that he would beg her for help within a week. No! A *day*!"

Another round of agreeing harrumphs followed, whereas Regina shrugged and nestled back down in her lounge.

Tory found all this unsettling. Favoring Her Majesty over the king. Pitting the prince against the queen. It was all too much. She had never been one for politics in general, but something about the sentiment of favoring one of the royal family over the other did not sit right to her.

She rubbed her temples and asked, "May I be excused? I'm not feeling very well."

"Nonsense, Tory," Serina replied. "It will pass."

Suddenly, she clapped her hands together and sat on the edge of her chair, as if she had just thought of something. "Now, let's talk about—"

"Please, Serina. I think the morning chill has gotten to me." Tory had spoken without thinking, more desperate to leave than suffer any more of her sister's tea party.

Serina sprang to her feet and clasped her hands together. "Please excuse us for a moment, ladies.

"Tory, may I speak with you for a moment?"

Serina stormed toward her bedroom, her skirts swishing furiously with every step. Then she jerked the crystal doorknob and caught the swinging door before it slammed against the wall. When Serina looked over her shoulder, Tory found her practice smile gone and her cold, disappointing eyes had returned.

Tory followed like a condemned prisoner about to be thrown to a steel-fish. She held her hands in front of her and kept her head hung a little as she walked into the bedroom and braced herself. *My first scolding of the day.* She quietly sighed. *And it's not even midday yet.*

Serina's bedroom was as immaculately organized as her sitting room. All her trunks had been unpacked and stored away, and the three wardrobes against the wall, adjacent to the sitting room, were undoubtedly filled and organized. Her spacious bed was neatly made with the blue and gold trimmed blankets that Tory despised because they were too hot, and the white, silk bed curtains hung neatly against the varnished bedposts.

"Please excuse us, ladies," Serina said again. "This shan't take long."

Tory's heartbeats sped up when the door closed, and then tension grew in her shoulders as Serina marched in front of her.

She started to raise her head and, in a weak voice, said, "Serina, I—"

Serine grabbed her by the chin and violently jerked her head up. She sneered down at her, eyes burning with rage. "What are you doing, you little *chit*?" she hissed soft enough that she wouldn't be overheard by the ladies in the next room but still fiercely. "Are you trying to humiliate me?"

Of course you'd think that.

"No," Tory replied, hoping short, simple answers would make this end sooner.

"Then, what is wrong with you? Are you so inept you can't read a room?" Serina sighed in frustration and let go of her chin, scratching her with her fingernails. She took a deep breath then asked, "Now, why were you speaking with the prince?"

Tory rubbed her chin. "I told you! He came up and started talking with me before session. That's it!"

"I told you *not* to talk with anyone unless I introduced them first."

"He's the prince!"

"Especially *him*!" Serina almost yelled. Her face became a thunderclap as she thrust her finger in Tory's face. "Don't speak with him. Don't speak *of* him. And don't *ever* defend him! He's not worth it, and everyone knows it. You understand?"

Tory pressed her lips tightly together to hold back her desire to scream. She knew Serina only wanted to use her for a laugh with her friends, despite her talk about educating her. However, being chastised for *not* mocking someone whom she barely knew infuriated her. Tory barely stopped the impulse to slap her sister.

It's not right. Her hand began to tremble as she rubbed her chin. *It's not fair.*

But Serina was hardly ever fair, and Tory knew she would only take more of her anger out on her and their maids if she failed to answer correctly.

She dropped her head so her hair could cover her face. "I understand."

Serina sniffed dismissively. "Good. Remember your station. You have just arrived at court with older, unwed siblings. Do not ever let me hear you talk of him or hear you spoke with the prince again. Go to your room. I shall make an excuse for you. You have caused me enough disappointment for one morning."

Serina brushed past her and toward the door. Tory followed behind with her head down. Being led out like a naughty child in front of Serina's friends left a foul taste in her mouth, like bad squid, but she couldn't pass up the opportunity to escape her sister's tea party.

"Sorry about that, ladies," Serina announced. "Turns out my dear sister is not feeling well and needs to rest."

"Oh my," Regina said in feign concern. "I do hope you feel better soon."

"Thank you," Tory weakly replied with a nod then reached for the door.

Serina clapped her hands and, as Tory stepped into the hallway, she caught her saying, "Now, we each have letters from Emelie Faviann to design dresses for us, and Her Majesty needs our support. We should arrange a luncheon in honor of all the hard work she is doing and show her our new dresses!"

"That's an excellent idea!" one of the ladies cheered just as Tory closed the door.

The hallway was quiet, almost defining. And she loved it. She breathed a sigh of relief from finally being free.

Candlelight gleamed off the floor's polished blue tiles from mounted candles on the wall, and a lone, arching window at the end of the hallway casted long shadows across the walls.

Stepping into her own sitting room, which was only across the hall from Serina's, though she wished it were farther away, Tory found it in disarray. The maids had picked over her furniture and had moved the best pieces over to Serina's to ensure all her guests had a place. Tory's sitting tables sat alone and at an angle, as if randomly placed aside with the single crimson lounge sitting against the side wall. She suspected the maids had left it because they knew Serina hated red.

She ignored the desolation and went straight to the bedroom. Its state was in even more of an upheaval, but that was her own fault. Neither she nor Nina had taken the time to unpack her trunks at the foot of her bed, and several of her dresses lay across them from where Tory had tossed them. Her unmade bed was stripped of blankets and left with only the sheets. The blankets were folded in the corner of the room. Despite the cold mornings, the nights were muggy and too hot for them. Tory loved the fluffy pillows, however.

With another deep sigh, she threw herself onto the bed and buried her face in them. Their silk cases smoothly rubbed against her cheeks as her head sunk into their plushy stuffing. *I can sleep on these all day.*

She didn't care her dress was wrinkling, and she kicked off her slippers to hang her feet over the edge of the bed. She wiggled her toes as the fresh air seeped through her socks, closed her eyes in the darkness of the pillows, and focused on her slowing her breathing. Right away, she started to feel herself float into sleep.

Then there came a loud banging knock on her door.

Tory's longed-for bliss was shattered in an instant, and she let out a frustrated yell into her pillows, muffling it. Then she squirmed on her bed, hit the mattress with her fists, and kicked her feet in the air.

"Go away!" she yelled, but again into the pillows.

Another loud knock came, this one sounding more insistent than the other.

Tory groaned and rolled over. She rubbed her eyes and steeled herself before getting to her feet.

The knocking came again as she reached the door.

"I'm coming!" she called, turning the knob. "Yes—"

A musical trill filled her ears when she opened the door. Jerro stood with a hand propped against the doorframe, as carefree as if he were still on his ship.

"I knew I'd catch you sleeping." He chuckled, grinning broadly at her disheveled hair.

Tory pursed her lips and ran her fingers through her hair, straightening it where she could. "Please, don't tease me, Jerro," she begged. "I just got free from Serina."

"Apologies, baby sister," Jerro said with a wave. "I figured, with session not being called today, you'd be free."

She folded her arms and studied him. He wore finer clothes than he would on his ship. The sleeves of his cream-colored shirt and blue vest with black embroidery were neatly pressed. His black trousers were clean, without a smudge of ocean spray, and his knee-high boots shined.

She arched an eyebrow. "And, what brings *you* here, if it's not for session? Met another lady to call on?"

"Now, Tory, that's harsh." Jerro lifted a large, wooden birdcage. "I wanted to bring a friend to see you."

Harpo sat in the center of the cage with his forewings tucked in, his plumage ruffled, and his tail and head crest feathers drooped. He twittered weakly when he saw her.

"Harpo!" Tory seized the cage, wrenching it from Jerro. It was heavier than she had thought, and she almost dropped it.

Harpo squawked and flapped his wings, bits of red feathers flying up from the bottom of the cage.

"How could you, Jerro? You know Harpo molts and gets sick if he's caged."

Jerro rubbed the back of his head and gave her an apologetic look. "I know, but it was for his own good. A few of the fishmongers were complaining that he'd stolen a fish or two from them and . . ."

"*And . . .?*"

Jerro shrugged. "One of the other captain's complained his ship's cat is missing, and it and Harpo were seen fighting a couple times."

Tory's breath caught, and she turned a scowl on the pytre hawk. "Harpo! Bad boy!"

It was well-known on the Isles that pytre hawks and cats despised each other. Tory wouldn't call either predators of the other but, from her experience, they would both maim or kill the other, if given the chance.

She whisked the cage into her sitting room and put it on a table close to the balcony. She then threw open the curtains and the balcony door, letting in the sunlight and fresh air, but ignored the chill. She opened the cage door and looked inside.

Harpo sat in middle of the cage, his head drooped against the cage floor, which already had a thin layer of his smaller feathers around him.

"Come on," she beckoned with a wave. "You can come out now."

When he didn't move, she gave her best imitating trill. Harpo didn't step forward, but he at least raised his head and blinked at her.

"You and your pets," Jerro tutted, closing the door behind him and shaking his head. "It's a good thing you didn't try to smuggle all of them with you."

"I didn't smuggle *any*!" Tory gathered up her skirts then smoothed them before kneeling to watch Harpo. "Harpo perched himself on the mast before we sailed." She imitated a chirp again, but the pytre hawk only turned his head and hid it under his forearm feathers.

Tory narrowed her eyes at him and puffed her cheeks. "He's pouting."

"Your room is very . . . empty," Jerro commented.

She turned her narrowed-eye stare on him as he plopped down on her remaining lounge and stretched out.

He noticed Tory glaring and guessed, "Serina?"

She nodded. "Serina."

Jerro sighed. "Well, we knew this would happen. Sorry, Tory."

She frowned and sat back on her haunches. She wrapped her arms around her knees and looked back into the cage at Harpo still burying his face in his feathers.

"I thought it'd be different here," she said. "I hoped she would busy herself with her friends or letters to Harris Fauman and let me enjoy being somewhere *new*." She pushed her face into her skirts. "At least, back home, I could talk with whomever I wanted."

"Serina got mad at you for talking with someone?" Jerro asked, confused.

"Mmhmm . . ." She pulled her face out of her skirts and set her chin on her knees. "Lady Malthas told everyone she saw me and the prince talking the first day of session, and Serina scolded me for it."

"He wasn't rude to you, was he?"

Tory shook her head. "*No*! He was very polite. And our talk was very . . . boring." She sighed. "I just don't see why some people seem to hate him."

"Well . . ."

Tory gave him sideways glance.

"Everyone has expectations," Jerro finally said. "People expect me to be a commander of the seas, and I'm happy to oblige, while also being gallant and roguish." He flashed a smile, and Tory rolled her eyes. "As for the prince, everyone expects him to be more than a friendless shut-in. And, for some, like Serina, if you don't live up to *her* expectations, she's mean to you forever." He shrugged.

Tory pursed her lips. "That sounds like her. Jerro?"

Jerro grunted.

"Are all the people here like that?"

"Some. Most are here because court is here, and they've come to get what they can out of it."

Her frowned deepened. Neither type of people sounded good to her.

"I guess, in her own way, Serina is right about who I get to know." *But I don't like the people she's introducing me to, either.*

"Tory."

Tory turned and found Jerro sitting upright.

"If you get to wanting to go home, just let me know, and I'll send you back, no matter what Serina says." He gave her a wink.

She smiled, despite herself. "Thanks, Jerro, but I can't go back after only two days. Father might be disappointed. And Mother might never let me leave home again."

Jerro barked a laugh and slapped his knees. "That's the spirit, baby sister. Never make them turn your sails." He grunted as he got up then turned to leave. "Now that you have your pet, I have other matters to tend to."

"Calling on one of your *lady* friends?" She grinned mischievously.

Jerro was halfway out of the room when he gave her a glance over his shoulder. "Just upholding *my* expectations. Now, don't stay in your room all day. Take advantage of Serina being occupied with her tea party and get out on your own. There has to be something fun around here." He started laughing. "A knight was chasing some poor recruit around the battlements and hitting him with a stick. Something about the recruit saying 'sorry' too much. That was funny to watch! See you later, baby sister." Just like that, Jerro was gone, and the empty room felt depressing all of a sudden.

Tory's grin quickly faded, and she turned back to Harpo. The pytre hawk was sniffing around his cage and slowly working his way to the open cage door. He noticed she was looking at him and made three quick chirps. He chattered his needlelike teeth and scraped at the cage floors with his forearm claws.

"Hungry, huh." She felt the urge to scratch his head but knew, with him being hungry, he might take her finger as food.

She glanced at the open balcony door and thought to close it, but she didn't want Harpo to feel shut in. Her balcony hung over a small courtyard, which was closed off, so if he did go outside, there was little chance he would be able to fly off.

"All right, I'll get you some food."

Harpo's head perked up.

She shook her head. "Of course you understood that." Tory giggled and went to fetch her slippers.

When she came back, Harpo was out of the cage and hopping on the sitting room table, taking in the sights of his new surroundings. Thinking about it, Tory quickly closed her bedroom door.

Best we keep this closed so you don't make a nest out my pillows. She was the only one going to make a nest out of those.

Then she took her brother's advice and slipped out of her room, with Serina none the wiser.

Chapter 10

Kalleb hurried down Kanestown's South Main Street, his bootheels thumping against the boarded sidewalk. He continuously stretched out his new uniform by flexing, straightening, and rolling his shoulders. He rubbed his neck in vain to relieve the itching from his jacket's starched, tall collar.

He was already sweating heavily. The back of his linen shirt clung to his back. The oppressive Easterly Sun was turning a normally mild morning unbearably humid. He clung to the meager shadows of the brick, two-story workshops and their awnings lining the left side of the street. Kalleb felt like he had been riding a week straight and hadn't spared the horses.

Assembly day, and I'm going to be late.

The morning after receiving his parole, Ma had cut his hair, and he had shaved for the first time in two months. Then began the rush across Kanestown to order his uniform and ready his supplies to muster out. Everything he had was new—his uniform, boots, and saddle. He knew, though, he wouldn't have been able to afford any of them without his family's help.

Another blessing of lost pride, Kalleb resigned, straightening his pa's saber hanging on his hip. He was running late from retrieving it from the blacksmith. He'd had to get it before reporting to muster; otherwise, his superior officer would have to allow him to get it. And given his situation, he doubted they would have let him get it.

"Officer!" a store hawker, a boy not thirteen, called in a high-pitched, unbroken voice. "Officer!"

Kalleb stopped mid-step and checked the street for an officer. The street was empty, and few strolled the sidewalk, especially this close to the blacksmith and tanner quarter. Kalleb's nostrils still burned with the combining stench of coal smoke and fish oil.

"You, Lancer!" The boy pointed at him. "Do you need a new saddle or an old one repaired?"

Kalleb frowned at him then glanced at his saber. *Kid must think anyone with a saber is an officer.*

"Sorry, boy," he said, "I'm not buying anything. Excuse me."

"Oh," the boy said sheepishly. His smile dropped, and the color left his freckled face. He swallowed nervously, uncertain of what to do since his opening sales pitch had been slapped down.

I probably should have been nicer. Regardless, he said nothing as he hurried on his way.

"If you do need a new saddle," the boy called after him, "or need repairs, bring it by The Hennessey's. We're the best in town!"

You and everyone else on this street.

"And I like your saber!" the boy yelled.

Kalleb smiled, despite himself.

Was I ever that innocent?

He had first enlisted at fifteen. His excitement, his brothers' frightening jokes about hours holding up lances without resting and drills, his ma's fussing and silent worries, his pa's quiet pride—all another lifetime to him now. Those naïve dreams had been shattered five years ago.

Remembering his tardiness, Kalleb broke into a jog.

Running parallel to him, on the opposite side of the street, was the Great Stable of Kanestown, the largest horse barn in the world. Its red brick foundation sprawled over two hundred thousand square feet of the city's southern quarter and stood two stories tall on its massive, red wood timber supports. The slanted rooves made sure the rain slid off and into the city's streets, drains, and alleys. A company's worth of stable hands, to keep clean, feed, groom, and wash the nearly two hundred and fifty horses, were stabled within at any given time.

I could have sworn there were more doors, he huffed.

The Great Stable surrounded parade grounds and, unfortunately for him, was the mustering spot for companies inside Kanestown. He began to think he would have to run the entire length of South Main before finally finding an entrance.

Kalleb's uniform jacket was stained with sweat by the time he reached a large opening, one tall enough for a rider on horseback to ride through. He dashed across the street and staggered to a stop as soon as his boots skidded across the stable's red brick floor.

He doubled over and clasped his knees, gasping greedily for air. His shoulders rose and fell. He coughed and spat from his throat turning scratchy. The farm might have kept him fit for labor, but he had clearly lost a step if a small run had taken so much out of him.

"Good morning!" a young stable hand greeted from a small, brick office to Kalleb's left. His curly, blond hair was a disheveled mess from either a horse thinking his hair was dried grass or just waking up that way. He wore a leather apron, over his worn, gray tunic, and his boots were scuffed and worn from years of use; possibly handed down to him by older siblings.

"Morning," Kalleb groaned out. He then straightened, put his hands on the small of his back, and stretched. His back didn't pop, but he gave a loud sigh, nonetheless. The smell of horse, manure, hay, and the sweet, flowery scent of henipha grass—a purple grass horses became gluttons over—filled his nose, and he snorted.

"You with the company assembling today?" the stable hand asked.

"Yes," Kalleb replied. He took a few deep breaths to steady his breathing. "Do you know if they are still on the parade grounds or if the officers have arrived?"

"You're the only officer I've seen, sir," the stable hand replied, retreating into the office.

Kalleb watched over the office's closed half-door as the stable hand dug through a mess of stained paper on a shelf. The hint of coffee drifted out from the office but couldn't compete against the odors outside. The stable hand then returned, flipping wide, weathered pages of a large, leather-bound book with grimy pages filled with names, numbers, and paragraphs of scribble.

"If you give me your name," the stable hand said, setting the book on top of the half door, "we can get your horse ready, sir."

"No," Kalleb replied dryly. "I'll be back to get my troop assigned horses. And you don't have to call me *sir*." He gave the stable hand a nod then started toward the parade grounds.

Despite the smell, he enjoyed the cool of the stables. The soft draft drifting through the passageways tempted him to linger before stepping back outside again.

You're late to report! he reminded himself. *Get your ass out there!*

Kalleb ran his fingers through his hair, straightening it back after his run. His pa's words came back to him. "An officer, no matter how low in rank, must be an example to his men." He wiped his hands free of sweat on his trouser legs before straightening his jacket, smoothing the front, adjusting his shoulders, and leveling his saber belt.

He stepped out onto the hard-packed dirt of the parade grounds and stopped, stunned. He had expected the men to be divided into their individual troops of twenty-five, organizing themselves before their superior came to inspect them. Instead, five hundred men loitered across the grounds like a disorganized mob.

Why haven't they formed up? Confused, Kalleb watched clusters of young men laughing and carrying on conversations as carelessly as if they were in a beer hall.

He spotted a group of nineteen lancers gathered away from the mob, showing off their uniforms to each other like childhood friends. Most of them had sabers, too. One, in the center, had his propped against his shoulder and stood smirking with his chest puffed out. The glint of bronze lance pins on their collars and the yellow cords on the shoulders of their uniforms caught Kalleb's eye.

"Oh God!" Kalleb staggeringly said under his breath. He looked over the whole mob again. "It's a company of kids."

He doubted a razor had touched many of their fresh, young faces. Some of the lads still had freckles on their cheeks. As a rule, the Storm Cavalry required all potential recruits to be fifteen years old or older but rarely enlisted more than a hundred at one time. Kalleb wasn't sure if there were more than fifty out of the five hundred over nineteen, and most of them were in the strutting group of lance corporals.

Konner had mentioned the company was newly formed, but this was unheard of.

Kalleb shook his head. "Whoever agreed to *this* should be sent to that damn farm."

Dirt crunched under his boots, despite the rain from a few days ago, as he approached the cluster of youthful lance corporals calmly, clutching the hilt of his saber. The hilt's black wood rubbed against his palm's hard calluses and the brittle scar lines as he fought the urge to bark an order. That brought a small smile to his face.

Funny. Wouldn't have guessed I'd ever feel that again. The desire to take charge was another thing frowned upon on the farm.

His smile faded, though, once he overheard their conversation.

"Two years, guys!" the stocky young man in the middle, with the saber on his shoulder, declared. He waved two fingers defiantly against his fellows' grumbles. Then he ran a hand through his shaggy, sandy-brown hair with a laugh. "In two years, we'll be up for promotions!"

"Two years for you, maybe." A lanky youth with stringy red hair laughed. "I'm going to make lieutenant before any of you!" He smirked, scrunching his dark freckles together at his fellows' grumbles and kicked clumps of dirt with his boot.

"It might not be smart to talk about promotions so soon," a dark, sun-tanned man with square shoulders and jaw, pulling at his stretched jacket in vain attempts to make it fit better, said. "We've only just enlisted, and if a higher officer were to hear us . . ."

"Don't tell us *you're* scared of the officers on your first day?" another mocked. "Isn't one of the lieutenants your brother?"

The group dissolved into shouting.

The Storm Cavalry had their own method of recruitment and enlisting, separate from the city peace of Daincliff and the guards of Dain Castle. Its internal organization was different from aristos' personal guards and the multitude of Knight Brotherhoods. Its ranking system and requirements for promotion based on merits had become foundational staples of the cavalry.

Yet, despite that, a recruit's family and experience were looked at to see if they were officer material. Upon enlisting, if one had family already in the Storm Cavalry and were officers, they would often be made corporals in their recruiting troop. It appeared the recruiters had taken it a step further and had made them lance corporals instead.

Kalleb shook his head.

"Excuse me!" he shouted, stepping up to them.

Several jumped, and startled looks spread throughout the group. The stocky one's saber came off his shoulder, and the blade sliced through the air, alarming several close to him. Bewildered, he snapped to attention once he saw Kalleb.

"At ease," Kalleb said with a wave. "Where can I find Squadron Five?"

Confused looks passed among them, and a few glanced to the disorganized crowd filling the yard around them.

The big lancer stepped forward. His square shoulders loomed over Kalleb's head, and his uniform stretched over a broad chest. He held his narrow chin in the air and kept his blue eyes straight. He would be an impressive sight riding down a bushwhacker from horseback, but this close, Kalleb could see nicks in his chin where he had shaved, and his legs wobbled slightly. He was also one of the few who didn't have a saber.

"Lance Corporal Stew Bowden, sir, of Squadron Five," he said, sounding like he was trying to make his voice lower. "We haven't received orders to gather them yet."

"I said at ease, Stew," Kalleb said. "I just wanted to know if the company had been divided into their squadrons yet."

"Hey!" the lance corporal with the lanky red hair shouted. He shoved past Stew, pointing at Kalleb. "He's a lance corporal, like us. Look at his shoulder!"

Surprise spread among the lads as they finally noticed the yellow cord on his uniform's right shoulder, without any knots, marking him as a lance corporal.

A few sighed and relaxed from realizing he wasn't a higher officer.

Lanky Red-Hair, though, sneered at him and spat off to the side. "Finally decide to enlist, Grandpa? Or did you do some dumb shit and find yourself demoted?"

Their smirks and chuckles rolled off Kalleb like falling leaves. A little wise ass's cracks were nothing compared to what he had endured for years. Besides, it was a fair question.

"I might have done some dumb shit," he replied, smirking at their struck faces.

First, one snickered. Then another. Someone snorted. And then they all burst into laughter.

Kalleb let the moment of comradery pass. It had been so long since he had been in the company of other lancers and talked like ordinary people without a stain on his name.

Was it this simple back then? His smile slipped as it dawned on him that this wouldn't last, either. They would hear his name, and the stories would spread, and this will be gone. *Might as well stomp it out now.*

"But not as dumb as the shit you were talking," he said dryly.

The laughs stopped. They passed questioning glances at each other, their faces stuck between furled brows and mouths hanging open.

"You"—Kalleb pointed at the stocky lad—"put that saber away *now*!"

The lad repeatedly blinked his beady eyes, and his saber wobbled in his shaky grip as he stuttered, "But—"

"It's plain to see you haven't been trained on how to use it. Put it away before you stab someone!" Kalleb fixed him with a commanding glare, and the stocky lad's shoulders slumped as he fumbled to put his saber in its leather scabbard at his hip.

"Hey!" Lanky Red-Hair barked. "Who are you to give him orders?"

Several grumbled as their eyes were drawn to his father's saber.

Kalleb defensively patted the saber's hilt. "I'm someone who knows what he's doing." That said, he turned on his heels and headed toward the company.

"Where are you going?" Lanky Red-Hair's nasal, whiny voice was starting to grate on Kalleb's nerves.

He ignored him and turned his attention to the larger problem.

The mangled gathering filling the center of the yard was unworthy of being called a company. They grouped together, laughing and joking, as if they thought they were going on an adventure. Their burgundy jackets and cream-colored pants were all too clean, even though a few were sitting on the ground.

Children. Hopefully, they remember their troop and lancer assignments.

Kalleb took a few deep breaths.

Hope I still remember how to do this.

He took a few more deep breaths. He hadn't raised his voice in years. The punishments for doing so were harsh. As an officer, however, even the lowest-ranked officer, he had to overcome the fear that had been drilled into him. Kalleb sucked in one great breath, pulling it deep in his gut and puffing out his chest.

"Form up!" he yelled as loud as he could.

Startled looks spread throughout the mingled crowd, but most of the conversations kept going. There were too many people. Those in front of him simply stared at him, unsure of what to do. They needed something more to get them moving.

Kalleb drew his saber and thrust the blade into the air, its curved edge catching the sunlight and drawing more eyes to him. He glared back at them.

"Form into your squadrons! You"—he pointed at a cluster of lancers—"spread the word! Form up into your squadrons! I especially want Squadron Five over there! *Move!*" He pointed his blade to his right then began walking down the crowd, repeating his order. He waved his saber, drawing more attention from that than his yells. His voice was going hoarse by the time a sizable part of the crowd had started moving, and more confusion followed.

Cattle are easier to herd than recruits.

The scene quickly fell into madness. Men were yelling to form up, followed by questions of how, why, and where. Several even began talking with each other, asking which squadron they were in and who to ask if they weren't sure.

Kalleb didn't care about most of them. Each company was formed of five hundred lancers, divided into five squadrons, each of which were broke down into four troops. He yelled at them to get in their squadrons but, in truth, he was just trying to sort out twenty-five men.

"Squadron Five!" Kalleb stood with his saber again in the air, at the far end of the shifting crowd. "Squadron Five! Form up in front of me!"

Recruits finally started to gather in front of him, but they were as slow as water being squeezed from a leaf. While the others milled about, trying to figure out where the other squadrons were supposed to gather, one by one, those assigned to Squadron Five massed in front of him.

He glanced toward the other lance corporals and saw they were still standing around. Some watched him, some watched the company, while the rest continued to talk amongst themselves. His old instincts told him to command them to their squadrons and troops, but he bit his tongue. He had no right to order about his fellow officers. Those who did were the ones everyone came to hate.

I'm going to be an outsider, anyway, once they learn who I am. Might as well not be hated on top of that.

A sizable gathering had formed in front of him. He wasn't sure if there was a full squadron but figured there were enough.

"Squadron Five!" He jabbed his saber toward them. "Divide into your troops! I want Troop A here, followed by Troop B, and so on. Form four rows of five! Step to it!"

More scrambling, shoving, and even cursing followed as the men finally started to resemble lancers.

Kalleb sheathed his saber as he strolled to the center of the four columns. It was obvious each troop was missing men, but they were still trickling in, and Kalleb wanted to speak with some of his troop before Vallant arrived.

"I am Lance Corporal Kane." He cut off their spreading murmur with a look. "Yes, Kane. You've all enlisted in the Storm Cavalry and were going to meet lancers with the name sooner or later. Shut it!"

The whispering stopped, much to Kalleb's liking.

"I have been assigned as the lance corporal for Troop D. The other lance corporals will be with us"—he looked over his shoulder at the others still milling about—"someday. Troops A through C, stay in your troop until they do."

Kalleb finally turned his attention to his troop. He noticed more were missing from it than the others; only fourteen had formed into ranks.

They were the most unlikely recruits that he had ever seen. Several appeared frail, with fair complexions, as if they had never worked a day under the suns in their lives. Others were as sun tanned as him, clearly the sons of working hands who thought life in the Storm Cavalry would be better than lives behind a plow or herding cattle. *Depending on the farm, they might be right.*

Still, he estimated only a few had ridden a horse in their lives but doubted any of their families owned one.

Not a usual troop of recruits.

One recruit, standing in the front row, caught his eye. He stared at him in disbelief, standing nearly a head taller than the rest, with bronze, coppery skin and blond streaks running through his black hair. With his close-set, hazel eyes, he watched Kalleb's every move, and despite how wide they were, Kalleb could make out the wrinkles surrounding them. He looked older than most in the troop but seemed more anxious.

Certainly not the usual troop recruits.

A few more hurried to take a place in the back rows, bringing the count to seventeen.

"I have been assigned as your lance corporal," Kalleb said, his hoarse throat grateful to be addressing a small group, even though his voice now had a low growl. "This troop will be under my direct command for the duration of your training and onward. Have any of you been assigned as corporals?"

The men turned and looked at each other as two more stragglers joined the back of the troop, and when the men asked them, they didn't respond, either.

"I guess they haven't been assigned yet." He shook his head. "Each troop will have five corporals. The lieutenants will choose them when they get around to it. If you are promoted to corporal, you will serve under me and carry out additional duties." Kalleb let them chew on that before continuing.

"The rest of the time, we will be training you to be lancers. None of you have done what we're about to put you through. You will be riding every day, physically pushing your bodies to fight both in and out of the saddle. You'll get up before dawn and go to your bedrolls after sunset. And any man I don't think is able, I *will* recommend be sent home. Any questions?"

An arm shot up from the middle of the troop. "Are we given horses, or do we have to buy our own?"

"If you have a horse, you can ride it," Kalleb replied, "so long as it is not an old nag."

A few snickered at that.

"Otherwise, you'll have to request one from the stables. I'll help with that at the end of the day. Next?"

Another hand went up. "When do we get paid?"

Kalleb barked a laugh, along with everyone else in earshot.

"You'll be paid when the paymasters come around," he replied, searching his memory to remember a time he received pay and shrugged.

"When that'll be, I'm sure you'll hear about it before I tell you. Anything else?"

The troop got quiet again. He gave them a minute.

I suppose I can teach them to stand at attention before Vallant shows up.

He was about to speak when—

"When do we get our sabers?"

Kalleb searched the troop, but no one had raised their hand. He checked for a look, a smirk, a twinkle in the eye, something mischievous marking the jokester.

Finally, he spotted a lad in the back row, one of the stragglers who had just taken his place. Muscularly built, with an olive complexion from working in the suns, his dark hair was a spikey mess. What caught Kalleb's attention, though, was his shifting green eyes, as if trying to avoid his gaze, but he forgot not to grin.

"You!" Kalleb pointed at him. "Smart ass! Front and center!"

The recruit's shoulders tensed for a moment before he pushed through the rows to stand in front of Kalleb.

Kalleb put his hand on his hips but didn't stick out his chest and get in the recruit's face. Such a show would mean nothing to a recruit like him.

"Name?"

"Rence Coup," the recruit replied.

"Well, *Lancer* Coup, you can buy a saber with your pay."

Rence blinked in surprise, and a few others excitedly smiled to each other.

Kalleb stepped away from Rence so they could all see him. "And, if *any* of you do during training, I'll break them over your dumb heads."

He directed himself back to Rence. "You don't even know how to hold a lance; what makes you think you're worthy of a saber?"

Rence looked upward, clearly thinking of a response. Kalleb was sure it would be another joke, so he yelled before Rence could speak.

"You're *not*!"

He turned back to the rest of the troop. "The lance will be the first thing you're trained with—holding it, charging with it, aiming it. Next will be the mace. After you've each learned to wield those weapons, you will be trained with a saber. Understood?"

Weak replies and nods rippled through the troop.

"That's *Yes, Lance Corporal*!" Kalleb bellowed. "Yell out!"

"Yes, Lance Corporal!" the troop shouted in unison.

Needs to be louder. But he accepted it as a start.

"So"—Rence raised his hand—"we *can* buy a saber once we've saved enough, right?"

Kalleb gave him an unamused look. "If *you* buy one, I'll ram it up your ass. Get back in line."

Rence smirked as he strolled back through the troop to the back row while ignoring the others laughing at him.

"As for the rest of you, forget about buying a saber."

The smiles disappeared, to Kalleb's liking.

"Spend your money on your horse, their feed, their shoes, and your saddle *first*. After that, look to your boots, pants, and anything special you can fit in your bedroll to make the nights more comfortable. None of you know just how much riding you're about to do, and a saber isn't going to mean shit when you have blisters on your rears because you only have one pair of worn-out pants.

"And, if I catch any of you with a saber before you're allowed to have one"—he smirked darkly—"you *won't* enjoy the punishment."

Kalleb let them chew on his words, sure that some would test him, despite his advice. *A sorry lancer he'll be, though.* He spotted Rence in the back, still smirking. *Maybe.*

"Eighth Company! Form up!"

Six riders trotted their horses out into the yard. They wore their dress uniforms—black trousers and gold cords hanging off the shoulders of their burgundy uniform jackets. The five lieutenants were marked by the single knot on the yellow cord on their uniforms' shoulders and wore helms without visors.

In their center rode a man on a white horse. His helm's red plume flapped from the bouncing of the horse. Kalleb could make out the man's hawkish features, even from this distance, especially as he held his hooked nose in the air and rode with his right hand on his hip.

Vallant.

Their appearance, though, finally sent the other lance corporals scrambling to their troops. Kalleb noted several of them copying him by guiding recruits with their sabers, dividing their squadrons into troops.

He turned back to his troop. After a quick recount, he was relieved to see the last of his stragglers had found their places, as he found twenty-five men formed in five rows.

"All right, stand at attention!" Kalleb ordered. "Back straight, head up, snap your heels together, and keep your feet at an angle. But don't lock your knees! If any of you faint your first day, you'll never live it down."

He turned and snapped his heels together as his troop followed his instructions. He had stood at attention more at the farm than he had ever done while previously in the cavalry.

Maybe, we won't have to stand here for hours. He frowned deeply. *If Vallant is still long-winded, though . . . Crap.*

The orders to form up continued but were quickly dying down.

Kalleb heard the crunching of boots against the crusty ground and glanced out of the corner of his eye to spy his squadron's lance corporals taking their places.

"Form ranks, Troop A!" one shouted.

Kalleb's angle prevented him from seeing who yelled, but he figured they were trying to show off in front of the higher officers.

Lance Corporal Stew Bowden's tall shadow cut across the yard as he looked over Troop C. Kalleb watched him looking between his troop and Kalleb's for a moment before he nodded with a grunt and stood at attention.

I might actually get along with another officer.

"Excellent, Squadron Five!" a rich voice boomed.

Kalleb looked up in surprise as his squadron's lieutenant trotted his gray dun horse in front of them. He had a striking resemblance to Lance Corporal Bowden—tall in the saddle, broad in the shoulders, with square features. His thin, dark hair, though, was receding. He wore a big smile, surveying the squadron.

"It makes me proud to see you formed up and at attention." He barked a laugh and slapped his thigh. "I am your lieutenant, Craig Bowden, and I promise to mold you all into the best lancers you can be!"

Kalleb raised an eyebrow and glanced to his right at Stew, who was beaming proudly and nodding.

Brothers. Definitely brothers.

"Now, stand at attention!" the lieutenant ordered, moving his horse around to the end of the rows. "The captain has a few words."

The other lieutenants took positions around the company. Despite the yard being enclosed, addressing five hundred men was difficult. The lieutenants began relaying Vallant's words as soon as he started speaking. Kalleb could hear Vallant's voice in his head, though, and it was still as pompous as he remembered.

"Men of the Eighth!" Vallant yelled. "It is my honor to be your captain. And make no mistake, it is my intention to make this company not only the finest in the country, but the finest in the history of the Storm Cavalry! I swear, the names of lancers in this company will be written in the annuals of the cavalry and the history of New Hartland itself!"

Kalleb furled his brow. *Laying it on a little thick for these boys, aren't you, Vallant?*

Some of the lancers around him seemed to agree by the sound of shifting feet grinding into the dirt behind him.

"You are each a member in the formation of a brand-new company!" Vallant continued. "In the past, the Storm Cavalry would only recruit new lancers based on need, sometimes no more than a squadron full at a time, to fill in for retiring lancers or casualties from assignments. The recruits were sent across the country, to different companies, commanders, and needs.

"But, all of you will be different. You will be trained together, ride together, fight together! The success of this company will reshape the very organization of the Storm Cavalry. And I promise you, promotion and glory await all who assert themselves. Work hard and succeed!"

Scattered cheers went up from the company. The few who came from behind Kalleb sounded unsure, like afterthoughts, as if they had heard others cheering and thought they were supposed to cheer. Kalleb simply remained silent.

Promotion and glory. He grunted. *What are we, mercenaries and knights?*

"Lance Corporal Kalleb Kane!" Vallant yelled. "Front and center!"

Kalleb tensed. He looked over his shoulder and saw the hulking lieutenant frowning down at him with a hint of pity in his eyes.

"Captain wants you up front, Lance Corporal," Lieutenant Bowden repeated.

Kalleb drew himself up, keeping his chest out and chin up, stepped out of formation, and then headed toward Vallant. He felt every lancer watching him as he walked out into view. His shoulder blades grew tighter and tighter with each step, as if they were threatening to fold together. He gripped the hilt of his saber for balance. His eyes, though, were fixed on Vallant.

Vallant was as long-legged and lanky as Kalleb remembered. He sat in his saddle with his boots rammed inside his stirrups, as if he would slide off if they didn't cling fast to them. His pointed chin and hawkish nose jutted down at him, with a harsh-eyed squint from under his helm. His tall face had sharp angles, with his high cheekbones pointing inward, toward his nose. He frowned with contempt as Kalleb snapped his heels at attention in front of him.

"About-face, Lance Corporal," Vallant growled, walking his horse around Kalleb.

Kalleb turned on his heels and kept his chin up as he prepared himself. *I am a lancer again. Not a deserter. No matter what he says, I will keep my head and show them what a lancer looks like.* He bit his tongue just in case, though.

"This man is Kalleb Kane!" Vallant yelled, gesturing down at him. "He has been assigned to Squadron Five as lance corporal of Troop D. He is *not* a recruit. He is a deserter!"

The faces of the men before him lit with stunned expressions. A few stared at him in shocked disbelief while, here and there, he could pick out the old scowls of disgust. Kalleb bit his tongue harder but couldn't stop from glaring up at his arrogant prick of a captain.

"Lance Corporal," Vallant growled, "admit what you did to your company."

Kalleb thought quickly then took a few deep breaths before yelling, "I rode to Haemsville!"

The yard grew still. The stunned expressions shifted to confused frowns, even those who had been scowling before gave him unsure looks. A couple lieutenants didn't repeat his words.

Vallant, however, glared and sneered down at him. He jerked his horse's reins and walked it in front of Kalleb, blocking him from the sight of the rest of the company.

"This man abandoned his post!" Vallant bellowed. "When he was ordered to stand firm to his duty, he left to in pursuit of his personal desires! He spat on the oaths we have *all* taken and was imprisoned for his crime!"

Kalleb clenched his fists until his knuckles turned white and ground his teeth together until his jaw ached. He wanted to scream.

The image flashed in his mind of pulling the fool from his horse and smashing his face into the hard dirt. He almost took a step, but taking a breath saved him.

"The brigadiers, however, have granted him parole," Vallant continued. "They have allowed him to return to service, but he will remain a lance corporal for the remainder of his service. I want each of you to strive to be the best lancers in the Storm Cavalry, but a company is only as strong as its weakest troop. Any lancer who fails in his training, lacks in his duty, or is disrespectful to his superior officers will be assigned to Lance Corporal Kane's troop and will remain there until he improves. Those who show commitment to being worthy lancers will be transferred out and be put back on the path of promotion and fame."

Kalleb stared dumbfounded up at Vallant. *Basically, my troop is a punishment troop?*

Setting aside lancers who were ill-fit or bad influences into one troop was not an uncommon practice. It meant the bad apples could be looked after easier and disciplined better. Then again, it also left a reputation on those officers who had to lead them.

Bastard. You've made them hate me, and now you're saddling me with all the screw-ups.

Vallant turned back to him with disdain clear in his eyes. "Return to your troop."

Kalleb felt the temptation to tell him to shove a lance pole up his smug ass. He wanted to rip off his jacket, throw it on the ground, and curse the day he had first put one on. Then the hair on the back of his neck stood up. He sensed something familiar.

Back on the farm, the overseers would occasionally start a conversation with an inmate, and the inmate would suddenly snap and say or do something the overseers would use as an excuse to punish them. They would make them mad on purpose. Kalleb had grown a sense for when they had tried to make him mad, and he felt it now.

You're trying to make me mad, you pompous prick.

Knowing that, he smirked and surprised Vallant by snapping his heels together. "Yes, sir," he said then calmly walked away.

Vallant remained silent longer than Kalleb had thought he would before he finished his address.

"We ride for Tradon in two days!" Vallant said. "Each man should see to his affairs before we depart. Your lieutenants will make sure each squadron is prepared for departure. Until then, I salute you, men of the Eighth!"

There were more cheers to that, but mostly from the squadrons on the far end of the formation.

As Kalleb walked farther down toward his troop, he found them more somber, despite their lieutenants taking their time to address their individual squadrons. They mostly went over what to pack and how to prepare for the journey, but Kalleb's focus was more on the men's attitude, especially those in Squadron Five.

None of them were happy, and it seemed Troop C stood a little farther away from Troop D than when he had left them. Despite Lieutenant Bowden's jovial speech to the squadron, it appeared the other troops disapproved of having the weakest troop singled out as being with them.

Kalleb took his place without a second glance at his men. They'd had enough shock for the day. Fortunately, their lieutenant wasn't as long-winded as their captain.

"Lance Corporals," Lieutenant Bowden said, "see to it that each man in your troop has a horse! Men, if you don't have your own horse, make a request with your lance corporal before we depart. Also, Lance Corporals, be on the lookout for quality corporals. If you have any recommendations, give them to me on the way to Tradon. That's all I have! See you all here, bright and early, in two days!" He flashed a broad smile at them and saluted them, flipping the back of his hand against his forehead, as if lifting a visor, before trotting away.

The other lance corporals went to work, enjoying being left as the highest-ranking officers, and began introducing themselves to their troop.

Kalleb, however, took in his troop. He had never seen such defeated lancers. They stood with hunched shoulders, lowered heads, and deep frowns. Most weren't looking at him. He had seen the reflective look in their eyes before. It filled the eyes of many on the farm, and he had seen it in his countless times washing his own face after long, hard days in the fields.

They're demoralized. Told they're at the bottom of the heap, and they haven't even started training yet. They're just kids . . . but they're my men. They may not have any respect for me, and they'll probably not take anything I say to heart now, but I'll make lancers out of them. Better lancers than Vallant could dream of.

He raised his head and cleared his throat. "All right, gentlemen, how many of you need a horse?"

Chapter 11

27th of Petrarium, 1109 N.F. (e.y.)

CRACK!

CRACK! CRACK! CRACK!

Alindale's hands stung each time his wooden practice sword struck Master Montaigu's. After three hours with only small rests, he was eager to toss the practice sword away and let his burning palms breathe. However, the scarred master knight showed no signs of calling it a day.

Montaigu raised his practice sword above his head and gave a stern nod. Alindale stifled a groan and mirrored him, gripping the sword tighter and raising it above his head. His sweat-soaked shirt clung to his aching sides and back. The heat of the Easterly Sun beating down on them wasn't helping.

He watched Montaigu's eyes and face intently, waiting for another nod. The knight's dark eyes flickered for a moment, and then came the nod. Alindale stepped and swung . . . right at Montaigu's head.

CRACK!

Montaigu's sword met his and, using the momentum of the repulse, Alindale swung the sword over his head and back around from the left, again toward Montaigu's head.

CRACK!

Again, Montaigu parried, and Alindale continued the form to its final strike by swinging the blade high. He saw Montaigu's sword wasn't already up to block, and he committed to his swing.

I got you!

A sudden jolt shot up from his left ankle, and his swing went wide to the left. He was falling and—

Montaigu's sword struck him across his chest. The force of the blow spun him in the air until Alindale crashed down on the brick of the battlement.

He groaned and gasped as he rolled on the floor. Everything was hurting now. His palms stung, his left ankle burned excruciatingly, and his chest throbbed. He coughed with every attempt to breathe.

He rolled onto his back and looked up to see Montaigu standing over him, staring down impassively. His white tabard, bearing the black skull of the Enderval cross-skull boar and broadsword on its chest, might as well have been pristine compared to Alindale's disheveled outfit. Not a drop of sweat stained the tabard, and only a lit sheen shined off the master's scarred face.

"What—" Alindale violently coughed. "What . . . did I do wrong . . . this time?"

Montaigu narrowed his eyes, and Alindale winced. That was usually a sign he should already know.

Montaigu slapped his left leg with his sword.

Alindale raised an eyebrow. "My stance was off?"

Montaigu nodded.

Alindale rubbed his chest and winced again. "And you had to strike."

Montaigu turned the sword in his hand, motioned the handguard across his neck, and then pointed at him.

Alindale just nodded. "Yeah, I know. I'm dead." He closed his eyes and wished he could be like the dead and get some rest. Clopping bootheels against stone killed that fantasy, though.

He listened to the footsteps come to a stop beside Montaigu, but he was in too much pain to look.

"We should toss the body over the oceanside and get to the stables," Brother Revel whispered. "We can be ten miles away by the time anyone notices."

"I'm not dead!" Alindale groaned.

"Ah! Good." To his credit, Revel sounded pleased about that.

Alindale opened his eyes to see the square-jawed knight smiling down at him.

"Then you can go for another run before we turn you over to the Kanes for your horseback riding lessons."

"Damn you," Alindale growled.

That got a snort out of Montaigu, who was picking up the training swords.

"Damn me when you're king," Revel said, nudging Alindale's leg with the toe of his boot. "Up, Prince! You'll never keep the young ladies at court gossiping lying on the battlements."

Alindale rolled his eyes at Revel's attempt at encouragement. For the past two weeks, he had put up with that kind of encouragement. Maybe for Revel, the admiration of women for his knightly physique came naturally to him, but to Alindale, his experience of indifference from the ladies at court made the promises sound vain.

"Can't," he said. "Broke my left ankle." His left ankle was still throbbing, and he had done his best not to move it too much. He doubted it was really broken, but he would say anything to get out of running again.

"No, it's not." Revel tapped Alindale's left foot with his boot toe, and Alindale jumped up at the sudden pain. "I've broken my ankle before. You're not in enough pain. It's just sprained."

Alindale grimaced up at the knight and tried to rub his ankle. He saw no choice, though, but to take Revel's hand and let the knight haul him to his feet. He sucked in the salty taste of the ocean as he put more weight on his ankle and had to hop a couple of steps before he could properly walk.

He took a moment to enjoy the feel of the ocean breeze sweeping around his damp clothes. The ocean was calm today. He watched the waves leisurely make their way toward the harbor from on top of the northeast turret of the battlements surrounding Dain Castle.

Montaigu found the large, square, open space perfect and preferred to train out of the way, hidden behind the castle's lone tower, the abandoned prison tower, from distracting onlookers. Revel enjoyed forcing Alindale to climb up the stairs every day for sword training. Alindale took solace at there not being an audience to watch Montaigu continuously pound him into the stones.

Montaigu snap his fingers and gave Alindale a dismissive wave.

"Thank you, Master Knight," he said with a small bow.

Montaigu snapped his fingers again, making Alindale straighten his back. He then unsheathed his long sword, raised it above his head, and swung once. Alindale understood.

"Sword strokes tomorrow," he said. "How many?"

Montaigu held up five fingers.

"Five hundred?" His arms already ached at Montaigu's sharp nod.

Up until this point, Montaigu had only allowed him to do sword strokes with an arming sword, trying to get Alindale used to swinging a sword with each arm. At first, Alindale thought the routine simple and a waste of time, but he soon learned the constant swinging took its toll on his arm muscles, building up strength. He could already feel them throbbing, thinking of swinging a two-handed long sword five hundred times without a break.

What else you got to do tomorrow? He frowned at the repeating question that he put to himself each time the knights or Amadus added to his new routine.

"Yes, Master Knight."

Montaigu snapped his fingers again, and Alindale felt close to yelling in frustration. Yet, when he turned back, Montaigu was finger-talking with Brother Revel. Alindale hadn't been able to pick up the knights' hand signals to each other, and they hadn't saw fit to teach him.

Brother Revel watched Montaigu's fingers flash intensely until he stopped. "The master wants you to rest your ankle," Brother Revel said. "No more running for today."

"Well, thank the Last God for that," Alindale breathed softly.

"You still have Colonel Kane waiting for you." Brother Revel slapped him on the back then pushed him toward the stairwell.

Alindale got the feeling he was being pressured to leave. Normally, he would be curious, but he was more than eager to be relieved of the knights' tutelage for the rest of the day.

He walked over the turret's wall and picked up his gray jacket he had left on the stool. The jacket was just something he could throw over his shoulders, with worn elbows and thin in several places for his training and running exercises. Despite the heat, it was better for him to wear it than having everyone in the castle gawk at his sweaty visage. His wet shirt clung to his back the moment he threw the jacket on.

As he stepped down the wide stairwell, he glanced over and saw Montaigu and Revel hand-gesturing to each other. Their fingers both moved faster than Alindale could read, but by the frown on Revel's face and darkened grimace on Montaigu's, it wasn't good.

He climbed down the steps, walking gingerly to get the sprain out of his ankle, and into the large, square room of the turret. Then he walked out the door and onto the eastern wall instead of down the steps to the courtyard below.

To his left, the crashing ocean waves breaking upon the cliff face, three hundred feet below, distantly echoed over the wall. He glanced over the side and gripped the battlement's thick, gray stones instinctively at the sight of the sheer drop. The eastern castle wall followed along the cliff wall until the cliff protruded outward. The distance made him feel lightheaded, so Alindale stepped away from the battlement then walked hurriedly to the next turret.

He walked down the turret's stairs and exited out into trimmed hedges of the Queen's Gardens. Alindale didn't remember which queen they were originally made for, but every queen since had used them as their own private domain inside the castle.

He continued along the east wall and the tall hedgerows of the garden's perimeter until he found the tall, open archway leading out onto the jutting cliff itself. He stopped right in front of the archway and looked out at the cliff. Lush, green flax covered the cliff top and hung over the cliff's edge. White and blue blooms dotted the cliff top, soaking in the summer's warmth.

The ocean breeze gently swept in and wafted the flowers' sweet scent over him. The musky smell brought back the memory of his mother kneeling among those flaxes in mourning blacks for hours. She had wandered out there the moment word of Adam's death had reached the castle those five years ago. Every day, she would stroll out onto the cliff top, and no one went to her.

Alindale's father had stoically told him not to worry when Alindale had voiced his fears that she might throw herself from the cliff. His father had merely said, "When a child is lost, each parent must grieve in their own way."

A high-pitched, crescendo trill drew Alindale out of the memory. Down a hedgerow path, he saw a young woman in a dress of shimmering, yellow silk.

"Hush, Harpo," she whispered up into a pink blossom tree, scolding at a bright-red pytre hawk perched nimbly in its branches. "You're going to get us *both* in trouble." She puffed out her cheeks and folded her arms across her chest. Her deep red hair lay over her right shoulder.

Alindale recognized her instantly. Young Lady Syros, who he had spoken with the day he had been . . . exiled from court. Although, as much as he racked his brain, he *still* couldn't remember her first name.

At first, he stepped back, intending to avoid being seen, but stopped. *Did she just say she's in trouble?* he thought.

"Do you need help?" he asked softly, walking down the hedgerows.

***

This was a disaster.

Not only was Tory being forced to spend her whole day with Serina. Not only was she expected to be a meek prop in the background of Her Majesty's luncheon. Not only was she wearing the absolute worst shade of bright yellow. Now Harpo decided to escape her room and somehow found his way into the Queen's Garden.

His high-pitched tweet was unmistakable, and so Tory had slipped away to find him.

"Hush, Harpo!" she whispered. The pytre hawk had perched himself in a pink blossom tree, and Tory had no idea how to get him down or sneak him out. "You're going to get us *both* in trouble."

She puffed her cheeks out and folded her arms across her chest.

Maybe I can make an excuse? she thought. *Say the sun's getting to me, and I need to lie down?*

Tory shook her head, immediately disregarding it. The excuse might work for these northern ladies, but Serina would know it was a lie. If a woman can get sick from too much sun, she wasn't a woman from the Isles. They would also be curious as to why Tory would dash into the garden for a few minutes before leaving. And if Harpo decided to be difficult . . .

"Do you need help?"

Tory glanced out of the corner of her eye and saw a sweaty, shabbily dressed man—probably a gardener—approaching down the hedgerows.

She grimaced. She hadn't even been able to try an escape plan, and she had already been caught.

"Sorry," she said. "My pytre hawk decided to be more adventurous today. He's been roosting on my balcony and has been good not to wander too far. I didn't mean for him to get into Her Majesty's gardens."

The gardener looked up at Harpo. The hawk was contently perched on his tree branch, looking about the garden in sharp, twitching motions and ignoring the two humans below. Tory hoped the gardener didn't go in search of a rake or shake the tree.

"Is he hurting anything?" he asked.

Tory shook her head. "No. I know he's not supposed to be here, but he's just curious. Please, don't call the guard or whoever on him."

"Why would I do that?"

"Well, aren't you a gardener . . .?" Her words died on her lips. His voice sounded familiar. She looked up at him and, despite his worn cloths and sweaty visage, she knew that face. Her eyebrows rose higher and higher, and then her breath caught. "Your . . . *Highness?*"

Prince Alindale winced, and his cheeks lightly flushed. He dipped his head and backed away bashfully.

"Yes, My Lady," he said. "I beg your pardon about my clothes. I know they are not very proper."

"No, it's okay," she replied, feeling her own cheeks warm. "People dress like this in the Isles because of the heat. I was just surprised that it was you."

The prince's new hobbies hadn't gone unnoticed by those at court. Serina complained about him and his new entourage marching through the castle every morning before dawn to demand he see his father. Many of the other ladies laughed and whispered about his new exercise obsession. Tory, however, had to admit that his color was better, tanner now after weeks of sunlight, and no longer pasty white. He stood straighter and wasn't as soft-looking as he had been when she had first seen him. He seemed to be taking his removal from court rather well. Tory almost envied him.

Harpo shrilled again, as if reminding them that he was still there.

"Quiet, Harpo!" she snapped.

She then turned to the prince. "I'm so sorry, Your Highness. I know he's not supposed to be here."

"It is fine," Alindale said with a wave. "He adds another splash of color to the gardens."

"I'm not so sure." Tory frowned worriedly. "If anyone tries to handle him, other than me or my brother, he may bite them."

Alindale took a step back, cautiously watching Harpo. "Good to know."

Tory snickered. Harpo wouldn't bite or scratch so long as he wasn't threatened.

Harpo suddenly hopped completely around on the branch. He bobbed his head side to side sporadically and ruffled his feathers. Tory knew he was about to spring into flight by the way his shoulders hunched, and before she could say anything, Harpo flapped his forearm feathers, stretched out his limbs, and caught a current of air to glide away.

Tory reached out for him, but he was gone.

"Now where's he going?" she said with a huff. She looked through the hedgerows, but there was no clear path to follow him.

"He should be fine," Alindale said. "If he bites anyone, you could let your brother take the blame for letting him loose."

Tory blinked at him.

Alindale hung his head, a small smile on his face. "Whenever Adam's dog got loose, he would always say either me or Amanda let him out. Sometimes we took the blame."

She smiled mischievously. "Your Highness, you're not exactly how my sister described you."

Alindale grunted and arched an eyebrow.

"Serina said I should not talk with you, that you were unsociable and lazy from just reading and lounging in your room all day."

Alindale's small smile slipped, and he stepped away. "Well, if you will excuse me, My Lady; I should be going."

Tory's heart fluttered, realizing she might have insulted him.

"Your Highness!" She reached out to him. "I didn't mean to offend you. I only wanted to say I am glad she is wrong. And, while I'm not entirely sure why Her Majesty threw you out of court, I'm glad she didn't force you to leave the castle."

Alindale's half-smile looked forced as he stood, half-turned, as if wanting to walk away but was hesitant. Tory tried to smile back to reassure him, but an awkward weight hung in the air and grew heavier the longer the silence dragged on.

Tory dug the toe of her shoe into the grass and tried to think of anything to make the awkwardness go away. Anything to break the silence so he wouldn't go away feeling insulted.

"Are those your running clothes?" she asked and immediately regretted it.

His clothes? She inwardly groaned. *Really?*

Alindale snorted and looked down at himself. "Just my training clothes, you could say."

"I see you running every morning." Her small smile felt less forced. "It looks like you are getting better. You are also tanner now." She giggled softly, her cheeks warming again.

Alindale touched his face and snickered. "Brother Revel would probably agree with you. I'm not collapsing every time he says I can rest."

Tory laughed at that, but the conversation soon died again. Fortunately, Alindale spoke first before the awkward silence returned.

"Your dress is very pretty," he said. "And shiny, too."

Oh no. I got him talking about my clothes now. She noticed him look away, frowning and shuffling his feet, and smiled. *Guess he's just as awkward as me.*

"It's an Emelie Faviann dress," she said, smoothing the front of her skirts. "They say he's the foremost designer in modern fashion. And he really does have a way with silk."

"You do not sound convinced," Alindale noted.

"Oh no, he's a good dressmaker." She frowned at the shimmery, yellow silk in her hands. "It's just . . . this is one of my sister's dresses that he made for her. She forced me to wear this one today, even though she knows I hate yellow. It was either this one or the red dress, and she *hates* red."

Alindale gave her a confused look. "Why would she force you to wear her dress?"

"Oh"—she waved, annoyed—"Her Majesty invited her ladies to luncheon, and Serina suggested they all wear their Faviann dresses to see how the shimmering silk looks among the flowers in the garden."

The color drained from Alindale's face, and his eyes went wide. "What?"

"Tory!"

A chill ran up her spine as Serina, in her shimmering, silver dress, walked out from behind a hedge toward them.

"I told you to stay where I—"

Serina stopped when saw Alindale. Her thunderclap expression changed to shock and disgust in an instant.

"Serina," Tory said gently, holding up her hands, "this is—"

Serina screamed, shattering the garden's serenity. "Your Majesty!" she yelled in alarm. "Trespasser in your garden!"

"Sister, please!" Tory cried insistently and flailed her arms in a vain attempt to calm her.

Serina grabbed her by the arm and harshly pulled her away, nearly tripping Tory over her own skirts. "Stay away from my sister!"

It suddenly dawned on Tory. *She doesn't recognize him!*

"Halt!"

Two Sunrise Guards suddenly appeared behind him, charging down between the hedgerows, the sun reflecting brightly off their shiny breastplates.

"Wait!" Alindale said in surprise, raising his hands.

He gasped in pain when the guards seized him, forced his arms behind his back, and then kicked his knees out from under him.

"Stop!" Tory begged.

"Shut up!" Serina hissed softly, digging her fingernails into Tory's arm as she dragged her back. Her heavy breath burned in Tory's ear as she said, "What did I tell you about talking with strange men?"

"Serina, you don't understand!" Tory winced and tried in vain to get free of the stinging fingernails. "He's—"

"Who is trespassing in my garden?" Her Majesty demanded, her voice cutting through the hedgerows.

"It's me, Mother!" Alindale yelled.

Serina stiffened, and everything fell still.

"Alindale?" Her Majesty said, sounding as surprised as everyone else.

Tory breathed a sigh of relief. Now the guards would release him. As for herself, Tory was sure she was in for another scorching scolding later. At least Harpo had flown away.

She only wished she had wings, too.

***

The Sunrise Guards loosened their grips and lifted Alindale to his feet. Through their visors, he saw them looking at him with suspicion and caution. He realized they hadn't recognized him when they had seized him.

Swishing skirts announced his mother's arrival as she gracefully strode through the thick grass. Alindale frowned uncomfortably at seeing his mother's violet silk dress. The silk shimmered as she walked, and the dress left her shoulders bare and the neckline outlined by lace. Her dark hair was pulled behind her, as usual, revealing her pearl necklace around her neck.

Her bosom wasn't exposed because of the lace, but she was his mother! The sight of her in such a dress didn't feel right, especially with his father still wasting away in sickness.

"What are you doing wandering in my gardens and scaring my ladies?" his mother asked softly through a forced smile.

Alindale could tell his presence was not wanted, though he wasn't sure if it was because of what he was wearing or his mere appearance in her gardens.

"Simply passing through," Alindale replied. "I did not mean to ruin . . . whatever it is you are doing." He looked around nervously, hoping to be lightly but quickly scowled then sent on his way.

His mother frowned disappointingly before smiling again at the Syros sisters. "I am terribly sorry, Lady Syros," she said to Lady Serina. "Could you and your sister go join the rest of my ladies? The servants were just serving tea."

"Yes, Your Majesty," Lady Serina said, hastily bowing before pulling Tory, the younger sister's name he heard Lady Serina yell, by the arm back the way she had come. As they left, Alindale caught Tory faintly whimpering her apologies, but Serina scolded her back, refusing to accept any explanation or apology.

"Alindale," his mother brought his attention back to her. Despite her smile, she looked him up and down. Her thin eyebrows were raised, showing her disdain for his clothes. "Since when did you take to sneaking through my gardens? And wherever did you get those *rags*?"

"These are not rags," he replied, looking them over.

"They are not worthy of a prince," she said. "I forbid you to wear them again."

"They are my training clothes, Mother." Alindale strained to keep his voice down. "They are the best clothes I have for it."

"Training?" She dismissively waved her fan, as if she found the thought ridiculous. "For whatever would you train for?"

"Self-improvement." He shrugged. "And so no one will forget I am still here."

"No one has forgotten you, dear." His mother's smile slipped for a moment before she regained her composure. "Everyone knows you are still the royal heir. It is just . . . you know how to behave at court. You know better than to falsely accuse an aristo."

Alindale balled his hands into fists at his sides. This was the first time in two weeks he had been able to be alone with his mother. Any other time, she was busy at court, surrounded by her ladies, or too indisposed to see him. He was busy, as well, but now they were finally alone. And everything he wanted to say came bubbling to the surface.

"*Why*?" he asked firmly yet softly enough so only she could hear him. "Why are you doing this? Why did you welcome Haemin back? Does Father's illness mean nothing to you?"

His mother shook her head and raised her hand, as if to hush him. "It is not like that—"

"Have you forgotten Adam *already*?" Alindale yelled.

Color drained from his mother's face. She stared at him, wide-eyed, unmoving, as if she had been slapped. Her color slowly returned, and as it did, she narrowed her eyes, her eyebrows tightening and lips becoming a thinly pressed line.

Alindale had only received this look once before, when he had been younger, but this time, he held his ground.

She reached up and grabbed his shoulder firmly. Alindale wasn't much taller than his mother, but the way she held him and the look on her face made her seem twice as tall.

"I command you," she whispered fiercely, "to stop this nonsense *now*. You will go to Lord Haemin and apologize. Afterward, this evening, both of you will come before me and say you have resolved your differences. For that, I shall lift your banishment and allow you to attend court again, and you can stop"—she waved her fan at his clothes—"this. Do you understand?" She squeezed his shoulder, emphasizing her words.

Alindale's initial feeling was to agree and do as he was told, but that feeling was crushed suddenly within him. He couldn't explain it, but a fire within him told him to hold firm. He would no longer be told what to do and disregarded afterward.

He leaned in close and whispered just as fiercely for only her to hear, "No."

His mother jumped back. Her eyes were full of surprise for a second before they were replaced by anger. She gave him her disapproving look and replaced it with her smiling mask.

"We'll speak of this later," she said with a wave of her fan.

No, Alindale thought, *we won't.*

"Come," she instructed. "I cannot have you wandering around, dressed like a vagabond and scaring my guests."

Alindale followed behind her, listening to the Sunrise Guards' clanking armor behind him. She led him back to the stone path, at the archway, and into the garden proper. He could see the castle's door down the path, calling him to freedom.

Unfortunately, four steps into the garden, they came upon his mother's ladies seated around white, circular tables to the right of the path, sipping tea and fanning themselves. Servants in gray and blue livery stood behind them, patiently waiting to refill their cups.

He felt his skin crawl from the multiple looks of shock, discomfort, and even disgust the ladies tried to hide behind their teacups. Unsurprisingly and undoubtingly, none of them found his sweaty visage, coupled with his plain clothes and lacking physique, appealing as Brother Revel had joked.

He glanced toward the castle and felt the urge to run for it, but the entrance felt a hundred miles away.

"Ladies," his mother announced, joining them, "please pardon His Highness. He has not interrupted one of my luncheons since his wet nurse begged me for assistance because he was a fussy eater."

Alindale's face reddened from the ladies' giggling.

"Me and my ladies are simply having tea and enjoying Emelie Faviann's latest dress designs," she told him, smoothing out her silk skirts and sitting down in the largest chair with a high back and red cushions on the back and seat. "He is a renowned dressmaker from Silkhaven who has recently come to the capital and graciously made dresses for me and my ladies."

Alindale envisioned the gathering of ladies, watching and whispering among themselves behind their teacups, as bundles of silk, sitting in the same cut dresses, all in different colors.

"His Highness," his mother said, gathering the ladies' attention to her while leaning back in her chair and holding her teacup out for a servant to fill, "has taken up running on top of the battlements to take up his abundance of spare time.

"Prince Alindale, do you have anything to say to my ladies?" She took a long sip.

Alindale's heart was pounding, and his legs were stiff, as if he had been standing for hours. He looked over the party of judgmental stares behind their fluttering fans and felt ill . . . until he saw Lady Tory Syros sitting in the back, with her hands folded in her lap. She looked at him with pity, but that made the pit in his stomach worse.

"You all are very lovely," he said with a small bow. "If you will excuse me, Your Majesty."

"What about our dresses, Prince Alindale?" His mother picked at her skirts with a clear smile on her face, enjoying his embarrassment. "Are they *lovely*, too?"

He forced the best smile he could. "All of your dresses are beautiful. If that is all, Your Majesty?"

His mother took another sip of tea. "First, apologize to Lady Syros for giving her a fright and the rest of the ladies for interrupting their tea."

Alindale felt the heat rising in his face and pushed down the urge to overturn a table.

"Lady Syros, I am sorry for scaring you." He added another small bow. "And ladies, I'm sorry for interrupting your teatime."

He turned and bowed deeply to his mother. "May I please be excused now, Your Majesty?"

He remained bowed over for a moment before she finally said, "We excuse you."

Alindale didn't even look from his bow. He turned and walked hurriedly down the pathway to the safety of the castle.

He heard the conversation of the ladies start again behind him. His ears twitched at the sound of their muffled giggles behind their fans.

Those giggles haunted his every hurried step. He could still hear them, even as he stormed up the steps, rammed his shoulder into the castle's east door, and then slammed it closed. Even the cool of the castle's interior did little to calm him.

"All things considered, that could have been much worse."

Alindale jumped, finding a man sitting on one of the wide windowsills near the door looking out into the gardens. The man's tall height forced him to press his right leg against his chest to sit on the sill as he let his lanky left leg hang down to the floor. His position showed no care for his tan, silk jacket, with lace and silver embroidery on the cuffs of his sleeves, and trousers being wrinkled together in such a tight space.

"Who from Oblivion are you?" Alindale demanded, making no attempt to hide his irritation.

The man gave him an amused smile, but it didn't touch his brown eyes. His long, angular, high cheekbone face fit his tall, lanky body, but his nose wasn't too large to stand out.

Something about his amused smile did strike a memory, though. *Wait. Is he the aristo who kept smiling at me when session was convened?*

"Forgive me, Your Highness," the aristo said, suddenly leaping from the windowsill and deeply bowing, flailing his shaggy, sandy-blond hair. "I am Nolen Ingman of Inglworf." He rose from his bow like his back was a spring. It felt too showy for Alindale's taste. He was also head and shoulders taller than him, but as thin as a post. "And, as I was saying, that could have been a lot worse."

"I beg your pardon?" Alindale asked.

"Well"—Nolen shrugged—"sneaking into Her Majesty's gardens, disguised as a laborer, to spy on her lovely ladies, I would have thought the punishment to be something more serious than a *motherly* reprimand."

"*Motherly reprimand?*" Alindale growled through gritted teeth.

"I meant no offense, Your Highness." Nolen raised his hands defensively. "I have an overbearing mother myself and know a scolding when I see one. And I must say, you're handling your banishment much better than most thought you would. I believe many were wagering whether you'd have left the castle by now."

"Thanks," Alindale grunted dryly. He then sighed, tired and not wanting to be drawn into another conversation. "Sorry, but I have somewhere I need to be. Excuse me." He walked by him, careful not to brush his shoulder against Nolen's arm.

"They're planning to kill you."

Alindale stopped, his last footfall echoing down the hall. He turned to find Nolen leaning against the windowsill, still smiling that amused smile.

"What?" he asked.

"I said, they're planning to kill you," Nolen replied. "Or, at least get rid of you."

"Who?" Alindale asked, lowering his voice and cautiously keeping his distance.

"Maybe Lord Haemin. Maybe Lord Fauman. Maybe a couple of others. Either way, it's obvious there are lords who have designs on the kingdom in His Majesty's absence. And those designs naturally put you in a dangerous position, whether they realize it or not."

Alindale balled his fists. "And how do you know this? Are you a new minister, or does the table openly talk about me during session?"

Nolen laughed. "I have not risen so high in Her Majesty's or Lord Haemin's eyes to be appointed to a seat at the table. I'm only here to avoid any duties that may be forced upon me in Inglworf. As for open talk, no one's mentioned you since Her Majesty removed you."

Alindale got the feeling he was being toyed with. "Then, may I warn you, Lord Ingman, that making such accusations without glaring proof did not go well for me. They most likely could be worse for you. Good day."

"No one's that bold or that stupid, Your Highness," Nolen called after him. "But I know that, when two opposing forces are building up to something, sooner or later, they're bound to clash against each other."

"The Table of Ministers are building up to something?" Alindale stopped, his curiosity piqued. This could be the first hint anyone's given him on what was going on behind those close doors. However, another possibility occurred to him. "Or Lord Haemin?"

"Ah-ah." Nolen wagged a finger at him. "Sorry, Your Highness. You're banished, remember? And that question was much too obvious. I don't want to get banished from court. Then I'd have to go back home." He chuckled.

"Then, why tell me any of this?" He gave Nolen a sideways glance. Something felt off. From the way the man looked and behaved, Alindale would have thought him someone who would be against him. He worried this was all a plot to get him in more trouble.

"Maybe I'm bored. Maybe I'm a jilted lord who no one wants to share anything with. Maybe I'm a known backstabber and nobody trusts me."

Nolen shot him a sideways glance and smiled. "Or maybe you could use a real friend."

Alindale grunted, annoyed. "I have enough friends."

"Really?" Nolen called after him. "How many? A few former ministers? An ancient old man? Two knights? Some Kanes?"

Alindale determinedly shut out his voice as he listed his few allies and walked away. Obviously, this Lord Ingman had been watching him closely since his banishment. Then again, that was the idea—to make the courtiers *watch* him.

"How about the youngest Syros sister?" Nolen's happy voice pierced him like a knife. "She a friend, too?"

"Sir"—he glared a warning back at the smug, lanky aristo—"if you mean harm to her . . ." Alindale's face grew warm again as his face contorted in controlled anger.

"Not at all, Your Highness." Nolen held up his hands defensively again. "I only wanted to point out that your friends are few and known. And you desperately need more."

"Why?" He wasn't sure why he kept humoring this new annoyance, but if did mean harm to those few around him, he could at least try to hear everything.

"Because you need every friend you can find," Nolen replied. "Especially to repair that damaged reputation of yours while making a fight out of being banished."

"Who says I am looking for a fight?"

"Oh please, Your Highness!" Nolen laughed, flamboyantly flailing his long arms then pressing his hands against his chest. "Don't insult me so. We've only just met. Putting everything together, staying here in the castle"—he began counting things off with his fingers as he listed them—"exercising, practicing swordplay, horseback riding with Kanes, studying with an ancient master, yelling at the top of your lungs each morning to know how His Majesty is . . ." Nolen trailed off for a moment, clearly trying to think of something else while holding his fingers in mid-count. "How is His Majesty by the way?"

Alindale folded his arms. "The same."

"My condolences. *But*, in the meantime, you're still planning something. And I just can't believe you're doing everything you can to improve your standing. Never fear, though! I, Nolen Ingman"—he bowed with a flourish again—"know just what you need to do."

Alindale gaped, unsure of what to make of him. Save for annoying. "That's okay."

"Now, now . . ." Nolen wagged a finger at him again. "I've made up my mind. And if you survive, you can thank me later."

"I doubt that."

Nolen barked a laugh. "Sarcastic humor! Perfect. You'll fit right in. I noticed you don't run on Almsday mornings; that means your Lasterday nights are free. Yes?"

Alindale felt he was being set up for something and was quickly losing touch with the conversation. He got the urge to leave as fast as possible.

"I really don't have—"

"Splendid!" Nolen cheered. "I know a place where lords, ladies, ministry officials—you name them—gather on Lasterday nights and talk about everything. Even court matters. It is the perfect place for a banished prince, eager to improve his standing, to mingle and talk."

Alindale felt uncomfortable by Nolen's eager grin and realized he was trying to invite him to something. "I do not think I have the time. Besides, you are forgetting everyone is *forbidden* from talking with me."

"Here in the castle." Nolen chuckled. "But, if you meet me by the stables at eight o'clock Lasterday night, I'll take you to place they'll talk with you about anything, without fear of your mother learning about it." He suddenly strode away, his long legs taking him down the hallway faster than Alindale would have expected. "I'll make all the arrangements!"

"I didn't say I would show!" Alindale shouted after him.

"But you will!" Nolen's voice echoed back as he turned the corner and out of sight. "I promise you'll thank me later, Your Highness!"

Alindale stared down the hallway, uncertain how many minutes had passed while he tried to make sense out of what had just happened. He wasn't sure if he had been threatened, warned, fooled with, or given an invitation.

He rubbed his forehead in frustration and finally went on his way, adding the odd encounter with his previous ones as things to worry about later.

Chapter 12

28th of Petrarium, 1109 N.F. (e.y.)

Kalleb blinked the dust out of his watering eyes and fought the urge to slump in his saddle. The dust hung thick in the air, kicked up from the passing horses and shielded from the wind by the tightly grown trees and thick undergrowth of ferns, vines, and bushes along the highway. Branches hung over the road, almost blocking out the Easterly Sun with a looming presence that threatened to swallow them. The low-hanging ones caused havoc among the lancers, constantly snagging the ends of the ten-foot-long practice poles that they carried.

Worse still, Kalleb's troop was the rear of the column.

I don't remember this ride being so exhausting.

He dipped his head, sucked in air through gritted teeth, and then lifted his rear off the saddle by pushing up against the saddle horn. His thighs were sore and chaffed from the days of riding. His years kept out of a saddle had not been kind to him.

"You all right, L.C.?" Rence Coup yelled. "Saddle sore in *your* old age?"

A few rounds of chuckles followed as Kalleb begrudgingly lowered back down and sat up straight.

"No," he grunted. "I'm still recovering from the ride your ma and me went on the night before we left." He whistled salaciously and smirked as the men behind him, and some of the troop in front of him, burst out in laughter.

Officers trading snide remarks with their lancers was frowned upon, a potential cause of strife between a leader and his men, but this was it for Kalleb. Not to mention, everyone already knew he wouldn't be rising in the ranks any further, so he had to show his rowdy bunch that, no matter how hard they bucked, he bucked harder.

"Look alive there, Lance Corporal!"

Lieutenant Bowden bound around the bend in the road, and Kalleb winced at the sight of his bulk bouncing in the saddle and his speckled horse snorting heavily. The lieutenant wore his broad smile, as if this was his first time on a horse, but Kalleb frowned. *He's going to ride his horse into the ground.*

Lieutenant Bowden whipped his horse around to ride beside him. The poor beast's nostrils flared, and it shook its head, its brown mane swaying.

"Evening, Lieutenant," Kalleb said with a nod.

"How's everything in the rear, Kane?" the lieutenant asked in his typical, jovial manner.

"Nothing to report, sir," he replied dryly. "The horses will need a rest soon, though."

Lieutenant Bowden grunted in agreement. "Vorge Township is a few miles up. The captain's gone on ahead to request we camp there. I believe Lord Renald also wants to spend the night in their inn instead of a tent, like the rest of us." He barked a laugh.

"Right." Kalleb faked a half-smile.

He had been surprised to learn that not only was he being deployed back to Tradon after his imprisonment but escorting its returning lord. Kalleb had a rule before being sent to the farm that, when it came to the nobility, mind his manners, stand at attention, and avoid them whenever possible. As a lance corporal, he didn't think he would have to worry about interacting with them, but his old rule still applied to Lord Julian Renald. He didn't dislike the man. It was more because of bad memories.

"Anyway"—Lieutenant Bowden cleared his throat and waved dust out of his face—"we'll be riding through the township whether we make camp there or not. The captain wants every lancer to ride in with backs straight, poles held tall, and heads held high." He sat up and threw his head back.

Kalleb frowned. "He wants a parade."

"Yep." The lieutenant's cheerfulness was becoming grating. "He wants the townspeople to see the Eighth as Lancers of the Storm Cavalry, alongside the Twelfth. So, make sure Troop D is formed up and no straggling rear guard. We can't have the whole column ride in like professionals and a handful in the back come in like farmhands on a Lasterday night. Am I right?" He boomed a laugh and slapped Kalleb's shoulder, his broad hand nearly pushing him out of the saddle.

"Yes, sir," he replied, bracing himself against his saddle horn.

Lieutenant Bowden smiled in approval. "Good man! Make sure your troop's in order. I have to get back to the head of the squadron." The lieutenant gathered his horse's reins and whooped loudly before slapping and kicking it into gallop.

Kalleb turned his head to block any dirt from flying into his face. Then he shook his head again from how hard the lieutenant rode his horse. *He's going to kill that poor animal.*

He turned his horse out of the column as the road curved to the left and pointed it toward the rear, allowing his troop to ride past him.

"Hey, L.C.!" Rence yelled as he rode by. "If we're camping near a town, does that mean we can have a night out on it?"

The rest of the troop let out hollers and laughs in agreement.

Kalleb rolled his eyes and picked the smirking recruit out from the column. "Just for that, Rence, get out of line and come with me."

"*What?*" Rence squeaked.

The rest of the troop laughed even harder at his high-pitched yelp.

"That's an order, Lancer," Kalleb barked. "Corporal Trevor!"

"Here, sir!"

Kalleb caught the sight of one of the poles wobbling in the air before finding the lancer waving it. Trevor Elkan was as thin as the pole he carried. His uniform hung off his body, as if a size too big for him. He was also ugly, the poor lad. He attempted to keep the few bald patches in his light brown hair covered by keeping his hair long and combed over. He claimed they were caused by a serious illness when he had been a young boy. His bulbous nose gave him the look of a drunkard, and his crooked grin made it appear his jaw was sinking into his neck.

The young recruit did have one standout quality that Kalleb liked, despite not appearing like a typical lancer. He had initiative. He took every order without question and volunteered to take on any extra duties required of him.

Kalleb had to take advantage of such actions, especially with the troop he had been given, so he had recommended Trevor to be a troop corporal. He needed at least one working hand who he could depend on.

"Ride at the front of the troop while I'm gone, Corporal," he ordered. "We're going to fetch the rear guard."

"Yes, sir!" Trevor shouted, clumsily maneuvering his red gelding out of line and nearly dropping his pole. His horse snorted and shook its head as Trevor frantically tried to right himself in the saddle.

"Ease up on the reins, Trevor," Kalleb yelled, "or he's going to buck!"

Trevor's horse danced and neighed loudly, threatening to rear up, but Trevor fortunately got his horse back under control and galloped toward the head of the troop.

"Why did you make *him* a corporal?" Rence asked, trotting up behind him.

Kalleb glared at him from over his shoulder. "Watch your mouth, Lancer."

Rence glowered and slouched in his saddle. He refused to look at Kalleb, staring into the forest like a petulant kid.

As the rest of the column passed them, the last lancer caught Kalleb's attention.

Zoren was a terrible rider. He rode out of line, nearly five feet back from the rest of the column. An agonized grimace marred his face as he tried to ride standing in the saddle, using his practice pole and saddle horn to prop him up. His coppery skin glistened with sweat from his constant effort, and his mixed-colored hair clung together.

His poor blood bay mare chomped at her bridle and shook her head in frustration. Zoren was holding her reins too tightly while bearing down on his saddle horn.

"Zoren!" Kalleb called.

Startled, the lad's eyes went wide at hearing his name, and he flopped down in his saddle. His horse snorted and softly whinnied from the sudden weight dropping on her back.

"Fall in with us, Lancer," Kalleb ordered, nudging his horse back onto the road. "We're going to fetch the lads playing rear guard."

Zoren glanced behind his shoulder, and a brief pained expression crossed his face before he meekly nodded his head. "Yes, sir."

Kalleb kicked his horse into a trot, riding past him. "You're holding her reins too tightly. Give her some slack, or your rear's going to be bruised from being thrown off instead of saddle sores."

He heard a grunt and snort behind him. He figured Zoren tensed and Rence snickered, but Kalleb let it slide. A little embarrassment would stick with Zoren better than him constantly correcting him on his riding.

The sounds of the forest slowly returned as the rumble of the column grew farther and farther away. Whistles and tweets from birds played in the air. Up ahead, three gliding lizards leapt from trees on their right. Their yellow, leathery wings, which were round, thinly stretched skin sprouting from their sides, sliced through the air as they sailed then disappeared into the tree branches on the other side of the road.

"Why does it take more than one person to tell three other guys to hurry up?" Rence complained.

"'*When there are men to spare,*'" Kalleb recited, "'*a commander will send more than one lancer to deliver messages.*' For the security of the messengers and the message. Besides"—he pulled his horse to a stop at a bend in the road—"Zoren and his horse need a rest."

"Thanks, Lance Corporal," Zoren said, slightly out of breath, "but I'm all right."

Kalleb gave him a skeptical look. "You're about to fall out of your saddle. Dismount and stretch your legs."

Zoren opened his mouth to object, but then he just sighed and slowly dismounted. He leaned his practice pole against his horse and grunted in pain from lifting his leg up and over his saddle. When he finally stood on the ground, his legs wobbled as he stretched.

"Why does it take *three* of us, though, to tell them to hurry?" Rence asked, slumping in his saddle with his elbows on his saddle horn and resting his chin in his palms. His practice pole hung in the crook of his arm and slid down to rest in the dirt.

Kalleb rolled his eyes. "It doesn't. You're just my favorite lancer to pick on, so you'd be doing this, anyway."

"Thanks, L.C.," Rence said dryly.

Zoren snickered.

"Besides"—Kalleb surveyed the thick foliage close to the road—"you don't want to be riding alone, even in a forest like this one."

He had always found forest rides pleasant before he had been sentenced to the farm. He knew there were some dangers in the wilds, but they had never haunted him. Even in his ride to Haemsville, he hadn't given a second thought about them. But, as everything else, the farm had changed that.

Every spring and summer seasons, they'd had to battle the encroaching jungle from overrunning the fields. The thick brush allowed the plumed rippers to get in close and hunt the workers. Kalleb could still hear the whistles and caws that they made to each other and how the brush would grow still and silent before a shriek always cut through the air.

A quiet brush was an ill omen in the south.

Quiet like the forest around them.

Kalleb sprang up. The chirps and whistles were gone, and the dense foliage prevented any breeze from stirring the leaves. A creeping chill crawled up his back, as if something was watching them. He checked the horses, but none of them were wide-eyed, snorting, or stomping the ground nervously.

Maybe I'm just imagining things.

A twig snapped to his right.

Kalleb turned too quickly in his saddle, wrenching the reins back, and his horse neighed in protest and stomped its hooves from his head being roughly pulled back. By the time he calmed the animal, the brush was still again. The tall ferns were packed together with thorn-covered vines and prevented most of the light from piercing the shrubbery. The longer he looked, though, he thought he caught a faint glint, as if from a reflection. However, he couldn't make out a shape.

"Finally!" Rence groaned in relief. "They're coming."

Kalleb heard them laughing before he saw the three recruits trotting up the road. They rode their horses alongside each other instead of in the triangle formation that he had taught them. They were so deep in conversation, like three boyhood friends riding out to sow wild oats, that they failed to notice him or their fellow lancers waiting ahead of them.

Kalleb snorted in frustration. Then he gave a last glance to his right, but the glint that he had focused on before was gone.

Nerves. And bad memories. He shook his head to focus on his duties.

"Rest over, Zoren," he said. "Mount—"

A blood-curdling shriek pierced the air.

Kalleb looked back at the horrific sight of Roy's, the lancer riding closest to the left side of the road, horse having its entrails ripped out. He then froze at the sight of an enormous creature slicing through the poor mare's belly with its saber-like teeth.

Gorro!

The gorro stood over three feet tall with most of its body still concealed in the brush. Its head was the length of a man's arm, and its jaw muscles bulged out of the side of its head as it slammed its mouth shut. Its short, bowed front legs were sprawled firmly on the ground, pulling the mare's guts into the undergrowth and spilling them out onto the road. All within a single breath.

Roy stared in shock as his mare flailed under him, her eyes wide and roving madly. The lancer didn't even have time to leap out of his saddle before she collapsed on her side, pinning his leg under her weight. He screamed in pain and clawed at the road but couldn't crawl free.

His companions were stunned, as well. Their horses neighed and pranced violently under them, desperate to run. The recruits fought with their reins in the vain effort to control them.

The gorro bellowed as it leapt out of the forest, its long, slender body landing on the mare's head. Its deep green skin and the black stripes running along its flanks blended perfectly into the undergrowth. Its gaping mouth flashed its half-a-foot-long saber-like teeth, stained with the mare's blood.

Kelly, the lancer closest to the right side, yelled in terror and threw his practice pole at the monster, more in desperation than with intent to fight. Then he turned his horse around and kicked the panicked animal into flight. The sight of the recruit racing by, terror-stricken eyes full of tears and face white and contorted, snapped Kalleb out of his shocked stupor.

"Zoren!" he yelled, snapping the young man out of a similar daze. "Get back to the company as fast as you can and tell them we need help! *Go!*"

Wide-eyed, Zoren shook his head then frantically tried to turn his horse but fumbled with his practice pole.

"Drop the damn pole and move!"

The gorro roared again as Zoren galloped away.

Avery, the last lancer, was desperately trying to back his mount away from the growling beast without being thrown off. He held his practice pole down in front of them, the long shaft wobbling in the recruit's shaky grip.

The gorro hunched lower to the ground. Its hind legs, though shorter than its front, were planted on the ground. Its short, lizard-like tail stiffened in the air.

It's going to lunge!

Before he could act or yell a warning, Rence galloped past him. He leaned froward in his saddle, holding his practice pole like a lowered lance, but he was leaning too far forward, almost against his horse's neck. His pole was braced under his arm instead of against his side and bounced violently, making it impossible to aim.

"No, Rence!" Kalleb shouted, but his voice was lost in the roar of battle.

As Rence sped forward, the gorro remained planted, preparing to spring up until the moment the end of Rence's practice pole speared the road two feet beside it. The pole bowed from the force of the collision and splintered with a loud *crack*.

The gorro swung its head around, its fangs narrowly missing Rence's horse's hind leg. His horse wailed in terror and leapt in the air, clearing the fallen mare's corpse. By some miracle, Rence stayed in his saddle, but his horse refused to turn around and continued to gallop down the road.

Avery, though, had taken advantage of Rence's failed charge and backed his horse away from the gorro, far enough that he could turn to flee. Roy, however, remained whimpering on ground, covering his face with his arms. He twisted against the saddle in a desperate bid to free himself while trying to avoid the gorro stepping on him.

The gorro began turning toward him.

"Get out of here, Avery!" Kalleb shouted as he threw his practice pole away before drawing his saber from his saddle.

Better an actual weapon than a long stick.

He kicked his horse into a trot and held his saber behind him, readying to swing the curved blade as he passed.

Avery was still trying to control his mount, uncertainty clear on his face, as he looked between Roy behind him and safety ahead of him.

"Ride, Lancer!" Kalleb roared, kicking his horse into gallop and thundering past him.

The gorro was focused on Roy, rocking its head back and forth, looking curious about the pinned man and slowly shifting its body.

Kalleb lowered himself in the saddle, dangerously low. He only had one swing and had to make it count. He urged his horse onward even as it bayed at the scent of death ahead.

A few more feet.

He pulled back as far as he could behind him, focusing on the gorro's striped back.

The beast unexpectedly leapt around faster than Kalleb could believe, its mouth gaped wide. Its jutting fangs were thrust out like pikes, especially those upper saber-like teeth.

And it bellowed!

The gorro's roar deafened Kalleb and made his horse skid to a halt and rear up. The last thing he saw was his horse kicking with his front hooves before sailing backward. The presence of his saddle disappeared out from under him. The reins were no longer in his hand. He floated in the air.

No. He was flying backward *through* the air!

Frick me.

Kalleb slammed into the ground, bouncing, flopping, and then skidding against hard dirt. His vision went white to black. Time slowed to crawl. His hearing also disappeared momentarily, but as it returned, all he could hear was the blood pounding in his skull. His body was numb and refused to move.

Tell me . . . I didn't break my back.

Feeling returned to his arms then his legs. He gasped in relief when he felt his feet in his boots but groaned from the growing pounding of his head. He strained to lift his head and blinked to clear his vision.

Kalleb's breath caught.

The gorro was a foot away from him. Its black, moist nostrils flared as it breathed in his scent, its stiff whiskers flickering. It moved its narrow head from side to side, as if confused.

No, not confused. Kalleb noticed its left eye was glassy. It couldn't see him clearly.

Kalleb's heart thundered in his chest. He made a fist and discovered his saber was gone. He frantically looked around to no avail. He must have let go of it when he had been thrown.

Snarling snapped his attention back to the gorro. The beast's head was angled so that its right eye stared at him. The black slit dividing its golden eye narrowed as it peeled its lips back and began to hunch its shoulders.

I'm dead.

Kalleb raised his right arm defensively as the gorro opened its jaws.

POW!

The gorro lurched sideways, a high-pitched whine whistling between its fangs as it shuffled on its feet. Suddenly, its front right leg gave way, and it collapsed on its side. Its flanks rose and fell rapidly as it tried to raise its massive head but, with a gasping whine, it flopped to the ground and breathed its last.

Kalleb stared, stunned.

"Lance Corporal?"

Kalleb hesitantly tore his eyes away from the gorro and to Roy, still pinned under his horse and as distraught as him.

"What happened?" Roy shakingly asked.

Kalleb shook his head. "I . . . don't know."

"Ha!" a deep, grunting voice barked. "Got the bastard!"

Kalleb looked over his shoulder and sat stunned from another shock.

The brush itself was moving. An entire grove of mixed ferns, vines, and grass rose higher and higher between two trees, and a haze floated in the air, tendrils of smoke drifting through the leaves.

Kalleb's nose wrinkled from the burning smell of sulfur.

Then came another shock.

A leg rose from the foliage and brush and stepped out into the road, as if part of the forest had taken the form of a man.

"What the *shit?*" Roy screamed as he frantically pushed and kicked against his saddle, his face stricken with panic. "What the *shit!*"

"Easy there, boy," the standing bush grunted. "You're going to mess your leg up even more."

A green-covered arm reached up and grabbed its head. Leaves and foliage twisted. Then, with a grunt, they peeled back like cloth, revealing the face and head of a wild man. Dirty, blond tangles from his long hair and beard fanned over his shoulders. His cheeks and forehead were smeared brown from what Kalleb assumed was dirt as the man beamed, staring proudly at the downed gorro with his hazel eyes.

Kalleb glanced at the body of the hulking beast, still disbelieving that it was lying there, dead, but his body ached too much to move.

"How?" he asked.

The wild man barked a laugh. The shrubbery around him shuffled and shifted until there was a sudden *snap*. The leaves, grass, and vines fell away, as if he was discarding a cloak, leaving him standing in clothes mixed with a patchwork of leathery animal hides, stained cloth, and worn leather belts holding it together.

Despite the dozen small knives lining his waist belt and heavy, bleached-bone handle tomahawk hanging off his hip, Kalleb's eyes were drawn to the smoldering weapon in his fist. It resembled a club, made of wood, but with a long, metal barrel fixed into the wooden stock, smoke drifting out of the end of the barrel. Intricate metal contraptions were fixed to the other end before the wooden stock formed a smooth, round fist, and hanging off it was a white fuse.

"Got this baby down south," the wild man said, patting the strange club. "They said it'd be better than a crossbow. Bigger punch and faster, too. Wish you lancer boys had gotten out of the way sooner." The wild man's footfalls thumped against the earth as he stepped forward and stood over his kill.

Kalleb pushed himself up with a groan then snorted from the sudden pungent smell coming off the man. "Who are you?" he asked.

"The greatest explorer alive, boys!" The wild man laughed as he kicked the gorro's body. "The greatest explorer alive! Let's get you out from under there."

Kalleb ignored the pain in his back and forced his wobbling knees to get him back on his feet. He hobbled over to Roy as the wild man leaned his strange weapon against the gorro's corpse then knelt beside the mare. Being this close, Kalleb realized the man was nearly twice his size.

"Take the lad's shoulders," the wild man instructed. "I'll lift, and you pull him out."

Kalleb nodded. Then his memory sparked! The wild man's words echoed through his head repeatedly. "The greatest explorer alive."

I've heard that before.

He studied the man as he reached under the dead mare. His broad shoulders went taut and forearm muscles bulged. He took a few deep breaths then lifted the horse's body, grunting through gritted teeth, his face turning red.

Roy gasped as the weight lifted off his leg, and Kalleb grabbed him under his arms, dragging him out.

"Dammit!" Roy yelled, squirming.

Kalleb laid him down in the road a few feet away from the dead animals and looked at his leg. He winced at the bones poking through his trouser leg at different angles. It was broken in at least three places.

Roy began whimpering, reaching down to it as the feeling started to return.

"Don't do that, boy," the wild man said, picking up his weapon. "Best leave it be until we can splint it."

Roy whined and fell back in the dirt, tears streaking down his face.

Kalleb studied the wild man for a moment more. Whatever was smeared on his face prevented him from getting a good look. The wrinkles and bags under his eyes were new, but his high cheekbones, his manner, his voice—they all stirred Kalleb's memory further and further back to his childhood.

"Olivar Trike?" he asked.

The man perked up. "That's me! Do I know you?"

Kalleb stared back at him. "I'm Kalleb Kane."

Olivar blinked at him with a blank look. "I know many Kanes." He shrugged then turned back to the gorro before Kalleb could say more.

Including Konner, he thought, remembering Konner had been a running mate with Olivar when they had been younger. Olivar was older than Konner by six years, yet he had befriended him and had gotten them both in more trouble than Ma had liked.

"Stay still, Roy," Kalleb said to his wounded lancer. "We'll get you fixed up."

He looked around, but his horse was nowhere to be seen. He caught a glint from the side of the road and walked over to find his saber impaled in a hedge. He pulled it out and sighed in relief that it wasn't broken.

"*Guys!*"

Kalleb jumped around in surprise, holding his saber in front of him until he saw Rence running up the road, still carrying his broken practice pole.

"I'm . . . coming?" Rence slowed to a stop, taking in the scene with confusion on his sweat-drenched face. He gasped for air and doubled over, clutching his knees. "How?"

"We got some help," Kalleb replied, glancing at Olivar. "Where's your horse?"

Rence growled in frustration. "Stupid animal wouldn't turn around! It ran nearly a mile before I could stop it. Had to tie it to a tree because it wouldn't come back up here."

"It smelled death and wouldn't come." Kalleb frowned, slapping the dust off his trousers. "Mine's gone, too." He nodded toward Roy. "Let's find the other practice poles and make a splint for Roy's leg while we wait for rescue."

"*Damn!*" Rence hissed at the sight of Roy's broken leg. "That looks bad."

"Piss off!" Roy snapped.

Kalleb shook his head as he went in search of the discarded poles. *Haven't even made it to Tradon, and my troop's down a lancer. Vallant's going to be a boil on my ass about this.*

<div align="center">~~~</div>

Kalleb sat on a chest and waited outside the tent for the township doctor, who was treating Roy's busted leg. He stared down into his own reflection from his saber sitting in his lap. His horse still hadn't been found, leaving him with the clothes he wore and his saber as his only positions.

This has been a shit day.

The camp bustled around him. With their horses seen to, tents pitched, and belongings stowed away, most of the recruits were anxious to go into town. Some, though, were curious about what had happened on the road. The rumor mill was working overtime, and Kalleb had little doubt that Rence was somewhere, making them grow. Kalleb, however, had little desire to go into town.

There were more lancers surrounding Vorge Township than there were residents. Lord Renald had convinced, or more likely paid, the mayor to let them camp in and around the town. His company had pitched tents and pickets along the creek on its western edge.

The township itself sat in the middle of a valley, with the main drag intersecting with the highway leading through a hedge of spikes from timbers surrounding the town instead of a wall. Stables, forges, and shops lined the drag to a square with the courthouse, inn, church, and market.

Music from whistling flutes, singing fiddles, and laughter drifted from the square where the townsfolk celebrated around the dead gorro that they had carted in.

Kalleb's saber started shaking, and he realized his leg was trembling. His nerves kept flaring up. No matter how many deep breaths he took, every time he closed his eyes, he could still see the gorro creeping closer, its huge fangs bared, and Roy struggling to free himself. He gripped his saber tighter and forced his leg still.

"Lance Corporal Kane!"

Vallant's grating voice made Kalleb grit his teeth. The captain was marching straight toward him, his beak of a nose high in the air and face a thunderclap. Lieutenant Bowden and another man followed on his heels. The lieutenant wasn't smiling.

The third man, Kalleb had never seen before. He strolled behind with a hand propped on his saber. His uniform was pristine, without a hint of sweat or dust on his jacket, trousers, or boots. His reddish-blond hair was combed and straightened, like he was attending a dance instead of having been riding all day. He looked over the pickets with hazel eyes, smirking at everyone he saw.

This won't be good.

Kalleb pushed off his knees and stood up with a grunt. He snapped his heels together and raised then lowered his saber in salute.

Vallant stormed up to his face, eyes blazing. "You lost one of my lancers!"

"Sir?"

"One of my lancers is laying up somewhere, unable to ride!" Vallant narrowed his eyes and jabbed Kalleb in the chest with a finger. "And *you* are responsible." He then gestured to the unknown man. "This is Jentrey Hunt. He will be Troop D's lance corporal from today on. Do you have anything to say before I go to the major and demand you be stripped of your uniform and whipped?"

Kalleb could think of several explanations for what had happened. They hadn't known the gorro was on the prowl. The gorro had ambushed Roy's horse before they could react. They had done their best, and no one had died. Nevertheless, they would all fall on deaf ears.

His saber arm trembled, the curve blade brushing against his trouser leg.

Jentrey smirked at him. No gold cord hung from his shoulder to identify his rank, but having a saber and fresh uniform to change into after a day's ride proved he had money.

Kalleb knew he had to remain calm, but the day's events weighed on him like a mountain.

"With all due respect," he said softly, "go—"

"Kalleb!"

To Kalleb's relief, his brother, Konner, was approaching with an entourage of his staff and officers from the Twelfth. Olivar Trike tagged along, as well, beside him, carrying a small keg on his shoulder and a mug in his hand.

The explorer was all cleaned up now; no smudges of filth on his face and his hair and beard were combed. Both he and Konner wore big grins, as if they had been out on the town. They probably had. Olivar was the toast of the town after having hauled in the gorro.

Vallant, Lieutenant Bowden, and Jentrey snapped to attention as Konner and his group walked up.

Konner waved them away, a burning hela cig between his fingers.

"I heard you've had quite a day. How's the wounded lancer?" Konner asked, pulling a deep drag from his hela cig then blowing the smoke through his nose.

Kalleb saw Vallant's lips tighten out of the corner of his eye. He didn't know. He hadn't even asked.

"The town doctor is still with him," he replied, nodding to the tent beside them.

Konner grunted and frowned. "Tough luck."

"Good luck, actually." Olivar burped. "Ol' Bushwhacker's been hunting around here for two years now, killing men and horses alike and dragging them off to damn knows where. But I finally got 'em." He beamed proudly then took a big swallow from his mug.

"If only you'd killed him sooner," Konner said, shaking his head teasingly.

Olivar snorted into his mug. "Damn big woods! Besides, if all these green soldier boys would have stayed out of the way, I'd've shot the bastard sooner."

"We were trying to save our man," Kalleb growled.

"No offense there." Olivar waved his mug, splashing some of the malty, yellow contents on the ground. "Took balls to charge that beast. Especially the idiot with just a stick!" He barked a laugh. "At least you had a blade. Then again"—he elbowed Konner—"someone in this half-wit's family had to have some brains. I knew I recognized you, lad!" He winked at Kalleb before refilling his mug from the keg on his shoulder.

Kalleb gave him a blank look. *No, you didn't.*

"Major," Vallant interjected, exhaling in frustration, "now that you are here, I feel it necessary to discuss the appropriate discipline for this lance corporal's failure to ensure the safety of his recruits."

It was Konner's and Olivar's turn to give Vallant a blank look.

"Damn," Olivar grunted. "You got a stick up your ass, don't ye?"

Kalleb strained to hold in a laugh but smiled despite himself. *All right, that makes up for everything.*

"Captain," Konner sighed out after taking another drag of his cig, "I understand you are strict with your new command. However, no one could have seen this happening. It would destroy their troop if their lance corporal were to be punished for saving one of his lancers."

"With all due respect, Major," Vallant objected, "if he'd trained his troop in proper rear-guard tactics, they'd likely not have been ambushed in the first place! I recommend he be removed from his post and a more proper officer be elevated in his place."

Konner gave him a stern look, and Vallant visibly stiffened.

"Whose idea was it to put green lancer boys with sticks in the back, anyway?" Olivar burped again after taking another swig from his mug.

Vallant turned his frustration toward the explorer. "This is Storm Cavalry business, Mr. Trike, and not—"

"Stop yelling!" Roxanne Quell fumed as she stormed out from the tent. With her freckled face and a stern grimace, she glared at each man with blazing gray eyes.

The township's doctor was a handsome woman in her late thirties. Her chestnut hair was wrapped back in a cream-colored scarf, matching the apron she wore over her gray dress. Despite being a head shorter than every man there, they all took a step back as she planted her fists on her hips.

"I just spent two hours fixing that lad's leg up *and* fighting a sudden fever, to boot," she hissed. "So, if you *gentlemen* would piss off and let him rest, I'd appreciate it." She pulled the tent flap back to go inside.

"Will he ride?" Konner asked.

Halfway inside the tent, Roxanne snorted. "He won't be riding for a while. In fact, I'd get him to a city surgeon in a hurry to make sure he doesn't lose his leg."

She was about to go back in the tent when she paused. Then she burst out and rushed up to Olivar Trike, snatching the mug out of his big fist. She gulped down the contents, holding the mug in both hands and leaving most of the men, including Olivar, watching her in surprise.

"Ah!" she sighed, pulling the mug from her lips then shoving it into Olivar's chest. "I needed that." She wiped her lips with her sleeve before retreating back into the tent.

Olivar stared down into his empty mug. "I think I'm in love."

"Again?" Konner asked, giving him a sideways look.

Olivar smirked and shrugged as he went to refill his mug.

Konner shook his head as he turned to Kalleb. "How does the rest of your troop look?"

Out of the corner of his eye, Kalleb glanced again at Vallant. His captain's face was red from being ignored.

"Besides Roy," Kalleb replied, "the rest of the troop have no injuries, but a few are shaken up. We lost two horses, though. Roy's and mine."

Olivar chuckled. "Yours is halfway home by now."

Konner nodded then considered for a moment, taking a last drag from his cig before dropping and stomping it out on the ground. "Lord Renald is taking the Timsberg route to Tradon. Most of us will be taking the long route around the Ralmae River, but the Twelfth's Squadron Two is going with him as additional escort." He frowned deeply with his hands on his hips. "We'll send your troop with them and take Troop D from Squadron Two to ride as our rear guard from now on."

Vallant's eyes went wide. "But Major—"

"*Captain*," Konner cut him off, "your request is denied. Go procure a wagon to carry our wounded lancer. Since you're out a horse, Kalleb, you can drive it."

Grimacing, Vallant saluted then turned on his heels to go. As he did, he flashed a narrow-eyed glare at Kalleb before he marched away, Jentrey

Hunt on his heels. Lieutenant Bowden saluted, as well, then gave Kalleb a pat on the shoulder before following his captain.

Kalleb watched them go and, for once, was grateful for being under one of his brother's command.

"Did you lose everything with your horse?" Konner asked with brotherly concern.

Kalleb frowned. "Everything except . . ." He held up his saber.

"Well, just make it to Tradon, and we'll get your kit replaced."

Kalleb snapped to attention. "Thanks, Major."

Konner nodded. "Get some rest, Kalleb."

After watching them pass, Kalleb sighed and sat back down on the chest, putting his saber back over his legs. He didn't have a tent to go to, because it was still on his horse.

He slumped his shoulders, wanting to lay back, but there was only a tent's canvas behind him. He hung his head, and his eyelids began to drift close.

Just a quick rest. I'll find a bunk in a minute.

Chapter 13

1st of Andril, 1109 N.F. (e.y.)

I'm surprised by you, Your Highness," Nolen said as he lounged in the backward-facing seat of the coach. "I was beginning to give up on you. I never took you for a man who shows up fashionably late."

Alindale folded his arms. The coach bounced on the cobbles, flickering the small, enclosed lantern illuminating the inside of the phaeton carriage from the opening by the coachman. He sat tensely in the corner of the seat, watching every move the strange lord made. He was still apprehensive about this. Part of him begged him to order the coachman to turn around and go back to the castle.

But the cryptic warning of those plotting to kill him had lingered in the back of Alindale's mind for the past four days. He also had the grating feeling that he wasn't doing enough after his mother had embarrassed him in front of her ladies. Even though he believed he was making efforts to improve himself, it was undeniably true that he still lacked interaction with people at court and the castle in general.

When he had brought this up to Amadus during a tutoring session, Amadus had shrugged and said, "It's a disadvantage we have to work with." And when Alindale had further asked if there were places outside the castle where courtiers might be inclined to speak with him, Amadus had laughed said, "If there were such places, they aren't places you should go. Besides, you wouldn't fit in."

The lack of confidence was irritating. Alindale couldn't see how he was supposed to improve his standing if no one supported him. Amadus's quick dismissal of the idea hadn't helped, either.

Then again, Alindale found little comfort sitting in a coach with a strange, untrustworthy lord, going to an unknown destination. Fortunately, he'd had the foresight to leave a letter for his knights and Storm Cavalry retainers, detailing if anything should happen to him, that Lord Nolen Ingman was responsible.

"I had to see to a few things first," he replied.

"I'm sure," Nolen said with a grin. "Guards can be annoying when you're trying to sneak off to have some fun." He peeled the window curtain back with his long fingers then peeked out. The street lanterns flashed by, shinning on his face. "The city's getting livelier. Are they here for the Abundant Harvest? We don't celebrate it in Inglworf."

The Abundant Harvest holiday was celebrated once every four years, with the Easterly Great Spring. The long months of warm weather and moderate rainfall were highly favorable crop weather. The celebration usually occurred around the beginning or second week of the season, close to the first harvest or the planting of the second, which was a boom for stockpiling foodstuff.

"I have never been to Inglworf," Alindale said dryly. New Hartland's northernmost coastal city's dubious reputation offered little incentive to visit. "But I find it hard to believe you do not celebrate the additional harvests."

"Everyone mostly lives off lobster, fish, and harpooning the occasional serpent whale," Nolen uncaringly replied, his attention focused outside the carriage. He then threw back the curtain and smiled broadly. "Leaving the boring aside, made any plans for a grand entrance to Her Majesty's ball?" It was tradition for the queen to host an Easterly Great Spring Ball during the Abundant Harvest celebrations. Yet another official gathering Alindale wasn't fond of. And usually avoided.

He groaned. "A banished prince is not welcomed."

Being surrounded by mocking aristos for a whole night? I would rather Master Montaigu beat me until I forget my name.

"I haven't heard that," Nolen replied, rubbing his narrow chin. "Her Majesty only banished you from court; she didn't banish you from *every* royal engagement. Besides, you can't waste such a golden opportunity to show off."

"Show off?" Alindale raised an eyebrow.

"From all that running and sword swinging." Nolen ridiculously mimicked swinging a sword. "You're not as soft as you used to be."

Alindale squirmed in his seat and ran his hand down his front, straightening out his clothes. "If you say so."

"I'd wager you've dropped half a stone or so. And you're certainly not as pale as before. With the right clothes and lady on your arm"—Nolen chuckled, looking out the window again—"you could drive some arrogant lords mad."

The sound of the horse hooves and thumps of the carriage wheels against the cobblestones changed. They sounded far off instead of close from echoing off the nearby buildings or manor house walls.

Nolen's mention of clothes gave him a bad feeling.

"We aren't going to a tailor, are we?" he asked.

Nolen snorted. "We won't find any tailors where we're going." Nolen reached behind him, pulled out a dark cloak, and then threw it in Alindale's lap before throwing his own cloak around his shoulders. "By the way, you don't mind me calling you Alin, do you? It'll be safer that way."

"Safer?" Alindale passed a confused look between Nolen and the cloak in his hands.

The carriage slowed and made a sharp turn. The creaking of the wheels and clomps of the horseshoes sounded much closer now. The buildings were closer now.

"Halt!" someone outside shouted. "Halt and present yourselves!"

"Put your hood on," Nolen whispered as the carriage slowed to a halt.

Alindale apprehensively did just that before a sharp knock rapped against the carriage door.

"What is going on?" he hissed. Something was wrong. He had expected to arrive somewhere with a footman, but the orders to halt wasn't right.

"Please, keep your voice down," Nolen whispered, pulling Alindale's hood lower and making it cover his face. "Just let me do all the talking. It's best you're not recognized."

The coach door was wrenched open, and light spilled in from a guardsman thrusting a lantern into the coach. The guardsman's faded gray tunic over the chain mail marked him as a guard of the city peace. He cautiously studied Alindale and Nolen, shifting his head back and forth and jingling his chain mail. All the while, he clutched his sword in his free hand.

"State your business," the guardsman demanded.

Alindale jumped and looked to Nolen, uncertain of what to say.

"Just a couple of gents out for the night," Nolen replied casually.

The guardsman grunted. "Do you gents know where you're going?"

That's the question of the night, Alindale thought, drawing his cloak around him and pressing deeper into the seat corner.

"We're heading for Red Mansion," Nolen cheerfully replied, tossing a small pouch from under his cloak. It struck the guardsman in the chest.

The guardsman quickly fumbled to catch the pouch. Coins jingled together every time the pouch bounced in his hand before he finally caught it. Then, feeling the weight, the guardsman again gave them both cautious looks.

"Open you cloaks, please," he ordered, now more courteous, stuffing the pouch in his pocket. "I must ensure no swords are allowed in South End."

South End! Alindale broke into a cold sweat and swung around to look at the small rear window of the coach.

"Of course," Nolen replied, lifting his cloak and letting the guardsman check him.

From the small window, Alindale looked around and recognized instantly they were in Alpheaus Square, the center of Daincliff.

In the faint light of the streetlamps surrounding it, he spied the carved, stone pillars of the Ministry of Justice, the highest court for all the kingdom's magistrates, in the center of the square. The Grand Cathedral of the Last God rose in the corner, towering over the Ministry of Justice, its marble walls separating North End from West End. They were surrounded by various ministry buildings, banks, and magistrate offices. Beyond them, Alindale could barely make out the small dots of light hanging above the city to mark Dain Castle. He also saw a faint red glow emanating from somewhere ahead of them.

"Open your cloak, sir," the guardsman demanded.

Alindale swallowed then turned around to find the guardsman holding his lantern closer to him. He felt warmth on his face as sweat ran down it. He nervously spread back the cloak and shivered from the night air swooping in, feeling much colder than before.

The guardsman barely glanced at him before nodding and pulling back out of the carriage. "Do not stray out of the Red District," the guardsman warned. "Stay in streets where the lamps are lit. If you go down to the wharf or stray deeper, the city peace is not responsible, and we will *not* come searching for you. Understood?"

"Yes, sir," Nolen replied with a nonchalant wave.

The guardsman slammed the carriage door shut. "They're free to pass!" he shouted.

Alindale pulled back the window curtain and tensed at the sight of the dilapidated gate standing open in front of the carriage. The rusty hinges of the lanterns mounted beside the gateway squeaked in the night breeze. Their faint light revealed gray and green steaks staining the looming stone wall. Ahead still, was that red light, brightly creeping out of the darkness.

He only realized they were riding toward the ominous glow when they slowly passed by the gray blockhouse beside the gateway. The guardsman and two more members of the city peace muttered to each other, watching them roll by. One spat against the side of the blockhouse.

"We need to turn back," he said, his voice shaky.

South End was Daincliff's ancestral residential district but had degenerated into teetering slums and notorious gambling houses, brothels, fighting rings, and black markets centuries ago. The city peace constantly requested more money and men to police it, and Alindale remembered arguments at court about flattening parts of the district, but the costs and potential for riots always tabled the topic. It was also the last place he would have thought of walking into at night.

"We can't turn back now," Nolen replied, waving behind them. "Not when we're almost there."

"Almost *where*?" Alindale snapped as he lunged and grabbed Nolen by the clasp of his cloak around his neck. "You said you knew a place where I could meet people of the court without word getting back to my mother. You said *nothing* about going to South End!"

Nolen snickered. "Well, of course I didn't say anything about that. You wouldn't have come."

Alindale couldn't stand his nonchalant attitude, especially as the red light filtered through the small windows of the carriage and the faint sounds of music and laughter drifted in from the coachman's opening.

His grip tightened, and his forearm began to shake. "We can't come here. Neither of us will walk out!"

Nolen arched an eyebrow. "You really believe all the stories, don't you? About all the good people staying away because it's just not fit? Maybe you should look for yourself at what it's really like." Nolen gave him his crooked grin, motioning to the window.

Alindale released him then nervously watched the flickers of red lights from passing buildings. Getting over his reluctance, he then pulled back the curtain and looked.

Squat buildings loomed around them, each with windows painted over so the light from within gave the street its red glow. Muffled laughter, dim music, and the occasional shout came from the buildings as they passed. Some had louder music than others, and more shadows walked by the windows, while some buildings looked abandoned.

When the dirt street turned into a boardwalk, the carriage wheels reverberated on the wood and the street got brighter, along with the noise. People began appearing on the street, walking from one establishment to another. Men and women walked as couples, arm in arm, or groups of people laughed and wobbled by on shaky legs.

"Welcome to the Red District, Alin," Nolen said, stretching out across his seat again. "I must say, as notorious places go, you do have an impressive one."

Something slammed against the carriage door.

Alindale jumped and spied two men spilling out of a tavern, grappling with each other as they rolled down the steps and onto the boardwalk. Patrons followed them, laughing and raising their cups at the spectacle as the two men punched and choked each other.

"I don't care much for taverns," he said, hoping to dispel Nolen of any notion of getting him drunk.

"You won't find the kind of people you need to mingle with at a common tavern," Nolen replied. "Besides, if I was after good liquor, I'd have tried to use you to raid the royal wine cellar."

Alindale frowned as he checked to make sure the brawl wasn't bringing trouble their way. Luckily, the onlookers were pulling the men apart.

He sat back in his seat, but his attention kept drifting back to the passing buildings, to their red-tinted windows and the unsettling atmosphere. His mind drifted with the plaguing question of where their destination was.

Red Mansion, he remembered Nolen saying to the guardsman. *That's not helpful in a place called the Red District! Why is everything red?*

The red glow from the windows made the boardwalk appear as if it was running red with blood, casting everything in light and shadow at the same time. The disorienting appearance made Alindale's stomach roll. If they weren't going to a tavern, he quickly thought of another option and considered the color and South End's reputation.

He seized Nolen by the arm and growled angrily, "I am not going to a brothel!"

Nolen gaped as he blinked down at him. Then he smiled so wide that it pushed his high checks farther up his face. He laughed.

His loud, high-pitched guffaw made Alindale let go and glance about, hoping they weren't drawing unwanted attention from the few people whom they passed outside.

"You are . . ." Nolen wheezed, trying to catch his breath, "the most prudish . . . person . . . of your stature I've ever met! I wouldn't take you to a brothel even if your life depended on it." He wiped away tears and wheezed again. Then he threw his head back and breathed deeply to calm down.

The carriage slowed then came to a halt. The red light flared and glared into the carriage.

"Red Mansion," the coachman grumbled.

"Ah," Nolen sighed out, opening the door, "finally."

Alindale shielded his eyes from the blinding light and watched as Nolen climbed out of the carriage. Before them was an outlandish, four-story building. It illuminated the night as if the center of all the hedonism surrounding it. Red and gold striped pillars lined the front of the building, holding up the second-floor balcony full of laughing, drinking people. Lanterns hung off its third-floor banisters, casting haunting shadows from the people on the balcony down on the boardwalk in front of the building.

"Thank you, kind sir." Nolen dropped a couple coins into the coachman's outstretched hand. The metal *clinked* together as the coachman quickly clasped his fare then whisked it into his jacket.

Alindale hesitantly stepped down from the coach and grimaced from the heavy aroma drifting across the boardwalk. The mixture of yeast, dozens of perfumes, incense, and undercoated with the strong smell of sewage made him cough and cover his mouth.

"What's that smell?" he asked through his hand.

"The smell of a city." Nolen chuckled, taking him by the arm. "Come on, Alin. Now comes the fun part of the night!"

Alindale longingly gazed over his shoulder and watched the coachman crack his teams' reins and pull away. His apprehension heightened, especially now that he was out in the open and watching his only way home drive away. The pit in his stomach grew tighter with each step up the Red Mansion's steps.

"I have ten gold mints on this fight," a man on the balcony pleaded. "You have to come watch it with me."

"I needed some air," a bored-sounding woman replied. "Besides, watching a dockworker and Syrosi sailor punch each other is boring."

Other conversations mixed in with each other, muffled by the ceiling and the roar coming from behind the door.

As Nolen banged on the enormous, twelve-foot-tall door, Alindale studied the strange slots carved into it; one at normal eye level and another, much large one at waist height. They waited a moment, and nothing happened.

Nolen grunted and banged again, even adding a kick for good measure.

The eye-level slot slid open. The din from within became louder as a pair of shifting eyes looked them both up and down.

"Do you belong?" a deep voice asked.

"Most certainly," Nolen replied with a lopsided grin.

Alindale looked between the two. He wasn't entirely sure what was going on but presumed, being where they were, this was some sort of code.

The waist-level slot slid open with a *thud*. Then a broad hand with thick, scarred fingers reached out. Thin wisps of smoke leaked out of the slot, as well.

"Ten silver mints," came the deep voice. "A piece."

Alindale tensed. He hadn't brought any money. One thing about being the prince and living in the castle all his life was he never really needed it.

Nolen plopped a small purse into the broad hand. It was quickly seized, slid back through the slot like a snake retreating into its den, and then the slot was closed.

Minutes of relative silence dragged by.

Alindale felt an itch growing between his shoulder blades and fought the worry to check the still boardwalk behind them for people creeping up on them.

A loud series of *clicks* broke the stalemate. The thick door was pulled inward, and a dense haze of smoke flowed out around their ankles. Nolen again dragged him inside by the arm.

Alindale shuffled into a den of deafening madness. Only when the door closed behind them did he notice the brawny doorman in a gaudy, stretched-out red suit standing off to the side.

"Welcome to the Red Mansion," he grumbled.

The large body of patrons mingled together around tables lit by oil lamps, smoking and drinking in huddled conversations. A few people mingled at the long bar in the back of the room, and the rest surrounded a railing, gazing down a large opening in the floor, cheering and yelling at some spectacle below. The yelling and cheering filled the place, making talking into someone's ear the only way people could speak with one another.

The heavy scent of smoke from tobacco, hela, and numerous other weeds mixed with the heavy smell of beer and the hint of wine. The mingled smoke formed the haze along the ceiling and the floor. The light from the myriad of candles on golden candlesticks, hanging from gilded mounts on the walls, reflected off it.

SLAP! SMACK! SMACK!

"Oh!" the crowd collectively groaned before breaking into a multitude of yells and cheers. The wall of sound was much bigger than to have come from the spectators around the railing. There had to be more somewhere else.

Alindale stood motionless, surveying the room as a tight ball formed in the small of his back. It grew tighter and tighter until his back ached from merely standing. Furthermore, his ears began to ring from all the noise.

He might not have liked the look of the place from the outside, but now he was certain he did *not* want to be here.

This was a mistake. He swallowed nervously. *No one from court comes to a place like this. No prince should be in a place like this!*

He stiffly turned to leave, hoping to sneak away. Unfortunately, his captor for the evening still held him by the arm, dragging him deeper into the frenzy.

"What do you think of the place?" Nolen yelled.

I never want to see it again.

"Strange . . . establishment," Alindale lied.

"It has its charms."

Nolen smiled at a serving girl as he nimbly snatched a glass off her tray without her noticing as she maneuvered between the tables. He took a sip of his pilfered drink. "Oh!" Nolen's eyebrows shot up. "Brandy!"

He's a thief, too . . . I'm not surprised.

"Oops. Sorry," Nolen begged his pardon from everyone whom he gently slipped by, giving Alindale a small window each time to slip in behind him. "Didn't mean to brush against you."

Alindale stepped through a cloud of vapers of various perfumes blended in the tobacco smoke, and his eyes watered from the sweet yet burning scent in his nostrils. He rubbed his eyes clear then found himself standing in front of the railing before a large hole in the floor.

SMACK! SMACK!

Below, a tall, muscular Syrosi man pounded the sides of a burly man holding his thick forearms in front of his face and chest to keep the Syrosi from hitting his face. Both men were stripped to the waist and fought in the middle of a circle.

Alindale rubbed his sides at how red the burly man's sides were. He had received similar marks himself after a few sparring sessions with Montaigu. *Those will be painful bruises in the morning.*

The burly man took a swing at the Syrosi, but the Syrosi nimbly danced away. His red, twisted braid of a beard flung around him as he bobbed from side to side. He kept his arms up and occasionally jabbed with his left to keep Burly Man at a distance.

Nolen elbowed him then excitedly pointed at the Syrosi. "That's Lord Jerro Syros! He's the brother of the Syros sisters."

"Lords are *fighting*?" Alindale asked, shocked.

"Never seen the other man before," Nolen said with a shrug. "With those muscles, he could be a dock loader or warehouse worker."

Alindale gave him a disbelieving look. "That's impossible! A commoner would not fight a lord. They would be convicted of a felony, if taken in front of a magistrate."

The slender woman beside Nolen threw her head back and laughed, flinging her hair off her bare shoulders. "Why, what strange company you're keeping, Ingman." Droplets of wine sloshed over the rim of her glass as she pulled her shawl hanging off her arms tighter. "Since when did your fellow rogues start caring about magistrates?" The woman's cheeks were flushed from the wine as she squinted at Alindale, trying to peer under his hood. Alindale lowered his head and kept the light away, but that made her peer even harder.

"Lady Malthas!" Nolen said cheerfully. "My apologies for not seeing you there. Alin, this is Lady Regina Malthas, a lady to Her Majesty herself."

"Enjoying the spectacle, I trust?" he asked her.

Alindale felt the urge to run. In his vainest of hopes, he wanted to speak with someone who had attended court recently and let them tell him what was going on. Not one of his mother's ladies! Especially after the incident in her garden.

"Hmm . . .?" Regina hummed, blinking. "Oh, yes! Jerro's putting on quite the show tonight." She chuckled then sipped her wine, returning her attention back to the fight.

Nolen leaned in closer to Alindale and said, "Anything goes in Mr. Norris's ring. He's the owner of this establishment. And anybody can fight anybody, so long as they pay and are willing to take the risk."

Below, Burly Man lunged forward, reaching to snatch Jerro's beard. Jerro slapped Burly Man's face and nimbly sidestepped away.

Regina and several around them laughed, but down below came the rumble of booing. There must have been a hundred people down there from the sound of it. And, from where Alindale stood, he could see many angry faces pressed up against the ring.

"Rip that scrap of hair out of his chin!" someone below yelled.

"Trip him and break his legs!" another screamed. "That Syrosi high-wash won't dance so good then!"

Nolen sighed, finishing his brandy before setting the glass on a nearby table. "No wonder the woman on the balcony found this boring. Jerro's toying with the guy."

"Maybe Jerro's just not her type," Regina piped in, sipping her wine.

"'*Arrogance is an opening an opponent doesn't have to make, because you bring that into the battle yourself,*'" Alindale quoted. It was a proverb from a manual on leadership that he and Amadus had discussed the day before.

Nolen and Regina gave him strange looks. Regina squinted with a look that told Alindale that she found his comment off-putting. Nolen's expression simply conveyed: *Why?*

"What are you?" Regina asked. "Some sort of knight admirer?"

Alindale's mouth suddenly went dry. He was grateful for the hood covering his face, but it didn't stop Regina from drawing out the pause for an answer.

"My compatriot is a stage actor, actually," Nolen interjected. "He performed in Inglworf only once before heading west. Saw him in the city and thought to warn him of certain audiences here."

Alindale stared at Nolen. *A stage performer? Seriously? And what if she—*

"What plays have you performed in?" Regina asked suspiciously.

Several play titles came to mind, but Alindale knew they hadn't been performed in years. The few he did know that were performed recently he had seen in Daincliff. If Lady Malthas had seen them, as well, she could remember him being there, or easily find out later.

"A few out west," he lied, slipping into slang speech. "I'm not sure you'd know them."

Regina frowned, unimpressed. "I've never known an actor to be so reserved."

"At least he's not like Minister Baltaer." Nolen laughed, having mysteriously acquired another glass, this time with wine by its red color.

Regina rolled her eyes. "Speaking of, he's sitting in the corner with his *usual* number."

A minister? Here? Alindale followed Regina's gesture to a booth behind him, nestled in the corner.

Simon Baltaer, Minister of Proclamations, sat in an arching booth with his back nestled in the corner, surrounded by five women. Despite the noise, the ladies were hunched over, as if transfixed on his every word.

The middle-aged aristo had become a performer in his youth but returned to his family after his father had died. He put his oratory skills to use for the ministry once he had gotten a taste for hearing the laws of the land in his own voice.

"Maybe we should introduce ourselves," Alindale suggested.

Nolen frowned and shook his head. "He has no time for us. Besides, all the quick information you want is right here."

The crowd groaned collectively as Jerro delivered a hard right into Burly Man's gut. The loud slap of fist against abdomen made Alindale flinch. Burly Man kept his feet, but his right fist dropped its guard, and Jerro's left hook into his jaw sent him spinning away.

Before Alindale could ask Nolen what he meant, Nolen leaned closer to Regina.

"I take it everything is going boringly well at court?" Nolen asked. "Since I'm not part of any ministry, I don't get the inner secrets as much."

Regina sniffed dismissively, more intent on the fight below now. "As if any ministry would have you, Ingman. I doubt you'd be picked for anything."

"Lords are being picked then?" Nolen probed then winked back at Alindale. "Should we expected Baltaer to make an important announcement soon?"

"Damn," Regina sneered at her wine. "I hadn't realized I'd drunk so much." She deposited the glass on a table behind them then wrapped her arms about herself in a huff.

"Oh, come on now," Nolen urged, elbowing her. "You've slipped, so you might as well say it."

"By the Last God, you are annoying," Regina groaned, rolling her eyes. "They're about to announce a commission of lords and magistrates to go straighten out Urwald. Perfectly boring and not something *you'd* be interested in."

Alindale straightened then leaned in, trying to hear more. It was the first official news that he had heard in nearly a month. But Regina had frustratingly stopped there.

Nolen shrugged. "I guess not. But it might interest His Majesty when he recovers. Or perhaps the prince in case . . . you know."

A chill ran up Alindale's back, and he glared at Nolen from under the hood. *You're asking* that*? Here?*

"Either of them might," Regina replied, returning the shrug. "But it won't matter. Despite what *some* of my fellow ladies think, it's not about who's appointed at the top, but delegated to do the everyday work. Even if His Majesty recovers and dismisses the ministers who weren't in his favor, or even if . . . the unthinkable happens and the prince is crowned, neither of them will be able to go through every ministry and dismiss or revoke the appointments of every aristo being appointed now. It's just impossible." She snickered, shaking her head and appearing impressed. "Avera really is taking hold of the kingdom."

Alindale shuttered and rolled the implications over in his mind. *Even if Father recovers and gets rid of Haemin . . . or if I . . . we might never be rid of his cronies. Mother, what are you doing?*

"How many have been appointed?" he asked, unable to stop his curiosity. "Did they mention any names?"

Regina raised an eyebrow. "What's it to you?

"Tell your friend, Ingman, that he should stay out of affairs above him."

"Absolutely," Nolen agreed with a nod. "They're such taxing things, really. Just take yourself. With your duties as one of Her Majesty's ladies, you must sneak away to this fine establishment to relieve yourself of anxiety."

Alindale snorted, smiling within his hood at watching someone else receive Nolen's snarky remarks.

"My duties, I can handle," Regina said. "It's actually Serina Syros who has been taxing me of late. She's only been here a month and thinks we all must attend her when Her Majesty has no need of us."

Nolen chuckled. "So, you sneak away to watch her brother instead?"

Regina pursed her lips as she looked down at the fight below with a twinkle in her eyes. "I wouldn't mind if Lord Jerro attend me every now and again. Although, I don't think he's playing by house rules tonight."

Burly Man wobbled on his feet, wiping away the blood running down the side of his head from a cut beside his eye. Jerro bobbed from side to side, waiting. Then Burly Man charged in with a yell, slamming his shoulder into Jerro's middle and punching his sides furiously.

Jerro held firm. He raised his arms above his head, ignoring Burly Man's punches. Then, with a roar, he slammed his fists down on Burly Man's back, grabbed his belt, and kicked him in groin.

"*Coi!*" Burly Man yelled, losing his grip around Jerro's waist as his knees gave out and he clutched his groin.

Jerro grabbed Burly Man by the hair, and then a crashing right blow to the jaw sent Burly Man sprawling unconscious on the floor.

The crowd erupted. All around Alindale, they cheered and clapped. Down below came a mixture of boos and some chanting cheer that he couldn't make out because of all the yelling. Many of the angry South End dwellers even stormed off, out of sight.

Jerro strolled around the ring, holding his arms out wide and smiling broadly. "What you think of Syros now?" he roared over the crowd while his opponent was dragged away. "We don't let fat merchants buy captains' births or give them out to someone with a family name! If you can't hold the lines in the eye of a hurricane with your crew or wring the neck of a snake whale with your bare hands, then you don't deserve to call yourself Captain!" He beat his chest, and the chanting became clearer as the crowd's yelling died.

"Captain! Captain! Captain!"

Jerro spread his arms out again and walked out of the ring and into the chanting crowd, all Syrosi.

"Brought his crew with him," Nolen noted, nodding approvingly. "Smart."

"And there goes my entertainment for tonight." Regina sighed then turned to leave. "Good evening, gentlemen."

"Good-bye," Nolen said happily with a wave.

Alindale looked between them anxiously and hissed, "We need more information!"

"That was probably all we're going to get from her. Probably got what we did because of the wine and distracting entertainment. I didn't expect one of your mother's ladies to be here, anyway. Still, the night is young and—Ah!" Nolen pointed at a table where a couple of men had recently vacated close to the railing. "Perfect!"

In the three long strides, he seized a vacant seat and sighed contently while vicariously leaning back in it.

Alindale slunk along behind him and, despite his misgivings about the place, was grateful to sit down. He groaned as his legs gave out the moment he sat and felt the soles of his feet pulsing inside his boots. Training all day and standing around all night didn't go well together, apparently.

He straightened his back against the chair and saw the door over Nolen's shoulder. Regina had wrapped a shawl over her shoulders. The enormous doorman grinned and shyly waved to her as she walked out. Following her was another group of well-dressed men and women, who had come from upstairs, and Minister Baltaer with his entourage of ladies.

"People are leaving," he commented.

"More people will come," Nolen said while trying in vain to wave down a waitress. "They may have been like Regina—only here to see an actual lord in fisticuffs with a commoner."

Alindale folded his arms and leaned on the table. "I thought you said anyone can fight here?"

"Well," Nolen huffed, flopping an arm against his side as a waitress passed them without a second look, "allowing anything is one thing. But there's always a risk in allowing aristos and commoners to fight. The commoners get to vent some built-up resentment, sure. But, if they lose . . ." He trailed off, glancing down below.

The boos had died down, but the grumbling remained like a roiling boil. The *clank* and *ting* of coins being counted and rolling on the tables added punctuation through the din.

Alindale frowned. "Disgruntled about taxes is one thing, but you make it sound as if they hate aristos enough to *want* to hurt them."

"Surely, you're not this naïve." Nolen chuckled. "I hear most in South End have had at least one run-in with the city peace. I doubt you could find one who has a pleasant word to say about the magistrates, North Enders, or even you, frankly."

Alindale gave him an offended look. "What have *I* done?"

"The city peace keeps the South Enders in South End or drags them in front of magistrates. The magistrates fine them, punish them, or sentence them. The well-to-do in North End demand the people here be locked in together. And which family sits at the top of it all?" Nolen glanced at him. "The royal family."

"That's not how it works!" Alindale protested.

"Just how they see it," Nolen said with a shrug.

That's not fair. Alindale hung his head. Talks about urban renewal in South End did come up in court every now and again, but besides money, the logistical question was always the same: where do you move thousands of people?

They don't have to stay here. They can move . . . can't they?

"That was unexpected!" a bald man shouted, stepping into the ring and clapping loudly as the crowd quieted down. His pearl-white clothes made him stand out in the dark background below. Even his boots were white. "I applaud you, Captain Jerro," he said, adjusting the monocle on his sharp nose. "Few have given a performance like that in my ring."

"That's Mr. Norris," Nolen whispered helpfully.

"Now," Mr. Norris shouted, "the next fight is going to be a little different. I'm sorry to tell you, especially all my lovely guests on the second floor"—he waved with a flourish toward them, revealing his large eyes and narrow face—"that the books will be closed for this."

A chorus of boos and groans came from below.

Alindale saw several people around the railing shrug and leave for the bar, and others gave up seats close to the railing.

"I know!" Mr. Norris replied to the crowd. "I know. We are all here for the sport. But, being a sporting man myself, I couldn't cheat my good friends."

The crowd below exploded into laughter, almost cruelly.

"Because this next fight"—Mr. Norris's jovial tone became darkly serious—"will be for more than just your entertainment. Someone has broken a rule of my house. We caught a thief last night!"

The crowd groaned ominously.

Mr. Norris gestured, and two darkly dressed men, with belts lined with knives, dragged out a smaller man in shackles and tossed him in the middle of the ring. The shackles on the man's wrists and ankles rattled against the floor.

"This isn't good," Nolen said, his jovial attitude gone. "I'm sorry, Alin, but this might not have been the best time to bring you here."

"What do you mean?" Alindale asked, ignoring Mr. Norris's continued speech.

"No one's going to be in the mood to talk freely after this," Nolen replied. "That's why people were leaving. They're going to make an example."

"An example?" Alindale gave him a flat stare. "You mean they *intend* to kill that man?"

Nolen nodded.

Alindale leapt from his seat, but Nolen grabbed his shoulder.

"No!" Nolen hissed. "Revealing yourself to stop it would be insane!"

"Then we should leave and inform the city peace."

Nolen's grip on his shoulder tightened. "Leave now, and we'll be noticed. We'd never make out of South End. We must wait until everyone leaves. That way, we can blend into the crowd."

"So," Alindale growled, "to keep ourselves safe, we must watch a man be murdered?"

Nolen's eyes hardened. "Sometimes you have to sacrifice others to keep yourself safe, even when you're simply passing through."

Alindale sat back, disgusted and unable to look at him. He folded his arms and grimaced down at the spectacle below.

The shackled man stood alone in the ring, ignoring the crowd cussing at him. He pulled his shoulder-length, midnight black hair back and looked casually about. He likely stood barely four-and-a-half-feet tall.

"Is this necessary?" Shackle Man asked. "This all feels excessive." He stretched, reaching up in the air and leaning back while standing. Alindale winced at the sound of Shackle Man's back popping. Then Shackle Man squatted, keeping his arms outstretched and parallel to the floor in front of him.

"Shitting your pants already?" someone in the crowd jeered.

Shackle Man said nothing as they laughed at him. He sprung up to his feet, chains striking the ring floor as he kept his balance. He turned his arms and cracked his knuckles with interlocking fingers.

Montaigu's training of observing an opponent awoke, and Alindale found Shackle Man to appear calm. He also noticed Shackle Man's exceptionally long fingernails, as wretched-looking as he was. His shirt was littered with small holes, the knees and hems of his trousers were worn to thin threads, and he was shoeless. Alindale expected Shackle Man's life to be a poor, harsh one. *Those fingernails don't fit.*

Four darkly dressed men entered the ring from four directions, each carrying long knives.

Alindale groaned. Not wanting to watch, he made to get up again, but Nolen took him by the shoulder and restrained him again.

"Stay," Nolen whispered, nodding to a few similarly darkly dressed men around the room watching everybody. "Clearly, Mr. Norris wants everyone to understand what happens to people who steal from him."

"I will just have to tell a magistrate then and show Mr. Norris what happens to people who murder," Alindale growled under his breath.

"But, who will you call as witnesses?" Nolen raised an eyebrow before turning back.

Alindale felt a pit grow in his stomach. He looked around at the other people watching, and the pit grew. He had come here in hopes of finding people willing to talk with him about things going on in court because he was promised no one would admit to being in such a place. That same logic held that no one here would testify that they had seen a crime occur here, either, no matter how heinous.

No one will say a word for him, he thought, looking down at Shackle Man with pity.

Shackle Man looked around at his four killers. "*Really* excessive!"

"Do you wish to beg for your life?" Mr. Norris asked from the crowd.

"Beg! Beg! Beg!" some in the crowd chanted.

Shackle Man dismissively waved. "No."

The crowd exploded in jeers, shouts, and laughs. They stomped their feet and pounded on tables.

Alindale's cheeks grew redder and redder as their laughter filled his ears. *Four men are going to murder another in chains* and *head and shoulders shorter than all of them. And they're laughing!*

"Begin!" Mr. Norris yelled.

The four men began circling Shackle Man. They held their knives, ready to thrust in a single leap. Shackle Man slowly knelt in the center of the ring, resting his hands in his lap.

The crowd booed.

"Coward!"

"At least try to run!" a woman leaning over the railing yelled.

Alindale bit his tongue. *His ankles are shackled!*

The four assassins sprung. The one behind Shackle Man reached him first, bearing down to drive his knife into Shackle Man's skull.

Alindale looked away before he heard a loud yelp then gargling noise. The sound of a body crashing against wood followed but was swallowed by the crowd roaring. He glanced back, but instead of seeing Shackle Man dead, two assassins were piled in a heap in front of him. The one on top clutched his throat, blood running between his fingers.

Shackle Man flung his arms to the left. Something flew from his fingers, and then a long knife embedded itself in the second assassin's chest. The assassin fell to his knees, staring down at the knife in shock before rolling over on the floor.

The third assassin rushed in from the right. His knife held low and ready to thrust. As he did, Shackle Man leaned back. The third assassin collided with Shackle Man, and their hands grappled together. Suddenly, the third assassin shrieked, and his body flew up in the air in a roll before coming down on the ring floor on his back.

Alindale groaned on reflex with every man in the crowd when he saw the third assassin's knife sticking out of his groin. The third assassin clawed at it, screaming.

Shackle Man leapt up with a bound, twisted in the air, and then landed on the third assassin's chest. He planted his feet on either side of the third assassin's head, cutting off his screams by choking him with his ankle shackles.

The last assassin finally pushed the first would-be killer's body off of him and roared. The first assassin was no longer moving.

The last man found his knife and charged in to save his choking compatriot, but before he reached him, Shackle Man arched backward, almost folding himself in two, and with his bound hands, he grabbed the knife in the third assassin's groin. He then sprung forward in a sudden jerk, throwing the knife into the fourth assassin's head. The fourth assassin collapsed in a heap, inches away the third, who was still jerking and gasping as Shackle Man's shackles continued to strangle him.

The crowd watched in silence.

The third assassin didn't seem to know what to do. He held his groin with one hand while reaching around Shackle Man's leg with the other, trying to loosen his grip. He kicked out then folded his legs in on his groin.

His gasps became louder and louder. Alindale could see him opening his mouth wider and wider, desperate for air.

Finally, Shackle Man reached down, grabbed the back of the assassin's head with one hand and the assassin's forehead with the other, and twisted.

CRACK!

The third assassin jerked then went still.

Alindale's mouth hung ajar. *By the Last God, what is he?*

Everyone around him appeared to be thinking the same thing, yet no one said a word. Nolen's eyes gleamed, and he smiled with his mouth agape.

Shackle Man dropped the assassin's head then sighed. He crouched down, and there came the sound of something scratching against metal. Two loud *clicks* cut through the silent building, making many people jump.

"Was all this necessary?" Shackle Man asked. He rose, carrying both pairs of shackles that he had somehow unlocked, twirling them in each hand. "I just won a few games of dice." He paused then shrugged. "True, I won four nights in a row, but was all this *really* necessary?"

The crowd remained silent. Alindale could see some below shifting uneasily. Many of them were looking in the same direction into the crowd.

"Kill him!" Mr. Norris roared.

Shackle Man looked up. His bright, narrow-set eyes sparkled as a smile split his oval-shaped face. Spinning the shackles faster and faster, he flung them in the air in two directions.

Glass shattered loudly, one right below where Alindale sat. He peered over the railing to discover the shackle had destroyed one of the oil lamps hanging around the ring. The oil sprayed everywhere, caught the flame, and was raining fire down below. Across the way, the other shackle found its mark, breaking another lamp, and it, too, sent burning oil everywhere.

A man's piercing screams sent everyone running.

Alindale jumped to his feet as the smell of burning wood and flesh filled his nostrils. In the panic, Shackle Man had disappeared.

"We got to get out of here!" Nolen yelled, grabbing Alindale by the cloak and surprisingly hauling him to his feet.

Nolen pulled him by the cloak and into the crowd forming around them. He pushed men and women alike out of their way, but people were already making for the door, pushing and shoving each other. A woman screamed and fell. Men swore in panic to get the door open.

The smoke was becoming thicker, and even though they had gotten a good head start, people closed in around Alindale, grinding his strike for freedom to a halt.

His eyes began to water, and he tried in vain to rub the smoke out. He coughed and wheezed at how thin the air had become. The world narrowed to the scrambling, desperate people shoving him and the growing flames behind.

A rush of air swept in suddenly, and the densely packed throng heaved forward, carrying Alindale along with him. He had lost sight of Nolen but, in this situation, it was run with the flow or be trampled. He rushed forward.

He gasped when the cool, fresh air hit him. Only the change in the air told him that he had made it outside . . . only to be hit in the center of his back.

Alindale grunted and arched his back from the sudden blow. He paused, but another blow sent him stumbling, desperate to keep his feet. Then the Red Mansion's front step appeared out of nowhere, and he missed it.

He fell, disappearing under the frantic mass of people. He rolled down the steps and hit the boardwalk hard on his hands and knees. Pain instantly shot up his knees, and he toppled over.

People rushed by, screaming and crying. He threw an arm over his head when he was kicked in the side then in the leg.

From out of the darkness, long arms wrapped under him and dragged him away.

"Can you move?" Nolen asked, rescuing him from out of nowhere.

Alindale tried to stand and winced. His entire body ached like he had been pummeled by Montaigu all over again. At least he got to his feet. He then gasped in relief once he checked and found nothing broken.

"Good," Nolen said. "We have to get to the docks."

"The docks?" Alindale asked.

"Chaos is about to sweep this place. The docks are our safest bet to get out of here than the way we came."

Nolen took the lead again, sprinting into the night, with Alindale struggling to follow. People began flooding out of the taverns and brothels as cries of "Fire!" spread. Alindale didn't dare look back, out of fear of losing his guide.

At least all that running is finally good for something, he jadedly thought, panting and struggling to keep up.

The red glow of the district's buildings began to fade. The dark void in front of them was only broken by the flickering lantern lights hanging from the dozen rickety fishing boats and smaller boats bobbing at their moorings. Fewer ships docked at the old docks' wharfs than the others, but Nolen kept running down the dock as if he were looking for something.

Alindale's legs started to burn, along with his sides. Sweat ran down his face, and his hood finally flew back, the brush of ocean air giving him some relief.

"Where are we going?" Alindale finally cried out.

"Ah-ha!" Nolen exclaimed then pointed. "There!"

Alindale heard men drunkenly laughing before he followed Nolen's outstretched finger down a wharf, to a group of men stumbling, about to fill two longboats.

"Come on, men! Let's get out of here before these northern bastards become sore losers!"

Jerro Syros! Alindale recognized.

The lord's men laughed even harder, but they were still stumbling about, and a few were resting on the wharf before filling the boats, one by one.

"My lord!" Nolen shouted, waving his arms in the air once they had turned down the wharf. "Lord Jerro!"

The laughter ceased, and the men still on the wharf formed a line, shoulder to shoulder.

Nolen slid to a halt, and Alindale nearly ran into him.

His thighs throbbed, and he doubled over, panting for air. Nolen, though, seemed fine.

"Lord Jerro, please!" Nolen craned his neck to look over the defensive crew. "We're in great need of your help."

"Ingman," Jerro snorted, his heavy footsteps beating on the wharf as he pushed through his men. He had tossed a jacket over his shoulders, but he was still shirtless. He folded his arms and gave Nolen a disinterested look. "What do you want?"

"Just safe passage across the bay," Nolen replied sheepishly, rubbing the back of his neck. "Some place close to North End, perhaps."

Both men were roughly the same height, but they couldn't be more different. Where Nolen was long and lanky, Jerro was broad and muscular. His looming presence added an air of confidence to him. The fact that he was also Lady Tory's brother was a little surprising to Alindale.

"Find your own way across the city," Jerro said, turning to leave.

"A fire has broken out at the Red Mansion!" Nolen exclaimed. "The entire boardwalk is a nightmare right now. It'd be suicide getting through it."

Jerro kept walking toward one of the longboats. "You'll find a way out. You're from Inglworf, after all, right?"

A few of Jerro's crew chuckled at that.

"If I were alone, yes, but . . ." Nolen frowned and gave Alindale a sideways glance.

Alindale hadn't said anything and, with barely any light, he figured they had yet to recognize him. It now seemed he had little choice of remaining secretive now.

"Lord Jerro," he called, stepping forward, "I need safe passage to North End."

Jerro stopped and looked back. He squinted his eyes to cut through the gloom, and then they went wide.

"I am Alindale Dain, and we would appreciate your assistance. I promise, I will never tell anyone about this."

Jerro grimaced and stayed silent for a moment. Then he noticed something behind them, and his expression softened. "I'll take you in my boat," Jerro finally agreed. "Ingman, you can go in the other."

Alindale covered his head with his hood the moment he sat down in the longboat. He sat in silence as they shoved off, trying to keep out of the way and not draw any more attention to himself.

A great *whoosh* cut through the night, followed by wood cracking and groaning. Alindale looked back to see the Red Mansion's roof collapse. Lights flickered on across South End as the screams of "Fire!" were carried through the narrow streets.

He had taken a risk to finally get some news about what was going on at court, and what did he have to show for it? Nothing.

Alindale wrapped his arms around himself and hung his head.

Chapter 14

2nd of Andril, 1109 N.F. (e.y.)

Kalleb planted his feet against the wagon's footrest to settle his stomach against the swaying of the ferry. The paddles of the horse-driven ferry churned through the Ralmae River's strong current, giving him a sprawling view of Tradon from the coachman's seat.

The white, plaster buildings stretched for miles up and down the river, reflecting the Easterly Sun's rays back over the river. River boats cruised and maneuvered in and out of the dock in front of them while giving the ferry room. Many sat low in the water, loaded with goods from the west to send to the coast. The rich, exotic goods would find their way to Daincliff or Silkhaven, while goods valued by a working man would slowly trickle their way to surrounding provinces.

Who'd've guess I'd return here again.

His gazed drifted to the polished, black carriage in front of him, owned by the man whose purse was filled by every trade in that city—Lord Julian Renald. The carriage and its six black thoroughbreds took up half the ferry's length. Trunks with heavy iron locks were stacked on top of each other and strapped to the back with smaller trunks on the carriage roof. It was wide enough for someone to lay in it, with glass windows, curtains, and a covered, raised seat for the coachman.

An approving whistle cut through the air, startling Kalleb.

"Can we hit the town before the captain and the rest of the company get here, L.C.?" Rence asked, grinning longingly over the river to the city's tightly packed buildings.

"There'll be no hitting the town, Lancer," Kalleb said dryly. "After I get Roy to a doctor, I'm acquainting you and the rest of the troop to the barracks."

Rence frowned, looking back at the covered wagon. "How is he today?"

Kalleb glanced over his shoulder at the sleeping lad in the back of the wagon. His dark hair was drenched with water from a cloth over his forehead and his own sweat. His chest rose and fell smoothly, with a blanket covering only his legs. His uniform sat folded neatly off to the side, leaving him in his undershirt and small clothes.

"His fever's broken," he replied, "again. As for his leg . . ." He frowned at Rence.

Roy's condition had worsened, which made Kalleb split nurse maid duties up among the troop. Each member had spent time caring for Roy during their journey from Vorge Township. Sometimes, his spirits were high, and it looked like he was recovering. Then a new round of fever had hit him a few nights ago, and several attending him, including Kalleb, had noticed an odor coming from his leg. The township doctor had said the break was the worse she had tried to mend, and they needed to get him to a big city doctor fast.

We might not have been fast enough.

"Lance Corporal!"

Lancer Ian Holtan snapped to attention and saluted up at him from next to Rence. He held the posture without wavering, save for the mess the wind was making of half his midnight hair. He tried to keep it parted down the center of his scalp, but the wind wasn't cooperating, flailing his right side wildly. His square features, though, gazed unfazed and sternly at him, his eyes squinted.

As serious as he always seemed to be, Kalleb knew Ian would stand there until his salute was returned and gave him a dismissive wave.

"What is it, Ian?" Kalleb asked.

"Will we be stationed here long, sir?" Ian asked. He had lowered his arm but remained as rigid as a board.

"We'll be here through the course of your training," he replied, raising an eyebrow. He had figured Rence would ask such a question, but not Ian. "After that, we'll be sent on patrols through the back roads. As for how long we stay here, that's up to our orders. And our patron."

"I see." Ian's eyes grew distant, deep in thought.

Rence gave him a pat on the shoulder and smiled cheerfully. "Don't let it get you down. We'll just have to enjoy it while we can."

Ian scowled at him. His glare made Rence step back, as if he had been slapped.

"Why do you ask, Ian?" Kalleb brought his attention back to him.

Ian's scowl disappeared as soon as it had appeared, and his serious frown returned. "Forgive me, sir, but I didn't know how big Tradon was. If I'd known, and if we were going to be stay here for a long time, I would have asked my wife to come and live here, too."

Kalleb's jaw dropped. He hadn't learned much about the personal lives of his lancers in the short time that he had been with his new troop, but he would never have supposed one was married, especially given how young most of them were. Most who recruited to be lancers were drawn to the promise of traveling the provinces, being away from lives that they thought boring and seeing the Storm Cavalry as an adventure.

"Well"—he struggled to think of a response—"you can move your wife to Tradon, but with things as they are, I would hold off on it for now." He nodded, figuring the advice was good enough. Then he noticed Rence.

"You okay, Rence?"

Rence stared at Ian, his face contorted between disbelief and disappointment. "You're . . . *married*?"

Ian glared at him again, but it didn't faze him this time.

"You mean," Rence continued, "a woman *actually* married you?"

Ian sneered. "My personal life is none of your business. Go back and relieve Kelly! He's been holding your horse and waiting his turn to walk around."

Rence looked to Kalleb for some support, but Kalleb just gave him a dry look and slowly shook his head. Rence slumped, and then he headed toward the rear of the ferry, making a rude gesture behind Ian's back.

Ian waited for him to leave before saluting Kalleb again. "Thanks for the advice, sir. I'll consider it."

Kalleb nodded, and then a thought came to him.

"Ian," he called before the lancer walked away. "A thing about women; it's best to talk with them on where they want to live instead of making a decision on where they should."

Ian's eyes drifted back into deep thought for a moment before he grunted and walked away.

Serious. Almost too serious. But he does have a commanding presence and is willing to give orders. He chuckled. *And he won't take any shit from Rence. I should talk with Lieutenant Bowden about making him a corporal later.*

The thumping of multiple boots alerted him of an approaching group.

"You have my personal guarantee, My Lord, that I will have the rest of your escort ferried across the river by nightfall."

Jasun Darloc, the ferry boat captain, led Lord Renald toward his carriage, followed by two of the lord's personal retainers and Storm Cavalry lieutenant, Heath. The ferry boat captain strolled cheerfully along, clutching the hems of his leather vest, as if strutting down Main Street and showing off a new suit of clothes. A Blood Islander, his coal-shaded skin soaked up the Easterly Sun's rays and made his light red and gray hair, ringing the bald crown of his head, stand out. Despite his portly belly, his muscular arms showed a life of rigorous work on the river. His loose-fitting trousers and lack of footwear stood out against the richly dressed man beside him.

"Thank you, Captain Darloc," Lord Renald told him. "Your ferry is truly a novel, and the horses look fit enough. You have my complete faith."

Lord Renald had changed little since Kalleb had seen him last. His face had a few more age lines, but the way he carried himself, his calm confidence, was as strong as ever. He wore a rich, emerald doublet and trousers, as if defying the heat.

Kalleb sweated more just looking at him.

As Lord Renald approached his carriage, one of his retainers reached to open the door when Renald paused. After a moment, Kalleb realized Renald was staring back at him and, to his horror, the lord then headed toward him.

Kalleb dropped his head. *Crap!*

There were several in Tradon whom he hoped to avoid. Lord Renald was second on that list.

"You there, Lance Corporal," Renald called. "Have we met before?"

Kalleb chewed back his nerves before replying as humbly as he could, "Forgive me, My Lord, but I think I'd remember if we had."

Renald walked up beside the wagon steps, studying his face with calculating eyes. Kalleb hoped his weeks-old beard, from having no razor, thanks to his former horse running off with his belongings, and his years of imprisonment, made him unrecognizable.

As the minutes tortuously passed, Renald's retainers flanked him. Their shiny breastplates reflected the Easterly Sun's rays into his face, and their helmets' black plumes flapped in the breeze. Their matching tunics with flaring, green and black stripped sleeves were uniform styles from over a century ago, but Kalleb knew the swords on their hips weren't for show. And they both watched him, as if waiting for their lord's order to seize him.

"Interesting choice of words," Renald finally said, turning back toward his carriage. His retainers shared a confused look before one shrugged, and then they both followed their lord.

Kalleb winced. *That can't be good.*

He ran his fingers through his shaggy hair then fiddled with the wagon reins, hoping Renald wouldn't give him a second thought. In his heart, though, he knew Renald was probably turning his face over in his mind.

"Are we going to have a problem, Lance Corporal?" Lieutenant Heath asked.

The lieutenant of Squadron Two of the Twelfth was a gruff, soft spoken man of middling years. A typical officer, he had little to do with Kalleb or his troop, besides issuing regular orders in breaking and making camp. He and his fellow squadron officers kept to themselves for most of the journey, and Kalleb preferred the distance.

"No, Lieutenant," Kalleb replied.

Heath grunted. "When we disembark, drive your team off to the side and wait for the rest of the lancers to get off. Follow in behind us to the barracks. I'm sure you remember the way." That said, he went back to the rest of the lancers before Kalleb could even acknowledge the order.

Soon after, the ferry's paddles slowed as they approached the wharf. The gears of the treadmill squeaked under the deck boards. Kalleb intently watched the ferrymen guiding the ferry's horses with interest. Two stalls on both sides of the ferry housed a horse that walked along a spinning treadmill that powered the paddles. The two ferrymen guided the horses, slowing them down or speeding their trots, by pulling on the horses' bridles and encouraging them with carrots and apples.

Amazing, he thought, having never seen a ferry boat like this.

The ferry churned past wide riverboats, heavy-laden with goods and floating low in the water, as their crews with long poles moved away from the wharf to the strong currents to take them east. Here and there, smaller boats and single-person fishing boats hurriedly paddled out of the ferry's way as it aligned with its berthing dock.

Orders and curses from the dockhands drifted from the wharf as more riverboats were loaded and unloaded. Kalleb's nose wrinkled at the potent scent of fish from the small market at the far end of the wharf.

Ten riders cut through the bustle of the city street beyond the wharf, heading straight for the ferry dock, parting the crowd and flapping the Tradon banner—a gold coin against a banner horizontally divided between green and black.

A welcome party. Great.

Kalleb sighed at the prospect of being held up as Renald shook hands and shared smiles with whatever stiff shirt wanting his favor, especially for Roy's sake.

The ferry's berth was an extended dock away from the other river boats. It crawled into the dock's sloped center until its hull scraped up against it and the ferry lurched to a halt. The ferrymen guiding the horses pulled on their bridles until they stopped.

"Secure the moorings!" Darloc bellowed. "Lower the ramp!"

The crew hurriedly tossed ropes to the waiting dockhands. As the lines were secured, the ferrymen then took up their stations at the cranks at the ferry's front. The cranks creaked, and their chains rattled, as the men turned the handles and lowered a raised ramp until it fell on the dock with a *bang*, rocking the ferry.

Kalleb's horses snorted, and the dapple gray, hitched on the right, struggled against his rigging. He gripped the reins and pulled them tight.

"Whoa!" he yelled. "Calm down, boy! We're gettin' off here in a minute. Impatient thing." The stud had shown his spirit the first time Kalleb had slapped the reins when the wagon team had been purchased from different village folk in Vorge Township.

A loud *crack* split the air, and then Lord Renald's carriage rolled forward.

Kalleb released the wagon's brake—a lever beside the coachman's seat—and waited until Renald's retainers were off the ferry before he slapped the team's reins. He drove the wagon off the ferry then slowly off the wharf.

As Renald's carriage headed toward his welcome party, Kalleb guided his wagon around pallets loaded with sacks so the lancers behind him could disembark. Lieutenant Heath followed at the head of his Troop A, their lances' steel heads gleaming in the sunlight as their horses clomped along the wharf's boards.

The last to get off the ferry were the five lancers of Kalleb's troop who had been allowed to accompany their wounded comrade. Kalleb had chosen a couple whom he wanted to keep an eye on, and the other three because it was their turn. He had left Trevor to look after the rest.

His lancers lack of lances and beaming faces, taking in the sights of the city, made them stand out from the Heath's.

"Thanks for waiting for us, L.C.," Rence joked as they passed.

"Shut up, Rence," Kalleb replied. "And watch where you're going."

Before he could drive his wagon in line with the column, Renald's carriage had stopped in front of his welcoming committee.

"We just got off the boat," Rence whined, standing up in his saddle to look over the heads of the lancers in front of him. "Why've we stopped?"

"Sit down, Rence," he replied, annoyed. Then he leaned forward with his elbows on his knees as he prepared to sit there for a while.

"I just want to see what's going . . ." Rence softly whistled approvingly and stilled his voice. "She's *definitely* worth stopping for."

Kalleb's heart skipped a beat, and he jerked his head up. His breath caught.

Sitting on a black thoroughbred beside the welcome party's bannerman was the woman who had haunted his dreams for the past five years—Amanda Dain Renald.

Her ivory skin and smooth face stood out against her dress's dark emerald silk. Her sky-blue eyes sparkled, adding to a smile that any man would wish to see again and again. Her poise was perfect, leaving no doubt she was a lady. She appeared to float while sitting side-saddle. Her dress and skirts were modest and didn't cling to her figure. Her hat, tilted on the side of her head to keep the sun out of her face, was as pale as her complexion, with three flowers sewn on the right side. Their red petals waved in the breeze, along with her midnight hair.

Kalleb's mouth suddenly felt dry, and he realized his jaw was trembling when his teeth started chattering. He clenched his teeth together and swallowed, dropping his head to hide his face again. *Don't look this way. Please, don't look this way.*

The carriage door was swung opened, and Lord Renald stepped out. "Amanda, darling," the lord greeted joyfully. "This is an expected surprise. But, my dear, you needn't have come to fetch me. I know the way, I assure you."

"Welcome home, My Lord Husband." Amanda laughed. "You coming home early was something I had to see for myself."

Her laugh is still the same. Kalleb felt a chill hearing it—honest and mirthful, with a hint of a tease.

Peering through loose strands of hair, he watched as Lord Renald helped her off her horse. They shared a smile before he kissed the back of her hand and they embraced.

"That it?" Rence whispered disappointedly to Kelly beside him. "Some fancy kiss on the hand and a hug?"

"Aye," Kelly agreed disbelievingly. "That's a crime, if you ask me."

"No one is!" Ian whispered furiously. "She is a *lady*. Both of you show some respect!"

Rence gave him a disrespectful look. "We were just talking—"

"*Rence!*" Kalleb hissed.

Rence turned in his saddle then swallowed from Kalleb's glare. He hung his head and turned back around.

"Where are Maxemon and Andrea?" Lord Renald asked.

"Maxemon is with his tutor," Amanda replied pridefully. "Arithmetic, of course. You'll be so pleased. And Andrea is with her nurse. I thought about bringing her, but she was sleeping so peacefully that I couldn't wake her."

Kalleb smiled. She had been pregnant with her first child when he had left those years ago. Now she was a mother of two.

Always knew you'd make a good mother.

"Would you wish to ride with me in my carriage?" Lord Renald requested with an outstretched arm toward the open carriage. Amanda smiled and wrapped an arm around his, permitting him to escort her a few feet to the open door.

As Kalleb started to breathe easier at the prospect of finally getting a move on, Rence slowly leaned sideways out of his saddle. Kalleb followed the young man's gaze. It was clear he was watching Amanda's figure as she climbed into the carriage.

Rence grunted approvingly, straightened back up, and leaned over to Kelly to whisper, "I'd like to go for a carriage ride, too."

Kalleb's face grew hot when both lancers shared a laugh. His team's reins shook in frantic waves from his tight grip. Growling in frustration, he then stood up in his seat and yelled, "One more word, and you're both *out* of the cavalry! Is that clear, Lancers?"

Rence and Kelly cowered in their saddles. They timidly glanced over their shoulders, their faces pale.

"What's the problem, Lance Corporal Kane?" Lieutenant Heath hollered.

Kalleb blinked, only now realizing that the wharf had gone quiet. The work had stopped around them, and everyone was still. And watching him.

Apparently, he cut an intimidating figure standing in his wagon seat and looming over his lancers.

He nervously raised his head and found every lancer, all of Lord Renald's waiting retainers, and Lord Renald himself looking at him. Amanda poked her head out from within the carriage and stared curiously back at him with a hand on her hat so it wouldn't catch the breeze.

"Sorry, Lieutenant," Kalleb coughed out, trying to deepen his voice. "Apologies, My Lord. A recruit spoke out of turn and needed a firm hand." He lowered back onto the wagon seat, and when he looked again, Amanda was studying him. He pretended to arrange the team's reins again and kept his head down.

Please, don't recognize me. Please, don't recognize me!

"Apologies, My Lord," Lieutenant Heath spoke. "We are traveling with a troop of new recruits, and some may still need a lesson in proper discipline."

"That's quite all right, Lieutenant," Lord Renald kindly replied. "Soldiers may talk among themselves. I'll leave them to their officers."

Kalleb risked a peek and watched Lord Renald climb into the carriage. Amanda, thankfully, had disappeared inside.

"Drive on," Lord Renald commanded just as he shut the carriage door.

"Make way!" the coachman yelled with a snap of the reins.

The distracted wharf workers came to their senses and made way for Lord Renald's leading retainers and his carriage. The Storm Cavalry's column shuffled and prepared their horses to follow.

As Kalleb was about to whip his team into motion, he caught a glimpse through the carriage window when it turned toward a busy street. Amanda's face sudden appeared, and she stared out intensely. Kalleb froze the instant their eyes met. His chest felt a piercing, heavy weight from powerful mixture of shame and regret hitting him at once, harder than any horse could kick.

And then she was gone.

But, even as he whipped the wagon into motion, Kalleb was certain of the look in her eyes.

Recognition.

<div style="text-align:center">~~~</div>

"Will he be all right, Doctor?" Kalleb asked.

Roy lay on his back, in a wide bed with a lumpy, stained mattress. His splinted, wrapped leg was propped on a pillow. They had stripped his sweat-soaked shirt off him and placed a fresh, wet towel on his forehead. Still, sweat ran off his body and dampened the mattress under him. His breathing was hoarse, his chest rising and falling sporadically.

"Hard to say," Doctor Ross Hephbern replied, grimly studying Roy's leg. His bushy muttonchops twitched as he snorted and rubbed his hooked nose. "This is shoddy work. Utterly unacceptable!"

Doctor Hephbern had been called immediately after Kalleb and his troop had arrived at the Storm Cavalry compound. He had become incensed the moment he had seen Roy's condition and had become as demanding as a brigadier. Once he had torn Roy's splint and bandages away, he had stepped back and begun studying it.

Roy's leg was red from ankle to hip. He had two sewn-up gashes where broken pieces of bones had stuck out of his leg; one above his ankle and the other along his shin. Yellow pustule balls boiled along his shin and along the sewn-up gash.

Doctor Hephbern shook his head. "All of this has to be redone. First, I'll need to cut out and clean all the infection I can find. Then I'll need to make sure the bones are set properly. I'll make sure there are no bone splinters, as well. But, if we don't get this infection under control, he may not live to worry about saving the leg." The doctor turned to fetch his large, leather bag from a chair beside the bed. The bottom of the bag bulged and jingled and clanged, as if stuffed with silverware, as he set it on the mattress.

Kalleb clenched his fists as he watched the doctor pull out a rolled-up assortment of knives, scissors, and pliers. The room's lamp light reflected off the sharp metal. He hoped there was no bone saw in there but, deep down, he figured there was.

If we'd only gotten here faster.

"Do we need to tie him to the bed?" he asked.

Doctor Hephbern snorted. "What do you take me for? A *butcher*?" He pulled out a corked, thick, black-glass bottle and glass cup out of his bag. Kalleb felt unsettled watching the doctor's spindly fingers wrap around the cork and pop it open.

"What's that?" he asked.

"Jael bulb extract," the doctor replied, carefully tipping the lip of the bottle over the glass. His hands remained steady as a milky, yellow substance gently flowed from the bottle. He only poured a small draft, barely a swallow, before tipping the bottle up and cutting off the flow. "I'm going to need you to hold his head."

Kalleb nodded, walking to the head of the bed and clasping the sides of Roy's head.

Doctor Hephbern gently put the bottle in the chair before moving up beside Roy. He squeezed Roy's nostrils shut and instantly poured the yellow extract into his mouth. Roy's body shook, and a cough gargled in his throat.

The doctor tossed the glass away once the last drop was poured into his mouth then forced Roy's mouth shut. The young man thrashed, and Doctor Hephbern put his elbow on his chest while he and Kalleb held his head up.

Finally, Roy started to gulp and settle down.

Doctor Hephbern sighed in relief as he let go of his mouth, allowing him to breathe. "That'll dull the pain and keep him asleep. Tastes horrible, though." He got up and started sorting out his instruments.

Kalleb let go and wiped his hands of Roy's sweat on the mattress. "Will you need anything else, Doctor?"

"If I do, I'll yell for it." The doctor kept picking up his small knives, one by one, and looking them over like a snob choosing a knife for dinner.

I'm sure you will.

Kalleb gave Roy a final look before leaving. The extract must have worked fast, because his chest rose and fell gently with deep breaths. His pained grimace was gone, replaced by calm and occasional eyelid flutters.

"Save him, Doctor," he pled. "The best you can."

Doctor Hepburn grunted.

Kalleb left before the doctor began cutting. The sight of blood and broken bones didn't bother him—he had seen plenty. The boils of puss, however, stuck in his mind, and he forced down a lump of bile forming in his throat.

The infirmary had doubled in size in the four years that he had been away. In fact, their entire compound had expanded. The Renalds had a standing commission for a Storm Cavalry company to be garrisoned in Tradon for close to four centuries now. They were traditionally barracked in the western district of the Old Settlement in the city.

The arrangement had changed, however, after Amanda's marriage. Being a child of the royal family, she was due an honor guard by the Storm Cavalry. Therefore, Lord Renald had purchased several city blocks of the Gentry District, next to the Renald's city estate for a new compound. When Kalleb had driven the wagon up the wide street in the district, he had noticed an additional block had been raised and added to their barracks.

As he walked out of the infirmary, he collected his saber from a knob on the wall-mounted hat rack, stretched over several feet along the wall. His saber's new sheath was mix-matched leather that he had sewn together from scraps around the camp while traveling. It was a poor substitute for his pa's old scabbard, but it was better than walking around with the edge exposed and risk cutting himself.

"Lance Corporal!" Trevor greeted, snapping to attention.

"At ease, Trevor," Kalleb told him, sliding his saber through his belt. "Have the men stabled their horses?"

"Yes, sir," Trevor replied, relaxing. "They're waiting outside."

"Good."

The rest of his troop had arrived three hours after Kalleb's party. He had still been waiting for Doctor Hephbern to arrive and had left orders for them to wait for him.

"Were there any problems crossing?"

When Trevor didn't answer, Kalleb looked to find him glancing at his feet with a distant look in his eye.

He stopped. "Trevor?"

Trevor blinked and shook his head. "No. But . . ."

"But?"

"Did I do something wrong, sir?" Trevor hung his head. "Was I not doing a good enough job as a corporal?"

Kalleb knit his brows. "What—" It suddenly struck him. "What did Hunt do now?"

Kalleb might have avoided Vallant's first attempt to remove him, but the next day, he had received transfer orders for Jentrey Hunt to be placed as a new corporal to his troop, and Hunt had quickly made his feelings toward the men known.

"He kept the men mounted while we waited to be ferried across," Trevor answered. "Even when they started complaining and the horses grew restless, he wouldn't listen to me or anyone about dismounting. He kept insisting they'd let us on the ferry faster if we looked ready."

Kalleb choked back a growl. *Idiot.*

"How are your horses?" he asked.

"They're fine." Trevor shrugged. "Several of the men are a bit saddle sore, though."

"Did he pick on Zoren?" Hunt had a particular habit of finding lancers at the worst time and scolding them over something. Zoren especially.

Trevor shook his head. "No, sir."

Kalleb set his shoulders. "You did nothing wrong, Trevor. Hunt and his rank were transferred in on orders, so don't be self-conscious. You just tend to your duties. I'll tend to Hunt."

Trevor seemed to accept that. "Yes, sir. I'll do my best."

"Good." Kalleb nodded. "Let's go check on the men."

The night was still and relaxingly cool but smelled of horse, iron, and men living in close quarters. Lamps from windows and hanging off the side of every buildings' doors lit the open yard with flickering orange light. The compound's gate was shut, and a lancer with a polearm stood guard beside the gate's blockhouse. The stable hands were performing the last of their nightly chores across from the blockhouse.

His troop, which was scattered around the yard and the porch of the infirmary in small groups, perked up upon seeing him.

"Troop! Assemble!" Hunt, who had been waiting beside the infirmary door, unseen by Kalleb, barked. He stomped on the porch with his hands on his hips, his saber slapping against his leg.

The men grumbled as they slowly began gathering in ranks in front of the infirmary.

It's too late in the night for this, Kalleb groaned.

"That's all right!" he said, nudging Hunt aside so he could address the men. He could see most of their faces, despite the casting shadows. They were tired and, being soldiers, they were most likely hungry. He needed to keep it short.

"Roy's going to be okay," he told them. "The doc says he's going to try his best to save his leg but should be able to save his life." Kalleb put on his best, reassuring smile, even though Hephbern hadn't been that reassuring. However, he needed to give his men some comfort, and some of them did brighten and stood at ease.

A hand went up in the back. "Excuse me, sir?"

The men parted to reveal Rence glowering at Kalleb. His clenched jaw made him appear like he was biting back from cussing. He had been like this since Kalleb had yelled at him on the wharf.

I need to do something about that.

"Yes, Rence?"

Rence dropped his hand. "We were told there was a saloon on the grounds. Could a few of us go and drink to Roy? Sir?"

Drago's Saloon belonged to a former stable master who had somehow convinced the officers at the time that cooping several companies of lancers across town from the closest tavern was a rowdy disaster waiting to happen.

I wonder if the old horse thief is still there?

"Recruits are not permitted in the saloon," Hunt said sternly, crossing his arms. "Captain Vallant will expect his lancers to wait for him at the barracks, not get drunk."

"Figures," a lancer in the back grumbled, followed by agreeing grunts and nods from several of the others.

Rence's head fell, and his shoulders slumped.

I need to clear the air.

"Rence," he said then scanned the gathering until he found the other man. "Kelly. Front and center."

Kelly timidly shuffled to the front, whereas Rence grumbled and scowled angrily as he joined him.

"I was a bit harsh on you two today," Kalleb started.

"Not really," Rence said dismissively. "If the captain's set on seeing us as trash he can lump together, guess, sooner or later, we'll be thrown out."

Kalleb frowned. *Trash? Who said . . .?*

He glanced at Hunt, the corporal didn't say a word. Considering Vallant held their troop as his 'punishment troop,' Rence's feeling wasn't completely unfounded. *Still . . .*

"Rence, you're not trash. None of you are. I lost my temper and didn't behave as an officer should. I . . . was wrong."

Rence lost his scowl and stared back him, as if Kalleb had grown two heads. "But . . . you were so mad . . ."

"Because what you were doing was dangerous, not just stupid." Kalleb had to choose his words carefully. As hard as it was to apologize, it was impossible to admit the true reason. This lesson was one the rest of the men needed to learn anyway.

"All of you listen." He raised his voice. "When it comes to the aristos, we take their assignments, we serve for its duration, and we wait for the brigadiers to reassign us. *That's it!* They give us our pay, and we go home. Don't *ever* talk about, or even *look* at, their women!"

Kelly's shoulders slumped. "She was pretty, though."

Kalleb's eyebrow twitched, but he let the comment go.

"You were saying it too much, and *leering*. Just remember, we only get these barracks because Lord and Lady Renald built them for us. If they wanted, they could build a small blockhouse for Lady Renald's guard and order the rest of us to camp in the woods outside the city. It's the same everywhere. And many aristos have taken their anger of one lancer out on all of us before."

Rence shuffled his feet and hung his head as he thought over Kalleb's words.

"Just watch your mouth next time," Kalleb warned, giving him a stern look. "*And* your eyes."

Rence nodded. "Yes, sir, L.C."

Kalleb grunted in approval. And, with that taken care of, he figured their morale was next.

"Ian!" he shouted.

"Sir!" Ian barked back, stepping out then stomping his heels together with a salute.

"At ease." Kalleb tiredly chuckled. "If I entrust them to you, can you look after whoever goes to the saloon and make sure they don't get too rowdy?"

The men perked up then, smiles and eager caught breaths all around.

Ian blinked at him, startled. "Yes, if it's an order, sir. But I'm not much of a drinker."

"That's a shock," Rence joked, to the amusement of many around him.

"Hush, Rence," Kalleb said then turned back to Ian.

"All the better. Ian, until I finalize it with the lieutenant, you're a newly acting corporal. Any of you men who want to go to the saloon, follow Ian. But don't drink too much! We're going to work on each of your riding until the rest of the company gets here."

Some of the men laughed, and some of the men groaned, but over half of them broke away, heading toward Drago's Saloon, Rence and Kelly both at their head.

"Sir!" Ian snapped a hasty salute before rushing off after his charges.

"Corporal Trevor," Kalleb called, "take the rest of the men to the barracks and get them sorted. You boys get first pickings of the bunks." He grinned at the whoops and laughs from his remaining lancers.

"You heard the lance corporal, guys," Trevor said, rushing down the steps. "Let's claim those beds!" He corralled them like a sheep dog and got the rest of the recruits heading toward their barracks . . . leaving Kalleb alone with Hunt.

Hunt stepped down from the infirmary porch, but Kalleb grabbed him by the shoulder.

"I didn't dismiss you," he said lowly, waiting for the rest of the troop to be out of sight.

Hunt regarded him coldly, jerking his shoulder free. Then he stepped back, crunching gravel under his boots as he put distance between himself and Kalleb.

I guess we can stop pretending to be nice, Kalleb thought. *Good.*

"I know you hate me, Hunt," he started. "And I know you're Vallant's man in my troop. But it's still *my* troop." He narrowed his glare, and his voice took a harsher tone. "If I see you berating my lancers unfairly, if I catch you beating on them, if I hear you call any of them *trash*, then, by God, I'll send you every time the lieutenant orders a work detail. *Every* dirty job. *Every* back-breaking job. You'll do it, too. Trust me; I know how to make a man work." He clenched his fists, rubbing his scarred calluses together. The work on the farm wasn't pleasant, but if the threat of similar punishment would save his men from an abusive officer, then he would gladly use it.

Hunt clenched his jaw so tightly that Kalleb thought his teeth would crack.

"May I speak?" Hunt snarled. "*Sir*?"

"Go on."

"You should never have been allowed back in uniform." Hunt straightened and stuck his chest out. "Your incompetence has already cost us one recruit. And now you've let nearly the whole troop go get drunk. The captain will hear of it. You can trust *me* on that."

Kalleb snorted at the threat. "Why wait? Why not go to the officer's quarters and make your complaint right now?" He pointed at the four-story brick block of a building at the head of lane from the compound's entrance. The headquarters was the tallest building in the compound but stood out like a farmer at an aristo ball compared to the grand houses and mansions filling the district. "I'm sure there are plenty of officers who'd love to hear a corporal go above his officers' heads."

Hunt didn't respond. He remained tense and motionless, glaring at Kalleb.

"No?" Kalleb asked. "Then go. I don't want to see you for the rest of the night."

Hunt turned on his heels, without even a salute, and marched away, kicking up gravel and dust on his way.

Kalleb sighed and rubbed his temple. *What am I going to do with that one?*

He didn't see Hunt being promoted or transferred to a new troop for good behavior because he was Vallant's man. No matter what, it seemed Kalleb was stuck with him.

He sighed again then began to stroll the compound. The nostalgia he had kept at bay because of Roy's condition flooded him. Memories of going out on patrol floated back as he strolled down the lane toward his company's barracks.

He walked by Drago's Saloon and stopped momentarily to listen to men laughing and singing inside. He shook his head, though, at the thought of peeking in and kept walking.

Chapter 15

3rd of Andril, 1109 N.F. (e.y.)

Tory gazed out the carriage window, watching the various people traversing down the sidewalks and shops of North End.

"*Gah*!" Serina groaned, flopping back in her seat. "Why does there have to be *so* many people out? If I don't get fitted today, the ball will be a complete catastrophe. Could you not have gotten dressed quicker this morning, Runt?"

Tory silently took the snide remark and unjust blame for the hundredth time. She had been eating breakfast when one of Serina's maids had rushed over and said her sister wanted them ready to depart the castle in ten minutes. The opportunity of being free of the vast stone walls had been too alluring to pass up, but no amount of rushing would have satisfied Serina.

She returned to people-watching while their carriage continued slowly down the street. She more than enjoyed the leisurely pace, getting to see more of the city than when they had first arrived and was in no hurry to return to the castle.

Most of the people strolling up and down the sidewalks were women, window shopping at all the latest displays of bonnets, hats, dresses, skirt hoops, skirt lace, shoes, and jewelry. Signs displaying prices and advertisements for the Great Spring Harvest filled every window, each more elaborate than the other, as if every shop was competing to make the most alluring sign.

Tory did a double-take, making sure she read one sign correctly. *"Ladies Corsets, Hose, and Undergarments in the Back. NO Gentlemen Allowed!"*

The shop had two benches in front of it, where several gentlemen lounged, checking their pocket watches and all looking incredibly bored.

Her cheeks warmed as she sat back, clearing her throat and eager to get that latest image out of her mind.

"Why do you need to be measured again?" she asked. "Emelie Faviann made you a few dresses just a few weeks ago."

"Tory, Tory, Tory," Serina sighed out, shaking her head dramatically. "You are almost a *hopeless* case. You do not simply give a master tailor and designer your measurements like she, or he in this case, is nothing more than a common seamstress! Every Faviann dress is a work of art, and if he is crafting a dress for me, I intend to be the muse for that art, too. Besides, I want to make sure he does what I want."

Tory folded her hands in her lap and huddled in her seat. Once again, Serina was on a selfish mission, and Tory was being dragged along to be kept an eye on. After the disastrous chance encounter with Prince Alindale in Her Majesty's gardens, Serina had barely given her a moment's peace, insisting Tory remain close. She had learned quickly it was just to remain under Serina's thumb, since Serina hadn't introduced anyone new to her since.

"I suppose I'll just wait in the carriage, then?" she asked.

Serina snorted disdainfully. "Don't be ridiculous. Your wardrobe is sorely lacking anything worthy of Her Majesty's ball."

My clothes aren't that *bad*, Tory sulked.

The street began to tilt, as if rolling downhill, the crowd grew thinner and, on their left, the clothing shops turned to cafés with outdoor tables for patrons to sit and eat.

The carriage slowed before pulling to a halt, gently rocking once it stopped. Serina surprised her by reaching for the door and opening it *herself* instead of waiting for the coachman.

She must seriously be in a hurry.

"Come on!" Serina insisted, waving Tory out.

She carefully watched her step, making sure her slipper heel found the carriage step instead of her toe. Tory could just imagine tripping and spilling onto the cobblestones, and then she would have Serina throwing a fit over how clumsy she was.

She glanced around the street, finding it incredibly quiet, even though they had passed a lot of people on their way here. She then saw their destination, and her breath caught.

The large, three-story building in front of them covered an entire block. Most of the shops they had passed were small, but this one loomed over them all, casting a wide shadow. Its display windows were full of dresses in styles that she had never seen before, or like the other shops they had passed. There were also bonnets, hats, and shoes. Her cheeks warmed again, seeing a pair of corsets displayed at the far window. Serina hadn't deemed Tory worthy of bringing along for her first fitting, such a blessed day, but Tory had to admit the shop was impressive.

A large sign hung from the second floor, its letters emblazoned with metal, that read: *"Emelie Faviann, Renown Master Tailor and Ladies' Fashion Extraordinaire!"*

"Don't gawk, Tory!" Serina hissed, paying off the coachman.

"Come back in two hours," she instructed him. "If you do not, or if you are late, you shall not receive a tip."

Tory frowned, listening to the coachman's mumbled reply. No matter where she went, Serina refused to be nice to any of the servants.

The carriage rolled away, and Tory wondered if she would have been better off staying in the muggy box all day.

"Come along," Serina ordered, swooping by and toward the establishment's door.

Following close behind, Tory spied another sign hanging inside the glass door and quickly read: *"Fittings by Invitation Only! NO Gentlemen Allowed!"*

As the hair on the back of her neck stood up, she tugged on Serina's sleeve as she reached for the door handle. "Serina! I don't have an invitation!" She was surprised that she had forgotten about that after all of Serina's gloating.

"Don't worry about that," Serina replied dismissively, pulling her sleeve away. "It's all been arranged." Serina reached for the door handle, but instead of the door opening when she turned it, a bell jingled from inside. Moments later, a tall woman in a lavish, maid livery strolled up to the door.

Her blonde hair was combed back and tied up in a tail, trailing down to her waist. With gray eyes, she critically studied them for a moment before they flickered in recognition at Serina. Then she hastily opened the door.

"Good morning, Lady Syros," the woman greeted, holding the door open while bowing her head. "Master Faviann is gracious for your returned patronage. He has been expecting you."

"Thank you," Serina replied, swaggering in.

Tory hesitantly stepped to follow, the scent of linen, yarn, and shoe varnish leaking from within, but the woman blocked her with the door.

"I'm sorry," the store clerk said, "but I'm afraid only ladies who have received an invitation from Master Faviann may enter."

Tory stared back, stunned. "Serina!"

Serina was perusing some of the displayed dresses, oblivious to her sister about to be shut out in the street.

"Hmm . . .?" Serina mused, glancing in Tory's direction before the door shut. "Wait! My sister was invited by Mr. Faviann. The letter came this morning."

"Forgive me," the woman apologized, looking between the sisters, but kept the door firmly between them. "There must have been an oversight. I was only aware of the invitation sent to you, Lady Serina. Would you, or your sister, have the invitation by chance?" The woman held out her hand, waiting.

Serina searched her small bag dangling from her hip, but as the seconds turned to minutes, her search became more frantic and her frown irate.

"I must have left it in my rooms," she huffed. "Is there any way to check your records?"

The woman dropped her hand and gave Serina a leveled look. "We can, Your Ladyship. However, your sister will have to wait outside until we can verify the invitation. It's the rules of the establishment. I hope you understand."

Tory raised an eyebrow. *I'm going to have to wait out here!*

The street was almost deserted, except for two gentlemen drinking coffee across the way and appearing to be in a serious conversation. The lack of people felt unsettling.

"Very well, then," Serina sighed out. "Wait right there, Tory. No backtalk! We shan't leave you out there for long."

The woman nodded then closed the door, leaving Tory to gawk while Serina was led farther out of sight and into the shop.

She stalked down the storefront and attempted in vain to follow them through the glass, but they disappeared somewhere toward the back.

"Well, this is just *great*!" Tory fumed, half-heartedly kicking the side of the building. That only made her shoe feel tighter so, instead of another kick, she folded her arms and began to pace back and forth.

I couldn't finish breakfast for this!

When Serina had ordered that none of their maids could come, Tory had feared she would have to take on their duties. That's what she had expected at least.

What if they can't find my invitation? she pondered. *What if I'm stuck out here for however long Serina's being fitted?*

She stopped mid-step, realizing she had been left outside while Serina was busy inside. She was all alone, without having to wait on Serina's every whim.

She grinned. *Might not be so bad.*

"Lady Tory?"

Tory spun around, expecting the tall store clerk, but the door remained closed. Instead, a shorter lady stood steps away from the door, holding the floppy brim of her aqua-blue bonnet against the breeze. The brim rose, and Lady Regina Malthas gave her an inquisitive look.

"Whatever are you doing wandering the streets?" Regina asked. "Does your sister know where you are?"

Terrific. Tory slumped. *Now I'll have to spend the day not only with Serina but with one of her friends, too. Why'd it have to be her?* She still held a smoldering resentment at Regina for snitching on her during Serina's first tea party.

"Good morning, Lady Malthas," she replied, putting on her best face. "Serina's inside. I'm afraid we forgot my invitation at the castle, so I'm having to wait for the store clerk to check on it."

"Ah!" Regina sympathetically cooed. "And they left you here all by your lonesome?"

Please, don't patronize me.

"Rules are rules." Tory shrugged. "I guess . . ."

Regina pursed her lips and looked across the street. "Come on; I'll buy you some coffee while we wait."

"That's okay," Tory said hesitantly, her hand half raised as Regina stepped off the curb. "The woman told me to wait."

"She is probably going to be a while," Regina said from over her shoulder, heading toward the small café. "Especially if they are serving Serina."

Tory tried to protest, but it died on her lips. *She's not wrong.*

The sudden prospect of standing around on the sidewalk in her uncomfortable shoes also aided her decision to join her. She might be one of Serina's friends, but at least she could sit down.

The conversing gentlemen suddenly broke off their conversation as the ladies approached. They stood up and respectfully smiled and nodded, first at Regina then to Tory. They had returned to their conversation by the time Regina claimed the table farthest away from them and sat down.

"Best to keep some distance between us and those two," Regina said, swooping off her hat and setting it in the chair beside her, allowing her chestnut curls to bounce free.

"Why?" Tory whispered, straightening her skirts while sitting and raising an eyebrow at the two men. "Are they the bad sort?"

"Hmm . . .?" Regina gave her puzzled look before shaking her head. "Oh no. Nothing like that. Gentlemen conducting business hardly ever like to be eavesdropped, even by accident."

"Conducting business?"

"Good morning, Ladies," a serving boy greeted, his smile making his dimples stand out. "How may I serve you?"

"Coffee!" Regina replied, suddenly perky, her button nose standing out from how broadly she grinned. "A cup for me and my friend, with sugar. Syrosi, if you have any."

"Yes, My Lady." The server nodded. "Anything else?"

Regina glanced at Tory, who shook her head, waiting for the server to leave to tell Regina that she had no money.

"Do you have any chocolate swirls left?" Regina asked.

Tory sat up straighter. Not because she liked chocolate swirls—she didn't know what they were—but because they would make the bill that much higher.

"Yes, My Lady!" the server happily replied.

"Bring two," Regina requested, winking at him.

The server nodded then sped away.

Tory stared at Regina, not really sure what to say after having watched that.

"Never be afraid to flirt with waitstaff," Regina whispered. "It helps make them work faster." She giggled.

Tory folded her hands in her lap, unsure of how to respond. Yet, true to her boast, the server did return quickly with their coffees, the cups clattering on their saucers from him rushing. He returned soon after that with a small bowl of sugar cubes, the small red blocks marking them from Tory's home Isles. Lastly, he brought two large pastries, the dough baked in a coiling swirl with melted chocolate between the layers.

Tory's eyes went wide. The large pastries nearly hung off their saucers, and her mouth watered at the chocolate's sweet scent.

"Thank you!" Regina said sweetly to the server, dropping a couple sugar cubes into her coffee. She blew on it a couple times before taking a sip, only to add another cube afterward.

With the server gone and the treats before her, Tory suddenly felt guilty.

"Thank you for being so kind, Lady Malthas," she whispered, "but . . . I'm afraid I don't have any money."

Regina wagged a finger at her. "Think nothing of it. And please, call me Regina. Standing on ceremony outside of court is exhausting, don't you agree?"

"I suppose," Tory replied, unsure if she had any other choice. She barely knew the woman but, at the same time, if she said no, she could take offense . . . and tell Serina.

Regina dug into her chocolate swirl with a fork, carving out a slice in the coil then stirring it in the chocolate that flowed from the breach before eating it. "Mmm . . ." she hummed then giggled.

Tory bit her lip, but it was too infectious, and so she giggled, as well. Thoroughly convinced, she took up her own fork and copied Regina.

Her entire world brightened the moment the hot chocolate touched her tongue. The dough was crunchy along the rim from where it had baked in the open, but the inside was soft and soaked in the heavy, sweet, yet with a touch of bitter flavor of the chocolate. As she chewed, the chocolate filled her cheeks, and she had to swallow a couple times to get it down.

Regina watched with a big smile, as if they were sharing secrets, and Tory had to giggle again. In turn, it reduced Regina into giggles, as well.

"Oops," Regina said, glancing toward the gentlemen. "I guess we're not far enough away."

Tory risked a look and caught one of the gentlemen watching them from over the other's shoulder.

"I would apologize," she said, cutting another piece of swirl, more toward the center where the dough was softer, "but this is too good!" She barely chewed. The dough was so soft that she gulped it down then ran her tongue between her teeth to get at the remaining chocolate.

"So"—Regina blew on her coffee then sipped—"are you enjoying Daincliff?"

Tory shrugged. "I've barely seen any of it. This is the first time I've been out of the castle since I arrived." She poked the swirl with her fork, trying to fish out its gooey center.

"Oh my!" Regina's eyebrows shot up above her coffee cup. "You mean, you have been at the castle this whole time?"

Tory slumped in her chair, embarrassed. She was beginning to feel the onset of cabin fever from the mundane days that she had spent behind those gray walls. Besides going to court and getting lost in whatever they were talking about, or being dragged to Serina's excruciating get-togethers, there was *nothing* for her to do!

"Serina insists I learn court culture, but everything is just so . . . *frustrating*," she complained. "I'm not really sure what's going on in those long, dull meetings, and I don't know who anybody is! Serina said she would introduce me to people, but the only people I have met are her friends." Her breath caught, and she glanced, wide-eyed, at Regina, remembering she was one of those friends.

The chocolate's cursed! she thought as the excuse in how she had become so forgetful.

"I'm sorry," she whispered. "I . . . I didn't mean—"

"It's okay," Regina dismissed. "It can be very frustrating your first time out in society, and court life is notorious for running over anyone who doesn't know what's going on. Everyone here knows their roles and positions and doesn't have time to help strangers figure out theirs."

Tory easily related to that. She wasn't sure if she even had a role, other than Serina's trailing younger sister.

She picked at her chocolate swirl, unsure of what to say or if she should remain quiet.

"But, since I have the time," Regina continued, setting down her cup then folding her arms on the table, "is there anything I can explain for you?"

Regina smiled and waited, but Tory was still unsure. Being one of Serina's friends, she had to assume most of this would get back to her sister, and so she had to be more careful than before.

"Were you frustrated or run over the first time you came to court?" she asked, hoping asking questions about Regina would keep her out of trouble.

"Worse," Regina replied, rolling her eyes. "Not because I didn't know my station, mind you, but a land aristo will always be overlooked by everyone here."

Tory arched an eyebrow. "Land aristo?"

"Yeah," Regina sighed then chuckled, "a land aristo as one of Her Majesty's ladies. Most are usually stunned when they trace my family."

I have no idea what she's talking about! Tory tried not to panic or look flustered, dreading to appear hopeless.

"Oh?" She hesitantly poked at her chocolate swirl with the fork while trying to appear natural. "Is that uncommon?" She swirled the fork's prongs in the chocolate smeared on the saucer and waited, expecting Regina to give a long list of personal accomplishments in how she had reached her feat. Instead, the silence stretched on.

She chanced a glance at the other lady and found her staring, dumbstruck. Regina's grin soon returned, though, crooked, and then she planted her chin in her palm and leaned against the table.

"My, my, my," Regina said, "you *are* an innocent."

Tory felt cold sweat run down her cheeks but resolved to keep her head up. "I beg your pardon?"

"We're both ladies," Regina urged, reaching across the table to cup Tory's hand, "and can be honest with each other. You really don't know what I mean when I say I'm a land aristo, do you?"

Tory tried to keep her composure, but Regina's gentle squeeze of her hand made her sigh and her shoulders fall.

"No," she replied.

"Don't feel downhearted." Regina grinned, obviously trying to cheer Tory up. "You are here to learn, after all. And, since Serina can't be bothered, I guess I can give you your first lesson."

Tory nodded, preferring the encouragement rather than a scolding and being called names.

"Good." Regina took her hand back and straightened, enjoying having a captive audience. "Well, when I say I'm a land aristo, I mean my family's titles and income come from owning land. My uncle is the head of the Malthas family and oversees the control of over thirty-thousand acres in Sevier Province, just south of here, in fact."

Tory listened and tried to understand, but she still felt a few things sailed past her before she could read their signals.

"Thirty-thousand acres," she said. "That must be a lot."

Regina shrugged and sipped her coffee. "It's modest. However, my family is really just rent collectors for the farmers who tend it and look after a few province aristos' estates when they're away. I don't own an acre in my name, of course. My father left a trust for me, and my uncle graciously adds to it so long as I also represent the family at court."

"So, an aristo is a land aristo if their family owns land, even if they themselves don't?" Tory questioned, trying to sort it all together in her head.

"That's right!" Regina's eyes sparkled. "See! Learned something new already. And sadly, land aristos are the lowest aristos one can be."

"How's that?" Tory frowned. "You're one of Her Majesty's ladies."

"Only *because* I make myself indispensable"—Regina shook her head, swinging her curls—"and don't have any land in my name. If I owned one acre and drew a single mint from it, I wouldn't have a place in court."

"Why?"

"It's the law, I'm afraid." Regina rolled her eyes. "An aristo can't earn income from land and hold an appointment."

"Oh." Tory wrapped her hands around her coffee cup. The black liquid rippled but was no longer steaming, and the porcelain was starting to cool.

Even though this all seemed new, she still felt she should have known. Back home, though, hardly anyone referred to her by title. She was simply *Tory*.

She mulled it over, thinking about home. Something didn't sit right.

"But my family holds an appointment," she said, "*and* owns land. I mean, they are called the *Syros* Isles." She snickered, finding it all obvious.

Regina blankly stared at her, her mouth slightly ajar.

"Oh, no, dear"—she shook her head—"you don't. Your father is Lord Governor, but your family doesn't own the Isles. You just govern them."

Tory's brow furled. "But the Isles are ours. My father and everyone always said so."

Regina winced. "Your family is what we call old aristos. There are only a few left—yours, the Vannis, the Faumans, and . . . the Renalds. Your family's historic, just below the royal family, but . . . you govern your province like every other province aristo. Serina complains about it all the time."

Serina complains about a lot of things, Tory thought. Upon reflection, however, she realized that Serina hadn't about this sort of thing. At least, not to her.

She gazed back into her coffee again. *So, is our home even ours?*

"But you shouldn't let it bother you," Regina said cheerfully. "Just like I tell Serina, you're an *old* aristo, just below the royal family, remember? You can practically do whatever you want!"

Not if Serina has anything to say about it.

Tory shied away. She shook her cup and made her coffee ripple.

"Kind of like"—Regina grinned teasingly—"having a secret rendezvous with a certain prince."

Tory's eyebrows leapt up into her hairline, and her ears grew warm. "I wasn't having a secret rendezvous!" she protested then quickly raised her cup over her mouth to hide behind, clicking the cup's porcelain against the saucer from her shaky grip.

This is just like last time! she fumed. Fortunately, Serina and the other ladies weren't around.

Tory sipped her coffee and instantly regretted it. It was bitter, biting her tongue and making her nose wrinkle from its pungent smell. She lowered it then reached for the sugar cubes but stopped halfway to take up her fork to finish off the rest of her chocolate swirl.

"Are there any other aristos I should know about?" she asked between nervous nibbles on her pastry, grateful for the chocolate's sweetness to replace the coffee's bitter aftertaste and hoping to change the subject.

"Aw . . ." Regina cooed. "You're no fun."

"You wanted to teach me, right?"

Regina hummed as she cut into another piece of her chocolate swirl. "Well, I've told you about those of us at the bottom and you at the top. In-between, there are the province aristos, the lord governors, the local magistrates and ministry arms, and city lords. Most of the aristos here in the capital, though, are bureau aristos. They run the ministries."

Tory nibbled some more on her chocolate roll. The gooey center was all gone, and the chocolate was a sticky syrup. She listened and thought back to home and the other aristos who worked with her father. She had grown up around them, and most acted more like family than government officials. She didn't see any of the differences Regina did.

"Something wrong, Tory?" Regina asked.

Tory jumped, realizing she had sat there quietly for a time while her mind was miles away. "Sorry, just thinking. It all just seems rather complicated."

"The royals thought this up, dear." Regina shrugged. "It's all part of ruling, and they made sure to make it as complicated as possible."

Tory tensed. There it was again—the unflattering talk about the royal family out in the open. She couldn't say why, but it made her uneasy. A crawling itch creeped up between her shoulder blades, and she had to rub her back against the chair to ease it.

"Luckily for you"—Regina slid the remains of her chocolate swirl away, only the center eaten—"you have me, and there're really only three rules to follow." She started ticking them down with her fingers "Learn what an aristo does and how they live. That will tell you what class of aristo they are. Then learn how important they are, either by their family or position. The most important thing, though"—she grabbed Tory's arm, dropping her voice to a whisper—"learn who their *friends* are. Most important. Their friends will tell you everything you need to know."

"Right." Tory weakly nodded.

Memories returned of Serina's tea party back with them all clustered around her sister, gossiping and laughing. None of it had felt genuine.

Depends on what we mean by friends, *I guess.*

DING!

Tory snapped her head around, looking down the sidewalk where the sharp ring had come from. Three men walked together, clearly not North Enders. Their trousers were stained and threadbare, and they wore robes with rope tying back their wide sleeves. One held out an open purse to anyone passing by, while the one in the center rang a bell every few steps.

DING!

"Funds for the poor!" the last one yelled out. "Spare funds for the hungry!"

"Brother Priests," Regina informed her, pursing her lips and turning in her seat so she wasn't facing them as they walked up. "Probably collecting for the fire survivors."

"Fire survivors?" Tory questioned.

"There was a fire in South End a couple nights ago," Regina replied. "Nearly reached the old docks and destroyed a good section of the district close by, and a few tenements farther in before it was put out."

"That's horrible." Tory remembered the shabby look of the place when they had sailed into harbor. "Those poor people. Does anybody know what happened?"

"Someone must have forgotten to blow out a candle," Regina said on a sigh, "or fumbled a lamp, or who knows what? I would never go to such a place. However, some at court are saying this could be a great opportunity."

"For what?" Tory grimaced, finding the comment a bit heartless. "People lost their homes, didn't they?"

Regina calmingly shushed her. "It's all right! They're just thinking this could be a good opportunity to build newer, better ones. South End's been needing renovations for centuries, and there are some who are looking at this as a chance to do it." Regina winked.

What was that for? Tory gave her a perplexed look, figuring it meant something, but she didn't know what.

DING!

"Funds for the poor!" the priest said, walking past them.

Tory shrank back in her seat, watching the offering purse pass by. *Sorry. Please, don't look at me. I don't have anything.*

She fumbled with her hands in her lap, but the priests passed without a glance at the ladies. Instead, they stopped by the gentlemen's table.

Their conversation stopped, and one of them fished out his purse to drop a few spare coins into the priests' purse. The other gentleman shook his head when the priests turned to him, and then they walked away. The gentlemen paid their bill, leaving coin on the table, and left.

"Upstarts," Regina mumbled, sipping on her coffee after they walked far enough away.

"Hmm . . .?" Tory grunted.

"Those gentlemen were merchants," Regina replied with a sideways glance over her cup. "One was trying awfully hard to look like an aristo, probably from a newly formed company selling who cares what." She set her cup down and rearranged her seat back.

Tory looked after the two men, but they were gone over the rise of the street.

"You know them?" she asked.

"Nope." Regina sniffed, flicking at the crumbs on the table.

"Then, how do know they're merchants?"

"Their *shoes*, dear," Regina replied matter-of-factly. "Always check a gentleman's shoes. The one who ignored the priests was dressed well enough, but his shoes were stained and needing a shine. The other gentleman's were so worn that I don't know how they were still together."

Tory hadn't noticed their clothes. She just assumed everyone in North End were aristos, or at least in their employ. That was what Serina made the place out to be, after all.

"And you don't like them?" she asked, folding her arms while sitting back.

Regina ran her tongue between her teeth then rolled her jaw. "Not generally. Several years back, a few owners of large trading companies were *actually* allowed to buy titles for themselves. And, ever since then, more and more merchants have been trying, as well."

"People can *pay* to become an aristo?" Tory whispered, leaning in closer.

"They've been trying to call themselves *merchant* aristos." Regina snickered and shook her head. "Ridiculous. Of course, this is all Lord Renald's fault."

"Lord Renald?" The name was familiar, but Tory couldn't quite place it.

"Yep." Regina nodded. "Our former Minister of Treasure started it all. The merchants pay a special fee and taxes and are just granted titles. Of course, it's only a coincidence that over half of those trading companies are headquartered out of Tradon, and those merchants are provincial aristos now. Still making money from their companies while *I* can't own a single speck of land!" She slapped the table, making the cups and saucers bounce and clatter.

Tory jumped and rocked in her chair.

"Apologies, Tory." Regina sullenly bit the inside of her cheek and ran her fingers through her hair. "That wasn't very lady-like."

"It's okay, Lady Regina," Tory said. "I get upset sometimes, too." *Although, it's usually about whatever Serina's up to.*

She inwardly groaned. *I'm still not sure what all this means.*

"I'm sure." Regina fluffed out her hair. "I just get a little upset when I've worked *so* hard to get where I am today. The things I have to do . . . And yet others—" She snapped her mouth shut, clicking her teeth together, as if about to say something she shouldn't.

She must really dislike those merchants. Or maybe . . .?

"Lady Regina, may I ask you a personal question?"

"Careful, Tory," Regina mused, "personal questions can be frowned upon in polite society. Unless, of course, they're really juicy." She giggled.

"Do you . . . like my sister?" The back of Tory's throat tightened, as if something inside her tried to cut her off, but it was too late.

Regina's eyes never wavered, but the corners of her smile twitched for a brief second.

"Yes," she finally answered. "We're old friends. I absolutely adore her!"

Lie, Tory instantly recognized. *That's definitely a lie.*

"She's your sister," Regina continued. "You must love her, as well."

"Absolutely," she strained to say.

"Absolutely."

Both ladies stared at each other, eyes locked, while their smiles strained to remain.

Tory was sure Regina knew she was lying, too. Just as certain as Regina knew Tory understood she did not like Serina.

Finally, Regina let out a practiced chuckle, but Tory couldn't stop herself from genuinely laughing.

"Lady Syros."

"Yes?" Tory flung her head up and blinked tears from the corners of her eyes.

The woman store clerk was suddenly there by their table, arms folded in front of her like a servant randomly appearing to tell them the time of day.

"So sorry for the wait." The woman nodded. "We found your invitation. However, your lady sister required assistance with her measurements and requests. Master Faviann is ready for you now."

"Oh well." Regina shrugged. "How time escapes us. Don't worry about the bill, dear; I'll take care of it."

"Are you sure?" Tory asked, concerned despite not having any money.

"I said, don't worry about it." Regina dismissively waved then stood up, leading Tory to follow. Then Regina took her by the hand before the store clerk could lead her away.

"If you have any more questions about court life," she said, squeezing Tory's hand, "don't hesitate to ask. We should really do this again some time."

"Sure!" Tory agreed, squeezing her hand back. "I'd love, too."

This was the first conversation that she'd had where she felt she was being talked with instead of talked at. Well, except for those times she bumped into Prince Alindale, but those conversations had always been interrupted, somewhat awkward, *and* had gotten her in trouble.

"Thank you, Lady Regina."

She turned to go, but Regina tightened her grip.

"One last thing, Tory," she said softly. "If you find you have a better, happier life waiting for you back home than whatever someone offers you here in Daincliff, my best advice is to choose the happier life." Regina gave her hand one more squeeze then let go. Her practiced smile never wavered, but it didn't touch her eyes.

"I'll keep that in mind," Tory replied.

"Off you go, then." Regina gestured toward the shop. "Can't keep Serina waiting."

Tory rolled her eyes. "No, I can't."

They shared a final giggle, and then she joined the store clerk, heading back to the master tailor's shop.

"Oh! Lady Tory!"

Tory stopped halfway across the street and looked back.

"If you see your brother around, I know he must be terribly upset about some of the South End establishments burning down. Can you tell him, if he gets too bored, he can always call on me?"

Tory's mouth fell open, and she felt her ears and cheeks warm again, enough that they might burn.

Did . . .? Did she . . .?

Regina suddenly burst into laughter and pointed at her. "You are so *fun* to tease! We really need to do this again soon." With that, she grabbed her bonnet and went back into the café, assumingly to pay their bill.

Tory shook her head and tried to put it off as a joke while she crossed the rest of the street, but she couldn't be entirely sure.

As she walked into the shop, surrounded by the glamourous dresses and patterns, Tory compared the complex weave of the court life that Regina had described and the simple nature of everything back home. The Isles certainly felt more appealing.

Chapter 16

15th of Andril, 1109 N.F. (e.y.)

Alindale tugged at his jacket's high collar. *I can't believe I was talked into this.*

He kept finding something about his new suit to fuss over, from his jacket's itchy collar to his new boots squeezing his feet.

"It's best to leave the collar alone, Your Highness," Colonel Kenith Kane advised. "It feels like it's too tight at first, but the feeling goes away once you get used to it."

Alindale growled, smoothing the front of his dark blue jacket then running his hand down the gold buttons on the jacket's right side. The sides overlapped, similarly designed like his retainers' dress uniforms.

His immortal tutor had been incensed after hearing about Alindale's venture to South End, calling it a crazed risk, with nothing meaningful to gain. Amadus had gone so far as to reprimand Kenith in front of him, because his guards had failed to stop him. Since then, Alindale could never find a moment alone without a few Storm Cavalry guarding him.

And tonight, Kenith took it upon himself to command Alindale's retinue.

"Is that so?" Alindale asked. He glanced over his shoulder to his usual shadows—lieutenants, Holt and Malory.

Holt grimly faced forward, stomping along behind. Malory, on the other hand, comically grimaced and shook his head.

Alindale grinned. "Well, at least it's better than armor."

"That, it is," Kenith agreed.

Complementary grunts followed behind them.

Amadus had insisted he attend his mother's ball. Alindale needed to elevate his presence. It was more important now than ever for him to show the courtiers, the ministers, *and* his mother that he wasn't going anywhere and use the ball to demonstrate how many improvements he had made in the face of his banishment from court.

Yet, Alindale couldn't help but feel this was a little punitive for his ill-thought-out excursion to South End. Still, even if he should be punished, he didn't want his escort to be punished. Therefore, he had authorized Kenith and the rest of them to wear dress uniforms and sabers instead of armor. He was trailed by an entourage of burgundy and the sound of steel slapping against their sides, with the sound of music getting louder ahead of them, just around the corner.

He breathed heavily, trying to steady his nerves. With trembling fingers, he traced the gold, embroidered swords on his sleeve cuffs.

I can do this, he assured himself. *I'm only here to be seen.*

But he could see the lords' mocking looks from the day he had been banished. He could hear his mother's ladies giggling from his embarrassment underneath the faint music drifting from the ballroom.

Alindale had been hiding his fear of someone learning he had been in South End the night of the fire and telling everyone. This would be a perfect time for it to come out.

He took a deep breath to calm his nerve . . .

And failed to watch where he was going.

He turned the corner and walked right into someone. He gasped and jumped back in surprise from a stunned yelp from Lady Tory Syros.

She stepped back, catching the gold, embroidered stars on her shimmering, black skirts in the hallway's lamp light. Her deep red hair was spun up to show off the high collar of her dress, while also leaving her shoulders bare.

"Your Highness!" Tory gasped. Then she sighed with a half-grin, amused but trying not to laugh. "Why is it you startle me every time we meet?"

Alindale felt his cheeks flush. "Pardon me, Lady Syros. I didn't see . .
. I mean, I didn't mean to . . ." His tongue twisted into knots, and his words
became incoherent.

Tory winced. "Did I startle you, too?"

"You didn't startle me, Lady Syros," he lied, straightening his jacket
again. "I was lost in thought for a moment."

"Oh?" Tory raised an eyebrow, and he got the impression she didn't
believe him. "What were you thinking about?"

Alindale thought for a moment, but his mind had gone blank. "I . . . To
be honest, I can't remember now."

She gave him a concerned look. "Did I scare you *that* much?"

"You didn't scare me!" Alindale shouted before recognizing the
twinkle in her eyes, telling him that she was teasing him. He cleared his
throat to stall and collect himself. Then he remembered his escort.

He glanced at his guard. Kenith was noticeably facing away from him,
while Holt and two others sweated heavily, their placid frowns appearing
strained. Malory, though, grinned like a fool.

Alindale felt his face getting warmer and cleared his throat again.

"Colonel," he said, trying his best to sound commanding, "will you
and your fellow officers go on ahead? I would like to speak with Lady Syros
alone—I mean, in private."

Kenith faced him then obediently nodded. "As you wish, Your
Highness."

Despite Kenith's disciplined demeanor, Alindale caught the bushy tips
of his mustache trembling.

They're going to have a good laugh about this, he thought, watching
them file away. *They're supposed to be on my side!*

"Excuse me, Your Highness," Tory said, respectfully nodding. "I
didn't mean to tease you, or embarrass you."

"You didn't embarrass me, Lady Syros," he lied again then quickly
thought to change the subject. "What are you doing here? You are"—he
looked at her dress—"beautifully dressed for the ball. Where is your
escort?"

Tory's smile slipped, and she shifted her feet. "Truth is . . . I am
supposed to have an escort tonight."

"*Supposed to?*"

"Serina said she had arranged an acquaintance of Lord Harris Fauman's to escort me. A magistrate from . . ." She blinked then shook her head. "I can't remember."

Alindale looked down the hallway for her sister's party or a stranger looking for his wandering date, but the hallway was empty.

"Did he not show?"

"Actually"—Tory winced, rubbing her hands together, doing her best to avoid looking at him—"I snuck out of my room before anyone came to get me." She glanced up at him, her mouth twisting into a suppressed smile.

Alindale smiled with her and tried to hold in a laugh, but when air escaped Tory's tight lips, they both ended up laughing together. They laughed loud enough that they drowned out the distant music.

"But now"—Tory coughed nervously—"I'm not sure what to do. I don't know what kind of attention I will get if I go in unescorted, and Serina is going to be mad no matter what I do." She folded her arms and anxiously looked down the hallway toward the ballroom.

Alindale frowned, rubbing the back of his head, unsure, as well. "I wish I could help, but I'm afraid I don't know that many people."

Tory straightened and looked up at him, as if seeing him standing there for the first time. "Are you escorting anyone?"

Alindale stared at her, his body tense. He worked his mouth, but no sound came out until he cleared his throat.

"Lady Syros, I am . . . not sure I can," he said reluctantly. "It may not be good if we are seen together."

Tory physically tensed, and her eyes widened. She folded her hands together in front of her and lowered her eyes. "Forgive me, Your Highness. I was not thinking of my place. I'll go." She hastily walked around him, head down, eyes downcast, and arms folded in front of her.

Alindale felt a sinking feeling grow in his stomach. *What just . . .? Did I . . .?*

He threw his head up, eyes wide, as realization hit him.

"Lady Syros!" he yelled after her, but she kept walking, almost reaching the hallway curve and out of sight. "Lady Syros, please wait!"

Tory stopped mid-step but didn't look back at him.

He rushed to catch her, his ears ringing with the beating of his heart and stomping of his bootheels against the stone floor. When he reached her, she turned her head so he couldn't look at her.

Alindale winced, embarrassed.

"I'm sorry," he finally said.

"You do not have to apologize," Tory said quietly. "I know what they would say. A young lady, so recently welcomed to court, isn't important enough to be escorted by the royal heir."

"That's not what I meant!" he yelled. "I do not treat people like that, and to Oblivion to whoever does!"

Lady Syros jerked her head up, blinking tears out of her eyes.

Alindale's breath caught at seeing her in tears. He blushed, feeling awkward again.

"Forgive me for my outburst, My Lady. I should not have yelled, or cursed."

"Stop apologizing!" she snapped. "You're the prince! You should stand up for yourself!" She suddenly gasped and covered her mouth then began to wipe her eyes. "But you shouldn't curse, either. You're terrible at it."

Alindale gave her a level look, which she gave right back. He felt a growing urge to smile the longer they stared at each other but didn't. The corners of Tory's mouth twitched. Alindale tightened his face, attempting to keep from smiling, but something deep down kept growing until he grinned and began to laugh. Tory burst into laughter with him.

"Well, this has been"—he gasped, taking several deep breaths to recover—"a terrible conversation."

"Yep," Tory agreed, smiling again.

He smiled back. *I suppose I should be the gentleman now.*

"Let us start over, then." Alindale smoothed the front of his jacket before making a small bow, formal but not too deep. "Lady Tory Syros, may I escort you to the Easterly Great Spring Ball?"

Tory curtsied and replied, "I humbly accept, Your Highness."

As Alindale straightened, he presented his right arm, which she gracefully took.

"You know," Tory said as they walked, "if you had just asked me in the first place, we could have avoided all that."

Alindale nodded before realizing what she had said. "Wait. *You* asked *me*."

"Probably best if you don't tell anyone that," Tory whispered.

He grunted and gave her a sideways look. The mischievous light sparkled in her eyes, and her pursed lips held in another giggle.

The faint music grew louder as they walked down the curved hallway. His old fears of what the other lords and ladies were going to say began to return.

What's Mother going to think? He almost stopped from the spark of fear the thought sent through him.

"Relax," Tory whispered, squeezing his arm. "Never show weakness in your own house, Your Highness. That's what my mother says."

Alindale took a deep breath, trying to relieve the tension built up in his shoulders and loosen his arms, especially his right.

"Thank you," he said. "You may call me Alindale. It would be too tedious to walk in there and keep using titles."

"I agree." She nodded. "And you may call me Tory."

As they turned the bend, the castle guards flanking the ballroom's large doors snapped to attention, slapping their polearms against their shoulder plates. The doors, however, were closed, without a line of guests waiting to be announced, as Alindale had expected.

Kenith and the rest of his escort stood off to the side. More grins sprouted when they saw him walking arm in arm with Tory. Kenith stroked the triangular tuff of his beard approvingly.

Alindale tried not to let them bother or embarrass him again. If he couldn't take the looks of his own guard, how would he be able to handle the looks the aristos would give them?

"Are we late?" Tory whispered.

Just as Alindale shrugged, the right door slowly opened and out stepped Thomas. The old steward's thin eyebrows shot up upon seeing them.

He quietly shut door then fumbled with his scepter, the shaft sliding through his white gloves.

"Your Highness?" the steward gasped. "Lady Syros? You are both late!"

"Late!" Tory squeaked, squeezing Alindale's arm.

"Do you mean my moth—I mean, Her Majesty is here already?" Alindale asked. By custom, the king and queen were the last to be announced, and it was considered rude to arrive after them.

This could be bad, he thought.

"No, Your Highness," Thomas replied. "Her Majesty has not arrived, but the Table of Ministers and Her Majesty's ladies have."

"Then, how are we late?" Tory asked.

"It is customary," Thomas explained, "for the royal children to be introduced before the Table of Ministers. And you, Lady Syros, were supposed to have been escorted by Magistrate Holden."

Tory pursed her lips and glanced off to the side.

"That is my fault, Thomas," Alindale interceded. "I asked Lady Syros if I could escort her tonight, but I also asked her to keep it a secret. I didn't want my banishment from court to reflect badly on her."

Tory pulled on his arm and shook her head. "No. Don't you remember, Your Highness? I suggested we go together and surprise everyone. Sadly, we lost track of time."

"Is that what happened?" he asked.

Tory smiled at him and nodded.

"Oh." He shrugged. "I guess that would be right, then."

Thomas stared at them with his mouth agape, flashing his eyes between them, as if he didn't know what to say.

"But"—Thomas shook his head in frustration—"you're late, Your Highness."

"Thomas," Alindale said warningly, "unless you want Her Majesty to arrive and have to wait, you better announce us."

Thomas sniffed sharply. His chin trembled for a second before he humbly bowed. "At once, Your Highness. Your guard must enter before you when I strike my scepter." Thomas then turned on his heels, his scepter turning without hindrance.

Alindale leaned down to whisper in Tory's ear, "This is your last chance to back out."

Tory grinned. "Wouldn't dream of it."

Thomas pushed open the large doors without them making a sound. They were engulfed in bright light from inside the room. The music softened as Thomas entered. He stepped to the side and struck his scepter three times on the marble floor, the loud cracks drowning out the music. Kenith led other Storm Cavalry officers into the ballroom, taking positions on the descending steps.

"Here we go," Alindale said under his breath, loud enough for Tory to hear, and then led her into the ballroom.

"His Highness!" Thomas announced, cutting through every conversation in the large, oval room. "Prince Alindale Dain! Royal heir to the Sunrise throne and the crown of New Hartland!"

Alindale and Tory stopped at the top of the round, seven-step stairs, bathed in the light of the room's five crystal chandeliers. Alindale took a deep breath as the menagerie of lords, ladies, magistrates, knights, merchants, and other dignitaries gazed up at them. He felt Tory's arm shake and squeeze around his.

"His Highness escorts," Thomas continued, "Lady Tory Syros! Second daughter of Lord Guamalto Syros, Lord Governor of the Syros Isles!"

Alindale took a hesitant step then stopped. Tory looked flabbergasted at the sight of the glittering beauty of the chandeliers and the six granite pillars holding up the room. She snapped out of her daze as the musicians began to play in the far back of the room and followed Alindale's lead down the stairs and into the crowd.

Before taking their final step, Alindale saw the tall figure of Nolen Ingman standing beside the far-left pillar, just away from the tables serving food and drink. Despite being dressed in bright orange, he got the impression that Nolen was trying to stay out of sight by the way he leaned against the pillar.

Alindale had avoided him since returning to the castle. Although he hadn't seen him since, Alindale had feared finding the lanky man around any random corner.

Nolen raised his glass of wine, like a salute, before Alindale lost sight of him as he stepped into the crowd.

The crowd parted for them. Lords and gentlemen mumbled and nodded. Ladies watched the couple over their fans and whispered to each other behind their hands. None stepped out to greet them while they moved deeper into the room.

Alindale began to tense again, unsure of where to go.

Tory tugged his sleeve and whispered, "What do we do now?"

"Honestly," Alindale grunted nervously, "showing up was as far as I planned. I'm still not very good at mingling." He glanced around at the watchful stares and didn't find a familiar face. Kenith and the others had wandered off, probably somewhere with a drink.

"Is there a refreshment table?" Tory asked. "My brother, Jerro, always says people mingle better around food. And alcohol."

"I guess that would be better than standing around—"

Alindale saw Tory's older sister flowing her way toward them. Her glittering, red ball-gown's wide hoops made people step out of her way. She had made her way to them before Alindale could even warn Tory.

"Your Highness," Serina greeted, making a deep curtesy.

"Lady Serina." He nodded. His cheeks flushed, and he awkwardly averted his eyes to avoid seeing her revealed cleavage that her gown's square neckline exposed from her pose.

"I must thank you, Your Highness," Serina said as she straightened and brushed a strand of wavy hair out of her face with a gloved finger.

"Thank me for what, My Lady?"

"Why, for escorting my sister, of course," Serina replied, gesturing to Tory. "I was beginning to fear she would not be joining us. Although"— she turned to Tory, her eyes a veiled blaze—"I was expecting her . . . *earlier*."

Tory kept her head up, but she clamped her hands on Alindale's arm tightly.

"I didn't mean to worry you, sister," Tory said. "We just thought everyone would like the surprise."

"Yes, but Tory, you could have at least told *me* beforehand." The corners of Serina's smile twitched. "And poor Maddox Holden. He had to come all alone. It was quite embarrassing."

"I'm sorry, sister." Tory pursed her lips, and Alindale recognized the mischievous look in her eye. "I didn't mean to embarrass you."

Serina covered half her face with her fan. "You embarrassed Maddox, Tory, not me."

"I'm sorry. I meant Magistrate Holden, too."

Serina narrowed her eyes, and her hand trembled, shaking her fan.

Tory smiled smugly up at her older sister with a look a younger sibling made to goad an older when they couldn't do anything to them.

As for Alindale, he wanted to slip off to the other end of the room . . . far away from them.

"Serina," a man carrying two glasses of sparkling wine called. He stood a little taller than Serina, and Alindale guessed he was around Serina's age. His light brown hair was combed back to show his M-shaped hairline, and he had a thin mustache under his prominent nose. His red coat, with silver embroidered sleeves, and black trousers and belt matched Serina's ball gown.

"Thank you, dear," Serina said, closing her fan as she took a glass with a beaming smile. "Your Highness, may I present Lord Harris Fauman, son of our Minister of Treasure."

"Prince Alindale," Harris greeted with a bow while holding his wine glass steady. "It's an honor to meet you, Your Highness. May I just say I'm glad you aren't how people described you."

Alindale gave him a respectful nod. "And, how are people describing me? That I'm a bumbling fool or an unfit royal heir?"

Color drained from Harris's face. "No!" he stuttered. "Your Highness, no. I assure you that no one is saying such things."

But they are thinking it.

Alindale frowned as Harris apologetically winced. He wasn't sure what to say, and so an uncomfortable silence settled over them. Serina stared, wide-eyed, over her wine glass at him.

Alindale felt a tug on his sleeve and looked to see Tory frowning up at him. She shook her head with disappointment in her eyes.

"Forgive me, Lord Fauman," he apologized. "I am afraid my current worries have made me forget my manners."

"I understand, Your Highness," Harris replied. "I pray His Majesty recovers." A shadow fell over his face. "There is no greater loss than a family member."

Alindale was slightly taken aback by his sincerity. He had received few well wishes for his father, and most of those had felt obligatory. He hung his head, more embarrassed by his rudeness.

"Thank you," he said softly.

Four loud *cracks* rang out, silencing all the conversations. The musicians stopped mid-notes, and the trumpeters stood. They sounded a cadence as the Sunrise Guard filed in and took flanking positions on the ballroom steps.

"Attend!" Thomas yelled. "Attend! Her August Majesty, Queen Avera Dain!"

Everyone in the room bowed as Her Majesty entered, glowing in white.

"Wife and consort of His Majesty, King Richman Dain the Third, Lord of the First Kingdom, King of New Hartland, and Defender of Humanity! God Bless Their Majesties!"

The crowd rose in applause.

Her Majesty waved at them from above. Her ruby earrings and her hair's dark curls stood out from her white gown as she smiled at the room full of guests. The clapping continued for another moment until she finally motioned with her hands, and the clapping slowly stopped.

"Welcome!" she called out. "In the name of His Majesty, My Royal Husband, I welcome you all to the Great Spring Ball. Tonight, we celebrate the bounty that we have raised and the long months of continued warmth to raise more. We celebrate the seed growing in the ground and the harvest that will feed the people in need of salvation from the long drought. So, eat, drink, and let us dance in this long spring night."

Her speech was greeted with more applause, which continued as she descended the steps.

"That was pretty," Tory commented.

Alindale shrugged.

"I think she might have borrowed some lines from a poem," he said, making Tory snicker. "Although, I can't remember its name."

The applause slowly died, and the musicians resumed as his mother made her way through the parting crowd. Men bowed and women curtsied.

Alindale leaned down and whispered, "This would be the perfect time to slip away to the refreshment table."

"But your mother's coming right toward us," Tory whispered back.

"That is why it is the perfect time."

Tory giggled, but Alindale knew it was too late. His mother paused, saw him, and then headed their way, her welcoming smile never wavering. He bowed at her approach, and Tory curtsied.

"Alindale," his mother said happily, "this is a most pleasant surprise." She took him by the shoulders, making him rise, and then lightly kissed him on both cheeks. "If this is a gift to me, then I will gladly accept it."

Alindale strained to keep smiling, despite the whispering lords and ladies around them. "I am glad you are happy, Mother," he said respectfully.

"I am merely happy that you have taken up your princely duties." She glanced over, saw Tory standing arm in arm with him, and then turned her attention to her.

"Lady Syros the younger, correct?"

"Yes, Your Majesty," Tory replied with a small curtsy.

His mother looked her up and down, as if seeing her for the first time. "Do I owe you my gratitude, as well, my dear, for bringing my son away from . . . What was it?"

She turned toward him. "Your training?"

"Well, actually—"

"I asked to escort her, Mother," Alindale interrupted Tory.

His mother passed a look between them, her mask never wavering, making it hard for Alindale to guess what she was thinking.

"Your jaunt through my gardens must have left an impression," his mother teased, causing them both to blush. "Would you mind if I borrow her for a moment?"

Alindale raised an eyebrow. "Borrow?"

"Only for a moment." His mother beckoned to Tory. "A talk between ladies that would certainly bore you. Go to the tables and get a refreshment. I promise not to keep her long."

Alindale gave Tory a worried looked, but Tory simply patted his arm before slipping hers away.

His mother swooped in and took Tory by the arm, pressing her forward into the crowd. Alindale tried to watch them as best he could, but they soon disappeared.

He suddenly felt strangely alone. The din of different conversations surrounding him blended to the point that he couldn't tell one from the other. With Her Majesty's arrival, the guests now spoke freely in their own groups, leaving him alone in the middle of them. Even Lord Harris and Lady Serina had disappeared.

This feels familiar, he thought, slowly making his way toward the refreshment tables.

***

Tory's heart fluttered. She, a newly arrived lady, was accompanying Her Majesty herself through a throng of the highest dignitaries and aristos of the kingdom. This night was turning into a whirlwind of excitement, no matter how she tried to steady her sails.

She hadn't planned on coming across Alindale and going to the ball with him. She had actually been thinking of finding some corner to hide in and hoping Serina was too occupied with Harris to notice when she ran into him. Tory bit back a grin, remembering how flustered Serina had gotten.

And there was nothing she could do to her about it! She was almost giddy and desperately trying not to laugh. *And she had to wear red, too!*

That was what their last-minute fitting with Emelie Faviann had been about. After Tory had returned from her fitting, Nina had told her that, when Serina had discovered Harris Fauman's only suit worthy enough for Her Majesty's ball had been red, she had raged through her rooms, throwing aside furniture and almost smashing her bedroom mirror. Tory was so used to her sister's foul attitude of late that she hadn't thought there might have been a particular reason for it. It tickled her more now, adding a spring to her step.

"Tell me, Lady Syros," Her Majesty spoke, snapping Tory back to reality, "how are you finding your time here at court?"

"It is going well, Your Majesty," Tory half-lied. She had enjoyed a few days, but most, she was either bored or felt like an outsider watching people do things.

"Have you met many interesting people?" Her Majesty asked, nodding to another group of bowing and curtsying aristos. "Ministry officials, perhaps? They are always looking for young lords and ladies to induct in promising careers."

Tory paused to think of the best way to answer. "I have met a few new people, Your Majesty. My sister has introduced several of her old acquaintances. However, I do not know if any of them worked in any of the ministries."

"That is a shame." Her Majesty gestured to a passing servant carrying a silver tray with glasses of sparkling wine. "It is vital for a young lady entering society to think of her future. It would not do for others to think you weren't taking every advantage being offered to you, or stepping outside her bounds."

The hairs on the back of Tory's neck stood up. Something inside her, an instinct she had grown from being around Serina, stirred. Its warning whisper told her to take care and mind what she said and how she reacted.

She watched Her Majesty take her time to inspect each glass on the servant's tray before plucking one to her liking. Meanwhile, Tory noted a small space had formed between them and the other aristos and dignitaries, as if everyone was keeping their distance from the pair, save the two escorting Sunrise Guards at their backs.

"How long have you known my son?" Her Majesty asked before sipping her wine.

While her poise was excellent, as always, Tory caught her studying gaze leering at her from over the glass's rim.

"Not long, Your Majesty," she replied, clasping her hands together in front of her to ensure they didn't fidget. "We have only spoken a couple of times."

"And yet, he offered to escort you tonight?" Her Majesty raised an eyebrow while leisurely swirling the remaining wine in her glass. "Those must have been quite the conversations."

Tory's heart fluttered again, only this time she was not excited. She tried to keep as calm an appearance as possible.

Oh no! she internally panicked. *She's testing to see if I'm a proper match or not. I didn't mean for that! If I tell her that, though . . . will she be insulted?*

"They were really spur of the moment talks." She bashfully laughed. "I am kind of surprised His Highness even remembered me." She tried to make herself look humble and innocent. That was what her instinct told her to do. Same as if she had to guard herself against one of Serina's tirades. Only, Tory had no idea how Her Majesty would respond.

"Yes," Her Majesty said, her shoulders falling slightly, "my son's pursuits have often made him aloof to the ladies at court, which has also left him innocent in many ways. He may be of need of protection from those who would deceive him."

Tory swallowed under Her Majesty's hard stare.

Deceive him? She felt a sinking feeling in her gut. *Is she saying I'd . . .?*

Anger and disgust boiled inside her, but there was also fear. This was the queen.

"I promise, Your Majesty," she said, lowering her head, "I am not trying to seduce your son, or deceive him. Alindale—His Highness—has been nothing but kind to me."

"That is good to hear." Her Majesty stepped closer and lightly took Tory by the chin, raising her head. "Perhaps you can perform a service for a worrying mother to prove it?"

Tory stifled a cough from Her Majesty's heavy perfume of hibiscus and cloves. Unfortunately, she knew there was only one response she could give.

"What do you wish, Your Majesty?"

Her Majesty frowned sadly. "As you know, my son is being . . . stubborn about a little misunderstanding. It would only take a small apology for him to be forgiven, but he refuses. And I fear it has torn a rift between us."

What does that have to do with me?

"That is terrible, Your Majesty," Tory said out loud.

"Thank you, dear." Her Majesty brightened. "He may not be willing to listen to me presently, but perhaps he would listen to a friendlier voice. If you could convince him to apologize, we would be most grateful." She took a long sip of wine then smiled.

"Yes, Your Majesty," Tory agreed nervously.

Why would Prince Alindale listen to me? She didn't know how to fulfill Her Majesty's request, or even if she could. Or should.

Alindale had called First Minister Haemin a murderer in front of everyone. Tory didn't see how such a thing could simply be handwaved away with a simple apology.

"But, if you are unable to, I shall understand," Her Majesty told her. "You are still new to court, and young, as well. I only ask because, being a newly arrived young lady, being in my good graces would be an excellent opportunity. And I do wish to be a gracious host."

Tory squeezed her hands together. If she were any other young lady, she would probably be jumping at this offer. Her nervous instinct, though, told her to be careful. There was more here than she understood.

"If you cannot"—Her Majesty finished her wine—"then I suggest you not get ahead of yourself, *young* lady. Do not forget your station. Enjoy the ball."

Moments passed. The musicians began a new movement before Tory finally moved. By then, Her Majesty had moved off, gathering a crowd around her as she went. No one noticed Tory anymore, standing shocked and wide-eyed in the middle of the room, surrounded yet alone, heart crushed and replaced with a heavy weight in her chest.

Did she . . .? Did she just . . .? Her thoughts were a jumble, but Tory understood. Her Majesty's opinion of her was clear.

Unworthy.

She watched Her Majesty laugh with the other ladies flocking to her now that she was available, one of them being Serina, naturally.

Part of her wanted to scream. Instead, she wrapped her arms around herself and slunk away.

***

Alindale meandered around the serving tables, realizing only upon reaching them that he had no idea what Tory would like. He didn't know which drink was the best, despite the occasional wine with meals.

Dodging the occasional servant stacking drinks on trays to deliver across the room, he instead took the moment to people-watch. He could tell the social rank of the different groups by the drinks the servants were serving them.

Servants served wine and the occasional glass of brandy to the wealthy merchants discussing business ventures and magisters. Lords ordered multiple glasses of wine for their ladies waiting in their gossip circles for them to return.

The knights were the easiest to spot because of their ceremonial tabards bearing the sigils of the different brotherhoods. Some of the masters ordered brandy and port, along with the magistrates and merchants, but the reek of yeast hung over the rest being served mugs of dark beer.

As he suspected, Alindale spotted Kenith and the other Storm Cavalry officers among them, but no sign of Master Montaigu and Brother Revel.

"A toast to you, Your Highness!"

Alindale flinched, finding Nolen suddenly standing beside him with his wine glass raised. His cheeks were flushed, and he wobbled on his feet.

"Lord Ingman," he greeted dryly. "Are you drunk already?"

Nolen smiled even bigger. "Of course, Your Highness, of course. The lovely servant girls are serving Alsarian wine like water. Why aren't we all drunk by now?" He sipped his glass's bubbling orange content.

"That used to be outlawed," Alindale remarked, "along with the Staphli grapes, because people got intoxicated by simply eating them."

Nolen smacked his lips and squinted, as if he couldn't focus. "Sounds like exactly what you need."

"How many of me do you see?"

Nolen blinked and wobbled more. "Four. Which is good. Remember, you still need all the friends you can find."

"After last time, I think I am fine." Alindale hoped Nolen would take his meaning and remember the disastrous night in South End.

Nolen took another wincing sip. "You surprised everyone with that grand entrance." He tried to wave at the crowd but wobbled and tipped backward. Alindale leapt and caught him by the shoulder. Nolen leaned forward, so close Alindale could smell the alcohol on his breath. "But making such a statement," Nolen whispered, "that you're above the Table of Ministers. If you didn't have enemies before, you certainly have them now."

Alindale studied him for a moment. "Are you really drunk?"

"Of course I'm drunk!" Nolen snorted then sprang back. "A knight has absconded with my lady, and I am distraught. Only this fine wine can console me." He lifted his glass to his lips and glanced around. "Where's your lovely lady?"

Alindale grunted, and his cheeks grew hot. "She is not my lady."

Nolen pointed at him and softly laughed in a high-pitched trill. "You escorted her, so she's your lady. At least to everyone here, she is."

Two loud *cracks* came from the center of the room. The musicians stopped while the crowd dispersed to the sides of the room, leaving a wide, open space in the center. One by one, gentlemen led their ladies onto the floor.

Thomas signaled the musicians once twenty couples had taken their places. As the musicians pulled their bows across their strings, the men and women bowed to each other before coming together and beginning to dance.

"Alindale!"

Amadus strolled through the crowd with his arms outspread. The immortal's beaming smile shined through his trimmed whiskers. He had gone through a transformation in the weeks since Alindale's banishment. He appeared to be a man in his fifties or early sixties, with black hair replacing his old, stringy white strands, and his aging wrinkles had vanished. He walked among the gentry as one of them, without a hint of frailty, dressed in elegant, violet silk robes.

"I am so *proud* of you!" Amadus declared, clasping and shaking Alindale by the shoulders.

Alindale was taken aback by Amadus's jovial behavior. "For what?"

"For that grand entrance!" Amadus replied. "Even I didn't think you were ready to make such a bold statement. I was as surprised as everyone. I'm so proud to finally have a pupil who . . ." He glanced about. "Where is your lady?"

Alindale gave him a flat stare. "She is *not* my—"

"She was stolen by a knight," Nolen interrupted.

Alindale turned his ire on the lanky lord. "That was *your* lady!"

"Oh. Right." Nolen shrugged then drank his wine.

Amadus squinted up at Nolen, finally noticing him. "Who are you?"

"I am—" Nolen tried to bow with a flourish but pushed against a passing lady and sprang back up. "Apologies, dear lady, apologies."

The lady scowled at him then walked away.

"Did your mother invite jesters?" Amadus asked softly to Alindale.

"That career would suit him," he replied, "but no. Amadus, this is Lord Nolen Ingman."

"That's me!" Nolen said happily, raising his glass. "It is a pleasure to finally meet the legendary immortal."

Amadus grunted and frowned, unimpressed. "Nice to meet you, My Lord. Please, excuse us." He pushed Alindale forward, but Nolen stepped in front of them before they could get away.

"I'd like to ask a question, if I may?" Nolen asked.

"You've already asked one," Amadus growled.

Nolen chuckled, leaning forward unsteadily. "You're tutoring His Highness on leadership, I assume, the knights are whipping him into shape, and the Kanes are making sure he doesn't fall off a horse. I'm just wondering: are you preparing him for the throne, or preparing him for war?"

A tight knot gripped the small of Alindale's back. *Where did that come from?*

Amadus glared back at Nolen, and the two men stared at each other.

The music stopped, and the crowd clapped at the end of the first dance.

Nolen suddenly grimaced and grabbed his belly. "Pardon me . . . Your Highness," he strained to say, wincing as sweat appeared on his face. "But it seems that Alsarian wine has a stronger kick than I thought. I need to find a chamber pot! Excuse me!" He dashed away, striding carelessly through the crowd to the curtains in the back of the room, behind the musicians, where the chambermaids waited.

Alindale laughed. "He would make a good jester, if he wasn't so weird."

"Do not trust him, Alindale," Amadus growled.

Alindale glanced and found Amadus watching the curtains, as if looking to see if Nolen had really left. He had intentionally left Nolen's involvement in his trip to South End out of his story, figuring the less people who knew about him, the better.

"I don't," he confessed. "I know he is not as big a fool as he pretends."

"He's a murderer, Alindale," Amadus snapped, squinting darkly at him.

"What?"

"Three years ago," Amadus began, lowering his voice, "there was an incident at a gambling house in Inglworf. He was brought before a magistrate and acquitted, but there are still those who are fairly certainty it was murder and that the magistrate was paid off."

"How certain are you?"

"A knife in a man's back doesn't sound like self-defense to me."

Alindale swallowed. *That would have been nice to know two weeks ago!*

Trumpeters opened the next movement, bringing him out of his thoughts as new couples formed on the dance floor.

Amadus grunted and waved. "Never mind. I'll keep an eye on him. You best return to your lady."

Alindale followed Amadus's line of sight and saw Tory watching the dancers alone. Her black dress stood out in sea of the bright, lively colors of the other guests.

"Enjoy tonight, Alindale," Amadus said, clapping him on the back. "Back to routine after tomorrow."

"Thanks for reminding me," Alindale grumbled.

He carefully brushed through the meandering crowd, making his way toward Tory. He sniffed and wiped his nose from the heavy mix of fruity aroma of wine, the grain scent of beer, and perfumes of saffron and clove.

Most were absorbed in watching the dance and talking among themselves while waiting for room on the dance floor.

"I am afraid I forgot to ask what you wanted to drink," he told Tory bashfully when he finally reached her.

Tory jerked, as if she had been in deep thought. "What?" she asked, blinking. "Oh! Thank you, but I don't want anything." She looked back at the dancing couples, swaying her shoulders to the music. "So, this is what it means to be the queen."

Alindale's mother gracefully spun in the arms of an older, shorter gentleman in the center of the dance floor. She danced like she loved it, her back straight, head up, radiating an unwavering smile.

A knight in the red ceremonial tabard strolled around the other couples on the floor and toward her. Her partner stopped and exchanged pleasantries with the knight. Then the two men bowed to each other and Her Majesty and exchanged places. Alindale thought his mother's smile brightened when she started dancing with the knight.

He glowered. *And Father's left sick and alone in his chambers.*

"My mother enjoys her duties," he said dryly.

"No, I meant"—Tory's lips trembled, watching every graceful move his mother made—"being the center of the world and admired by everyone surrounding her, no matter what she asks."

Alindale glanced at his mother then back to Tory. "What did my mother say to you?"

"She wanted to compliment my dress," she replied. "She found it lovely." She gave him a small smile, but her eyes were red and puffy.

Alindale drew himself up and glared across the dance floor at his mother. *You should be ashamed, Mother.*

He pulled out a soft linen handkerchief from his pocket and handed it to her. Tory snatched the handkerchief and dabbed the corners of her eyes.

"Thank you," she said.

The dancers spun to a stop as the musical movement ended. They bowed to each other at the final note then clapped.

"My lords and ladies!" Thomas announced, striking his scepter on the floor before couples could change places. "This next dance is reserved for the royal family and the Table of Ministers. Would the ministers please bring their lovely ladies and join Her Majesty on the dance floor for the next movement?"

As the dance floor cleared, Alindale caught sight of Haemin walking through the press, to the center of the room. The new first minister's beard had grown since Alindale had last seen him. Dressed in silver and white, he and his mother looked like a matching pair as he bowed to her and she accepted him as her new dance partner.

Alindale gritted his teeth together and turned his head away at the seeing Haemin wrap his arm around his mother's waist. *Father is upstairs!*

He felt his shoulder tugged on and snapped around to see Tory gleaming up at him.

"Shall we dance?" she asked.

Alindale winced, nervously looking at the clearing dance floor and growing crowd of spectators watching his mother and the other nine couples take their places.

"I am . . . not sure Thomas meant us to. It might be terribly rude."

"He said the dance was reserved for the royal family," Tory pointed out. "Besides, we've been rude ever since we arrived." She suddenly gave him a knowing look. "You don't know how to dance."

"I know how to dance!" Alindale looked away.

Tory giggled.

The ministers and their ladies were at their places, in a ring around Her Majesty and Lord Haemin. The dance floor was clear.

Alindale trembled, feeling the moment growing short.

Thomas did say the royal Family, he pondered.

He struggled in his mind for a reason to step out on the dance floor and the hesitation not to. Then he looked back at his mother, excitedly waiting in the arms of the man responsible for his brother's death.

I came here to be seen, he told himself. *Let's show them that I'm a better prince now!*

He took a deep breath then stepped out on the dance floor.

Faint hushes went up around him as the crowd watched him intently. He put all those forgotten etiquette lessons to use and held out his hand to Tory, who was smiling at him from the edge of the crowd.

She took his hand, and then he led her onto the front of the dance floor, near the musicians, in a hole where the first minister was supposed to be. Alindale didn't look at his mother, but he could feel her glaring at him. The back of his legs trembled, and he did his best not to shake while he and Tory waited for the music to begin.

"Your Highness," Thomas whispered.

Both Alindale and Tory snapped to see the steward looking at them anxiously.

"Yes, Thomas?" Alindale whispered back.

Thomas's bushy brows trembled as he looked back toward his mother then back to him.

"If there's no problem, Thomas," Alindale said, louder for those around him to hear, "then begin the dance."

Thomas frowned and turned away.

Tory grinned proudly as the flutes and trumpets opened the next movement, followed soon by the strings. He bowed, and she curtsied. Then they came together by raising their right hands and placing their left behind their backs. Their right hands met, and they spun around each other when the trumpets fell silent, followed by a solo flute whistling over the strings. After a few spins, they switched to their left hands.

As they spun, Alindale glimpsed his mother and Haemin from the corner of his eye. They were dancing closer to each other and slower than the rest of them, as if intensely drawn to each other.

Alindale and Tory stopped spinning, bowed, and came together again, his left hand in her right, and his right on her hip, while her left held her skirts. His shoulders and back began to tighten from trying not to stand too close or hold her too tightly.

He knew the movements expected of him, remembering he had to lead. He took a step forward, she took a step back, and so on. He kept his eyes on her face, but his mind was on his steps.

Don't step on her skirts, he repeated to himself. *Do not step on her skirts.*

"You're tense again," Tory whispered. "Relax."

Alindale took a deep breath, trying to ease his shoulders and nerves. "I do believe I told you that I'm not much of a dancer."

Tory's smile widened. "That's because you're thinking about it too much."

"*Thinking about it too much?*"

"When you dance, don't think about your steps; follow the music."

Violins took over the melody from the flutes, strumming low, soothing chords, harmonizing with the rest of the strings and woodwinds. Alindale listened closely and slowed the pace of their dance. The tension in his shoulders disappeared. Before he realized it, they were dancing closer together.

"Much better," Tory said, seemingly pleased at the change in pace.

Alindale gave a small laugh. The violins' rhythm quickened, and the trumpets and horns joined the woodwinds. As the music became grander, so did their dance. Their steps felt light following the rhythm, as if their tiptoes were treading on water. Everything faded away as he listened to the music and watched Tory's gleeful face.

They wrapped their arms around each other's and spun to the fanfare of the trumpets. They swayed with the flurry of the flutes and clarinets, their decrescendo slowing the pace until the strumming violins took up the melody again.

Alindale never wanted it to end. Here, away from his troubles. Here, in the music, in the dance, not only was there escape but a joy he had never experienced.

He sighed disappointedly when the movement ended with the drawn-out pull from the basses' strings and low, long notes of the woodwinds.

He and Tory bowed to each other as applause filled the ballroom in place of fading music. The peaceful world that Alindale had envisioned faded with it.

"I think I'd like a drink now," Tory said, breathing a little heavier. She took his arm, and they maneuvered through the shifting couples walking out to replace them for the next movement.

Alindale glanced over his shoulder to see if his mother and Lord Haemin were preparing to dance again, but they were gone. He scanned the room but still couldn't find them.

They left?

The image of his mother storming out, livid, raced through his mind, and he nervously scouted the path to the refreshment tables, expecting her to be waiting for them.

The musicians began again when they had returned to the tables. Tory slipped away to the head of the tables.

"Careful," Alindale warned when she took a glass of bubbling Alsarian wine. "That is the strongest they are serving."

Tory's eyelashes flickered. She leaned in and whispered, "Don't tell my sister." She grinned, took a sip, and her eyes flew wide.

Alindale pressed his lips tightly together, forcing himself not to laugh as she winced and coughed.

"Do you"—she coughed again—"want anything?"

"I think one of us should stay sober and watch after the other," he teased, making her giggle into her glass.

"Alindale," Amadus gruffly interrupted, coming up behind him again.

Alindale gave the immortal a small, acknowledging nod. "Amadus, may I present Lady Tory Syros."

Tory gave him a wave. "Lord Amadus."

Alindale spotted Amadus's deep frown, and his left eyebrow twitching.

"What's wrong?"

"Would you please excuse us, Lady Syros?" Amadus asked.

Tory glanced at them over her wine glance, taking a small sip. "Okay," she said, making a small curtsy. "Your Highness. Lord Amadus."

Alindale grunted, watching Tory walk away. The carefree, simple joy of the dance seemed to have vanished with her.

"What is wrong now?" he sighed out.

Amadus's eyes grew dark and misty as he took Alindale by the shoulders and said, "The king is dead."

The world deafened around him, leaving only the thumping of his heart to echo in the void. Alindale's chest suddenly felt tight. He gasped for breath, struggling to breathe. All the happiness he had felt moments ago crumbled into pain.

"Calm yourself, Your Majesty," Amadus hissed, shaking him by the shoulders.

Alindale shoved him away. "No!" he shouted, not carrying for the startled stares he drew. "I'm not . . . Father's not . . ." His cheeks began to sting from his face contorting, holding in the surge of emotion. "He can't be!"

He stormed past Amadus, ignoring his pleas, and plowed through the crowd. He shoved lords out of the way and pushed past ladies without apologies or concern for decorum. None of them mattered.

He can't be! Not after fighting to live for so long!

Alindale burst through the crowd and ran up the ballroom steps two at a time. He startled Thomas, who was speaking intently with two Sunrise Guards at the top of the steps, but didn't slow.

"Your Highness!" Thomas yelled after him, but he kept running, too focused on reaching his father's room.

Once out of the ballroom, he ran straight down the hallway toward the southwest stairwell and continued running up to the third floor. He ignored the familiar burning in his chest. He tried to take longer breaths, but he was too frantic to calm down.

Not again! The hot sting of tears ran down his face. *I couldn't say good-bye again!*

His brother had left without a word, and Alindale hadn't spoken to his father since the day before he had fallen ill. Both memories combined in his mind, urging him on.

He dropped his head, grabbed the walls for added purchase, and then pressed forward as hard as he could. As he passed the second floor, the sound of his bootheels against the stone steps matched the beating of his heart.

"I'm innocent!"

Alindale stopped short, nearly tripping over his feet as three castle guards dragged Lord Bernold Vanni down the steps. Two held his arms, while the third pushed him from behind. Bernold struggled in their grips, disheveled and in disarray.

"What is the meaning of this?" Alindale demanded.

"My Prince!" Bernold cried, trying to rush toward him, but the guards held him fast. "Your Highness, please! You must help me!"

"Silence!" the guard behind him said. "Keep moving."

"I demand to know what is going on!" Alindale yelled, stepping in front of them.

"Her Majesty has ordered Lord Vanni taken to the northeast tower," the guard replied.

Alindale was stunned. The northeast tower was the castle's derelict, old guard tower and hadn't been used for nearly a century.

The guards began dragging Lord Vanni around Alindale while he was complacent.

"Why?" Alindale stuttered. "For what reason?"

"For the murder of the king!"

"It's a lie!" Bernold shouted, reaching out Alindale, tears streaming down his face. "I found your father dead. I swear it!"

The guards shoved him against the wall then continued to drag him down the stairs.

"Please!" Bernold begged. "I must speak with Her Majesty. The assassin is still loose! The assassin is still loose, Your Highness!" The guards paid him no heed, continuing to drag him around the bend of the stairwell.

Alindale pressed himself against the stone wall of the stairwell, clutching his chest, while Bernold's pleas and warnings filled his head.

Murdered . . .? Murdered!

He hurried up to the third floor, his legs aching from how hard he was pushing himself. Small clusters of servants bowed to him as ran past, ignoring them as he sped through the royal quarters of the castle. Finally, turning a corner, his father's room came into sight. Its large, oak door stood open with two Sunrise Guards still at their post beside it.

And his mother and Lord Haemin were coming out the room.

His mother was in tears with her arms wrapped around herself. When Haemin tried to touch her shoulders, she jumped away from him. "Leave me!" she screamed furiously at him.

Haemin stepped back and bowed hesitantly. He glanced at Alindale as he began to walk away then paused. His face was a blank mask, without a sign of grief, remorse, or fear, before leaving in the opposite direction.

Alindale's focus returned to his father's opened doorway. He slowly approached, as he had done so every morning for the past six weeks.

As he drew near, his mother threw her arms around his neck, pulling him into a tight embrace. She was shaking, and tears ran down her face, smearing her makeup and staining his coat as she pressed her head against his shoulder. "Don't go in," she cried, her voice shaky and cracking. "He's gone."

"What happened?" Alindale asked.

She pulled back from his shoulder and cupped his face in her hands. Her dark eyes were flickering and unfocused, and the corners of her mouth trembled. "You must be brave," she whispered. "You must be brave."

Alindale pulled her close and held her tightly. She dissolved into quiet sobs against his chest, trying, even in her grief, to compose herself but couldn't. The last time Alindale had seen her cry was when they had brought his brother's body home. She had wailed openly then.

Alindale's nose wrinkled at the whiff of something strange. His mother's perfume wasn't that strong, and so he quickly traced the scent coming from his father's open bedroom. He took another deep breath then coughed. It smelled like a mix of perfume with rotting meat. The scent burned his nostrils and made his stomach pitch.

Something down the hallway moved.

The flamboyant orange, lean frame told Alindale who it was peering around the corner. Nolen's lean face was rigid, and his eyes wide. In the dim light, Alindale read him mouth three words.

You. Are. Next.

Chapter 17

26th of Andril, 1109 N.F. (e.y.)

Kalleb struggled to keep Cloud in line with five other lancers of his troop. He had registered the dapple gray stud as his to their barrack's stable officer the day after arriving in Tradon and learned the horse was more spirited saddled than in a team. The stud snorted and pulled against his reins, impatiently flaring his slivery mane with the desire to spring into a gallop.

"Keep the line!" he yelled through his helmet's visor and over the thumping hooves.

They rode toward a line of straw-stuffed dummies, shaped like the upper bodies of men by sack cloth. The dummies were spaced, allowing horses to ride between them, but the problems for the recruits was riding in formation and effectively using their lances.

"Gallop!"

Kalleb nudged Cloud with his heels, and the stud sprang forward. He had to pull him back so he wouldn't get too far out of line. The distance began to close fast. By the time he regained control of his horse, he cursed at nearly missing the next order.

"Lancers! *Charge!*"

He held his lance crouched under his arm, but a couple of lancers in his line had been holding theirs high the last he had seen. He couldn't look to help or correct them, though, as Cloud thundered toward the dummies.

He yelled and focused on the dummy coming up on his right. He changed his hold on his lance, dropping it from being crouched to holding it only with his hand. He aimed for the dummy's right side, where a man's lungs would be. Thrusting for the center or the left risked breaking or pulling his lance from his grip on impact.

He leaned forward in the saddle and pulled his arm back. He thrust before Cloud reached the dummy. The steel point speared through the dummy's left side, higher than Kalleb wanted, but it was too late. The jarring impact ran up his arm as he clutched the lance shaft tighter to prevent it from slipping out of his grasp. Then he twisted the lance, and its tip ripped through the dummy, flinging strands of straw and spinning the dummy around from the force.

Kalleb exhaled and struggled to reel Cloud in. He still instinctively held his breath when he charged, despite it being years since he had practiced charging in formation. The sound of his heavy breathing echoed inside his helmet.

"Form on me!" he yelled, raising his lance in the air.

The other lancers were still regaining control of their mounts, snorting and stomping after the charge.

"Lancer Zoren!" Corporal Hunt bellowed. "You broke your lance! You lanced your dummy with your lance crouched, didn't you?"

Kalleb shoved his visor up and turned in his saddle. Hunt bore down on Zoren sitting slumped in his saddle with his head hung, hiding his eyes under his helmet's rim. There was no hiding his broken lance, though. More than half of the shaft was snapped off, leaving him with only four feet of useless wood in his hand.

Kalleb looked back and found Zoren's dummy knocked on the ground with the remains of Zoren's lance impaled in its center mass.

Only one way that could've happened.

"Yes, Corporal," Zoren replied sheepishly. He shifted his eyes nervously, his face strained from his tight frown, like a child preparing to be scolded.

"The lieutenant ordered *no crouching!*" Hunt snapped.

"I'm sorry—"

"No excuses!" Hunt slapped the butt of his lance against his boot. "Your thrusts and flings are still pathetic! If you can't learn the technique and follow orders, then—"

"That's enough, Corporal Hunt!" Kalleb roared, charging Cloud between him and Zoren, their horses snorting and nipping at one another. "He struck his target; that's good enough for now."

"With all due respect, Lance Corporal," Hunt sneered, "we've been practicing for weeks. Any lancer who can't follow orders now—"

"I said *enough!*" Kalleb bristled, knowing what he was implying. "I *warned* you not to berate the men. Return to the rest of the troop."

Hunt grimaced but didn't protest. He wheeled his mount without a salute and galloped back toward the rest of their waiting troop.

"Sorry, Lance Corporal," Zoren apologized. "By the time we started galloping, we were too close, so I just aimed my lance and . . ." He held up the sorry remains of his lance, and a couple of his comrades snickered.

Kalleb cleared his throat to get their attention. "It's all right, Zoren. It was partially my fault for not giving the commands properly. At least you struck your target."

More snickers followed, but Kalleb passed a careful look across the rest of them. He thought he caught a hint of nervousness in their chuckles. Lancing something, even something not moving, wasn't as easy as it looked. Many thrusts either missed their marks or their target altogether.

He gently tossed his lance up and caught it again. "You boys just need more practice. It's not enough to ride down someone and spear them. You need to instinctively thrust, twist, and fling." He made a thrusting motion before turning the lance by the wrist and flicking it. "It must be all in one motion; otherwise, it'll get stuck. And if that happens to you at full gallop, you're going to be in more trouble than snapping your lance on impact. Understand?"

His lancers grunted and nodded.

Kalleb nodded back then tucked his lance under his arm. "I know it feels right to crouch your lance under your arm, but as Zoren's shown, it may help your aim, but you're also likely to break your lance doing that. And, since you're all still new to using maces and don't have sabers, you're more likely to get your fool selves killed. So, at least for my sake, learn to thrust and fling. Keep yourselves alive and off my conscience. Got it?"

"Yes, Lance Corporal," the lancers barked in unison.

Content that he had performed his officer's duty in begging them not to get themselves killed, Kalleb turned Cloud away and led them around the field, back to their waiting troop.

Hopefully, that's enough warning for now.

The days of drills slowly brought Kalleb's old training back, like a farmer grinding rust off an old sickle and finding it still had an edge. Their company's training ground was a large field, north of Tradon; flat and surrounded by gently sloping hills to the south, fenced pasture to the east, and the sprawling trees of the Renwood closed around them from west and north.

Drumming *thumps* bounced around the field from dozens of practice charges. Squadron One stood in a massive square, practicing thrusting their lances and shouting in unison, as if they were footmen. Across the field, Squadron Three practiced mace-wielding, where several lancers sat on wooden horses and swung maces down on the heads of the dummies that their comrades rushed up to them. That had quickly become the favorite training assignment among the men.

The men from Squadron Four were running laps around the field, while Squadron Two practiced their riding. That left Kalleb's squadron practicing lance charges in the center of the field.

As the drill masters reset the practice dummies for the next line, Kalleb spat when he saw Captain Vallant inspecting his troop, with Lieutenant Bowden beside him.

That can't be good.

Save for the five lancers waiting in a line for the next charge, the rest of the troop was dismounted with their horses picketed behind them, waiting for their turn in line. Loose grass and dust coated their trouser legs and rears where many of them had been sitting. From their grim faces, Kalleb knew Vallant was scolding them for it, along with many other things.

"Lance Corporal!" Lieutenant Bowden boomed, waving to him. His jovial smile bore a hint of relief at seeing him.

Vallant swung his mount around with his nose in the air.

Kalleb pulled his horse to a halt, with his lancers behind him, and raised his lance instead of saluting as Vallant trotted toward them.

"Afternoon, Captain," he said, trying to remain pleasant. "Is everything all right?"

"Everything is *not* all right, Lance Corporal," Vallant snapped, halting his horse in front of him. "Half of your troop was lounging in the dirt when I arrived and barely taking note of the exercises. This is unacceptable!"

Kalleb dipped his head. "I apologize, Captain, but you know the men should rest whenever they find the chance."

"*Your* troop is resting too much, and it shows."

Vallant raised an eyebrow and eyed something behind Kalleb. "What did you do to your lance?"

Zoren's face turn red, his hand trembling with the shattered remains of his lance. He opened his mouth but said nothing.

"He struck his target with his lance crouched, sir," Kalleb interjected. "I failed to order lances lowered in time. But his lance struck home."

"And a fine strike at that!" Lieutenant Bowden barked, but his smile slipped at Vallant's glare.

"He broke his lance," Vallant growled dismissively, "and left himself vulnerable and useless to his fellow lancers if they needed to charge again. If he crouches his lance again, make him run sprints." He glowered back at the men. "Lancers are dismissed. Lance Corporal, you remain."

"Yes, sir!" the lancers said in unison then guided their horses toward the picket line.

Kalleb crouched his lance and set his shoulders, preparing for a further scolding. He took the time to study the other men as his lancers walked their horses to the picket line.

Vallant's dismissive frown remained as he narrowed his eyes and watched the lancers closely, as if judging their growing distance. Lieutenant Bowden's eyebrows twitched as a light sheen of sweat ran down his forehead, staring apologetically at Kalleb.

"Kane," Vallant finally said gruffly, "Lancer Roy Parr's leg had to be removed early this morning. He will be discharged as soon as he recovers and his name struck from the company roll."

Kalleb's jaw dropped. Roy had begun trying to walk when he had last checked on him two days ago.

"I'll have another lancer assigned to your troop shortly," Vallant continued uncaringly, leaning forward in the saddle and fixing him with an intent stare. "You should remember this the next time you fail in your duty. Is that understood?"

In other words, I've lost a good lancer and am going to be saddled with another of yours.

"Yes, sir," Kalleb replied, defeated.

Captain Vallant smiled, smugly satisfied, and gathered up his horse's reins. "Excellent! Back to your troop's training. I expect better results. I expect . . ." His brow wrinkled as he looked past Kalleb, confused. "Who's that?"

Kalleb tried to look over his shoulder, but his back protested. He took care with his lance and gently turned Cloud around, despite the horse pulling against his bridle in protest.

Two men on horseback were riding through the field toward them. One was a Renald man-at-arms, standing out among the training lancers in his shining breastplate over his green and black uniform, his silver helm with a black plume, and his arming sword on his hip.

Lancers pointed and gawked at the man leading the soldier. His black suit was unfit for horseback riding, and his straight back posture in the saddle marked him as a gentleman. He was an older man, with thinning, honey-colored hair, who held his hooked nose in the air while surveying the field. He turned this way and that, studying each man he passed.

"He seems lost," Lieutenant Bowden pointed out.

No, Kalleb thought, *he's hunting for someone.*

As if the man had heard him, the gent suddenly sat forward in his saddle, his gaze fixed on them. He kicked his horse, catching the man-at-arms off guard when his horse sprang toward them, and then they both galloped up to them.

"Good evening, gentlemen," the gent greeted with, a proper accent with every word. "Could either of you point me in the direction of Squadron Five?"

Kalleb shifted in his saddle and shared a questioning look with Bowden.

Vallant sat taller in his saddle. "I am Captain Vallant, commander of this company. What business do you have with one of my squadrons, sir?"

"Ah! Pardon me, Captain, allow me to introduce myself. I am Mister Vidont Luttrell, an assistant to her Ladyship, Lady Governor Renald. I do not have business with the entire squadron. Rather, I am under orders from my lady to find Mister Kalleb Kane. I understand he is a junior officer in that squadron."

Kalleb sat, dumbstruck. *Amanda's sent for me? Why now?*

After the incident on the ferry, he had worried this would happen, but nothing had come of it. Then, as the days turned to weeks, his fears had faded.

Captain Vallant's jaw hung open. "Forgive me, but how could one of my most junior officers be of interest to our Lady Governor? Has he committed an offense?"

The leather of Kalleb's reins dug into his palms. He set his jaw, refusing to give Vallant the satisfaction of a glance. The arrogant ass's voice had dripped with hope when he had asked the second question.

"No," Mr. Luttrell replied. "I am simply on an errand to locate Mister Kane. Please, point him out."

"I am Kalleb Kane," Kalleb interjected. He knew Vallant was probably sneering at him, but he enjoyed cutting him off before he could speak.

"Ah!" The gent's eyes lit up when he turned to him. "Mister Kane, Her Ladyship is currently hosting a picnic with several guest and requests you join her."

The hairs on the back of his neck stood up, and the sweat on his face suddenly felt cold. His lance shook as his hand trembled. He had interrupted Vallant for sport, only now realizing he had charged off a cliff.

"I . . . can't."

"Her Ladyship is waiting," Vidont bullied through, "and it would be rude to prolong it further. Please, collect your things and follow me."

Between going with Vidont or remaining with Captain Vallant, Kalleb chose the first. He trotted Cloud over to the lance rack and dismounted without a look at his commander. He racked his lance then his helmet. Raking his fingers through his damp hair, he then saw Ian and Trevor walking toward him. He fixed them with an intense look and shook his head, making them stop in their tracks. Rumors were bound to spread, but he didn't intend to start them.

"I expect you to be on your best behavior, Lance Corporal!" Vallant warned. "If I hear you dishonored Her Ladyship or the company's good name in any way, I will drum you out of the Storm Cavalry!"

Galloping hooves marked the captain's departure.

I'm sure you look for that every day.

Kalleb took off his padded, gambeson jerkin and left it on the ground beside the lance rack. He straightened his uniform the best he could before remounting, but there was no chance of removing the wrinkles and sweat stains under his arms after practicing charges all morning.

"I'm afraid this is the best I can do," he told Vidont.

Vidont sniffed deeply, his nostrils flaring, and frowned, disapprovingly looking Kalleb up and down.

"Very well." Vidont wheeled his horse around. "Please, this way."

Kalleb felt the eyes of his troop boring into his back as he trailed behind Vidont and the man-at-arms. Lancers from other troops gawked at them, nodding and whispering too low for him to make out. Being lancers, he could guess there would be a hundred stories as to why he was being escorted off the practice grounds by the time they got to wherever he was being led.

Vidont turned them south, leaving the practice field, and then they galloped over two of the gentle, sloping hills. The charging hooves thumping became distant behind them.

As they crested another hill, the top of a large, gold and burgundy striped tent, open to the air, with streamers flapping in the breeze, on and around its posts, came into view. Ten Renald men-at-arms stood guard around the tent, armed merely with swords. Their horses, along with the horses of the servants who scurried around the tent, were picketed a short distance away.

A group of Storm Cavalry lancers patrolling around the picnic broke off to meet them. Vidont raised his hand upon seeing them, and they formed an escort around them as they trotted into the picnic.

Kalleb caught the laughter of women and giggling of girls growing louder as they approached.

"Come on, Sofie!" a woman yelled. "You have to catch one!"

"No, she can't!" A girl laughed, followed by a mass of playful squeals.

A group of girls, from six-year-olds to teens, raced around a blindfolded maid flailing her arms, trying to catch one of them. The girls' white skirts tossed everywhere while they ran in circles. Their slippers kicked up grass, and the ribbons in their hair trailed behind their heads like banners. While the maid in the center tried to catch one of them, other maids formed a circle around the playing girls, laughing and keeping them from running outside the circle.

Vidont led Kalleb toward the pickets, and the lancers and soldier who had escorted them peeled away.

"This way, sir," Vidont instructed after they had picketed their horses with the others.

Kalleb's legs suddenly felt stiff with every encroaching step. His heart began to beat harder in his chest. He would see Amanda's passing eyes in his sleep at night, those mere glimpses before the carriage had rolled out of sight, and he knew for certain that she had recognized him.

He ran his hands through his hair again, straining the sweat with his fingers. Then he wiped his hands on his pants legs after feeling how damp they were and paused. He looked down at the dark outline of fingers on his pants and sneered.

Dammit! What's the matter with me?

When he looked back, Vidont was staring back at him, waiting beside the tent with a raised eyebrow and giving him a queer look.

"Sorry," Kalleb said hesitantly and tried to act like he was fussing over his uniform again. He made a show of straightening his jacket and collar as he approached.

At least I shaved. He had shaved the beard he had grown between Vorge Township and Tradon after he had arrived.

Vidont raised his hand and gave Kalleb a pointed look to remain outside the tent. Kalleb's eyes watered from the heavy, mixed scent of jasmine, lilac, and honeysuckle when a breeze blew the potent wave of perfumes from under the tent.

"Pardon me, Your Ladyship," Vidont announced loudly upon entering.

"Vidont!"

Kalleb felt a chill at hearing Amanda's cheerful voice.

"Welcome back," Amanda continued. "Were you able to return with our special guest?"

"Yes, My Lady," Vidont replied, pulling back the tent canvas.

Kalleb slowly entered the tent. He kept his head up and stopped himself from clenching his fists so they wouldn't shake.

Amanda sat on the blanket-covered ground, surrounded by seven other ladies forming a half circle so they could sip their tea and watch the little girls play tag. Her dress's white skirts were smoothed over her legs. The sleeveless dress was modest and didn't cling to her figure or have a low neckline, but Kalleb eyes didn't wander.

When her blue eyes lit up under the brim of her white bonnet, his chest tightened the instant their eyes met. Her smiling lips danced around the edge of her porcelain teacup.

Kalleb jumped when Vidont cleared his throat. He realized he had frozen when he had seen her.

As the women around her started giggling, he lowered his head and tentatively made his way around the skirts of the other ladies. They each wore a variant of light cream, gold, and white dresses, with white bonnets laced with gold ribbon. He figured they all dressed the same to imitate Amanda. When they had been younger, visiting aristo girls to Daincliff would dress the same as her to befriend her.

Kalleb clicked his bootheels together and snapped to attention in front of Amanda. "Lance Corporal Kalleb Kane, of His Majesty's Storm Cavalry, reporting as requested . . ." He paused. *How do I address her again? Your Highness? My Lady? Your Ladyship?*

Once again, his years of imprisonment had ebbed away another memory from his former life. It had taken him years to learn how aristos liked to be address. In most cases, he wouldn't give a damn. Amanda was the exception.

Damn it all!

He dropped to a knee and bowed his head. "Your Highness."

The tent fell silent. Kalleb stared down at his boot. Sweat ran down his back, and he resisted a chill as the quiet seconds dragged by.

The ladies then burst into giggles, and he felt his cheeks warm.

"You needn't stand on ceremony, Mister Kane," Amanda said. "And we mustn't tease him, Ladies. Mister Kane is an old friend who has been away south, training lancer recruits in Alenice. He recently decided to return and grace our recruits here in Tradon with his skills."

The ladies' approving hums around him made his heart feel even heavier in his chest.

Kalleb frowned. *Please, don't lie for me.*

"You can raise your head, Mister Kane," Amanda said. "It has been far too long. How many years has it been?"

Kalleb swallowed his pride and did so, forcing his frown away. "Five years, My Lady. The day before I rode to Haemsville."

Amanda's smile slipped, and her teacup clanged onto the small plate she held in her other hand. Several of the ladies sat up straighter, concern on their faces. Amanda then slowly set the plate and cup beside her, clattering the porcelain together.

"Yes, Haemsville." She lightly brushed her face and put on somber expression for the rest of the ladies. "Mister Kane's father led the Storm Cavalry company with my brother to Haemsville."

The ladies' eyes lit up and a few nodded and *awed* with realization.

Amanda gave him a sympathetic look. "Did you . . . make in time to . . . to . . .?" Her words died in her mouth.

Kalleb set his jaw. He had been asked countless times what he had seen that day during his first couple of years on the farm. However, he knew, from the pained look in her eye, she was only asking about one thing.

I shouldn't. He hung his head. *This really isn't the best of company.*

He glanced up, and those pleading eyes were waiting for him.

I can't lie to her.

"I saw it all," he replied, "from start to finish." He hoped she would be satisfied with that, but Amanda looked at him more intently. Kalleb sighed and tried his best to give her his most reassuring smile. "They both fought bravely . . . until the end."

Amanda clasped her trembling hands together and pressed them against her chest. She hung her head, her face covered by her bonnet. Kalleb thought he heard a faint sniff.

"Your Ladyship?" Vidont asked.

Amanda threw up her head, smiling, but her eyes were closed with faint tears hanging from their corners. "I'm fine." She nervously laughed, wiping the tears away. "I'm fine. I'm sorry, ladies. I invited all of you for a nice picnic, yet here I am, bringing up bad memories."

"You have nothing to apologize for," a lady to Amanda's right said.

"Perfectly understandable." The one to her left nodded.

"Is there anything we can do for you?" another asked.

Amanda gave them each a thankful smile. "Well, if you dears wouldn't mind, I think I need to walk a turn in the sun to collect myself."

The ladies nodded in agreement as Amanda smoothly rose to her feet.

"Mister Kane, will you kindly accompany me?"

She strolled past him, skirts swaying and swishing by, before he could respond.

"As you wish, My Lady," he grunted, pushing himself to his feet.

Amanda raised a hand to Vidont as she walked out of the tent. Kalleb avoided meeting the servant's warning stare.

He walked along behind her, his mind spinning, trying to think of something to say. "My Lady—"

Amanda smirked at him from over her shoulder. "You don't have to stand on ceremony now that we're alone, Kalleb."

"I'm not sure I have that right anymore," Kalleb said hesitantly. "Not after leaving you."

Amanda took him by the arm, ignoring the sweat, and squeezed it comfortingly. "You never have to apologize for that ever again. Least of all to me. Understand?"

Kalleb swallowed, chills running up his arm from where she held him.

She looked up at him, her eyes like pools of spring water, calling for him to dive into her.

Amanda, I wanted to be this close to you for—

He tore his eyes away from hers and buried that thought deep inside of him. She was a married woman. More than that, such thoughts belittled their long friendship.

"I understand," he finally said.

Amanda nodded and, still holding his arm, pulled him along with her. "I should have thought better than to ask you about what happened. You've suffered enough on that account."

"I managed," he lied.

"Did you? Your skin's the color of leather, and there is some white in your hair. You have aged fifteen years in five." She reluctantly snickered. "When I recognized you with that beard, I thought, *God, what have they done to you?*"

Kalleb remained firm, determined to keep a brave face. "It was a sentence of hard labor. I doubt I'd look any better with the other option."

Amanda sniffed sharply and slapped his chest. "Don't *joke* like that! I was halfway to Daincliff to petition the Minister of Justice *and* my father to intervene on your behalf when I heard they were going execute you."

"Well, that'd've been something." Kalleb gritted his teeth to prevent himself from smiling.

He didn't know much about legal stuff, or if she could have intervened, or got anyone to intervene for him.

Her father is the king, though.

Amanda gave him a dry look. "Nice to know I'm appreciated."

"You are!" Kalleb winced from how loud he was. "Thank you."

She gave him nod, but then she took on a serious look. "I still thought they sentenced you too harshly. I knew my father, and anyone else I could go to, would likely call it an act of mercy and not intervene. I considered going to your brigadiers and offering them the alternative of indenturing you to me."

Kalleb stopped, his body stiffening.

His pa's words echoed in his head. *"No Kane man would ever become indentured."*

They were thought of as Slave-debtors in Kanestown while Kalleb had been growing up. People who couldn't pay off their debts and chose to contract themselves to work for whoever held their contract until their debt was paid. A rarity nowadays and more fit for people from the Daincliff's South End.

"You didn't?" he asked. Kalleb wasn't sure what bothered him more—being indentured or Amanda asking the brigadiers, including his grandpa, to indenture him.

Amanda nudged him with her elbow. "It's good to see you still have that Kane pride. That's the reason I didn't do it. I knew you would put on a strong face and say you were grateful, but you would hate it all the same."

"I could never hate you."

"You would never *say* it but, deep down, you would."

Kalleb snickered. "That'd be a shame. You're the only friend I have left. If I hated you, I'd be shit out of luck." He sucked in air through his teeth and timidly glanced at her.

Amanda cupped her hands against her mouth and laughed. "*There* he is! The honest Kane boy I grew up with. I was starting to worry they worked him out of you."

"I did have to learn to watch my *honest* mouth more over the past five years." Kalleb grimaced, mostly at himself.

"I doubt that." Amanda snickered and folded her arms, looking him up and down. "Does it feel any different? Being a lancer again?"

Kalleb looked over his wrinkled, saddle-ridden uniform then thumbed the lance pin on his collar. "I do my duty and carry out my orders. It feels like home, but . . . not. Everyone knows who I am, knows what I've done.

I see the looks and hear them talk about me behind my back. My own captain despises me, by the way."

Amanda's face ebbed from a concerned frown to pity. "Why did you agree to this, then?"

Kalleb swallowed. He had thought the same question late at night, particularly after Vallant had issued orders targeting his troop. However, he would close his eyes, remember the farm, and knew this was paradise compared to that. There was also another reason . . .

"I am a Kane," he replied. "And the Storm Cavalry is my family. No matter what, I serve and love my family."

Amanda smiled in agreement. "Family is the most important thing in this world." She turned and watched the game of tag.

A girl around nine or ten was now blindfolded and running in circles with her arms outstretched in front of her. She screamed and laughed with the other girls and the few maids running around her.

Seeing Amanda happily watch the girls chase each other reminded him of something.

"Did I hear right that you have a girl now?" he asked.

"Hmm . . .?" At first, Amanda raised an eyebrow. Then her face lit up. She lifted her chin and stood straighter, her eyes sparking. "Yes. Andrea is nine months old now. And oh!" She softly laughed. "She's a handful! I guarantee she will learn to run before she walks." She shook her head then watched the game of tag for a moment longer.

Kalleb remembered how excited she had been when pregnant with her first child and how her moods had swung between moody and anxious.

She seems to have taken it well. Though, it was hard for him to see her as a parent. Probably from growing up with her.

"Oh!" Amanda clapped her hands together. "Since you're going to be stationed here for a while, you can teach Maxemon to ride!"

Kalleb reeled back. "Your son?"

"Mmhmm . . ." She nodded. "He's turning five soon and needs to know how to ride a horse. Julian says he never learned, but I think he decided he *wouldn't* because he prefers to travel by carriage everywhere. So, I'm going to make sure my son doesn't take after him on that. Can you please teach him?"

"I . . ." He stopped before denying her.

When they had been younger, it had been hard to say no to her. Being the princess, she could get anything she wanted, and she could be persuasive when she wanted to be. Kalleb's current standing was also undeniable.

"Amanda, I'm just a lance corporal now," he explained, "and stuck with the greenest company to boot. I don't think I'm going to have the time—"

"Of course you can!" Amanda waved her hand dismissively. "I'll send the request to your brother and have him order your captain to give you the time." She giggled with a hint of maniacal glee.

Kalleb sighed. "I don't think . . . it's a good idea to let *me* teach him."

Amanda's smile slipped, and she fixed him with an intent stare. "Kalleb Kane, you cannot hide yourself away. I *refuse* to allow you to live in shame, understand me!"

He swallowed and wilted under her glare. "Yes, ma'am!"

Amanda gave him a snap nod. "Good. You will instruct my son how to properly ride, and that's the end of it. Understood?"

Kalleb straightened to attention. "Yes, ma'am!"

Amanda stared back at him. Her nose wrinkled, and her mouth tightened, struggling against her lips curling. She trembled until she snorted then burst into laughter.

Kalleb remained standing at attention but smiled as she laughed. She had laughed the first time that he had snapped to attention in front of her, too. Something else that remained the same.

Amanda pushed against his chest, forcing him to step back and catch himself. "All right, enough of that," she said, breathing deeply to stop laughing. "So, you will teach my son?"

"If you order it," he surrendered.

"Excellent!" Amanda took him by the arm again to continue their walk. "It's only natural, of course. Your father taught me how to ride. Now you, his son, can teach my son to ride. It's all perfectly poetic."

"Perfectly."

Best to just agree.

"And you really mustn't let being a lance corporal get you down, Kalleb."

"Mmhmm . . ." He felt a lecture coming on, so he just nodded and let her talk.

"You're a natural, experienced officer with a good name." She shrugged. "Even though you were imprisoned, any reasonable person would understand your reasons. You just need someone to look after you."

"Mmhmm . . ." Kalleb wasn't paying attention, catching the hint in her voice saying she expected him to respond. Instead, he scanned the horizon, taking in the rolling grassland and the breeze bending the tall grass stocks in flowing waves. A glint to the south caught his eye, but he couldn't make it out.

"It's time for you to marry," Amanda continued.

"Mm—"

Kalleb stopped short and snapped around to face her. Her sideways glance and mischievous grin made the hairs on the back of his neck stand up.

"Oh no!" he shouted, shaking his head furiously. "We're not starting this again!"

Amanda had always been a secret matchmaker. She keenly noted who was courting who when they had been kids, and it had gotten worse when she had married by actively taking a hand to introduce couples.

Kalleb had been her special project. He remembered her introducing countless young women to him, both in Daincliff and while he was first stationed in Tradon. His patrol duties then became his saving grace.

"*And*"—Amanda grinned, not taking the hint—"I just so happen to have brought someone with me on the picnic who would be perfect."

Kalleb groaned.

"Don't start that." She slapped his arm. "You haven't even met the girl."

"I'm thirty, Amanda. I can't be courting a girl."

Amanda rolled her eyes. "Jessica's not *that* young. She just turned twenty-three."

"That's still young. And a thirty-year-old lance corporal can't court ladies. That's stupid."

"Didn't I tell you to get over being a lance corporal?" she hissed. "Besides, she's not a lady. She's a daughter to an upcoming banker who I'm entering into a very lucrative talks with, and a very sweet young woman."

Kalleb frowned. "You wouldn't be trying to us me in your aristo dealings, would you?"

Amanda pulled away from him and gave him a hurt look. "You should know me better than that, Kalleb."

He winced. "Sorry. Who is she, then?"

I just have to meet her and be polite. Then get back to my company as quickly as I can. Crap. That means I have to go back to Vallant. He wanted to wring his fingers through his hair to get the frustration out but held it in.

"She's the second one on the left." Amanda pointed back at the tent. "I was planning to introduce you earlier, but . . . Well, it wasn't the right time."

Kalleb hesitantly looked, trying not to draw attention to them while searching for the woman in question. Despite the distance, he found the slender young woman still sitting on the blanket and watching the ongoing game of tag. She wore a cream-colored dress with a wide belt, which wrapped tightly around her waist. The distance obscured her face, but the hint of pale skin and midnight hair caught his eye, and his shoulders tensed. He was certain she bore a resemblance to Amanda.

He had admitted that he loved her when they had been young, on his enlistment day into the Storm Cavalry. He had gone to show her himself in uniform and became so overcome with emotion that he had declared his love as soon as he had seen her. She had smiled and told him that she understood, but she didn't feel the same. Afterward, most of the women whom she would introduce him to bore a resemblance to her in some way.

Kalleb glanced down at his boots and shuffled his feet in the grass. "I'm sure she's nice."

"Julian has sent someone for me," Amanda said abruptly.

Kalleb's ears twitched at the sound of hooves, and he shot his head up. Five Renald men-at-arms rode hard up to the tent, skidding their horses to a halt. The leading soldier leapt off his horse and rushed to Vidont.

"That's not good," Kalleb said under his breath.

Amanda was already moving. The maids were collecting the girls together, and Amanda strode right through them. As Kalleb followed, he spotted the lancers, who had been patrolling the area, were riding in, as well.

"Vidont!" Amanda called. "What's happened?"

Vidont turned from the soldier, clutching a folded letter. His face was pale, and his hands shook as he held out the letter to her.

Amanda snatched the letter away from him then quickly unfolded it.

Kalleb kept a careful distance, making sure not to stand too close for her servants, guests, and the men-at-arms, as he watched her read the note.

At first, Amanda's eyes smoothly ran across the page then stopped and widened. Her mouth dropped open. Her entire body tensed, and the paper crumpled in her grip. Her pupils frantically flickered, as if reading whatever it was all over again. She looked up and glanced at everyone staring at her in turn.

"My father . . ." She stopped as her throat clenched. Then she dropped her hands to her sides. "The king is dead."

The ladies gasped. The men-at-arms and lancers muttered to each other.

Amanda took a few quick breaths before turning to Vidont. "We must return to Tradon," she ordered. "Everyone, prepare to leave!"

The small picnic became a flurry of activity, leaving Kalleb standing alone in the storm. Amanda had requested him, but with the news, he found himself forgotten.

The tent came down easily enough, and the children were loaded into a carriage that he hadn't seen when he had arrived. With his eyes, he followed Amanda as she took charge of every little thing, from where to stow the teacups to ordering the horses saddled, that fateful letter still clutched in her hand.

Someone clearing their throat beside him brought him out of his daze, and Kalleb turned to find Vidont standing beside him.

"Her Ladyship thanks you for your time, Lance Corporal," the gent said, "but she has pressing business to attend to. You may return to your company. Should she have need of your services again, she will send for you." With that, Vidont stepped back, clicked his heels together, and then made a sharp bow before joining the rest of the decamping.

Kalleb remained still for a while more afterward. It was awkward. For a moment, he had caught a glimpse of the old life he used to have, one he thought he would never have again. And then it was gone.

He maneuvered his way, avoiding frantic riders forming a column, to get back to the picket line. Cloud pawed at the dirt and snorted when he saw him. The animal felt something was going on and seemed eager not to be tied in one spot.

As Kalleb mounted, Amanda and a column of men-at-arms, followed by lancers, thundered south, kicking up a cloud of dust behind them. He followed the dust with his gaze for a few moments before it crested a hill. And then she was gone.

Chapter 18

27th of Andril, 1109 N.F. (e.y.)

Alindale shook his head at the lines of people shuffling past his father's closed casket. He saw a few sorrowful looks in their passing glances, but most were simply paying their respects before returning to their lives.

"Sit up, Alindale," his mother whispered from beside him. "We cannot have our subjects looking up and seeing you bent over, frowning at them."

Alindale grunted and sat back. Their gallery seats obscured most of the people below from view.

He glanced sideways, trying to see his mother's face, but it was obscured by a black veil tied to her bundled hair. The voluminous skirts of her mourning dress spilled out around her seat. Her fan, though, was noticeably absent. Alindale figured she would be sweltering under the weight of the black silk, along with the long sleeves and high neckline, lined with white lace.

"This is wrong," he said under his breath.

"It is tradition to let the people pay their respects to their former king," his mother replied.

"Not the procession." He shook his head. "We are holding the funeral too soon. Amanda has not even had the chance to get here."

"Amanda knew he was ill," his mother replied dryly. "None of us knew the extent, but we knew it was serious. If she wanted to check on him or be close, she could have come to see him." She sniffed and turned her head to wipe her nose under her veil with her handkerchief. "Besides, I sent her an invitation to the Great Spring Ball, to her *and* her mercantile husband." Her voice cracked, and then she groaned. "Why did she not come? It has been so long since I have seen my grandchildren." She pushed her handkerchief back under her veil and softly sobbed.

Alindale rubbed his palms and shrunk into his seat. He then reached to comfort her, but she jerked away.

"Everything's going to be all right, Mother," he said, still trying to be comforting.

She cleared her throat and sat up straight. "Yes, dear, I know. We will all be fine . . . once this all passes."

"It is all right to cry, Mother."

"Thank you, dear," she said, taking his hand and squeezing it, "but we must show strength to the people."

But you wailed at Adam's funeral. Alindale remembered her unable to control herself, even leaving the gallery to cry next to his brother's casket.

"The people especially need to see it now." Her tone turned dark. "His Majesty being murdered in his sickbed by one of his closest friends has shocked them."

Alindale shifted in his chair. "Mother, you and I both know Lord Vanni—"

His mother slapped his leg. "Don't you dare say his name! Not here! Not now!"

Alindale leaned forward, trying to peer under her veil. "Are you sure you're all right, Mother? You've been locked in your rooms for days. You didn't even come to tell me we were having Father's funeral today. You sent *Thomas*!"

"Quiet, Alindale!" she hissed. "These galleries echo."

He frowned and jerked away.

You can at least cry for Father like you cried for Adam.

He glanced over the gallery railing and at the casket below. The light of the cathedral's long candles reflected the people's somber faces off the bright varnish of the casket's cherry wood. Alindale's eyes began to mist at the sight of the Sunrise banner where his father's face should have been.

"The casket should be open," he said, his cheeks trembling. He took a deep breath and sat back, pulling his head back to stop any tears from falling. "Why is the casket closed? He was shut away for so long. It needs to be . . ." He ground his teeth together and rubbed his eyes, wiping the tears before they could fall.

It needs to be open.

His mother offered him her handkerchief, but he shook his head.

"The illness withered him in the end," she said. "He wouldn't want the people to see him like that."

I wanted to see him, Alindale thought, yet he bit his tongue.

"Pardon, Your Majesty, Your Highness," a Sunrise Guard said, "Father Finrie is asking if he can be of service again."

"We thank the father," his mother coldly replied, "but we don't require his services at this time. As we have told him, he is to focus on his priests and making sure the viewing and vigil are conducted smoothly."

"Yes, Your Majesty." The Sunrise Guard bowed then stomped away.

"We should let Father Finrie see us, Mother," Alindale said. "That's the seventh time you have sent him away."

"No need," his mother said dismissively. "I'm in no mood for religious platitudes."

"That's unfair, Mother. He only wishes to pay his respects."

"He can show the proper respect by making sure your father's funeral continues without incident. He could have shown us more respect by cleaning these galleries more thoroughly before we arrived." She bushed her sleeves and skirts.

Alindale ground dust under his boot as he spied a recently swept pile of dirt in the corner. Sheets covered the pews and seats in the gallery on the other side of the sanctuary, the formerly white linen tanned with age.

"I'm going to see Father Finrie," he said as he stood.

"You will do no such thing!" his mother furiously whispered, grabbing his wrist. "You need to remain here and let the people see you."

Alindale gently pulled his wrist away, trying not to make a scene. "Mother, no one is looking up here. Their following the line so they can pay their respects and go about their lives. I am going to see Father Finrie and stretch my legs."

"*Alindale*," she hissed warningly.

"I'll be right back, Mother."

Alindale went to the nearest Sunrise Guard lining the tight walkway behind the gallery and asked, "Where is Father Finrie?"

"He just went down the stairs, Your Highness," the guard replied, pointing down the walkway.

Alindale rushed down the back of the gallery to the stairs, where he found Father Finrie slowly taking one measured step at a time, clutching the stair's stone handrail. His robes, stained from years of wear and frayed in several places, made him appear like a beggar instead of Head of the Faith of the Last God.

"Father Finrie," Alindale called after him.

The portly elder's sincere smile came warmly. His white, curly hair reflected a golden hue from the sunlight streaming through the stained-glass windows lining the aisles below.

"Alindale," Father Finrie rumbled in his deep voice. He shuffled around and clasped his broad hands around Alindale's, looking up at him over his prominent, hooked nose. "My condolences for your loss."

"Thank you, Father," Alindale replied, stepping down to his level.

"Is there any more I can do for you or your mother?"

Alindale shook his head. "You have done plenty."

"If only that were true." Father Finrie's long face drooped as he looked over the handrail. "We've sparsely seen your family these past five years. I sent a priest when I first heard of your father's illness, but he was turned away. I should have gone myself, but"—he sadly looked at his bulk—"the thought of my old knees climbing that steep cliff and all those stairs . . . I'm afraid I failed my faith."

"You could have sent for a carriage," Alindale jokingly suggested.

"I could never have done that, Alindale." Father Finrie shook his head. "No. No, a simple man as I can't demand for carriages."

Still the same Grandfather Finrie.

Adam's nickname for the old priest leapt into Alindale's mind at his sincere humbleness. Adam had referred to the father by the name, and Father Finrie would chuckle and pat the boy's head, regardless of their mother telling him not to.

"Forgive me, Father," he said, "but I was joking."

"Oh yes . . . a joke." Father Finrie blushed, putting on his gruff smile. "I'm glad you're able to keep your spirits up. Do you remember what I asked of you five years ago?"

Alindale furled his brow. "I am . . . afraid—"

Father Finrie gripped his arm. "Grieve first. No matter what worries or troubles, you must grieve first. Then move forward."

"You do not have to worry, Father." Alindale hung his head. "I have been grieving for days."

"But did you ever move forward five years ago?"

Alindale froze.

"Do not shut yourself away this time," Father Finrie urged, gripping Alindale's shoulder.

Alindale's eyelids and chin trembled. His inner core shook, teetering on an edge. Something he had been holding in cracked, refusing to be ignored any longer.

"I didn't get to say goodbye," he gasped. "Again!"

His sight blurred, and his cheeks throbbed and burned from the flowing tears. His legs became weak, and he dropped to sit on the steps. The cold of the wood seeped through his trousers. He slumped forward, hanging his head and cupping his face with both hands, trying to muffle the sounds of his sobs and prevent anyone from seeing him. Nevertheless, he couldn't stop the tears.

Father Finrie grunted and, with a shuffle of fabric, eased himself down, holding his robes in one hand and gripping a banister with the other. The elderly priest gasped when he sat down and patted Alindale on the shoulder. "Do not be ashamed to grieve, Alindale," Father Finrie said softly, "for this is a time to grieve. As it was your father's time to die, now is your time to grieve. And after will be your time to live on."

Alindale sniffed then wiped snot on his shirt sleeve. "It wasn't my father's time to die. He was *murdered*!"

Father Finrie drew a deep breath through his nostrils. "It is written that the Last God knows our time, but there is no guarantee on the *manner* of our deaths."

Despite the father's attempt to be tactfully comforting, Alindale felt hollow.

"Forgive me, Father"—he balled his shaking hands together, but their shaking only grew worse—"but I find that lacking on the Last God's part."

Moments passed. The scraping feet of the moving procession through the cathedral's nave filled the silent void as the seconds dragged on.

Alindale's eyes lost and regained focus multiple times, following the colorful cascades from the stained-glass windows.

"Then I have failed again," Father Finrie finally said.

Alindale snapped around and found the father crying.

"The teachings of God are all I have to give to all of you," Father Finrie rumbled, tears rolling down his round cheeks. "If I can't bring any solace with it, then I am truly sorry."

The hollow feeling in Alindale's chest became heavy. He had never seen Father Finrie cry.

The old priest gently rocked back and forth with his hands in his lap, fingers interlocked. The wrinkles around his eyes and mouth from smiling drooped like melted wax. The sight flooded Alindale with guilt.

"I never . . ." He swallowed. "I never meant to hurt you."

Father Finrie forced a smile and shook his head. "You didn't hurt me, Alindale. I am called to bring the teachings to you. Should you fail to find solace in them, then the failure is mine." He patted Alindale on the arm. "I only wanted you to know God is with you. He is always with you. Grieve and believe, and you shall not be alone. You will find peace."

Alindale smiled, despite how strained his cheeks felt. "I guess I can try."

Father Finrie nodded as he dried his eyes. Alindale sniffed and did likewise. His face burned as if it were raw.

"I need to step outside," he sighed out, rising to his feet. "Get some fresh air."

"Good," Father Finrie agreed. "May I ask a favor before you go?"

"Of course."

Father Finrie frowned sourly at his bulk and rubbed his knees. "Could you help an old, fat man up, please? I'm not sure I can get up by myself."

Alindale snickered, trying not to laugh. He then knelt and took Father Finrie by the arm. Father Finrie winced, grabbed the stair banister, and set his feet. Alindale grunted and gently eased him to his feet.

"*Gah!*" Father Finrie groaned, steadying himself against the stair's railing while he wobbled to keep his balance. "It's getting to the point I can't climb one flight of stairs. Soon, I'll be confined to the ground floor of the cathedral."

Alindale chuckled as he helped him take slow steps down. "You would hate living in the castle. All the living quarters are above the second floor."

"I'll say a prayer for your knees, then."

Alindale stayed two steps ahead, letting the priest brace himself against his shoulder and the railing. He shaded his face against the Easterly Sun's light shining brightly through the stained-glass windows as they trekked down the steps.

The windows running beside the aisles told the various stages of when the Last God had saved humanity from Oblivion and brought them to a new land. With the gallery stairs being close to the main doors, only the last panes of the story threatened to blind Alindale. In one pane, a black void was threatening to swallow two groups of people; one kneeling, the other a mass of panic, anguish, and anger. In the next, the void swallows the mass group, while light surrounds the kneelers. And in the final pane, the kneeling group are on a green hill, raising their hands up to a blue sky with two suns in each top corner of the pane—one yellow and the other white.

"Thank you," Father Finrie said, breathing a sigh of relief after making the final step.

"You are welcome, Father," Alindale replied, trying to roll his shoulder without the priest noticing.

"Walk with God, Alindale, and you will never be alone." Father Finrie gave him a reverent smile and nod before walking away, down the side of the north aisle.

Alindale watched him leave, seeing some of the crowd watching him. A few bowed while a few knelt. Alindale shied away, worried about his appearance.

One of the side doors creaked open and a castle guard peeked in.

"Your Highness!" the guard exclaimed with a bow. "Is everything all right?"

"Fine," he replied, heading for the open door.

The guardsman stepped aside and returned to his post, scraping the tip of his arming sword against the cathedral's outer stone wall.

Alindale shaded his eyes against the blinding sunlight reflecting off the white stone.

"Keep the lines moving," a castle guard by the main doors urged.

Squinting, Alindale watched the people entering the cathedral with bowed heads beneath the guards' large halberds. *That's not right.*

He hesitated for a moment, the size of the crowd coming into view as he adjusted. The line stretched down the cathedral's steps and into the masses filling the square below. Their individual chatter and mingling filled the air like the waves of the ocean. Lines of city peace formed around the cathedral, funneling the giant crowd into cohesive lines before the castle guards ushered them through.

"Keep moving!"

Alindale jerked out of his daze as one of the castle guards shoved a man through the doors.

"Guard!" he shouted, drawing startled looks from both the guardsmen and the people in line, as he marched up to sternly stare up at the guardsman. "What are you doing? They are paying respects to my father; don't mistreat them!"

"I beg your pardon, Your Highness," the guardsman replied wearily over the mumbling whispers of the people in line, "but Her Majesty was explicit that we must keep the procession moving."

Alindale glared up at the guardsman. "Do not shove anyone else." That said, he turned on his heels and stormed away.

"Your Highness!" a guardsman called as he walked down the steps. "Where are you going?"

"Tell Her Majesty I shall be back!" he yelled from over his shoulder.

He walked around the cathedral to its cloister built in a space between its main body and the wall separating North End. The din of the crowd echoed between the two walls, but the city peace kept the crowd away.

He walked through carriages kept in the reserved pocket until he found Holt and Malory sitting on a bench against the cloister's wall. Both men were sleeping. Holt was leaning against the cloister's wall, breathing loudly and blowing the ends of his bushy mustache up every time he exhaled. Malory, however, sat folded in on himself, as if he had a stomachache. His arms were wrapped around his waist, and his head hung between his legs, trying to keep the sun out of his face.

Alindale smirked as he crept up on them.

"You two bored?" he yelled.

Malory sprung to his feet, only to waver and fall back down on the bench, his saber clanging against the stone. Holt groaned and loudly stretched before standing.

"Sorry you had to stay here with horses and carriages," Alindale said.

"Don't mention it, Your Highness," Malory said, scratching his head and squinting up at him. His freckles stood out on his suntanned face.

"Won't be long till you don't have to worry about us following you around everywhere," Holt replied gruffly, straightening the saber on his hip.

Alindale's smirk slipped.

I haven't even thought of the coronation. His mind had only been on his father's death and Bernold.

Malory yawned and stood back up. "Are you wanting to return to the castle, Your Highness?"

Returning to the castle did sound tempting. He could be alone and away from the worried courtiers and his mother, but not his problems.

He squinted and looked up at the sky. It was not yet midday. "What would two say to a ride outside the city?"

The men's grogginess disappeared instantly in eager Storm Cavalry fashion.

~~~

Alindale leaned against the horn of his saddle, feeling the warm westerly breeze on his face. He basked in the sunlight on from a hill a mile outside of Daincliff and let Marcie leisurely graze. He had taken a liking to the blue roan mare's easy-going attitude once Colonel Kenith had started giving him riding lessons. He trusted in her calm demeanor now, too, while he marveled at the other animal grazing on conifer shrubs scattered on the hillside.

"I have never seen a shoulder-spiked rockback before," he said, recalling the name from an old book depicting native wildlife.

The rockback chopped off the top of a small shrub with its beak, its scaly cheeks bulging as it chewed. The sun reflected off the boney nubs of its back's carapace. Alindale kept following the parallel rows of spikes down its neck to the long, curved spikes jutting out from its shoulders. *They have to be four feet long each.*

Lieutenant Holt had spotted the cow-sized beast from the road, toward Amadus's manor. Alindale had welcomed the chance to watch the strange animal and forget his troubles for a time.

"Would a lance through the side bring it down?" Malory asked Holt. "Or the head?"

Holt grunted. "Head's too small. And it would be dangerous for a horse if you got too close with those shoulder spikes and tail."
~~~

The rockback's tail gently wagged back and forth as it ate. Its nubby carapace ran all the way down the length of the tail, ending with two spikes protruding at the tip.

"What if we approached on foot?" Malory asked.

"Then it would just run you over," Holt replied dismissively.

"Why would it run *me* over?"

Holt snorted. "I'm not getting near that thing on *foot*!"

HONK!

Alindale jumped in his saddle, and Marcie jerked her head up. The rockback studied them from under its boney eye ridges. Its spiked tail hung stiff in the air. It lifted its head and sniffed sharply a few times. Then it snorted and gave them another deep-throated honk, this one halfheartedly, before returning to carving the remainder of shrub. Its tail resumed its gentle swaying.

Alindale exhaled a heavy sigh of relief and gave the Storm Cavalrymen a long look. Both men sat on edge, reaching for their sabers.

"I'm not sure if he said, '*Leave me alone*,' or '*I'd like to see you try*,'" he quipped. "Either way, I think we should leave."

The Storm Cavalrymen nodded in agreement.

Alindale gently tugged on Marcie's reins to stop her from grazing again and turned her back toward the road.

They were carefully cutting through the bushes when the sound of hoofbeats on the hard-packed road caught their attention. Holt drew his saber and kicked his horse into motion, placing himself in front of Alindale while Malory stayed by his side.

Alindale kept a tight grip on his reins until he saw the maroon-uniformed rider ahead of two burgundy-armored riders with lances.

"Your Highness!" Colonel Kenith yelled, waving his arm.

Holt sheathed his saber and turned his horse aside.

Kenith pulled sharply on his gray horse's reins, making it skid to a halt. His horse's nostrils flared, breathing hard, along with the horses of his fellows. His hair was in disarray, worry evident on his face.

"I'm glad to find you well, Your Highness," the colonel said.

Alindale felt a sinking pit grow in his stomach. "What's wrong?"

"I don't know," Kenith replied, straightening his hair. "We've been receiving strange reports. A lot of castle soldiers and city peace have been called out. I rushed to ensure your protection."

"Your pardon, Colonel," Holt said, "but we haven't heard anything—"

"I just got the reports in!" Kenith grimaced then glanced at Alindale. "His Highness requires more vigilance. Understand, Lieutenant?"

"Yes, Colonel," Holt snapped.

Alindale noticed a look pass between the two men and felt uneasy at the way Kenith sat in his saddle. He kept his reins in both hands, his back straight, and legs tense, as if he was ready to kick his horse into a gallop. The cavalrymen behind him were watching the trees and bushes lining the road in quick jerks.

There's something else.

"Sorry, Kenith," he said, "I needed to get out of the city. If there is no urgent call to return to the castle, would you please join us? We were on our way to Amadus's manor."

"No urgency, Your Highness," Kenith replied with a respectful nod. "We'll gladly join you."

"Good." Alindale pulled Marcie's reins and set her course up the road. "Ride with me, please."

They rode in silence, the smell of cedar pine filling the air, through the shade of the tall trees. Alindale watched Kenith, who watched the tree line, his eyes jumping from one tree to the next as they went by. Alindale then looked over his shoulder and saw Holt, Malory, and the other two cavalrymen doing the same.

"What are you *actually* worried about, Kenith?" he whispered, moving Marcie closer to Kenith's mount in case the colonel didn't want the others to hear.

Kenith drew himself up in his saddle and breathed deeply through his nose. "Two magistrates came to Storm Hall this morning, accompanied by two Sunrise Guards and a complement of castle soldiers."

Alindale gave him a confused look. He had never heard of such a group before.

"Did they say what they wanted?"

"They demanded to speak with the brigadiers," Kenith replied. "They stormed out after two hours, and I was ordered to report to the brigadier marshal himself. He wouldn't tell me what they wanted, but he did order me to double your guard. I was trying to gather more lancers when I heard you were riding out of the city."

"What could they have said to make the brigadier marshal believe I need more retainers?"

"Whatever it was, the last time I saw him that mad was"—Kenith's face grew grave—"five years ago."

Alindale grimaced. He wasn't the only one who remembered what they had lost at Haemsville.

"One more thing to talk with Amadus about." He kicked Marcie into a trot, and the rest quickened their pace to follow.

The road twisted as the forest thickened. Distant tweets and caws made the cavalrymen shift in their saddles and their horses snorted, feeling the tension of their riders.

Why did you have to live so far away from the city, Amadus? Alindale complained for the hundredth time.

The forest began to thin, and the road bent into a straight path uphill. The conifer trees were cut back, passed the ditches. Evenly spaced thin cypress trees lined the road up to the remnants of an iron gate at the crest of the hill. Several cypress trees were brown, and a few scattered open spaces marked where a tree used to be.

"Wait!" Kenith shouted, pulling his reins and causing his horse to neigh in protest.

Alindale grunted when he fell forward against his saddle horn from pulling Marcie to a sudden halt. The lances, armor, and sabers of his retainers behind him clattered loud enough to spook the entire forest quiet.

"What?" he gasped.

"Fresh tracks," Kenith replied, "in the dirt going through the gate. Several horses and two carriages at least, heavy-laden."

Alindale squinted at the road ahead, focusing on the crest of the hill. He blocked out the sun with his hand for a better look, but he couldn't make out any tracks. "I don't see them."

"They're there," Holt grunted.

"Lieutenant Holt, scout ahead," Kenith ordered.

"Yes, sir."

Alindale's breathing quickened the closer Holt trotted up the hill. He checked behind each cypris he passed until he almost reached the crest then dismounted. Crouching, Holt approached the crumbling brick gate posts, holding his saber to prevent any rattling.

Alindale held his breath as Holt peeked past the posts. Marcie snorted, startling him. He let out a deep breath and blushed in embarrassment, but neither Kenith nor his remaining retainer appeared to have noticed.

Holt crouched his way back to his horse then kicked it into motion once mounted. His horse's hooves threw up dirt on the way back.

"Two castle carriages and a guard wagon are outside the manor," Holt reported. "Six mounts, as well, but no sign of their riders."

Alindale turned to Kenith. "Those magistrates who came to Storm Hall this morning, did they come in carriages with riders?"

Kenith shook his head. "Only one carriage for the magistrates. The rest rode horses. They certainly didn't have a guard wagon."

"What should we do?" Holt asked.

Alindale hung his head. *What is happening?* Then he glanced at Kenith, whose stern frown pushing his blond mustache up told him he was thinking of leaving as fast as they could, but the bigger group and the guard wagon worried him.

I can't abandon Amadus, Alindale thought. *Not after everything he's tried to do for me.*

"Let's find out who they are," he said.

Malory rushed forward to join Holt at the head of their column.

The weathered, brick chimneys of Amadus's three-story manor rose into view halfway up the hill. Broken bricks lay scattered around the gate wall. The iron hinges were the only thing left of the gate itself. The grass had grown up since Alindale had last visited, and the hedges lining the manor's extended wings needed trimming.

He grimaced at the sight of the black guard wagon in front of the manor's door. One of the two castle soldiers standing in front of limestone doorway rushed inside when they rode through the gate.

"Who goes there?" the remaining soldier shouted. Three more appeared from around the carriages and spread out in the round circling the manor lawn.

"His Highness!" Kenith shouted back. "Prince Alindale Dain! What goes on here?"

They rode onto the lawn with the cavalrymen flanking Alindale and Kenith in the center.

"Magistrate business," the soldier replied. "Begging your pardon, Your Highness"—the soldier bowed to Alindale—"but we are under orders not to let anyone enter."

The soldiers scowled at the Storm Cavalrymen. A couple clutched their sword hilts.

"By whose orders can *I* not enter?" Alindale demanded.

The soldier who rushed in returned, followed by two Sunrise Guards and Lord Haemin.

"Your Highness!" Haemin said in surprise, stepping out of the manor, flanked by the Sunrise Guards. "I was of the understanding that you were attending His Majesty's vigil with Her Majesty. Why are you outside the city?"

Alindale gaped at the sight of him. "What are *you* doing here, Lord Haemin? On magistrate business?"

"An investigation into the charges of treason concern the table, Your Highness," Haemin replied.

"*Treason*?" Alindale exclaimed.

"Unhand the master!" a man from within the manor yelled.

Moments later, castle soldiers dragged out Stevens, Amadus's manservant and manor warden, who was kicking and resisting with every forced step. The long strands of the middle-aged man's combover flung about. He snarled at the soldiers holding his arms behind his back.

"Your Highness!" Stevens desperately shrieked, leaping when he saw Alindale, but the castle soldiers held firm and pulled him toward the guard wagon. "Save him, Your Highness! They think the master plotted to murder His Majesty!"

"Quiet!" one of the castle soldiers snarled.

They tossed him carelessly into the back of the guard wagon. The wagon rocked, and chains clanged from within.

Before Alindale could demand an explanation, two more castle soldiers brought out Amadus. He gasped at seeing the old man hanging limply in the soldiers' arms, his legs and feet dragged behind him.

"Amadus!" he cried, nudging Marcie froward, but Kenith grabbed his arm.

Kenith's eyebrows twitched, and Alindale followed their line of sight to the castle soldiers fanning out around them, bolstered by the two Sunrise Guards in the center. They all grimly stared back at the Storm Cavalrymen.

Alindale glared at Haemin, standing defiantly with his arms folded. "Lord Haemin," he growled, "you go too far."

"No, Your Highness," Haemin replied. "I am here under the authority of Her Majesty and the table as First Minister to uncover the whole truth behind the king's murder. And evidence has led me to this very door!" He emphatically gestured behind him as Amadus was taken to the guard wagon.

Two magistrates followed, barely giving the standoff any thought as they climbed into the coach behind the wagon.

Alindale's hands trembled. *Why? Why is this happening?*

He watched helplessly as Amadus was put in the back of the guard wagon, the scraping *clicks* of the guard wagon's lock ringing in his ears.

"Your Highness," Haemin said, making Alindale jerk, "it is my duty as First Minister to advise you to return the castle and leave this matter to the table and Her Majesty."

Alindale looked back at the wagon, searching for any sign of Amadus through the iron-barred windows.

What do I do?

"We should leave, Your Highness," Kenith whispered tensely.

Kenith's mount stomped the ground and flayed its mane at the Sunrise Guards in front of them. They were edging closer, along with the eight castle soldiers, spread out in a half circle around them. They wearily eyed the cavalrymen's lances while the cavalrymen tried to keep their horses calm and watch all the castle soldiers at once.

"Fine," Alindale said, pulling on Marcie's reins to slowly back her up, but the mare shook her head. He had to wait for Kenith to back up his mount before he could wheel Marcie around. Holt and Malory joined them at their sides while the cavalrymen that Kenith had brought watched the castle soldiers as they made their way back toward the manor gate.

Mother, he thought. *Mother can put a stop to this.*

The sound of rushing hoofbeats made them stop before they had reached the gate. The sun glared off the armor of another Sunrise Guard leading a column of ten more castle soldiers behind him. They peeled off to the left and right, blocking their way.

What now?

"Colonel Kenith Kane!" the leading Sunrise Guard shouted, pulling out a roll of parchment from his belt. "By order of Her Majesty, I have a warrant for your arrest!"

Alindale's eye went wide as he snapped around to Kenith, whose jaw tightened as blood drained from his face. Holt and Malory moved to block the Sunrise Guard's path.

"Stand down!" the guardsman shouted, "or we shall arrest you, as well, as accomplices. Drop your lances and sabers and stand aside. Kenith Kane, drop your saber and dismount!"

Holt and Malory exchanged glances with one another then looked to Alindale. The cavalrymen behind him shifted uneasily in their saddles, their lances wavering.

Alindale turned to Kenith, who stared blankly at the guardsman with his arrest warrant.

"Your Highness!" Lord Haemin yelled.

Alindale turned in his saddle and saw Haemin walking toward them, flanked by the soldiers who he had brought with him.

"Please, stand aside," Haemin requested. "Let the Sunrise Guards do their duty. The castle soldiers can escort you back."

Alindale looked back to Kenith. The Kane glared at the guardsman holding the warrant, his pale visage gone.

"It is the Storm Cavalry's duty to protect the heirs of the throne," Kenith said, glancing to Holt and Malory, "no matter the threat."

Holt and Malory nodded, their faces grim.

"Kenith," Alindale said warningly.

Kenith took a deep breath. "Forgive me, Your Highness."

"Don't just stand there and be *surrounded*!" Amadus shrieked with his crackling voice.

Alindale snapped around in his saddle, finding the immortal clutching the guard wagon's bars, snarling at them.

"Run!" Amadus yelled.

Kenith seized Alindale's reins and yelled, "Charge!"

Holt and Malory wheeled their horses around and charged the mounted Sunrise Guard. The guardsman cursed as Holt's saber struck him before he could reach his sword. The blade slashed under the guardsman's arm, causing him to yell and fall from the saddle.

Malory's saber narrowly missed a castle soldier's head. The soldier toppled from his saddle in a failed attempt to wheel his horse around.

Kenith kicked his mount and dragged Marcie with him. Alindale yelped as Marcie lunged forward. He felt his balance pulling him backward and scrambled to grab his saddle horn. His fingernails scratched the horn's leather, finding enough purchase to pull himself up before his saddle slipped out from under him.

"Stop them!" someone yelled.

A shriek followed a *crack*.

Alindale and Kenith burst through their line and darted for the manor gate, horses and men screaming around them.

"Ride, Alindale!" Kenith yelled, tossing him his reins.

Alindale fumbled with them at first then slapped them against Marcie when he finally caught them. They sped down the hill, their horses' hooves throwing clods of dirt in the air. As they reached the trees, he glanced over his shoulder but didn't see any of the other cavalrymen behind them.

"Don't look back!" Kenith yelled, his face contorted in a twitching scowl. "We have to reach Kanestown!"

"Kanestown?" Alindale questioned.

"It's the only place I can keep you safe!"

They galloped down the winding forest road. Trees became blurs as they rushed past. Alindale's heartbeat drummed in time with the horses' gallop. The hoofbeats bounced off the trees and echoed in his ears. They were getting louder.

He glanced over his shoulder and saw four castle soldiers closing in behind them.

"They're behind us!" he yelled.

"Faster!" Kenith yelled back.

Alindale cracked Marcie's reins, but the mare was breathing hard and fell behind as Kenith began to pull away.

"Faster, Alindale!" Kenith urged. "Faster!"

Alindale kicked Marcie in the flanks, but she shook her mane, refusing to go any faster.

"She can't!"

Kenith threw a grimace back at him and to the soldiers behind them. Then he set his jaw and drew his saber. "Don't stop until you've reached Storm Hall!"

Alindale's eyes went wide, realizing what he was planning. "No, Colonel! I can't leave you, too!"

"You must!" Kenith looked back, his green eyes resolute. "For His Highness!"

Kenith pulled back on his reins. His horse reared up, neighing loudly as Alindale dashed past him.

"Ride, Lancers, ride!" Kenith roared, charging the soldiers.

Alindale turned a bend in the road before he could look back to see the result of Kenith's charge. The clanging of steel against steel and angry yelling filled the forest behind him. Then the sounds of fighting faded, and Marcie's hoofbeats filled the void the farther away they galloped.

Alindale hung his head. *I lost another friend.*

He snapped his head back at the sound of charging hooves. A lone castle soldier was closing in behind him.

No!

He had let Marcie slow, but now he kicked her back into gallop. The mare's breathing was labored. She snorted louder with each sprint, and Alindale worried how much longer she could last.

"Come on!" he urged her, leaning into the saddle and patting her neck. "We make it out of the forest and—"

Alindale's breath caught. The shoulder-spiked rockback was grazing on the saplings in a ditch row ahead of him. Its bulk blocked half the road, and its shoulder spike jutted out over the other half.

Or most of it.

Alindale thought he could see just enough space between the tip of the spike and the trees on the other side of the road. He looked over his shoulder and found the soldier bounding forward, focused on him and ignoring the rockback.

He looked back at the rockback. They were closer. Much closer.

The rockback ripped a small limb off the sapling then turned its head toward him, chewing the limb, stem and all. It shifted its weight, waving its left shoulder spike in the air.

"We can make it," Alindale said under his breath. "We can make it."

He leaned more in his saddle and aimed Marcie at the space between the spike and the trees.

HONK!

The rockback's deep bellow reverberated off the trees, and Alindale felt it deep in his chest. It lowered its head and rolled its shoulders, waving its spikes as it stuck its tail into the air. Marcie snorted and tried to pull back, but Alindale pushed her toward the gap.

"We can make it," he chanted. "We can make it! *We can make it!*"

HONK!

The rockback pivoted just as Marcie leapt through the gap. Alindale yelled and watched the shoulder spike slice through the air, missing the mare, but cutting through his pants and slicing his shin.

A piercing pain shot up his left leg. The hairs on his leg stood up as trails of warm blood ran down into his boot. He gritted his teeth, and tears formed in the corners of his eyes. He tried to reach down and see if he could stop the bleeding, but Marcie's bucking made it impossible.

"*Ah!*"

Alindale looked over his shoulder at the shriek. The soldier had tried to follow him through the gap, but the rockback now covered the entire road. The soldier's horse had refused to charge and violently veered away, throwing the soldier forward under the rockback's feet. Alindale grimaced and turned away before the hulking beast stepped on the screaming soldier, crushing him.

He slowed Marcie from a sprint to a gallop then to a trot.

"We made it," he groaned out, patting Marcie's neck then rubbing his leg. He couldn't tell how deep it was, but it stung. "We have to get back to Daincliff."

He remembered Kenith telling him to get to Storm Hall, but there was only one person who Alindale knew who could help him, and she was at the cathedral.

~~~

Alindale limped through West End's bustling Main Street. He kept his head low, trying not to draw attention to his sweaty visage and winces of pain at each step he took. His eyes, though, remained fixed on the cathedral's flying buttresses in the distance.

"Kanestown is under martial law!"

"I heard castle soldiers have seized Storm Hall!"

"The city peace is talking about closing the gates!"

Alindale ignored the frantic alarms. When he had left the forest, he had found a platoon of castle soldiers patrolling Kanestown's palisade wall,
~~~

reinforcing his only choice was to reach his mother. He had left Marcie at the West End gate. The city peace had been too distracted with the city's uproar to notice him tying up his gouged leg and limping into the crowd.

Get to the cathedral, he told himself. *Just get to the cathedral!*

He slogged through the panicked crowd, doing his best not to get caught between two groups of whispering housewives.

The crowd continued to grow the closer he got to the square. He could see its wall ahead of him, but the West End's entrance was packed with no visible way through or around it.

The funeral procession! Alindale groaned, wiping his face, sweat drenching his hands and dripping off his chin.

A shooting pain ran up his left leg. He gasped and made himself limp to the nearest building to brace himself against it. He propped his back against the wall and looked up at the cathedral looming over the square wall, so close yet unreachable.

Alindale breathed heavily through his nose and gritted his teeth. Sweat dripped from his eyebrows and into his eyes, blinding him. He clenched his eyes shut hard enough to make blood rush to his ears and deafen the sounds of the crowd for a brief second.

Move, he told himself. *She's right there! I can't stop now. Move!*

Alindale pushed off the building and limped into the densely packed crowd.

"Please, let me through," he said, ignoring the pain in his leg.

"Sorry," he said, ignoring the looks people gave him as he brushed past. "I need to get through."

The square's wall was getting closer, but the crowd thickened around its gate.

Alindale dove deeper into the crowd. He ignored people shouting at him and pushed them aside to inch ever farther. The chattering of a hundred voices filled his ears in a cacophony of noise. The compressed body odor of thousands made him want to vomit.

A sharp tug on his clothes brought him to a halt. He groaned and struggled to rip free from their grasp.

"Stand aside," he growled. "*Move!* In the name of His Majesty!"

The people around him fell silent and stared at him with stunned expressions. His clothes fell back on his body. He took a step, free of whoever had a hold of him. The crowd in front of him began to part as, little by little, he limped pass.

He blinked tears of relief as the cathedral finally came into view and limped through the crowd to its marbled steps. Upon reaching them, Alindale saw the city peace were no longer holding the people back. His heart sank at seeing not one castle guard at the cathedral's entrances.

The cathedral doors were closed. The people shut outside.

No.

Alindale began climbing the steps, dragging his left leg as the calf muscle throbbed in protest. He fell to his knees after the second step and looked down to discover he had left a trail of blood in his wake. He had lost his makeshift bandage somewhere along the way.

Got to keep moving.

Alindale turned back to the climb. The cathedral's doors looked so far away now, and blurry.

"Got to keep moving," he said out loud, on his hands and knees, climbing up the steps. "I walked up these steps hours ago . . . There can't be this many."

He climbed to the landing and dragged himself to the doors, where he flung himself, clinging onto the door handle to pull himself to his feet. He pushed, trying to open them with his last ounce of strength.

They were locked.

"No," he groaned. He pushed again, but they wouldn't budge. He hit the doors with his fist and pushed.

Nothing.

"No. No! *No!*" Alindale began hitting the doors, not even trying to open them as he wailed, "Mother! *Mother!*"

One of the doors opened, and Alindale fell through the doorway. He crumbled onto the chapel tiles and gasped. He felt like he was floating.

"Alindale?" came from a familiar, deep voice.

He tried to see who it was, but his vision was becoming blurrier.

He felt strong hands wrap around his shoulders, and then Father Finrie's concerned face came through the fog.

"Alindale," he said, "what happened?"

Alindale tried to think of a way to explain it all but only shook his head.

"Help me," he begged weakly. "Help me."

His vision distorted further, and then the world faded away.

Chapter 19

30th of Andril, 1109 N.F. (e.y.)

The air in Tory's bedroom smelled stale, like brine water after sitting in the sun for days. Despite burying her face in her pillow, the scent leaked through, but she refused to get up and open her balcony door.

Her bed's stuffing had molded perfectly to her body, as she lay curled up on her side, her arms wrapped tightly around her legs with her pillow between her knees and face, holding it tightly. The bedsheet snuggly covered her from head to toe, and the temperature was just right, comfortably warm where she nestled with a hint of coolness around her.

Tory simply felt too good to get out of bed. If she got up to let air in, she risked never returning to her peak comfort. She would also have to face another morning again.

Nina should be coming any second.

On cue, she heard her sitting room door unlock and a breakfast tray roll in.

Tory rubbed her face into her pillow, feeling the soft silk against her nose and cheeks while ignoring the faint stings in her scalp from strands of her hair catching against the mattress.

But I don't want food.

Her stomach growled, and she pulled her legs tighter. Her knees started to feel sore. Her back, as well. The shoulder she was laying on and her arm under her legs both felt numb and asleep.

Don't all of you start betraying me all at once! There's no point in getting up, so let's just stay here!

Her legs started to twitch in response, and her stomach rumbled again. Her serenity shattered.

Tory growled in frustration and slowly rolled over onto her back. As she did, her back and legs pulled her into an instinctive stretch, arching her back and stiffly shooting out her limbs in every direction, flinging her bedsheet off in the process.

A soft squeak escaped her when she flopped back down on the bed. She took a few deep breaths, hoping she could lull herself back to sleep, but it was in vain.

Her nose wrinkled from directly smelling the room's stale air, and she reluctantly blinked awake. Despite having the balcony curtains drawn, invasive rays of sunlight streaked across the bedroom ceiling.

"Great," she huffed out. "Another terrific start to another terrifically boring day."

Tory ran her fingers through her hair and found a few bed knots that she tried to gingerly untangle as she slipped out of bed. Some strands came loose simply enough, others would need the comb, but she felt little need of it.

I'm not going to see anyone but Nina today, anyway.

She dug her toes into the carpet before standing and hobbling through her bedroom toward her sitting room door, dodging a few scattered trunks on her way. They had never managed to get her fully unpacked, and with everything going on, she had decided it was best to start preparing to pack again.

As she opened the door, sunlight blazed in. Tory squeezed her eyes shut against the piercing glare and was forced to turn away. Tears formed in the corner of her eyes, and she had to rub them away, along with the crusts of sleep.

"Lady Tory!" Nina gasped from somewhere in the sitting room, the heel of her shoes thumping against the floor.

As Tory blinked her vision back, she felt her maid's comforting hand gently rub her back.

"Are you okay?"

"I'm fine, Nina," Tory reassured her, despite still wiping away the few remaining tears. "It's just very bright this morning."

"Oh, in that case, Miss, shall I close the curtains?" Nina was already moving before Tory could respond.

"No!" She waved after her as her eyes finally adjusted to take in the bright room. "No, Nina, I think it'll be fine. Besides, Harpo likes it bright and open. Has he been feed today?"

Taking in her sitting room, she saw a few of its chairs had found their way back, but there were still plenty of open spaces where furniture was clearly missing. In the center of the room, a small loveseat and two armchairs surrounded a short coffee table where Nina had set out her breakfast tray.

"Yes, Miss," Nina replied, glancing over at the pytre hawk nestled in the remains of ripped open lounge cushion that he had turned into a nest in front of the closed balcony door, with feathers, both his and the cushions, scattered about him. "He was mighty hungry this morning. I'm surprise his screeching didn't wake you."

Tory faintly smiled and shrugged. "I'm used to it. And he probably wasn't crying for being hungry as much as he's a prisoner, like the rest of us now."

Nina tensed, holding her arms to her chest. "You shouldn't talk like that, Miss," she whispered.

Tory found it undeniable, though. The morning after the ball, she had woken to find herself locked in her rooms, with Nina and Harpo, as well. Nina had informed her that Serina had ordered it, and only she and two of Serina's maids had a key to unlock the door to bring them food.

Most of what had happened at the ball was a blur after she had danced with Prince Alindale. Tory figured she was being punished for that, and ruining Serina's plans. Although, she had expected Serina to claim she had made a scene after drinking that strange liquor. She couldn't be certain, though. Serina hadn't come to scold her yet, despite it had been a couple of weeks already. That was the most worrisome thing of all.

"What's for breakfast, then?" She stifled a yawn, shuffling her way to an armchair.

"Well, today they brought—"

The door lock clicked before Nina had lifted the tray lid. Tory and Nina looked back together as the latch was slid back and the door flew open, Serina storming in with it.

She marched in, heels thumping against the carpet and skirts swaying in crisp strokes, her hair curls bouncing in time.

Serina's scorching glare made Tory swallowed hard. She felt the urge to hide behind her chair when her sister stared aghast at her.

"Why are you *not* dressed?" Serina hissed.

Tory meekly pulled back. "For what? I just woke up."

"You stupid little fool!" Serina shook her head in disgust then rubbed her temples before yelling behind her, "Get in here! There's work to be done!"

Serina's maids rushed into the room, half of them branching off and hurrying into Tory's bedroom, while the rest gathered behind their mistress. Serina, though, reached down and took Tory by the arm, jerking her to her feet, and started dragging her back toward the bedroom.

"*Ow!*" Tory hissed. "Serina! What's going on?"

Serina ignored her, pulling her along, even overcoming Tory's attempt to dig her heels into the carpet with surprising strength. She paused at the bedroom's doorway and sneered inside. The maids who had rushed in before were digging through every trunk in a near frantic frenzy.

"Why are your clothes still in your trunks?" Serina growled.

Tory winced, both from Serina's tone and her tight grip on her arm. "I was getting ready to be sent home. That's what you were planning, wasn't it?"

"You'll be lucky if that happens."

Tory was dragged into the room and thrown into the chair in front of her dresser. The dresser's mirror showed she did look quite the sight. Her hair was sticking up in more than one place, her eyelashes were flat and knotted, and there were bags under her eyes.

"Clean her up," Serina ordered the maids who weren't searching through the trunks. "Make her look presentable but also humble. Nothing bold. Same with her clothes!"

Tory's pulse quickened as the maids closed in around her. *Presentable? Who am I being presented to?*

"Serina!" she yelped as a maid picked up the hairbrush and started furiously combing. The maid forcefully tore through the few snags of hair, snapping Tory's head back. The others took their turn to torment her, as well.

One brought a towel and wash bowl to scrub her face until her cheeks and forehead felt raw. Tory gnashed her teeth as another preened and even plucked a few of her eyelashes, while the maid with the brush finished combing her hair. Last came the makeup.

"No lip rouge," Serina ordered. "She needs to look modest, as well."

Tory hardly recognized herself in the mirror when they were done. They had combed her hair until the ends curled and completely covered her bags with makeup. She almost looked prepared to attend another ball.

"This grey dress will have to do." Serina examined a dress that a pair of maids held up for her and were smoothing out a few wrinkles. "It would have been better if it had longer sleeves, but at least it appears somber. Get her in it, and hurry! They could be here any minute."

"*Who*?" Tory cried in frustration as she was hoisted from her chair and pulled behind the dressing screen in the corner of the room.

The maids stripped her of her nightgown and began fitting her into a corset and the dress. Serina watched coldly with her arms folded, as if appraising her.

"Stop yelling, Tory," Serina said softly. "A magistrate is on his way with a royal summons. Her Majesty has taken it upon herself to investigate the king's murder and"—Serina pressed her lips together tightly and glanced at the mirror for a moment with a haunting, heavy look—"there appears to be evidence that Prince Alindale was behind it."

Tory's gasp turned into a grunt when the maids tightly laced up the corset and drove the air out of her. Tears formed in the corners of her eyes.

"That's impossible!"

"Do *not* doubt Her Majesty!" Serina snapped, waving a fist, as if making a rousing speech. "She is taking this very seriously and personally. We must stand firmly behind her! It is our duty as she searches for the truth."

Tory wiggled about on her feet, trying to keep her balance as the maids slid on her leg hose.

"But, what does that have to do with me?" she asked.

"You silly girl," Serina sighed out, rubbing her temples again. "Everyone knows you were with His Highness, even after I told you *not* to talk with him. You even attended the ball with him on the very night the king was murdered. It looks suspicious."

"But we weren't *doing* anything!" Tory stumbled from the maids forcefully sliding on her slippers then winced from the tight soles squeezing her feet.

Serina let out a long, comforting hush and reached over the screen to cup Tory's face. "You didn't do anything, of course not. But that prince has been fooling us all for years. Being capable of this is just dreadful. You just need to go in front of Her Majesty and tell her the truth to prove your innocence. Just answer her questions. And I will try to be there to help."

Tory frowned, the whole prospect not sitting right with her.

You're trying to calm me *down? Why? You never cared before.*

"Lady Tory Syros!" a man from outside her sitting room announced.

Tory breathed in sharply as she snapped her head toward her open bedroom door.

"I am Magistrate Maddox Holden," the man called again, "and I bear a royal summons from Her Majesty. Are you decent enough for us to enter?"

Tory's mouth fell open, but she couldn't draw enough air to speak.

"She is almost ready, Magistrate!" Serina called. "We will be out in a moment."

Tory shook her head, starting to tremble, looking back at her sister pleadingly.

"Shh . . ." Serina shushed her again and gave her cheek one last pat. "Just tell the truth, do as I say, and everything will be all right. Okay?"

Her small smile didn't calm Tory's nerves.

She wanted to call back to her when Serina left the bedroom for the maids to finish, but again, words failed her.

I want to go home.

~~~

Tory and her escort's footsteps echoed down the castle's deserted hallways. They hadn't come across anyone since leaving her room, and Serina had ordered her entourage to remain there.

Magistrate Holden had brought two castle guards, yet despite his pleasant demeanor, Tory felt a grim presence around them. They both flanked her as they walked through the hallways, and she thought she
~~~

occasionally caught them giving her sideways glances, as if expecting her to run any second.

I feel like I'm under arrest.

The image of being led to a dark cell with cold manacles and chains on the walls and rusty iron doors flashed into her mind. Goosebumps ran up her bare arms, like prickly waves, and she began to furiously rub them until she folded and pressed them tightly around her.

"Stop that," Serina hissed from behind her. "We can't afford to look nervous. Unfold your arms."

But I am nervous!

Tory reluctantly did as she was told and stiffly pressed them against her sides, clenching her fists to stop them from fidgeting.

Magistrate Holden was the only member of her escort who looked remotely relaxed. A head taller than Tory, and younger than she had expected for a magistrate delivering a royal summons, he wore the black velvet robes of his station well and walked lightly, almost happily. He also bounced the rolled parchment with the summons in his hand like a ball.

Tory frowned at his back. *Why is he so happy?*

The distraction faded away when they reached the castle's foyer, the first place she had walked through when she had first arrived.

The trepidation of seeing those stairs leading up to the throne room hit her like a gale. Her heart started pounding in her chest, and her legs stiffened at the first step.

The guards paused when they noticed she was no longer following. However, her legs were as stiff as anchors and refused to budge.

"Is something wrong?" Magistrate Holden asked.

Tory jumped and looked up to find the magistrate already at the top of the first landing, looking down at them. The guards, however, were still on the second step, watching and waiting.

"Everything is fine," Serina replied, firmly taking Tory by the shoulders and sending a chill straight down her spine.

Serina's hot breath brushed against the back of her neck as she whispered, "Her Majesty is waiting. Stop wasting time, or it will look bad on us." She pushed her from behind, forcing Tory to either walk up the stairs or be thrown down on them. Hesitantly, Tory chose the former.

The thundering in her chest only roared louder with each step until it filled her ears and drowned out the sounds of their footsteps. Serina kept a firm hand against Tory's lower back, ensuring she kept moving. Tory's stomach rolled when the throne room's closed doors came into view, and she felt bile trying to form in the back of her throat.

I guess it was a good thing I overslept breakfast.

Her stomach rumbled in protest.

The guards stopped her before they reached the looming doors. Tory watched them, feeling cold sweat running down her back. Her legs started to feel stiff again.

The doors were flung open.

"You can't do this!" a man from within roared.

Tory clutched her hands together at the sight of guards restraining and dragging an elderly man in magistrate robes through the throne room. The man struggled fiercely, flailing against the guards' grips, his shoes scraping and squeaking against the tiles, to no avail.

"Your Majesty!" he yelled. "By the Carta, this isn't right! None of this is right!"

"Away with him!" Her Majesty shouted back. "We will deal with his contempt at a later date."

The guards dragged the poor gentleman out of the room, even as he began to cough and slump in their grasp, trailing his feet behind them, the fight clearly out of him. Tory caught sight of the poor man's sagging, sweat-drenched face. The wisps of his gray hair were in disarray, and his eyes wild.

"Lord Justice Blakwell!" Serina gasped under her breath.

Tory looked over her shoulder and found she had pressed herself against her sister without realizing. She started to shake, and her breathing became short and loud.

"I want to go home now," she said frantically, her lower lip trembling as her vision became glossy. "Serina, I want to go home."

Serina spun her around and hushed her again. "It's too late for that." Serina fished out handkerchief from somewhere and dabbed the tears pooling in the corner of Tory's eyes. "Just go in there and tell the truth." She then turned Tory around and ushered her in with the guards.

The throne room was quiet, although its galleries were full. Everyone was dressed in different shades of black. The large table for the ministers had been removed, and a testifying podium box had been erected in its place. A man stood in the box. His clothes, once fit for court, were wrinkled and worn with brown smudges ringing his trouser legs. His knuckles were white from clutching the podium's railing, and he hung his balding head.

Everyone's attention was divided between the man and Her Majesty, sitting immaculate as ever on her throne, which now sat center-forward on the royal dais in front of her husband's empty throne. Her dress was as black as night, the glossy silk sparkling, as if stars were woven in it. Her eyes were covered by a veil, but red, rouged lips were visible for all to see. She sat straight back, lightly fanning herself, facing down the man before her.

With everyone's attention so divided, no one blessedly noticed Tory being guided to a small, empty bench to the side of the room, close to the dais. The guards left her once she was seated, as did Magistrate Holden, who left to join a table filled with four other magistrates across the room.

"Magistrate Orvein," Her Majesty called, "kindly read the statement you were about to read before His Lord Justice lost his senses and rudely interrupted our inquest."

"Yes, Your Majesty." Magistrate Orvein bowed, rising from his seat. His portly belly knocked against the table's edge as he walked around in front of it, sliding a sheet of parchment with his pudgy fingers.

"This"—he held up the parchment above his wide head for everyone to see—"is a statement, written and found in the cell of one Michal Stevens, manservant to the illustrious Amadus, where he writes, '*I have failed in my service to my master and country. I should have convinced my master against this dreadful scheme. For on the night of the eleventh of Petrarium, in the year 1109 N.F. (e.y.), my master entertained a conference with his lordship, Lord Bernold Vanni; his lordship, Lord Julian Renald; members of the Enderval Brotherhood; members of the Storm Cavalry; and, alas, His Royal Highness, Prince Alindale Dane. There, I overheard them plot to bolster His Highness's esteem in the preparation of him ascending to the throne with the death of his royal father. I am ashamed of my failure to act to prevent this horrible tragedy and of all who were involved. May the Last God have mercy on my soul.*'"

The onlookers gaped at Lord Vanni, still standing with his head hung low as Magistrate Orvein slammed the parchment down on the table.

Tory wrapped her arms around her waist. *It can't be true.*

"Lord Vanni," Her Majesty spoke, breaking the silence, "you were found over my royal husband's murdered body. Do you have any response to this statement?"

Tory joined everyone else in the room as she looked at the wretched man in the podium box.

"A response?" he hoarsely replied. He slowly raised his head, and Tory covered her gasping mouth at his visage. His eyes were bloodshot, and his pale cheeks sagged. There were deep bags under his eyes, and a red rash around his neck, showed off by his jacket's unbuttoned collar. "Not a word of it is true!" He turned his scowling eyes to Magistrate Orvein. "Not even the signature on the page."

Magistrate Orvein scoffed. "Your Majesty, this statement was the last written testament of Amadus's manservant, a man named Stevens, before he sadly took his own life. It *screams* his remorse!" Magistrate Orvein emphatically gestured down at the parchment before jabbing his finger at Lord Vanni. "And it declares the guilt of *this* man and everyone involved in His Majesty's murder."

"And, how convenient it is that Stevens died in *your* custody!" Lord Vanni spat. "*And* made your case for you in the process!"

Magistrate Orvein threw up his hands. "Spare us, Lord Vanni. Your guilt has been obvious since your capture. Just admit the treachery of your confederates!"

Lord Vanni slammed his fists against the podium's wooden railing and turned his blazing eyes up to Her Majesty. "My word may be worthless to you now, Your Majesty, but I swear on my life that your son did not plan, or have any part, in King Richman's death." Tears streamed down his cheeks as he shook his head. "Prince Alindale has always been an honest lad. It's impossible for him to have done such a thing! You *must* know that!"

Her Majesty remained motionless, apparently unmoved from Lord Vanni's plea.

"Guards, take Lord Vanni back to his cell," she finally said.

Lord Vanni slumped his shoulders and offered no resistance, as the old Lord Justice had, when the guards marched up to the podium and seized him. He followed their insistence and walked meekly from the room.

Tory's right leg began to furiously tremble, lightly tapping her slipper's heel against the floor tile. *Am I next?*

A firm hand squeezed her shoulder, and she looked up at Serina. Despite her soft smile, Tory found little comfort from it.

Her Majesty tapped her fan against the arm of her throne. "Steward, call Lady Tory Syros."

The steward step away from his place beside the dais and tapped his scepter against the tiles. "Lady Tory Syros, present yourself before Her Majesty's inquest." The steward pointed at the podium box with his scepter.

Tory rose hesitantly to her feet, her wobbling knees threatening to drop her back on the bench if Serina hadn't caught her. Serina took her by the arm and gently led her out to the podium.

"Just keep your head down and tell the truth," Serina whispered.

Tory found keeping her head low easy. A knot was growing in the center of her back from the thought of everyone looking at her with the same accusing looks that they had given Lord Vanni.

Once she made it to the podium, she eagerly gripped a hold of the railing for support.

"If you would allow, Your Majesty," Serina spoke, "may I be allowed by my sister's side? She is still ignorant and innocent of these proceedings, and I am afraid to leave her alone without anyone to council her."

Through her hanging bangs, Tory spied Serina curtsying and bowing her head. She dared not to look up at Her Majesty, though.

"You may remain," Her Majesty granted. "But *she* must answer for herself. You cannot answer for her."

"You are kind and gracious, Your Majesty." Serina stepped back and took a place beside the podium.

Tory took a deep breath of relief from not being left alone in the box. However, her sister looked calm, much how she had looked the first day they had been welcomed in court.

Wait. Is she acting again?

"Magistrate Holden," Her Majesty called, "proceed with the inquest."

Magistrate Holden walked around the table and bowed before Her Majesty. "Yes, Your Majesty." He then rose and addressed the rest of the court onlookers.

"As we have all heard, the statement provided by Mister Stevens reveals a sinister motive behind the recent actions of His Highness of late. According to the statement, those involved conspired not only to murder the king but also raise the prestige of Prince Alindale. Therefore, all of his actions from the time indicated in the statement must be thoroughly examined."

Tory's chest tightened as he turned his dark eyes on her.

"Lady Syros," he continued, "the date in the statement also coincides with the day you arrived in court, and you have been seen publicly with His Highness on three separate occasions since your arrival. Please, explain to Her Majesty the relationship you have with him."

Tory's heart skipped a beat, and her mouth gaped open. *My . . . what!* She flickered her eyes between the magistrate and Her Majesty, who was staring down at her. *But I already told her?*

"I don't have one," she replied hoarsely then swallowed to force moisture back into her mouth.

"Really, Lady Syros?" Magistrate Holden frowned as he began pacing, his hands folded behind his back. "You expect us to believe you have no relationship with Prince Alindale, despite accompanying him to the Spring Ball?"

"It's true!" she protested. "We have really only spoken to each other by chance."

Magistrate Holden paused to give her a speculative look and shook his head. "One meeting maybe, but *three*? Everyone should be so lucky to get so many chances."

Low rumblings of chuckles with a twitter of giggles filled the room, and Tory felt her cheeks grow hot.

"What of your first conversation?" Magistrate Holden grinned smugly, enjoying his joke. "Who introduced you to Prince Alindale?"

"No one," Tory replied.

"No one? Do you mean His Highness introduced himself to you?"

"No." Tory shook her head. "I was studying the mural on the ceiling, and he was the first person to walk up to me, and I just asked him who they were. It wasn't until he started talking that I recognized—" She gasped as the memory struck her, and she grabbed Serina's shoulder. "You remember, Serina. I talked about it at your tea party the morning after!"

Serina waved her away. "Yes, yes, I can confirm my sister's story. She described His Highness going on about the history of late kings depicted on the ceiling. Going on about things of the past was a hobby of his that we all know well.

"But, if I may interject on your logic, Magistrate." Serina smiled cleverly, and a hint of mirth dripped from her voice. "His Highness's behavior did not start to change until he was banished from court. Perhaps only then did he fully embrace the conspiracy and merely targeted my sister for that purpose, because she is still a novice to court life and showed he could drone on without her being rude and rejecting his presence."

Magistrate Holden narrowed his eyes, looking between Serina and Tory, as if weighing them. "That might explain the first meeting, Lady Serina," he replied lowly, "but what of their second meeting? Lady Tory, is it not true that you and Prince Alindale were caught secretly together in Her Majesty's gardens? Discovered by your very own sister, no less!"

Tory clutched the handrail, her eyes wide from the sudden outburst. "We weren't secretly meeting!" she protested.

"Then, why did you leave Her Majesty's party to meet him?" His shout rang in her ears while he glared up at her.

"I didn't!"

"Lie!" He pointed up at her, his eyes gleaming, as if she were a fish on a hook. "You did leave Her Majesty's party. This is a known fact!"

Tory shook her head in frustration and slammed her hand against the railing. "That's because of Harpo!"

"Harpo?" Magistrate Holden blinked rapidly, his confidence gone. "Who's Harpo?"

"He's my"—Tory paused upon noticing Serina rubbing the corners of her eyes—"my pytre hawk. He came with me from home. He was squawking in my room when you came for me, Magistrate. He was the animal my maid was trying to put in the cage."

A few scattered snickers popped up here and there, too fast for Tory to pinpoint.

Magistrate Holden's face flushed, his lips twisting, as if he had just tasted something vile. He paced away from her and cleared his throat, his composure regained by the time he turned back.

"And, how did your pytre hawk find its way into Her Majesty's gardens?"

"Because he's a rather clever pytre hawk." Tory smiled despite knowing she shouldn't. "I figured he'd be okay out of his cage, but I should have known he'd look for places like those gardens. Pytre hawks love gardens, or places with dense foliage and trees with lots of color. They like to sit in branches and wait for something small to run under them, and then they either dive or glide down on their—"

"Let's get back to the matter at hand," Magistrate Holden interrupted dryly.

Tory clenched her teeth once she realized she had just rambled on about her pet in front of the entire court. A sideways glance revealed Serina's steely-eyed glare directed at her.

"If you were after your *pytre hawk*, as you claim"—Magistrate Holden folded his arms across his chest—"how did you come to meet Prince Alindale?"

"He"—she drifted her eyes upward, trying to remember—"just appeared."

"*Just appeared?*"

"Mmhmm . . ." She nodded. "Although, I didn't know it was him at first."

"And why was that?"

"He wasn't dressed like you'd expect a prince would be." She winced apologetically up at Her Majesty. Truth or not, she could still take it as an insult to her son. "I mistook him for a gardener at first. He wore—"

"We remember how he was dressed that day," Her Majesty interrupted. "We reprimanded him for it. What interests us is what you and he were talking about, alone in our gardens."

Despite her veil, Tory knew she was glaring at her, and goosebumps ran up her arms again. She bit her lower lip to stop herself from rubbing them and remembered their brief talk. She hadn't even tried to do what Her Majesty had requested. And she likely wasn't pleased that Tory and Alindale had danced instead.

"I apologize, Your Majesty." Tory lowered her head. "I don't remember most of it. From what I can recall, it was rather casual. He asked me how I was doing. I asked how he was doing. I mentioned his clothes, and he talked about his exercises. I think he complimented me on my dress that day, and I told him about your luncheon. He seemed surprised by that. And by Serina calling the guards on him, too."

Chuckles floated around the room again.

Tory glanced through her hair for any reaction from Her Majesty, but apart from shifting her legs under her skirts, there was none.

"You mentioned His Highness was surprised by Her Majesty having a luncheon in her own gardens," Magistrate Holden said, stepping back into her view. "Do you know why?"

Tory shrugged. "I suppose he didn't know she was having one."

A sharp cackle made her jump and jerk to her right.

The people in the gallery shifted nervously as they collectively gazed at a lankly lord sitting next to one of the throne room's pillars. His long fingers were covering his mouth, and he sat with his shoulders hunched, like a child who had been caught being mischievous.

Magistrate Holden cleared his throat, drawing attention back to him.

"Lady Tory, you have testified that two of your public discussions with His Highness were mundane in nature. How do you expect us to believe that a man of Prince Alindale's station and proven intentions would escort you to the Spring Ball? A young lady, by your own testimony, he barely knows?"

"That should be obvious," Serina interjected with a dismissive wave. "She is new to court and was easily swayed by his position alone to accept his invitation."

"Lady Serina!" Her Majesty snapped. She aimed her closed fan down at her like a lightning rod, causing Serina to instantly drop her head. "We explicitly stated you may stay as comforting counsel to your sister, but *she* must answer, not you. Are we clear?"

Serina curtsied. "Yes, Your Majesty. Please, forgive me."

Her Majesty sniffed sharply before aiming her fan at Tory. "Answer our magistrate's question, Lady Tory. Why did Prince Alindale escort you to the Spring Ball? Or do you feign ignorance to that, as well?"

The instant Her Majesty pointed her fan at her, Tory's head filled with the echo of Her Majesty's words to her at the ball. *"Don't forget your station."*

She clasped her hands in front of her and rubbed sweaty palms together.

I could just lie and say he invited me earlier that day. She glanced to her sister and noted her warning glare.

"Actually," she replied timidly, "Prince Alindale didn't invite me."

Gasps and coos rose about the room. Serina and Magistrate Holden both stood, wide-eyed and surprised. Her Majesty even tilted her head and, for a brief second, pursed her lips.

"Then, how did His Highness come to escort you?" Magistrate Holden asked.

"Well"—she winced and snickered, the obvious pattern too coincidental even for her—"we kind of bumped into each other on the way and discovered we were both alone. He wasn't escorting anyone, and I"—

she hunched her shoulders and apologetically glanced at Serina—"didn't know who my sister had arranged to escort me, so I snuck out early. Being we were both without an escort, we simply went together." A nervous laugh escaped her before she could stop it.

A drawn-out pause suddenly seized the room. Magistrate Holden narrowed his dark pits for eyes at her again. Serina's face appeared to be carved from stone. Her eyes, though, glared with a flame that made Tory shake. The rest of the onlookers looked at her as if she was a mythical beast. Her ears twitched from the soft sound of restrained snickering.

"Steward," Her Majesty called, breaking the stillness, "who was scheduled to escort Lady Tory to the ball?"

The elderly man stepped up to the dais and lowered his head as he replied, "Magistrate Holden, Your Majesty."

Tory's eyes flew open wide, taking in the magistrate in a new light. "*You?*" she squeaked, pointing at him.

"*Ha!*"

The sharp, laughing bark made Tory snap around again, but this time the disturbing lord was nowhere to be seen. The outburst opened the floodgates, though, as more chuckles and murmurs erupted around the room.

"Silence!" Her Majesty roared, springing from her throne. She slapped her fan against the throne's armrest and scowled the onlookers into silence.

The gale in Tory's head, though, refused to calm. *If he was supposed to take me to the ball, then . . .*

With trepidation, she turned to Serina. Her sister dipped her head, hiding her face under her curls, but her shoulders were shaking as she held her arms stiffly against her side, gripping her skirts tightly in her fists.

He's one of her friends.

She spied the ladies grouped together in the gallery, hiding their faces behind their fans. *One of them.*

"Lady Tory!" Her Majesty snapped.

Tory's breath caught, and she yelped, "Yes, Your Majesty!" She hurriedly bowed her head.

"We will tolerate no more distractions," Her Majesty scolded. "You will answer our magistrate's questions directly from now on."

"Yes, Your Majesty," Tory replied.

"Finish this, Magistrate Holden." Her Majesty sat back on her throne, smoothing out her skirts as she lowered herself.

"Yes, Your Majesty." Magistrate Holden stepped up to the box, still scowling at her. "Lady Tory, you claim every interaction you had with Prince Alindale was innocent, but how can we believe that? We have this sworn statement stating it was Prince Alindale's intentions to act princely to pull a veil over everyone's eyes in court while he and everyone supporting him plotted their scheme. How can we be sure you, who claim to be new and simple, are not trying the same thing?"

Tory gaped. Her mind spinning. *How am I supposed to prove that? Alindale lied to them, so now I must be lying to them? That doesn't make sense!*

"Because I'm *not* lying to you!" she replied in frustration. "Nothing ever happened when Prince Alindale and I were together. You must believe me!"

Magistrate Holden's expression remained cold, unmoved.

Tory looked over the gallery and found the same disbelieving eyes staring back at her.

"But, how can we, Lady Tory?" Magistrate Holden pressed. "How can Her Majesty believe you? If we know Prince Alindale's motives were sinister, how can we trust you did not conspire with him, despite being seen together multiple times?"

Tears began to form in the corners of Tory's eyes. Her chest rose and fell as the sound of her sharp breaths filled her ears. Her mouth fell open to respond, but the only thing she could think of was the same response.

How can I convince them if they won't believe me?

She felt as if she was caught in a whirlpool with no hope but to be sucked down to the depths.

"What if she swears to it?" Serina suggested.

Tory straightened with a start.

"Swear how, Lady Serina?" Magistrate Holden asked.

"It is possible His Highness was using my novice sister to further his charade in front of the court." Serina's voice dripped with mirth again, and it gave Tory a chill. "My dear sister can swear a statement of her own, proclaiming her innocence before Her Majesty while His Highness carried out his conspiracy, using her in part to raise his prestige, as Mr. Stevens's statement said. Right, Tory?" Serina turned her smiling face up at her.

Tory swallowed hard. There was a fiery gleam in her sister's eyes, and her broad smile wasn't comforting, more akin to the one she wore when she gained something for herself.

Her ambitious smile.

Magistrate Holden turned to Her Majesty. "Would Your Majesty be satisfied with such a statement?"

Her Majesty tapped her fan against her palm in consideration. "If Lady Tory swears upon penalty that is what happened," Her Majesty replied. "But, if proof of her lying emerges, then her punishment will be the same as if her name was listed with the other conspirators."

Tory squeezed her hands together, sweat oozing between her fingers. The goosebumps on her arms were starting to burn, and the air felt so heavy around her that it was almost like being underwater. Her mind, though, continued to spin.

I simply swear and sign a piece of paper, and I go home? She frowned. *Something's not—*

"Tory?" Serina whispered. She had taken a hold of the box's railing beside her. "We are waiting, dear. Just agree to sign the statement, and I promise you will be on your way home tomorrow. Okay?"

Tory's pulse wouldn't stop racing. She desperately wanted to go home, to be away from this retched place. Then there was Serina's ambitious, hungry smile.

She started turning her words over in her head. Her frown deepened. "Are you wanting me to swear my meetings with Prince Alindale were innocent?" she asked. "Or are you wanting me to swear he was plotting something evil? I'm a little confused."

Serina dismissively waved and shook her head. "Don't overcomplicate things, dear. Her Majesty needs to know you are innocent. Say you will swear your encounters with His Highness were innocent, as he attempted to build his prestige, and you will be free."

Tory gritted her teeth. "But . . . that doesn't make sense!"

"Lady Tory," Magistrate Holden snapped, "are you willing to swear out a statement, or are you not?"

Tory threw up hands. "How? I don't even know what you want me to swear *to*! I tell you I've done nothing wrong, and you won't believe me. Now you want me to say something else!" Tears ran down her cheeks, and she tried in vain to wipe them away, but they kept flowing until she was rubbing her eyes. "It's not right."

Magistrate Holden sighed and bowed his head. "I tried, Your Majesty, but I remain unconvinced."

Tory blinked the remaining tears away and watched him join the other magistrates.

Her Majesty gazed down her, still tapping her fan in her palm. Tory thought she caught her head turn, as if looking into the gallery, but she quickly turned back.

"Since you are confused, Lady Tory, perhaps you need time to think over your choices," Her Majesty said, her voice cold, emotionless. "You are confined to the castle's tower to think on them. We still have a trial to conduct; perhaps you will come to a decision before or during it.

"Guards, take her away."

With a swish of Her Majesty's fan, castle guards began to stomp toward her.

Tory's body spasmed, frozen in place.

"Serina," she whimpered, but her sister walked away. "Serina?" She reached out for her, but a guard grabbed her by the wrist instead.

No!

The thundering crashed within her when the other guard grabbed her, as well. Her breaths came so fast that she began to pant. The image of the old magistrate being dragged from the room flashed in her head, and tears sprung from her eyes again.

"*Serina!*" she cried as they hoisted her from the podium box and began to drag her toward the doors. "I want to go home!" She tried to dig in her heels, but they skated effortless across the tiles. She wrenched her neck around to look behind her, her cheeks aching and throbbing as more tears came. "Please! I want to go home!"

But Serina didn't look back at her. Nor did any words of comfort or words of reprieve come before the throne room doors boomed shut behind her.

Chapter 20

1st of Iam, 1109 N.F. (e.y.)

Kalleb hustled through the torrential downpour, clutching his jacket's collar tightly and hunching his shoulders to keep from being completely soaked through.

It had been raining for the past night and day, and the heavy rain showed no signs of letting up with the oncoming of night.

He struggled to keep his balance on the wood planks crisscrossing the muddy lanes of their compound. One false step, and he would lose a boot to deep pools.

If this isn't important, Konner, I swear, somehow, I will find a way to fill your bed with horseshit.

Kalleb and his troop had certainly shoveled enough of it over last two days. The rain hampered their company's normal training and put their horses at too great a risk, so they were confined to barracks while Vallant found tasks for each troop to do around the compound. Neither Kalleb nor any in his troop was surprised when they had been assigned to the stables.

The awning of Drago's Saloon called to him as relief from the rain, but just beyond, he could make out the flicker of lanterns from outside the officers' quarters.

Kalleb clenched his teeth and braced himself against a gust of wind blowing water in his face. *Just a little farther.*

After finally being relieved from duty from another miserable day in the stables, the only thing he wanted was to strip out of his smelly clothes and sleep. Instead, he had found written orders from his own brother, ordering him to report to the officer's quarters as soon as he got them. He hoped the note was still dry in his uniform's inner breast pocket.

Upon reaching the door, Kalleb didn't bother with knocking. He pulled the latch and bulled on through, slamming the door closed behind him then sighing with relief from finally being out of the wet. Water dripped and ran off him, pooling on the floor around him. His hair clung to his face, and he fought the urge to shake himself dry like a dog.

"You there, Lancer!" A lieutenant who Kalleb didn't recognize came storming down the hallway, pointing at him. "You better have business here and not drying yourself off in the officers' doorway, or I'll report you to the company's commanders."

"I do, you idiot," Kalleb grumbled under his breath, shaking off more of the rain.

"What was that?" The lieutenant was closing, and his ears were sharper than Kalleb had thought.

The officer's scowl warned he was either going to throw him out or berate him for not properly respecting his superior officers. And Kalleb didn't have the patience for it.

"I have orders, Lieutenant," he said, performing a hasty salute before digging inside his jacket. "Major Kane is expecting me."

The lieutenant stopped in his tracks; his scowl replaced with confused disbelief. "Major Kane?"

Kalleb nodded, but his blood ran cold when his fingers felt wet paper. He pulled out his orders, and his heart sank at discovering they were indeed soaked through.

Hopefully, the ink didn't wash away, too.

He held the note out for the lieutenant, who quickly snatched it. The lieutenant ripped the paper while unfolding it and grimaced. He then squinted, trying to read it.

"This could be the major's signature," the lieutenant grumbled before he frowned up from the page. "A shame you couldn't have kept it dry, Lance Corporal . . .?"

Kalleb stomped his bootheels together. "Kane. Lance Corporal Kalleb Kane."

Recognition flashed in the lieutenant's eyes, and he crumpled up the orders in his fist. "Follow me."

Kalleb expected to be led up to the top floor, to his brother's quarters, or one of the operation rooms reserved for the garrison commander. Instead, the lieutenant led him farther down the hallway, never once toward the stairs.

The only difference between the officers' quarters and the regular barracks was there was less men to share space with. The building smelled the same—of wood, polished boot leather, and men's living quarters.

Turning a corner, they found two lancers standing guard by the officers' common room, their double doors strangely closed. The sight of the lancers wearing their armor instead of merely their uniforms also caught his attention.

The lieutenant ignored the guards and knocked on the door.

"Enter," Konner ordered.

The lieutenant opened one of the doors and stepped inside, leaving it slightly a jar. "Lance Corporal Kane is outside, Major," the lieutenant informed him.

"Get him in here."

The lieutenant opened the door wider and beckoned to Kalleb.

The room was originally meant as a gathering place, where the lieutenants or captains could rest and talk as men instead of officers. It had quickly become a trophy room, with various banners tacked up on the wall; some in tatters, while others were pristine. Most were from disbanded Knight Brotherhoods who had turned to banditry that this Storm Cavalry garrison had put down. Candlelight glinted and danced off suits of armor displayed beside the banners, most from the commanders of their bands or renowned outlaws.

Konner stood in the middle of the room, leaning over an oval table, with an old map pinned down on it. He wore his dress uniform, although, from the wrinkles, the jacket could use a press. Kalleb was more concerned by the serious look on his face as he stared down at the map.

He was flanked by two captains whom Kalleb recognized. On his left were Captain Galen of the Fifteenth and Captain Morsey of the Twelfth. Both men were likewise in their dress uniforms and grimly studying the map on the table. To his right was Olivar Trike, standing back from the group, with his big arms folded across his chest. He gave Kalleb a bored wave as he entered the room.

"Lance Corporal Kane," Kalleb announced, snapping to attention, "reporting as ordered."

"Return to your post, lieutenant," Konner grunted.

The lieutenant nodded and closed the door behind him.

A stillness settled after him. Kalleb wasn't sure what to expect. Any other officer, he would wait for a sneer or attempt to make him mad. Konner, though, kept running his fingers across the map, as if planning a route. A distant clock chimed, nine light gongs echoing through the wooden and plaster walls.

"It'd be a damn miserable ride, to say the least," Konner groaned, scratching his head.

"It's the only way around," Olivar grunted.

Konner sighed and glanced up. "Drop it, Kalleb," he snapped.

Kalleb frowned and wearily eyed the captains. "Sorry, Major, but I'm not sure—"

"Drop the damn ranks and get over here." He waved him toward the table then dug a hela cig from breast pocket. "The world's going to Oblivion, and we're practically on the far side of the world to do anything about it. And we're being frickin' drowned, to boot." Konner picked up a candle and lit his cig. His heavy puffing nearly blew the candle out.

Kalleb kept an eye on the captains and moved closer to the table, but their grim attention was fixed on the map. He glanced at it, but it was merely a map of the northern provinces and roads of New Hartland, from the ocean to the Tradon. Nothing important or new had been marked on it. Unless . . .

I'm missing something.

Konner coughed and waved a thick haze of hela smoke away. Dark bags ringed his eyes, and his chin and the side of his cheek had a nick from shaving.

"Well, if we're dropping ranks"—Kalleb took a deep breath to settle his nerve—"you look like crap, Konner. What's going on?"

Konner took a long drag on his cig, half of it was already ash, despite just being lit. He flicked the ashes away and snorted a cloud of yellow smoke. "Kenith's been arrested for killing the king."

Cold sweat broke out on Kalleb's forehead. He searched for any hint in Konner's eyes that he was joking or mistaken, but his brother merely puffed more on his cig until it was a mere butt.

"They'll kill him," he muttered under his breath. He wasn't sure of the circumstances, but a crime like that meant only certain death.

"There's more."

"How can there be *more*?" he asked, knots beginning to grow in his belly.

"I received orders today," Konner explained, "ordering all Storm Cavalry personnel to stand down and remain in our assigned posts. Any signs of mustering toward Daincliff will be seen as aggressive and will be met with force, under the queen's authority."

"The queen?"

"The orders didn't come from the brigadiers," Konner growled. "They came directly from the table and the queen. Even had the first minister's signature and the queen's seal on them."

"Why didn't it come from the brigadiers?" The knot in his stomach tightened. "Has something happened to them?"

Konner scowled at Olivar.

Olivar stroked his beard and snorted. "I stopped by Vorge Township a few days ago, for reasons, and there was a big ruckus going on. Some boy had ridden his horse to death outside of town, claiming Kanestown was under martial law."

"*What?*" Kalleb exclaimed.

Olivar grunted. "He said soldiers from Dain Castle have sealed the gates and won't allow anyone in or out."

"Too bad you didn't stick around to hear more," Captain Morsey grumbled, glaring at the explorer through his bushy eyebrows. The ends of his mutton chop beard shook from how tightly clenched his jaw was.

Olivar snorted. "You're lucky to hear that much. If I'd stayed around to hear more, those knights would have bottled me up with the rest of the town."

"Knights?" Kalleb straightened, startled from how things kept piling up.

"Two groups of 'em." Olivar waved a couple fingers. "Came riding in, bold as brass, and started barking orders and everything. So, I got out of there quick."

"Leaving the poor people of Vorge alone," Captain Morsey quipped.

"What was I supposed to do against two hundred of those tabard-wearing bastards?" Olivar threw his hands up. "Even *I* can't face that many of them when they're in their heavy suits and got the drop on me!"

Konner stepped between them. "The important thing is you got here to tell us. You said the last thing you saw was them cutting down trees across the road?"

Olivar nodded. "The woods were full of axes. Doubt there'll be good hunting around there for a year or two."

"More importantly"—Konner tapped Vorge Township on the map—"they cut the road off at its narrowest point on our fastest route to Kanestown."

Morsey slammed his hands on the table. "We can't let that stop us, Major! We can break through two hundred knights easily with the garrison we have."

"I'm not so sure," Kalleb said without thinking.

Morsey grunted, and the rest turned their attention to him. Kalleb simply pointed at the map.

"If they barricade the road and fortify the woods and fields around it, you'd basically be riding into a death trap. Our first charge will fall apart upon making contact, and the thick woods would prevent us from using our lances and any flanking moves we try. If there are many wearing full plate, our sabers will also be at a disadvantage."

Silence fell as the older men stared at him.

Captain Galen stroked the fine point of his gray beard, while Morsey hung his head, leaning his haunches against the table.

Konner smirked. "Good to know you still have your Kane know-how."

Kalleb smirked back, but he drifted back to the map as something began to bother him.

"Seems odd that they'd cut the road after sending us orders *not* to ride on Kanestown."

Someone sharply knocked behind him.

"Enter," Konner called.

Kalleb stood up straighter as Amanda strode into the room, her legs kicking and flaring the divided skirts of her dark green riding dress from her path. Dried mud clung to the hem of her dress, rain cloak, and shoes.

She bore a cold expression, but her eyes were clear instead of red from crying, as people would expect from someone who had lost a loved one.

She's mad.

He knew the pain of her loss but had neither the rank nor station to ask about her.

The Renald mansion had been a flurry of activity in the week after hearing of the king's death. Everyone assumed they were preparing to depart for Daincliff, but no official word had come from either Lord Renald or Amanda. Then the rains came, and everything stopped.

Kalleb realized he was not prepared to meet with her. Despite walking in the heavy rain, the scent of horse manure from the stables still lingered with him. Also, his uniform jacket was crisscrossed with wrinkles and bore its own musky odor, like moldy corn, from going unwashed for a couple of weeks.

He stepped away from the table as she approached.

"Apologies for making you wait, gentlemen," she said. "I had to speak with my husband's messenger."

She nodded at Kalleb. "Have they informed you of everything?"

Kalleb suspected they hadn't.

"I've been told my oldest brother's been arrested and two Knight Brotherhoods have cut the road between here and Kanestown," he replied. When her frown darkened, he hung his head. "My lady—"

"We don't have time for that," she stopped him, shaking her head then turning her ire on Konner. "You haven't told him *anything* yet."

Konner defensively raised his hands. "I was waiting for you to return in case something happened to His Lordship."

"My husband is fine." Amanda took a deep breath, as if trying to calm herself. When she looked up at him, her eyelids wavered warily as if she had been up for days.

"Kalleb, your other brother wasn't the only person arrested for the death of the king. They are claiming it was a plot, that your brother helped *my* brother kill my father for the throne."

The knot in Kalleb's belly grew so tight that he thought he was about to be sick. A cold sweat returned and began running down his face. His collar suddenly felt tight, and he braced himself against the table.

Royalty and nobility killing each other. This is too much.

"They have also accused my husband," Amanda said, her voice barely louder than a hush.

Kalleb snapped alert.

Amanda gripped the edge of the table, her fingernails digging into the wood as her hands and arms shook. She kept her head up and jaw clenched, her nostrils flaring. Still, there was no hint of tears in her eyes.

In that brief second, Kalleb forgot about his oldest brother, Kanestown, the knights, the accusations, even Lord Renald. All he saw was her struggling to keep her emotions within while maintaining her dignity.

"Did they . . .?" He swallowed, finding his mouth dry. "Have they accused you?"

"No," she replied coldly. "But they will. They will come after all of us, eventually. That's why we must strike first."

Kalleb frowned, confused. "What—"

"My husband has reported," she bullied on, addressing Konner and the others rather than him, "that the chief magistrate and the majority of officers in Tradon support him and me. Without my support as Lady Governor, *he* won't be arrested by anyone in this province. Nevertheless, we still must move quickly."

"How long can you keep the city gates open?" Konner asked.

"Traffic is down, because of this deluge, but once it lets up, I will have to close the gates to try to stall any correspondence to Daincliff. I suggest the companies depart before dawn, even if it's still raining."

Konner folded his arms and frowned down at the map.

"Depart?" Kalleb asked, startled.

He could tell by the way Konner studied the map that he was thinking of riding on Kanestown. The old calling from five years ago was still there, under the surface. It was also his oldest brother who had been arrested, and their mother was likely living under martial law. But this was different from five years ago. To ride against Daincliff screamed suicide.

"Konner, we know that's impossible!" he urged. "Even if we break through the knights at Vorge, who's to say they won't have more waiting down the road? And when they send word back to Daincliff, then what?"

"My men's families are still in Kanestown!" Morsey shouted. "So are yours. So are many of ours. Are you, *Kalleb Kane*, saying we should just follow orders and sit here?"

"I *didn't*!" he snapped. "And it cost me five years! Where was this understanding when *I* was dragged before the Drumhead? Or spat upon in the streets?"

Morsey recoiled, and a grave look shrouded everyone's face, while Kalleb's chin trembled from the grimace twisting his face.

"This is different," Amanda said calmly. "This involves *all* our families. And possibly, the kingdom itself."

"Desertion is desertion," Kalleb said, balling his fists and feeling the scars on his palms and the hot field sun on his back.

"Not if we pull this off," Konner interjected. "There is more than one way to reach Kanestown and Daincliff." He smirked at Olivar.

"There's a trek I know," the smug explorer announced, pressing a thick finger on the map, tracing his path. "A little ride north toward Timsburg, cut off the path through these woods, and then between the dikes at the bottom of Siegman's Success and the Northern Bog. Once around them, link up with the road to Inglworf and come down on Daincliff from the north. None of those high and mighty lords would have thought of that!"

Olivar barked a laugh and knocked on the table. His smirk drained away, though, when he looked up and remembered Amanda was with them.

"Present company excluded," he hastily said, "Your Ladyship."

"No offense taken," she replied, waving away his concerns, although Kalleb caught the hint of a smile.

He looked over the route again. On the map, it appeared possible, but he had never ridden through that country before. He doubted anyone would expect cavalry from using the route. Then he thought of something else.

"Your trek might be good for you, Olivar, but how will it fare for four companies of lancers?"

"Two companies," Konner corrected. "We can't manage to send the entire garrison in case there are spies watching us, as well as Lord Renald. We do have an idea, though, on how to get two companies out of Tradon." He nodded to Morsey.

"In the morning, the Twelfth and Eighth will muster, as if riding to the training grounds," the captain explained. "If anyone asks, we'll be doing joint exercises. The older, more experienced company showing the green boys how it's done." He chuckled at that.

"That's why you're here," Amanda cut in, catching Kalleb off guard as she rounded the table and stepped closer to him, her eyes intense. "We need someone we can trust to take command of the Eighth . . . should the need arise."

Kalleb pondered for a moment, turning her words over and over in his head. He couldn't look away, yet her meaning slowly dawned on him.

"Take command of the Eighth? Are you suggesting—"

"Kalleb," Konner cut him off, "you've served under Vallant for a couple of months now and knew the arrogant prick long before that. If he hears about the order to stand down, would he obey them or ride with us to Kanestown?"

Kalleb frowned. The answer was obvious. "He'd side with the person who gave him the fastest promotion."

"And I have no doubt my mother would be that person," Amanda said. "If not her, then Lord Haemin. We can't trust this mission to men who are not loyal."

"But I'm just a *lance corporal*," Kalleb protested.

"You're a *Kane*!" Amanda snapped back and charged up to him. "And it's time for you to get over the guilt of not making it to your father in time and start acting like one!"

Kalleb reared back on his heels. Amanda's face was a thunderclap, and her blue fire glare couldn't be argued with.

A crack of thunder roared outside, shaking the building and sending him back to that cliff overview five years ago, his pa and all his lancers crushed and broken under Téions' hooves.

"You're a natural born officer, Kalleb," Amanda continued, "despite being humiliated as you are. Use this opportunity to say, '*be damned with that ridiculous restriction*,' and take the rank that's rightfully yours!"

Olivar barked another laugh.

"Now that's a lady," he grumbled to Konner, failing miserably at trying to whisper.

Kalleb took a deep breath. "I can't promise the other officers of the Eighth will back me."

"They might if me and mine do," Morsey said. "And only if needs be."

"I'll give Vallant orders that this expedition is part of the joint training exercises," Konner said. "If he goes along with it until you reach Daincliff, he may fall in line to break the martial law without you needing to remove him."

That brought a new worry to Kalleb, one he had never thought he, or any of them, would have considered.

"Attack Daincliff with just a thousand lancers? Half of which had never been in a real fight?" He shook his head. "That's suicide! Even if we got inside the walls, we'd never seize control of any part of the city before being thrown back."

"The mission isn't to take Daincliff," Konner said. "Just cause enough panic to break the martial law in Kanestown. If word reaches them that Storm Cavalry lancers from the outside have come riding through Daincliff, the people of Kanestown will remember their Kanes, too, and start messing shit up."

"*And*," Amanda added, "free as many people as you can."

Kalleb assumed she wished they could free her brother, as he desired to free his, more than the other people. The odds, though, were still weighed against them.

"What say you, Kalleb?" Konner asked. "Are you willing to ride against orders again?"

The two brothers shared a look. Kalleb returned his brother's grim expression without blinking.

Desertion is desertion, echoed in his mind.

His calluses ground together in his palms, bubbling up the rigors of the farm again. The long days of menial labor. The hot, oppressive nights. Working like an animal for no reward, for a punishment undeserved. The constant reminder of his crime in the sneers from his fellow officers when his back was turned.

What was it all for? I didn't make it last time. And, even if we do pull this crazy plan off, what can we accomplish with only a thousand men?

The image of Kenith swinging from the gallows flashed in his mind.

"For family," he replied, setting his shoulders as his chest tightened.

Konner nodded in approval. He stood a little taller, with a cocky smile spread across his face.

"Here's your man in the Eighth, Captain Morsey," Konner said. "Your companies leave at dawn, rain or no. I'll have special orders sent to Vallant with our cover story." He hit Olivar in the arm. "Try not to get 'em lost, Trike."

Olivar snorted. "I'll do my best."

"Very well, gentlemen," Amanda said, satisfaction and confidence in her voice, "I will leave this matter in your hands. I must return to my manor and see to my children. Kalleb, please walk me out." She started for the door before he could respond.

Kalleb hesitated and looked to his brother help. Konner, though, his eyebrows raised, pointed after her. Olivar was smiling broadly, a snarky joke clearly on the tip of his tongue.

He gave a hasty salute before rushing to follow Amanda, who was already out of the room. The two lancers previously standing guard were now escorting her.

As they turned a corner, Amanda paused momentarily, allowing him to catch up.

"Thank you for agreeing with our crazy plan," she said.

"Family is at stake," he said. "That's when we all do crazy things."

"Quite."

The hallways were quiet; quieter than Kalleb remembered. He took passing glances in the rooms as they passed, but most of them were empty.

Where are the lieutenants?

None appeared as the approached the door.

Amanda stopped and pulled out gloves from her pockets. "This seems all too familiar," she said, tugging them on. "You back, members of our families in danger, and now riding off again." She laughed nervously as one glove gave her trouble. "Only, this time, you're heeding my advice and not going alone."

"As I recall, you said I shouldn't go because it was foolish to go alone," he chided back. "Not to take more people with me."

"Of course I told you to take more people with you. That's what I meant by it was foolish to go alone."

"Oh." Kalleb rolled his eyes. "Well, thanks for being more direct this time."

Their eyes met, and a few moments passed. Then a smile bloomed on her face, and he cracked, the laughter pouring out of them.

"Oh . . ." Amanda breathed deeply, regaining her composure. "I missed teasing you."

Kalleb shook his head, not sure what to say to that. He wanted her to enjoy this little moment, but his chest felt heavy, as if someone was standing on it. He couldn't keep it in.

"I might not come back this time, Amanda," he said.

Amanda drew herself up. "Don't talk like that. A doomed mindset only leads to failure."

"If they see us and close the gates, or if they're keeping all the gates closed"—he shook his head—"there's nothing we can do. And, if we make it inside, there's no guarantee any of us will make it out again."

"But you will make it in. I have faith."

"And if we do, I won't rest until I find my brother. Even if I must break into every cell in Daincliff. That's what I'm trying to tell you." He frowned, seeing only one outcome. "There's little hope of coming back from that."

Amanda took him by the hand and squeezed. The velvet cloth rubbed and pressed into his rough calluses.

"Cling to that hope," she told him. "Cling to it with all your might and don't let go. You didn't get there in time to save your father or my youngest brother. This time, you *will* get there to save your brother, and maybe even my other one." She gave his hand another firm squeeze.

The tactic and odds mounted in Kalleb's head. Like the towering cliff of Daincliff itself, disaster waited at the end of the road, and they were going to go charging off it. But Amanda's sparkling blue eyes stared up at him, confident and unafraid.

I still can't say no to you.

"Yes, Princess," he replied, forcing a smile.

She gave his hand one last squeeze before throwing her hood over her head and motioning her lancer escort toward the door. One of the lancers passed between them and stepped outside. The heavy rain drenched the man in seconds as he gazed into the darkness before waving back at her.

"Ride, Lancer," Amanda said from over her shoulder, stepping over the threshold. "For family or me, ride."

Kalleb stared at the shut door minutes after she had gone. His chest swelled again. He knew she didn't love him as he loved her, but that friendship was enough.

The image of Kenith on the gallows flashed again with the lightning, and an urge grew inside him, like the growling rumble of thunder from the storm outside. The urge to ride.

Chapter 21

9th of Iam, 1109 N.F. (e.y.)

A small draft pulled a current of air across the floor of Tory's cell, turning the wooden floorboards to ice and making them slippery in the early morning hours, forcing her to stay in the lumpy bunk of a bed. She wouldn't have cared about the bed's pungent smell, if only she could stretch out instead of sleeping with her legs curled up to keep her feet from dangling off the edge, or if it was *actually* comfortable. After all, she didn't have a busy schedule.

The Easterly Sun's morning rays shined through the small window near the ceiling. Tory could feel them on her back and knew they would soon force her up.

Another day in this humid, suffocating box.

She squeezed a lump of mattress stuffing together through its thin fabric. The temperature was already rising, the area under her was getting warmer. Soon, her hair, which was now stringy and flat, would start clinging to her face and neck.

Why couldn't it have kept raining?

She groaned in frustration and forced herself to sit up. The flimsy sack cloth blanket fell from her shoulders as she leaned against the stone wall of her cell.

Her prison cell was larger than she had imagined one would be. She had smaller quarters on a few boats back in the Isles. It was also bare and, after a day thinking about it, because she had little else to do, she realized the cell was meant to have two bunks. She only had the one, and her chamber pot.

Sensing she was up, Tory's morning necessities suddenly demanded release.

"*No!*" She grimaced and rolled her head in protest of the task ahead of her.

She kicked her skirts out so she could walk and began the frustrating process of getting out of some of her dress enough to use her chamber pot in the corner of the room. Part of her wanted to strip out of the thing and be done with it, but that would leave her only in her shift, and between being free of the dress but at the mercy of the guards was a risk she wouldn't take.

The chamber pot was no more than a bucket and bore its own humiliation. Even though she had used chamber pots all her life and learned how to use the necessities aboard ships without them, there was something disgusting about using a bucket and having to live with the stench in a closed in cell.

Tory had relieved herself and was doing up her dress the best she could when her cell door rattled with a hard knock.

"Lady Tory Syros?" a guard called.

"I'm still alive," she replied, hopping to the other corner of the room, behind the head of the bed.

She knew the routine. Two guards came to check on her every morning. They had to knock and call out because the peep slot was rusted shut. One would change out her bucket of a chamber pot, and the other would bring her what passed for breakfast for a rationed deckhand.

They wouldn't have any news for her, and she didn't want to be alone with them for any amount of time. As long as she kept quiet and out of the way, they changed things out then left. And that was how she wanted it.

Keys rattled outside against the door's iron lock. Metal scraped against metal as each tumbler was forcibly turned with a hard, tooth-grinding *click*. Tory was certain that, one morning, they would try to unlock the door and the key would break right off, leaving her trapped in the barren, dingy cell forever.

A hard *thump* shook the door, the warped wood clinging to the stone mantle.

Tory's cellmate, Lord Justice Blakwell, in the cell across from hers, had told her that the cells were in such a decrepit state because they hadn't been used in over a century. It was amazing the cells could even lock.

Another heavy *thump* burst the door in, its iron hinges screeching as the door swung around and slammed hard against the wall.

Tory covered her ears in a desperate effort to stop them from ringing.

"These cells are a disgrace," someone said from behind the guard, his voice muffled by Tory's hands and the softening ringing.

The guard stepped back, and a plump man pushed around him, hesitating from entering the cell. He surveyed the room with a grimace, his nose wrinkled, and then he waved his hand in front of his face. The silver buttons of his waistcoat strained against his girth sticking out of his suit.

Something about his round face seemed familiar, but Tory couldn't place him. She knew he had to be someone important; otherwise, how else would the guards have let him in.

The man stroked the curly remains of his chestnut hair that ringed the sides of his bald scalp then flopped a leather satchel on her bed.

"Lady Syros, I am Magistrate Orvein. I was a member of the panel at Her Majesty's inquest the day you came before her. Do you remember me?" He raised his flabby chin and cupped the collar of his waistcoat. He might have thought he was sticking his chest out, but his belly stuck out too far for that. Tory felt uneased by how his pudgy cheeks made his eyes squint as he grinned.

"Vaguely," she replied, folding her arms. "You were the magistrate asking questions when I was first brought in." Before she had been turned over to the other snake.

"Correct!" Magistrate Orvein bounced on his heels. "And I know this must be a very difficult ordeal for you. A young lady, as yourself, should never be caught up in all this."

Tory squeezed her arms, feeling goosebumps again, and tried not to rub. She narrowed her eyes at him, not believing his words of concern.

"Thank you. Does that mean I can go?"

"About that . . ." Magistrate Orvein wagged a sausage finger in the air then turned to his satchel. He pulled out a writing board and flopped it on the bed. Then came out a bottle of ink and quill. Lasty, he brought out a roll of thick parchment. "Her Majesty believes you've had sufficient time to think on the matters discussed during the inquest and your"—he glanced around the cell—"current situation. She hopes you have come to a decision and, in the interest of justice, will do the right thing." He held out the parchment to her.

Tory stared at it, as if it were a wriggling steel-jaw fish pup, held out toward her with his blade jaws snapping closed too fast for the eye to follow but making the unmistakable slicing grinding sound when their jaws came together. Then she gingerly took the parchment carefully and unrolled it.

The script had too many flourishes for Tory's liking, as if the writer wanted it to be more of a work of art, yet she could still read it.

> *I, Lady Tory Syros, doth solemnly swear before Her August Majesty, Queen Avera Dain, and the Honorable Table of Ministers, that I took no part in the conspiracy, which took the life of the king, that every encounter I had with His Highness, Prince Alindale Dain, was genuine and platonic on my part, and that I had no intention for my encounters with His Highness to be used to or further His conspiracy. This I swear and affirm through my allegiance to Her Majesty and before the Table of Ministers, the lords of the kingdom, and the laws of New Hartland.*

Tory's head spun from the legal jargon. The words ran together and were more tangled than any sailor's knot. There was also a blank line at the bottom of the page, and she suspected what it meant. She thought it best to pry, anyway.

"What is this?" she asked.

"Why, it's your proof of innocence," Magistrate Orvein replied jovially, wrapping his arms around his belly and lacing his fingers together. "This is the statement Her Majesty wished you had signed at her inquest, and we—the magistrates on her panel—did wonder why you would refuse her. One of us suggested that maybe, if you held the statement in your hands and read it yourself, you'd be eager to change your mind."

Tory tried to match his explanation with her memory of that horrible day but only grew more confused. Underneath the flowery words, she came to a detail she couldn't get around.

"Wait. I recall my *sister* asking if I could make statement, not the magistrate." She refused to say Holden's name, not unless she was free to add a few choices swear words with it. "Are you saying you had a statement prepared before that?"

Magistrate Orvein threw his hands up. "Not at all. We were merely performing our duties to establish key facts before any sort of trial could proceed. But, being authors of the law, we could have written up a statement then and there at the inquest, if only you had agreed."

"Oh." Tory supposed that made sense, being this was their profession, after all.

Looking over the statement again, she wished they could have done a better job. The wording began to bother her, though, the more she read and thought it over.

"But, while you were considering your decision to sign or not"— Magistrate Orvein took up the writing board and pulled the stopper out of the ink bottle before setting the quill in it—"we of the panel took the initiative to make the statement as clear and concise as possible that it screams your innocence."

This is clear and concise? she winced. *I'd hate to see their sloppy and confusing writing.*

Magistrate Orvein cleared his throat and held out the writing board and the quill, its end dripping with ink. "Just sign on the line, My Lady."

Tory plucked the quill from his fingers and hovered its dripping tip over the line before she paused. She kept being drawn back to the words, turning them over in her head and trying to sort them out. A still voice told her that she was being asked to say one thing while saying something else, just as she had back in the throne room.

"Before I sign, could you explain why I have to say I'm innocent while His Highness is not?" she asked.

Magistrate Orvein's left eyebrow twitched. "What?"

"Well"—she flattened the parchment on the writing board and presented it him—"I understand me saying I didn't murder His Majesty or having a part in any plot to, but saying I had no intentions to further Prince Alindale's plot sounds like I'm saying *he* did plan to kill his father. I can't *say* that. I don't even know if he *did*! It's all hard to believe."

"But you *do* know he planned it," Magistrate Orvein insisted, his cheeks shaking in frustration. "You were at the inquest. You heard me read the confession from one of the plotter's servants. Surely, that must convince you. It certainly is enough for Her Majesty and the court, which is why you must sign this statement. It's the only way we'll all know you were not involved and be assured you're innocent."

He turned the writing board back toward her and pushed it closer toward her, smiling his pudgy-cheeked smile over the top of it.

The quill shook in Tory's hand. The magistrate's insistence of her signature made the cell feel even smaller. The ink on the tip had almost dried on the end as it hovered over the blank line.

If I sign this, I go home, she told herself.

The image of the Isles bloomed in her mind—ships sailing around every horizon, the land covered with red foliage, the waves gently washing against the beaches, and the constant, warmth of the suns. Paradise.

It all faded as the memory of Alindale came to her from when she had first seen him, alone and sad.

She dropped the quill. "I can't. It still just doesn't feel right."

Magistrate Orvein's smile slid away, his jowls drooping like hanging water bags.

"Well," he sighed, yanking both the writing board and statement away. "We'd hoped that your time here would have given perspective. Without your sworn statement, it might be you will have to remain here until called to trial with the other conspirators."

The hairs on the back of Tory's neck stood up.

"Trial?" she asked weakly. "But I wasn't part of it! That servant didn't write my name down!"

Magistrate Orvein shrugged, snatched the quill from her, and put his things back in his satchel. "True. Still, we must be certain you didn't join afterward. While, in normal circumstances, we could give you more time for . . . reflection and give you another chance to sign later, I'm afraid time is of the essence." He paused to give her a squinty-eyed stare. "Perhaps, though, you don't have a full understanding of the magnitude of this conspiracy."

Tory took a step back, not liking how he was looking at her. It reminded her of a xerao homing in on its prey. They hunted more by smell than by sight, and they would angle their heads and squint to make sure they knew where their prey was before they struck.

"Guard!" Magistrate Orvein barked, closing his satchel and making Tory jump.

One of the guards entered.

"Please, escort me and Lady Syros up to the fifth floor," he said. "There is something she needs to see."

Tory was surprised when the guard simply nodded and waved to her to follow Orvein out of the cell.

She hastily put her slippers on, having to hop on one foot to set her left one correctly after mashing down the heel. Then she took a long, drawn-out breath once she was in corridor. She wasn't entirely free, but at least she was out of that cell.

Those feelings of relief didn't last long.

Once upon the spiraling staircase, she glanced over the railing to the freedom below and how brighter each lower level became. The guard shoved her forward and, as she followed behind Orvein's puffing bulk, the stairs grew darker with each step up.

The top of the stairs was encased in darkness, save for the faint glow of a candle sitting on a small table outside a closed door that was warped worse than Tory's cell door.

Orvein waddled up to the door and knocked, still taking long, gasping breaths.

The door's small spy window slid open with a piercing *shriek* of iron sheering against iron.

"Magistrate Orvein," he gasped, "of Her Majesty's Special Inquest. I'm here to join today's interrogation, with a witness."

Today's interrogation?

Tory watched with trepidation as the guard inside and the guard who had escorted them worked together to shove and heave the door open.

The wood scraped and cracked against the floor. A gust of air from the stairway whooshed around them into the black abyss inside, pulling her dress toward it. She instantly clapped a hand over her mouth and nose after catching the powerful stench of human waste and something rotting leaking out. She took a step back and pondered if it was better to make a mad dash down the stairs than take one step inside.

Orvein dragged a handkerchief from his waistcoat's pocket and covered his face. "Come along, young lady," he called, nudging her to follow. "It's time for some real education."

Tory really wanted to bolt then, but the guard reappeared and took her by the arm before she could try and escorted her in. As they dragged the door shut, cutting off the light from outside, she felt as if she was trapped in a capsized ship disappearing under the waves.

It took minutes for her eyes to adjust. A dim light winked somewhere far ahead, but it didn't help much. Her breathing felt close, as if the walls were closer than those in her cell. When she heard a deep pant, she jumped and realized the guard was standing right behind her.

"This way," Orvein's voice echoed. "Just come to the light."

A shove from behind got her moving.

As Tory walked closer, she glanced around, trying to take in as much as she could. At first, she couldn't pick out where the wall began. She assumed she was walking down another cell block, but she couldn't pick out the doors. Every now and then, a flicker of light casted strange, tall, parallel shadows, and her mind spun, trying to puzzle out what they were.

Her ear twitched at the sound of sliding bootheels against stone from her left. A chain rattled to her right. Then a harsh, wet cough shattered the silence up ahead. It went on for over a minute as she got closer, reminding her of a sailor who had caught something aboard ship. He had coughed for days down below, spitting up bile.

"Guard!"

Tory froze, and her breath caught. To her right knelt a middle-aged man clutching the bars where his cell door should have been. His hair and beard were unkempt and clung to his face. His eyes were sunken in. The remains of what looked like a uniform jacket hung open.

"My grandpa's been coughing for days," the man said. "Please, he needs medicine."

"No medicine for traitors," the guard grunted.

"We're not traitors!" the man yelled back, shaking the bars. Another wet coughing fit followed them. "Help him, damn you!"

By the Last God! Tory trembled. *That was the man leading Alindale's escort the night of the ball. These are the conspirators!*

She couldn't steady her heart now. She really was trapped under the waves, and there was no escape. Her vision adjusted. These cells didn't have warped wooden doors, but iron bars. And the reason it was so dark was because there were no windows. She heard the moans and breathing of the men, spread out down the block, and still, the guard hurriedly pushed her forward.

As she got closer to the light, she saw a small lantern hung outside a cell, facing down the block, and the only one with a wooden door. She finally reunited with Orvein.

"Finally," he grunted then knocked on the door.

This door unlatched and pulled back smoothly, without scraping or dragging against the ground, or its hinges screeching. Light shot out from inside, and Tory shielded her eyes.

"Magistrate Orvein," came a familiar voice, "Amadus is about to recover. Did Tory Syros sign the statement?"

"Apologies, First Minister," Orvein replied. "But she is still hesitant. Since time is of the essence, I thought a glimpse of what we're fighting against would help her come to the right decision."

Minister Haemin stood in the center of the room with his hands behind his back and fixed her with a weighing stare. His shirt was unlaced at the top, and his sleeves were rolled up at the elbow. Flanking him were two other magistrates.

A chill ran across Tory's shoulders at seeing Magistrate Holden on his right.

"Lady Syros, are you well?" Minister Haemin asked.

Tory stood up straighter, her teeth knocking against each other when she snapped her mouth shut. She hadn't realized it was gaping.

"Considering where I am, My Lord, no," she replied, shaking her head and nervously looking around, trying to avoid anyone's eye.

"Understandable," Minister Haemin said. "This is not a place for a lady."

A gurgling moan came from behind him.

"First Minister," someone in the back corner said, "he's reviving."

"This will be unpleasant," Minister Haemin told her. "But, if you are as innocent as you claim, this will convince you of the evil that has been lurking in the corner of our nation, and why we *cannot* allow it to keep controlling us."

He beckoned her in and, once again, Tory was given little choice as the guard behind her gently shoved her into the room. It was bare, without a single furnishing. A set of lanterns in every corner kept the room lit.

It was tighter quarters than Tory ever wanted to be in, surrounded by five strange men—that she could see—especially with Holden being one of them. She didn't want to be near him ever again. At least they kept the door open.

That tiny bit of comfort evaporated when the first minister turned away and revealed the horror hanging behind him.

An old man dangled from chains in the ceiling, his wrists scraped raw and red from the manacles. His ankles were chained to the wall behind him, keeping his feet from touching the floor. He hung, stripped to his undergarments, which barely even covered his genitals. His hair and beard were bone white and hung in strands off his gaunt face. His body was almost skin and bones, his belly sunken into his ribs, and crisscrossed with lacerations and scars.

A dark pool stretched out beneath him. Tory swallowed when realizing it was blood. Multiple pools had mingled into one. Some were still wet. It was too much blood for someone to lose and still be alive. In fact, she couldn't tell if the poor soul was breathing, and she prayed he wasn't.

Two guards nestled themselves in the back corners. They stood over the lanterns, encasing themselves in shadow. One held a whip, while the other held an arming sword with three feet of the blade streaked with blood.

Is this what I'm supposed to see? Sign or they'll hang me from the ceiling and torture me to death? This is—

The old man jerked. His head flew back in a wet, gargling gasp.

Panic gripped her. She clasped her hands to her mouth and screamed.

"Don't be afraid," Minister Haemin said, giving her a stern look. "This evil can't harm you. Or any of us. Never again." He turned back to the wretched man with contempt.

The old man started swinging in his chains, gargling even louder. Tory caught a glimpse of a hideous wound on his left breast. The long gash was bubbling, as if blood boiled under his skin, but it wasn't pouring or running out of it.

Finally, the old man heaved forward, his back hunching to the point that Tory believed it would snap. The gargling grew its loudest until he heaved and vomited a long trail of blood on the floor, adding to the pool beneath him.

"Lungs growing back," the old man coughed out in a raspy voice. "Still the worst part. What day is it?"

"Why is that *always* the first thing you say?" Minister Haemin asked in annoyance.

"*Heh,*" the old man cackled. "Because I'm hoping, one day, I'll wake up and someone will tell me it's been a hundred years, and then I'll know all of you are long gone." The old man raised his head with a big smile on his face, teeth stained red.

Tory's eyes went wide, finally recognized him.

Amadus!

The immortal eyed the room, taking in each person's face, before stopping on her.

"You're new," he said, narrowing his eyes. "Obviously, Syrosi. Name escapes me, though. What new game do you have for me today, Henri? Hoping beating a young woman in front of me will make me give up my secrets?" He snickered and hung his head. "Seen that before, too."

With her hands still pressed to her mouth, Tory's eyes danced across the room at the men surrounding her, and she began to shake.

Beat me!

"Oh, that's very clever!" Orvein said cheerfully, squeezing his bulk to maneuver around her to Holden. "He revives, sees her, and instantly says he doesn't know her while also making a shocking comment to throw us off the scent. A clever way indeed to try to pull suspicion away from an *unmasked* conspirator, eh?"

Orvein's high-pitched chuckle reminded Tory of Harpo's happy trills that he usually made after being fed.

It all came rushing together in her mind. Their impatience for her to sign the statement, locking her up, bringing her to the top of the tower to see the horrible state the other prisoners were in, and now this. They were still accusing her of being involved in killing the king.

"I'm not a conspirator!" she blurted out, unable to hide the fear in her voice.

"While we sadly only have your word for that, Lady Syros"—Minister Haemin turned his annoyed look to Orvein—"that is far *too* clever, Orvein. And too much effort for this old monster."

Orvein slumped, deflated like a child who had been told he wasn't getting a treat.

"An old monster now, am I?" Amadus cackled. "Me? Long cast from society, not those arresting and torturing the innocent?"

Minister Haemin suddenly backhanded him with a fist. Amadus's head jerked around, blood spraying out of his mouth and onto the wall. His frail body sagged and squirmed in his chains.

"You are *not* a man!" Minister Haemin roared. "Nor are you as feeble and outcast as you pretend to be." His harsh grimace made Tory step back, afraid of his glaring visage.

"Here's the truth, Lady Syros." He reached into his trouser pocket, drew out a polished, oval stone, as big as a man's hand, and the room burst into a brilliant, white light. It was smooth as polished glass and clear enough to see through. Light hung in the center, like a trapped star, throwing roving sparks crawling over its insides.

"This is from the Téionaropi," Minister Haemin explained. "Fashioned from pure crystal, they call them *astras* in their arrogant language. And they are the key to their magics."

"Wrong." Amadus snickered, shaking his head.

Minister Haemin sneered at him as he pressed the crystal against Amadus's chest.

The immortal seized, his head springing back, his body turning rigid, and then he began to spasm. The sparks within the crystal merged, focusing directly at where the crystal touched Amadus's skin. As the seizure intensified, every cut on his body began to steam, especially the gash over his left breast.

Tory's eyes widened as the wounds closed, replaced by fresh, pink skin.

"If I'm wrong," Minister Haemin growled, "why are you healing? How does this magic work? Why does this work for you when it didn't for those Téionaropi soldiers we slew five years ago? *Speak*, traitor!"

A pained growl slid past Amadus's clenched teeth. He gripped his chains, turning his knuckles bone white, and thrashed in the air. The crystal grew brighter with each passing second.

"Understanding . . ." he groaned, his voice strained, as if being choked, "beyond—Ah!" His scream was cut off as he coughed up more blood. "Blessings . . ."

Minister Haemin pulled back.

Amadus fell forward, slumping in the clanging chains, his chest expanding and deflating in haggard breaths. His body was covered in sweat, but his wounds were gone.

"Blessings?" Minister Haemin spat. "Do you worship them, as well?"

Amadus's eyes rolled back in his head. His gaunt, haunted appearance had been refreshed. It was as if years had been peeled away, and now he was much younger than the near skeleton that he had been when Tory had first entered the cell. Even his hair had darkened to gray.

"*This* is the truth!" Minister Haemin thrust the crystal in front of her. "This wretch is no longer a man. And just as his continued life is tied to the Téionaropi's influence, so, too, have they kept the progress of our entire nation tied down! We are weak. And every time quick action is needed, we're stopped as crisis after crisis grows in every province. And why? Because *they* want it."

Tory knew little of the Téionaropi. She had never seen one. They never traveled the world. They never sent merchants beyond their own borders. One had to sail to their ports to trade with them.

The stories that sailors brought back were of little note, save for their cities being filled with light and the few they had encountered had a strange glow about them. Other than that, the Téionaropi kept themselves at a distance, and sailors could only talk and interact with a few of them.

"Please, My Lord," she said, giving him a pleading look, "I don't understand what this has to do with me or why I'm here. I just want to go home."

"Your home is in just as much danger as all of ours," Minister Haemin replied. "Who do you think stripped us from owning the land we aristos govern? Who made it so we had to beg and kneel to be appointed the masters of our own homes?" He jutted a finger at Amadus. "This traitor right here. And why? So his real masters can control us from afar while he works his poison into every king who comes to the throne, to be as lethargic and wasteful as they can be."

He tossed the crystal in the air and caught it before sliding it back into his pocket. Its bright light gone, only the red glow of the lamps with their long shadows remained.

"Her Majesty realizes this," he said. "She's witnessed it for years. And when we acted to finally correct centuries-old wrongs, this immortal spy conspired to place another useless fool on the throne as fast as he could. Well"—he lorded over Amadus—"we caught you this time."

"The only thing you've caught," Amadus sneered up at him, "is the delusion of your own importance."

Minister Haemin motioned to the guard with the whip, who stepped out of the corner and cracked its multi-tailed prongs across Amadus's back.

Amadus arched his back as fresh blood rained from his new wounds. His mouth flew open in a silent wail, but he gnashed his teeth together and struggled to swallow his pain, his nostrils flaring and eyes a fiery glare at the first minister.

"*You* want the throne," Amadus hissed. Then his clenched teeth broke into a wide smile, and he cackled. "Or rather, what's in the—"

Minister Haemin nodded to the guard again, and another lashing followed.

This time, Amadus gasped, and a strangled groan escaped.

"I want nothing from *them*," Minister Haemin spat.

He left Amadus hanging as he stomped over to Tory.

"Are you innocent, Tory Syros?" he asked lowly. "Are you loyal to Her Majesty?"

"Yes," Tory replied, frantically nodding her head. "Yes!"

Minister Haemin reached out, and Orvein placed the writing board with Tory's unsigned statement in his hand. She hadn't even seen Orvein take it out again.

The first minister turned it around and aggressively shoved it toward her. "Sign," he ordered.

Like magic, Orvein was at her side, holding out the quill with its tip again dripping with ink.

When she took the quill, the cell felt even smaller. Every eye was on her, waiting. They could all have been watching over her shoulders from how close they felt.

Her fingers trembled, holding the quill over the signature line. Small black dots dripped from the tip like the drops of blood dripping in the pool underneath Amadus.

"Sign that, and you'll die!" Amadus shouted.

Tory seized. Her entire right arm began to shake, and her legs locked.

"You *dare* threaten her?" Holden snapped, speaking for the first time.

Amadus barked a laugh. "She is no more than your third *proof* for your false trial and the proclamations afterward. You plan to do to her the same as you did to Stevens!"

Tory gazed up into Minister Haemin's face. The shadows made it hard to see but, up close, she could make out the hard resolve in his eyes, the crow's feet around them, and the deepening wrinkles on his brow. He was tired but determined.

"We are not as heartless as you," he said to Amadus. "Your man, Stevens, gave you up and hanged himself because he couldn't face his shame. You may have killed key witnesses in your time to hold on to power, but we are patriots here. We would never murder those who are loyal and innocent."

Amadus hung for a moment, speechless. Then he snickered. And then he threw his head back, laughing. It grew louder and louder, almost maniacal.

"You think you're special?" He gleefully swung in his chains. "You think you're different? Fools! I've been on both sides of this. *None* of you are different! We all have blood on our hands. Innocent blood that will never wash off." His laughter spiraled into sobs. "You believe you're on the path of liberation, but you're only heading for destruction."

Minister Haemin shook his head in disgust. "You're insane."

He nodded to the guard, and the whipping resumed. The guard set into a rhythm, pacing out each lash between thirty seconds apart.

Amadus reeled only once before slumping in his bonds, his body twitching only when he was struck. Then he weakly raised his head, his pitiful, tear-streaked eyes burning right at her. "Poor little fish," he said weakly. "Poor little fish."

Tory drew in on herself, his words striking her core.

On the Isles, mothers told their children the story of the *Poor Little Fish* that grew up in the shallows around the Isles. The shallows had plenty to eat and plenty of safe places to swim and play. One day, though, the little fish saw the great blue ocean beyond and wanted to play out there, to explore and dive as deep as it wanted.

So, it swam out, farther and farther away, until all around him was deep blue, the ocean floor nowhere in sight. That was when the monsters came. Snake whales with their serpentine necks and heads full of long teeth, and giant steel-jaw fish as big as ships that could swallow the fish whole. And they devoured the poor little fish before he could turn back to the shallows.

It was a cautionary tale told to children on the Isles. They could play in the shallows, but they were never to venture near deep water. Whenever tragedies struck, especially to children, people would shake their heads and say, "Poor little fish."

In this room, Tory felt like the poor little fish, and everything inside her screamed she was surrounded by monsters. With the story running through her head and the wet, sickening sound of the whip in her ears, she looked back to the parchment.

The tip of the quill rested on the line.

Her hand still shook as the ink blot grew.

Part of her screamed for her to sign.

That still voice yelled back, *They'll kill us!*

Tory tasted salt on her tongue. She had started crying, and a tear had run down to the corner of her mouth. Her mind spiraled. She was still in that capsized boat, and it was about to touch bottom. She was running out of air.

And there were monsters swimming outside.

Amadus finally screamed.

They don't want me, she rationalized. *They want Alindale.*

They clearly enjoyed having Amadus. If she signed, they might go back to enjoying their actual prey and let this little fish go. Could she do that though? Condemn others just so she could run away?

I want to go home!

She started to sign.

"Lords!" a voice roared from back in the cell block, followed by iron bars crashing loudly. "Magistrates! Guards! *Anybody*!"

Tory gasped for air as the whipping stopped and the men surrounding her turned toward the cell block in confusion.

"Shut up, Revel!" Orvein yelled. "We don't have business with you today."

"Well, I have it with you," Revel called back. "Or at least any of you who are interested in a confession."

The first minister, Holden, and Orvein perked up in unison. Tory caught a nod from Minister Haemin before Orvein slipped out of the cell.

"You wish to confess?" Orvein asked. "To what?"

"Everything," Revel replied. "The conspiracy, the plot, the murder—everything you claim. Just let the girl go, and I'll write the whole thing."

"Don't be a fool, Revel!" Amadus yelled, his face a raging torrent. "That won't save any of you!"

The guard whipped him again, and he gasped. The pool underneath him seemed to have doubled in size.

"It might save her!" Revel shouted back. "Let the girl leave, released completely, and I'll confess. I'll take Lord Haemin's word as an *honorable* patriot, and you'll let her go. She's an innocent in all this!"

Tory was numb. She could barely feel her legs anymore, and her grip on the quill was so tight that her fingers were starting to sting. She glanced up at Minister Haemin through cloudy eyes. He seemed to be thinking it over.

"Holden, get fresh parchment," he finally said, taking the writing board and statement away. "Orvein! Take Lady Syros to her brother."

Tory jerked her head up, her burning fingers dropping the quill.

Orvein returned, confused. "My Lord?"

"You heard me," Minister Haemin replied. "A confession from a conspirator for the release of an innocent. That's just."

Orvein nodded, though he still didn't look convinced. "As you wish, First Minister."

He took Tory by the arm and began dragging her out into the cell block.

"And, Lady Syros," Minister Haemin called.

"Yes?" she replied weakly, turning to see the other guard hand him a sword.

"Stay loyal. Stay innocent. Understand?"

She timidly nodded. "Yes, First Minister."

"Take her away, Orvein."

Orvein began to drag her away in earnest, and the guard who had escorted them up fell in behind. In the final moments, Tory watched the first minister plunge the sword into Amadus's left breast, directly into the heart. No scream or cry of pain came. Just the sickening sound of steel sinking into flesh and sliding against bone that made her want to vomit.

Tory didn't look at the dark cells this time, not even to catch a glimpse of the man who had offered himself in her place. She followed as if adrift.

When they opened the cell block door, the rush of air made her shiver. She swayed on the stairs, barely feeling the steps beneath her as her knees wobbled from staying locked for so long.

Tory paused upon reaching the third floor, a part of her believing they were simply taking her back to her former cell. The guard persuaded her otherwise, pushing on.

"Tory!"

Tory blinked. Her eyes were still clouded, though she wasn't sure if she was still crying. As they cleared, she found herself on the bottom floor, the tower's thick, wooden and iron door open in front her. A figure stood a distance away. She blinked again and realized it was Jerro.

"Tory!" he yelled again, his face a thunderclap of concern, eyes wide, head bobbing and searching. His big fists shook like tempests at his sides, and he was practically bouncing on his toes in the middle of the open yard.

With the door open in front of her and her brother in sight, Tory bolted. She left nothing to chance, hiking up the skirts so as not to trip. If Orvein, the guards, or anyone else yelled after her, she didn't hear it. She refused to stop and didn't until she slammed into Jerro's chest, burying her face in his shirt.

"Tory!" Jerro cried, wrapping his strong arms around her and cupping the back of her head with his big palms. "What did they do to you?"

Tory failed to think of any words horrible enough to describe what she had seen. Hence, she simply shook her head, dragging her tear-streaked face deeper into his chest, and wailed.

Chapter 22

11th of Iam, 1109 N.F. (e.y.)

Alindale's legs were asleep, and a back-biting twinge dug into the curve of his spine. He sat slumped forward in a pew with his arms braced on his knees and head hung low. Only the sound of his breathing kept the sanctuary's maddening silence at bay. It warped his sense of time, breaking apart all his trail of thoughts along with the heavy hollowness he felt deep in his chest.

I can't stay here . . .. But where am I to go . . .? I can't abandon everyone . . .. But I can't even help myself. . ..

BANG! BANG! BANG!

Alindale didn't flinch at the pounding of steel against the cathedral's thick doors.

Must be the hour.

"Prince Alindale Dain!" The Sunrise Guard's yell was muffled, but Alindale still heard him. "By order of Her Majesty, you are ordered to come forth and deliver yourself before her! You have been named in connection to a conspiracy in the murder of His Majesty, your royal father! We demand you come forth!" The guard hammered on the doors again.

After a few minutes, the beating stopped, and the cathedral's silence returned.

He'll be back next hour. Alindale assumed it was the same Sunrise Guard. *And I'll still be right here.*

"'*Do not dwell on your troubles,*'" Father Finrie recited, his deep voice rumbling through the cathedral's nave, "'*nor face your transgressions alone. In all things, lean upon God, and you shall know peace.*'"

Alindale remained motionless.

"Please, go away," he droned lifelessly.

"I cannot," Father Finrie replied, ambling closer, his sandaled feet scuffing along the floor.

"Please, don't," Alindale groaned, sensing a sermon. "There must be people who need you right now. Go help them."

Father Finrie's shadow crept over him in the candlelight. "No one else needs my help more"—the father groaned as he gently sat down next to him—"than you."

"I'm beyond help, Father." Alindale sunk lower in the pew.

He waited for a typical response, some menial words of comfort, but the moments dragged by. The sound of loud breathing grated on his ears each passing second. From the corner of his eye, Alindale saw Father Finrie sitting back in the pew with his hands folded in his lap and his eyes closed.

"Are you asleep?" he asked disbelievingly. "Or praying?"

"Neither," Father Finrie coughed out. "Only waiting."

"Waiting for *what*?"

Father Finrie opened his eyes and looked down his long nose at him. "On whether you believe you are beyond help or not."

"Everyone is gone," Alindale replied. "My father is dead, and my mother is sending guards proclaiming I'm wanted for it." He snickered, surprisingly smiling despite himself. "The only reason they don't drag me out of here is because there're probably showing off to a crowd outside. What help is there for me?"

"There is always God's help, Alindale," Father Finrie replied.

"You would say that." Lifelessness returned to Alindale's voice, and he dropped his head again. "It's all you know to say."

"I would say that," Father Finrie admitted, "but it is not all I know. Every man has his own advice to give. Even me." He grunted as he leaned forward, his robes rustling and sliding as he moved. "But as I look back, I find my words lacking. Failing."

Alindale studied the father out of the corner of his eye. He sat with his arms propped on his legs, like Alindale, with his round belly puffed out the sides of his robes. The elder priest's face drooped, his lips pressed together in a deep frown, and he stared forward with a disappointed look in his eyes.

"A young woman came to me once," Father Finrie spoke. "Told me she'd received two letters from two men wishing to court her, and she wanted my advice on which man she should favor. I told her to follow her heart and court the man she could love to bring her the greatest happiness. Years later, I learned the man she chose beat her." His round cheeks quivered.

"Then there was a man in great debt," he continued. "I found him weeping on the altar, not knowing what he should do. He feared for his life and his family's, and I told him to go to his family and work to repay the debt." Tears ran down Father Finrie's face. "He left and went to the gambling houses instead, increasing his debt. He lost his family's home and is now indentured while his family lives destitute in the gutters of South End."

Alindale straightened, popping his back while watching the most pious man he knew sob beside him.

"One woman brought her husband to me once," Father Finrie recounted. "They were having trouble with their marriage, and she'd been trying to bring him to sermon for years. She finally convinced him to come, and I withdrew the first time he flinched when I quoted the Texts. I told them to talk with each other, discover their problems, and find a solution together. Instead, the husband went home and shut himself away. He drank himself to sleep and forgot to extinguish the candles that burned down his home, with him and his wife inside."

Father Finrie took a deep breath, his eyebrows, cheeks, and chin stiffening. Then his eyes hardened. "I should have told the woman to pray and court the man who would follow the Texts to love and cherish her as he loves himself." He grabbed his knees and pushed himself to his feet, shaking.

Alindale reached to steady him, but Father Finrie slapped his hand away.

"I should have offered the indebted man charity from the church's offerings," Father Finrie continued, "and told him to follow the Texts and deliver himself from his debtors, to humble himself and pray. And if he still worried for his family, to bring them here for sanctuary."

Father Finrie gazed upward at the cathedral's vaulted ceiling. "And I should have never let the husband and wife leave that night. He needed to hear the counsel of God and pray together with his wife!"

He sighed and looked down at Alindale, disappointment in his eyes. "My advice is meaningless, Alindale. The Texts are all I have, because the advice of God is your only hope that I know!"

Alindale gripped the side of the pew, its wooden edge digging into his palm. He wanted to shrink down in his seat. He wasn't sure if Father Finrie's disappointed stare was meant for him or the father himself.

"What advice does God have then?" he asked sheepishly.

Father Finrie gripped his shoulder comfortingly. "Pray first, Alindale. As it is written, '*Give your burdens to God, and your soul will find rest.*'"

"And that will stop from sending the guards to arrest me, and this will all go away?" Alindale asked cynically, without thinking. Then he winced. "Sorry, Father Finrie. I know you are just trying to help."

"Pray," the priest urged, squeezing his shoulder. "I can't promise a miracle will come, but it may give you something you need much more—peace."

Father Finrie gave Alindale his most grandfatherly smile then patted him on the back. "Then come eat. The city peace has allowed us to resume feeding the people again, and we have fresh food, as well."

"So, no more bread, honey, and rice?" Alindale half-heartedly joked.

"There'll still be bread and honey," Father Finrie joked back, giving him a final pat before ambling away.

Alindale watched the father leave, and the gloomy hollowness returned. His shoulders felt heavy, and the urge to lean forward came again.

Get up, he told himself. *Don't give in again.*

He braced against the pew and dragged himself up, careful to keep weight off his left leg. The rockback's spike had sliced across it. The leather leg of his boot had blunted the blow and, luckily, the spike had missed his shin bone and didn't tear his leg muscles. He no longer limped, but his leg still stung, the stitches pulling and tugging with each step.

He walked to the front of the sanctuary, bracing against each pew for support. His father's coffin still sat in the center of the cathedral. Alindale ran his hand down the coffin's smooth finish, limping to its head. He played with the idea of opening it and finally seeing his father's face after so long but grimaced.

He's been in there for over two weeks.

The heavy scent of pine from the incense candles made him wonder if the priests were worried about the same thing.

"Isn't it funny?" he mused out loud. "They demand I come out. That *I* had something to do with . . . with your death. And yet, no one's come to lay you to rest." He rubbed the head of the coffin, his vision threatening to blur. "Did they ever care about you, Father? As much as they ever cared about me, perhaps?"

Alindale gripped the wood until he heard his fingers squeak against it. Then he drew himself up, tears dripping on the coffin, and turned away.

A large stone altar sat in front of the grand pulpit, a heavy slab of granite, weathered and gray with time. Small cracks and fissures spread across it like vines, almost creating strange glyphs, but the priests said they were tricks of the eye. Despite the cracks, the slab was solid. Carved across the mantle of the altar were the words, *"God Delivers The Faithful From Oblivion."*

Alindale looked at the altar hesitantly. *Not sure if I know how to pray anymore.*

Begrudgingly, he took the last few steps to it and winced when lowering himself to his knees. His leg throbbed for a moment, and a dull pain rose from his knees pressing into the hard floor.

Alindale stared at the altar's bare surface. Minutes dragged, his mind blank and unsure. He clutched the sides of the altar, as if dangling from the edge of a cliff, the coarse stone biting into his skin.

"What am I even supposed to say?" he asked under his breath.

His eyes unconsciously drifted shut and, as the minutes grew longer, they tightened. Shutting everything out, Alindale felt adrift, with only the altar holding him to reality.

Help me! The plea echoed in his mind. *Help me! If you can save anyone from Oblivion, then O' God, help me! I'm so . . . so tired. Tired of failing. Tired of not being good enough. Tired of being . . . alone. Please, help me.*

He begged and prayed, unaware of bowing his head and pressing his forehead into the altar's surface. Small pools formed underneath him from tears squeezed out through his pinched eyelids.

~~~

Alindale walked out to the cathedral's cloister, scratching the crust from the corners of his eyes. He rubbed his forehead, trying to loosen the skin after being pressed against the altar. He had lost consciousness but didn't remember when. His problems still remained, waiting for him, but that hollowness was no longer crushing him from within.

He stopped mid-step at the sound of children laughing.

"Everyone needs to be clean before they eat!" a woman yelled at a gaggle of children chasing each other through the garden's bushes.

Ten women sat on stools, with large washing pails next to them, scrubbing the children's faces and hands before sending them into the monastery. Alindale quickly counted over thirty children milling together in the middle of the garden, while several ran around the edges. The kids running around wore better clothes than the children being scrubbed, who eagerly dashed for the monastery door once they were set free.

"Hello, Brother," came from a boy's soft voice.

Alindale's breath caught. *Adam!*

A little boy hiding in some bushes jumped out and waved up at him, his curly, dark hair filled with leaves and small twigs.

Alindale sighed deeply, remembering he was wearing a priest's robe. The clothes that he had worn the day that he had collapsed in the cathedral doorway were in tatters; one leg of his trousers was blood-soaked and in shreds, and pieces of his doublet had been ripped out.

"I'm not—"

The boy giggled and scampered off.

Probably wouldn't understand.

He shook his head as he watched them play. They seemed happy, carefree. Alindale listened to them laugh and, for a brief moment, it was a blessed relief.

But it didn't last.

Alindale slowly walked around the garden, his shoe heels thumping against the brick floor of the cloister. He paused outside the monastery's door at the churning din of voices inside, as if there could be over a hundred people.

Maybe I shouldn't.

"Hello, Brother!" a girl running into the monastery said, followed by two others.
~~~

Alindale grunted and scratched the days-old stubble on his face. *I should just stay in back. Maybe they'll all think I'm a brother of the church, too.*

Sweat formed on his brow, and his nose wrinkled at the scent of boiled meat coming from the monastery's dining hall.

He hiked up his robes and walked down the steps. Three of the seven long benches filling the hall were already full of people, hunched over wooden plates, their wooden spoons scraping against their plates as they scooped rice into their mouths or ate their boiled pork.

Alindale kept his head low as he walked around them, hugging the wall. The scent of body odor mixed with the salty tinge from the docks and hint of smoke reminded him of his excursion to South End—the cramped debauchery, the brutal fights, and the burning building.

He shook the memory away but glanced and saw a few people watching him while they ate in silence. Swallowing hard, he nodded and walked on.

Brothers shepherded people into the monastery through a wide door on the right, in a long line to the food tables at the head of the hall. The children from the gardens slipped in between the adults here and there. Alindale followed one.

"Hey!" the middle-aged woman, who he had cut in front of, complained.

"Pardon me," he said to her, pointing to the child in front of him, trying to pretend to be with him.

The woman pursed her lips, making a mole on her cheek throb. Alindale tore his eyes away before she saw him wincing at it.

"Did you wash your hands?" the woman asked.

Alindale forced a smile at her and nodded.

With his eyes, he followed the line of people to the monastery's outer door and saw more brothers pouring water over each persons' hands then wiping them off with cloths.

The woman huffed and folded her arms under her chest, annoyed but fortunately not making a scene.

The line crawled forward.

The priests had brought food to him the first couple of nights, and he had eaten with them the previous night.

Brothers filled his plate for him, a spoonful of rice, a slice of pork, a sausage, a spoon of greens, and a hunk of bread, none of which looked appetizing. Only the rice steamed.

At least it's not just bread and rice, Alindale told himself.

He took his cup of watered wine then slipped out of line.

While the line of people filed to fill up the fourth table, he instead headed to the seventh. He sat at the far end, hoping to be finished by the time the line reached the table. Although, as he poked at his food with his spoon, Alindale suddenly lacked an appetite.

Maybe just bread and rice would have been best.

He sniffed the sausage then turned his head to repress the impulse to gag at the smell of boiled meat. He tossed it aside and picked up the slice of pork. Pressed juices dripped out of the lukewarm meat as he brought it to his mouth. Its smell didn't make him gag, and so he timidly took a small bite.

The pork was tough, and the overuse of salt made him push the meat away with his tongue. It had gone stale, with barely any flavor, and as he chewed, he bit down on a piece of gristle. He instinctively spat the squishy flesh out then rubbed his mouth with his robe sleeve.

Yes. Just the bread and rice would have been better.

Alindale grimaced, cupping his face in his hands. Pleading his soul out had momentarily lifted a weight from his shoulders, but the poor food was souring his mood again.

"Are you not going to eat that?" came from a crackling voice over his left shoulder.

Alindale snapped around. A tall, hunched figure hovered behind him, his face hidden under a hood. The wide sleeves of his green and orange striped shirt hung off his body, as if meant for a much larger man. His trousers were too short, exposing his pale legs from his ankles to the middle of his shins. The leather of his shoes was cracked and in desperate need of a cobbler.

"I . . . don't . . .." Alindale hesitantly replied.

The hooded man cackled. "Haven't made up your mind?" He set his plate and cup down then slid his long legs between the table and bench. "If you don't mind, I'll sit here until you have!" The man plopped down on the bench then elbowed Alindale a few times, as if he had told a joke that

Alindale didn't understand. Alindale tried to scoot away from him, but he was already on the edge of the bench.

The man's long fingers contorted around his spoon as he scooped up spoonful after spoonful of rice, shoveling it up into his hood. Alindale grimaced at the sounds of the man humming and smacking his lips after each bite. He slurped his wine to wash down his hunk of bread, and Alindale clenched his teeth to stop from yelling.

"If I give you my pork and sausage, will you sit somewhere else?" he asked lowly, attempting to hide his annoyance.

"Hmm . . .?" the man hummed while chomping on a green. "What a tantalizing offer. But, don't you need to eat? After all"—his cracked voice changed—"a condemned man needs to enjoy every meal he gets."

Alindale sat up straight, recognizing the flamboyant voice. "Nolen?"

A cackling chuckle came from under the hood and with a long finger, he pushed it up to reveal Nolen's grinning face. "Good evening, Your Highness. Glad to see you're well."

"How in—" Alindale choked off his curse as people slid onto the bench behind him. He lowered his voice and whispered, "What are you doing here?"

"Got curious again," Nolen replied, finishing another green. "I wondered if you were actually in here or in the tower with Amadus. Since sneaking into the tower is insane, I decided to sneak in here. It was . . . a little disappointing." He frowned, taking a sip of wine, thankfully without slurping this time.

Alindale gave him a flat stare. "Disappointing because I was here and not . . . in the *tower*? Why would I be in the tower?"

"I just told you, because Amadus is there," Nolen replied nonchalantly. "But it was disappointing sneaking in here. Sure, castle soldiers and the city peace are watching the doors and everybody coming in, but they're not searching them. A real lack of effort, I must say."

"Wait until you go out," Alindale huffed, but the news that Amadus was being held in the castle tower was disturbing. He should have been taken to the holding cells under the Ministry of Justice. It didn't make sense.

He picked at his food again, his appetite still eluding him, and tossed his slice of pork on Nolen's plate.

"I don't want that," Nolen refused.

Alindale dropped his arm against the table, clattering their plates and cups. "You said you did!"

"Shh!" Nolen waved his hands for him to lower his voice. "Part of the act. I'm a hungry beggar, and I saw the food wasn't to your liking." He cackled in his vagabond voice.

Alindale rolled his eyes and took a drink of wine. It was more water than wine, with barely a hint of grape and not a bite of alcohol.

"What's going on outside?" he asked lowly.

"The city's not fun anymore." Nolen shrugged, pushing his remaining rice into a small hill with his spoon, like he was bored. "The good spots of South End are all burned down, and with the city peace evicting and moving people around, what's left is practically under martial law. Kanestown *is* under martial law, by castle soldiers. The castle feels almost deserted without them all."

Alindale frustratedly groaned. "That's not what I meant." He leaned against the table, folded his arms against it, and kept his head low. "You mentioned Amadus was in the tower. Who else?"

"Lord Vanni, of course," Nolen began, "for the assassination—"

"He didn't do it!" Alindale hissed.

Nolen raised a hand defensively. "I'm not saying he did."

Alindale sighed. "Go on."

"Colonel Kenith Kane and Knight Brother Revel are imprisoned for conspiring with Lord Vanni. They've also imprisoned the brigadier marshal of the Storm Cavalry, with a few other officers. The magistrates are claiming Amadus is the mastermind behind it all"—Nolen shrugged—"but they've yet to bring them to trial. Her Majesty also sent—"

"Trial?" Alindale sprang up, nearly jumping off the bench. "They are having a trial *now*?"

"Yes." Nolen frowned, confused. "That's why the Sunrise Guard have been pounding on the cathedral's door for the past two weeks."

"They have demanded I come before my mother." Alindale gripped the sides of the table, squeezing until the wood groaned. "No one said anything about a *trial*. Not even the sound of a crowd outside the Ministry of Justice."

"Trial's not," Nolen mumbled around the last of his bread and had to swallow, "being held at the Ministry of Justice."

"What?"

"Your mother is presiding over the trial at the castle."

Alindale stared disbelievingly at him, his mind racing at the implications. "She . . . she can't do that! The Carta states such trials are to be conducted by the Ministry of Justice!"

"The Lord Justice, unfortunately, thought the same." Nolen swirled his wine lazily. "Your mother sent *him* to the tower for contempt."

Alindale buried his face in his hands. All the time dwelling on himself, and he had thought his supporters were in the same situation, only locked away in a different place. This, however, was far worse than he could have imagined.

How did this happen so fast? He ran his fingers through his hair, thick and oily from a few days going without a wash. *Mother shouldn't be doing this!*

"Has she gone insane?" He recalled her reaction to mentioning Bernold, the vitriol in her voice. And yet, she had acted stately and distant when it had come to his father's death. "Nothing makes sense."

The table shook as people began to fill it. Conversations were starting to grow louder on the other side of the room from the first wave of people finishing their meals.

"She's not insane," Nolen whispered. "If anything, she's more firmly in control than ever."

Alindale shook his head. "She can't be. None of her actions make sense. She wouldn't send the Sunrise Guard and castle soldiers after me." He glowered at the obvious conclusion. "Haemin. This all started with him, and he was there when they took Amadus away. He must be behind all this."

"You sure?"

Alindale looked at Nolen from out of the corner of his eye. The table was filling up, and he questioned the safety of their conversation.

Nolen leaned in a little closer. "Can you *really* be sure your mother is not involved? She is presiding over the trial. She is sending people to the tower. She is sending the Sunrise Guard, demanding you surrender. To everyone watching, *she* is seeking justice for her dead husband on her own and naming *you*, her own son, responsible."

"Be very, *very* careful, Lord Ingman," Alindale warned lowly.

"Same to you." Nolen glanced around nervously. "People are starting to talk. Some talk as if the line of Dain kings may be at an end. They are acting like steel-jaw fish, circling a dying serpent whale, waiting for the feeding frenzy to start so they can each slice off the biggest chunk for themselves."

"And what about you? You circling, as well?" Alindale edged away, teetering on the edge of the bench. His arms stiffened as he gripped the table harder. His legs began to shake, ready to spring up.

"Why?" Nolen replied nonchalantly. "They don't have a high opinion of me. Everybody knows I stab people in the back, so there's no point in it. You're the one in dire straits here."

Alindale maintained a little distance, still ready to leap up and run, the suspicious twinge in the back of his mind still unsatisfied.

"And what is your advice?"

Nolen drained his cup then pushed his plate away so he could lean on the table and hunch closer. "Get out of the city."

Alindale snickered, despite himself. "Daincliff's under martial law; you said so yourself. The cathedral itself is surrounded. There is no getting out."

"I got in," Nolen pointed out. "And I'll get out the same way with the rest of these people. The soldiers will most likely be checking us, but I can still note the different ways to get in and out. I can try to arrange something. Things happen when you pass the right mint into the right hands."

Alindale's memory flashed back to the night that Nolen had taken him to South End and the different people he had paid off. Getting out of the cathedral and able to move might give him options. He wouldn't feel trapped any more, at least.

His thoughts, though, switched back to his supporters, still locked in the tower.

"I can't just leave them," he mumbled.

"Alindale," Nolen whispered, wrapping his long fingers around Alindale's forearm and squeezing, "some at court want you dead, others merely want you out of the way, but there is no denying the fact that they're all using this opportunity to ensure you never sit on the throne. The longer you stay here, the more you play into their hands."

Alindale's skin crawled from the feel of Nolen's grip as he tried to pry his fingers away.

"I know how serious this is. But, even if I did manage to escape, I have nowhere else to go."

"Anywhere is better than here." Nolen let go of his arm and thought, "Tradon! To your sister."

"Amanda has two children. And I won't put her or them in danger." Alindale hung his head. "I actually haven't seen her in years. There is no guarantee she would take me in after all this." He couldn't think of a reason why she would. They had never really been close because of their age difference and their different personalities. She easily took to court life, while he . . . was himself. There was no guarantee Julian would help, either. Julian might have offered help in the beginning, but he was a calculating man. Proclamations must have gone out by now, accusing him of murder throughout the entire kingdom.

All the while, Alindale wallowed here, alone and trapped in his own failings. He couldn't think of anyone left who could help him. Despite Nolen's advice to escape, there didn't seem any place he could escape to.

"You are the most stubborn, negatively-minded person I've ever met," Nolen groaned in frustration. He hunched his back and moved like he was about to get up. "And that's saying something. *Gah!*"

Suddenly, Nolen was hoisted off the bench and slammed down to the floor. A large man in a stained hood loomed over him, holding Nolen's left arm behind his head. Nolen yelled and squirmed on the floor, kicking his long legs wildly, but none reached the man holding him.

"Stop!" Alindale yelled. He jumped from the seat and grabbed the hooded man by the shoulder. His breath caught at the scarred visage glaring back at him. "Master Montaigu?"

Dark bags hung under the master knight's sunken eyes. Dried mud caked his boots, and grime stained his trouser legs. His cloak was riddled with holes, his tunic threadbare and missing one sleeve. His tabard and sword, though, were nowhere to be seen.

"Ahh!" Nolen screamed in his crackling voice again. "You're breaking my arm! I was only asking if he wanted his pork!"

The conversations died. People jumped up from their seats and gathered at the end of the aisle between the tables. They focused on Nolen screaming under Montaigu and Alindale standing beside them.

A deathly thought shot through Alindale's mind. *The screaming will bring the soldiers!*

"Montaigu!" He grabbed the knight's arm, but his grip was iron. "Montaigu, let him go!"

"What is this?"

Father Finrie shuffled through the parting crowd. Alindale had never thought it possible that the father could scowl, but his bushy brows were contorted, his prominent nose flaring, and there was a blaze in his eyes. Montaigu, however, didn't flinch.

"A misunderstanding, Father," Alindale replied, nervously checking the entrance, praying the soldiers wouldn't come.

Nolen's shoes thumped against floor, his flailing legs going still. His face was red, and his head wobbled back and forth on the floor. Tears ran down the corners of his eyes, and he let out a low, high-pitched whine.

Father Finrie loomed over Montaigu. "These are sacred grounds, and in the name of the Last God, there will be no violence here! Release that man!"

Montaigu glared up at Father Finrie, and the father sternly stared back.

With a grunt, Montaigu grabbed Nolen by the collar and hoisted him to his feet as easily as an empty sack. He reached into Nolen's clothes and slammed something black on the table.

Alindale's breath caught, his eyes wide. A black-sheathed dagger.

Nolen's words echoed in his mind. *Everybody knows I stab people in the back.*

Father Finrie looked from Montaigu to the dagger then to Nolen. He picked up the dagger and put it in his robes. "Let him go," he told Montaigu softly.

Nolen gasped and cradled his arm after Montaigu released him. He collapsed on the bench, rubbing it and whining, hunched over.

Father Finrie patted his shoulder. "No weapons are allowed in the cathedral."

"It's only"—Nolen coughed and cackled in his vagabond persona—"for protection."

"But you are safe."

"Prince Alindale Dain!"

A chill ran down Alindale's spine.

Haemin!

Anxious looks spread among the people closest to the doors. They spread out, as if in a hurry to get out of the way. Everyone else in the room looked at him.

Alindale, though, watched the entrance. With no sunlight to shine shadows into the room, his only warning would be the soldiers filing in. He expected Haemin to be at their head, with the Sunrise Guard at his back, like when he had arrested Amadus. However, as the minutes passed, no soldiers came.

"Prince Alindale Dain!" Haemin yelled again.

Alindale passed a worried look between Montaigu and Father Finrie. The master knight's sunken-eyed glare remained, his face a scowl carved from rock. Father Finrie gave him a reverend look and stepped aside, clearing a path. Alindale tentatively stepped around Nolen, still hunkering over his arm.

The people watched his every step and huddled away from him, as if he had a plague.

Alindale expected Haemin to be in the doorway with soldiers ready to rush in and seize him. Instead, he stood outside the monastery and away from the door, Sunrise Guards flanking him with soldiers behind.

"Prince Alindale Dain!" he shouted, holding up a rolled parchment. "I have in my hand a warrant for your arrest, for the conspiracy, regicide, *and* patricide of His Majesty, King Richman Dain!"

The people murmured around him, and the soldiers behind Haemin shifted on their feet, their eyes hard set on him.

More theater.

Sweat ran down Alindale's face, and trickles ran down his back, under his robe.

"By order of Her Majesty and the Table of Ministers, you are to surrender yourself and be brought to stand trial for your crimes!" Haemin folded the warrant into his belt.

Alindale held his gaze. The crowd inside and outside the monastery watched in silence. The soldiers remained outside, waiting.

"Well?" Alindale asked. "I'm unarmed. Aren't you here to arrest me?"

Lord Haemin set his jaw, as if agitated. "I will not send soldiers into the cathedral and risk the safety of the people inside. If you have any concern of the people inside, or the security of the kingdom, *you* will come out!"

Alindale looked for any sign of comfort or advice from Father Finrie, but the father frowned somberly, his eyes full of pity.

It would all be over, he considered. *No more hiding. No more waiting. Just over and done with.*

Master Montaigu stepped up beside Father Finrie, his defiant scowl a sharp contrast to the father's.

It'll all be over. He remembered the talk of a trial and what Nolen had said before, but he had tried to knife him. Everything Nolen had said could have been a lie.

"You mentioned standing trial," Alindale commented. "I assume proper advocates will be appointed and the Lord Justice will be presiding?"

"This matter has been deemed too serious for the Ministry of Justice alone," Haemin replied. "Her Majesty herself will preside."

The crowd broke out in dozens of whispered conversations, like an audience at a show at the prospect of his mother sitting in judgment over him.

"That is not what I'm guaranteed by the Carta," Alindale argued.

"The Table of Ministers has found the severity of your crimes, and those of your co-conspirators, too great to be left to one ministry." Haemin's expression gave nothing away, but he sounded bored. "The Table of Ministers has seen fit to suspend the Carta in this case so that justice may be fulfilled. Now, Prince Alindale, come out!"

Alindale balled his hands into fists at his sides. Nolen had told the truth. If he stepped outside, if he did surrender, it would all be over.

They've already made up their minds, he boiled. *They want their show now.*

A dull pain grew on the left side of his jaw from grinding his teeth too hard, and his body began to shake. The hollowness returned and threatened to crush his chest, only to be met by raging frustration. *Why should I go along with it?*

"No," he growled lowly.

"What?" Haemin demanded.

Alindale took a deep breath. "I will not surrender! I will not be falsely accused and stand before a trial where my rights are taken away! If you wish to seize me, I'm right here." He raised his arms. "But I refuse to surrender to the man who killed my brother."

Members of the crowd gasped, and several women dashed around, picking up children and hoisting them away.

Haemin's eyes flared, and he pressed his lips tightly together.

"Good people of Daincliff!" he yelled. "I will not risk your lives by sending soldiers among you. But, if you are law-abiding people, I ask you to drag that man out!"

Blood drained from Alindale's face. Several people around him looked between him and the monastery entrance.

"A hundred gold mints to the man who brings him out!" Haemin added impatiently.

People seemed to leap at him as one. Alindale couldn't react before hands seized him from all directions. He pushed and flailed his arms, hitting anyone he could reach. He kicked at them in the vain attempt to drive them back, but the mob soon grabbed his legs, too.

"*No!*" he yelled as they raised him off the ground, ripping his robe while he struggled in their grips.

Just as the mob hoisted him toward the entrance, a loud roar ripped through the monastery. Women screamed as the cluster of holding hands wavered. Someone below Alindale vanished, the world spun, and he plummeted backward, dragging the poor soul holding up his legs with him.

He hit the floor then bounced. The back of his head slammed against the stone floor, knocking the breath out of him, and lights flashed before his eyes. He rolled on the floor, grasping for a way out, only for a foot to slam into his side.

Alindale blurted a croaking gasp and curled around his stomach, coughing and dry heaving.

Someone tripped over him, and bodies fell on top of him.

CRACK!

"*Argh!*" a man screamed, following the snapping crack.

"Don't harm the prince!" someone yelled.

"Get the—*Gak!*"

THWOMP!

SMACK!

Alindale caught his breath and pushed against a weight on top of him. He rolled off an unconscious man, who had blood running out of his bent nose and the corners of his gaping mouth. Alindale flinched at the bleeding holes where teeth should have been.

He rolled over and found six men struggling with someone in the center. Men were strewn unconscious or wailing from injuries, like the man Alindale had pushed off. Another man lay against the monastery wall, holding his broken right arm, the bone jutting out from under the skin. Another lay under the wrecked ruins of a table end, blood pooling around his head and splinters from the cracked wood littering on top of him.

"Hold him!" a man in the group yelled.

SMACK!

"*Gah!*" A man stumbled out of the pack, clutching his face, blood squirting from between his fingers.

"I can't hold—*Ahh!*" Another man toppled out of the group, clutching his bent knee and revealing Master Montaigu in the center.

The master knight roared at his assailants, his mouth wide, showing he had no tongue. Two other men let go of him and scrambled away; one ran out the monastery in a panic, slamming through the castle soldiers.

"Wait!" one of the remaining men yelled after him before Montaigu drove his fists into his and the other man's bellies.

As they doubled over, Montaigu grabbed the sides of their heads with his broad hands, his eyes blazing as he pulled them back and—

"*Enough!*"

Montaigu stopped mid-motion before he could slam the last two men's heads together.

Father Finrie stormed into the midst of the carnage, tears streaming down his red face, a distraught scowl distorting his features. "What are you people *doing*?" he demanded, wrenching the men from Montaigu's grip. "This is the house of the Last God! Not a gambling house in South End!" He turned about the room, giving anyone who met his gaze a disappointed stare.

"Father Finrie!" Haemin called from behind the soldiers. "Those good people only seek to bring a fugitive to justice. It is not your place to interfere with the laws of the kingdom!"

Father Finrie rounded on Haemin. "Nor is it yours to incite the people to drag out those who seek sanctuary in this holy place!" He gave Alindale a pity-filled look. "Especially this poor, lone young man."

Alindale withered on the floor. He clutched his sides in a futile attempt to dull the throbbing pain of his ribs. A pulsing drum grew louder in his ears from pressure building in the back of his head. He refused to look around at the people staring down at him and forced himself not to curl up in a ball in front of them.

"Father Finrie, are we to understand that you would give sanctuary to the murderer of His Majesty?" Haemin asked warningly.

Father Finrie folded his hands in front of him. "This cathedral is a sanctuary to all, from the desperate of South End to the lords and ladies in the castle, content with their titles and ignorant of their souls. None may be turned away here."

"So, you stand in defiance of Her Majesty and justice."

Father Finrie shook his head. "I stand not in defiance of you. Neither I, nor any brother, would stand against you should you order your soldiers in to seize this young man." He raised his head, his weathered face turning hard and fixing Haemin with a steely gaze down his long nose. "But I will not stand by and allow the people who came to us, seeking alms, turn into a greedy mob. I will not condone violence or assassinations under this roof!" Father Finrie pulled out the dagger from his robes and slammed it on a table.

Alindale sat up slowly, still holding his stomach, and searched for Nolen, but he was nowhere to be seen.

With puzzled eyes, Haemin looked back and forth from the dagger to the people's watchful eyes. They had lost their attention on Alindale, it seemed, and now waited on what Haemin would do.

"Prince Alindale," Haemin finally said, "will you come out?"

"No!" Alindale spat, but he no longer had strength left. If the soldiers came, not even Master Montaigu would be able to stop them for long, unarmed as he was.

"Very well." Haemin drew himself up, and Alindale prepared for the worst. "Prince Alindale, in fifteen days, the verdict will be read against your co-conspirators. If you haven't vacated the cathedral by then, we will enter and seize you! If you care at all about the safety of the people of this city, of this kingdom, you *will* come out!" At that, Haemin turned on his heels and stalked away, Sunrise Guards trailing at his back. The castle soldiers, however, spread out around the entrance, forming a perimeter.

The crowd burst into small, clustered groups as brother priests came out of their corners to see to the injured men still scattered along the floor.

Alindale's head was pounding, demanding he remain still, but he couldn't curl up in the middle of the floor in front of all these people.

He crawled on hands and knees back toward the cloister, ignoring the few offers of assistance and wrenching himself back to his feet by using the doorframe. Soon, all sound was drowned out by the pounding in his head. He lumbered, shoulders slumped and head hung, back toward the sanctuary. Back to his pew. And collapsed.

Chapter 23

12th of Iam, 1109 N.F. (e.y.)

U p and at 'em, boys!" Kalleb kicked a lancer in the rear after he curled back up in his bedroll. "Get up before I roll you into the swamp!"

He had performed that duty several times already once his troop's eagerness had worn off and they had become increasingly difficult to stir about. He shamelessly enjoyed it each time, too.

The poor lancer groaned and rolled begrudgingly out of his bedroll while a few other lancers laughed at Kalleb's threat. Kalleb gave them each a commanding look, and they hastily threw off their bedrolls to get ready for another day of slugging it through the edge of the Northern Bog.

Damn, we better get through this today. He missed the feeling of firm ground under his feet, even more so under his horse's.

Olivar was leading them on a winding trek through the marshlands. Their camp stretched out for over a mile in individual pockets of men and horses on the highest ground they could find. A humid mist hung in the air, obscuring the individual camps down the line.

Difficult to see or not, it was Kalleb's duty to rouse his whole troop, even if he had to kick every straggler out of their rolls or dunk them in water. And he couldn't trust all his corporals to pick up the slack for him.

"I'm going to wake the others up," he said to those he had just roused. "You men better be packed, dressed, and eating something by the time I get back."

"Yes, Lance Corporal," one said on a yawn.

Kalleb settled for that probably being the most enthusiastic response he was likely to get this morning then cautiously made his way toward the next pocket in line. Already, groans and mumbles of waking lancers hauntingly whispered through the mist.

The wet and humidity made lighting morning fires impossible, or at least they took too long to try. Moss and vines hung off the spindly branches of the trees, their thin limbs stretched out over the water with sparse foliage on the tips, like dangling fingernails.

The bank started to slope suddenly, and Kalleb felt his foot slip before he caught himself on a low-hanging vine. Still, his boot splashed and kicked a little water. He grimaced and rested his hand on his saber for comfort. The mist was bad enough, but the murky, still water was unsettling, especially since no one knew what was lurking in the shrouded pools. He used the vine for balance to quickly find the mossy incline and jogged up it.

"Pack it up, Lancers!" Ian ordered, his stern voice cutting through the mist. "The lance corporal will be here soon and want us moving!"

"The lance corporal is here," Kalleb announced, striding up on the small camp.

Ian snapped to attention and saluted. He stood in the center of the camp, fully dressed and surveying his small group of six other lancers fumbling in stages of undress. His uniform was much cleaner than the others, including Kalleb's, with only a few smudges of dirt or moss speckled here and there. Kalleb didn't know how he managed it.

"Morning, Ian," he said with a wave.

"Morning, Lance Corporal," Ian replied. "We're just about ready here."

By the sluggish pace of his fellow lancers, Kalleb found that quite the understatement.

"Hurry it along, then," he sighed out. "You men need to get something to eat before we press on."

"Back in the shit," a lancer mumbled. With them all bent over, Kalleb couldn't tell who had said it.

"Who said that?" Ian snapped, but no one replied.

Kalleb understood their feelings. Their eagerness to finally be on a mission and riding with armor had quickly disappeared once they had entered the bog. Their morale had plummeted in the humidity, the wet, and the biting insects.

It made it all the worse with the Twelfth dogging them, urging them to quicken their pace. They knew the real mission, while Kalleb's company still believed they were on a training exercise. Kalleb didn't know how long Captain Morsey could keep up the ruse.

"Let it go, Corporal," he said. "Just get everything packed and—"

"Kane!"

Kalleb stifled a growl. Captain Vallant was the last person he wanted to see on any given morning. His annoyance of the bog, and their slow march, dwarfed the men's complaints. And with his rank, he let everyone know and suffer because of it.

Kalleb heard the hoof plops in the shallow water before Vallant came trotting out of the mist. He frowned at how irresponsible it was to the horse but snapped to attention, regardless.

"There you are, Kane!" Vallant snapped down at him. He wore his brigandine armor over his uniform instead of having it stowed. Another stupid move. "Why is your troop not with your squadron?"

"Begging your pardon, sir, but as far as I know, the rest of Squadron Five is rising, too," Kalleb replied. "I haven't heard the call to muster."

"Wrong, Kane!" Vallant spat. "Squadron Five was assigned to scouting duty with the Twelfth's Squadron One. The order went out last night for your squadron to muster an hour early."

Damn change in orders! The messenger either got lost or . . .. Who am I kidding? They didn't tell me.

"Apologies, sir," he replied, straining not to swear. "The orders must have gotten lost."

"I don't care what happened. Get your men up to the front! The sooner we get moving, the sooner we're out of this *damn* bog! I am not spending another night in this miserable shithole. Do I make myself clear?"

"Yes, sir." Kalleb would agree to anything to get rid of Vallant.

"See to it, *Lance Corporal*, or your troop's camping in water tonight," Vallant sneered before wheeling his horse around, slinging mud from the poor beast's dancing hooves, and disappearing into the mist.

Kalleb listened to the splashes from the hooves as the distance grew and waited. He hoped to hear a yell or sudden splash.

Come on. Just one slip, and the dumb ass could be thrown off and drown in that armor. It'd be a waste if he breaks that horse's leg, though.

Fortunately for the horse, no sounds of an accident came. Unfortunately for the rest of them, Vallant was still going to be giving stupid orders.

Kalleb turned back to his men and found them hanging their heads with their gear in hand. No breakfast for them this morning. For his mood, Kalleb didn't have any words of encouragement. He knew nothing could cheer up a hungry belly.

"Afraid shit's going to be worse today, men," he said.

~~~

Cloud snorted in protest as Kalleb dragged him by the reins through knee-deep water. The ground was solid enough, although slippery, and the mud stuck to the bottom of his boots. He couldn't risk taking his time or stopping to catch his breath while trudging across a runoff from rice fields into the edge of the bog. He risked his feet getting stuck in the mud if he did, and then he would really be in a bind.

It would be worse for Cloud. The horse was loaded down with Kalleb's saddle, lance, saber, mace, armor, bedroll, and a stash of food in the saddlebags. The poor beast was more pack mule than lancer's mount, and the extra weight made this crossing even more dangerous if he got stuck.

But on the other side of the runoff was dry land. The opposite bank rose into a grass and conifer field, sparsely dotted with pockets of pine trees. They were finally out of the bog.

"Come on, you stubborn thing," he growled, putting his shoulder into a forceful tug of Cloud's reins. "I know you're sick of being wet, too. We get to the other side, and I'll let you graze for a bit."

The promise of grazing didn't improve Cloud's unwillingness to hurry, and Kalleb was forced to steadily pull and coax him across. When he took his first step out of the water to solid ground, though, Cloud perked his head up, his ears stood on end, and his nostrils flared before jolting forward.

Kalleb yelped and leapt aside before Cloud nearly ran him over to rush up the dry bank. He rolled on his shoulder and came up, sitting on his rear, looking up at the Easterly Sun with his boots splashing back in the water.
~~~

Laughter erupted around him, from the men crossing in line behind him, the men crossing in lines farther up and down the runoff, and the men already across.

"Looks like we're not the only ones happy to get out of that damn bog, aye, L.C.?" Rence, who just happened to be the lancer crossing behind him, laughed.

"Very funny, Rence," Kalleb said dryly, flicking the mud and grass off himself.

As Rence made it to the bank, he let his horse trot after Kalleb's and stuck his hand out. "Need a hand?"

Kalleb took his hand and winced from a stinging pain in his knee as he stood up. He rubbed the momentary pain away with a grunt.

"Getting old, L.C.?" Rence snickered.

Kalleb shooed him away. "Get your horse and find the rest of the troop!"

"Okay." Rence threw his hands up defensively and backed away. "Do you want me to get your horse, too, since you can't chase him down if he runs away?"

"You're about to be—"

Over the small rise, two lancers galloped out of the trees beyond the small field. Their hunched postures and them kicking their horses' ribs told Kalleb they were being pursued. One was missing his lance.

Before they were a quarter across the field, three men on horseback burst from under the trees after them. Two instantly pulled their reins once they were in the clearing. The third, who carried a peculiarly long lance, stopped his horse after charging in a few yards.

"Who are they?" Rence asked. The lancer shaded his face with his hand and squinted at the new arrivals.

Rence wasn't the only one curious about the commotion. More than half the two companies were across the runoff now, scattered about and disorganized. Many had remained dismounted, as well, and were letting the mounts rest. The sight of lancers being pursued, though, had killed their relaxing moment.

Kalleb focused the best he could. He made out the telltale glints of sunlight sparkling off the riders as their horses danced in place, a sign the riders wore armor. The one in front with the large lance turned his head, and light reflected off a bucket-shaped helmet. They all wore blue and white tabards, but Kalleb couldn't make out a pattern from the distance. He didn't need to, though.

"Knights," he replied. "Those are knights."

"What are knights doing here?" Rence asked.

"They're not supposed to be . . ." Kalleb's words died under his breath as the knights turned and galloped away, disappearing back into the trees the way they had come.

His mind reeled. They were getting away, and there was no time to stop them. He had no idea where they were going or how many of them there were. The lancers they had been chasing had peeled off to the left, possibly going to report to Lieutenant Ryne, the Twelfth's Squadron One commander. The possibility of knights being stationed here meant only one thing—their mission was doomed.

"L.C.?" Rence was looking at him with concern.

"To your horse, Lancer!" Kalleb snapped, his heart racing. There was still time, if they moved fast. "All of you! To your horses! To your troops!"

Rence stared, wide-eyed, his mouth agape.

Kalleb gave him a shove toward his horse before spinning around to the men still crossing.

"Hurry, men!" he shouted, waving his arms and beginning to pace back and forth. "Pick up the pace! Kick your horses' asses if you have to, but get them across *now*!"

Stunned and confused, the crossing slowly became frantic. He could pick out the men in different companies by their reactions. The lancers in the Twelfth began pulling their mounts across with heedless determination, almost recklessly. They all knew hearing an officer, no matter how lowly, yell for everyone to hurry across and form their troops was a bad sign, especially with their squadrons so divided. The Eighth's lancers, young as they still were, seemed to slow down.

One especially caught his eye.

"Hurry, Zoren!" Kalleb yelled, making the poor lad jump. He had been walking with his head down, taking slow, deliberate steps, despite not being able to see where he was walking. He was also holding up his line. "If I have to wade in there to drag you across, I will!"

"*Lance Corporal!*"

Kalleb snapped around to find Lieutenant Bowden clomping toward him, dodging a lancer and his horse scurrying out of the water.

"What's going on?" the lieutenant demanded, looking over the chaos with a mixture of concern and confusion. "They can break their horses' legs if they're not careful. Who ordered you to hurry the crossing?"

Kalleb frowned. He hadn't told anyone in his company about their true mission or goal. He had fought with himself to pick out a select few in his own troop the first few days after they had departed Tradon, but the risk of one of them letting something slip was too great. He settled for the hope they wouldn't have to reveal their true intentions until they were in sight of Daincliff and Kanestown. Still, he should have known that was too much to hope for.

He saw no other choice now, other than control who got told what and how.

"Forgive me, sir," he replied, "but our situation has changed. Did you see those knights chasing, what I assume, were a couple of the Twelfth's scouts?"

"I did, yes." Bowden nodded. "Very peculiar. I was on my way to speak with Lieutenant Ryne when I found you doing . . . this." He gestured to the lancers dragging their horses across the runoff. One horse slipped, splashing water everywhere, and nearly dragged his lancer with him before righting himself and wading across.

"Then we shouldn't wait," Kalleb said, making his way toward the direction the Twelfth's scouts were riding. "Once you talk with Lieutenant Ryne, you'll know what's going on."

"Hold up there!" Bowden yelled, storming after him. With a strong hand, he jerked Kalleb around by the shoulder. "You're not going. This is officers' business. And how would you know what's going on?"

Despite serving under him for a short amount of time, Kalleb fought the reflex to snap to attention and obey. He had been surprised by how quickly he had picked up the drilled habit. This time, however, he stared defiantly at the man.

"With all due respect," he replied firmly, "I can't tell you that. At least, not here. You'll understand the situation better from Lieutenant Ryne than from me. I have to warn you, though . . . it's going to be hard to swallow."

~~~

Lieutenant Bowden grimaced, as if he had swallowed a rotten egg, with his chin pressed against his chest. His thick arms stretched his
~~~

uniform's sleeves, threatening to rip them with his arms folded. He took deep, long breaths, nostrils flaring.

Kalleb stood back, letting him think over the truth. He had taken it much more quietly than Kalleb had guessed. Bowden's blusterous demeanor had made him worry he would yell with surprise at every reveal. Instead, he hardly said a word until the end when he had asked for proof. Fortunately, Lieutenant Ryne had written orders from Konner explaining everything, as well, including the possibility of Kalleb being made Captain of the Eighth should Vallant choose not to fulfill the mission when the time came.

Kalleb wondered what was hitting Bowden the hardest—that their mission had been a lie, that the Twelfth had known all along, or that *Kalleb* had known all along and had kept the truth from him. In his position, Kalleb would have chosen the third option. It was hard to rely on the men under you if they kept things from you.

Lieutenant Ryne, however, was writing out a hasty message for one of his lance corporals to rush to Captain Morsey. Shaded under a pair of trees, they were far enough from earshot of most of the men assembling into their troops. The lancers of the Twelfth were hastily getting into their armor and using the rest time to feed their horses.

The young lancers of the Eighth stood away from them, huddled in their troops, and watched the more experienced lancers arming themselves. They likely knew something wasn't right with the tension in the air but, without orders, they stood around, uncertain if they should be following the other squadron's example.

"Get this to Captain Morsey as fast as you can." Lieutenant Ryne handed a note to a waiting lancer.

The lancer saluted before hastily running off.

"You all right, Bowden?"

Bowden looked up, appearing slightly dazed from being pulled out of his thoughts.

Ryne sighed. "It is a lot—I'll grant you—but let me make this simple. *My* family is in Kanestown. The families of most of my lancers are in Kanestown. We are riding to Kanestown. You with us?"

Both lieutenants stared each other down. Bowden towered over the older, stout Ryne, but neither of them wavered.

"I suppose," Bowden said, "that's understandable. Me and my brother only have our grandpa back in Kanestown. I can see why you're all up in arms about this." He worked his lips and gave Kalleb a sideways glance. "Never let it be said that the Bowdens, or lancers of the Eighth, let other lancers down."

"Much obliged," Ryne said with a nod. "Best get your squadron ready, then. Trike's already gone ahead to track down those knights, but we can't wait for the rest of our companies. We've got to ride after them and make sure they don't tell anyone they saw us."

"What were they doing out here?" Kalleb asked.

Ryne stopped in his tracks. "One of my boys thought they were foraging, but neither of them are sure. They just rode up on them."

Bowden remained quiet as they returned to their squadron. While Kalleb was curious to know what he was thinking, he knew better not to ask. He still grimaced as if holding back a seething rage, and Kalleb preferred to return to his duties and give him space than face it. He worried, though, if the lieutenant still had reservations that might change his loyalty later.

Kalleb left for his troop as the other lance corporals nervously walked out to meet them. He let Bowden choose what to tell them while he took care of his own curious and nervous troop of lancers.

"What's the situation, sir?" Ian asked, snapping to attention.

"Did you really get chewed out by both lieutenants, L.C.?" Rence asked, grinning in the back.

"Did we get you in trouble by not crossing fast enough?" Zoren asked, hunched over with his head bowed apologetically.

"Why's the Twelfth's lancers putting on their armor?" Avery asked, standing on his tiptoes to watch them.

"Should we be arming ourselves, too?" Trevor asked. "Or should we feed the horses?"

Kalleb threw his hands up. "Hush, dammit! Bad as kids."

His troop chuckled, either from his comment or seeing him flustered. Their eager and curious faces reminded Kalleb that many of them *were* still kids. Though, they had come a long way since that first day at muster. They at least knew how to mount a horse and hold a lance. Then again, they had only been doing so for three months, and none of them had charged another man or been in a real fight. None of them had faced death.

They might today. Kalleb grimaced. *Can't keep it from them anymore.*

"Troop D," he said, "I got something to tell you, and you're not going to like it."

As he explained the truth of their mission, their eager and curious expressions faded. Pale and shocked looks spread to replace them. Even Rence stood in the back, his mouth agape but silent. Blessedly.

Kalleb did leave out a few details, like how his brother had been arrested and the charge. He left the whole matter of the prince being accused of conspiring to kill the king entirely; simply telling them that Kanestown was under martial law and the families of those who still lived there were being held.

Many took the news hard. Their eyes danced wide open like a gutted stud. A few worked their mouths to speak but couldn't get the words out, the confusion of the news too much for them.

Ian took the news the worst. Kalleb saw him slip away from the rest and disappear behind the horses, his head down and shoulders slumped.

"I know you're all asking why this is happening or how this happened," Kalleb said, trying to sound reassuring, "but those are questions for later. All you need to know is that we are riding to lift Kanestown, one way or the other. And those knights we saw a moment ago cannot reach Daincliff and tell them we're coming. So, feed your horses and get your armor on. Move."

The men broke up in small groups, clustered together, as if afraid to be alone.

As they returned to their horses, loud demands and yelling erupted from the other troops in their squadron. The other lance corporals were telling their men close to the same thing that Kalleb had told his, and they were all taking it differently. Poor Stew Bowden, the lieutenant's younger brother especially, held his big hands up defensively, trying to calm the insistent and frantic demands from his lancers.

"Excuse me, Lance Corporal."

Kalleb gave a start. He hadn't noticed Jentrey Hunt still standing there.

"What is it, Hunt?"

"Just curious. Does Captain Vallant know about all this?"

Kalleb paused. He had kept Hunt at a distant during the march, finding odd jobs to keep him busy. The hard terrain had kept Vallant's man in his troop occupied. In the excitement, though, Kalleb had forgotten him and now felt suddenly apprehensive. In their current situation, Hunt could be dangerous.

"Yes," he lied. "All the officers have known all along."

Hunt raised an eyebrow. "Really? The captain hasn't acted like this exercise, or mission as you say, was important at all."

"He's been a very good actor," Kalleb explained. "Even fooled me."

He hoped his lie wasn't too transparent. Vallant's attitude toward this whole mission since they had entered the bog had been that it was a waste. And he wasn't shy about letting people know.

"Get to your horse, Hunt," Kalleb ordered, walking around him. "I got to make sure mine hasn't wandered off."

Hunt grabbed him by the shoulder, and Kalleb turned on his heels, flinging his hand off. Hunt pointedly ignored his glare.

"Has any word been sent to the captain?" he asked insistently. "Why are the lieutenants hurrying us? We need to wait for the rest of the companies."

You mean, wait for Vallant, Kalleb mentally finished.

If Hunt had simply let him go, Kalleb would have wondered if he had bought the lie. Now he was sure he hadn't. Fortunately, he was just a corporal, and Vallant was an hour or more behind them.

"There is no time," Kalleb said firmly, making sure to keep his voice low. "A messenger has already been sent to the rest of the companies, but we have a mission to complete. And *nothing* is going to stop us. Now, tend your horse! We got knights to catch!"

Kalleb took him by the shoulder this time and shoved him forward. He gave him a stern, officer's look that said he didn't have the rank to say no.

Hunt shook his head, found his horse among the mounts, and began tending to it, with Kalleb watching every step of the way.

It's starting. Kalleb took a careful glance at the other troops and found they were slowly arming and tending to their horses, as well. He found Lieutenant Bowden next to his, still grimacing like a rock. *Some are thinking there are two sides to this and wondering which side to pick.*

As he tended to Cloud, the stud eager to munch down some grain, he figured chasing down knights to be a great distraction from worrying if the lancers around him were thinking of siding against him.

~~~
~~~

The lancers rode through the trees, spread out in four columns, trying to keep in formation while also spreading out their search. The lancers from the Twelfth took the right, leaving the Eighth on the left. Kalleb's squadron was divided into two, with his troop and Troop C in the farthest left column.

They rode around every tree in their path, with their lances crouched and eyes sharp, studying every moving bush and fern they rode past. Stealth was impossible. Their armor, weapons, and kits *clanked* loudly while their horses stomped through the wood.

The knights will hear us long before we find them.

Kalleb rode at the head of their column with the other lance corporal, Stew Bowden. They tried to keep in sight of the other half of their squadron, fifty yards away, but they had lost sight of them shortly after entering the trees. He caught Stew standing up in his saddle, anxiously searching for sight of his brother before flopping back down, discouraged.

"Take it easy," Kalleb told him softly so their men wouldn't overhear. "We'll join back up with them soon. Just act like we know what we're doing, for the men's sake."

Stew grunted, but his worrying frown remained.

As they rode on, the forest grew quieter. The distant trills, chirps, and hoots from animals faded away.

Cloud snorted and shook his mane, making Kalleb take a firm grip of his reins in case he bolted. The memory of the gorro ambushing Roy crept up on him, and he checked over his shoulder at the lancers behind him.

They were a lot more nervous than before. Many sat on edge, and some pushed themselves up by their stirrups, barely touching their saddles. They looked behind every tree and warily watched every large fern and bush, regardless of if something moved. Kalleb even saw a few flashes from lance points thrusting into them to check the bushes.

His ear twitched, and he spun in his saddle.

Was that a clang?

He listened harder, leaning forward in the saddle and squinting, trying to see farther through the woods ahead of them.

Nothing.

Kalleb was about the sit back when he definitely heard something. A faint clanging of metal against metal. It was so faint that he couldn't tell if it was one clang or many.

"Do you hear that?" he asked.

"Yeah," Stew cautiously agreed. "It's too quiet."

Kalleb frowned and realized Stew hadn't heard anything. He was nervously looking behind every tree and bush, like the men.

"Not that," he said. "Something's happening up—"

A long barrel lowered from behind a tree, aimed right at his head.

His eyes went wide.

He pulled Cloud up sharply and threw his head back. The stud wailed angrily in surprise from the sudden, harsh treatment.

Surprised cries rang through the column like a wave.

Kalleb almost fell out of his saddle and would have if he hadn't righted himself by the stirrups. Only then did he see Olivar Trike stepping out from behind the tree.

"Dammit, Trike!" he growled.

Olivar frowned up at him. "You're all too noisy. I heard you coming a mile away."

"And you couldn't wait for us where we could see you?" Stew growled.

"Had to make sure you were who I thought you were and not get snuck up on," Olivar replied. "Where are the rest?"

"We split into columns and spread out," Kalleb informed him before waving to his right. "The rest are over there."

Olivar glanced that way and spat. "Too far. They might ride on by. Send riders to turn 'em this way. While we wait, I'll show you where those knights went. It's something to see."

~~~

Kalleb had never seen a siege before and had never expected to find one out in the middle of nowhere.

A large company of knights and soldiers surrounded a centuries-old castle set on hill, overlooking the forest and a small road trailing around it. By the number of recently cut tree stumps around its outer wall, Kalleb figured the owners hadn't planned defensively for a long time. The stones were worn gray and patches of moss had grown up in several long stretches.

Two banners flapped in the soft breeze above the outer gate and the castle's keep. One was royal banner of Daincliff, and the other had a yellow background with a black crisscross skull of what Kalleb thought was a cross skull boar.
~~~

"Those are the knights we saw earlier," Lieutenant Ryne confirmed, studying the knights besieging the castle with a spyglass.

All the officers of both squadrons studied the battle hidden behind the forest's tree and brush line. Ryne's focus was on the large camp at the base of the hill instead of the soldiers assailing the castle's outer walls with ladders and arrows from two directions, that they could see. Their camp also waved two banners—the royal banner of Daincliff and a light blue banner, striped with white bars.

"A whole brotherhood, I figure," Olivar noted. "Maybe more. At least they have more men than the poor bastards bottled up on that hill." He pulled out a strip of jerky meat from somewhere and ripped off a piece.

The whistle of arrows and snapping of bow strings cut through the air, followed by the missiles arching over the outer wall. No return volley came, not even when the ladders were set. From their angle, Kalleb couldn't see how many defenders were on the wall. The lack of defense made him wonder if there was any.

"Why are they fighting?" Lieutenant Bowden asked.

"Who knows?" Ryne shrugged. "All we know is they saw us." With his spyglass, he scanned the camp then suddenly stopped.

"There!" He pointed off to right. "Knights are mounting."

Ryne passed the spyglass to Bowden, who looked around before he saw them and grunted.

"Close to a squadron size, I'd say," Bowden said.

"If such a heavily armed force takes the runoff before our companies can cross, it'll be a blood bath," Ryne said.

Kalleb shuddered. *It would be a disaster.* He figured it would be worse with his company being inexperienced and having little faith in Vallant.

"How can we be sure?" Bowden asked. "If the knights are fighting each other, how can we be sure they're going to fight us?"

"They chased after my scouts!" Ryne snapped. "That's all the proof I need."

"But it would be best if we avoided a fight if we could!"

The two lieutenants locked each other in an unblinking stare, both obviously unwilling to give up their position but neither with the rank to order the other to obey.

Kalleb grimaced in frustration. From behind his tree, he spied the knights mounting and some forming into a column. They would be heading toward them soon, and they needed a plan. Their numbers brought one to mind.

"May I make a suggestion?" he insisted.

Both lieutenants snapped around toward him, and Kalleb caught the faint rustles of his fellow lance corporals shifting uneasily around him.

"And what would that be?" Bowden growled warningly.

Kalleb ignored it. They didn't have time.

"Entice and Encircle," he replied.

The lieutenants shared a curious look before Ryne broke away and moved closer, intrigued.

"Go on." he said.

"We have two squadrons; they only have one," Kalleb explained. "One squadron rides out to meet them under a flag of truce. If the knights parley and tell us they don't wish to fight, we wait for the rest of our companies and move along. If they do wish to fight, we lure them in with one squadron and, upon contact, the other squadron charges in from the flanks."

A quiet pause set in. Ryne toyed with his saber's hilt, drifting into thought, his eyes dancing, as if watching the tactic play out. Bowden, though, stared blankly at him.

Kalleb understood and drew back in surprise. His fellow lancers only knew him as a lance corporal, training in the fundamentals, like them. Not in complex maneuvers they have yet to be taught. Yet, the tactic had naturally come to him.

He shrugged it off to deal with their current situation.

"Kane," Olivar grunted, happily chewing on a thick piece of jerky.

"It could work," Ryne finally admitted.

"Too complex," Bowden disagreed, shaking his head. "It requires a lot of discipline and timing. The squadron that entices must be disciplined enough to meet a charge at the right moment. They can't charge too early or break. The squadron that encircles must charge before the knights can react. My squadron's not ready for either task."

"We can encircle," Kalleb insisted. "We charge, we hit them, and we break away before they can hit back. It all depends on when the order to charge is given."

"Or who gives it," Bowden added.

"Better make up your minds." Olivar burped, nodding toward the knights' encampment. "They're heading this way."

The column of mounted knights was riding out of their encampment, kicking up dust, straight toward them. The Easterly Sun glinted off their armor, helmets, and lances.

"My squadron will entice," Ryne said. "If they give battle, encircle them. No matter what, they can't stop our mission. For Kanestown!" He left them, rushing back into the woods with his lance corporals on his heels.

Bowden watched him go before giving Kalleb a worried look. "We'll have to divide the squadron to encircle. I'll lead the two troops on the right. I suppose there's no use asking if you'll be leading the left?"

His fellow lance corporals mumbled confusedly to each other, but there wasn't enough time to explain. Kalleb could tell Bowden had accepted the idea of him taking command, if not reluctantly.

"I'll lead my troop and Troop B on the left," he replied. "Troop A and C can stay under your direct command."

Bowden perked up. He took a deep breath, his broad chest swelling, and held his chin in the air. "Agreed." He nodded, and Kalleb took it as a thanks for suggesting his younger brother stay with him. "To your troops! We have a battle to prepare for!"

As Kalleb joined his fellow officers, Olivar grabbed him by the shoulder.

"You're taking over easily," he chuckled. "Better than Konner thought you would."

"Thanks, Olivar," Kalleb said begrudgingly, "but we really got to go now!"

"But you didn't tell me where I fit in."

Kalleb looked over his shoulder. Those knights were getting closer, and from the bushes rustling and snapping behind him, Ryne's squadron was coming up behind.

"Just find some place to watch," he said. "I'm sure you can take care of yourself."

"Sure can." Olivar barked a laugh then threw his rifle over his shoulder. "But I promised Konner I'd look after you. Since you have no place for me, I'll make *myself* useful and see what's holding the rest of your lancers up. You can never have enough cavalry, right?"

Kalleb grinned. "Right."

~~~

We should have trained more calming techniques.
~~~

Kalleb worried the heavy breathing from the fifty nervous men behind him would give them away. It had been hard enough finding the grove of trees on a hill slope to hide them and their horses from the advancing knights and those still in their camp.

The mounted knights broke their column as soon as they saw Ryne's squadron trotting out of the woods. They formed two long lines, fifty knights each, with a space of ten feet dividing them.

Ryne, though, kept his squadron in troop columns, each of the four troops formed into four separate columns of five and spread out facing the length the knights' line. The formation confused Kalleb. Their tactic would require them to engage the knights' entire line. If they charged, the Twelfth's current formation would put more force in breaking the knights' line in several points and lessen the advantage that the knights' heavier armor gave them.

But the space between them would let some of the knights' ride and threaten to encircle each troop individually. If either Kalleb or Bowden charged too soon or were seen, some in that second line could turn to meet them. Their encirclement could fail.

What is Ryne thinking? Kalleb thought.

"They've been talking for a while," Timothy, lance corporal of Troop B, said. "Maybe they're talking it out."

Kalleb didn't have it in him to crush his fellow officer's wishful thinking. The stocky boy had lost weight since the first time he had met him back at muster. His beady eyes were squinted as he tried to read the faces of Ryne and the knights talking in the middle of the field between the two forces under flags of truce.

As Timothy bobbed his head about, trying to get a better angle, Kalleb glanced at the saber bouncing at his hip. The same saber he had shown off so proudly to his fellow lance corporals at muster.

"Did you put in any training with your saber yet?" he asked.

Timothy swallowed and defensively clutched his saber's hilt. "Some."

"Don't use it unless you have to," he advised. "Rely on your lance, mace, and fellow lancers."

Timothy puffed his lip and hung his head. "Okay."

The young man was shaking. The length of his saber wobbled as his hand shook.

Kalleb looked over his shoulder. Most of the men stood with their shoulders hunched, their arms folded with their lances propped under their arms, and horses' reins clutched tightly in their fists. The horses felt the tension of their riders and held their ears up in the air, turning them this way and that, listening for danger.

"Come on," Kalleb told Timothy. "We got to talk with the men."

He took Timothy by the pauldron plate on his shoulder and led him back to their men. The men in front saw them coming, and their eyes lit up. The wide-eyed dread from several of them reminded Kalleb again that many of them were still just boys. There would be no playing lancer after today.

"Listen up!" he said firmly but didn't shout. "Those of you in the middle, relay what I have to say to those in back. This is going to be a real fight. A real charge with an enemy at the end. Keep your training in mind. If we surprise them, thrust your lances under their shoulders or in their thighs. Don't go for their necks, because you're likely to miss. If you crouch your lance, you will hit them harder but risk breaking it. If you do, use your mace and bash your way out.

"We are going to hit them *hard* and hit them *fast*, and then get out. Hit them and pull back. Do *not* get in a melee with them! Do *not* go off on your own! Stick with your comrades and look out for one another. If you see a knight's been unhorsed, but so has a fellow lancer, pick up the lancer and get out of there. No glory hunting, or you're going to get yourselves killed.

"You have your training and your fellow lancers. Stick to them. We can do this. I promise I won't leave any of you out there alone. All right?"

"Yes, sir," the men in front said, and then the response rippled down the column.

Kalleb nodded then turned to find Timothy saluting him.

"Thank you," he said, "sir."

Kalleb waved him down. "At ease."

Back on the field, the talk between Ryne and the knights had taken a turn for the worse. They were pointing at each other, gesturing toward the men behind them, and their shouts barely reached where Kalleb and his men were hiding. The short, demanding tones made Kalleb suppose they were yelling for each other to stand down while trading threats and cusses.

That's that.

He rushed over to Cloud, untied his reins from a tree branch, and took his helmet from his saddle horn.

"Mount!" he ordered. "Spread the word down the line. We charge only when I order it. Follow the man in front of you and remember what I told you."

Kalleb's helmet was snug. It pushed in his ears, and no amount of wiggling made them any more comfortable. *Serves me right for just taking what was handed to me instead of trying it on first.*

His entire company had been outfitted with armor in a rush before they had headed out on their mission. He wouldn't be surprised if most of his lancers had complaints about their armor not fitting right. Another worry Kalleb had to push down as he climbed into his saddle.

He lowered the face guard, which many of his fellow lancers didn't have, and took up his lance from leaning against a tree, crouching it under his arm.

In the field, Ryne and the knights shared their last insults before turning their mounts and riding back to their troops. They mirrored each other, shouting orders to their men. The front line of knights lowered their lances, while the second line drew swords and waved them in the air, yelling battle cries.

Ryne's squadron stayed in troop columns, their front line lowering their lances.

"Ride, Lancers, ride!" the whole squadron shouted in defiance.

This is it.

Kalleb checked Timothy behind him, hearing his loud breathing echoing out of his helmet, his face guard a mere bar curving down his face. He was also holding his lance high.

"Crouch your lance," Kalleb ordered. "You'll get it caught on a branch."

Timothy jerked then briskly did as he was instructed.

Kalleb turned in his saddle and saw other lancers holding their lances high, too. "Pass the word back. Crouch lances until we clear the trees."

"Yes, sir," a lancer said, and then the order trickled backward. Lances fell like a ripple, shafts knocking against saddles as they did.

Kalleb took one last look at his men. There was still fear there. There was no way one talk would make it go away. None of them had ever been in battle, and Kalleb had never been in a fight like this. He was merely going off training and instincts passed down to him by his family.

He caught Zoren looking at him from a few horses back, sitting hunched over, too tense in the saddle, and hugging his lance to his side as if it were holding him up.

Kalleb looked right at him. "Stay with me. We knock these shiny pricks out of their saddles then ride on to Kanestown."

Grunts echoed, and a wave of nods flowed down the column close to him. Several leaned forward in their saddles, preparing to kick their horses into a gallop. The horses snorted and pawed at the dirt, sensing their riders were about to turn them loose.

Maybe this is how I should have done it five years ago.

The rumbling of hooves cut him off. He whipped around in his saddle to find the two groups beginning to charge. Their formations unchanged, Ryne appeared to be countering the knights' heavier armor by putting more numbers to break points in the knights' line.

Kalleb swore at seeing it.

He's supposed to be drawing them in so we can encircle them, not break their line so they'll scatter!

It was too late. They were charging. Maroon-clad lancers thundered down the field toward the galloping blue and white knights, their lances each aimed at the other's guts.

Kalleb leaned forward in his saddle. His focus narrowed to the distance between them. His heart pounded, beating in time with the hooves.

Fifty feet . . . Forty feet . . . Twenty . . . Ten!

He kicked Cloud. "Charge, Lancers!" he roared. "*Charge!*"

Cloud screamed, or it could have been Timothy, or the lancers behind him, and leapt forward. Their crashing through the woods was drowned out under the sounds of Ryne's squadron's and the knights' lines colliding together. Screams and wails cut over the thumping of horses slamming against each other and steel scraping against plates. Lancers were lifted from their saddles, impaled on the ends of the knights' thick shafts. Knights in turn tumbled from theirs, grasping at their gushing throats or bleeding armpits, skewered from a well-aimed lancer thrust.

The field was in chaos moments after Kalleb had ordered the charge. He hadn't reached a quarter of the distance and the knights' lines were already fractured by Ryne's troop formation. Now it was a jumbled mess with knights trying to hit the flanks of the columns while the troops made a dash to avoid getting caught in a melee from all sides.

Kalleb saw no choice, so he pointed Cloud toward where the knights' line used to be.

"Level lances!" he shouted over his shoulder.

Timothy was still riding with him on his right and following his lead, leveling his lance. A lancer from behind pushed his horse too hard and began sliding between them. Kalleb gave him space and let him. This was no time for a reprimand and their charge would have greater effect if there were more of them at the front than two.

Glancing to his left, he saw another lancer ride up and join him.

The knights spun and whirled, trying to rally for another charge after Ryne's squadron. One pointed his sword at Kalleb and his lancers.

Kalleb aimed for that one.

Leaning in his saddle, he looked down his lance's shaft, right at the knight's side.

Other knights wheeled around.

Too late.

A knight turned just as Kalleb and the lancer beside him crashed into him. His horse wailed, and the man cried as the poor beast was thrown sideways, crushing its rider under him.

The jostling from the hit threw off Kalleb's aim, and instead of hitting his chosen knight under the arm, he struck his shoulder pauldron instead. His lance point grazed against the plate, throwing the knight back but not unseating him. The blow to his shoulder did prevent him from striking back with his sword before Kalleb stormed on by.

The world suddenly shrank now that he was in the fray. Cries of pain, cusses of anger, and pleas swirled around and by him. The wretched stench of blood, piss, shit, and bile filled his nostrils. Metal hissed against metal. Here and there came the faint, gut-wrenching sound of metal sinking and slicing into flesh. All of it passed him by within seconds of each other.

Kalleb couldn't slow down. He refused to slow down, or he would get pulled into a melee, or trampled over by the lancers behind him. His odds of surviving a melee were slim. And he could only hope there were still lancers behind him.

A dismounted knight slowly rose to his feet ahead of him, stumbling on shaky legs. His breast plate was caved in with a massive dent, but there was no hole or sign that it had been punctured. He shook his head, clasping his bucket helmet as if to remove it.

Sorry, Kalleb thought, *but you should've stayed down.*

He leveled his lance again and steered Cloud directly at the knight. The distance closed fast. He aimed his lance at the knight's chest below the neck.

CHUNK!

The knight never moved to dodge.

His helmet was halfway off when Kalleb's lance point speared through the left side of his neck. Hot blood sprayed Kalleb's leg and Cloud's flank as they rode on. Kalleb didn't even glance back to see the knight fall.

A mounted knight suddenly appeared in front of him. His lance, dripping in gore, leveled right at him.

No time to wheel or angle Cloud. No time to draw back his lance to aim another thrust. On instinct, Kalleb crouched the lance under his arm and leaned forward in a desperate attempt lower himself into Cloud as much as possible. In the last second, their eyes met through their visors, eyes wide with near madness.

CRACK! SHING!

The knight's lance slammed into Kalleb's right shoulder, ripping off his pauldron and throwing him back in his saddle.

He yelled from the jarring impact. His lance was ripped from his hand as it struck the knight's plate and slid down to his belly, impaling there and getting stuck. Both lances exploded and cracked. Splinters showered them.

All within a blink of an eye, and then they were beyond each other's reach.

Kalleb entered a daze from the pain in his shoulder. His vision became blurry, and when he came to, he found himself on the other side of the field. Cloud slowed to a trot then to a stop, panting and wheezing.

Kalleb lacked any strength to wheel him around. The flaring pain from his shoulder drove any of those crazy thoughts away. His right arm hung limp at his side. He was slightly amazed it was still there. He could still move his fingers, but there was something wrong with his shoulder.

He rubbed it and gasped from the stinging pain. Tears ran down his face. He cupped it and realized it didn't feel right.

Dammit. Dislocated. Or broken? If only slightly. He could feel the bone out of the socket.

He gritted his teeth and pulled until he heard a dizzying *pop*.

He gasped and slumped in his saddle. His shoulder was still sore, and he would probably have trouble swinging anything.

Cloud snorted at him.

"I'm alive," he told the stud, patting him on the neck. He chuckled as the horse shook his mane. "We're alive. We made it through our first—"

Kalleb glanced around. He was alone.

"Where—"

He jerked back toward the battle, and his heart sank at finding what he feared the most.

A disorganized melee churned in the center of the field. Battle lines were gone. Cohesion on both sides were gone. Knights and lancers battled each other in groups and individually. On horseback, knights hacked with their swords as lancers flailed back with their maces. Here and there came the pings of saber against arming sword. And underneath, the ground had turned to mud from dismounted knights and lancers wrestling with each other.

And the dead piled around all of them.

More thundering of hooves tore him away from the horror of his green lancers being hacked to pieces by the knights playing in his mind.

To his right, another long column of lancers, led unmistakably by Lieutenant Bowden because of his bulk, were charging into the fray.

"Now?" Kalleb cried in anguish. "You're charging *now*!"

Bowden and the head of his column crashed into the melee, bringing only more confusion to it as men and horses screamed. Their column was so long, though, that the charge slowed to a crawl by the time the lancers in the center reached the battle. Those in back stopped altogether and began trotting around the melee like lost sheep.

Kalleb shook his head.

Cloud snorted and pulled at his reins. Three knights were riding toward him, swords waving in the air.

"Yeah, I guess you're right," Kalleb told him. "We shouldn't be sitting here!"

He wheeled Cloud around and kicked him into a gallop. His shoulder throbbed in protest with every bounce. He didn't bother glancing over his shoulder to see if the knights were chasing him. He steered straight for the closest group of lancers and hoped they would see.

"Knights on your flank!" he yelled, charging in.

A lancer turned and pointed his lance at him. Several of the lancers who had been trotting around the melee grouped together and charged, hopefully at the knights following him. However, they charged too close together for Kalleb and Cloud to pass through them.

Sucking wind through his teeth, Kalleb turned Cloud sharply to the right, dashing out their path.

And straight into the melee.

Horses and riders bumped and shoved against each other as if the world was shaking apart. The sounds of battle mixed and drowned everything out. Swords, sabers, lances, and maces clashed against each other as men and horses cried, yelled, and struggled against each other.

Kalleb kept his head down and kicked Cloud forward, trying to find a way out. He thought of getting his mace, but his pulsing right shoulder was strongly against the idea.

The knights and lancers around him lashed out at anything that came near them or tried to hit them. The knights especially, with their limited visors, could only react back if a lancer attacked them, giving Kalleb an edge to slip by them so long as he didn't touch them and draw their attention.

We need to get out of here! he growled in frustration at the slow pace. His mind raced for a way out. *We need . . . to rally.*

Cloud stopped and flailed his head. Their path was blocked by a lancer and knight grappling together on the ground. The knight flipped the lancer on his back and fell on him. Holding his sword by the hilt and blade, the knight drove the point into the lancer's breastplate, trying to skewer his guts. The lancer cried out.

Kalleb's own words came back to him. *Save the lancer!*

He kicked Cloud forward, and the stud rammed into the knight, sending him and his sword flying. He reached down to the wounded lancer with his good arm.

"Come on!" he yelled.

The lancer's face was covered by his visor, and he struggled to his feet, holding his middle. Nevertheless, he finally grabbed hold, and Kalleb pulled him up. Cloud snorted and whined under the weight of two riders. Kalleb ignored him.

"Hold on to me!" he ordered the lancer, who in turn wrapped his arms around him.

The melee was getting worse. Lancers were falling to knights' swords as they hopelessly tried to bash them with their maces. They needed to get out. If someone didn't order it soon, they would be cut to pieces.

Cutting through the pain in his right shoulder, Kalleb reached across and drew his saber. While his hands exchanged the saber and reins, the knight that Cloud had rammed had gotten back to his feet and was rushing back in, trying to grab the horse's reins. Kalleb kicked him in the helmet for his effort.

"Get out of my *frickin'* way!" he roared, waving his saber in the air. "Lancers, to me! Lancers, to me!" He kicked Cloud into trot then into a gallop. "Rally, Lancers! Get out of here! Lancers to *me!*"

The closest lancer joined him. Then another. A few to his right broke off their fight with some knights and joined them. More followed. They became a stream, galloping out of the desperate fighting. Kalleb let Cloud gallop, not caring where he was going so long as they got out with as many lancers as they could.

They finally burst out of the melee . . .

And found a column of infantrymen with pikes marching toward them. They had broken out in the worst possible place. They were in the middle of the field, facing the besieged castle, and the knights' soldiers had finally noticed the cavalry battle behind their camp. Those pike and spearmen could turn the melee into a rout.

Kalleb threw up his saber and yelled, "Wrong way!"

He tried to steer Cloud to the left, but the horse reared, nearly throwing him off. His shoulder screamed when he came back down. Cloud panted and snorted, foaming around the corners of his mouth. The stud was tired. He had slogged through the bog all morning just to be thrust into a battle with only a short rest and small bag of grain. The breakout from the melee was probably the last bit of strength he had left.

Lancers pulled up beside him, worn out and hanging in their saddles. Several saw the infantry coming and were able to gallop away. The rest formed around him. Their horses, too, were spent.

Kalleb looked at the lancers beside him and didn't recognize either. By how young the one on the left was, he suspected him to be a member of his company. The one to his right was older, blood staining his beard.

"I'll stick with you until the end, men," he promised, holding out his saber to the advancing infantry. The older lancer grunted and drew his own saber, while the younger shook his mace in his hand.

The first rank of infantry lowered their pikes.

Just then, a horn blew from the castle, and the front gates opened. Mounted knights, carrying a yellow banner in front of them, charged out. Their small number dove into the camp as soldiers with red and yellow tabards rushed after them, clashing with the besiegers and arches left to harass the walls.

The infantry marching toward Kalleb kept advancing. He knew they would likely kill Cloud first then kill him once he was on the ground. Or perhaps they would try to kill him first and give him an opening to kick Cloud into them, just enough to be around them so they couldn't use their pikes. But, even if Cloud had the strength for one last gallop, Kalleb would be pulled from his saddle and torn to pieces.

Sorry, brothers, Ma. I didn't make it this time, either.

POW!

The small eruption cracked over the battlefield. The fighting continued. The pikes were getting closer, but Kalleb grinned.

From his left, three columns of lancers, each two squadrons strong, charged out from the woods. One column wrapped around the melee, the second thundered off toward the knights' camp, and the third blessedly slammed into the infantry's flank.

The infantry column rippled. As the far left shattered under charging lancers, the far right and rear saw their camp was being attacked. Pockets of men broke formation and made a run for it. The center held firm, forming a defensive ring of pikemen as more and more lancers thundered and whooped around them.

Kalleb and the rest around him stayed where they were and let the battle continue around them. He joined in a collective sigh of exhaustion and relief and deflated in his saddle.

Men around him began to laugh. An infectious laugh. Slow to start but impossible to stop as one realized they were about to die, but now they were alive.

Kalleb felt the pull to join in, but he was too tired.

"I think we should all rest for a bit," he said. "What do you lads think?"

The lancer with the bloody beard laughed loudly and slapped his shoulder. His injured shoulder.

"*Ow!*" Kalleb cried and nearly crumbled out of his saddle.

That just made the lancers around him laugh harder.

He shook his head and struggled to sheath his saber.

He suddenly realized he felt lighter and thought he shouldn't be. As he was sheathing his saber, he noticed no one was holding on to him like before. He glanced over his shoulder and found the lancer who he had saved lying on his back behind Cloud. He must have fallen off when the horse reared.

And he remained on the ground.

"Lancer?" Kalleb cried.

He swung out of the saddle, wincing and groaning from the sharp pain in his shoulder when he hit the ground. He cradled his arm and wobbled over the fallen lancer. As he fell to his knees beside him, he shook the man's breastplate, getting his hand wet with blood. It was running from the puncture in the lower middle of the plate.

In a frenzy, Kalleb wrenched the stubborn face guard up then reeled back.

Ian stared back at him with glassy, unfocused eyes, blood running down the corners of his mouth.

Kalleb fell back and, with trembling hands, raised his own face guard. The cries of victory as the last knight and their soldiers dropped their weapons swept by him like a forgotten breeze. He remembered Ian being standoffish after being told the truth of their mission, that they had to get to Kanestown to at least try to lift the martial law. He had a wife there, and now she would never see him again.

"I'm sorry, Ian," he said, closing the man's eyes. "I'm so, *so* sorry."

Chapter 24

"Alindale?"

His name reverberated, as if spoken underwater. Something cool and damp pressed against his forehead, but his world was still black.

A groan bellowed from deep within him. Everything was numb. He couldn't move his limbs.

"Alindale?" someone called out to him. "Can you hear me? You need to open your eyes."

Alindale groaned again. His head was swimming, but he felt consciousness returning. Sharp stings ran down his spine and his limbs. The numbness was fading. His fingers twitched and legs spasmed. His eyelids fluttered and soft candlelight pierced through the cracks.

When his vision finally cleared, he looked up, a damp cloth was on his forehead, and he saw Father Finrie standing over him with a concerned look on his face.

"Alindale!" the father said excitedly. "Thank God. You must stay awake. Can you speak?"

Alindale weakly opened his mouth, but only a small gasp escaped. He felt suddenly lightheaded, his sight becoming blurry. He smacked his lips together, his throat dry.

Father Finrie reached down beside the pew and brought up a cup.

"Shh . . ." the father hushed, gently sliding his hand underneath Alindale's head and tilting him up. "Drink slowly."

The cup was pressed to his lips, and before Alindale could swallow, the wine's sharp, alcoholic tingling ran down his throat, spreading a fire throughout his insides.

He coughed. His head spasmed, throwing off the cloth on his forehead as he struggled for breath.

"There," Father Finrie said. "The wine will get your strength back. You had us worried."

Alindale coughed again and laid his head back, finding a pillow waiting for him. "What's happened?"

Father Finrie frowned and concerningly glanced to the side before turning back. "You've been laying in the sanctuary for a day and a night."

Alindale squinted at him, but Father Finrie's worried look remained.

Realization hit him, and Alindale's breath caught. He grabbed the head of the pew and jerked up, immediately regretting it. The lightheadedness returned, harder than before, sending his vision swimming. His head bobbed, unable to remain steady from the sudden rush of nausea.

"Slowly, Alindale," Father Finrie urged, taking a hold of his shoulders to steady him. "The back of your head is still swollen. Don't rush yourself, but you must stay awake now."

The cathedral's windows were dark. The chapel filled with shadows cast by the various candles spread about. Those surrounding his father's casket were small nubs, the little melted wax left hanging from the holder's edges.

Alindale took in the empty chapel and spotted the shadowy, bald figure of Master Montaigu sitting in the back pew, close to the doors.

"Sorry, Father," he said. "I must have fallen asleep in the pew."

"Rather, you must have hit your head harder than we realized," Father Finrie corrected. "Your knight found you lying here soon after, unconscious with the back of your head terribly swollen. We thought it best not to move you. But now that you're awake, we can breathe easy. It's good"—he slowly sat down and sighed once he was in the pew—"to know people can find rest here, especially when I'm not preaching."

Father Finrie beamed a smile, and Alindale tried to not to laugh at the obvious, old joke.

They sat a moment in silence, allowing his nausea to slowly wear off. He turned his aching body around and rubbed life back into his numb limbs. The curve in the pew offered a great nook to curl oneself up against and block out the light, but the hard wood left him stiff.

A whole night and day? he reeled, thinking of the time. *Must have been right after . . ..* The events in the monastery came back to him bit by bit.

"Sorry," he apologized, "for the trouble I caused."

"Think nothing of it," Father Finrie replied.

"But they were here for me," Alindale insisted, leaning forward with his arms against his knees. "None of those people would have been hurt if it wasn't for me."

"They were here for you," Father Finrie agreed, "but they could have come for any of those other poor souls, as well."

"Haemin wouldn't have put on such a show if he were after one of them. Probably would have sent the city peace in and just arrested them. He *could* have simply done that to me." Alindale took deep, steadying breaths to keep the nausea from returning.

"Why didn't he, you think?"

"He just wants to keep humiliating me."

It was the only explanation that Alindale could think of. He didn't see Haemin, or anyone left in court, caring about him hiding in the cathedral. They could have seized him with a simple order. The theater of the hiding prince, though, was something Alindale was sure they were enjoying.

Father Finrie exhaled loudly and folded his arms. "So, what do you intend to do? You defied them yesterday, you and your knight. Do you intend to keep on fighting?"

"I don't know," Alindale sighed out. "It seemed like the right stand to make at the time, but when the people tried to carry me out . . .."

That had been the most terrifying moment in his life. All those hands dragging, holding, and pulling him along. No matter how much he would have struggled, they would have still thrown him out.

"You can still surrender," Father Finrie suggested.

Alindale hated to admit it, but at any other time, he probably should have, just plead his case and hold fast to his innocence. He had done nothing wrong. Therefore, logic told him there was no proof that he had committed a crime. Nolen's story, however—if he could even believe the sneak—told him otherwise. Everyone in court had already made up their minds, even his own mother.

"I can't," he replied. "I can't just give myself up to be falsely tried and executed." The back of his head pulsed like a dull heartbeat as he drifted his gaze toward his father's casket. "Is there really any hope?"

The pew creaked as Father Finrie sat back and said, "Remember, I only have the Last God's immutable counsel."

Alindale turned to hide his smirk. *Well, I shouldn't be surprised.*

"And what does the Last God counsel?" He set his shoulders for another long sermon that he would have to piece together later.

"Hmm . . .." Father Finrie hummed, as if he were having to piece it together himself before giving it. Then, surprisingly, he grabbed the pew in front of him and, with a wrenching groan, pulled himself up. "Come with me," Father Finrie instructed, patting him on the shoulder before walking away. He even waved at Master Montaigu to follow.

Alindale watched Father Finrie shuffle to the cathedral's side door and pick up a lantern he must have left when he had first entered.

"Get up, Alindale," Father Finrie called from over his shoulder. "You've sat in that pew long enough."

Alindale grunted and carefully rose. He braced himself against the pew for a moment, steadying himself against the last wave of nausea. Then he walked out of the sanctuary, with Master Montaigu trailing behind, checking behind every door they passed. They caught up to the slow-moving father easily without having to rush.

The cathedral's grounds were quiet, but while walking around the cloister, Alindale picked out lumpy rows crossing the open ground. Distant lanterns and candlelight leaked from windows, revealing people curled up in blankets, and mothers huddled with their children, with notably few men among them.

"Has something happened, Father?" he whispered. His breath then caught from a sudden thought. "Are the soldiers not letting *anyone* out?"

Father Finrie stopped, casting his lantern's light on the sleeping people. "No. These poor souls came seeking sanctuary after being evicted. The castle and ministries are putting South End through a renovation after that devastating fire a few weeks ago.

"Many people have come here, seeking sanctuary rather than going to the camps outside of the city. But we only have so much room and had to limit the space to families with children. Most of the men, though, are out searching for work, if they can find any."

Father Finrie turned and hobbled on his way, whereas Alindale stared at the huddled forms on the ground, remembering that night in South End.

I was there, he thought. *I could have said something; made it stop before it happened.* He had kept quiet because Nolen had told him it was for his own safety, and no one would have listened to him, anyway. Looking at the consequences now, however, Alindale felt only shame.

Montaigu nudged him and pointed after Father Finrie. Alindale said nothing, following until they were led around to the rear of the monastery.

"Where are we going?" he whispered.

Father Finrie remained silent until they came to an old, cracked door. A large iron lock dangled from its handle, covered in rust along with the door's hinges. He set his lantern down and fetched a ring of long, old keys, clinking together as he pulled them out of his robes.

Alindale gritted his teeth from the squeal of the lock's stubborn tumblers. Red and clay colored dust flaked off the lock by Father Finrie's mere touch. When the latch finally came loose, it popped off and the lock fell apart.

"This door hasn't been open for over a century," Father Finrie commented.

Montaigu grunted.

Father Finrie pushed on the door, but it didn't budge. He tried again, to no avail.

"Master Knight," he begged, giving Montaigu an apologetic look, "if you please?"

Montaigu pressed against door then rammed his shoulder into it. The wood groaned and popped, but the door held. Montaigu grimaced and pulled back a little farther before slamming against it again with a grunt.

CRACK!

The door flung open and banged against the wall. In the light, Alindale could make out a landing and steps leading down into darkness.

"This is all I can do for you," Father Finrie told him, handing the lantern to Montaigu. "May whatever you find serve you well. God be with you, Alindale." He began to shuffle away. "And don't forget your prayers."

Alindale watched him go before turning toward the black stairwell. A stale musk escaped from below, like someone exhaling after holding their breath. Montaigu held the lantern low, checking the doorway with suspicion.

"Father Finrie wouldn't lead us to harm," Alindale attempted to assure him.

Montaigu gave him a long look before cautiously starting down the steps.

The air grew staler the farther they went. The stairs led straight and narrowed. Montaigu's shoulders brushed the walls as they approached the bottom. When he did, he stopped, preventing Alindale from joining him. Alindale watched the lantern's orange glow, catching glimmers of things below.

"Is everything all right?" he asked.

Montaigu walked forward without a gesture or grunt.

Alindale stepped down into a large room. His eye caught a glint from his left, and he jumped. As his eyes adjusted, he found a metal plate hanging on a wooden peg.

Armor?

He ran his hand over the chest plate and found a long crack running through it. The edges were frayed and bent.

Decayed armor.

He frowned then explored more.

Tables lined the walls with piles of old plate armor stacked on them. The lantern casted an ominous glow on the racks of forgotten instruments of war from the center of the room. Montaigu ignored the armor to search through a pile of swords on the other side.

"Where did all these weapons come from?" Alindale questioned. He walked by a spear rack with scattered spearhead around its base and splintered remains of rotted shafts.

Something caught his eye in the far back. He walked closer and discovered another rack holding armor plate. Brushing away the dust, he saw this plate had held up better than the previous. He ran his hand across the breastplate, feeling indentations, like a design, but couldn't make it out in the dim light.

"Master Montaigu, could you bring the lantern over here?" he asked.

A grunt later, the light moved closer and revealed a man holding aloft a sword with a white disk around the blade.

"The Knights of Adam," Alindale recognized. He looked to Montaigu and found the master wide-eyed for the first time. "These weapons are from the Disarmament."

In 898 N.F. (w.y), a question had arisen on whether knightly orders should be beholden to the church or the kingdom. Many brotherhoods had tenements of faith in their own codes, but none so symbolically as the Knights of Adam. Alindale recalled they were the predecessors to the Sunrise Guard, but because they had invoked Adam Dain the First, they had been seen to have a religious affiliation. In the end, the Disarmament of the Church decreed the church could not have its own knightly orders, so any brotherhood affiliated with it had to change their charters or disband, including the Knights of Adam.

Montaigu lowered the lantern and found a sword hanging off the armor. He pressed the lantern into Alindale's chest, giving him no choice but to take it. Then Montaigu took the sword off the rack, frowning critically as he examined the sheath. The wood was weathered, but not cracked.

Montaigu took it by its hilt and slowly unsheathed it. The lantern's orange glow flickered off the blade's dull steel. The sword was a little longer than a regular arming sword and had a finer tapered tip.

"Is it usable?" Alindale asked.

Montaigu shrugged as he rubbed the side of the blade then motioned against its edge with his fist.

"Needs cleaning and sharping?"

Montaigu grunted then walked to the center of the room. He squared his shoulders and took a stance, holding the sword out in front of him with both hands. He swung, slicing the air with a loud *swoosh*. He remained motionless for a moment before breaking his stance and turning back to Alindale.

"Master Montaigu, I haven't thanked you—"

Montaigu pressed the sword against his chest and held it there.

Alindale gave the sword a confused look before looking back at Montaigu. "You want me to take it?"

Montaigu nodded.

Still confused, Alindale set the lantern down then held up the heavy weapon.

Montaigu stepped back and took a stance, holding his hands together, as if clasping an imaginary sword.

Alindale squinted at him. "Make a stance?"

Montaigu nodded.

The weeks of training came back to him, and Alindale realized what the master knight meant.

Once he did, Montaigu walked around him, correcting his shoulders and feet. When he was finished, the master knight hand motioned *"forms."*

"You want me practice my sword forms?"

Montaigu nodded.

"How many times?"

Montaigu shook his head then flashed *"five."*

"Fifty times?"

Montaigu grunted and slapped his arm, making Alindale wince. He flashed *"five"* again.

Alindale rubbed his arm and swallowed. "Five . . . hundred times?"

Montaigu nodded.

"Seriously?" Alindale complained. "I've been unconscious for a night and day. My head still *hurts!*"

Montaigu grabbed him by the shoulders and glared at him, his dark eyes made even darker from the shadows of the lantern. His nostrils flared from his heavy breathing.

Alindale swallowed hard. "I only have fourteen days."

Montaigu nodded again then let go.

It had been over two weeks since Alindale had last swung a sword, and his arms were already beginning to protest holding another. Nevertheless, he took a stance, raised the old blade, and swung. The long steel wobbled a little in the hilt on the down swing but remained firm. So, he swung again, ignoring the dull pain in the back of his head. He stepped and made a thrust. Then swung again. And again. And again.

***

Tory floated in darkness. Everything swayed bank and forth. Staying in place but always swaying.

Sound was a vacuum, muffled but humming, as if in a void.

Or water.

I know this feeling.

She was underwater, just barely under the surface. She saw the ripples of the surface, but no light source. She seized, holding her breath, but her lungs weren't burning. There was . . . air?

Where am I?

She tried to turn her head but couldn't. She tried to spread her fingers to catch the water, to stroke with her arms and kick with her legs, but they didn't move. She felt them yet didn't. Her entire body felt pressed together, as if bound.

Why can't I move? she thought frantically.

Her world thrashed. Or maybe it was her body. She couldn't tell for sure. Her breathing became short and fast, panting through the vacuum.

But her body was turning. Or, at least her vision was. She rotated around, the rippling surface sliding away, and then she was gazing into the black abyss.

Tory thrashed again.

She knew where she was. She knew she shouldn't be there. Only death lurked here.

Deep water.

"Poor Little Fish."

Tory's eyes bulged, and her throat tightened, as if something was strangling her. She gasped, desperate for air. That wasn't her voice. It echoed from below.

"Stay loyal. Stay innocent."

From the depths it came. The massive, thirty-five-foot-long monster steel-jaw fish rushed up at her. Its mouth gaped wide enough to swallow her whole. Its armor plates clinked together. Its jaw sheers gleamed in unholy light. And as those jaws sliced around her, Tory's world went white.

~~~

Tory screeched. She was falling and instinctively reached out to grab anything she could find.

And landed hard on the deck, her elbows slamming into the boards and driving air out of her lungs.

"Ow!" she groaned, wrapping her arms around herself. She clutched her throbbing elbows and rolled over onto her back, stray splinters snagging her hair.

"Miss Tory!" Yuba Linch cried out.
~~~

As feet slapped against the deck, Tory's sight and senses finally cleared enough for her to make out her brother's first mate kneeling over her with concern. He cradled the back of her head and put his knee under her.

"Are you well?" he asked, checking her up and down for injuries. "Was it another nightmare?"

Tory swallowed hard. She had slept little in the days after her release. Every time she closed her eyes, she was back in that horrible cell where an immortal was endlessly tortured, and towering figures surrounded her, demanding she sign a piece of paper. Every time she tried to sign, her hand wouldn't move. The demands would grow louder until the figures turned into monsters.

This time was different. This time, she was already in the deep water for the monsters to devour.

"Yes," she said on an exhausted sigh while brushing her hair out of her face, pulling it behind her ears. "I'm sorry if I scared the crew."

After her release, Jerro had immediately taken her to his ship. She refused to step foot back in the castle, which Jerro completely understood. Although, now that she was aboard, she tried to stay out of the crew's way.

"You didn't scare any of them," Yuba said. "Except the watch, the rest are asleep below."

"Asleep?"

Tory lifted her head and looked around. Night had fallen, and the lanterns were lit. Even at berth, the crew lit them all from bow to stern.

She looked back at her hammock, erected on the forecastle because she refused to return to her quarters below deck. They were too cramped, reminding her of the closeness of the cells. Her hammock was twisted into knots like a stowed sail. She didn't remember laying down, though.

"How did I get here?" she asked.

Yuba rubbed the back of his head and puffed his cheeks. He nervously looked away, avoiding her eyes. He was a few years younger than Jerro and barely had any red in his hair. His coppery skin tone marked his heritage from Crescent Bay rather than directly from the Blood Isles, but Jerro trusted him and his navigational skills. Although, Tory did notice he was awfully shy around her.

"You sort of . . . collapsed." Yuba winced.

Tory sat up straight. "Collapsed!"

"Yes, miss." Yuba nodded. "One minute, you were walking the deck. The next, you . . . fell. The captain said it was because you haven't been getting enough sleep."

Tory cupped her face, more out of embarrassment than anything else. She had thought these northern ladies were weak, fanning themselves wherever they went, and yet she had fainted in front of everyone. In front of her brother's crew!

"Where is my brother now?" she asked.

"The captain's not here, miss," Yuba replied. "Was summoned to the castle, he was."

Tory perked up. For days, she had feared Jerro would get in trouble with Serina or someone from court for bringing her back here. She didn't trust any of them to let her go.

"How long has he been gone, Yuba?" she demanded, seizing his shoulders. "Did he say who summoned him? Or why?"

Yuba leapt back and stumbled to his feet. Tory wasn't sure if it was because she surprised him or because she had touched him. The crew treated her differently, being the sister of the captain. Somewhere between fellow brothers, or friends of her brother, they tried to watch their manners around her.

"Sorry, miss." Yuba bowed his head. "I don't know who summoned him, but—"

"Officer of the Watch!"

Jerro's voice made them both perk up.

Yuba immediately scrambled off, toward the forecastle's steps. "Here, Captain!" he yelled, running along the deck railing toward the gangplank.

Tory picked herself up and straightened her clothes, a comfortable cotton blouse and trousers. They were loose-fitting from being borrowed, but they were better than a choking corset and tripping skirts. She rubbed her elbows, still a little sore after having fallen on them, walked over to the railing, and peeked.

Jerro was waiting at the gangplank with a trunk resting on his shoulder. Behind him was a man in a coachman's outfit, struggling to carry another trunk with two hands, his back bowed over it. Another man, carrying yet another trunk, followed from a carriage parked at the end of the wharf.

Tory's eyebrows leapt upward. Nina was getting out of the carriage with a bag and large cage.

Tory ran down the forecastle steps just as the gangplank was being lowered.

"Baby sister!" Jerro thundered at seeing her and ran up the plank the moment it struck the wharf.

Tory and the gangplank crew stepped aside to make sure they weren't run over.

Jerro dropped the trunk with a heavy *thud* on the deck and instantly took her by the shoulders. "Are you all right?" he demanded, looking her up and down before cupping her head and running his fingers into her scalp. "No head wound? No trouble speaking?"

Tory giggled from his fingers tickling. She saw the crew watching them, though, and her cheeks warmed.

"Stop it, Jerro!" she complained, pushing his hands away. "I was just a little tired."

Jerro snorted. "You wouldn't be tired if you slept in your quarters."

Tory's smile slipped. "I . . ."

"Lady Tory!" Nina yelled.

Her maid servant bobbed behind the coachman, who was now climbing up the gangplank with his heavy burden. The plank shook from the coachman's painstakingly slow pace and Nina's impatient bouncing. Tory worried the plank would slip from the wharf.

When the coachman made it on board, he dropped the trunk with a loud *thud* and gasped in relief. Nina gave him no time to rest, pushing him aside to rush up to Tory. Dropping both her bag and the cage, her maid leapt and wrapped Tory up in a tight embrace.

"Oh, Lady Tory!" Nina cried, pressing her face into Tory's shoulder while squeezing her. "Thank the Last God you're safe!"

Tory would have laughed, happy to finally see Nina was safe after being separated for so long. Instead, all the air was forced from her by Nina's stranglehold.

"Nina," she gasped, "you're . . . choking me."

Nina jumped back, her eyes misty with tears. "I'm sorry, My Lady. I'm just so glad to see you're well!"

Tory took deep breaths, slumping her shoulders from the sudden excitement. "I'm fine. Barely."

She meant it as a joke and halfheartedly laughed. Concern grew on Nina's face, though, as she studied her. The maid brushed Tory's hair back, her eyes dancing across her features.

"What did they do to you, Lady Tory?" she finally asked.

Tory bit her lip. She was sure she looked horrid. Her hair was stringy and flat, her face was gaunt from lack of appetite, and her eyes were likely redder than normal, with bags under them because of the nightmares. She glanced at Jerro and shook her head.

"It doesn't matter," she said. "I'm . . ." Her eyes unconsciously wandered down to the cage, and she realized she hadn't received someone else's greeting.

"What's wrong with Harpo?"

Nina grimaced at the cage, and Tory's heart sank. She dropped to her knees and peered through the bars. The dim lantern lights barely helped, but she could see her pytre hawk, curled up in the center of the cage, surrounded by a fluff of discarded feathers. She chirped a weak imitation, but he didn't chirp back.

"He's alive, My Lady," Nina said. "But he's in a bad way. Your Ladyship's sister made me keep him locked in the cage, and when you didn't return, he refused to come out. He hasn't eaten in a couple days."

Tory balled her hands into fists against the knees of her trousers. Her eyes then finally adjusted, and she made out Harpo's sides expanding and deflating, weakly.

"Fetch me some meat from the galley," she ordered, picking up Harpo's cage and heading back to the forecastle. "I'll take care of him."

"Yes, My Lady," Nina said. "But, why are you heading up there?"

"I'm staying on the forecastle for now," Tory called back.

"But—"

Tory glanced over her shoulder and saw Jerro take Nina aside. Jerro briefly whispered to her, cutting off the obvious concerns she had, and waved her away.

They're probably going to team up on me, she suspected. *Try to make me go to my old quarters.* She could hardly follow Nina walking to the opening to go below. The sight of the narrow corridor gave her chills and forced her to look away. She instead turned back to poor Harpo.

"Stow these trunks below," Jerro ordered to his crew. "Once everything's on board, raise and secure the gangplank."

"Yes, sir!" the watch crew said.

Tory set Harpo's cage on a barrel and opened the cage door. Her poor pytre hawk trembled from a small breeze swept in from the harbor and buried his head deeper into his forearm.

"Anything to report, Yuba?" Jerro asked.

"Nothing, Captain," Yuba replied. "Harbor's been quiet since the city peace patrols swept through."

Jerro grunted. "Still, make sure the watch keeps a sharp eye out. Those South Enders are becoming more desperate to stow away anywhere if it saves them from being put out in the camps. I'm afraid they'll riot if their markets are closed."

A chill ran up Tory's spine. She looked across the harbor and made out a few more columns of smoke than there had been the night before, rising from the derelict part of the city. During the day, the sounds of hammers, saws, and winches filled the harbor, followed by the occasional collapse of buildings. At night, fires lit the sky, filling the harbor with the smell of smoke.

The worst part was the people. Nights before, the docks had been full of homeless South Enders, huddled in the corners and alleyways between the fishmongers and warehouses. Some had tried to sneak aboard ships. That had alerted the harbor masters, who in turn brought the city peace to run them out.

Tory's ear twitched from the sound of Jerro's boots walking up the forecastle steps.

"How is he?"

Tory shook her head. "He's lost a lot of feathers and is weak from not eating. Probably dehydrated, too."

She spied a coil of rope on the deck and decided not to wait for Nina to get back. Carefully, she reached into the cage.

"*Tory*," Jerro warned.

She ignored him. Harpo was her pytre hawk, and she knew what he needed—food, water, and someplace warm. Someplace open.

I'm getting him out of this stupid cage!

She gently cupped Harpo's wings to his sides and slid her fingers under him to hold his legs. There were two things to watch out for in handling a pytre hawk—their teeth and their talons. She knew Harpo wouldn't bite her so long as she didn't surprise grab him or hold him too long. She just needed to hold his wings and legs in and move him to the coil of rope quickly.

She gripped him firmly. He was thin, and his breathing slow. She felt his head move underneath his forearm and knew she had to act. Tory picked him up before Harpo poked his head out. His talons scraped against the cage floor, and his head bobbed and weaved as she pulled him out. He blinked at her. More of his head feathers were gone, exposing more of his black scales. Tory felt his wings and legs try to stretch against her grip and hastily rushed to the coil of rope.

Harpo squawked at the sudden jolt, flashing his sharp, needle-like teeth just as Tory set him on the rope. She let him go and hopped back, hoping he would stay there.

Harpo plopped on the coil and flared his wings and fore-arm claws, letting loose another warning squawk. He bobbed back and forth, taking in his new surroundings, before collapsing on the coil. He tucked in his wings, blinking as if on the edge of exhaustion.

Tory exhaled. *At least he stayed.*

"Had another nightmare?"

The hairs on the back of her neck stood up. Jerro stood much closer behind her now, grimacing at the twisted state of her hammock.

"Yeah," she admitted, slumping.

"Same one?" Jerro asked.

"No," she replied, beginning to untwist her hammock. "And yes."

Jerro raised an eyebrow.

"It's complicated." That was about all she had told him about what had happened to her in the tower. It was easier that way than have two of them share her nightmares.

After finishing straightening the hammock, she sat down and rocked in it to make sure it was still firm. Seeing Harpo curled up on the rope gave Tory a way to change the subject.

"Thank you," she said, "for bringing Harpo and Nina back."

Jerro snorted. "No need for that. I couldn't free one prisoner and leave the other two, could I?"

Tory snickered.

"Pull!" Yuba yelled. On deck, the watch crew hauled in the gangplank with a loud rumble, threatening to wake the entire dock.

Hearing Yuba reminded her of something else, and she critically looked Jerro up and down.

"Yuba said you were summoned to the castle. What did Serina want?"

Jerro folded his thick arms. "How do you know I saw Serina?"

"Your clothes." Tory picked at the hem of her hammock. "They're not formal enough to meet Her Majesty or ministers, and they're not stylish enough for a . . . rendezvous."

Jerro didn't take her bait at the tease. Instead, his expression hardened. "Serina said your absence has been noticed at the . . . at the trial," he replied. "She wanted you to attend."

"*No!*"

Everything went quiet, the deckhands talking, the coachman and his lads heading to their coach, and the ship's rigging stopped moving. Tory's screech had startled even her.

She dug her nails into the hammock's fabric, her body quivering. "I will *never* go back there!" she hissed. "You hear me, Jerro? Even if they send every soldier to drag me back, I will throw myself into the harbor and take my chances *swimming* home!"

Jerro threw his hands up. "Easy, baby sister, easy. I told Serina the same. Except the part about you swimming home. That seems a little extreme."

Tory knew he was trying to comfort her, but she was in no mood for jokes. She hung her head, suddenly feeling so exhausted, yet her body continued to shake.

"I told Serina that I would not allow you to be forced off my ship," Jerro continued, patting her on the shoulder and kneeling beside her. "Especially after not telling me about the first trial when they sent you to the tower. And *certainly* not to make you a side prop at this second one."

"Thank you," she said weakly and did her best to give him a grateful smile. She failed to hold it long, though, before it slipped away.

Jerro took her hand and squeezed it. "There is a condition, though, Tory."

"Get more rest?" The quip just slipped out, not meaning to be a joke.

Jerro didn't laugh.

"No. I was able to stand against Serina from forcing you to attend the trial"—Jerro's chin trembled, and his iron grip got tighter, threatening to crush her hand—"but not the execution. The family can't have anyone notice you missing from that and think you're still disloyal. Not even a little."

Tory's eyes went wide. She worked her mouth, but no scream escaped.

With everything else, Serina wants me to watch that!

Jerro's reasoning brought the first minister's words back to her, "*Stay loyal. Stay innocent.*"

Jerro pulled her into his broad chest and wrapped his arms around her, cupping her head just like he had done when she had been released from the tower. "It'll be all right," he promised. "It'll be horrible to watch, but you will be *all right*. I promise, you won't be taken off my ship until that day. Then, on that very day, after all is done, I *will* take you home. I promise, you'll never have to come back here. You just have to be strong, baby sister. Syros strong."

Jerro squeezed her tighter, and Tory squeezed him back. She had never seen an execution before—her mother had forbidden it. But she saw no way out of this.

"I will," she whispered. "I'll be strong."

Jerro stroked her hair and held her for a few more moments before finally letting her go. He then patted her on the head as he walked away.

"And try to get some rest," he said from over his shoulder.

"I'll try."

On deck, Jerro gave some passing instructions to Yuba and the rest of the watch before retiring below, leaving her alone on the forecastle.

Tory glanced over at her hammock then sighed in relief at seeing Harpo still nestled on the coil of rope, his sides expanding and deflating, with his head underneath his forearm. When she straightened, she spotted the cage still sitting on top the barrel. She stood and picked it up, spilling the loose, red feathers on the deck while shifting it in her hands. She then went to the ship's railing and held it over the water.

We will never be caged again, she swore, releasing the cage. It made a small splash upon impact then sunk into the abyss. *Never again.*

Chapter 25

The thrill of victory had waned in the hours after the battle. The lancers had effectively taken over the besieging knights' former camp. A mixture of fatigue, worry, and excitement hung in the air after word had spread of their true mission.

But they weren't the only ones in camp. Knights of the brotherhood whom they had liberated walked in pairs or threes, thanking every lancer they met. Townspeople from Siegman's Success wandered about, searching among the living and dead of both brotherhoods for missing loved ones. Apparently, both had levied men from the township to fight in the siege.

Kalleb passed several weeping women and men, mourning over the bodies of dead soldiers laid out with the rest of the dead. Lines of men had been dragged from the battlefield and arrayed so they could be identified. They had only stopped after sunset. He was coming back from counting his own dead and avoided looking at grieving family members the best he could.

Seven lancers from his troop had died in battle, including Ian. Three others were injured, and two of those wouldn't be riding again any time soon. Lieutenant Ryne was also dead; killed in his initial charge. Over half his squadron were dead or wounded.

Lieutenant Bowden had been thrown from his horse and found comatose. No one was sure if he would ever wake up again. Of the thirty-six dead and injured in Squadron Four, over half of them were shared by Troop B and Troop D, Kalleb's troop.

Too many. He cradled his right arm, set in a sling. His shoulder still throbbed and was starting to bruise up to his collarbone, down his arm, and creeping across his chest the last time he had taken his uniform off to check it. *We lost far too many.*

Leaving the dead behind, the camp proper was lit by dozens of campfires, spread out in rows for the men to sleep around. The surviving tents from the captured knights had already been commandeered, but there wasn't enough room for most of the men. Laughing, crying, shouting, snoring, and even singing came from every direction.

Kalleb wanted to find his bedroll and crawl under it.

"Lance Corporal!" Trevor sprinted down a lane of tents, his unbuttoned uniform flapping behind him as he ran, revealing his sweat-stained, yellow undershirt. He had been one of the lucky ones in the rear of Kalleb's column. It turned out they had gotten bottled up, like Lieutenant Bowden's column had. Being in the rear, Trevor had ordered as many as he could back and not to charge into the growing melee, probably saving a few lives.

His concerned look added more weight to Kalleb's heart.

We lost another one.

Trevor stumbled to a halt in front of him, doubling over and clutching his knees as he sucked air in.

"Calm down, Trevor," Kalleb told him. "You're going to collapse after a day like this."

"Sorry . . . sir," Trevor gasped out, "but Captain Morsey sent a messenger requesting you join him and the other of Twelfth's officers in their new command tent. It's the large, blue-striped one." He pointed at a large tent near the center of the encampment, almost directly facing the castle.

"Fine," he sighed out, heading toward it. "No need to get out of breath over that."

"It's not that, sir," Trevor wheezed out as he fell in behind him. "I think something's wrong."

"We just came through a battle; a lot of things have gone wrong."

"Okay?" Trevor replied, confused. "But, sir, we're having trouble finding people."

"If you're asking about Kori, don't bother." Kalleb's grimace darkened. "I already found him." The back of the poor lad's skull was caved in, and not by a sword, either. The massive, round dent in his helmet could only have come from a mace. The melee must have been so intense that men swung weapons around, not caring who they hit.

"Oh." Trevor paused a moment. "But, sir, there's more. We can't find Captain Vallant."

That's a good—

Kalleb stopped mid-step.

"What do you mean, *we can't find Captain Vallant?*" Their captain had barely been in the battle, riding in with the rest of the companies to turn the battle into a rout. Knowing Vallant, he probably waltzed in *behind* the rest of the company so as not to get dirty.

"We just can't," Trevor replied worriedly. "Captain Morsey asked for him, as well, but we can't find him. We checked with the other squadrons, and he wasn't with them, either."

Kalleb broke into a cold sweat. "Is anyone from the other squadrons missing?"

Trevor straightened in surprise. "We can't find Lieutenant Horus or Lieutenant Mires when we went to their squadrons."

A line of sweat ran down the side of Kalleb's face. Those were commanders of Squadrons One and Two. Vallant especially favored Squadron One and spent a lot of time with them during their training drills.

His bad feeling reminded him that they weren't the only ones Vallant favored.

"When did you last see Hunt?"

Trevor's eyebrows bunched together as he glanced toward Troop D's encampment. "Last I saw him, he was getting situated with everyone else."

"How long ago was that?"

"A few hours."

"Was he there when Captain Morsey's messenger came?"

Trevor's mouth fell open to respond, but he paused. He then turned his eyes upward in thought. "I . . . don't recall."

Kalleb ground his teeth together. The last time he had seen Hunt was shortly after the battle. He had been preoccupied with Ian's death and trying to drag the man's body off the field, using one arm while his injured arm held on to Cloud's reins. His head had been so clouded by pain and exhaustion after the battle that he hadn't even asked for the other lancers to help him.

Hunt had ridden up to him, clean as if he had never charged. His lance's head, though, had been red with blood. He had requested they report to Captain Vallant, without a word about Ian. Kalleb had told him to piss off and probably would have thought to drag the ass from his saddle if he hadn't been injured.

Vallant knows something is wrong. He's getting everyone he trusts together to decide what to do.

The shadows between the tents leading toward the knights' castle looked darker and taller than they had a second ago.

Or maybe they've already decided.

"Get the men," he ordered Trevor. "Get Troop D together and bring them to the command tent. They need to bring their lances and maces, too." He cut off Trevor's incoming question with a wave. "Go! Now!"

Trevor frowned but saluted before running off through the camp.

Kalleb watched after him to be sure none of those shadows jumped out and grabbed him. Then he glanced down at his saber, hanging uselessly on the left side of his hip. There was no chance he could draw it if he were attacked. He suddenly wished he had kept his armor on.

His right shoulder naggingly stung.

Well, most of his armor, anyway.

He took a deep breath. *Let's take this slow and easy. And smart.*

Kalleb strolled into the Twelfth's encampment, figuring there was less of a chance Vallant would have sent someone to grab him among those lancers. He moved around and through their tents and bedrolls, making a wandering path, curving here, zigzagging there, toward the command tent.

~~~

"Who goes there?" a lancer posted outside the command tent demanded as Kalleb walked out of the shadows.

No one had grabbed or attacked him, but Kalleb still cautiously approached the tent, gravel crunching under his boots. His back itched as if someone was watching him. The sight of only one lancer standing guard did nothing to settle his nerves.

"Lance Corporal Kane of the Eighth, Squadron Four, Troop D," he answered softly to avoid shouting out his name.

"One moment."
~~~

The lancer pulled the tent flap back and poked his head inside. Instantly, Kalleb's nostrils flared from the scent of roasting meat mixed with wood smoke drifting out from the tent. His stomach growled, reminding him that he hadn't eaten a real meal all day, and his mouth watered.

"Lance Corporal Kane is here, sir," the lancer announced.

"Send him in!" Morsey shouted, his voice slightly muffled. Kalleb could guess why.

The lancer stepped back from the entrance and held open the flap.

Inside, Kalleb found a victory feast. Captain Morsey ate at a table—presumably captured with the tent—with his officers to his right and three knights to his left. He shared space with one knight wearing a white tabard crested with a black skull of a cross skull boar on his chest while his compatriots' tabards were stained yellow. The tent was lit by an iron cast, and a glass lantern dangling from a chain over the table.

Close to the opening, the spitted carcass of their meal still hung over the glowing coals of the cook fire. Kalleb thought it was a hog at first, but then he saw the feet sprawled out to the sides and four toes instead of hooves. Without a head, he wasn't sure what the animal was, but it still had some meat left, and it smelled better up close.

"There he is!" Olivar laughed, appearing from the corner of the tent with a mug in his fist. He slapped Kalleb on the back and nearly sent him sprawling over the cook fire. His right shoulder screamed in protest, and the sharp throbs brought tears to the corner of his eyes. Olivar caught him, though, wrapping his big hand around the back of his neck.

"This is the officer who thought up the plan that saved your knightly asses!" Olivar laughed again, tapping his mug against another knight in a yellow tabard.

The knight was a head shorter than Olivar, bald, with only curly mutton chops running down the sides of his face, along his jaw, and to his chin. His cheeks were bloodred. He pressed his lips together and squinted at Kalleb. Either he had taken offense to Olivar's boasting and was going to take it out on Kalleb, or he was really drunk.

"We'd've done okay." The knight burped, his breath so strong that it made Kalleb blink rapidly. "We Enderval knights are worth *ten* of those Aulbrone thieves. Come marching up and demanding our charter and keep." He spat and squinted at Kalleb. "But, you know . . . I was expecting him to be taller than you"—he slapped Olivar in the chest with his mug, splashing beer—"ye blond giant!" The knight burst into laughter, and Olivar joined him.

"More beer?" Olivar asked, throwing up his hands.

"Why not?" the knight replied, laughing his way to the rear of the tent where the beer barrels were situated.

Kalleb watched them wobble away and shook his head. *How does Trike find these people?*

"Kane," Morsey called, gesturing him over to the table.

Kalleb walked around the roast and saluted with his left hand.

"We can dispense with that," Morsey said before turning to the knight beside him. "This is Master Noa Blain of the Enderval Knights Brotherhood.

"Master Blain, this is Kalleb Kane. He's the surviving officer who led the charge today."

The master knight appeared to be a man in his mid-thirties, much younger than Kalleb would have expected for someone with his title. He wiped his mouth with a napkin as he methodically studied him with his hazel eyes, lingering on his slinged arm and saber. He bore no signs of a man who had just endured a siege. His black hair was slicked back and combed, his face clean shaven, and his tabard pristine. He sat straight back and poised in his chair, as if he could leap up at any time, but he also reminded Kalleb of something else.

He's an aristo. He had seen them eat together many times with Amanda, and their snobbish "table manners" always made him roll his eyes. *But, if he's an aristo, why is he a master to a Knights Brotherhood way out here?*

From what Kalleb remembered, aristos thought the Knights Brotherhoods as old commodities of the past, like a saber from a great-great-grandparent. They would hire them as guards or teachers for their sons in martial arts for sport, but few ever joined them.

Master Blain sipped water from his cup, his eyes lingering on Kalleb's wounded arm. "You should be wearing your saber on your right hip," he finally said. "It's useless with your arm in that sling. Is it broken?"

Kalleb pressed his lips together tightly to keep from saying something he shouldn't. They had just met, and Kalleb had been a part of the battle that had saved this knight from being besieged.

You could have at least thanked me first.

"No," he replied. "My shoulder was dislocated by a lance blow. The armor took the brunt, and the bone's been put back in place. It's just sore."

"Better get it looked at," Master Blain suggested. "At worse, your collarbone may be broken."

Who are you to give me orders? Kalleb wanted to yell, yet a warning voice told him that they were wasting time.

"What Master Blain means to say is," the closest knight beside the master interjected, roughly the same age, "thank you for coming to our aid. We didn't get to see the initial charge, but we're grateful you helped us crush the Aulbrones." He raised his mug, his red beard flaring as he passed a thankful smile across the table to all the Storm Cavalry officers.

"Here, here!" the other knights around the table cheered, lifting their mugs and cups. Even Olivar, with his newest friend, bellowed laughs and joined in raising theirs. Master Blain, though, folded his arms and sat back in his chair.

Kalleb frowned, watching them drink. They were too happy.

"Don't look so serious, Kalleb," Morsey told him. "Get you some food. We need to go over a few things. Master Blain and the Endervals are aware of our situation and have suggestions—"

"There's a problem," he interrupted, stepping closer to the table.

"Can it wait?"

"No." Kalleb glanced sideways at the knights, especially Master Blain, who leaned forward in his chair. The worrying voice was yelling at him that they didn't have time to bother with what the knights thought. "We can't find Vallant, and several of his closest officers are missing, as well."

Morsey shrugged. "So? Captain Vallant sent word to us that he was eating with his officers when I sent him the invitation to join us a little while ago."

Kalleb broke into a cold sweat again at the lie. "My men couldn't find any of them, *eating* or doing anything else."

Morsey's confused look told Kalleb he didn't see the danger.

"You talk as if you don't trust this officer," Master Blain noted, his eyes narrowed and his right hand casually slipping under the table.

"We had that fear when this mission started," Morsey admitted, nodding. "But when the word came of the battle with the Aulbrone

Brotherhood, I explained the situation to Vallant. He accepted the orders and ordered his company into battle with my own."

Kalleb found it hard to believe that Vallant would just accept the orders after learning he had been lied to.

"Did he not have any questions?"

Morsey shook his head. "He heard there was a battle and performed as a Storm Cavalry officer should. Maybe the mistrust you and Major Konner had for him was unfounded."

Or maybe Vallant settled for getting his questions answered later, when he had more of his men around him and time to think. A bootlicker he may be, but not a fool.

The fact their true mission had been kept from him should have irked his pride, at least. Given some time to think and talk about it with the men whom he trusted could also lead them to think there was more going on, as well.

"You only have one sentry guarding this tent," Kalleb said. "I think we need more men before—"

"Captain Vallant!"

Kalleb whirled in time to see the sentry being pulled away from the tent flaps as Vallant, followed by Lieutenant Horus, Lieutenant Mires, and five other lancers, stormed into the tent. The five lancers formed a line in front of the tent flaps, their hands resting on sabers. Kalleb spotted Hunt being one of them, and Vallant was still wearing his armor.

"Captain Vallant," Morsey started, "we were just talking about—"

Vallant kicked the roast, flinging it to the side of the tent, and then pointed at Morsey. "I'll get to you in a minute." Then he trailed his finger, like the tip of a lance, and pointed it, and his pointed-nose sneer, at Kalleb. "*You*! You got over a quarter of one of *my* squadrons killed today!"

Kalleb stood his ground, despite his injury giving him a clear disadvantage. "We had no other choice. Those knights would have attacked us no matter what we did. We couldn't risk them blocking the crossing out of the bog."

"No *choice*!" Vallant spat. "You forget your rank and sentence, Deserter. Of everyone here, you have no right to decide if *anyone* should go into battle! I'll have you stripped of that uniform permanently after this."

Morsey slammed his fist on the table, rattling the mugs, knives, and plates, and then jumped to his feet. "Enough, Vallant! I gave you the major's orders before we went into battle. You knew full well what we were riding into!"

"I knew one of my squadrons—my least prepared squadron—was in battle," Vallant replied coldly. "I left the matter of the orders for afterward. And now that the battle is done"—he pulled out a crumpled sheet from his pocket—"what is the meaning of *this*? Secret mission? A change in command?" He charged forward, pushing Kalleb out of his way to storm the table, and threw down the paper.

Morsey's lieutenants rose to their feet beside their captain. Kalleb backed away and, out of the corner of his eye, caught Lieutenant Horus stepping closer to him.

"You, the major, and this"—Vallant pointed at Kalleb again, grimacing but failing to spit out an insult—"planned to send my company riding against Daincliff. Are you all *mad*?"

"They have seized our families," Morsey growled. "What kind of Kanesman are you to think we'd hear our homes are under unjust martial law and do *nothing*?"

"Ah!" Vallant cheered. "I'm glad you brought that point up. Because, if I am to understand this right, Kanestown has been placed under martial law by royal authority. The reasons I am not sure yet, but tell me, if we are riding to lift the martial law, doesn't that mean we are riding against royal authority?" Vallant fumed, eyes blazing and sweat running down his face. He leaned in against the table, trying to bear down on Morsey.

Morsey leaned in, as well, glaring at the other captain. "Damn whatever authority it may be! No one holds our families hostage and thinks Kanesmen will do nothing!"

Vallant pulled back, straightening slowly and somewhat dramatically, a big grin on his face. "You evade the question. So, I must assume that was your intention. And such an intention is treason. Gentlemen!"

On cue, Vallant's two lieutenants and lancers drew their sabers. Morsey and his lieutenants reached for theirs as the knights, save Master Blain, leapt to their feet.

"Don't!" Vallant warned. "I have twenty more men outside, all with lances. Make a fight of this, and I will order them in here before any of you can sound an alarm."

Morsey and his lieutenants glowered at Vallant. Their hands remained on their sabers, but they didn't draw them. The knights stood still, a couple nervously glancing toward their master.

A glint out of the corner of his eye caught Kalleb's attention, and he turned to find Lieutenant Horus leveling his saber at his face.

"I don't want any bloodshed," Vallant promised. "Relinquish your sabers and surrender peacefully. We will sort out the proper course of action in the morning."

"We can't do that," Morsey snarled.

"You have no choice." Vallant smirked as he folded his arms across his chest.

"There is always a choice," Master Blain stated calmly, rising smoothly from his chair. He carried two swords on his hips; a regular arming sword on his left and a short sword on his right. He gazed over the lancers in front of him, as if they were holding sticks.

"This has nothing to do with you, Knight," Vallant said.

"I am Master Noa Blain of the Enderval Knights Brotherhood." Master Blain's voice was as cold as a True Winter chill. "Last disciple of Montaigu."

Vallant arched his eyebrows, and his mouth hung open. He looked over the Master Knight as if seeing a madman. "Well . . . that tells us nothing."

"Yes, it does."

Vallant and Master Blain stared at each other for several long, drawn-out moments. Vallant stared on in disbelief, while Master Blain's hard, uncaring glare bore back at him.

"Enough!" Vallant finally said, shaking his head dismissively. "Arrest the officers of the Twelfth. If the knights get in the way, take them, too." He pointed at Kalleb. "Start with the deserter."

Lieutenant Horus stepped closer, pointing the tip of his saber in Kalleb's face. "Your saber, Des—"

POW!

The sudden, mini explosion cracked through the night air, startling everyone and making Kalleb's ears ring.

The top of Vallant's head exploded. Brains, blood, and skull fragments sprayed the tent ceiling and the lancers behind him. His head jerked backward, and his knees buckled, sending him sprawling on top of the cookfire's ashes.

The acidic smell of sulfur filled Kalleb's nostrils. That, combined with the ringing in his ears, sparked his realization.

Olivar Trike.

The big explorer waltzed out of the corner, his smoking rifle in hand and his new drinking companion behind him with his sword drawn. The other knights, Morsey, and his officers were rubbing their ears while watching him walk around the table.

Vallant dead, his two lieutenants shared looks of confusion as the lancers guarding the entrance stared down at the body of their commander in shock.

Olivar dropped his rifle on the table, the *bang* loud enough to bring the lancers around as they trembled at the big man grinning at them. He pulled his ivory-handled hatchet from its holster on his pants leg and leisurely tossed it back and forth in his hands.

"Arrogant ass," he spat. "What do you think, boys? Was that a loud enough alarm for everyone?"

Cries from outside the tent were already popping up outside, men demanding to know what was going on.

Morsey and his lieutenants drew their sabers, followed swiftly by the rest of the knights.

"What's it going to be, men?" Morsey asked.

Horus and Mires still passed uncertain looks at each other, their failing attempt to come to a silent decision cutting into their meager time while the voices outside grew louder.

"What's going on in there?" someone shouted.

Kalleb's ears twitched. That was Rence, as loud as ever.

Horus had lowered his saber out of Kalleb's face and now held it out in front of him. Kalleb seized his wrist with his free hand and kicked out his knee. Horus hollered as his knee cracked and he crumbled down onto his side. Kalleb kept a hold of his wrist and twisted it as Horus fell, his grip loosening, making him drop his saber. Once on the ground, Kalleb put his knee on his back and held his arm behind him.

Kalleb's shoulder stung like something was biting him from the sudden movement, but at least the saber was out of his face.

"Drop your sabers!" he ordered. "Enough of us have died today."

Horus squirmed under his knee, but a little more weight and he slapped his fist against the ground and stopped.

Mires made a calculating glance at the steel leveled against him and dropped his saber by Vallant's body. The other lancers followed his example. The man who stood directly behind Vallant when he had been shot stared fixatedly on the blood and brains streaking his hand after wiping off his face, trembling.

"Collect their sabers," Morsey ordered to his lieutenants as he sheathed his. He then angled his head, listening to the growing noise outside. "We need to tell those men outside what happened."

"Tell them everything," Kalleb said, getting off Horus after his saber was picked up. "We might have a riot if we don't." He rubbed his shoulder to soothe it, but the pain flared even worse. It felt like it was spreading down his collarbone. He settled for squeezing it to try to numb the stinging.

Morsey frowned, thinking it over.

"Lies breed distrust," Master Blain recited from around his knights who had retreated to a corner of the tent for a conference of their own. "We will return to Erin's Keep and leave this to you. If you still need our assistance afterward, you can send a messenger there."

Morsey nodded. "Lieutenant Heath, call assembly for both companies. We'll settle all this tonight. Kalleb, we'll need you there with us."

That's frickin' obvious! Kalleb thought.

He let his eyes wander to Vallant's body and lingered on the pool of blood around his ruined head. He never liked the man and felt little grief over his death, yet the shaken lancer behind him reminded Kalleb of all the other battle-shocked green lancers who had barely managed to ride out of the melee that he had led them into.

Maybe he was right? he wondered. *Maybe I did lead those men to their deaths?* After all, he did tell Amanda he was likely riding to his.

~~~

"That's our mission!" Morsey bellowed as loud as he could, even though his lieutenants and several of their lance corporals, scattered around the over nine hundred men assembled in front of him, echoed everything he said. "We had to keep it a secret to ensure its success. Same with our route. We have to reach Kanestown with the least possible resistance!"
~~~

Kalleb watched the debacle, sitting on a stump off to the side. The men were assembled near the castle's eastern wall with Morsey using the slight slope up to the wall as a rise to talk with them.

The young men of the Eighth stood and sat around in a state of confusion, shock, and disbelief. Kalleb blamed Morsey for explaining events out of order. He had told them of Vallant's death first, which had started an uproar, and then he had gone into explaining the truth of their mission and why they had kept it a secret. He hadn't told them that the men whom Vallant had brought with him were being held under arrest, depriving the company of all their officers, save for one lieutenant.

Lieutenant Landier, Squadron Three's commander and the youngest lieutenant in the company, had been found under guard in a lone tent before the assembly had been called. Apparently, he hadn't expressed enough loyalty to Vallant to suit him, so he had ordered him under guard until he returned. The scrawny youth stared up at Morsey, dumbfounded.

"But, who killed Captain Vallant?" someone shouted.

"And *why*?" another added.

"Who cares?" a brawny lancer snapped, leaping to his feet. "I want to know how anyone expects us to charge against Daincliff? The frickin' city has walls!"

"Enough!" Morsey roared, temporarily catching everyone's attention again. "Captain Vallant was killed attempting to seize command of this force by Olivar Trike." Who was, for once, nowhere to be found. "His compatriots have been placed under arrest until we are certain if they are individually loyal to him or were simply following orders."

Lieutenant Landier hung his head, his wide eyes dancing. He was likely putting it together that he was the last remaining officer of the Eighth.

"So what?" the brawny lancer yelled again. "Who's crazy enough to send us charging into Daincliff? There are more soldiers there than I can count!"

"That's not very many, Kent," someone mocked.

"You son—"

A scuffle broke out in the middle of the company, as other lancers laughed. Those of the Twelfth watched, frowning with disapproval.

Kalleb rubbed his forehead as lancers with sense pulled the would-be fighters apart. *This isn't going to work.*

"I said *enough*!" Morsey yelled back, his face growing red. "Our mission is not to take Daincliff, but to relieve Kanestown. There're at least six thousand lancers bottled up in town. We lift the martial law, and we'll be able to make a stand of it to get our families released!"

The lancers of the Twelfth nodded in agreement, while most of the younger lancers of the Eighth grumbled, shook their head, and whispered to each other.

Kalleb watched them, especially the men of his squadron. Several were easily picked out by the bandages on their arms, legs, and a few on their heads. The others sat slumped and tired from needing rest after the battle. Kalleb could tell by their dull and haunted expressions that many were reliving it and going over the prospect of riding into another one, but this time against the walls and, by some miracle or joke, the streets of Daincliff. He knew their loud compatriot's reaction to their mission was silently spreading in their heads.

He looked over his battered squadron, picking out the grim faces of the men in his troop. He noted the missing faces from the crowd and saw Ian's dead eyes staring up at him in his head.

The older lancers of the Twelfth might have held on to the belief that they were riding to rescue their families, despite the odds, but Kalleb could see his company wasn't convinced. He didn't blame them.

"Pardon me, sir," Lieutenant Landier said. "With Captain Vallant . . . dead, who will command the Eighth?"

The question hung in the air. Most noticed Lieutenant Horus and Mires weren't there, but Morsey had yet to mention they were part of Vallant's followers, held under arrest.

Morsey shuffled his orders in his hands. He had been reading off the three wrinkly sheets of paper, as if they held all the answers and merely reading off them would convince the Eighth to completely fall in line. Their reluctance had him stumped, and he obviously wasn't used to it. He clearly had wanted to tell the men what had happened, give them their orders, and they would all go riding on together.

"It was decided by Major Konner Kane," Morsey said grimly, "that if Captain Vallant didn't have the conviction to carry out this mission, command of the Eighth would be turned over to Kalleb Kane."

Almost as one, the whole company turned to Kalleb.

He had never seen so many dumbstruck and disbelieving looks in his life. Not one accepting soul in the bunch. He was sure, if they were all struck by lightning, they probably wouldn't feel it.

"Captain Kane," Morey said, holding out one of papers to him, likely the orders that stated he would be given command, "care to speak with your men?"

You're wanting me *to convince them where you couldn't?*

It was obvious. Morsey wanted this over and done. He had the support of his company and probably thought that was all he needed to see this mission through. As for this rowdy, green company, he wanted to hand them off to someone else, since they failed to fall in line after he had barked orders at them.

Kalleb got to his feet with a grunt. His legs ached, and his body protested, telling him that he should sit back down and rest. He held his wounded arm as close and still as he could, so as not bother his shoulder that was still numbingly stinging.

He snatched the paper from Morsey's hand but couldn't read the words in the dim torch and lantern light. He tried, and as he did, he watched the faces of the young men in front of him.

Some sat back and slumped in confusion, reeling from the rules that they had been used to since muster suddenly being pulled out from under them. Some folded their arms and grimaced up at him, probably thinking him unworthy of command, either by his former crime, his lower rank, or— because it was impossible to ignore—being given command by an order from his own brother. The survivors of the day's battle stood out to him the most, weary and tired. A few stared down at the ground, cradling their wounded bodies.

Kalleb crumpled the paper in his hand and dropped it.

"They're going to hang my eldest brother," he said.

That brought many out of their stupors and those slumping to sit. The scowls of a few softened, not having expected his honesty.

"They say he plotted to kill the king," he admitted then continued over their murmuring, "But I know it can't be true. Kenith is the best of us and took after our pa in everything. All he cares about is his wife, his two little boys, and his honor. That's it."

Kalleb cupped his fist in his left hand to make sure his injured arm kept still. "I don't care what the aristos do or say," he continued, shaking his head. "They can plan and scheme all they like, but not Kenith! He'd ride, just like our pa did, into death itself if commanded! But he'd never agree to be part of some dark-alley scheme to kill one aristo just to put another's pampered butt in their place. *Never!*"

Nods and grunts of agreement spread around the lancers of the Twelfth. The young men in Kalleb's company remained quiet, listening.

"That's why I'm going to Daincliff," he sighed out. "And I'm not asking any of you to come with me."

The assembly went silent. Morsey and his company stared, wide-eyed and shocked. Most of the Eighth were stunned. Even the scowlers were taken aback.

Kalleb swallowed to put moisture back in his throat. "I am a deserter. You all know what I did five years ago. Today is no different. I have left my post, and I am riding to save a member of my family.

"As I told someone, though, before we left"—he snickered—"I don't think I'll be coming back, even if I get there in time. So, I won't order any here to follow me. I ordered over fifty lancers to charge today and barely came out with half." He hung his head and thought of the men he had left out there, many of whom he didn't know their names. Tears welled up in his eyes. "I will not order anyone else to follow me while I'm riding off for my own personal reason."

He turned and began to walk away, but Morsey stepped out and blocked his path, his face livid and stunned.

"What are you *doing*?" he hissed.

"What's right," Kalleb replied. "This company's been decimated. Nearly half of a squadron is gone. Their command structure, gone. And you expect them to ride into death after that?"

Arguing was already brewing behind him, men demanding to know what they were supposed to do now, questioning where they should go, or if there was anywhere they *could* go. The yelling started up again. A few spoke up, saying they should continue with the Twelfth, but not many.

Kalleb brushed past Morsey.

"Where are you going, Kane?" Morsey yelled back.

"To get my shoulder looked at," he replied. "It's killing me!"

~~~

"I can't *believe* you waited so long!"
~~~

Kalleb gasped as a pail of cold water was dumped over his head. He shivered from the icy water, stripped to his waist on a medical bench among the many wounded.

"You should have come straight away once you learned there was a field hospital set up," Sasha Holstimen, one of the nurses from Siegman's Success, fussed. She was the first to tend to Kalleb when he had reached it and had begun chastising him the moment he had taken his shirt off.

The slim brunette wore her curly hair tied in a light blue shawl. Oily sweat glistened off her tanned, freckled face while she stormed around him, looking him over, from head to toe, for more injuries with her sharp, dark eyes. The sleeves of her blouse were tied up past her elbows, and her apron was streaked with bloodstains.

"That is a serious break," she hissed, pulling up a stool beside him and dragging over a stack of bandages. "What did you do? Fall of your horse? Dive shoulder-first into a tree?" She gingerly grabbed his right shoulder. Her fingertips felt like five icy spikes being driven into his shoulder.

Kalleb ground his teeth and did his best to bear it. There was a noticeable lump pressing up against the skin along his collarbone. The skin was deep blue around the lump, and the shade grew lighter the farther away the skin was until it turned yellow. It was just as Master Blain had said. He had broken his collarbone.

"I was struck by a lance," he growled.

"You're lucky you're not dead," she returned dryly.

"Most of us are—"

Sasha set the bone with a *crunch*, without a hint of warning.

Kalleb threw his head back, and tears streamed from his eyes from the flare of hot pain searing through his entire body, leaving him shaking. By the time he gasped for air, she had already pressed something against the break and was wrapping his shoulder up tightly with bandages, tying them under his arm and over his collar bone.

"I set it," Sasha said unnecessarily, "but it may need surgery. I suggest you come back to Siegman's Success and see the township doctor."

"Just wrap it up as tightly as you can," Kalleb said. "I have to ride on in the morning."

"Out of the question!" She pulled the bandage extra tight, making him wince. "You won't be riding anywhere for six months. At *least*."

"I don't have that long." Kalleb turned to her, and something about the way he looked at her made her stern glare melt away. "Please, tie it as tightly as you can. I'll keep my arm in a sling. Promise."

Sasha frowned. "Okay."

"Thank you."

As she continued to bandage him up, Kalleb spied Lance Corporal Stew Bowden a distance away, slumped over with a blanket hanging from his shoulders.

"Has he been there long?" he asked, nodding toward his fellow lance corporal.

Sasha followed his nod, and a sad look came over her face. "He finally cried himself to sleep."

"Come again?" Kalleb raised an eyebrow.

"His brother died," she replied. "Must have taken a hard blow to the head. We couldn't wake him up. He stopped breathing a couple hours ago, and the lad broke down."

Kalleb wheeled around and found the covered body at Stew's feet. A big body by the outline of the sheet.

"Did you know him?" Sasha asked.

"He was my lieutenant," he replied, sighing, suddenly feeling so tired. "And I got him killed."

Sasha paused for a moment, staring at him blankly before carrying on with her work. "You shouldn't say things like that. You just feel like it because you came through it alive."

"Three of us led two hundred men into battle today. Only one of us came out alive, leading half that number."

He grunted as Sasha tied a bandage knot tightly.

"Feeling sorry for yourself is not going to help."

Probably not. But, as Kalleb listened to the soft groans and snoring of the wounded men around him, sorry was all he felt.

"L.C.?"

Kalleb hadn't heard them coming, but Rence and a few others from Troop D were tiptoeing around the wounded men laying on the ground. Rence was still in uniform, although the jacket hung open to reveal the stained shirt underneath. The right side of his head was bandaged up at an angle from being struck with a sword, yet he still carried himself as if he hadn't a care in the world.

"Shouldn't you boys be finding your bedrolls?" Kalleb asked.

Sasha ignored them, finishing up her bandaging. Already, the pain was dulling with everything bound tightly in place. It would probably get better if he could rest up a bit, but Kalleb knew that was impossible.

"I'll check on a few other patients while you men talk," she said, picking up her remaining bandages and stool. She gave Rence and the others a pointed look. "Don't be too loud."

Rence softly whistled through his teeth once she had walk away. "Where was she when I got doctored up? L.C., you sure are lucky."

"Was there something you wanted, Rence?" Kalleb growled. A twinge in his temple warned of a future headache, and so he rubbed his forehead in an attempt to prevent it.

"Well, sir," Rence started, "after you left, me and the rest of Troop D got together and . . ."

Kalleb looked up through his fingers and found Rence standing with his head down and hands in his back pockets, like a child working up the courage to ask their parent something.

"Rence," he groaned, "I really don't—"

"We'll ride with you, sir!" Rence spat out.

Kalleb stared up at him, his mouth hanging open. At first, he thought Rence was joking, one last laugh before saying "so long." But the moments passed, and his serious expression, and those of the other men's, didn't crack. That was when Kalleb cracked.

He snickered and grinned. "You need to sit down somewhere, Rence. That hit to your head is getting to you."

"We mean it, sir!" Zoren exclaimed, anxiously stepping out of the night. "If you're riding to Daincliff, we're riding with you."

"I'm riding to my death, Zoren," Kalleb said. "That's if I get there in time to try to stop the hanging. I might just get there and be too late." He puffed his lower lip. "Just like last time."

Rence stepped up and took him by his good arm. "Come see the men again. They're waiting, just a piece away. Please, L.C., they really want to tell you themselves." He kept tugging on his arm. No matter Kalleb's groans or dry looks, he stubbornly kept pulling.

Kalleb groaned. "Fine. I'll tell them all myself." He pulled his arm away then flung his sling around him shoulder and arm.

Rence, Zoren, and the others led him down the rows of injured men, toward the outskirts of the field hospital, walking excitedly. He saw a large group standing outside, ringed with torches and lanterns. The size alone told him it was more than Troop D.

As he got closer, he saw they were spread out in ranks, torchlight outlining formations.

"Company!" someone yelled. "Attention!"

The ranks snapped their heels together as one and saluted.

Kalleb stopped in his tracks, stunned. It wasn't only Troop D in ranks, but the rest of Squadron Four as well as Squadron Three, with Lieutenant Landier standing at attention in front of them. Rence and the others dashed off to join Troop D, leaving Kalleb standing half-undressed in front of half the company.

"What's all this?" he asked.

Lieutenant Landier stepped forward. "If I may, sir? After you left, the men of your troop began speaking very highly of you. Then the rest of Squadron Four began sharing stories of today's battle—"

"He charged headlong into the melee!" Rence yelled from the middle of Troop D. "Rode all the way through it and went back in for us! He said he'd stick with us, and he did!"

"He rallied us in the middle of the melee and got us out of there!" Zoren screamed.

"He fought a knight just to save another lancer!" someone else added from within the squadron.

"He stood firm against the line of pikemen!" another yelled. Kalleb barely recognized him in the flickering lantern light as the younger lancer who had ridden beside him when the infantry had been advancing against them. "He never once gave the order to retreat or surrender. Swore to fight with us to the end, he did!"

"What *more* can we ask for?" Rence shouted. "I'll ride with *Captain Kane*!"

"I'll ride with Captain Kane!" Zoren shouted back, pumping his fist in the air.

"We'll ride with Captain Kane!" the lancers of Troop D roared.

The chant grew until both squadrons were chanting it. Men raised their fists in the air until their throats went hoarse. Behind them in the camp, people stopped to watch. In the field hospital, men rolled over in their bedrolls to see what was going on.

Kalleb listened to the men chant, dumbfounded. He had never imagined hearing such a thing. Such a declaration of loyalty sprung to mind the hope of them charging down on Daincliff, throwing open Kanestown gates, and seeing dancing and celebration in the streets. But the cold reality lay spread out behind him, and he took a few deep, calming breaths to bring himself down.

He finally had to raise his good arm to get them to quiet down.

"Not that I don't appreciate it, men," he said, "but I've already told you that I'm probably riding on my way to die, one way or another. It's not right to drag all of you with me." His chin trembled. "Too many have died already."

"We're not afraid!" Trevor yelled.

"We made it through today," Zoren added. "We can make it through tomorrow!"

"We have family in Kanestown, too!" Lieutenant Landier said.

Nods and grunts of agreement spread through the ranks like a wave.

"But none of them are at risk," Kalleb pointed out. "Come with me, though, and they might be."

He let them chew on that thought and prayed they would see reason in it and back down.

Rence stepped out of line. "We could just follow you, whether you like it or not."

An infectious snickering laugh spread throughout the men and, by the way Rence grinned, Kalleb knew there was no point.

"I suppose Squadrons One and Two weren't convinced to come with you?" he asked Lieutenant Landier.

"Some are still thinking it over," Landier replied. "They're still getting over the shock, but some may come around."

Kalleb looked over the men, saddened to find his words of warning had apparently fell on deaf ears. Eventually, he met Rence's smirking eyes.

"You know," he spoke dryly, "we're probably all still going to die."

Rence beamed and threw his fist in the air. "Who will we ride for?"

"*Captain Kane!*" they shouted in unison.

Kalleb didn't know whether to call them fool kids or brave lancers.

"It's a rare thing," his pa had once said, *"for men to choose their own commander. It's the most sacred thing an officer could strive for."*

Kalleb saluted them with his left hand, and they cheered. There was no other response he could give them. After all, they were his lancers now.

Chapter 26

26th of Iam, 1109 N.F. (e.y.)

Alindale watched the Easterly Sun's rays creep over the horizon through his half-lidden eyes. The golden beams turned the ocean's rolling waves into sparkling stars, as if promising eternal tranquility beyond the sight of land. Such a promise had eluded him every passing night and had denied him completely the night before.

Come out . . . or they come in. He rocked the uneven stool, shifting his weight. His pulse quickened, and his throat tightened, forcing him to take a deep breath to calm his heart. *Best to get it over with, then.*

He pushed off his knees and reached up in the air, stretching. His back popped, his legs quivered, and his biceps spasmed and clenched.

Suddenly, a sharp pain ran up his right leg. Alindale doubled over and grabbed his calf, sucking air through gritted teeth.

"At least I won't have to run around the cloister today," he muttered, rubbing the cramped knot in the muscle.

Master Montaigu had drilled him relentlessly in sword forms and physical exercise until he had grown to miss Brother Revel. Revel, at least, gave him breaks to catch his breath. Montaigu struck his back with an old sword sheath whenever he paused.

He forced himself to walk, limping around the top of the cathedral's south tower to work the cramp out.

I finally stop limping on my left leg and start limping on my right. He chuckled as the knot started to fade and took longer steps, putting more weight on his right to push the cramp out more.

"What a mess," he sighed out, walking up to the open window.

Below, Alpheaus Square was still shrouded in pre-morning darkness. The lamps around the Ministry of Justice casted shadows of the recent constructions in front of it. Carpenters had descended on the square after Lord Haemin's ultimatum, and the sound of hammers, winches, and saws filled the air.

An observation box, over a story tall, for his mother and the ministers, stood in front of the Ministry of Justice with twelve rows of benches extended from both sides of the box. They curved around the tall gallows erected in the center of the square. Thirteen steps led up to long landing with places and hatches to hang five men at once.

The proclamation of the condemned still rang in Alindale's ears.

Bernold Vanni. Kenith Kane. Brother Revel. Brigadier Marshal Kane. Even Lieutenant Holt. She's going to hang them all.

He leaned farther out the window and squinted in vain to see if a crowd was forming. *Maybe everyone's still sleeping before seeing today's spectacle.*

Despite his hope, Alindale knew castle soldiers held their perimeter around the cathedral.

Heavy footsteps behind him announced Master Montaigu's approach. Alindale caught the whiff of bread and sausage before Montaigu walked up beside him, eating a muffin with a piece of sausage in it.

"Morning," Alindale yawned out.

Montaigu grunted, swallowing another bite. The dark circles under his eyes were gone, and he seemed well-rested in comparison to how Alindale felt. He finished his muffin and held out another to Alindale.

"Not much of a last meal," he joked, grimacing at the muffin.

Montaigu gave him a low growl and demanding glare.

Alindale winced.

"Fine." He took the muffin, his nose wrinkling after sniffing it. "They burnt it today."

He reluctantly bit into the muffin. The thick bread was stale, nearly flavorless. He carved his teeth into it until reaching the burnt husk of sausage and broke it off without any force, making himself swallow after chewing the brittle, crunchy chunk of former meat.

"At least the cathedral will receive fresh food after today." Or he hoped.

The soldiers had begun stopping anyone from entering the cathedral ten days ago, placing it under siege in all but name. They wouldn't even allow brother priests, who had left to bring back food or run errands, to reenter. Men who had left their families here for sanctuary were denied from seeing them and, as the food ran out, the mothers and children were forced to leave. While Alindale was sure this was an attempt to force him out, he was also sure they were doing it because of Father Finrie's refusal, too.

Montaigu stepped up to the window and surveyed the square below. He had stitched a misshapen skull of the cross-skull boar on a tunic in place of his Enderval tabard but had run out of string to finish the inside of the skull, leaving the right eye incomplete.

Alindale swallowed the remainder burnt muffin and sighed. "Master Montaigu, I've given this some thought and . . . when I go out there today, you should use the opportunity to slip out from the monastery or maybe—"

Montaigu struck the side of his face like iron. Alindale reeled backward, stumbling over his feet and trying desperately to keep his balance. He clutched the side of his stinging face and rubbed his jaw.

"What did you do *that* for?" he yelled, glaring at Montaigu.

Montaigu's dark eyes blazed, and his chin wobbled from his deep scowl. The veins on his bald head stuck out and emphasized his scars.

"They'll hang you, too, if you come out with me! Or worse!" Alindale tried to explain. "I won't have you die because of me!"

Montaigu backhanded him again on the other side of his face. Alindale spun and smacked against the windowsill, colors flashing before his eyes from the force of the strike. He patted the side of his face, and a sharp sting ran along the inside of his mouth. He rubbed the corner of his mouth then pulled his hand back to find blood on his fingertips.

He looked over his shoulder at Montaigu, standing behind him with a disappointed expression. His dark eyes were watery, as if deeply insulted.

"Why?" he groaned. "Indulging Amadus is one thing, but why stay with me? Why find me in the first place?"

Montaigu's disappointment melted. He snapped to rigid attention, his polished bootheels clicking together, and stuck his broad chest out and chin up.

Alindale shook his head as he frustratedly ran his fingers through his hair.

"I don't understand!" he shouted.

Montaigu knelt on one knee and bowed his head.

Alindale stared at the master knight kneeling in front of him, uncertain of what to do. People had bowed to him all his life, but more out of obligation to his position as royal heir than out of any love for him.

I'm not worth it.

But he doubted he could make Montaigu see that, knowing his stubbornness.

He turned away and looked down at the square below. The Easterly Sun's rays had reached it. Only the shadow of the Ministry of Justice kept the stands and gallows away from the light. Scattered crowds of people milled about here and there, and the castle soldiers' perimeter was clearly visible around the base of the cathedral. They were faint, but he caught the distant yells of proctors, proclaiming the execution on distant street corners throughout the city.

The North End gate opened, and two black wagons, driven by six-horse teams and flanked by more castle soldiers, rode out toward the gallows.

"Then I suppose we'll all hang together," he said.

***

The morning's humidity was choking. Tory's hair clung to her face and the back of her neck while she sweated through her dress. A blessed breeze stood little chance of reaching her in the crowded bleachers erected in a wide semi-circle in front of the Ministry of Justice. The lords and ladies of court, and Daincliff's well-to-do of North End, crowded them, packing seats, determined by stature and rank. Every few minutes, someone had to give up their seat to someone more prominent.

Unfortunately for Tory, no one more important was going to come and rescue her from having to sit and watch the ghastly spectacle.

450

"I thought there would be more people," Regina Malthas said disappointingly, sitting on the other side of Tory. She pouted at the crowd trickling in and gathering outside the perimeter of soldiers around the gallows. "Their former king's assassins are going to be hanged today; the people should at least come see justice is done."

"Well, he was a weak king," Serina whispered over Tory's head, smirking. "Weakness barely brings admiration. Now, if anyone *dared* to have harmed Her Majesty . . . well, I would expect to see the whole country rioting over it."

"Quite right," Regina agreed, chuckling.

Her Majesty and the Table of Ministers had yet to arrive. Their empty chairs in the royal box in the center of the bleachers forebodingly stood open to the gatherers, as if to say, *"These people are in charge, and when they arrive, men will hang."* And, from her seat, Tory would be forced to watch each of them drop.

The gallows were tall and long. Five nooses dangled menacingly in the air. There were more than five men convicted of conspiring to assassinate His Majesty, but Tory figured they would hang them by rank.

I must be strong, she reminded herself, squeezing her eyes shut. *I have to be strong.*

Tory missed the ship already, the gentle bobbing in the water while moored to the dock, the soft breezes swept in from the bay. Even the occasional smell of fish was better than the sweaty body odor of pressing bodies, the mixing heavy perfumes, and the lingering smoke from the fires in South End.

"Looks like Eugena and Maddox are getting along well," Serina cooed.

Tory's blood ran cold. She followed Serina's smiling gaze to a couple walking arm in arm together through the crowd. Even without his black robe, she instantly recognized Magistrate Holden. He smiled down at the young lady, no older than Tory, who was giggling into her hand at every word he said.

"That could have been you," Serina whispered into her ear, "if you'd just behaved."

Tory's stomach rolled, and she gripped skirts.

The nightmares still plagued her. Monsters came each night to either swallow her or demand she sign a piece of paper. One of those monsters was Magistrate Holden.

"I'm better off," she said softly.

"What was that?" Serina snapped.

"Nothing," Tory replied solemnly. She pretended to sulk, but it was really so she could divert Serina's attention elsewhere.

A sharp pinch stung her back and made her jerk. Then Serina pulled her against her seatback with a vicelike grip on her arm. "*Behave!*" she hissed. "Or you won't be going home today."

Tory clenched her teeth together so hard that she feared they would break. Tears clung to the corners of her eyes as the spot that Serina had pinched throbbed. It took all her restraint and effort not to grimace, but a storm raged inside her. She wanted to scream, spit the curses that she had overheard Jerro's sailors use, and slap Serina until her face matched the color of her hair.

Sleep might have been hard after her imprisonment, but being back aboard Jerro's ship was the first inkling of comfort she had felt since being in Daincliff. Once aboard, she had slowly relaxed and taken note of the life going on around the docks, the sailors, the ships, and the dockhands, all reminiscent of home.

Jerro had sailed out into the bay one day, and Tory had happily crawled out onto the bow's mast to enjoy the salty spray of the ocean. When evening had come, though, Jerro had turned back to port, and Tory had sulked on the forecastle beneath her hammock. Jerro hadn't taken the ship out again, but she had his promise to sail home today.

It was all she wanted. And she was getting tired of being threatened.

"She comes!"

Tory snapped her head up as a rider bearing the badge of the Ministry of Proclamations pranced around the gallows.

"Her Majesty approaches!" the rider shouted. "Attend! Attend!"

The rider circled the gallows once more then rode off toward West End.

Tory glowered. *Guess he wants a bigger crowed.*

Soon after, soldiers parted the crowd and carriages began riding down the street from the north. Each one drove up to the royal box and deposited a minister and their entourage of assistants and servants. Poor Lord Justice Blakwell wasn't among them, likely still locked in the tower.

Serina squealed when Harris Fauman stepped out of a carriage with his father, Rudmund. Tory again had to hold back from rolling her eyes.

The last minister to arrive was Lord Haemin, naturally. The crowd in the stands, and from North End, clapped when he stepped down from his carriage. He gave them a small wave then strode to the royal box. Strangely, he also carried a long, slender sword on his hip.

"Don't you think the first minister seems a little gloomy lately?" Regina asked. "He doesn't seem to be as cheery as he used to be. His fashion sense has been off, too. Too many blacks and dark colors for my taste."

"Don't be too hard on him, Regina," Serina said. "These are trying times, and he's doing so much to make sure Her Majesty isn't overwhelmed. Who knows what she would do without him?"

"I suppose," Regina mused, pursing her lips.

Tory's stomach rolled again. Despite his gracious, if not humble, appearance, she still remembered the man she had seen in that cell. The chief torturer himself, full of hate and no shred of mercy. His final words still haunted her. *"Stay loyal. Stay innocent."*

The implication was as clear and sharp as a blade. They would say she was innocent as long as she obeyed and stayed on their side. Tory wasn't sure what she hated more—that they had imprisoned her for it or that her own sister had taken part in it.

Or perhaps because I went along with it. But, what else could she have done? They could be hanging her today, too.

Trumpets blared, and everyone stood.

Serina took Tory by the arm and hoisted her up just as the Sunrise Guards rode by in their shining armor and capes, escorting an immaculate carriage with the royal crest emblazoned on its doors. The wheels were spotless, white wood with rims of gold. The Easterly Sun's rays bounced of the carriage body's sparkling silver paint.

When the carriage pulled to a halt before the royal box, three servants dashed off the back with a footstool and long purple rug. Two of them rolled the rug out from the carriage door to the royal box, while their fellow servant placed the footstool below the door. As they did so, the Sunrise Guards dismounted and formed an honor guard along the length of the rug.

Trumpets blared again once they were set, and then the carriage door was opened.

"Her Majesty, Queen Alvera Dain!" a proctor announced.

Her Majesty lightly stepped from the carriage, and everyone, Tory included, bowed or kneeled. Her dress was shimmering dark blue, almost black. Gone was her morning veil. She wore a silver crown on her head, which pulled her magnificent black hair behind her, the curvy waves spilling down her back. She strode toward the royal box, trailed by two handmaidens tending to her dress's train.

No one looked up until Her Majesty was in her box and had taken her seat. Then the ministers joined her, and the Sunrise Guards took up posts before the box.

"Well," Regina said after they had all sat back down, "*that* was a grand entrance."

"There could have been more fanfare," Serina fussed. "And certainly more cheers."

Regina giggled. "This is an execution. Not really a cheerful event."

"It will be to see those wretches get what they deserve. *All* of them."

Hearing the coldness in Serina's voice, Tory chanced a sideways glance. Serina gaze was fixed on the cathedral with an almost predatory glee. It was there and gone in an instant, but Tory had seen it.

The cathedral was surrounded and cordoned off by another line of soldiers, making sure the crowd didn't get too close. Jerro had joked about Alindale hiding there, finding it funny that he had run out of one castle to another one just down the hill. Jerro had said a smarter man would have run much farther, and if Alindale was clever, he would have tried to slip out at night long before now.

Tory doubted it. Everything she had seen of him told her that he wouldn't likely run from his home. Part of her wished he had, though.

Just stay in there, she prayed. *Stay in there as long as you can.*

She glanced back at the dangling nooses. *This is going to be a horrible day.*

***

"Make sure their *tight*!" Kalleb hissed through the stick he was biting down on.

Sweat poured down his face. His hair clung to his scalp, and his body felt sticky. His arms and legs shuddered despite the Easterly Sun bearing down on him, sitting shirtless on his saddle.

Trevor grunted and pulled the long strip of cloth tight under Kalleb's left arm then wrapped it around his back to tie it under his right. Kalleb's back popped as his spine was pushed in, forcing him to sit up and stick his chest out. He growled and bit down harder on the stick from another powerful sting from his broken collarbone, tears welling up in his eyes.

"Almost done, Captain," Trevor told him, tying the knots tightly.

Kalleb had slowly come around to accepting the rank. When they had departed Siegman's Success, it had taken him a minute to get used to being addressed as *Captain*. Now he hardly noticed. He had other things on his mind.

"L.C.!" Rence shouted, jogging toward them and dodging lancers saddling their horses and putting on armor. He ran clumsily with his uniform jacket flapping open and one hand propped on the hilt of his arming sword to prevent from tripping on the straight blade's scabbard. He had claimed the sword after the battle, and Kalleb didn't have the heart to take it away from him.

"He's the captain now, Rence," Trevor grumbled, finishing with his task.

"I know," Rence said with a crooked grin. "I'm just used to calling him that."

"What's the hurry, Rence?" Kalleb asked. He took deep, measured breaths to keep his head up. Part of him, though, wanted to find a tree and prop against it to sleep for a hundred years.

Rence winced. "You don't look so good, L.C. Sure you can ride today?"

"I'm fine," he lied. He felt like shit and was sure he was running a fever.

Before they had left Siegman's Success, Sasha had tracked him down and had given him some num bush leaves. They were thick, bright green leaves with sticky juice inside which, when sucked, numbed his pain. It also numbed his mouth, lips, and tongue and made him woozy in the saddle. At least he could ride . . . until two days ago when he had run out, fell from his saddle, and had to be dragged on a stretcher by a horse. But he had to ride today.

"What is it?" he asked.

"Those knights sent back some of their men," Rence explained. "They're talking with Captain Morsey now, and he's wondering if you're able to join."

Kalleb sighed, having wanted a few moments to get used to his newly wrapped bandages before he needed to move again.

"I'm able," he said.

He braced against the horn of his saddle with his good hand and tried to push himself to his feet. His legs wobbled, and before his rear lifted an inch off the leather, his foot slipped. He flopped backward.

Grimacing from the slip, he knew he wasn't setting an example of confidence for his men. They had all sworn to join him in the heat of the moment, all right after a battle and riding high off the adrenaline of winning. Now they were staring down the prospect of another one. A hopeless one. And their leader couldn't get to his feet, let alone lift his injured rear into a saddle unaided.

They must be having doubts, Kalleb feared. *They must be.*

"Let me give you a hand, L.C.," Rence said, reaching down.

With a grunt, Kalleb had to accept the hand up. He held his right arm as still as he could, pressing it tightly to his body. Any movement at all inflamed the injury.

He shuffled to his feet after being pulled up, stubbornly determined not to fall again. Trevor gently slid his uniform jacket, wrinkled as it was, over his shoulders.

"We'll saddle your horse while you're away, sir," Trevor assured him.

While Kalleb disliked being looked after, he lacked the strength to argue. He couldn't saddle Cloud, anyway.

"Very well," he said, sliding his good arm in his uniform's sleeve so the jacket wouldn't fall off. "Make sure you—"

"Feed him first so he'll let us," Trevor finished. "We know."

Kalleb frowned at Rence's cocky grin. "Let's go."

He brushed past Rence and headed toward the outskirts of the camp.

They had pressed on into the night, on the final leg of their journey. Daincliff lay just over the hill, with the camp obscured by the rise from any watchers along the castle walls and a crop of trees from anyone who might be traveling the northern coast road.

Men watched him as he passed. Some sat around one of the dozens of cook fires, eating the remaining rations of pork, beans, and whatever else they wanted to toss into the pots. The mixed smells of the cooking, along with weapon oil and horse manure, made his stomach churn. He wouldn't have thought a wounded collarbone would affect his appetite, but it did. Or perhaps it was the fever. Kalleb couldn't say. He just found it hard to be hungry today.

Dodging lancers leading horses away in preparation to be called to ride, Kalleb left the camp and spotted a group of men standing just below the rise. Captain Morsey and the other lieutenants were already in their armor and talking with a group of knights. The small group of forty-eight Enderval knights had joined them the morning they had left the castle, wearing the blue and white tabards of their fallen enemy to conceal their true identities.

As Kalleb approached, Olivar Trike nodded in recognition, standing apart from the group. He lazily swayed on his feet with his arms folded across his chest, as if he wanted to return to his bedroll.

"Kanestown's gates are barred and chained," one of the knights reported. "They're impossible to get in from the outside. Even the outlying homes have soldiers patrolling them."

"Were the other knights let in?" Morsey asked, standing with his head hung in thought and hands on his hips as he ground the dirt under his boot.

"The gates around the West End of Daincliff are open," the knight replied. "The soldiers there were very eager to get as many people as possible outside the walls to come to the execution. Master Blain didn't even have to lie about which brotherhood we belonged to, to get in. The guards seemed happy for more security."

A chill ran down Kalleb's spine at the word *"execution."* They hadn't known how much time they had when they had first left Tradon. And his worry of being too late again had dogged him each step of the way. Arriving just on the eve felt like a miracle. Although, they apparently needed another one to get in to try to stop it.

"If that's the case," Lieutenant Heath said, "even if we rode straight for those open gates, we'd get bogged down by the people in our way. Our charge will stall, and the city peace will regroup and counter."

"We'll be thrown back easily if that happens," Morsey agreed.

"What about the stockyards?" Kalleb asked.

The other officers snapped around, only now realizing he had joined them.

The stockyards lay in the southern outskirts of Daincliff, easily passible for horses, and connected to the gates into Kanestown and Daincliff's South End.

The knight shook his head. "There's a large encampment; over half the stockyard. We didn't get too close because there were a lot of soldiers there, too, but they looked to be guarding a large crowd gathered there."

"Besides, that's too far," Morsey said. "By the time we get there, the entire city, from the castle, the outskirts of West End, and Kanestown, would have seen us coming."

Kalleb deflated at the point. "We might as well charge at a wall and get it over with." He put his free hand on his hip and thought. Each time, he came back with the same answer—there was no way in. At least, no way by force. They could split up into groups and try to get past the guards that way, but timewise, they would be too late.

Kalleb groaned. *Again? I arrive but can do nothing. Again!*

"What about that gate at the bottom of the cliff?" Olivar asked. "The one facing the coast road."

Kalleb popped his head up and found Olivar looking over the rise, at the castle below.

"What about it?" Morsey asked dismissively. "That gate just leads to the castle."

"And around the rise to another gate into the city," Olivar pointed out with a grin. "Which I know hasn't been closed in . . . who knows how long?"

Kalleb joined the rest in giving the wily explorer a dumbfounded look. His brain ran through the route. They would have to get through the gate to the castle's lower defenses, ride across the round of the cliff, pass through the gate into North End, and then charge through North End to Alpheaus Square.

It was madness. Madness considering all the soldiers Dain Castle must have. Sheer and utter—

Brilliant, he thought, standing straighter, recalling how many of those soldiers must be spread out in different parts of the city, ushering people from West End, guarding the important people at the execution, watching people outside South End, and holding down Kanestown. That took a lot of manpower.

How many soldiers could be left at the castle?

"That gate is shut," one of the knights reported. "Unless you know a way to get the guards to open them, you're still charging into a wall."

Kalleb quickly jumped to the idea of scaling them after imagining there couldn't be a great number of defenders at the gate or to call on from the castle. Then again, that would take time. Time they didn't have.

"I once knew a woman in a town called Reenwalt," Oliver said. "Decent-sized town. Even had its own wall. This woman, though . . .." He whistled, and his eyes lit up as threw his large hands out.

Kalleb figured she must have been quite a looker, but Olivar had deeper feelings for her. Otherwise, he would have described her in detail.

"Anyway," Olivar continued, "let's just say she was worth knowing. But I had a small problem. Reenwalt's mayor liked her, too, and *didn't* like me, and had the town guard keep me out. So, what I did was—"

"Trike!" Morsey interrupted. "You can tell us about your conquests later. Do you have an idea to get the gate open or not?"

Olivar frowned at his story being interrupted before turning to the knights. "Got any more of those long, blue and white cloaks you're wearing?"

"Tabards," the knight replied dryly. "They're called tabards. And yes, we have a few. Why?"

Olivar turned to Kalleb, grinning again. "Got any more bandages? Or wounded lancers that can still ride and fight?"

Kalleb raised an eyebrow, getting a bad feeling from the way Olivar was looking at him.

"Yes," he replied, sharing a confused, concerned look with the knights. "*Why?*"

Olivar's grin grew bigger, and then he laughed.

Chapter 27

Alindale flexed his fingers and tested the grip of the gauntlet on his right hand. He thought it would feel like a thick glove, but the overlapping plates scraped together and made it difficult to fully close his hand.

Heavy pulsing boomed in his ears. He took a few deep breaths, trying to calm down for what felt like the hundredth time, to no avail. He coughed and braced himself against the table that held his father's coffin. A violent tremble ran down his body, clanking the Knights of Adam's armor plates together.

"Father," he rasped under his shaky breath and pressed his chin against the breastplate. "Adam, I will see you both soon."

"'*Fear not,*'" Father Finrie recited in his deep voice, "'*in the presence of thine enemies. For the Last God is always with us.*'" The father slowly walked around the coffin and comfortingly placed a hand on Alindale's shoulder.

Alindale stifled a grunt. A dull pain was growing in his shoulders and the center of his back from his armor's weight.

"The only thing I'm afraid of is nothing I do, or *try* to do, today will matter," he said.

The knot in his back began to twinge, and he had to straighten. The breastplate's tight strap under his arm and shoulder pauldrons prevented his attempt to reach around and press the center of his back.

Alindale groaned in frustration. "I am not sure I can move in all of this."

He also felt a little ridiculous. He wore three tunics in place of gambeson under the plates. He had oiled and scrubbed the Knights of Adam's breastplate between Montaigu's drills, rubbing out the scattered spots of rust. Nevertheless, the plate was clearly made for a taller man, extending below his waist, and the corners poked the sides of his hips if he turned the top of his body.

"Have faith," Father Finrie said, his gray eyes growing misty for a moment. "The Knights of Adam once believed every piece of armor represented a tenant of the Last God, as well as being a knight."

"I doubt no amount of faith will change what happens today," he said.

He knew Father Finrie was trying to be comforting, but what waited outside hung over him. The Easterly Sun shined through the stained-glass windows, lighting the nave to the cathedral's doors in a mosaic of dancing colors. Alindale only felt Oblivion, the dark void of nothingness, waiting whenever he glanced in the doors' direction.

He frowned at his mismatched armor. The shoulder pauldrons were from different sets; a few extra plates hung off the right, while the left's orange paint had faded and peeled in several places. He had found only one fitting gauntlet, so Montaigu had put a plate on the back of a glove for his left hand. His forearm braces came from different sets of armor, as well. The left one extended past his elbow and prevented him from straightening his arm. His shin guards held his ripped bootlegs together to keep them on.

"If I can get in front of my mother without being seized, it will be a miracle."

"You don't have to go out there," Father Finrie insisted. "I can go and try to speak with your mother or—"

"No," Alindale interrupted.

Montaigu stomped into the sanctuary, his chain mail jingling, carrying a spear against his shoulder's pauldron. Sunlight twinkled off the polished spearhead as he marched up the center of the nave, still wearing the tunic that he had sewn the Enderval sigil over his chain mail.

"I have thought about it for days," Alindale continued, "ever since they started building the gallows. After the execution, they will come and drag me out for everyone to see. My arrest will be another show at the time of their choosing. I may not be able to save anyone, but I can try to be taken on my own terms."

"Father Finrie!" A young priest dashed from the back of the sanctuary, his robes hiked up above his knees, and huffed for breath. "Father Finrie, the prisoners are climbing the gallows!"

Father Finrie's frown darkened.

Alindale's pulse quickened. His every instinct pleaded for more time, to stall as long as possible. His legs trembled, not wanting to move. He took a deep breath then breathed harder, clenching his fists to force his resolve back.

Time's up.

"They want a spectacle today," he said to Montaigu. "Shall we add to it?"

Montaigu slammed the butt of his spear on the floor with a loud *crack*. He made a deep growl, the veins of his neck popping, making the jagged scar across his neck wrinkle. A blaze burned in the master knight's eyes, and the corners of his lips slightly curved, as if he were smiling and scowling at once.

Alindale picked up the Knight of Adam's sword from against the table. He tossed its leather belt around him a couple of times before he caught the buckle and wrapped it around his waist. The old sheath slapped against his leg as he buckled the belt over his breastplate. A long crack ran down the length of the sheath, but Montaigu had sharpened the blade back to its former glory.

He let his hands linger at his belt. His fingers felt stiff in his gauntlet and glove. The lopsided weight of the sword hung like an anchor on his hip. His vision momentarily blurred and lost focus while staring at his wavering hands.

"Alindale."

He blinked and jerked up, finding Father Finrie watching him with deep concern.

He took another deep breath, dropping his hands away from his belt. "I'm fine," he lied.

Father Finrie nodded then pulled Nolen's dagger from his robes. "Since you couldn't find a worthy shield, maybe you should take this, as well."

Alindale frowned at the dagger. "I doubt it will make any difference."

He glanced at Montaigu, but the master knight shrugged then motioned frustratingly at the doors.

Alindale slid the dagger into the belt and wedged it against the edge of the breastplate.

"Go with God," Father Finrie bade him, his eyes still misty and his cheeks wobbling, "and don't be afraid. '*With God with you, why should you fear?*'"

Alindale gave him a small smile. His words of comfort did little, knowing the reality facing him, but he could give the old priest the thought that he comforted him.

"Goodbye, Father Finrie," he said, walking around his father's coffin to his helmet hanging on the end of a pew.

Flakes of gold remained sprinkled across the steel. The plume, or horsehair, that had once hung from the top of the helmet had rotted away centuries ago, leaving a lone notch on its cranium.

"I will be praying for you," Father Finrie called, "Prince Alindale."

Alindale paused, the helmet hovering over his head a moment before he slid it on. The slender eye-slit narrowed his sight, cutting off his peripheral vision. Another thin slit cut down the center of the helmet, forming a *T* shape with the eye-slit and separated the cheek guards. The cheek guards covered his entire face and extended down to protect his chin, but also prevented him from looking down unless he bent over because they would hit his breastplate.

"Let's go," he said.

Montaigu grunted and followed. Their footfalls and armor creaking and scraping filled the sanctuary on their way to the doors.

The doors' heavy beam had been removed and leaned against the wall earlier that morning. Nothing would have stopped the soldiers had they come to arrest him before the executions.

When Alindale reached for a door's iron ring, Montaigu grabbed it first.

"I should go out first," he said.

Montaigu shook his head.

"All right," Alindale conceded, finding it pointless to argue.

Montaigu heaved open the heavy door, his burly forearms bulging as he pulled. The door's iron hinges groaned loudly, like yawning beasts. Alindale had to shield his eyes from the sunlight flooding in.

Montaigu leveled his spear and strode out, stepping to the side once he was on the steps.

From the doorway, the welcoming sight of the glimmering bay with ships cruising in and out greeted him. The peaceful call of making for the docks to try to escape suddenly sprang to his mind, but Alindale discarded it. He knew what was waiting at the bottom of the cathedral's steps. Running was impossible.

I've done nothing wrong! he told himself with a few more heavy breaths. *I'm not going to run.* While his confidence in his chances remained low, that did give him the confidence to take the first step across the threshold.

The crowd was smaller than Alindale had thought. He had expected there to be tens of thousands packing the square, gawking, talking, and watching. Daincliff was home to that many. Instead, a rumbling murmur rolled up from the clearly divided gathering.

Crowding the northern end of the square, around the Ministry of Justice and the stands, was nearly everyone from North End and the castle. The fine display of upper-class fashion, fine suits, large-feathered hats and bonnets, and dazzling silk dresses made the event appear as a ball instead of an execution. Hawkers patrolled the outskirts of the crowd, calling out their retailing of food and drink—especially wine—to the wealthy patrons so their servants can fetch it for them.

The rest of the crowd was far humbler and stood away from the amused, almost cheerful North Enders. The people of the docks and West End gathered around the western part of the square, huddled together, as if nervous to spread out. Hawkers walked through the crowd, trying to sell food, water, and beer to the people, but most stood in groups and watched. Random groups of knights strode around the crowds, marked by their brotherhood tabards.

Alindale strolled along the step, following a line of spearmen at the base of the steps. Soldiers were everywhere, ringing the gallows, ringing the crowd, ringing the cathedral.

Are there any soldiers left in the castle?

His little curiosity cut off when he found the Sunrise Guards standing in front of the central box in the stands. His mother was there, along with the rest of the ministers, with plenty of room between the box and the gallows and perfectly clear of any crowd.

There, he decided. *That's where I need to get to.*

"Good people of Daincliff!" Simon Baltaer, Minister of Proclamations, roared, snatching Alindale's attention. The performer turned aristocrat strutted about the gallows in a blazing dark suit, as if he were the executioner. "Today, we gather for justice!"

Behind him, five men stood under hanging nooses. Facing the royal box, Alindale couldn't see their faces, but he was sure he could pick out each one of them. All their clothes were worn, tattered, and filthy. Their hair unkempt. Brigadier Marshal Kane stood out from the rest because two guards held him up from his armpits, with no support coming from his legs. Alindale had only met the man a few times in his life.

He doesn't deserve that. He squeezed his gauntlet tightly. *None of them do.*

He took a step down then stopped. The soldiers cordoning off the cathedral were facing the crowd, not one was watching it.

Alindale snickered and glanced over his shoulder to Montaigu. "We're not even worth looking for."

Montaigu snorted, which Alindale took as the closest thing to a laugh coming from the hardened master knight.

Alindale traced a path toward the royal box again. As they stood there, though, without anyone raising alarm, a thought occurred to him.

Can we just stroll out of here?

They could walk into the crowd and mix in like the other groups of wandering knights. If they kept calm and didn't draw attention to themselves, it could turn out like that night in South End—slipping away while everyone was distracted. It worked then. It could work again.

"These men have been found guilty before Her Majesty and her supreme court!" Simon continued. "Guilty of conspiracy, sedition, and the assassination of our beloved king!"

Alindale frowned at Simon's extravagant flare, remembering the people he would leave behind.

"Let's go," he said, slowly descending the steps.

He cautiously watched the soldiers, expecting one of them to glance backward or hear them approach and raise an alarm at any second; that at any moment, someone in the crowd would happen to see them and point them out.

"Here are their charges, oh noble subjects!" Simon shouted, holding up a roll of parchments. "The names of each of the accused and individual charges that Her Majesty finds them guilty of!"

Alindale tensely slipped into the crowd, walking behind a man gawking at Simon and standing in front of a guard. The minister's extra flare at least appealed to the taste of the North Enders, who watched the show as if they couldn't look away. With them fully engaged and distracted, Alindale and Montaigu did become another pair of wandering knights in the crowd.

I could have sworn we would be accosted as soon as we left the cathedral, he thought, surprised, as he pushed around a group of gentlemen, ignoring the calls at his back. *Maybe I'll reach Mother after all.*

"*For the crime of conspiracy to commit sedition,*" Simon read, "*Karson Kane, former Brigadier Marshal of the Storm Cavalry, is found guilty and sentenced to death by hanging!*"

He was never a part of any of this! Alindale wanted to yell, but he still had a distance to go, so he bit his tongue.

The old man groaned and coughed as the guards holding him up wrapped the noose around his neck.

Simon continued to read of the others' crimes individually while Alindale kept moving.

"*By his own confession, Marc Revel, of the now disfranchised Enderval Knights Brotherhood, has admitted to conspiring to assassinate His Majesty and formulate sedition against the crown!*"

Alindale stopped.

His own confession? The implications flashed through his mind like lightning, his racing heart thundered in his ears. *But we didn't! If they forced him to confess, then . . .. then . . . all this . . . is for nothing.*

A firm hand grabbed his shoulder, and he turned to find Montaigu holding his chin up, his face carved from granite. Alindale nodded and continued up the line of soldiers holding the anxious crowd back.

Most of them were young men and women, laughing and finding the whole thing a wonderful show. They were also the loudest members of the crowd, cheering and jeering after every name.

"Stay back," a guard ordered as Alindale approached, holding his hand out. "No one beyond this point, even knights."

"I'm not a knight," Alindale replied.

The guard tilted his head in confusion.

"I'm expected before Her . . . my mother."

"Your mother—"

Montaigu slammed the butt of his spear into the guard's face. The crushing blow sent the guard spinning and crashing down in a heap on the cobblestones.

Even Alindale was taken aback by the master's sudden ferocity as the people around them began to scream in shock. They had come up with a plan that Montaigu would disarm or deal with any guards who got in their way, but Alindale hadn't expected him to leap into action at the first encounter.

Montaigu kept moving, striking the guard to Alindale's left in gut, then cutting the legs out from under the guard to his right. As the guards reeled and the crowd pushed away from them, Alindale strode out into the open and toward the royal box, his legs feeling numb with every step as he gazed up at his mother.

The crowd in the stands pointed at the fight. People leapt to their feet to get a better view, but Alindale kept walking. He had to get within voice range, at least.

The soldiers in front of the stands were castle guards. They lowered their halberds as he rounded in front of the gallows, placing himself between them and the royal box. The Sunrise Guards reached for their swords. The sounds of fighting, screaming, and yelling was growing behind him, and people were shouting over each other, demanding to know what was going on.

"*Enough!*" his mother screamed, jumping to her feet.

The people in the stands slowly went quiet, but the fighting continued.

"Desist in the name of the queen!"

The sound of battle slowly stopped.

His mother's eyes were ablaze as she looked between him and Montaigu, finally coming to rest on him. "How *dare* you disturb these proceedings?" she sneered. "Identify yourselves or die where you stand!"

The Sunrise Guards drew their swords, and Alindale could hear running boots against stone in the distance. More soldiers were coming.

Alindale raised his head. He supposed she couldn't recognize him in his borrowed helmet and armor. He barely recognized himself. He also barely recognized her.

Gone was the gentile mask and practiced smile. Her narrow-eyed glare was colder than the darkest night of True Winter. There was no mercy or understanding in those eyes. No feeling in her expressionless face. She was akin to a statue, her poise perfect but without emotion.

"I am Alindale Dain!" he shouted, removing his helmet. "And I have come to respond to the lies and *false* accusations spread about me!"

A hush fell over the crowd. Ladies covered their mouths, and men gaped as everyone tensely watched his mother.

His mother trembled, looking him up and down. Her cold demeanor cracked as her eyes slowly widened and she shook her head.

"Alindale?" she gasped. "What are you doing?"

"I was told I was summoned before you, Mother," he replied. Then he searched the box until he found *him*.

Lord Haemin sat in the far right of the royal box, curiously the farthest away from Alindale's mother. He calmly watched Alindale without a hint of surprise or concern, one leg propped across the other, his arms resting on his chair's armrests, as if it were a throne.

"And I'm here to say"—Alindale turned back to his mother, inhaling deeply—"I did *not* kill my father!" His shout echoed across the square, bouncing off the stone walls and thick bricks of the surrounding buildings. His body began to shake at hearing his own denial reverberate around him.

The concerned look on his mother's face, and the dismissive expressions on the ministers surrounding her, made him grimace. He had tried to plan a rational argument but always got stumped on how he could even deliver it. The whole idea that he would even get here had felt impossible. But now that he was, his reason fled him as every depressed emotion, frustration, and heartache boiling inside of him burst.

"How could *you*, Mother?" he screamed. "How could you believe I would have *any* of my family killed? I gave up my place in line for the throne once for this family; you actually believe *now* I would kill for it?"

His mother took a step back but quickly regained her composure, folding her hands in front of her. "We have evidence, Alindale," she said coldly, with a trace of pity. "Confessions by people who say that you have."

"Confessions made by those thrown in a tower until they confess are no confessions at all!" Alindale threw his helmet to the ground in the rage of the moment, the metal clanging against the cobblestones. He instantly regretted it but left it at his feet.

"You have sat as magistrate and executioner over these men, and you had no *right* to! How many others have you locked in the tower? Did you give *any* of them a chance to defend themselves, or did you snap your fingers and order the gallows built? All just so you can have a grand spectacle to wear your shiny new crown!"

"Enough!" his mother screeched, slamming her fist on the box's railing. "I have every right and authority to find and pass judgment upon those who killed my husband. It is my power to see that justice is done. I am the queen!" She fixed him with her domineering glare, as if he were still a child.

Around her, ministers and others in the stands nodded.

"No," Alindale said. "You are the *queen mother*."

The crowd gasped.

He felt the sting of his callousness in his gut after he had said it but still believed it had to be said.

"Disgraceful!" someone from the crowd yelled.

"Shameful!"

More boos and jeers followed. All the while, his mother stood aghast, almost deflated. She reached behind her until she found the armrests of her chair and strenuously lowered herself onto the seat, her head bowed.

"How could you?" a woman from the stands screamed.

A wine glass exploded a few feet away from him, showering glass and wine across the cobblestones. The crowd eagerly threw condemnation at him behind the line of guards, but Alindale saw they weren't rushing him like that day in the cathedral's kitchens.

As he reached down to pick up his helmet, another woman screamed over the booing crowd, "Worthless prince!"

The hairs on the back of Alindale's neck stood up. He scanned the crowd, but as more people shouted in agreement, it was impossible to find the person who had started it.

They're finally admitting it, he reflected, straightening back up, holding his helmet. *This is what they thought of me all along.*

Alindale held his head up, frowning back at them and finding, deep down, he no longer cared.

His mother suddenly raised her hand.

The crowd again took a moment to realize and quiet down, but when they did, she lifted her head with tears streaking down her cheek.

"Prince Alindale Dain," she said, "we hereby place you under arrest. Please, submit yourself, and your remaining compatriot, to the guard."

As the crowd cheered and clapped, two guards began to approach him, hefting their halberds on their shoulders.

Alindale slid his helmet back on. *This is it.*

He had said his peace, what little there was. Now his reason returned, and he rolled his words over and over in his head, trying to look for the right things he should have said to make a difference. But, with the guards approaching, he shoved his anxiety away. None of that mattered. He only had two choices left, likely the last two he would ever make—surrender or make some fight of it that will likely be just as meaningless.

"Surrender your sword," one of the guards ordered, holding out his hand.

From their slack postures, Alindale assumed they thought he would just give in.

He reached for his sword, his hands again hovering over it.

Strike hard. Strike decisively.

He drew his sword and went into a fighting stance, swinging the blade with both hands. The blade sliced through the air inches above the guard's outstretched hand.

The guard jerked his arm away and stumbled backward. His shocked compatriot fumbled with his halberd, clumsily lowering it, but his footing was poor.

Yelling as loud as he could, Alindale swung again. His blade thumped against the halberd's shaft, slapping it out of the guard's grip and flinging it away on the cobblestones.

He turned to the other guard, who was clumsily lowering his halberd, but Alindale reversed his swing. Steel sang against steel as his blade caught the halberd's head, throwing it to the side before the guard could thrust.

As the guard struggled with his top-heavy weapon, Alindale rushed in and put his shoulder into the guard's chest. The loud *smack* of his shoulder's pauldron slamming against the guard's breastplate rang in his ears and sent the guard toppling backward.

Alindale took up a defensive stance, sword outstretched to control the distance in front of him. Sweat ran down his brow and into his eyes. He had to blink them away, thanks to the lack of room in his helmet. His heavy breathing made him fear his chest was about to burst. He thought the two guards would rush him quickly, but after blinking away the sweat, he saw they were backing and crawling away.

They're backing down?

That didn't make sense. Every ounce of Alindale's reason said they should be rushing him. That was what he had expected.

The sound of boots walking in step made him look up. The rest of the castle's soldiers were approaching in a line, halberds leveled. He glanced to the right and saw a line of spearmen advancing. Same to his left. He spun and found soldiers, who had been guarding the gallows, approaching.

"Oh," Alindale mumbled under his breath.

Montaigu was in the same situation, surrounded by a group of spearmen. Randomly, a soldier would make a thrust, and the master knight turned to parry. Montaigu kept turning in circles, making sure the spearmen kept their distance, but he was favoring his right side, and blood stained his left thigh.

He won't last long, Alindale surmised then looked at the number of soldiers closing in on him. *But we both knew we wouldn't.*

"Alindale!"

He spun on his heels to find his mother leaning over the royal box's railing in anguish.

"Don't do this!" she cried.

Alindale grimaced, feeling as if a spike was going through his heart. Despite all that had happened, she was still his mother and hearing her cry made something inside him quake.

He ground his teeth and set his stance, leveling his sword toward the advancing castle soldiers. Focusing on them brought him back to the moment at hand, and he pushed his conflicted feelings aside.

"I will *not* surrender!" he shouted defiantly.

The soldiers crept closer, keeping their lines straight. Everywhere Alindale turned, the glint of spear points greeted him. Surrounded, the bristle of steel inched nearer as the soldiers shuffled their feet, no one wanting to be the first one to dive in without his fellows.

This is it.

He changed his stance, bringing his sword high beside his head. No matter which way he swung or lunged, he would meet the end of a spear thrust. Or maybe one would heft their halberd and cleave him with the axeblade.

Alindale snickered. It was a little funny. He had probably walked past these soldiers countless times in his life. Now they were going to kill him. He laughed a little more and trembled, feeling strangely cold under all his armor and clothing.

I wonder if Adam felt the same thing before . . .

"Your Majesty!" Haemin shouted, suddenly standing below the royal box with his arm stretched high in the air. "Permit me, your humble servant, to disarm and arrest His Highness."

The soldiers halted. They were close enough for Alindale to make a lunge and attempt to knock a halberd aside and try to break through. However, he was as shocked as everyone else staring at Haemin. Even his mother gawked at him speechlessly.

"First Minister," she struggled, "your request is unwarranted. This dirty business rests on our shoulders."

"Permit me to explain myself, Your Majesty," Haemin begged. "It is true that His Highness should be arrested, but if he's arrested like this"— he gestured at the surrounding guards—"it is likely he will be killed in the struggle. Surely, this is something you don't wish. We can all see it."

What are you doing, Haemin? Alindale couldn't reason it out. This was his, and everyone else's, chance to get rid of him once and for all. It made no sense that they wouldn't watch and clap at the end.

Others in the crowd nodded in agreement with Haemin's heartfelt plea to his mother, but most were as confused as Alindale.

"Of course we do not wish this," his mother replied. "No mother would wish *this*!" Her chin trembled as she straightened her back and lifted her head. "But we have a sworn duty to uphold."

"This is not the only way to uphold your duty, Your Majesty," Haemin said. "I can disarm and arrest His Highness, for justice and for your heart's sake."

His mother frowned. "Lord Haemin, you are not armored. Your swordsmanship is renowned, but such a handicap would probably result in more needless bloodshed."

"I am willing to take that chance."

"But we are not!" Alindale's mother glared down at Haemin. "Only those found guilty of their crimes were supposed to face their judgments today. No one else." She gave Alindale a pain-stricken look.

"Then permit me to add one more thing?" Haemin persisted.

Alindale's mother took a deep breath. "Which is . . .?"

"His Highness has, on several occasions, slandered me by saying I caused the death of your second son. Permit me to disarm and bring him justice, alive, to clear that slight before all here and take this burden away from you."

Alindale's mother studied him as the crowd watched, sitting on the edge of their seats. Alindale, though, racked his brain, trying to understand Haemin's motive. There had to be more than what he was saying. This was all a show. Everything had been. A truer motive must—

He wants me alive.

It was so simple. If Alindale fought until he was overwhelmed, they couldn't drag him to his own trial then hang him next. It would be the biggest spectacle of all.

"Why so concerned now, Haemin?" he yelled, causing the soldiers surrounding him to jump, their spears and halberds wobbling in their shifting hands. "You plan on executing me, anyway. Just get it over with now!" Alindale pointed his sword at him.

His mother collapsed in her seat, her lips pressed into a thin line, and tears ran down her cheeks. "Lord Haemin," she said shakenly, "if you can disarm our son and turn him into our custody, we would be most grateful. Only, please, don't kill him."

Mother! That emotional sting to Alindale's heart returned at hearing his mother beg. It didn't feel like an act for the crowd or the courtiers. It just couldn't be.

Haemin bowed. "As you wish, Your Majesty."

He turned on his heels and approached. His coat was gone, leaving him in a tan vest over his loose-sleeved shirt. He wore no armor, but gracefully stalked toward Alindale with a confident air about him. A long, thin sword rocked on his hip.

The soldiers surrounding Alindale began to move, making him jump. He raised his sword, believing they were rushing him, but discovered they were backing away, keeping in their lines while also giving him space. As well as Haemin.

"Your Highness," Haemin called, putting on gloves that he had fished from his belt, "please surrender now. This whole thing has gone far enough." He got a few feet outside the reach of Alindale's sword and stopped.

"Haven't I made it clear?" Alindale took a two-handed stance, the first and simplest he had learned, leveling his sword and claiming as much distance as possible. "I'm not surrendering. Least of all to *you!*"

"But, why?" Haemin implored. "Why are you doing this? You must know you're rushing to your death."

"Of course I know that!" Alindale yelled, his voice bouncing off the stone walls around them. "I knew from the moment I stepped foot outside the cathedral. However, this is my only choice. My *last* choice. And this is the only way I can make it matter."

Haemin frowned disappointingly while placing a hand on his hip. "You are being ridiculous."

"Says the man without any armor, who volunteered to disarm an armored opponent," Alindale retorted.

"Fair point." Haemin shrugged then slightly turned his body sideways. "But you are missing something."

Haemin sprung forward, drawing his blade in a flash, faster than Alindale could see.

He raised his blade to parry, when something struck the tip of his blade, knocking it to the right. He tried to correct his stance when a sharp sting suddenly pierced his left eyebrow. The sting sliced like fire across his brow, followed by a clang of metal on metal as something struck his helmet, whipping his head left.

Alindale stumbled back. He shook his head, disorientated. His brow was burning. His left eye clouded red with blood, and he couldn't keep it open. He reached to stop the bleeding, but the glove on his left hand was too thick, making it impossible to get his fingers through the eye slit.

What was that? he panicked.

"I commend you, Alindale," Haemin said. "It was admirable of you to throw yourself into training these past months."

Alindale snapped around, thrusting his sword out to try to command as much distance between him and Haemin as possible. He blinked, but he could only see out of his right eye. The bleeding cut over his left made it impossible to keep it open for long.

Haemin stood out of reach again, keeping only half his body exposed while holding his long, thin sword outstretched and poised in a one-handed stance. Alindale's blood ran across the tip. It was at least a foot and a half longer than Alindale's sword.

"But that won't be enough against me," Haemin said. "Surrender. Now."

The stinging cut in Alindale's brow felt like it was digging into his skull. He wiped at it in frustration, but all he did was run his hand uselessly across the face of his helmet. Growling, he lunged with a sword thrust of his own. Haemin parried, and the square rang out with the sound of blade slicing against blade.

Chapter 28

Tory squeezed her eyes shut, jerking at every *ting* of metal and *boo* from the onlooking crowd. She wrapped her arms around herself, clinging tightly to the point she almost doubled over in her seat. She wanted to, but that would draw Serina's attention.

"Come on!" Serina groaned, her tone dripping with annoyance. "Why is he taking so long?"

"Minister Haemin did promise to arrest Alindale *without* killing him, dear," Regina said with a tipsy giggle. She had started drinking heavily since the duel had begun. "That takes more . . . finesse, I guess."

Serina slapped Tory's arm. "Don't be so squeamish. There's not *that* much blood."

Tory grimaced, cracking her eyes open. She instantly regretted it. The red smear running down the side of Alindale's helmet from the eye slit made her think he was crying blood. She wondered if Alindale had lost his eye by the way he held his head to the side, as if he could only see out of his right eye.

She had jumped in her seat at the ferocity of Lord Haemin's his first strike. In that same instant, the image of Lord Haemin plunging the sword into Amadus's chest, back in the tower, had flashed in her mind. She didn't want to see it repeated, especially to Alindale.

When the soldiers were closing in, she had screamed with the crowd around her for him to surrender. However, unlike the rest, she genuinely didn't want to see him die.

She had been just as puzzled as Serina and everyone else when Lord Haemin had stepped forward and offered to arrest Alindale personally. And when the duel had started, it had been clear that Lord Haemin had the upper hand.

Alindale sported more wounds now; small cuts on his arms and legs bleeding through his clothing between the plates of armor. His movements were starting to slow. Every step appeared sluggish, as if it were taking painful effort to move his armored limbs. Often, he reacted after Lord Haemin parried or struck.

Alindale dove forward, swinging in a downward slash to the right. That flowed into an upward slash to the left. Then he lunged straight forward, never once touching Lord Haemin.

The first minister was living up to his reputation, nimbly dodging and sidestepping Alindale's attacks, barely needing to lift his sword. The long, narrow blade sliced through the air faster than she could follow. The nimble thrusts and stabs reminded her of Harpo pouncing on his food, stabbing it with his talons, and leaping back to check the damage.

When Alindale lunged forward, Lord Haemin merely turned his body, letting Alindale's sword thrust by. As fast as a snake, Lord Haemin then leapt forward, his sword arm sprung out. Steel scraped against steel, and his long blade pierced through Alindale's shoulder, between where the breastplate and shoulder armor met.

Alindale jerked back his left shoulder. His helmet wobbled as his head rolled, and a gargled wail came from underneath.

Lord Haemin twisted the slim blade before pulling it free, blood trailing after it. Alindale stubbled back, sagging from his wound and clumsily clutching his shoulder while holding his sword toward Lord Haemin, shaking.

"*Impressive!*" Regina cheered, smiling broadly with a sparkle in her eye, her cheeks flushed.

A few in the crowd clapped, as if they were watching a game. Thankfully, the feeling failed to spread.

The duel paused. Both men held their swords toward the other, but neither moved. Tory thought she caught a faint word pass between them, but they weren't speaking loud enough.

Suddenly, Lord Haemin sprang forward. Their blades scraped together briefly before Lord Haemin knocked Alindale's sword aside, stepped in close, and slammed his sword's gilded hand guard into Alindale's face. Alindale's head snapped back. He backpedaled, reeling from the blow, and sent the soldiers behind him scurrying away as he backed into one of the legs supporting the gallows.

"This is over," Serina said confidently. "Lord Haemin might as well tell the soldiers to seize him; he can barely stand."

Alindale wrapped an arm around the gallows' supporting post and rested his head against it. His sword dangled in his grip as he visibly drew deep, exhausting breaths. Lord Haemin, for his part, kept his distance and waited.

"Do you think Her Majesty will rush him to trial?" Regina whispered behind Tory. "Or do you think she will lock him in the tower for a while?"

Tory tensed and dug her fingernails into her elbows. Those dark, moldy cells sprang into her mind. The stale air and the stench of filth. The wet, blood-gurgling cries filled her ears. This time though, when the wretched figure hanging from the ceiling lifted his head, it was Alindale.

"It doesn't matter," Serina responded. "Justice will be done either way."

Tory trembled as something inside of her snapped.

"I'm sure you and your friends will see to that," she spat.

"Hush, Tory," Serina scolded.

Tory ignored her. Nothing could stop her suppressed feelings from pouring out.

"I mean, that's what you did for me, right? You came the moment you heard I'd been summoned. Promised to stay with me every step of the way." Her giggle was borderline hysterical. "Every step *behind* me."

"I said, that's enough, Tory," Serina warned.

Tory snapped around and, for the first time in her life, saw Serina flinch.

"You going to give him the same trial you gave me? Demand he prove his innocence while refusing to ever believe him? Or maybe your friends, like Holden, will just throw him in the tower to torture until he signs a confession?"

Serina looked at her as if she were deranged, between glancing nervously at the people around them who had overheard the exchange.

"Torture?" Serina held out her hands. "What are you talking about?"

Tory lashed out, grabbing her by the arms. "Tell me! You were going to let them do it, weren't you? If I didn't sign, or if that knight hadn't signed for me, or . . . or . . . ."

Serina pulled back, her face a mask of unease and trepidation, but anger blazed in her glare. She tore Tory's hands away, but not before Tory scratched her as she lost her grip.

"Quiet, you stupid girl!" Serina hissed. "You're causing a scene."

"You'd have let them hang *me*!" she screeched.

Tory wasn't sure what happened first after that—the onlookers around them gasping or Serina slapping her across the face.

Flashes obscured her vision, and the loud *clap* echoed in her ears. Her head was violently whipped to the side, jerking her neck and leaving her right cheek burning. She slid forward on the silk of her dress and nearly tumbled out of her seat and onto the people in front of her, but Serina caught her by the arm in a vicelike grip, slicing her fingernails into Tory's arm, as if returning her scratches.

"Serina!" Regina hissed with concern.

"This is a family matter," Serina replied coldly, standing up before smiling and putting on airs to the people watching them. "Sorry. This is all too much for my sister. Come along, Tory."

Serina kept her iron grip as she hauled Tory out of her seat without waiting for a reply. Tory tried to pull out of her grasp, but that only made Serina dig her nails deeper into her arm. One even drew blood as Serina dragged her down the steps of the stands.

"Please stop, Your Highness!" Lord Bernold Vanni cried.

On the gallows, he was the only condemned member who didn't have a noose around his neck. He was more disheveled, and his features more hollowed out than when she had seen him at the inquest.

"Let your loyal subjects die," the lord pleaded. "Keep your dignity!"

When Tory's resentment for Serina had broken, she had missed Alindale walking out from under the gallows. He merely stood facing Lord Haemin, his sword half raised, as if he hadn't any strength left. She failed to catch any reply before Serina pulled her out of the stands and dragged her through the crowd to the stands' rear, where Serina flung her against a support post.

"You little *chit*!" she hissed, bearing down on her. "Have you lost your mind? Screaming like that and startling everyone. They are anxious enough as it is. What if Her Majesty had noticed?"

Tory clutched her arm, pressing tightly against the bleeding scratches. She returned Serina's glare. Her intimidation would have easily worked before she had come to Daincliff, but not now. Not after the tower.

"Yes, what if she had?" she hissed back. "Finally seeing Serina Syros show everyone just how nasty she is." She narrowed her eyes. "You *would* have let them hang me."

"I would not," Serina denied, rolling her eyes. "Despite still acting like a stubborn brat, you are my sister."

Tory snickered. "And you can't have your own sister make you look bad. It's always about you."

"I gave you every hint I could, short of yelling at you not to be stupid and sign the damn paper, letting everyone know you were innocent."

Tory threw her hands up. "Did no one tell you *why* they released me? That knight they're about to hang said he'd confess, and the magistrates decided to let me go right then and there. Even your friend, Holden, didn't hide it. You think I am stupid *not* to figure out all you wanted me to do was condemn Prince Alindale?"

"Of course I wanted you to condemn him, you little fool!" Serina snapped. "That was the only way you would be safe!" She groaned in frustration and rubbed the bridge of her nose between her eyes.

Tory was taken aback. No denial. No deflection. Not even a hand-waved excuse. Hearing the honest truth, though, didn't lessen the sense of betrayal that she felt in her heart. She had been accused in front of the entire court, thrown into the tower, left alone in that cramped cell, and made to watch a man tortured. All because her own sister wanted her to join in her flock's chorus to condemn . . . an innocent man.

She couldn't be sure of that. She couldn't explain Bernold Vanni being found with the slain body of His Majesty. She hardly knew Alindale, to say anything of his character or if he was the type of person to smile in public and abuse others in private.

Tory recalled the night of the ball, though, now seemingly ages ago. He had been rude and a little standoffish, at first. Then again, she had met him by chance and had made her request on a whim. His initial reaction had been more out of that sense of propriety that he tried to uphold instead of from a mean spirit.

No, she thought. *Alindale was kind . . . when he didn't worry about what other people thought.*

She had seen it that night. He couldn't have had his father killed. He just couldn't. Maybe that little intuition, nestled in the back of her mind, was the reason she couldn't have forced herself to sign.

"Alindale is innocent," she said.

"Don't be absurd," Serina said in annoyance. "His followers confessed. He is as guilty as they are, and we all know it. You would know it, too, if you had been properly schooled to understand the importance of associations. Now shut up while I think." Serina grimaced and rubbed her temples again, as if she were getting a headache.

The crowd gasped and shouted behind them.

She's thinking of how to get rid of me. She's already made up her mind on everything else. And by what she had said, Tory had figured everyone else had, as well.

She stood up straight. A thought flashed through her mind. It was dangerous, risky, but out of everyone here, everyone watching, there might be one person who had doubts, one person who might hear what had happened to her in the tower that would change everything.

Tory turned on her heels and began heading toward the front of the stands.

"Where do you think you are going?" Serina asked condescendingly, hurrying after her.

"To Her Majesty," Tory replied without looking back. "Maybe she'd like to hear what happened—"

Sharp nails raked Tory's scalp, snapping her head backward. Tears immediately sprang from the corners of her eyes as Serina wrenched her back by her hair.

"You will do no such thing!" Serina hissed, beginning to pull her away.

As Serina marched off, Tory cried out, twisting and doubling over, forced to follow along unless Serina pulled her hair out by the roots. She slapped Serina's arm, to no avail. She wasn't sure where she was being taken; all she could see were their shoes and the paving stones, but the sound of the crowd was getting softer.

"Let me go, Serina!" Tory desperately cried. "I'm telling Father!"

Serina stopped, and her grip slowly loosened. Feeling a little slack, Tory took her chance and ripped away from her, sacrificing some of her hair in the process. Strands snapped and stung her scalp from being pulled out.

She took a few steps back and ran her fingers through her hair, expecting to find bare patches. Fortunately, most of it was still there. She clutched her head and straightened, blinking the tears away.

She expected Serina to be glaring at her or preparing a fiery tirade. Instead, Serina studied her with cold, unfeeling eyes, like a fisherman who chopped off the head of any fish that they caught without regard to whether they should throw the small ones back or not. A few strands of Tory's hair still clung, stuck, in Serina's nails.

"You should really learn when to keep your mouth shut," Serina said softly and began looking around.

Tory found she had been dragging her toward the docks, and her heart leapt in chest.

Home!

"Knights!" Serina shouted, suddenly all smiles, and waved at a group of patrolling knights. "Brother Knights! A couple of ladies need assistance!"

The knights paused and looked between them and each other before approaching.

"What are doing?" Tory asked.

"Sending you back to the castle," Serina said cheerfully as she waved on. "And for that, you need an escort. I can't leave, but you most certainly can."

Tory went cold, and her heart raced. If she went back to the castle, she was merely a remark away from being thrown back in the tower.

I won't go back. She backed away a few steps. *I won't!*

She bolted, hiking up her skirts so not to trip on them.

"Tory!" Serina yelled. "Get back here!"

The knights watched her run by, confused, but didn't give chase.

Tory didn't look back and didn't stop running until she was back among the crowd. Even then, she pushed and shoved through until she once again was behind the stands. Once there, however, she discovered she wasn't sure how to get to Her Majesty.

If I go around the front, she thought, gasping with her hands on her knees, *Serina's friends will see me and probably stop me.* She looked down the back of the stands and saw they curved around, out of sight. *Maybe there's a way to reach her down there.*

Tory walked down the back of the stands, looking for a rear entrance or walkway into the royal box. Despite the large crowd on the other side, the back of the stands was eerily quiet. Sounds were muffled and muted.

She searched through the crisscrossed braces holding the stands up for a way around or through them. Occasionally, *dings* and moans bounced off the stone walls and pillars of the Ministry of Justice and howled through the passage like a gust of wind.

She stomped her feet and frowned in frustration after searching the length of the royal box's rear and finding no back steps or entrance.

"Do I really have to walk all the way around?" she complained.

The sound of approaching footfalls, hard heels against stone, made her break out in goosebumps. She swiveled around and saw a group of knights, larger than the ones whom Serina had called for, rushing toward her.

Tory's breath caught.

Serina sent them after me!

She hiked up her skirts again and began to run, but the knights were gaining closer and closer.

They're going to catch—

From the corner of her eye, she saw a gap in the frame, between where the royal box and the stands to the left met. Without thinking, she dashed into the gap but found it merely a wedged corner with no escape. The knights were getting closer, the clanging of their armor and weapons getting louder.

Tory squatted down in the corner, trying to get as small as she could. She wrapped her arms around her legs and buried her face in her knees.

Please, just run by, she begged. *Please, just run by!*

She waited, expecting any moment they would stop and order her out. She would go back to the castle, back to that cramped cell. Or worse.

"They can't hold them for long!" someone yelled.

Tory shook from how tightly she held herself and listened. The knights *were* running by, without even stopping. She clung to the corner, though, waiting and making sure it wasn't a trick. The footfalls became quieter and quieter. Tory held her breath then slowly exhaled.

She chanced a peek over her knees. The gap was clear. She even checked for shadows on the ground in case someone was waiting outside but couldn't see anything. She anxiously got to her feet and stuck her head out of the wedge, checking one way then the next. The knights were gone.

Tory took the chance and quickly pressed on, determined to get around the stands. She could barely hear the crowd, and she hadn't heard the *ting* of swords in a while. Either everyone was bored on the other side or the fight was over.

As she rounded the corner, finding only a small crowd on this side of the stands, a loud *boom* caught her attention.

On the square's south wall, down a long lane, a large group of knights and men of the city peace caught her attention. They milled around a gate, struggling and shoving against it in desperation to close it.

"No more evictions!" an angry voice beyond the gate yelled.

A guard of the city peace rammed a spear through the gap and was swiped at by a club and forced to back off.

"Food for our children!"

"What's going on?" a woman behind Tory asked, turning her attention away from the duel in the square to the fight at the gate.

Several in the back of the crowd looked to see what the commotion was.

A man chuckled. "Looks like the beginning of a riot."

Tory froze. His voice, or rather his chuckle, sparked a memory.

A tall, gangly man in the crowd pointed at the gate. His foppish blond hair was disheveled, with loose strands sticking every direction. He wore tan traveling clothes, suited for a merchant. Yet the crooked smirk on his narrow face looked familiar.

The laughing man at my inquest! Tory realized but didn't know his name.

"What are those knights doing over there by the Kanestown gate?" someone else asked.

As more in the crowd turned around to see what was going on behind them, the smirking man slipped away. Tory tried to follow him with her eyes, but it was as if he slid under the waves and vanished among the people.

Sharp scraps of metal on metal, followed by an ear-piercing shriek, snapping her back to reality. The crowd watching the fight shouted and cried, and she broke into a cold sweat.

Alindale!

She threw herself into the crowd, pushing and shoving her way through and ignoring their complaints. A few, though, were too stunned by what they saw to say anything.

She clawed her way forward, squeezing through the line to the front and stopped.

Tory covered her mouth with her hands and gasped.

***

Alindale stumbled back, fumbling to grasp his wounded shoulder that was screaming in pain louder than his shallower wounds. His forearm and bicep plates prevented him from fully bending his elbow. His glove's thick fabric made it impossible to press against the wound and stop the bleeding, anyway. A hot trail of blood ran down under his arm and soaked his undershirts.

He struggled to keep his sword up. His entire right side spasmed and shook from tension. He had to control some of the distance in front of him. Otherwise—

TING!

Alindale's blade was knocked to the side. His grip almost slipped because he was reduced to one hand. He turned his head back forth, trying to see where Haemin was coming from with only his right eye, his left already crusted over with dried blood.

Haemin was inside his reach!

CRACK!

Something slammed in the center of Alindale's face. His helmet's face guard caught most of it, but the blow still smashed against his nose, throwing his head back.

Alindale reeled back. Stars flashed before his eyes as his sense of balance slipped away. In a panic, he backpedaled faster and faster until, just as he was about to lose his footing, he bumped into something. His helmet knocked against wood. He stumbled and reached around, groping, as if in the dark, only to realize he had backed into one of the gallows' support posts. His aching legs found the extra support too alluring, and he braced against the wood.

He panted, long, haggard breaths, spitting out drool and coppery blood as he gulped down air. Rank sweat and blood were the only things he could smell. He worried that last blow might have broken his nose. But oh, the gallows support felt terrific to lean against.

He wrapped an arm around it, his sword dangling from his fingers.

Aches and stings plagued Alindale's entire body. He figured he must have a cut or prick between every joint of his armor. Haemin had danced around him the entire time, never committing or attacking, as Montaigu would. He would feint and thrust. Feint and thrust. Alindale hadn't even been able to see the thin blade.

Most of the cuts were shallow, but the wound to his shoulder was deeper. Steel had reached bone.

I'm not going to win this. He tapped his helmet against the wood and snickered. *Then again, I never expected to.*

"Your Highness," Haemin called.

It took effort for Alindale to turn his head. Through the eye slit, he saw Haemin standing off to the side, waiting, like a dance partner. He was sweating but not tired. His breathing was even and form still the same.

"It's time to surrender," Haemin said. There was no trace of malice or arrogance in his voice or expression. Only pity. "You have fought, you have tried, but everyone can see it's over. To carry on would be a disgrace."

Alindale tried to push off the post, but his legs nearly gave out, and he fell back against it. His muscles spasmed and quivered. If he made the wrong move, jerked too fast, turned too soon, he could easily pull a cramp from anywhere. If he could only rest for a bit.

A woman screeched somewhere in the crowd. Her words were unintelligible through his helmet, but the shriek was enough to make Alindale push off the post. The tip of his sword touched the paving stones, and he used them to slide his hand back down the hilt and better his grip.

I swore to never surrender, he reminded himself. *I won't give them their show.*

He walked out from under the gallows, dragging his feet, as if his legs were chained to weights. His armor thumped and clanked with ever painstaking step. He could only raise his sword halfway up, his forearm screaming and pleading to drop. His back wanted desperately to double over, and sweat dripped from his brow, threatening to blind his remaining eye.

"Please stop, Your Highness!" Lord Bernold Vanni cried from behind him. "Let your loyal subjects die. Keep your dignity!"

Alindale stopped. Let them die? Just give up and let the executions continue? He knew, that morning, he wouldn't be able to stop it. He could have simply waited in the cathedral, too. Let the others die in the hope that, if he held out long enough, *something* would set him free. Make a run for it and hope he blended in enough that no one would notice.

What a vain and hopeless thought.

"I have no dignity," Alindale said. "I am a disgrace. I have never been the prince anyone wanted. And try as I might, I never will be." He gnashed his teeth together, growling through the pain to grip his sword with both hands, and steadied his stance. "But today, I am the prince *I* want to be! And I will *not* surrender!"

Haemin pressed his lips into a thin line. He shook head as his expression shifted from pained, to pity, to resolute in the span of a breath.

He's coming.

Alindale didn't look for Haemin's sword. He focused only on Haemin, refusing to move even when his sword struck Alindale's, to turn away the blade. Alindale didn't follow up with a parry; he lacked the strength to, anyway.

He ignored the pain of Haemin's blade piercing the inside of his right elbow between his armor joints again. It was a graze, even though blood ran from the bend in his arm. Nevertheless, Haemin's blade had failed to strike the center into the tendons.

With Haemin inside his reach, Alindale put all his strength into a swing, cutting from right to left. Haemin's eyes went wide, and he tried to leap back, but Alindale caught something this time. He felt resistance against his sword's point and grunted as he followed through.

After Alindale reset his stance, Haemin stumbled back, checking his side with his free hand while keeping his sword poised.

Alindale's heart fell when Haemin pulled his hand away. His sword had only caught Haemin's clothes, ripping his vest and undershirt, but there was no sign of blood. Alindale checked his sword tip, but there was no blood there, either. He had missed. Barely.

The inside of Alindale's right arm stung and begged to fold inward. His left shoulder screamed from being forced to move.

My arms are losing strength, he realized. *I can't do this for much longer. I have to strike him!*

Haemin disappeared to his left.

Alindale shifted, desperately searching so he could aim his next swing—

BANG!

A hard strike cracked against his helmet, snapping his head to the side. As Alindale's world spun, a sharp pain stung deep into his hip, again between his plates. He yelped and turned in on his side, pressing his elbow against his burning hip.

Alindale shuffled clumsily, haggardly sucking down air and frantically looking for Haemin before—

Steel bit deep into the back of his right leg, just below the knee. He threw his head back and screamed in surprise. His knee buckled, and he crashed to the ground with a roar from his armor plates striking the stones. His leg trembled and spasmed.

As Alindale coughed and groaned, a shadow moved from his left. In desperation, he yelled through his body's agony, took his sword in his left hand, and swung backward with the last of his strength, hoping to catch Haemin in one last strike!

Steel scraped against steel, and Alindale felt his blade being batted away. His grip slipped. He fumbled and awkwardly tried to catch his sword in the air.

A blade swooshed through the air, followed by the sickening thump of steel ripping through flesh. Lastly, the final *clang* as the blade struck metal.

Alindale stared as his sword flew away, beyond his reach. Then he caught sight of something else tumbling end over end before plopping on the stones in front him. His blurry vision slowly cleared for him to discover a thick, clothed digit, oozing blood with something white sticking out of the ruin.

Alindale hesitantly followed the trail back to his ruined left hand.

His thumb was gone. Cut clean along the side of his hand.

Blood squirted from the stump, and then his entire hand suddenly erupted in pain, as if on fire. The new pain was beyond all the others, overtaking them and making the aches of his other injuries vanish.

Alindale wailed!

Doubling over on his knees, he clutched his injured hand with his gauntleted right and pressed it to his chest. Blood squirted through his fingers and smeared against his breastplate.

His thumb was *gone*!

Alindale's head was jerked forward as his helmet was pulled off and dropped unceremoniously in front of him with a *thump*.

"Prince Alindale Dain," Haemin started, "in the name of Her Majesty, you are under arrest."

Through blurry eyes, Alindale looked up and watched Haemin sheath his sword, the handguard clapping in his ear as it slid home.

Haemin gave him a final look of pity before turning away.

"Disarm the fugitive knight," Haemin ordered to the soldiers behind him. "Escort His Highness away and continue with the execution."

Haemin suddenly spun around as sounds of distant commotion grew somewhere south of the square.

The sounds of a struggle—grunting, punching, and knocking wood—sprung up behind Alindale. He glanced and found Montaigu set upon from all sides, parrying where he could, but a spear caught him in the hip. The master knight remained stone-faced but dropped to a knee. He parried another thrust, but a soldier struck him from behind with the butt of his spear, sending Montaigu sprawling on all fours.

Alindale winced, blinking tears and blood away, and looked back down at his butchered hand. He tried to make a fist and wrap his fingers around the stump where his thumb used to be, but they couldn't reach. Tears mingled with the blood on his face and dripped down onto his hands.

It was all for nothing! Alindale wanted to yell, to roar and curse until his throat went hoarse, and he lost his ability to speak. *They'll make a show of me. And mock me every step of the way!*

He folded his hands together and pressed them against his breastplate. The pounding of his heart boomed in his ears, drowning out the footfalls of rushing feet behind him.

To Oblivion with this. He growled. *To Oblivion with all of . . .*

His elbow knocked against something. He looked and found Nolen's dagger, still lodged in his belt. He had forgotten all about it, yet there it was. He had a way out. Or a way to keep fighting.

He glanced up through his eyebrows. Haemin stood in front of him. His back turned. His attention somewhere else.

To Oblivion with him!

Alindale drew the dagger before he could think and lunged with a vengeful yell. However, he had misjudged the distance in his haste and, instead of anywhere vital, drove the dagger into the back of Haemin's upper right leg.

Haemin cried out in shock and pain. He reached back to grab the back of his leg and fell head over heels over Alindale. Alindale rolled with him, their bodies mingling in thrashing limbs.

When Alindale came up, he found Haemin beside him, reaching for his leg again. Snarling, he balled his hands together and slammed his combined fists into Haemin's belly, making a hard *thump*. Haemin's eyes bulged, and he gasped as the air was driven from his lungs.

Alindale's rage boiled over, and he hit him again. And again!

"No more evictions! Food for our children!" Cries and shouts were getting louder around him, but Alindale couldn't stop hitting the man.

He crawled on top of Haemin, stumbled and rammed his shoulder against him before punching him in the chest with his gauntleted fist. Alindale then smashed his fist into Haemin's face, his nose crunching under the gauntlet's blow. It felt good!

The drumming in his ears grew louder, and he panted harder. Haemin's head rolled around, and he tried to lift it.

This was the man who had wanted his father removed.

Alindale hit him again, bending Haemin's nose sideways.

This was the man who had poisoned his mother.

Alindale hit him again, his gauntlet's iron knuckles cutting into Haemin's cheek and flinging blood.

This was the man who wanted him executed.

Alindale slammed his fist into Haemin's jaw. A tooth flew out.

This was the man who had gotten his brother killed!

More! He wanted more. It wasn't enough to hit him. Alindale wanted to see agony. He wanted to hear pleading. He wanted Haemin to feel the rage and pain roiling inside him!

Alindale spied his helmet off to the side. In a desperate lunge, he grabbed it and, using the last of his strength, pushed himself up, raised the helmet high, and aimed the crown to smash down on Haemin's head.

"For *Adam!*" he roared, bringing down his blow.

Only for a couple of soldiers to suddenly seize him under the arms and pull him away before he struck.

Alindale's narrow focus shattered. He gasped, as if he had been holding his breath. His lungs ached desperately for air as the pounding in his head froze over, sending icy spikes through his temple. More soldiers crowded around Haemin, who was groaning and rolling on the paving stones.

"No!" Alindale yelled. He tried to struggle, but his rage was subsiding and his strength abandoning him. He had been seized alive, and he knew they would hang him later.

"No!" he yelled again. "Don't do this! *Mother*!"

His protests were swallowed under a crashing roar rushing in from all sides. Panic screams, shrieks, raging bellows, and agonizing cries mixed with sporadic clashes of battle springing up everywhere. Officers shouted hasty, contradictory commands.

The soldiers dragged Alindale underneath the gallows, and the entire world fell apart around them.

Chapter 29

O pen the gate!"

The pleading knight reined in his galloping horse on the moat bridge before the closed northern gate of the Dain Castle's lower wall. Three of his brothers galloped up behind, their horse's hooves pounding across the wooden boards.

"Open the gate!" the knight shouted again. "We have wounded and are being pursued!"

The knights were playing their part well. Kalleb spotted a few soldiers rushing on the top of the wall to the gate's turret, the Easterly Sun's rays sparkling off their spears and helmets.

Kalleb and his sorry-looking troop of riding wounded trotted behind. They were lancers with minor wounds; some with bandages around their arms or heads. They sat slumped in their saddles, trying their best to give the impression they were about to collapse.

For Kalleb, it was easy to act as if he were about to fall out of his saddle. Every small bump or shake rippled up his saddle and jarred his collarbone, no matter how close he held his arm or how still he tried to keep it. It didn't help that Cloud wanted to gallop after the knights as soon as they kicked their mounts. The stud nearly *threw* him out of the saddle.

"This gate is closed to all travelers," a soldier through the portcullis's iron bars said dismissively. "Unless you have official letters of mark from either a minister or the queen, we cannot let you pass. Go around to the city entrances. You can find doctors there."

"There isn't time!" the knight cried. "They'll be on top of us any minute!"

"What?"

"Brother Harken!" another knight yelled from the back of their group.

Morsey's not wasting any time. Kalleb both felt and heard the thunder of hooves behind him.

Trike's plan was simple. An advance group would pretend to be a band of loyal knights who had escaped an ambush, with wounded, to get the guards to lift the gate. The rest of the lancers would charge as soon as the decoy knights reached the gate. Once the gate was raised, the decoy group would rush in, seize the gate, and ensure the rest charged in.

For Kalleb's part, he and seven others served as the group's wounded, while the knights with fifteen other lancers dressed in spare tabards of the slain brotherhood served as the surviving members. No tabards for Kalleb and his wounded, though. They were stuck with ripped undershirts and trousers. No armor. If this went bad, they would be the most vulnerable.

"Sergeant!" an alarmed soldier yelled from atop the wall. "There're Storm lancers! Hundreds of them!"

"And knights!" the knight yelled, feigning panic as he leapt from his saddle and slammed into the gate. "Rogue knights and Storm lancers ambushed us east of Siegman's Success. Our whole brotherhood was nearly wiped out! Please! You have to let us in!" The knight railed against the iron bars, forcing the sergeant to step away, startled.

"We can't," the sergeant stuttered, glancing between the knight and the oncoming lancers. "We don't have orders."

"You're going to watch them *kill* us?" The knight kicked the gate. The iron bars rang out as his boot slammed against them.

By the sound of hooves behind them, Kalleb knew they were closing in. If the gate wasn't opened soon, the charge would stall, and their ruse would be up. He would never reach his brother in time.

Grimacing, he slumped in his saddle and kicked Cloud forward. His shoulder screamed at him, but he channeled the pain and groaned loudly.

"Please," he begged through gritted teeth. "I can't keep in my saddle."

He kept a firm grip on his saddle horn and bent over a little farther, balancing precariously in his stirrups and making it appear he was about to fall off.

"My brothers can't fight back!" the knight screamed. "You must let us in! We're loyal!"

"They're almost here!" someone cried out from the back.

Kalleb looked through sweaty strands of hair to watch the sergeant. He was pale, in near panic, looking between them and the oncoming lancers. His eyes were wide and dancing as decisions likely spun in his head.

"Open the gate!" he finally yelled. "Quickly, men, or there'll be a slaughter! Sound the alarm!"

Winches started turning, sending grating screeches from inside the gateway. The portcullis shuddered and slowly began to rise.

Kalleb grunted in amazement. Olivar's crazy story and idea had worked. At least, so long as they got in.

Let's just hope there's not over a hundred soldiers on the other side of the wall.

He stayed slumped as he watched the rising gate as far as his poor position would allow. When it passed out of sight, he kicked Cloud forward.

"Look out!" the sergeant shouted.

The tip of a portcullis spike grazed Kalleb's scalp before he could stop. If he had reined Cloud, there was a chance of hitting the spike if the stud bucked. Kalleb had promised himself, if he made it through the gate, if he made it inside, he would only go forward.

Forward, he urged, pushing back on his saddle horn and sitting up. *Keep going forward.*

"Get in quickly!" the knight shouted.

Two knights rushed in behind Kalleb and flanked him on either side. The stomping hooves grew louder in the gateway, signaling the rest of the decoy group were following behind.

Kalleb glanced around, spotting murder holes higher up along, with holes for pouring hot oil, but he didn't see anyone manning them.

As he passed through the inner gate, he surveyed the other side. Four soldiers worked the gate winches, huffing and frantically spooling the ropes back as fast they could. Two more soldiers readied to close the inner gate's double doors. All their spears rested out of reach as they focused on their tasks. There were no guard houses or barracks for a large garrison, leading Kalleb to assume they rested somewhere in the wall turrets between duty.

"You well, L.C.?" Rence asked, walking his horse up to him. He played one of their wounded, with extra bandages wrapped around the side of his head. He patted Kalleb on his good shoulder and concerningly looked him over. Other disguised lancers gathered around them.

Kalleb couldn't help but grin. "We're in."

Rence's eyes lit up.

"Close the—"

The sergeant's order turned into a watery gargle.

Kalleb looked over his shoulder to see the knight sliding his knife out of the man's neck and the sergeant sliding down the wall.

"Seize the gate!" Kalleb yelled.

The lancers around him whooped and turned their mounts on the soldiers manning the winches. Two broke and ran at the sight of horsemen bearing down on them with lances, but they didn't get far.

"Don't kill me!" a soldier cried, throwing his hands up as a lance was leveled at him. Others joined him.

"Brother Knights!" the knight shouted, cleaning off his knife then drawing his sword. "Take the turrets and make sure they don't cut the ropes!"

The knights kicked in the turrets' doors just as a pounding alarm came from above.

"You men who are able," Kalleb said to the lancers stripping off tabards, "join the knights. Maces and sabers only! Don't let them cut those ropes!"

The lancers divided themselves between the turrets and threw themselves from their saddles. They stacked their lances by the door and stormed in after the knights, maces and sabers in hand. Shouts, cries, and the thumps of battle came from the windows and above.

The portcullis remained open.

"What should we do with the prisoners?" Rence asked.

Three soldiers sat on their knees with their hands behind their backs. One of them, no more than eighteen by Kalleb's guess, trembled and hunkered his head.

"Put 'em next to the wall and keep them there," he replied. "We just need to keep them out of the way."

"Yes, sir." Rence saluted then trotted over to relay the order.

The alarm suddenly cut off, replaced by a cry and the clangs of sword fighting. Kalleb spied men rushing across the wall to join the fight, but with the battle now on top the wall, the portcullis's ropes were likely secure.

The way was open, and Kalleb could see the head of their charging column coming down the hill.

They'll reach the moat bridge in moments.

He wheeled Cloud around, choking down the stinging across his chest, and took in the open, sloped ground of the cliff. Around that slope lay another gate, opening into Daincliff. Where his brother was.

Forward. His own promise called to him. *Forward!*

He nudged Cloud into a trot. His instincts and heart yelled at him to kick the stud into a gallop, but his broken collarbone pleaded with him not to. To distract his inner argument, Kalleb fumbled, exchanging his reins between his hands before clumsily failing to draw his saber hanging on his saddle.

Dammit. Why didn't I put this on the right side?

"Captain!" Rence yelled, galloping after him. "Wait!"

"Stay with the others, Rence!" Kalleb shouted back, growling at his stubborn saber.

"Can't do that, sir," Rence replied, rounding his mount in front of Cloud.

The stud snorted at the perceived challenge, and only Kalleb's quick pull on the reins stopped him from nipping at Rence. The sharp tug resulted in another stabbing pain, and he grimaced at the unruly lancer.

"Rence," Kalleb warned in a low growl, "get out of my way."

"Can't," Rence replied again. "Promised the others I'd look after you until we met up again. I may be a cut-up sometimes, sir, but I'm not about to break my word."

"Too bad." Kalleb grunted, finally sliding his saber free, although now he held it underhanded. "*I* swore never to watch another family member die. I saw my pa ridden under. I'm not about to stop after coming so far and push my way through just see my brother swinging! Get out of my frickin' way!"

"But you'll *die*, you stubborn bastard!" Rence roared, his face red. "You won't even make it into Daincliff. And others are just coming over the bridge. We rode here for *you*! Wait for us, dammit!"

Kalleb's ear twitched from hooves drumming on wood. He glanced over his shoulder to watch the first lancers, in burgundy armor and lances leveled, charge through the gate. The lancers on top the wall were waving their sabers, beckoning.

He sighed and looked over at Rence. The young lancer sat straighter in the saddle now, hardly the problem recruit Kalleb had taken him to be that first day at muster. He was probably right, too. A stiff breeze might be enough to push Kalleb out of the saddle.

"Rence," he said.

"Sir?"

Kalleb raised his saber. "Help me with my grip. I can't get it right with my stupid shoulder."

Rence grinned. "Yes, sir!"

He took Kalleb's saber by the blade and held it out so Kalleb could hold it right.

"You're still an ass," Kalleb grumbled as the first lancers galloped by in a column of four.

"Thank you, sir!" The smug ass even saluted.

"Well done, Captain Kane!" Morsey shouted, pulling his horse up beside them, along with three accompanying lancers. "The gate is ours, and no counteroffensive from the castle."

Morsey was right. The sound of galloping hooves was so loud that Kalleb couldn't hear an alarm banging up there or not. But there had to be. The castle gates were closed, but it was stupid to assume some form of garrison wasn't up there.

"Then we best move before they realize we're not aiming for it," Kalleb said.

Morsey grunted in approval. He was about to join the column when he paused.

"Kalleb," he said while taking off his helmet and holding it out to him, "something to protect your head."

Kalleb saw the determination in Morsey's eyes and knew he didn't have time to argue. He glanced at his saber and slung arm then hung his head. "Rence," he groaned out, "help me with the helmet." The hairs on the back of his neck stood up as it was slid on. He knew they were all smirking now.

"Ride, Lancers!" Morsey yelled, joining the column and raising his saber in the air. "For Kanestown!"

"For Kanestown!" the lancers roared.

"Troop D!" Rence called out, standing in his saddle and waving his sword in the air.

Part of the column lifted their lances, and Kalleb recognized his men's faces. He set his jaw and kicked Cloud into a gallop alongside them. He pushed down the tears and welling pain of his shoulder and raised his saber in the air, channeling his pain to battle fury.

"For Kanestown!" he shouted. "Forward, to the gallows!"

"To the gallows!" the men around him screamed.

Their horses kicked up dirt, grass, and dust as they ran across the rising cliff's curving slope.

The city came into view quickly with each second until they had finally cleared the horizon. Men were already fighting down below. The lancers at the head of the column had broken their charge, dismounted, and rushed the gate leading into Daincliff's North End. The fighting had spread to the top of that gate, as well, passed the turrets, and on the wall.

The gate, though, was still open.

Lancers were charging into the city. Daincliff lay open.

I'm coming, Kenith, Kalleb swore, leaning farther into the saddle, his adrenaline pumping, breathing hard. *I'll make it this time!*

***

"Let me go!" Alindale groaned. He tried to pull his arms free from the soldiers dragging him under the gallows, but they were sluggish and heavy. He could barely move in his armor. "Where are you taking me?"

The soldiers suddenly dropped him, Alindale's armor pulling him to the ground with a *thud*. The back of his head bounced on the paving stones, sending his vision into a spin. His world went numb. The sounds of running, screaming, and fighting all sounded far away.

His head rolled to the left. Knights in white and blue were fighting the soldiers surrounding Montaigu. The master knight was doubled over on his knees, leaning on his spear and holding his side. One knight cut a path through the soldiers, carving them with two swords, as if their spears had no reach.

Rolling his head to the right, Alindale found soldiers and knights struggling against a chaotic mob. Soldiers attempted to corral a mass of people with their spears, but the unruly rioters boiled around them, breaking up any line the soldiers tried to make.

A knight threw a man back, only to get struck in the back of the head by another man with a club. As the knight crumbled into a heap, a soldier speared the club-wielding assailant. The man grappled with the spear in his gut, and the people around them leapt at the soldier, swallowing him under a barrage of fists and kicks.

Alindale's hearing returned in time to hear the panicked screams.

"What do we do?"

Alindale blinked and rolled his head up. The two soldiers who had dragged him away were watching in shock. One kept turning in circles, jumping at every scream, yell, or sight with wide-eyed panic. The other stood still, mouth agape.

"What do we *do*?" the scared soldier cried.

"I don't know," the other replied softly.

"But we have to do something!" The soldier looked down at Alindale, his green eyes shaking with confusion. "What are we supposed to do with him?"

"I don't know."

Movement caught Alindale's eye. Someone was sneaking up behind the scared soldier. He lifted his hand and tried to speak.

"Wha—"

The soldier gasped. His head spasmed, and his eyes rolled back in his head.

Alindale's hand fell to his chest, his gauntlet cracking against his breastplate, and groaned while watching Nolen Ingman step out from behind the soldier.

Nolan coldly slid his dagger from the base of the soldier's skull then pushed him aside. As the body crumbled on the stones, he gingerly stepped over Alindale with his long legs, heading toward the fallen soldier's compatriot, who was slowly turning around.

And received a slash to the throat.

Blood sprayed the boards above. The soldier twisted away and fell, shaking violently and clutching his throat for a few gasping moments before falling still.

I have to get up, Alindale told himself.

He tried to move again but failed.

I need help.

He looked for Montaigu but couldn't find him in the fierce fighting on the left side of the gallows.

Nolen walked around him, looking out at all the chaos surrounding the gallows. He pulled a handkerchief from his pocket and wiped the blood from his dagger. Alindale barely recognized the sharp-tongued and smugly apathetic man.

Nolen squatted beside him, his cold, unfeeling demeanor making his sharp, angular features stand out more prominently.

"Well, Your Highness"—he looked Alindale up and down—"I bet you didn't expect to end up like this today."

Alindale glanced at the dagger still hanging in Nolen's hand. "I expected I'd die today," he said hoarsely, his throat scratchy from needing a drink. "Just not by you."

Nolen arched an eyebrow then suddenly snorted, as if he had heard a joke, cracking his cold mask.

"Why would I kill you?" Nolen asked.

Alindale laid his head on the stones with a deflating groan. "I'm too tired for games, Nolen. Just get it over with."

"Sorry"—Nolen smirked—"but this is no place for a prince to die." He gestured with his dagger at the gallows above them.

Alindale frowned, and when Nolen reached for him, he closed his eye and waited.

"No!"

A woman's piercing scream made Alindale snap both eyes open, breaking the crusty blood around his left eye but also opening the cut in his eyebrow.

He watched a woman shove Nolen aside through a tear of blood, and the lanky man rolled away with a surprised yelp, followed by the skidding *ping* of his dagger flying from his hand and sliding across the paving stones.

Tory Syros stepped between Alindale and Nolen with her arms outstretched defensively, her dark red hair a stark contrast against her gray dress.

"You can't kill him!" she said defiantly.

***

Tory glared down at the sprawled-out man who she had just pushed over. Her sense of time had slowed from the moment she had witnessed

Lord Haemin slicing off Alindale's thumb to narrowly avoiding being swallowed by the rioters pouring out of South End, and finally watching Alindale stab Lord Haemin from behind before being dragged under the gallows.

Her path to Her Majesty had disappeared once the Sunrise Guard had formed a defensive line in front of the royal box, and with the frantic fighting growing behind her, Tory had felt she had no other choice but to rush toward the gallows. And she had arrived just in time to see the tall man kill the two soldiers who had dragged Alindale away.

When she had seen the man—Nolen Ingman, she had overheard Alindale say—squat beside Alindale, she had panicked and leapt before she had given it a thought, shoving Nolen aside.

Her heart raced, pounding hard enough she thought it would burst from her chest as she stood over Alindale with her arms outstretched. She risked a glance down at him and winced. He was badly cut above his left eye. Blood, fresh and old, stained that side of his face. Every joint bore a cut or wound. But the black stump that had previously been his left thumb was the worst of all, as part of the bone was visible.

"I knew I should have brought another knife," Nolen said dryly, looking disheartened at the scuffle closest beyond the gallows. He then rolled around and blinked up at her, as if trying to remember her name. "Why, young Lady Syros, what are you doing here?"

"I was trying to speak with Her Majesty, but . . . this . . ." Tory waved at the fighting around them. Then she shook her head, recalling what she had just prevented. "Never mind that. I won't let you kill Alindale!" Although, even without his knife, Tory wasn't sure how.

"I'm not going to kill anybody," Nolen said as he sat up.

Tory and Alindale shared a disbelieving look. Then, together, they glanced at the dead bodies of the soldiers near them and back to Nolen.

"Else," Nolen added. "I meant to say, I'm not going to kill anybody *else*." He threw his hands up. "Everyone's going crazy right now, and I don't have time to figure out who's on whose side."

"And whose side are *you* on?" Tory asked, fixing him with a suspicious stare.

"His," Alindale coughed before Nolen could reply.

Nolen shrugged and smiled. "At least I taught you something, Your Highness. In all seriousness, though, we need to get out of here." His smile dropped, and he nodded behind her. "Even Her Majesty knows it's time to run."

Tory heard the horses before she looked over her shoulder to see the royal carriage grind to a halt in front of Her Majesty's box, forcing people around the stands to leap out of the way or be crushed under hoof and wheel.

The panicked screams were growing louder, and more people were running; most of them heading toward North End and the castle. The Sunrise Guard joined in the defense to hold back the growing mob, slashing and gutting anyone who got too close.

A grunt from Alindale tore Tory's gaze away from the carnage, and she gasped at seeing him push himself to sit up.

"This is an opportunity," Nolen said, springing to his feet faster than Tory would have expected. In three long strides, he slipped around her, squatted down at Alindale's side, and grabbed his injured hand. He pulled out a cloth from somewhere and began wrapping it around the stump.

He's helping? Tory gaped, confused.

Alindale, too, leaned away and watched Nolen with suspicion. His left eye squeezed shut again from the blood oozing from his cut, but his right flickered between Nolen and his injured hand.

"This is your only chance," Nolen said. "Use this chaos to escape. This kind of mess could take weeks to fix." He tied off the makeshift bandage then gave Alindale a serious look. "It's time to go."

Tory suddenly felt at a loss. She thought she was helping, but now she wasn't sure what she was doing.

An agonizing scream made her jump. The riots were getting too close, and the conversation appeared to be leaving her behind. She wrapped her arms around herself and knelt beside Alindale.

He stared straight ahead. At first, Tory thought he was watching the growing fighting, like she had, but then she followed his eyeline. He was staring at the royal carriage desperately trying to turn and flee.

"Where is Prince Alindale?" someone cried from above them. "We must find Prince Alindale!"

***

Alindale anxiously watched Nolen bind his injured hand. He winced when the cloth was pulled tightly and pressed the remaining bones in his former thumb's joint deeper into his palm.

His instincts told him not to trust Nolen, but his current predicament said it didn't matter.

Escape? he questioned, seeing no way out through the fighting mob and panicking crowd. *How? Where?*

A cracked whip and the bay from horses snatched his attention back to his mother's carriage. The coachman was desperately trying to turn the horses around, swirling his whip frantically in the air, lashing out at poor beasts and anyone who stepped too close. Behind the turning carriage, soldiers frenziedly tore down part of the stands to use as an impromptu wall against the rioters. A gang of rioters broke away from the main fighting and latched on to the other side of the stands, creating a game of tug-of-war between the two groups.

How did this happen?

"Where is Prince Alindale?"

Alindale looked up at the sound of Bernold's voice as running footsteps drummed on the boards overhead.

"We must find Prince Alindale!"

"I need to get up there," Alindale said.

Nolen coughed. "What?"

"I can't run," Alindale sighed out. He was too tried, too wounded to run now. He gave Nolen a wary look. "And I *can't* trust you. Not after you tried to murder me in the cathedral."

Tory sniffed sharply and stared in alarm at Nolen.

Nolen frowned questioningly, ignoring Tory completely. "Murder? I was going to leave you that dagger so you could have something to protect yourself. If I knew the priests could pray all this up"—he gestured at Alindale's armor—"I wouldn't have bothered and saved my arm from being wrenched out of its socket."

Alindale shook his head. The denial was expected, though the reasoning could be plausible. He didn't have time to sort it out.

He braced his good hand on the ground then gently pulled his legs under him to try to get to his feet. His leg muscles were stiff and throbbed. He barely suffered through the aches and pains just to get his left foot under him.

"Is the ground . . . shaking?" Tory asked, looking at the stones beneath her with a puzzled expression.

Alindale stopped.

There. A slight tremor.

"Lancers!" someone yelled.

They snapped around. The people fleeing toward North End began screaming and running back into the square. The royal carriage had finally turned around and was heading straight for the North End gate, with a few other carriages and wagons behind it, when the coachman suddenly pulled the teams' reins and the carriage swung down an alley and out of sight.

Before the following carriages could turn with it, Storm Cavalry lancers stormed out the North End gate, flooding the square at full charge. Alindale turned his head so he didn't have to see the men and women yelling and screaming in shock as they were swallowed under the lancers' hooves.

The remaining soldiers, who had been trying to cordon off the panicked crowd from the mob, were as blindsided as the people. No ranks were formed, or defensive lines attempted. They had no time before lances and sabers bore down on them. An unfortunate fleeing carriage overturned when its horses panicked and slid into the North End gate, slamming into lancers and fleeing people alike.

But the charging tide that had gotten through was heading straight for the gallows.

***

"Keep moving!" Kalleb yelled hoarsely. Sweat poured down his face and, while wearing a helmet, there was no way he could wipe it out of his eyes.

Their grand feat of charging into Daincliff had slowed to a crawl. The street was packed with lancers, horses, and people. Terrified, confused people.

"What's going on?" a balding, middle-aged man, wearing some sort of robe or gown over his clothes, bellowed from a second-story balcony.

"Stay in your house if you want to live, snob!" a lancer shouted back.

The balding man's face turned red before he stomped back inside. Where he stayed.

"Captain!" Trevor shouted, sluggishly guiding his horse around the lancers in front of him. "Someone overturned a carriage ahead. Some lancers made it into the square, but damn, sir, there's a lot of people down there! The streets are full of 'em running around, scared out of their wits."

Kalleb frowned and looked behind them. The buildings blocked his line of sight, but he was sure there was still fighting going on at the inner gate connecting Daincliff to the castle's approach. If they got pinched here, they were done.

"Find another way around!" he ordered. "There are other gates into the square. Break up into troops and find them! Move!"

Lancers barked acknowledgments and began spreading the order. They broke off from the main street in units then galloped down the side streets.

"Troop D rides with you, sir," Zoren said from behind him. The wide-eyed lad was still shaking in his saddle as he looked all around.

Kalleb grunted. "Keep your head, Zoren."

He turned Cloud east, down a connecting street. From the fancy dresses, clocks, and furniture decorating the gilded windows, he surmised they had found the street where the snobs and aristos did their shopping, with signs that read, *"Closed Due to Today's Execution,"* decorating many of their doors.

Kalleb ignored them as he searched for back alleys or side streets large enough for horses to ride through and lead them to the square, preferably one with a clear path. Lancers pushed on ahead, scouting their path forward.

Come on, he groaned inwardly after passing the sixth dead end. Time was running short. His adrenaline had stalled with the charge, and now the pain of his shoulder was starting to creep across his chest and his body's weariness was returning. He wouldn't be able to stay in the saddle much longer. *Come on!*

A loud *whoop* from up the street caught his ear. Then a lancer came galloping back, waving his lance before pulling his mount up in front of Kalleb. It was Kelly, bouncing with excitement in his saddle.

"We found another street to the square, Captain! It's a tight archway, but it looks like men and horses can ride through it. Doesn't look like anyone's there, either!"

"Zoren!" Kalleb yelled. "Go back to the column and tell the others waiting we've found a way through. Lead them to this street!"

"Yes, sir!" Zoren replied. Then he turned his mount around and galloped away.

"Kelly, stay at this corner and guide them down the right street," Kalleb ordered, to a salute from Kelly. "The rest of you, let's get into that square!"

The troop whooped and hollered as Kalleb kicked Cloud into a trot. They turned the corner and fanned out in the connecting street, where the storefronts changed to two- and three-story brick houses.

As the street rolled downward, Kalleb spied an open archway in the dividing wall to the square, standing open just as Kelly had said. Almost beckoning.

"Forward," he ordered, "at a trot."

Kalleb and his troop trotted steadily down the street, checking behind every corner they passed to every connecting street and alleyway. They had lost the element of surprise and so, despite wanting to rush and grab that archway, Kalleb didn't want to risk his troop being ambushed.

"Hurry!"

Kalleb pulled Cloud up short when a squad of ten or more soldiers led a terrified group of North Enders through the archway. The soldiers stumbled to a stop when they saw Kalleb's troop heading toward them. Many were without their spears, and several looked like they had been in a brawl, their faces bruised and bloodied, their clothes and armor mangled. They stared, tired and terrified, at the lancers. Especially at their lances.

"What should we do, Captain?" Trevor whispered. "Go around and look for a different street or . . .?"

Or charge and run them down.

The choices were obvious to Kalleb. It was likely the head of their column chose the same course of action. However, there were not only soldiers in front of them, but women, as well, pressing themselves against the archway, the wall, or the arms of another.

"They'll move," Rence said. "They'll move."

But not all of them, Kalleb knew.

"Stay here," he ordered then nudged Cloud forward. He trotted up near the crowd and pointed his saber at the soldiers.

"Escort these people out of the archway," he ordered, guiding his saber down the street to his left.

The soldiers shared confused looks with each other. One reached for his sword.

"If you do that," Kalleb yelled at the man, "the lancers behind me will run you down. All of you! But, if you move over, you'll live. You have my word. What'll it be?"

The soldiers looked at each other again, but as they tried to make up their minds, a few women burst from the group and sprinted toward the street that Kalleb had directed, with their skirts hiked up so they could run. Others joined, streaming across the street, and before the soldiers had moved. The soldiers followed them, a couple running with scared civilians, not looking back.

As soon as the archway was clear, Kalleb kicked Cloud, diving headlong into the square. He ignored the cries behind him. From the sound of rushing hooves, he knew his lancers were following.

He pressed Cloud into a gallop up the street, feeling the ground curve. He spotted the Ministry of Justice and weaved up a few side streets toward it. He passed clumps of people running aimlessly and groups of soldiers huddled together.

As Kalleb broke through an alleyway, a large carriage roared past him, its coachman cracking his whip frantically as the mad team raced away. He thought he had caught sight of the royal crest of Daincliff on the door, but it was gone too fast to take any real notice.

Kalleb gulped down air, gasping as he looked over the sheer madness.

The entire southern end of the square was engulfed in a frantic melee. Common people with clubs, hatchets, shovels, and everything else in reach, raged against soldiers and knights alike. The frenzied mob fought up the Ministry of Justice's front steps, some pounding on the doors to get in while soldiers tried to form ranks to push them back. Each time, they got flanked and surrounded by offshoots of the main mob.

The north side of the square resembled a panicked rout. People fled in every direction. The cathedral's doors stood wide, accepting a stream of people rushing in for safety. Others fled toward Kalleb but broke down another street as soon as they saw him. No gallows in sight, though, leading him to assume it was behind the Ministry of Justice, where the smoke was coming from.

Galloping lancers drew Kalleb's attention. They looped around a throng of panicked people, knocking over soldiers. He picked out the overturned carriage blocking the main street entrance to North End.

Dismounted lancers were trying to dislodge it and push it into the square, while people in the square were trying to shove it into North End.

"Sorry we're late, Captain," Trevor said as he trotted up beside him. "We ran into some soldiers and—"

"How in *Oblivion*?" Rence cursed, pulling up sharply on Kalleb's other side.

More lancers gathered around them, surveying the same chaos as Kalleb and realizing they were riding into something much more dangerous than a crazy relief mission.

Kalleb's heart urged him to keep his promise. The way in front of him was clearer than any path. The mob hadn't surrounded the Ministry of Justice yet. He could easily lead his troop around its north side and go around to the gallows. However, if the melee were to swallow the square and the North End entrance was still blocked, he had no certainty he could rescue his brother and lead his troop into Kanestown. They could be trapped.

Even in his tired state, Kalleb only saw one option.

"Rence, did more lancers follow us?"

"Yes," Rence replied. "Several other troops are using other side streets to get our entrance."

Kalleb nodded. "Split up the men, then. Take your half and push through to move that carriage." He pointed at the blocked entrance.

Rence frowned. "You sure?"

"You may have to ride down some people," Kalleb whispered grimly so only Rence could hear. "But it needs to be done, and you're the only man I got near me to give that order. Be an ass and get through that crowd."

Rence's frown darkened to resolve, and then he nodded.

As he turned back to divide the lancers, Kalleb turned to Trevor.

"The rest of you, follow me!" he ordered, pushing Cloud into a gallop one more time.

***

"Where from Oblivion did *they* come from?" Nolen asked, backing farther under the gallows as Storm Cavalry lancers looped closer.

Alindale smiled at Nolen's surprise, despite the worsening situation, but then he coughed.

"Are you okay?" Tory asked, lightly touching his shoulder. She nervously glanced at him then the fighting beyond.

Alindale coughed a laugh. "With the day we're having?"

Tory cracked a small smile and snickered. Then she looked out and said, "I left my sister out there somewhere. She tried to have me taken back to the castle, and I just left her."

Alindale followed her gaze to where the panicked crowd milled around the North End's blocked main entrance.

After the first wave of lancers had poured into the square, the people had tried to run in behind them. Several lancers were riding around the edge of the crowd and the gallows, as if uncertain where to go.

"Maybe she made it out," Alindale suggested.

"Maybe." Tory grimaced, turning her gaze away from the crowd to the east. Her eyes grew watery. "I was hoping to go home today."

Alindale looked away. Cries of agony and anger filled his ears. Everywhere he looked, someone was being beaten, stabbed, punched, or begging for mercy. He caught the scent of smoke and looked to see the stands that the soldiers had tried to use as a barricade ablaze.

Did I cause all this? he wondered.

"I hate to say it," Nolen started, taking him under the arm, "but I think your window of escape is closing."

Nolen gently tugged him, and Alindale used the added support to finally push himself to his feet, groaning from every straining muscle and stinging wound. He hobbled on his left leg to a support beam. The wound to his right knee refused to take any weight at all.

"Where are the steps?" he asked, searching for them through the gallows' support beams.

"There." Tory pointed.

Alindale followed her finger. The knights who had fought around Montaigu were now struggling with the soldiers remaining around the steps. Men struggled on every step. A soldier cried and fell with a *thud* off to one side of the gallows. He didn't get up.

"Might want to stay down here a while longer," Nolen suggested.

Alindale grimaced. He had been down here too long already. It would only take one battle-crazed soldier or rioter to rush in and kill him and the others.

He pushed off the support beam and hopped toward the nearest one, making his way toward the steps.

"To the gallows!"

The unified shout made Alindale glance behind him.

More Storm lancers trotted into the square from the east, divided into two columns. One headed toward North End's main entrance. The other headed straight for them, lances leveled in a steady, determined march.

***

"Lances leveled!" Kalleb ordered as his line rounded the Ministry of Justice.

Five lancers formed a wedge at their head. Trevor and several others demanded Kalleb not to ride at the head of the wedge, so he rode in the center to relieve their worries and give orders.

Rence's line was already forcing their way into the tightly packed group surrounding North End's blocked main entrance.

Kalleb ignored the cries and screams and finally took in the execution grounds and the gallows erected in the center.

Soldiers amassed on top of it, using the advantage of the higher elevation between the rioters to their south and knights and lancers closing in from the north. The familiar blue and white tabards of the knights told Kalleb that they were with Master Blain, but they were struggling to get up the steps.

Kalleb's breath caught at seeing the prisoners still there, nooses tied around their necks and ready to drop. He quickly found Kenith, his uniform stained and ripped, his hair and beard shaggy and disheveled. Nevertheless, it was his brother, and he was struggling with the soldiers holding him, yelling about something—

At the far end of the gallows hung Grandpa Kane.

A shocking chill ran up Kalleb's spine, and he trembled in his saddle.

No soldiers were holding him, and he hadn't been dropped, yet he hung there. His knees were bent forward, legs giving him no support. The noose stretched his neck. His face was blue. His eyes were bulged.

"Get to the gallows!" Kalleb bellowed.

"To the gallows!" the lancers around him yelled, waving their lances and moving forward in unison.

Kalleb wanted to dash froward, but being so tightly packed in, he could only move with the column. As they steadily trotted forward, other lancers, who had been aimlessly looping around, joined in behind, swelling their numbers.

"Some of that mob's broken through that line of soldiers," Trevor said, pointing toward a group of men who were hollering, as if possessed, and swinging clubs and hatchets over their heads toward the crowd still trying to push into North End. And right into their path.

"Run them down!" Kalleb ordered.

The head of their wedge sprang forward. Rather it was from blind rage or the fog of chaos around them, the rioters didn't even notice the lancers until their lances ran them through. Some of the angry mob tried to fight back, but against armored lancers with better reach, Kalleb's column rode over them without a pause.

Their intervention, however, alerted the soldiers on top the gallows. It was easy for them to see Kalleb and his men were heading straight for them. Some officer began running back and forth, shoving men to the sides of the gallows, where they lowered their spears in a bristling defense.

"Surround the gallows!" Kalleb ordered, and his column divided again, trying to engulf the gallows with lances leveled at the defenders. As they got closer, though, it became apparent that the guarding soldiers had height on their side.

Did they have to make the damn thing so high? Kalleb growled in frustration.

The first line of lancers grew closer and began thrusting their lances against the soldiers' spears, trying to knock them away and looking for openings.

Kalleb looked at his grandpa. The old man wasn't moving. His arms hung limply at his sides. Kalleb searched again and found Kenith staring right at him.

If someone pulls that lever . . . or even if someone gets hit and falls on it . . . Kalleb tried not to panic, but the soldiers on the gallows weren't giving up. They were cornered and scared, swinging their spears desperately to keep the lancers back.

They're right there! Kalleb gritted his teeth, wanting to shout but held back. *But, how do I get to them and not get them killed?*

"*Stop!*" someone shouted loudly from the other side of the gallows.

Kalleb couldn't see who it was, but the soldiers' officer paused and looked behind them. Despite the desperate situation around them, a small lull settled in the fighting around the gallows.

***

511

"I have to get up there!" Alindale declared defiantly as the lancers rode down a small party of rioters. He hopped to another support, inching closer toward the steps.

"You'll die if you go there now!" Nolen yelled.

Alindale fell against another support with a grunt, the steps just another hop away. "I've been expecting to die all day, Nolen. I'm just surprised it hasn't happened yet!" His exhaustion had him forgetting the decorum of his speech.

He didn't hear if Nolen made a snark response or not before he slipped out from under the gallows and was engulfed by the sounds of fighting, groaning, and struggling men. He tripped over the leg of a dead man just as something whooshed above his head, the air slicing through his hair. He crawled around shuffling feet until he finally reached the steps.

Alindale had no plan or idea of what to do if he made it up them. Even getting up there was uncertain. Regardless, he used the wooden railing to claw his way back to his feet, gasping through the pain in his injured hand and shoulder just to push past a knight and take his first step up.

Someone has to stop this, he told the part of him that agreed with Nolen. This was idiocy! Likely suicide. *This has to stop!*

A knight and soldier grappled with each other in front of him, blocking the rest of the way. One of them tripped, and as the soldier flipped backward, the knight fell on top of him. They both crashed through the railing, leaving a gap. Another knight pushed past him and engaged two more soldiers blocking the top of the steps.

From his higher perch, Alindale got a better view of the square. Fires were springing up along the southern end as the mob swelled against the weary soldiers. Another mass of people rioted out of Kanestown, but they were more fighting off the mob from South End than the soldiers. People were struggling to get into West End, while others desperately tried to close its gates. North Enders swarmed up the cathedral's steps, desperate for refuge since the North End was still blocked.

Soldiers, lancers, and knights fought each other around the gallows. And for what? For *what?*

"*Stop!*"

Alindale was surprised he had found the strength and air to yell as loudly as he had.

The steps in front of him creaked.

He looked up as a soldier bore down him, sword high in the air. Sweat glistened off his face as he wheezed for air, his shoulders rising and falling sporadically. Alindale was too tired to dodge the blow and waited for the sword to fall.

The soldier suddenly stopped, arms shaking with strain, keeping his sword above his head. His eyes went wide with surprised recognition.

"Prince Alindale," the soldier stated.

Alindale stared back at him. The struggle around the steps paused. Soldiers and knights shifted toward him and watched.

"May I pass?" Alindale asked. "If not, be swift."

The soldier panted. Just a simple swing, and he would have Alindale's head. Yet, for some reason, he dropped his sword to his side and backed away.

Another surprise, he thought, taking each step one at a time.

The knight and the other soldier, who were fighting at the top of the steps, gave him some space so Alindale could step up onto the gallows.

"Your Highness!" Bernold cried. "You're alive!" The former first minister was being held by two soldiers with a noose around his neck. Tears streamed down his cheeks as a great, joyful smile split his face.

Despite Bernold's hope at seeing him alive, Alindale noted the many soldiers on the platform. More than enough to make freeing the prisoners turn into a bloodbath. Enough people had died today already.

Alindale studied the soldiers as they watched him. They were tired and scared, panting and frightened. They appeared more as cornered animals, staring wide-eyed and lashing out at anything they perceived as a threat.

They would be my soldiers if I became king. My people. Perhaps I should speak with them like that.

"Enough, Soldiers of Daincliff," he urged. "No more need to die today. Release the prisoners."

"We can't," a soldier said from their center, clearly their remaining officer, wearing a hood of chain mail over his head. He had gray streaks in his beard.

"Why?" Alindale asked. "My mother has fled. Every minister of the table, every magistrate, every officer of the kingdom has fled! Who are you fighting for?"

"For ourselves!" The officer stomped on the boards and thrust his spear toward him. "Look around you, Prince! This isn't a battlefield. This is damnation, pure and simple. The only ones getting out of here alive are those who stick together. And so long as me and my men have this high ground, there's a chance we might survive."

The officer was right. Despite the area around the gallows being a concentrated battle between the soldiers, knights, and lancers, elsewhere else in the square were pitched fights against random groups. Soldiers against rioters. Knights against lancers. Even pockets where the city peace fought each other.

Something more needed to be done.

Despite being an inopportune moment, despite the bloodshed around him, a quote rang in Alindale's memory.

"'*When need arises to take command, take it,*'" he recited under his breath. It was from Master Ghiran Dewgen's Treatise on Authority, one of several that Amadus had him read.

The knight beside him grunted and nodded in approval. It reminded Alindale of Montaigu. Though, the knight never took his watchful eyes off the soldier in front of him, his sword still poised and his stance firmly on the steps. His tabard was splashed with blood, but the man in his mid-thirties didn't have a scratch on him, despite the chaotic melee. Even with sweat glistening on his face, his breathing was calm and steady.

If Alindale let him loose, he would likely carve into the tired soldiers, but these were *Alindale's* soldiers.

"Join me," he offered. "Join with me, and your men will survive today."

The officer spat and sneered at him. "Join *you*? You can barely stand. It'll be a miracle if you survive today with how much you're bleeding."

A groaning scrape reverberated from Alindale's left, and a cheer went up from the North End entrance. The remaining crowd of North Enders were rushing toward the docks or somewhere eastward, as more Storm Cavalry lancers claimed the main entrance, pushed away the overturned carriage, and rode in. They would join their fellows around the gallows soon.

The officer and the rest of his soldiers saw the same thing. Alindale needed to press him.

"You are running out of time!" he warned. "Release the hostages, especially Colonel Kane and the brigadier marshal, and the lancers will stand down."

The lancers kept pouring into the square, getting closer.

"I am your prince!" Alindale implored. "Join me and live! Or die for nothing! Make your choice!"

The soldiers watched their officer, many with pleading, tired eyes. They were all scared. Alindale knew that fear of death. He only hoped their officer hadn't given up and accepted it.

"Obey His Highness," the officer finally ordered. "Release the hostages. Soldiers of Daincliff, hail Prince Alindale Dain!" The officer then walked to the edge of the gallows, raised his spear in the air, and repeated the hail to the scattered soldiers waiting among the lancers and knights.

The soldiers within earshot raised their spears and yelled back.

As the soldiers stood down, the lancers around the gallows lowered their lances. The knights, as well, lowered their swords. The soldiers manning the gallows then began cutting the prisoners' bonds.

Alindale breathed a sigh of relief. He slumped and braced himself against the railing to keep his balance. If he slipped and cracked his head open after all this, it would be a sorry joke for the historians to record later.

"Your Highness!" Bernold cried, pushing through the soldiers. He rushed up to crush Alindale in an embrace.

He gasped as all his wounds screamed. It only grew worse after he breathed in Bernold's overwhelmingly stench of sweat, urine, and filth.

"Your father would be so proud!" Bernold whimpered.

Alindale awkwardly patted him on the shoulder. "Thanks, Lord Vanni, but this *really* hurts."

Bernold's breath caught, and he leapt away, wiping his face and straightening his clothes. "Forgive me, Your Highness! Today's been . . . rather emotional."

"That's putting it mildly."

Bernold beamed a smile and set his fists on his hips.

"How is he?" a lancer without armor, his right arm in a sling, demanded.

The lancer was halfway off his horse and clawing up onto the gallows toward Kenith, who was cutting Marshal Kane's limp body from his noose, with the help of Lieutenant Holt. They laid the marshal out on the boards, and Kenith shook his head.

The soldiers spread back, giving them a wide berth, and the lancers suddenly grew tense.

Before Alindale could inquire what was happening, a fiery groan of cracking timbers and crumbling stone boomed from the south side of the square. One of the buildings that had been set ablaze had fallen in, and now rioters were cheering around it. A great bulk of them were breaking off and running eastward into new parts of the city.

Their moment of reprieve was gone.

"It's not over yet," Alindale said under his breath.

Chapter 30

Tory breathed a sigh of relief when she heard the soldiers hail Alindale. She had waited below with her arms wrapped around herself, listening for that fateful blow. Something would happen. There would be a crash or a thud. And someone would have shouted, "The prince is dead!"

But, mercifully, or miraculously, it never came.

Now what? Tory contemplated, finding she had no answer.

She had tried to reach Her Majesty and the world had turned upside down around her. She thought she had saved Alindale, but now he didn't need saving. That left her underneath the gallows, unsure of what to do.

I could go up with Alindale now that the fighting has stopped, she considered, running her fingers through her hair in frustration. *But, what would I do there? Stand around and be in the way?*

"Lady Syros?"

Tory flinched at hearing name whispered so close to her.

She backpedaled, discovering Nolen had silently slipped close enough to hover over her.

"There's an opening," he said, pointing at the lancers, who had been crowding around the gallows, now pulling back, allowing light to shine underneath.

Tory's gaze followed Nolen's finger at the clear gap between the lancers riding into the square and the crowd hurrying away, toward the docks.

The docks!

Tory's heart leapt in her chest.

"This may be the last opportunity to get out before anything else happens," Nolen whispered. "And I'm going to take it. Want me to see you off at the docks on my way?"

Tory gave him a sideways glance and shied away from him, still remembering the bodies at their feet.

"If Alindale couldn't trust you, how can I?" she asked.

Nolen shrugged. "I'm taking my chance. Come if you want."

He strode toward the rim of the gallows, stalking on his long legs and glancing cautiously from underneath. Over his shoulder, Tory could see the path that he had pointed out. Still open. Still beckoning, *Stay and perhaps wander Daincliff or make for the docks and home?*

"Wait!" Tory took after him before she had realized. "I want to go home."

Nolen glanced over his shoulder and nodded. "Stay calm and walk," he instructed, taking her by the elbow. "Steady strides. Don't run unless I tell you."

Tory ducked her head under the rim of the gallows and followed. Her heart boomed in her chest, as if it were being crushed. They walked out between the lancers' horses with barely a word or glance from them. The lancers still seemed preoccupied with things on the gallows.

As they cleared the horses and walked out into an open space, Tory felt the urge to run, to follow that open path before her, all the way up the plank of Jerro's ship. Nolen, however, kept a hold of her elbow, keeping her pace steady with his. He flickered his gaze this way and that, alertly searching every corner and distant group of people.

Tory kept her head. She was finally setting her course for home.

***

"How is he?" Kalleb cried, desperately struggling to climb up on the gallows from his saddle.

A war raged within him through the entire lull. His pa's lessons of command strained against the desire to save his brother and grandpa. He needed to avoid his lads getting hurt if there was a chance the fighting

518

would stop, but pressure built every second that he was left staring at Grandpa Kane hanging at the end of the rope. He didn't even know why he was on the gallows!

He heedlessly tossed his saber onto the boards and tried to raise one leg over the top. He ignored the agonizing flare in his shoulder as he belly-crawled over the rim. Cloud neighed in annoyance while Kalleb struggled to get free of his stirrups.

"Captain!" Trevor cried in alarm. "Your injury!"

"Push me up, dammit!" Kalleb growled, finally getting a leg over the side.

He felt a slight push, but it was enough.

He awkwardly shuffled on his knees and good hand to clamber over to Kenith, who was kneeling beside Grandpa Kane's body. Kalleb reached them in time to watch Kenith close Grandpa Kane's bulging eyes.

"He caught sick in the tower," Kenith explained solemnly, his voice cracking. "He didn't even have the strength to stand when they hauled him up here. Had to hold him. Then *this* all started"—he shook his head—"and they just let him go."

"No," Kalleb gasped, sliding his helmet off, releasing a wave of sweat down his back. "No, I thought I made it this time. I *did* make it this time. It . . . it's not *right*!"

Kenith turned to him, misty-eyed and in wonder. "How did you get here, Kalleb?"

"It turns out I can't keep my post if I hear a family member's in trouble," he replied. "Only, this time, Konner and Amanda—Lady Renald—thought I'd better have a couple of companies ride along."

Kenith stared at him then glanced at the lancers watching them. A smile spread under his shaggy beard, and a chuckle grew from the back of his throat. He tousled Kalleb's hair, slinging droplets of sweat everywhere.

"Still the deserting baby brother," he said.

Kalleb grunted and brushed his hand away. He sulked for a moment.

"At least I don't have to worry about being court martialed again," he quipped.

Kenith snorted and shook his head. "No. Every lancer that rode in with you, and all of Kanestown, would have to be court martialed alongside you. Way too much paperwork."

Kalleb snickered.

There was still some fighting going on around the entering street to Kanestown. The lancers who had gotten around the blockading carriage were riding right toward it, though, and the crowd was breaking up. Thinking of Kanestown reminded Kalleb of their ma at home, waiting and certainly worried.

"Ma's probably going to kill the both of us for worrying her," Kalleb said.

Kenith grunted, and then his eyes lit up. "Let's tell her it was all Konner's idea."

Kalleb laughed so hard with Kenith that tears welled up in his eyes and his shoulder ached. The laughter seemed to grow louder around him, and it took him a moment to realize the other lancers were laughing with him.

Kalleb and his fellow lancers might have been too late to save his grandpa, but they had arrived in time to save his brother. They had gotten inside Daincliff and had relieved Kanestown. And they were still alive. It was something to take comfort in.

I made it, Pa. He hung his head and looked down at his grandpa. *I saved some of my family this time.*

***

Alindale, Bernold, and the soldiers around him started to relax as the lancers began to laugh. Alindale had feared they would seek revenge for the death of their marshal, as well as lacking the power to stop them. The reunion of the two brothers, though, seemed to have eased the tension.

"Brothers?" Bernold questioned. "I'll be damned."

"Fortunately for us," Alindale agreed before he took a wobbly step to speak with his former protector and suddenly felt lightheaded.

"Your Highness!" Bernold cried, steadying him.

"I'm fine," he told him, "I'm . . .."

Alindale's legs suddenly failed, and the world seemed to slip away. Hands grabbed him from every direction, bracing him under his arms, chest, and back until he was sitting on the steps.

"Water!" Bernold demanded. "We need water for His Highness!"

Alindale blinked to clear his vision, limited as he was with only one eye. Someone was tugging against his arm, and he turned to see Bernold struggling with the straps to his mix-matched armor.

"Don't do that!" a steely-eyed knight warned. "With as many small wounds as he has, his armor may be acting as tourniquets. Make the straps tighter. If you strip him now, he could bleed out."

"And who are you, Sir Knight?" Bernold asked.

"Master Noa Blain," the knight replied, stripping off his tabard, "of the Enderval Knights Brotherhood." Underneath the tabard, Master Blain wore a chain mail coat with plate across his chest, emblazoned black with the Enderval skull. He reached behind his back and pulled out a small water sack.

"Drink, Your Highness." Master Blain held out the water sack with a respectful bow.

Alindale took it, but his injured hand prevented him from pulling the stopper out.

"Permit me, Your Highness," Bernold requested, and Alindale begrudgingly accepted.

When Alindale squeezed out a gulp of water, he felt it run down his throat and flow through his body. He gasped and coughed from trying to drink too much with his second squeeze.

"Easy," Bernold warned.

Alindale nodded then froze. "Montaigu!" He looked up and found Master Blain grimacing.

"Master Montaigu fell," Master Blain reported. "Speared from behind. Even with surprise, we couldn't break through in time."

And yet, I lived. It felt cruel. Both him and Montaigu had thought they would die today.

"It doesn't seem fair," he said under his breath.

"Captain Monroe!" a soldier running up the gallows cried. "Captain Monroe!"

"What are you yelling about, lad?" the officer who had surrendered to Alindale asked.

"It's the mob, sir!" the soldier replied. "They're storming toward the warehouse quarter. We think they mean to raid the grain stores!"

"What do you think we can do about it, man?" Monroe demanded.

"Captain!" Alindale yelled. "What's going on?"

Monroe frowned and snapped to attention. "Begging your pardon, Your Highness, but the rioters are heading to the grain and food stores, and I fear we haven't many men to stop them."

Rioters heading toward the food stores. The reason was obvious. They were hungry. Possibly their families, too. Families he remembered being forced to leave the sanctuary of the cathedral from lack of food.

Alindale quickly noted there were only about twenty soldiers on the gallows. Maybe dozens more scattered and disorganized groups around the square. They would need a larger, swifter force to cut off the rioters before . . ..

"Kenith," he called. "Kenith!"

A moment passed before Alindale heard boots drumming on the boards behind him.

"Are you all right, Prince Alindale?" Kenith asked, kneeling beside him, Lieutenant Holt right behind him.

"I'm sorry for your loss," Alindale said. "And I'm sorry to ask you this—I have no right—but the rioters are heading toward the grain stores. Can you take command of every lancer you can and head them off?"

Kenith frowned. "And do what?"

"Head them off. And the first grain store you find, I want you to open it and give them all the food in it."

Kenith's mouth dropped agape. Everyone else seemed taken aback from the request, as well.

"*Give* them the food?" Kenith questioned.

"But Your Highness," Bernold protested, "the lancers and soldiers together might be able to stop the mob."

"They're hungry," Alindale gasped, "and angry. I saw it in the cathedral. Their markets have been closed, and they have been forced out of their homes. If we give them food to take back to their families, they might calm down long enough to save the rest of the city."

Bernold hung his head in thought, and Kenith's frown returned. The soldiers around them shuffled uneasily.

Alindale had to admit it was their only a hope. There was no other way, that he could think of, from stopping the mob taking the food and coming back for more. He lacked the manpower, possibly the authority, and the desire to order every soldier and soul with a weapon to run after the rioters and crush them, especially understanding their plight.

"Begging your pardon," Kenith's brother said. He wobbled over, his back bowing as he leaned toward the right, as if his slinged arm was a heavy burden. "I don't mean to interrupt or insult anyone, but most of us rode here for our families. Some lancers may object to leaving them." He hung back, as if nervous to approach.

With his shirt hanging half-open, Alindale saw redness spreading out from under the bandages. He tried to keep his eyes down, but every now and then, they would flicker up. Alindale took him for a smart but proud man, as most Kanes he knew. He was also in a lot of pain.

"Prince Alindale," Kenith brought the prince's attention to him, "this is my youngest brother, Kalleb. I hope he didn't talk out of turn."

"On a day like this?" Alindale asked. "Is that even possible?"

A chuckle spread throughout the lancers still mounted within earshot, and Kenith smiled.

"But he's right," Alindale said then thought briefly. The answer was obvious.

"Tell your men that, once they have emptied the first storehouse to the people and seen them stand down, go to the second grain store you can find and send it all into Kanestown."

Kenith stared agape at him again, him and all the other lancers.

"*Two* storehouses, Your Highness?" Bernold whispered anxiously. "That's a lot of food. And what of the merchants and property owners?"

"Do you see any merchants here, Bernold?" Alindale asked. "Do you see any magistrates or ministers?" He shook his head. "People are tearing themselves apart in the streets. If we offer them food, it may give us enough time to regroup and save the rest of the city from being torn apart."

"Give them food instead of steel," Master Blain summarized.

"And if they take the food and riot for more?" Bernold questioned.

"We'll still have our steel," Master Blain retorted. "And have regrouped and rested."

Alindale turned to Kenith. "Will you do it?"

Kenith looked toward Kanestown then pushed himself to his feet. "Your servant, Prince Alindale." He bowed then straightened, quickly returning to being an officer.

"A horse! I need a horse!"

He turned back and pointed up at his brother. "You stay! I forbid you from being in a saddle until that broken collarbone's mended."

Alindale watched him go, with lancers trotting behind him. His mind churned with thoughts on what to do and what needed to be done. It would take more than just the Storm Cavalry lancers to handle the mob.

"Captain Monroe!" he called.

"Here, Your Highness!" the captain replied, stomping his heel on the boards.

"Take as many men as you can spare and gather up every scattered soldier in this square. Have them support the lancers. Don't attack the mob unless you must. If they calm down, escort them back to their homes."

"Yes, Your Highness!" The captain stomped away, hopping off the gallows.

"Off the gallows, men! Gather up the stragglers!"

His men followed and began scouring the square for more lost soldiers.

Alindale turned his attention to Master Blain. "Master Blain, please gather your knights and search for any Knights Brotherhoods and every man of the city peace still left in the square. Try to get them to stop fighting, secure the square, and help put the fires out."

Master Blain slammed his fist into his chest and bowed. "As you command, Your Highness."

As he walked away and began gathering his knights, Alindale remembered Brother Revel. He looked for him, but he was gone.

"Master Blain!" Alindale yelled.

Blain turned from giving orders to his brother knights.

"If you find Brother Revel, please tell him that I do not blame him for what he did."

Blain nodded then went back to giving his knights instructions.

Alindale sighed and hung his head. He went over everything in his mind, trying to think if he was forgetting something. His eyelid drooped, and he felt the powerful urge to let it fall.

No! I'm not done. I need to stay awake.

"Your Highness?" Bernold asked with concern, shaking him gently. "We should move you some place safe."

"I *can't* move," Alindale raspingly replied. "Find Father Finrie. I think I need his services again."

"But I can't risk you falling unconscious if I leave you." Bernold shook him again, more fervently this time, and made Alindale open his eye. Bernold looked at him with a mixture of worry and pride.

"I'll stay with him," Kalleb volunteered. "I've suddenly found myself useless."

Bernold looked to Alindale for permission, and Alindale weakly nodded.

"I'll be back as fast as I can," Bernold promised.

"Make sure he remains awake!" he ordered as he stormed down the steps then sprinted faster than Alindale thought possible for a man of Bernold's age.

"Well, he can run," Kalleb joked.

They shared a small laugh as Kalleb sat down beside him on the step.

Alindale knew he had to stay awake, but his head and eyelid began to grow heavy again now that he, too, found himself useless.

"Your sister sends her regards," Kalleb told him.

That made Alindale raise his head. "You know my sister?"

"Well"—the lancer turned away, as if trying to avoid looking at him in the eye—"she kind of came up with our plan to get here. She asked me herself if, while I looked for my brother, I could look for you, too."

Alindale coughed. *Who would guessed she cared so much.*

He saw Kalleb lick his lips out of the corner of his eye and remembered the water bag.

"Here," Alindale offered, holding out the bag as water sloshed in his hand.

Kalleb shook his head. "Couldn't take your water, Prince. Wouldn't be right."

Alindale nudged him with his shoulder pauldron. "It's the least I can offer to someone who came to help me."

Kalleb grimaced for a moment, but Alindale kept holding out the water bag. Kalleb finally sighed and took it. He then lifted it to his lips but paused.

"To your health?" Kalleb asked.

Alindale arched his good eyebrow. "After a day like this, that might be a questionable toast." He pondered a moment, but nothing came to him. "What would a Kane drink to?"

Kalleb got a far-off look, and it only broke when a column of lancers thundered through the square, heading toward the warehouse quarter, with Dain soldiers running at their heels.

"To family," he finally said then lifted the bag back and gulped down a couple large squeezes of water. He gasped and held it back to Alindale.

When Alindale took it back, he shook it in his hand and figured from the weight that there might be one last swallow left.

Family, huh?

Alindale's father and brother were dead, his mother believed he was responsible for his father's death, while his sister had sent a company or two of lancers to try to save him. His family was a mess.

He held up the water bag, anyway.

"To family," he said, squeezing out the last gulp of water. Despite being lukewarm and barely a swallow, it was the best drink Alindale had ever had.

***

Tory fell to her knees, numb against the boards of the wharf. The numbness spread until she felt hollow inside. Her gaze remained locked on the clouds of canvas as every ship in the harbor sailed away. Jerro's ship sailed in the center of the desperately fleeing fleet. It was slinking ahead of the others, cutting through the incoming tide, thanks to her extra sails.

"He *left* me," she gasped.

You promised, Jerro! she screamed inside. *You promised!*

"He may not have had a choice," Nolen said. He then tapped on her shoulder and pointed back along the dock.

Tory had run across the wharf as soon as she had seen all the ships sailing away. She hadn't seen the carriages left empty, their horses abandoned along the dock. Her Majesty's carriage was one of them, its doors hanging open from the aftermath of a mad dash.

The implications were clear. Her Majesty, along with everyone who could reach the docks first, had commandeered every ship that could sail. And Tory didn't care.

"He still could have waited," she said, falling back on her heels. "Or sent someone to find me."

Nolen raised his eyebrows and dramatically glanced back the way they had come. "I rather doubt that." He then turned on his heels and strode down the wharf.

"Where are you going?" she asked.

"To find us something that floats," Nolen replied. "Something that can get us into North End or an entrance to the castle."

A chill ran up Tory's spine at the mention of the castle. "I'd rather drown than go back to the castle!"

"North End, it is!" Nolen waved, trotting down the wharf.

The docks were quiet, save for the sound of rushing water as the waves rolled in and out against wharf's supports. The hawkers were gone. The fishermen were gone. Even the animals were gone, save the abandoned horses.

Tory looked back out to sea, instantly seeking out her brother's ship. The other vessels had closed in behind it, though.

I wonder if Serina made it out?

A high-pitched shrill made her spin around in time to see Harpo's red wings spread wide, flapping hard, with his talons outstretched. He clearly was preparing to land on her shoulder before she moved.

"Harpo!" she cried, holding out her arm.

The pytre hawk gladly accepted the perch, his talons nicking and piercing her skin while he kept his forewings spread for balance.

"At least *you* waited for me." She smiled and stroked his head feathers, now healthy again after she had nursed him. She giggled at his happy coo.

A loud crash behind her shattered the eerie quiet. Tory leapt to her feet, fearing the rioters had reached the docks and now she had nowhere to escape. Harpo squawked in protest.

A barrel rolled out from an alley, curved onto the dock, and then stopped.

Tory watched, expecting a mob to rush out at any moment, but no one came. She listened but didn't hear anything.

Maybe a wharf cat? she pondered.

A low moan came from the alley, sending goosebumps up her arms.

That's no cat.

She cautiously walked toward the alley, holding Harpo close and listening carefully for another moan, but none came. She slipped around an abandoned carriage and stealthily approached the alleyway, her back hugging the building's wall.

When she reached the corner, Tory made a quick glance down the alley then pulled back. She hadn't seen anyone standing there, waiting to grab her or charge at her.

She looked again, this time studying the surroundings. The alley ultimately led to a dead end. Although, from the light, it appeared to connect to other small paths between the buildings. The buildings had no alley doors, though. No doors to any cellars, either. Nothing to say where the barrel had come from—

Tory caught movement.

Something was in the corner of the alley, trying to slink forward. It took a moment for her eyes to adjust and see a woman lying on her belly. Her silk dress was in tatters and streaked with mud and filth from the alley. From her outstretched arms, it appeared she had been pulling herself, inch by inch, through the muck. The woman's left leg was twisted badly, her foot misshapenly hanging to the side.

The woman let out another moan.

Tory clasped a hand over her mouth, dropping Harpo in surprise.

She's alive!

She ignored Harpo's chirps and rushed to the woman's side, kneeling beside her. She wasn't sure what to do, but she couldn't leave her facedown. Tory gently tried to roll her over.

The woman threw her head back and screamed. The piercing shriek echoed in the close quarters and nearly made Tory drop her. When the woman threw her head back, though, Tory was able to see her face.

"Regina?" she gasped. "Regina Malthas!"

Regina's once chestnut hair was caked in mud, and her head rolled around like a newborn's. Her eyes rolled back in her head as Tory tried to cradle her.

"What happened?"

Tory looked up to find Nolen dashing into the alley. Harpo squawked at him and made the lanky man recoil.

"I found her like this," she explained.

Nolen grimaced at the pytre hawk then at Regina's leg and shook his head. "We should leave her. I found a dingy but saw a group of men farther down by the warehouses. We must get out of here. Now!"

"We're not leaving her," Tory said firmly. She stared up at Nolen while cradling Regina's head firmly and refusing to blink. She had been left behind and abandoned, just like they were, and Tory wasn't about to let it happen again.

Nolen snorted. "Fine. I'll take her shoulders. You manage the legs."

Tory smiled triumphantly . . . momentarily. Then she realized she would have to manage Regina's mangled leg.

She tried to be as gentle as she could. Nolen, though, took Regina under the shoulders and didn't even count before picking her up. Regina gasped and mumbled as Nolen dragged her out of the alley.

"Careful!" Tory insisted.

"We have to hurry!" Nolen snapped back, determination clear on his face.

Tory took up Regina's good leg but dared not touch her injured one.

Nolen paused behind a carriage and peeked along the dock. "All clear," he whispered. "We need to move *fast*. Don't stop until we reach the dingy."

Tory nodded, and Nolen took that as his signal. He huffed as he dragged Regina along. Tory jogged to keep pace, holding Regina's good leg up.

As soon as they were clear of the carriages, the dingy came into view, tied up three wharfs down from where her brother's ship had been anchored.

"Come on, Harpo!" Tory hissed.

Harpo danced after them, hopping a few feet, then another, then running along beside her. His head bobbed around, curious of Tory's bundle.

"Why?" Regina mumbled.

"Be quiet," Nolen shushed.

Regina's head rolled around, and Tory caught the faint sight of the whites of her eyes. They were still rolled up in her head.

"She can't hear you," Tory whispered.

"Terrific," Nolen grunted. "The pain's making her delusional."

As they hurried down the dock, Tory looked for that group of men that Nolen had mentioned, but they were nowhere to be seen. The dingy was enough for two, sitting, but Regina wouldn't be able to sit.

"It's a little small," Tory commented.

"Don't be choosy," Nolen snapped. "You get in first, and I'll lower Regina down to you."

Tory gently laid Regina's leg down then hopped into the dingy. The small boat swayed violently, but the familiar feeling of deck beneath her gave Tory comfort. She stretched out her arms and balanced herself until the swaying stopped. Harpo wasn't so patient, jumping on her shoulder and refusing to budge from his perch.

"Here." Nolen slowly lowered Regina to her, pointedly ignoring their additional passenger.

Once Tory wrapped her arms around the woman's shoulders, she sat down with her.

"Why?" Regina groaned and grimaced. "Threw me out of the coach. Why?"

Tory gasped, and she looked at Nolen in alarm. "They threw her out of a coach?"

Nolen shrugged as he scooped her good leg into the dingy. Her mangled leg, he left hanging over the edge.

"It was a panic," Nolen explained, untying the boat from the dock. Then he hopped in as it started to drift and took up the oars. Long, smooth strokes, Tory noted, as if he had done this before.

"Just in time," he said, nodding behind her.

Tory glanced over her shoulder to witness a group of men rushing the abandoned carriages. Harpo ruffled his feathers at the abandoned horses' alarmed neighs and snorts, but the men were more interested in whatever they could find inside the carriages. They were so distracted that they took no notice of them rowing away, heading toward North End.

Tory turned back around to see Nolen smiling smugly. While she didn't believe the smugness was warranted, she couldn't be rude in denying he had likely saved her life.

"Thank you," she said.

"No thanks needed," he replied.

Tory shook her head as she stroked Regina's hair, trying to be as comforting as she could, while her gaze drifted back out to sea.

"I *really* wanted to go home today," she uttered.

Harpo cooed in her ear, and she patted him with her free hand.

"You made it out alive today," Nolen said. "*That's* the important thing. You still have a chance to make it home tomorrow."

"Alone?" She frowned. "Without my brother's ship or support from my family? They probably don't think I'm alive."

"Who says you need them?" Nolen grinned. "All your enemies have fled Daincliff, leaving you alone with friends. You'll see home one day, Lady Syros. I'm certain of it."

Tory wished she could be as certain.

She distracted herself with Regina, making sure her leg didn't fall into the water. She only looked back out to sea when the temptation, or desperation, grew too much. Her brother's ship was gone.

I'll make it home, she promised herself, tearing her eyes away.

A tall shadow swallowed them, and she looked up at the cliff jutting out over them, blocking out the Easterly Sun.

Someday, I will *make it home.*

Chapter 31

13th of Iohan, 1109 N.F. (e.y.)

Alindale braced himself against his walking cane to stay on his feet. He wished he didn't need it, but his right leg was still unable to bear his weight for long while standing. The stitches in his joints, knees, elbows, and left shoulder, along with the cut above his left eye, made his movements stiff and slow. Most no longer needed bandages, save for around his left shoulder and hand.

He tried not to think about his hand, keeping it tucked by his side. His fingers curled around the hem of the bandage but were prevented from curling fully to form a fist from the tight bond.

Many were surprised he was able to walk again after only two weeks of bed rest. Bernold was especially vocal about him needing a longer recover, but Alindale couldn't remain locked away forever. Responsibilities weighed on his mind and plagued him every moment he lay in bed.

The telltale tapping of Thomas's scepter signaled his approach on the other side of the throne room doors, and Alindale shifted off his cane to stand up straight.

Yesterday, I entombed my father, he reflected. *Today, I assume his throne.*

A chill ran across his shoulders, even as sweat dampened the small of his back and under his arms. Regardless, he shoved the anxiety away.

Thomas tapped on the doors, and a guard stepped up to open it, resting his halberd against his shoulder. The old man slipped through, dressed in his official regalia, his pristine white gloves keeping a tight grip on his scepter as he lowered his head.

"All is in readiness, Your Highness," the steward said. "The coronation may commence on your command."

The four Storm Cavalry lancers surrounding Alindale as his honor guard straightened to attention. Their sabers and brass buttons jingled on their burgundy dress uniforms.

Alindale wished he had the strength to stand as straight, but his arm was already trembling, and so he pressed down on his cane to keep him from stooping.

"Thank you, Thomas," he said. "Let's begin."

As Thomas turned, something pricked Alindale's heart as he watched the old castle steward perform his motions. One of those things that had weighed on his mind when he had awoken to discover himself back in his old room in the castle instead of in the cathedral after the day of the upheaval.

"Thomas," he called out, stopping him from slamming his scepter against the tiles. "Thank you for bringing me into the castle. Lord Vanni told me it was you who opened the castle gates after three days and declared me the rightful sovereign. I can't tell you how much that means to me."

Thomas gently lowered his scepter. "There is no need to thank me, Your Highness," he said from over his shoulder while also keeping his head lowered and his gaze angled downward. "It is my duty as steward to do what is best for Dain Castle in the absence of its sovereign. You were the only Dain remaining in the city after your mother failed to return. It was my duty to relinquish Dain Castle to you, as it is my duty now to announce you."

Alindale understood Thomas's response, despite it not being what he had expected. There was no malice nor regret in his voice. He was the dutiful castle steward, carrying out his responsibilities, while everyone else played politics around him.

I guess I can accept that.

"Carry on then," he said.

"Yes, Your Highness," Thomas replied then raised his scepter again. He slammed it down on the tiles three time, the loud taps echoing down the silent corridors around them. Alindale winced from their sharp ringing in his ears.

The guards pushed the throne room's doors open then snapped to attention before them, halberds raised.

Thomas entered first, treading on the blue carpet cutting down the center of the room and up to the steps of the royal dais.

"He comes!" the steward shouted with his scepter raised in the air. "He comes! All bow before His Royal Highness, Prince Alindale Dain!"

Trumpets blared from the trumpeters lined along the back of the throne room. Then Thomas moved to the side and bowed his head low, the signal for Alindale to enter.

He wished it were grander.

He kept his back as straight as he could, but his legs were stiff and his strides short. The trumpets fell silent before he had taken his second step inside. Fortunately, the carpet muffled the tap of his cane with every labored step.

Just keep moving forward, he told himself. *I shouldn't look around, either. I might trip.*

He started to sweat at the thought. Tripping on his way to his own coronation and after everything they had gone through, those who remained at court would surely lose their remaining confidence that they might have in him. It didn't help that the day was cloudy and humid, fogging up the ceiling windows and requiring lamps to be lit in the throne room.

Unable to heed his own advice, Alindale's curiosity got the best of him, and he glanced from side to side at the attendees. The seats had been removed, as per protocol, to allow as many as possible to witness the coronation. The room should have been filled with every lord governor, high-ranking bureau aristo and province aristo from every corner of the kingdom, wealthy merchants and land aristo who could travel or had a residence in Daincliff, masters of countless Knight Brotherhoods, and more.

Instead, hardly a quarter of the room was full. There had been no time to request and wait for lord governors, or anyone from afar, to travel. Nearly all the ministries were in shambles in some form or another. Some of the wealthy still in Daincliff were present, though most still feared more riots.

Representatives from the Knight Brotherhoods, who had taken part in the riots, were present, but their loyalty could not be guaranteed. All of them had made small encampments outside the city.

Alindale noted each group from how they separated themselves while trying not to let the small crowd size bother him. Even now, they clung together in their social associations.

None of that matters, he knew. *I have to be crowned to do anything. That's the important thing.*

Two men waited for him at the bottom step of the royal dais, Lord Justice Blakwell and Father Finrie. Both men stood out in stark contrast to each other.

The lord justice stood in his pristine purple robes, showing little sign of his confinement in the tower, except a thinner hairline and sunken cheeks. His hair, though, was slicked back and his face clean shaven. He held his head high with the Tablet of Oaths in his hands. The stone tablet bore the original oaths of New Hartland kings, required for all future kings to swear upon before being crowned, including Alindale.

Father Finrie was, of course, Father Finrie. His clothes were still the humble cotton cloth that he had worn in the cathedral. His hair and beard were unkempt, his belly rotund and, every few moments, he shifted his weight from one knee to the other with a wince, but he quickly forced it away. He held the royal crown on a blue pillow, its silvery shine flickering off the array of sunrays fashioned in metal.

Alindale took a long, relieved breath when he finally reached them. His legs were starting to quake from not only the walk but his stiffness in front of the attendees.

His Storm Cavalry honor guard snapped their heels then joined the rest of their delegation to his left, with Colonel Kenith in dress uniform, standing at their front.

Thomas had followed behind them and came to stand next Alindale's right. He tapped the end of his scepter twice again on the tiles. Then a great ruffle of clothing spread out behind Alindale as the crowd straightened and the throne room's doors boomed shut.

Alindale glanced up at Blakwell, who gave him a nod.

"Yesterday," Blakwell began addressing the audience, "we laid His Royal Majesty, King Richman Dain the Third, to rest. Today, we gather here to crown his heir and successor, His Highness, Prince Alindale Dain.

"Before the Oath of Kingship is spoken and levies are silent forever, is there any here who can lay claim against His Highness?"

A stillness fell over the room. A few shuffled their feet. Someone failed to muffle a cough. Bar that, no one spoke.

Alindale remained facing forward but frowned just the same.

They're afraid of me. They're all thinking about what just happened. But anyone who would say anything fled weeks ago.

He knew what it was like to be disliked. Quite used to it, in fact. But not feared.

His heart felt heavy. He didn't like it.

"Hearing no claims," Blakwell continued, "we shall proceed with the oath. May none bring any against him from this day forth."

Blakwell presented the tablet to Alindale. "Please place your right hand upon the Tablet of Oaths, Prince Alindale, and swear after me."

Alindale gingerly exchanged his cane from one side to the other to free his right hand. He grunted from his legs straining under his full weight and braced his injured palm against his cane. Without a thumb, he couldn't grip it. Instead, he steadied himself the best he could while placing his right hand against the tablet. His fingers outlined the chiseled words inscribed on the plate as the coarse stone dug into his hand.

"Alindale Dain," Blakwell started, "do you swear and affirm that you will honestly and faithfully take upon yourself the duties of the King of New Hartland?"

"I do," Alindale replied loudly.

"Do you swear and affirm," Blakwell continued, "to fulfill, carry out, and uphold the laws of New Hartland as set forth in the Carta, as your duties as King of New Hartland?"

"I do."

"Do you swear and affirm, by the Last God, you will preserve and protect the peace and people of New Hartland, cradle of humanity, as your duties as King of New Hartland?"

"I swear."

Blakwell lowered the tablet then stepped to Alindale's left. Alindale took the opportunity to switch hands grasping his cane as Thomas took the pillow from Father Finrie.

Father Finrie slipped in front of him, holding the crown above Alindale's head. "Alindale," he said in his fatherly way, "I know it is not traditional, but before I place this crown on you, may I ask you to swear something else?"

"Is this really the time?" Blakwell hissed.

"That wouldn't be proper procedure," Thomas added, shaking his head.

"Please," Father Finrie implored, "it would be for your own good, Alindale, and all here to hear."

What's one more oath? Alindale thought. He didn't expect Father Finrie would ask anything crazy. Spiritual, maybe. Enforceable by law, debatable. But probably not crazy.

"Go ahead," he agreed.

Father Finrie nodded then turned serious. "Alindale Dain, do you swear by the Texts and to the Last God that you did not conspire or have anything to do with the death of your father?"

A collective gasp cut through the room behind him. Alindale, though, stood stunned, staring up at Father Finrie. The father's fatherly manner was gone, and he looked down at him as if passing judgment.

Alindale felt a burning in his chest. They had settled this. He had strode out yelling his denial in front of everyone there in the square that day. He had fought, expecting to die denying it to his last breath. And now, about to be coronated, the question was still being asked?

Alindale tensed. *Or maybe he's asking so it can be said I swore it as I was crowned.*

He straightened the best he could so that no one could say he swore while appearing to look guilty.

"By the Texts and the Last God," he swore, "I did not conspire or have *anything* to do with the death of my father! I swear it!" His voice rang throughout the room.

Father Finrie nodded in approval. "Please lower your head."

Alindale leaned down.

"Alindale Dain," Father Finrie said, "by the honor given to me, I crown you, King of New Hartland."

The cool metal slid over Alindale's head like a tight hug. It was snug around the back of his head but slipped down without catching his hair. The rim of the crown dug into his brow, but fortunately stopped before reaching the cut healing above his eye. Alindale held his head steady; otherwise, the added weight threatened to pull it back.

"May the Last God bless him and his reign!" Father Finrie shuffled out of the way, clearing a path for Alindale up the dais steps to the throne. Even without sunlight shining down on it, the crystal vein running through the back and atop its head dazzled in the dim light.

Now for the hardest part. Alindale braced himself.

He led with his left, stepping up onto the bottom step, brought up his cane and, with two supports, raised up his weaker right. Each step took the same, laboring process. Sweat made the crown rub against his forehead by the time he reached the top. Once there, he looked at the throne, more for relief in being able to sit than the assumption of power. He did his best to avoid glancing at his mother's former throne beside it.

However, he knew there was one more thing that he needed to do before he could sit, so he placed himself in front of the throne and turned.

Alindale was struck first by the size of the throne room, which appeared larger from where he stood. The second thing was everything was facing him. The columns appeared to be angled toward him. The carpet stretched out toward him. The attendees gazed up, watching him.

He glanced up at the stained-glass mosaic on the ceiling, at the former kings and their swords looking and pointing at him.

I really want to sit down now.

Thomas tapped his scepter on the tiles five times, and then the attendees moved in closer, leaving space in front of the dais and a divide between them with the carpet.

"All hail King Alindale Dain the First!" Thomas announced. "Lord of the First Kingdom, King of New Hartland, and Defender of Humanity!"

"Hail!" the crowd shouted in unison. The men dropped to a knee and bowed their heads, the ladies curtsied low and lowered their eyes, and the soldiers snapped to attention.

Alindale's breath caught. The sight was intoxicating, regardless of the crowd size. The feeling incredible. It made him want to speak, but he was afraid to, as if everything he would say would be written into the hearts of everyone who heard them.

To shove the feeling away, he took the blessed opportunity to finally sit down.

The cool touch of the throne's stone seat seeped through his trousers. It was smooth, as well, polished by the rears of his forefathers, and hard.

I'll probably need a cushion after a while, he thought, arranging his cane by his side and leaning back. *At least I can—*

Alindale gasped.

An icy chill ran up the length of his back the instant he touched the back of the throne. The room suddenly brightened. The weight of his worries, his injuries, his insecurities with the crowd kneeling before him were all wrapped in a ball and shoved out his mind. In their place, he saw plans.

His plans.

Plans of what he had dreamed of long ago if he ever became king before he had become disillusioned by court life. Plans on what to do with the kingdom and how to answer its problems. Plans for what to do about the concerns of everyone in the room before him and how to restore security to Daincliff. Plans to answer with those who had fled and what they might be doing. Plans to find his mother.

He could do them all now. He could stretch out his hands, give his word, and lay out the foundations of New Hartland going forward. The future was his. All he had to do was lay the groundwork and the New Hartland of his dreams would be—

Alindale pulled forward, sucking down air as he hunched over and gripped the throne's arms.

What? he gasped. *What was that?*

The world darkened back to as before. The cloudy sky remained, casting a gray mugginess over the stained-glass windows on the ceiling. His worries and aches slowly trickled back, and whatever those visions had been began to fade into the corners of his mind.

He hesitantly glanced at the attendees, still on their knees, their heads bowed. The soldiers still faced straight ahead. All as if none had noticed anything.

What was that?

He peeked over his shoulder and briefly caught a strange, pure flicker of light wink out from the crystal rays ornamenting the top of the throne. Then again, that could have also been a glimmer from anywhere.

He didn't have the strength to get up, and he couldn't afford the gossip of the new king talking crazy about his first time sitting on his throne.

I have to make sure.

He sat back up, this time slowly pressing against the back of the throne. The same chill ran up his back, gently following his spine as it came into contact. His worries and insecurities faded away again, and his mind was left undisturbed. His plans were there, waiting, but didn't overflow him this time.

There is something about this throne, Alindale thought confidently.

However, the present called to him, and so his plans faded away, save for one—his thoughts on how to make this coronation answer all the concerns left with his ascension. Only, now he could see them—the outcomes and proper course he needed to make them happen.

Let's get to it, then.

"Rise," he said, his voice easily filling the room. "Proceed, Steward."

Thomas nodded then faced the attendees as they got to their feet.

"Change of the guard!" he shouted with a tap of his scepter.

Kenith Kane and the last remaining Sunrise Guard stepped out in front of the crowd then marched to the hems of the carpet, facing each other.

"The royal heir is crowned," Kenith called out. "The Storm Cavalry's charge is complete and turns its duties over to His Majesty's Sunrise Guard."

"The Sunrise Guard takes charge of the person and safety of His Majesty," the Sunrise Guard said.

Both men saluted each other, and then Kenith returned to the Storm Cavalry delegation. The Sunrise Guard, though, knelt at the bottom step. He slammed his fist over his heart and his other hand over his sword.

"Your Majesty," he said, "I, Juno Almarc, swear to defend, obey, and pledge to carry out my duty by every means necessary, even at the cost of my own life. My sword is yours."

"Your allegiance is accepted," Alindale said, the words seeming to come to him naturally. "Rise and take your post."

Juno stood to take his place to the right side of the carpet at the dais's bottom step. He was the only remaining Sunrise Guard left in Daincliff. Two others had been killed during the riots. The rest were assumed to have fled with Alindale's mother.

I will need to fill their spots later.

"We shall proceed with the Oaths of Allegiance!" Thomas announced. "Starting with the lords and ladies, please line—"

Matters of state should be addressed first. Appointments and justice.

Alindale tensed as the calling reverberated in his mind.

"Steward!" he interrupted.

Thomas stopped and turned about, keeping his head low. "Your Majesty?"

Alindale had planned on making a few appointments during the coronation, but those plans suddenly sprang in his mind, along with thoughts on how to set things right for those accused of conspiring to assassinate his father. They were both so clear, as if predestined.

"Because of the serious matters facing the kingdom right now, and this not being a traditional coronation," Alindale explained, "I want to move to important matters that cannot go unaddressed any further. Let us save the Oaths of Allegiance until after they are addressed."

"As you wish, Your Majesty," Thomas replied, nodding respectfully.

"Please call Lord Hugo Blakwell," Alindale ordered.

"Lord Hugo Blakwell!" Thomas shouted to the attendees. "Step forward and address His Majesty."

Thomas's shouting was unnecessary and more to do with his role, as Blakwell stood at the front of the crowd on Alindale's right, having turned over the Tablet of Oaths to a page already.

He strode onto the carpet in front of the dais, straightened his robes, and then knelt.

"Lord Blakwell," Alindale began, "I must offer you an apology. It was unjust for you to be locked in the tower."

"Your Majesty is kind," Blakwell said, "but you do not owe your subject an apology. After all, Your Majesty did not imprison me in the tower."

"I felt it was warranted," Alindale said. "After all, I would like you to remain Lord Justice and Minister of Justice, as you were under my father, and it was only right to apologize for your injustice before asking you to keep the post. Will you accept?"

"I humbly accept, Your Majesty," Blakwell replied without a moment pause. "And your kind apology is most gracious."

Alindale knew this was really all formality. Blakwell had immediately seized back control of the remains of the Ministry of Justice upon his release. From what Alindale had been told, magistrates were losing their certificates of practice and positions left and right or being reassigned.

Appointing someone else would amount to someone new inheriting a crumbled down building.

"Thank you," he told him. "Please remain, Lord Justice. The next few matters will require your counsel and opinions. Stand to my left, please."

"As you wish, Your Majesty," Blakwell replied, moving over as instructed.

Now for the hard parts.

Alindale set his shoulders. This was something he had to take care of now. Otherwise, doubts would linger, and his reign's foundation would have cracks before the real trials even started.

"Call Lord Bernold Vanni," he said.

"Lord Bernold Vanni!" Thomas shouted. "Step forward and address His Majesty."

Bernold stepped out from the middle of the attendees on Alindale's left. His gray suit hung on his body, and his trousers were slightly baggy, clearly showing signs of weight loss during his imprisonment. He had also let his beard and mustache grow out since the day of the execution.

He pointedly ignored the glances and expecting looks from the other attendees as he knelt by the bottom step.

Alindale took a deep breath to settle his nerve. "Lord Bernold Vanni, as you know, I opposed your removal as First Minister during my father's illness. Yet I cannot appoint you back to that position."

A surprised murmur ran through the crowd of attendees. Women whispered to one another while men grunted and nodded. It was evident that they had expected Alindale to sweep everything away and set it all back to before his mother had taken over. Alindale knew he couldn't do that, though.

With a few taps from Thomas's scepter, the attendees quieted down.

"You have been through a great ordeal, Lord Vanni," Alindale continued. "And, while I do not find the trial held against you, or any of the others involved, legal under the Carta, questions remain. And they must be answered. So, I offer you this: will you stand trial again, as written in the Carta, or instead demand it all be written as illegal and not stand trial at all. If you are tried again, the judgment found will stand. If not, you will be free to go, but neither I, nor this throne, will ever appoint you to any position ever again. I understand if you need some time to think about it."

Bernold wasn't as quick to respond as Blakwell.

Everyone's eyes slowly turned to him, waiting for his response and undoubtedly waiting to judge it for themselves. Alindale was sure most of them had attended the first trial. And they were all survivors of the execution day disaster.

More theater for them, he thought. *Please, Bernold, make the right choice.*

"I thank Your Majesty for your offer," Bernold replied, keeping his head down. "I have stated since the beginning that I did *not* kill your Royal Father. As your loyal servant, and *his*, should you wish me to stand trial again, I shall."

Alindale breathed a small sigh of relief. He knew another trial would be difficult, but to not have one would probably be worse.

"Lord Justice," he called, "I believe Lord Vanni's willingness to proceed with another trial is evidence he deserves parole. If he remains here in the castle, waiting for trial, will that satisfy the courts?"

"It will indeed, Your Majesty," Blakwell agreed. "The Ministry of Justice will hold Lord Vanni to his honor and grant him bail to remain free so long as he appears at trial. I'll set my clerks to make the docket."

"Thank you, Lord Justice," Alindale said. "And thank you, Lord Vanni. I hope for the best of outcomes. You may step away."

Bernold rose without another word and backed away, remaining bowed and low. Three steps, and then he returned to his spot in the crowd without ever looking up, as if practiced.

Alindale had to move on to the others.

"Call Colonel Kenith Kane and Lieutenant Lazar Holt."

"Colonel Kenith Kane!" Thomas shouted. "Lieutenant Lazar Holt of the Storm Cavalry! Step forward and address His Majesty."

Kenith and Holt stepped out of the Storm Cavalry delegation, respectfully moved around their four brigadiers in the front in the white uniforms, and marched before him. Their bootheels drummed in step together on the floor's tiles, only to be muffled by the carpet. They clicked their heels together before lowering to a knee, hands on their sabers.

I wish Malory was here, too, Alindale lamented.

"Colonel Kane," he said, "let me first give you my condolences on the death of your grandfather. What happened was a tragedy that I hope will never happen again."

"Thank you, Your Majesty," Kenith replied.

Alindale frowned and looked to Blakwell. "Lord Justice, it is my understanding that the only evidence against these two officers is a confession from a now deceased individual, and I find the confession itself questionable. What is your counsel on this?"

Blakwell bowed. "Your Majesty is correct. The previous confession, which named Colonel Kane as a conspirator, does have questions with its veracity. It is something that should have been investigated further before charges were made."

"So"—Alindale pondered for a moment, but again his mind cleared instantly, and he envisioned a way forward, his words seeming to flow naturally together—"is it possible that this confession should be investigated now, and we wait for a determination before anything else can be said? No trial?"

"That is correct, Your Majesty," Blakwell replied. "I'll personally choose new magistrates to investigate the veracity of the confession and the charge of conspiracy. Until I'm satisfied of their decision, no trial is warranted."

Alindale smiled. That made his decision a lot easier. "Rise Colonel Kane, Lieutenant Holt."

Both men stood then snapped to attention.

"Since no charges remain to clear up, I determine both of you are free to return to your homes and your duties. You are to remain posted in Kanestown as the investigation is underway, but I am sure you will both be happy with that." He snickered. "Maybe some light duty, right, Colonel Kane?"

Kenith's smile was faint, but Holt beamed.

"If that is your command, Your Majesty," Kenith replied.

Alindale nodded. "You may both return to your delegation. And the next time you see your brothers, Colonel Kane, tell them I am very grateful."

"Thank you, Your Majesty! I will," Kenith said.

He and Holt snapped their heels in unison again then marched back to their fellow lancers. Alindale saw a couple pat Holt on the back, but he let it slide.

One last thing, he steeled himself, his smile slipping. He set his shoulders and took a deep breath.

"Steward," he called, "call Brother Marc Revel."

"Marc Revel!" Thomas shouted. "Brother Knight of the Enderval Knights Brotherhood! Step forward and address His Majesty!"

Alindale searched the knights and quickly spotted the Enderval delegation. As he searched, though, he failed to find Revel. Others in the crowd looked back as Revel didn't immediately appear and looked at the knights. Alindale hadn't seen him since after the prisoners had been freed, and no one had news of what had happened to him after the battle, or at least he couldn't find anyone with news.

Did he die in the riots? he wondered as time dragged on. *Or did he run the moment he was freed?*

He was about to tell Thomas to carry on when a figure stepped out of the crowd.

Revel was in the black suit of a gentleman rather the tabard and arms of a knight. The suit was worn, fraying at the cuffs and the back hem of his jacket. He needed a shave and approached with his head down.

He merely dropped to a knee at the bottom step without a word or salute.

Alindale frowned. This wasn't the same cheerful knight who had laughed every time Alindale had groaned when he had forced him to run another mile. This wasn't the same knight who had stood proudly beside Master Montaigu. He looked like a haggard shell of that former man.

"Brother Marc Revel," Alindale said, "despite the legal leniency I was able to grant Lord Vanni, Colonel Kane, and Lieutenant Holt, you are a special case. Did you confess to conspiracy to murder my father?"

Revel swayed for a moment, like he was about to fall over, before finally replying, "Yes, Your Majesty."

Alindale's stomach rolled, like someone had punched him in the gut. He stared at the man whom he had thought had become a friend.

"Why?" he asked.

"Doesn't matter," Revel replied, shaking his head.

Thomas slammed his scepter on the floor. "Impudence! His Majesty asked you a question, Brother Knight! And you will answer!"

"I'm not a knight!" Revel yelled, visibly quaking. "A man who conspires to kill a king, or a man who gives false testimony, is not worthy of being a knight! So, I'm not one. Not anymore." His head dropped lower. His oily, unwashed hair hung down toward the floor.

Alindale felt sorry for him. Others seemed not to care by the way they avoided looking at the former knight or watched him shake on the floor with contempt. Either he told the truth, or he had given a false confession. To them, they didn't care why. To Alindale, though, that was all he cared about.

Come on, Revel, he groaned. *Talk to—*

Compassion.

Alindale's frustration was smoothed away, and he softly asked, "Please, Revel, for me. Tell me why you confessed."

Revel's trembling slowed, and he sniffed, clearing his nostrils. "They kept us in the dark. We only got food and water twice a day, if the guards remembered. When the elder Kane got sick, they did nothing. And they tortured Amadus every day. They killed him *every* day!

"One day, they brought a lady, and they made her watch. They demanded she sign a confession. We were innocent!" he slammed his chest and yelled. "She was innocent! While I had endured everything to that point, as a knight, I couldn't permit an innocent lady to suffer. So, I signed. I signed a confession, and they let her go."

A trial, Alindale concluded, spurred on by whatever power kept clearing his mind and making it easier to think. *A simple trial to throw out the confession.*

"Who was the lady?" he asked.

Revel paused. "Lady Tory Syros."

Alindale's heart sank, and he desperately searched for Tory among the attendees but, as expected, he didn't find her. Her brother's ship had been in the mass exodus from the city, and he hoped she had made it aboard. He could easily have Bernold and the others testify that that was what had happened, but it would be better if Tory testified herself.

"Thomas," he said, failing to find her, "call—"

"Your Majesty!"

Alindale turned sharply to his left and, amazingly, found Nolen stepping out of the far corner of attendees. In the turmoil, he had forgotten about Nolen and figured he had made good on his escape.

"Lord Ingman," he said, "this is a surprise. You have something to say?"

"Yes, Your Majesty," Nolen replied with a flourished bow. "It is about the whereabouts of Lady Syros. If I am permitted to approach?"

Alindale beckoned with his good hand. "Come forward."

Nolen took his usual long strides to stand beside the kneeling Revel and made another flourishing bow. "Lady Tory Syros is currently residing in a townhouse in the North End of Daincliff, Your Majesty," he happily divulged. "On the day of the great upheaval, she was unable to reach her family's ship in time before it departed. Finding her, I gave her lodging and sanctuary until the turmoil passed."

Alindale checked the crowd again but still didn't find her.

"Is she not with us today?"

Nolen gave a dramatic sigh. "Sadly, no, Your Majesty. Lady Syros was not the only poor soul whom we found left stranded that day. We discovered Lady Regina Malthus badly injured in the back of an alley, and Lady Syros has taken it upon herself to help mend the poor lady. Also, I believe Lady Syros was traumatized by her time spent in the tower and might be afraid of returning to the castle, Your Majesty."

That tower again. Alindale balled his good hand into a fist.

"Steward, take note," he said.

Thomas snapped his fingers, and a page came running over to him, writing desk in tow.

"The tower is now condemned," Alindale ordered. "And I want it demolished. See to it."

"Yes, Your Majesty." Thomas bowed, and his page wrote down the command.

Alindale looked to Blakwell. "Lord Justice, because Mr. Revel claims his confession was made in duress, and the witness to that is in this city, would you suggest a trial or investigation be proper to clear up this matter?"

Blakwell furled his brow and folded his arms. He studied Revel for a moment then gave Nolen a mere glance before responding with, "A trial, Your Majesty. A confession makes investigation pointless, and it would take a trial to rule the confession void."

Alindale would have preferred just an investigation to say the confession was void, but if his Minister of Justice said trial, then so be it. He was sure of the outcome so long as Tory backed up Revel's story.

Revel, though, remained on his knees with his shoulders slumped. He looked like a man who had given up.

"See to it, Lord Justice," Alindale said.

"Mr. Revel, you will remain here in the castle, with bail, as my guest until this matter of your honor is cleared."

"There's no need for mercy," Revel said. "You can throw me back in a cell if you want."

"Stop that!" Alindale grimaced at how the man was shaking and surely crying. It wasn't right he should want to be punished. "Steward, see Mr. Revel out and to a room to rest. He obviously needs it."

"Yes, Your Majesty," Thomas said then instructed the page to write something before striking his scepter on the floor. "Guard!"

Alindale watched the tense exchange as a pair of castle soldiers came over and picked Revel to his feet. Thomas handed one of them a slip of parchment and whispered them instructions before they carried Revel away. Alindale couldn't help but feel pity for the man.

I hope that will set things right, he prayed.

"Lord Justice," he said, "that should take care of everyone. You can prepare for everything you need after this ceremony."

"As you wish, Your Majesty," Blakwell replied, slipping back to his former place.

As he did so, Alindale caught movement from the corner of his eye. Nolen was trying to slink away back to his corner.

Another icy chill struck him.

A way with words can have a way with proclamations.

Alindale couldn't help but smile. The last thing he had to take care of was how to deal with those who had fled two weeks ago, those former ministers, Lord Haemin, and his mother. To do that, he would need to appoint a particular minister.

"Lord Ingman," he called, "where are you going?"

Nolen stopped mid-step, his shoulders hunched, and then he slowly looked back, the same smirk still on his lips, though now looking a little nervous.

"Forgive me, Your Majesty," he replied. "I assumed you had no further need of me too."

Alindale forced himself not to laugh. Nolen's choice of words was too good not use.

"Well, actually, I do." He beckoned to him again.

Nolen came back to stand before him, this time more hesitantly than before. He maintained the smirk, but Alindale could see he was avoiding the curious looks everyone else was giving him.

"The kingdom lost a couple of ministers in the chaos and confusion of the riots, Lord Ingman," Alindale explained. "Lord Simon Baltaer, the former Minister of Proclamations, was found dead afterward, and my new table has a special need to fill his place."

"Would you like me to give you a list of candidates, Your Majesty?" Nolen asked. He waved his hand then reached into his vest pocket. "Say no more. I'm sure I can come up with a few names in—"

"Lord Ingman!" Alindale rapped his cane against the dais's stone. "I do not need a list of names. I am appointing *you*"—he pointed his cane at the lanky man—"as Minister of Proclamations."

Alindale wasn't sure who was more surprised—Nolen or everyone else.

People stared in shook, but Nolen stood with his mouth agape and hand stuck halfway into a vest pocket.

Someone snickered. Another coughed. A lady giggled. Then the dam broke as the whole crowd laughed.

Nolen snickered and shook his head. "A fine joke, Your Majesty. But really, how many candidates would you like me to list?"

"None, Lord Ingman," Alindale replied and slumped a little. "You will do nicely."

Nolen clasped his hands in front of him, his smile appearing forced. "But, Your Majesty, I don't believe I'm qualified for such an . . . honored position."

"Why not?" Alindale shrugged. "You know people. You have a way with words. I am sure everyone can say you *certainly* have a dramatic flair."

The attendees laughed harder.

"You shall do fine."

Nolen waited for the laughter to die down, biting his lower lip yet preserving his smirk. After a moment, he finally shrugged. "As you wish, Your Majesty." He gave another flourishing bow. "But don't say I didn't warn you when I get in trouble."

"Trouble, we already have, Minister Ingman," Alindale said, sitting up. "Now, call a page; I have your first proclamation to send out."

Nolen searched the side of the wall before waving to one of the pages to come over.

Alindale waited for the page to be set before beginning. He had thought long and hard on what his first proclamation should be to try to fix the mess they were in. He had filled several pages, writing them over and over, until he had them memorized, and in such a clear mindset, they came naturally to him.

"First," he dictated, "to all lord governors, provincial lords, province magistrates, and Knight Brotherhood masters, they are to present themselves before me within two months to swear their Oaths of Allegiance.

"Second, if any of them receive news of the whereabouts of former ministers of the table—predominately Lord Haemin and the Queen Mother—they are to send messengers to Dain Castle immediately.

"Third, to all of those who fled Daincliff, should any of them wish to return, they will be permitted to do so, including former ministers of the table, Lord Haemin, and the Queen Mother, provided they swear their Oaths of Allegiance.

"Fourth, if any of those who fled believe they have committed a crime against the throne, they will be entitled to the rights and justice as prescribed in the Carta, just as the individuals here today were."

The throne room filled with the sound of scratches as the page wrote out his decree. He thought they were simple and rather expected. Follow tradition in calling those to declare their oaths while also trying to reconcile with those who had fled. Simple. Hopeful. Yet a pit in his stomach told him it wouldn't be.

Nolen was drumming on his chin and watching over the page's shoulder when he suddenly stopped his drumming.

"Pardon me from inquiring," he said, "but should we add that all those loyal to you gather forces in your name, just in case we receive word that those who fled are massing some form of opposition against Your Majesty's coronation?"

The page stopped writing. The room went still. Even the candles seemed to have stopped flickering. Nolen had a way with words, but Alindale and everyone else knew what he was talking about.

Civil war.

It was the unspoken specter haunting the castle, but Alindale knew it was being thought. The few remaining guests had remained sheltered in their rooms. The servants whispered in the corners. The castle soldiers gossiped in their barracks.

Soft, haunting quiet wrapped around Alindale, and the stares of the crowd bore into him.

Preparing forces would be prudent. Smart. However, it might also signal there was no turning back, no matter how many proclamations he sent out offering just reconciliation.

Civil war meant everyone had to choose a side. Civil war meant fighting between those sides. He would be on one side, and his mother on the other. To win meant he would have to—

Alindale threw his head back. A fiery brand ran up his spine instead of the icy chill. His mind became clouded with pain as all plans and thoughts fell away.

NO WAR!

Alindale gasped and fell forward. He gripped the throne's arm with his good hand and pulled himself all the way to the edge of the seat. The burning stopped the instant his back left the throne. Sweat dripped from his face as he sucked in air.

"Your Majesty!" Juno Almarc cried. The Sunrise Guard was up the dais's steps in an instant before Alindale got his wind back. "Are you all right?"

Alindale nodded and waved him away as he sat back up. Half the court, including the entire Storm Cavalry delegation, half the Knight Brotherhoods, and several of the lords were halfway up the steps.

"I'm fine," he said, though a little out of breath. "I suppose, I am pushing it with my injuries."

The crowd hesitantly accepted that before going back to their places.

Alindale sent Juno back to his post, as well, but it was comforting his oath of obedience wasn't just for show.

He nervously glanced behind him. The throne still appeared as it always had, sparkling with gold, steel, and crystal fashioned into the stone.

But Alindale was certain of what he had felt.

There is more to this throne. And, in his heart, he knew only one person who might tell him. However, he still had the coronation to finish. Alindale kept his back off the throne, though.

"Lord Ingman, at this time, I am not going to ask that. I still believe reconciliation can be made between the throne and those who fled. However, this city and castle have been through a lot recently, and Daincliff now stands vulnerable.

"Send out a separate proclamation to the surrounding provinces, their lord governors, and all Knight Brotherhoods, that they are to martial men of fighting age and gather food to provide for this city and kingdom. I do not know what will happen in the days ahead, but I promise everyone here that I will be the king you need me to be. That is all, Lord Ingman."

No great cheer followed; just more pen scratches from Nolen's page.

Nolen stood behind the man with his arms folded, drumming his fingers against his elbows now instead of his chin, as if he were bored. Alindale was sure he wasn't the only one.

"Steward," Alindale called, "that will be all I wanted to address. We may begin the Oaths of Allegiance now."

Thomas bowed. "As you command, Your Majesty."

Alindale's thoughts drifted elsewhere as Thomas went about instructing the crowd into lines, ordered by political office, social rank, and military standing. They would come up three at a time, kneel down, and swear the same oath over and over, but Alindale soon stopped listening.

He had completed everything that he had needed to, had assumed the throne, saw those tried in his name would receive true justice, and tried to set a path to heal the kingdom. His kingdom.

The crown rubbed against his sweaty brow, causing it to burn, but he endured it so the people wouldn't think he was getting bored. Alindale wanted to sit back, but that burning sensation worried him, so he endured the growing ache in his lower back, as well.

After some time, his gaze drifted up to the ceiling, to his forefathers depicted above him, their eyes and their swords pointed down at him, as if they were demanding him to measure up to their legends and names. As if they were demanding him to make everything right.

I will bring New Hartland together again, Alindale vowed. *I swear it.*

In the year 1109 N.F. (e.y.), King Alindale Dain the First came to the throne of New Hartland. Later, historians would also mark the day as the beginning of the New Hartland Civil War of 1109, the first of three events marking the Year of Upheavals.

Epilogue

15th of Iohan, 1109 N.F. (e.y.)

Wait here," Alindale ordered. "We are not to be disturbed."

His guard, a couple of castle soldiers, took up posts by the door. Having only one Sunrise Guard meant regular castle soldiers would have to be drafted for Alindale's guard duty. However, filling out that roster was the furthest thing from his mind.

He opened the door then limped into the sitting room. A heavy gust buffeted against the door, threatening to wrench it from his grip as the smell of sea salt washed over him. Alindale squinted against the glaring sunlight filling the room, making it difficult for him to find his quarry. He pushed the door closed with his shoulder and gave his eyes time to adjust.

"Amadus," he called, "are you awake?"

With his eyes adjusted, Alindale took in the room. The small guestroom was sparse, with only a few chairs and a table in the back corner. It didn't see many guests because of its placement on the northeast side of the castle, where it became uncomfortable during the hotter months of the summers from getting most of both suns and a terrible view.

An armchair sat in front of the open balcony, directly pointing outward into the Easterly Sun and the breeze. In-between the whistling of wind, curtains flapping, and the faint taps of hammers, Alindale heard heavy breathing coming from the obscured side, slow and steady breaths.

He's asleep, he mused as he began hobbling over, the carpet padding his cane drops as he limped along.

He paused at the table and raised an eyebrow at the sight of two, long-necked decanters half full of—what he assumed—wine; one deep violet and the other crystal clear. Between them was a smaller decanter with a glass stopper and pink liquid. Maybe a port or sherry. The amount of alcohol stood out from the empty soup bowl and half-eaten loaf of brown bread.

Why all the wine? he wondered but shook off the curiosity.

He walked around the chair and found Amadus sprawled out, basking in the Easterly Sun. His velvet robe hung open and splayed about him. His white undershirt and trousers hung off his thin body. Amadus had appeared to be in his late fifties the last time Alindale had seen him. Now he looked like a man in his nineties. With his shockingly white hair, his sunken cheeks, and his frail frame and limbs practically skin and bones, he resembled a corpse.

But the immortal happily snoozed away the day with his face in the sun and his chest rising and falling steadily. It was almost a shame to wake him. *Almost.*

"Amadus," Alindale called, shaking his bony shoulder.

Amadus grunted and rolled his head against the chair's cushioned back. He smacked his lips together and ran his tongue between his teeth while shifting in his seat. At last, he opened his eyes.

"Why, hello, Alindale," the immortal said with a raspy voice. He stretched, arching his back, followed by a series of pops. "I mean, Your Majesty. Sit down. The sun and fresh air do wonders for healing. As does a bit of wine and a good view."

The only thing visible from the balcony was the tower, where work crews were beginning the preparations for its demolition.

"Tell me everything about the throne," Alindale said pointedly.

Amadus looked at him as if he were joking. "I'm afraid you don't have that many lifetimes. Besides, you've just been crowned and can learn as you rule."

"I didn't come for advice!" Alindale stomped his cane down into the carpet. "The throne. There is something about it. Something else.

Something . . . other?" He clenched his teeth in frustration as words failed him.

Amadus grinned, leaning toward him with an inquisitive, near crazed look. "You experienced it, didn't you? What was it like?"

Alindale stepped back, disturbed by Amadus's change in demeanor. "You did know!"

"Of course I knew!" Amadus slapped the arms of the chair. "But that's irrelevant now. What did you *feel* when you first sat on the throne?"

Alindale thought for a moment, but his thoughts were all jumbled when it came to his experience. It left him with more questions on whether he experienced it in the first place than answers.

"Clarity," he finally said. "Certainty. As if all the things I wished to do were laid out before me, and I knew every word, every method, of how to say what I wanted and get the response I wanted."

Amadus sat back in his chair and chuckled. That led to a few snorts and snickers as his grin grew and shrunk. Finally, he threw his head back and loosed a high-pitched cackle, laughing until he was almost hysterical, when a sudden coughing fit cut him short. The deep, wet coughs alone were enough to make Alindale wince.

Has he gone insane? he feared. *Or is it me?*

"Good!" Amadus sighed and fell back in his chair. "Very good. The Blessing is still intact, and you have rightfully inherited it. That's very good."

Alindale gave the crazed immortal a confused look. "What are you talking about?"

"Did you ever notice the back of the throne, Alindale?" Amadus asked. "Looking from the seat up to the head, the steel and crystal widen up together and get lost in decorations. But, if you start at the head, you might notice the steel and crystal start together and perfectly slice down into the stone. Does that design seem reminiscent of something else?"

Alindale pictured the throne in his mind. He had seen it all his life and had gotten used to its awe-inspiring appearance early. He had simply assumed, along with everyone else, it was a sunray wedged in stone. As he thought about it, however, picturing the width between the steel and the long, narrowing length, another possibility came to mind.

"A sword?" he blurted out without thinking, confused. "No, that makes no sense. Why would anyone make a sword part of a throne?"

"To use its power with no one realizing it," Amadus replied.

Alindale gave him a blank stare, uncertain how to take such a response.

"Take a seat"—Amadus pointed at the closest chair, its back holding the balcony door open—"and let me regale you with some unwritten history."

"I don't want a long story, Amadus," Alindale sighed out, emotionally drained. "I just want an explanation."

"The story is part of the explanation," Amadus retorted. "Sit."

Alindale squeezed his fingers around the thick bandage. Although he was unable to form a fist, he swore he could still feel his thumb trying to curl. Relenting, he then flopped in the chair behind him. It denied him from facing Amadus by being turned into the room, but Alindale was annoyed with him for still treating him like a child and wanted to sulk.

Amadus didn't appear to notice.

"The Great War didn't just end in 556 because a new king was crowned and everyone magically wanted peace." Amadus snickered. "After ten years, the entire continent was fighting for survival, and peace meant very different things, depending on who negotiated with whom."

Adam the Great. Alindale recognized the history references and deduced that was the only person he could be talking about. He was the forefather who his brother had been named after, after all, and Adam had enjoyed hearing stories about him. Alindale figured he wouldn't like this one with the way Amadus was telling it.

"I guess you're going to say you were really behind it?" he inquired sharply.

"As a matter a fact, yes," Amadus replied. "Me and a couple of others like me got together behind battle lines and opened the doors to peace talks."

"You and couple of others *like* you?" Alindale snorted, but then he sat up straight. "Wait! Other . . . immortals?"

Amadus gave him a guarded look. "That's a story for another time. As for our current story, to get the Téionaropi to agree to peace, they needed assurances that humanity would honor it and, for that, they needed the assurance that the scattered human settlements and nations would follow as one in peace. So, they fashioned a special gift and gave it to our king. We were the first human nation, after all, and the Téionaropi have always viewed us above the others."

"And this special gift was . . . a *sword*?" Alindale arched an eyebrow, tumbling the idea around in his head. No matter which way he thought about it, it didn't make sense.

Amadus snorted. "We thought the same when they first presented it. Thought it was a joke. I still remember Telramond's smug face when he said, '*When mortals prepare for war, the only thing they listen to is a greater weapon. So, our Goddess Blessed a greater weapon.*' Arrogant, even though he's too sanctimonious to see it."

Alindale only half-listened, blankly staring at the sparse room. Most of it, he didn't understand, and it was clear Amadus was reminiscing about his past more than giving him an explanation.

Although a chance to hear Amadus talk openly about his past and events as they really happened centuries ago would have been too good to pass up months ago, now Alindale found it dull and meandering.

He rested his head back against the chair. His lids drooped from the temptation to nap like Amadus had been. Everything weighed heavily on him now.

If I'm not going to get an answer that makes sense, he thought, *I might as well—*

He snapped his head up, realizing something.

"Goddess?"

"Yes." Amadus chuckled. "I always thought that funny myself. What use could a race of immortals, who claim they are perfect, have for a religion?"

"Didn't you just say it gives them magic or something?" Alindale asked.

Amadus grimaced. "Not magic. They don't just pray and lights falls from the sky."

"Then, how does the sword, or now the throne . . .?" Alindale shook his head. "This is getting confusing. How does it work?"

Amadus leaned against the arm of his chair toward him. "As I understand it, they have a connection to a higher power that grants their race and society certain gifts, such as keeping their cities lit at all times. But the throne is something special. It grants the person who inherits the power to unify everyone within range of your voice."

"That's it?" Alindale sat back, honestly having expected there to be more to something Amadus spoke so highly of.

"What more does there need to be?" Amadus laughed and threw his hands up. "Everyone thinks power has to be something grand and larger than life. Yet, what can be more important to a king but the art of persuasion? Persuading the table to enact certain policies over others. Persuading conflicting sides to come to terms. Persuading those to agree to the appointments you want. It all guides the kingdom!"

The last one hit Alindale. *Like Nolen.*

After the ceremony, Alindale had retired to his rooms and thought back on everything that had happened. He had continually gone over what he had said to Nolen and how he had gotten him to agree to the appointment, and he couldn't have imagined saying or behaving like that even if he had orchestrated it.

Amadus suddenly grabbed his arm. "But there are rules, Alindale. You can't expect to decree anything you want and have the power to instantly convince everyone you're right.

"One, you must have an idea or thought of what you want before the throne can aid you. The power will not instantly give you an answer every time a problem appears.

"Two, you must be persuasive in everything you decree using the power. If you force or command what you want done, the throne's power will be less effective, especially if the person you're trying to force to do as you say is against you.

"Three, you, and only you, can now use that power. You swore the oaths and sat upon the throne after your father died, so no worries there.

"And lastly"—Amadus squeezed his arm harder than Alindale would have believed him possible of—"this is the most important one—*never* try to use that power to declare any type of war. Not against our fellow men or other races. The power is meant to unify and prevent war and will *not* allow itself to be used otherwise."

Alindale instantly remembered the ceremony, the searing burning up his back. "That explains why I couldn't sit against the throne when I knew I had to order forces to marshal here."

Amadus grunted in agreement and sat back. "And why your father failed to convince Lord Haemin to withdraw from Téionaropi lands. He kept demanding him to withdraw instead of persuading Haemin it was for the best. Haemin agreed in his presence, but the throne's power couldn't hold once he was outside its influence. Same for your own brother."

The hairs on the back of Alindale's neck stood up. Pieces fell into place in his mind as explanations for Haemin's motives became clear.

"Haemin knows the truth," he said, "doesn't he?"

"Him and many others who follow him," Amadus replied. "They distrust the power because it came from the Téionaropi and are likely jealous they can't use it for themselves. They'll claim they need to remove it, and *you*, for the sake of the country or the people, but it comes down to them seeing a power they cannot have. So, they must destroy it.

"And when they come, Alindale, you must promise not to face them expecting to die as you foolishly did that day in the square."

Alindale locked eyes with the glaring immortal. "I refused to run or surrender," he said. "I won't apologize for choosing to fight until the end." He also refused to be berated for what had happened that day.

"You should never have gone out expecting to lose!" Amadus yelled. "You're at war now. A king cannot go into war with his heart accepting he's inevitably lost."

"We are not at war, Amadus," Alindale said dryly.

"Alindale"—Amadus's voice took on a deathly serious tone—"we've been at war since that day the table began making arrests. The first blows were struck when your Storm Cavalry escort drew sabers. And, after everything else that has happened, I doubt there is any going back."

"*No!*" Alindale snapped, slamming his good fist against the arm of the chair. "It doesn't have to come to that. There is still time to talk. To come to terms—"

"*Terms?*" Amadus spat dismissively. "What *terms* can there be for those who falsely accused and usurped the rightful heir to the throne? What *talk* can be had with those who even now wish the destruction of our very manner of government?"

Alindale growled in frustration. Part of him knew it would be difficult, if not impossible, to reach out to those who had fled. It was likely they would never risk stepping foot inside the castle, or Daincliff, so long as he sat on the throne if they knew of its power. The more he turned it over in his head, the more the likelihood of war there seemed to be.

But Mother . . . he groaned inwardly. *Why is she with them?*

"Alindale," Amadus spoke softly, "you know this will likely happen. That's the reason you sent out the proclamation to gather forces and supplies here. But there is going to be more to plan and prepare for. It won't just be marching off to wherever Haemin and your mother are. There's recruitment, training, supply gathering, chain of command, proclamations, money, and more things than have ever been written and read in a mortal lifetime. It would be wise if you took the advice from someone who's actually seen a real war."

Alindale slumped in his chair. He had come here for answers and, while he had gotten them, he had also received more burdens. No matter how much he wanted to think of a simple solution or hoped to see the ships that had carried his mother away return in peace, he knew the hard truth was neither of those were likely to happen. Trying to put Daincliff and the ministries back together was daunting enough.

"What do you advise?" he asked.

"When you do declare war," Amadus replied coldly, "do it standing."

THE END OF

FOR THE PRINCE!
FOR THE QUEEN!

Almanac of Seasons

This world goes by many names, depending on whom you ask. Many of this world's inhabitants also have a different sense of time. For simplicity, however, we shall remain with the humans.

Humanity's arrival to this world has been long since soaked in myth, legend, and history, but it did not take them long to realize this was a far different world than the one they came from. It was both ancient but new; familiar but alien. It took years of adjusting until they finally calculated the changes in seasons and the passage of time.

This world revolves in an infinite pattern, exchanged between two suns, which humanity have named after the direction they rise—the Easterly Sun rises in the east and the Westerly Sun rises in the west—and this pattern of exchange revolves around a four-year cycle. Upon calculations, humanity also realized that the number of months are different depending on which sun the world revolves around, as are the seasons different. A new calendar was necessary, and a new system to track the year was established. The Easterly Year is marked as e.y., and the Westerly is marked as w.y. The seasons during this cycle are displayed as follows.

Easterly Year

Petrarium	Andril	Iam	Iohan	Filippum
4th - Exchange Ends (Cycle Begins)	13th - Great Easterly Spring Begins			
Summer				

Vartholo	Mattaeus	Alphei	Simem	Iouda
			22nd - False Fall Begins	

Thoma
18th - Short Summer Begins
25th - Exchange Begins

Westerly Year

Reun	Vell	Iuda	Esstonder	Zabulon
4th - Exchange Ends				
17th - Winter Begins				

Dane	Naphtal	Gad	Aster	Benjamine
8th - Short Spring Begins		12th - Great Summer Begins		

Josephus	Ephraim	Manas
		28th - Exchange Begins

Easterly Year

Petrarium	Andril	Iam	Iohan	Filippum
4th - Exchange Ends		11th - True Fall Begins		

Vartholo	Mattaeus	Alphei	Simem	Iouda
6th - False Winter Begins				3rd - False Spring Begins

Thoma
9th - Short Summer Begins
25th - Exchange Begins

Westerly Year

Reun	Vell	Iuda	Esstonder	Zabulon
4th - Exchange Ends	13th - True Winter Begins			

Dane	Naphtal	Gad	Aster	Benjamine
		5th - Spring Begins		

Josephus	Ephraim	Manas
	14th - Summer Begins	28th - Exchange Begins (Cycle Repeats)

About the Author

ZACHARY T. SELLERS is a licensed attorney in the state of Arkansas and currently works as a practicing attorney, serving clients by day and writing epic fantasy by night. *For the Bloody Marquesa!* is his second published work in his series, *The Conflicts*. He plans for the first three books in the series to center around their own conflicts spanning across the same continent at the same in universe time. Where they will lead, he doesn't know yet, much like the march of real-world history. He is eager to find out though.

Visit Zachary T. Sellers' official Facebook page to keep up to date with all his latest news.
https://www.facebook.com/Zachary-T-Sellers-108414535096643
https://www.zacharytsellers.com/

www.ingramcontent.com/pod-product-compliance
Lightning Source LLC
Chambersburg PA
CBHW030905300726

48970CB00001B/24